DA

John Pritchard was bor
career began with a su
tionist in his local hospital, after which eye-opening introduction he worked in administration and patient services. He currently helps to manage the medical unit in a large hospital in the south of England. *Dark Ages* is his fourth, and by far his most epic, novel following the highly successful *Angels of Mourning*, *Night Sisters* and *The Witching Hour*.

By John Pritchard

Night Sisters
Angels of Mourning
The Witching Hour
Dark Ages

Voyager

JOHN PRITCHARD

Dark Ages

HarperCollinsPublishers

Voyager
An Imprint of HarperCollins*Publishers*
77–85 Fulham Palace Road,
Hammersmith, London W6 8JB

The *Voyager* World Wide Web site address is
http://www.harpercollins.co.uk/voyager

A Paperback Original 1998
1 3 5 7 9 8 6 4 2

[Permissions coming soon]

A catalogue record for this book
is available from the British Library

ISBN 0-00-649637-7

Set in Postscript Linotype Goudy Old Style by
Rowland Phototypesetting Ltd
Bury St Edmunds, Suffolk

Printed and bound in Great Britain by
Caledonian International Book Manufacturing Ltd, Glasgow

For permission to reproduce copyright material the author would like to thank the following:

Lyrics from *Sell Out* (words & music by Simon Friend, Charles Heather, Mark Chadwick, Jonathan Sevink & Jeremy Cunningham) © 1991 Empire Music Ltd, 47 British Grove, London W4 for the World. Used by permission of Music Sales Ltd. All rights reserved. International copyright secured.

Lyrics from *The Fear* (words & music by Simon Friend, Charles Heather, Mark Chadwick, Jonathan Sevink & Jeremy Cunningham) © 1995 Empire Music Ltd, 47 British Grove, London W4 for the World. Used by permission of Music Sales Ltd. All rights reserved. International copyright secured.

Lyrics from *Forgotten Ground* (words & music by Simon Friend, Charles Heather, Mark Chadwick, Jonathan Sevink & Jeremy Cunningham) © 1995 Empire Music Ltd, 47 British Grove, London W4 for the World. Used by permission of Music Sales Ltd. All rights reserved. International copyright secured.

Lyrics from *Tell Me about the Forest*, by Dead Can Dance, © 1993, reproduced by kind permission of Beggars Banquet Music/ Momentum Music.

Lyrics from *The People who Stumbled in Darkness*, by Roger Ruston, reproduced by kind permission of the author.

Behind them, to divide the carrion meat,
They left the raven, dark and shadow-clad,
With cruel beak; the dun-cloaked eagle too,
With his white tail – exulting in the feast,
A hungry battle-hawk; and the grey beast,
The wolf of the deep woods . . .

THE ANGLO-SAXON CHRONICLE, 937

Watchman, what is left of the night?
Watchman, what is left?
The watchman replies:
Dawn is coming, and also the dark.

ISAIAH 21:11–12

To

Mum and Dad,
who laid the deep foundations.

Michael Wood,
who made the past alive.

and F.M.E.,
who's still my leading lady.

CONTENTS

PART FOUR HUNTERS

PART FIVE RAIDERS

PART SIX MARTYRS

PART SEVEN PILGRIMS

PART EIGHT WARRIORS

PART NINE RAVENS

EPILOGUE

Prologue

RISING SIGNS

(1989)

As touching the terrors of the night, they are as many as our sins. The night is the Devil's black book, wherein he recordeth all our transgressions.

THOMAS NASHE

She had no truck with horoscopes. No *way* could someone's future be predicted by the stars. And yet, as Frances glanced at them with casual disinterest, her own was written there for her to see.

The sky tonight was orange and polluted, but frosty sparks were showing here and there. The only shapes she recognized were two her mum had shown her – out in the back, one bedtime, long ago. From the flyover embankment, she could see them well enough. The Great Bear, rising upward from the dark fields to the north; and setting in the west, the Northern Cross.

Cars passed fitfully, racing westward through the night; the junction left behind before they knew it. In the lengthy gaps between them, the dark and silent countryside drew closer. Fran turned on the spot, then pulled back her glove to check her watch. Just past midnight. They'd got here first this time.

Wrapping her long coat closer, she went back to the car. It was parked up a service road, just short of the underpass. The others had sat tight; she didn't blame them. Paul leaned across to open the passenger door, and she climbed in, drawing a shivery breath between her teeth.

'Anything?'

Fran shook her head. 'Dead quiet.'

The CB crackled briefly, then lapsed into an empty, spooky hiss. She gave it a glance. The set was clamped below the dashboard, its digits glowing green.

'Nothing on that?'

His turn to shake his head. 'Not since Merlin.'

Ten minutes since that last, half-garbled contact. As if the silence of the night had clogged the airwaves. The sense of isolation was insidious: creeping up. Bullington Cross felt cut off from the world – a lonely, lamplit island in the murk.

'Want some coffee?' asked Marie from the back. Fran turned gratefully in her seat, and took the thermos cup she proffered. The coffee was too hot to taste: a gulp of scalding water. She wriggled as it seared its way down.

'So when are we going to meet this boyfriend of yours?' Marie teased in her ear.

Fran turned her nose up coyly. 'When I let you.'

'Knows about these midnight escapades, does he?' Paul murmured.

'Yeah . . .' said Fran. 'He knows.' Her eyes flicked down. She took another sip.

'And does he think you're mad?' Kate asked.

'He thinks I'm bloody crazy.'

Paul grinned at that, and raised the CB handset to his mouth. 'This is Catkin at Bullington . . . any news on the convoy, over?'

The edgy pause that followed made them all hunch forward: waiting. The radio snapped and squawked. And then a woman's voice came through – tone firm but faint with distance.

'*. . . call for Herbs and Watchers along South Route . . . Four launchers, two controls, out of Yellow by ten past twelve . . .*'

'Shit,' Kate whispered, shifting.

Fran swallowed. 'Twenty minutes . . .' She felt a tingle of relief: it wasn't a false call. Then her stomach hollowed out. *They're on their way. They're coming.*

Heart thudding, she climbed out; the others followed. Paul unloaded placards from the boot and passed them round. Glancing up, Fran saw that a police car had appeared while they'd been talking: it was parked on the flyover above them, watching the A34.

The four of them walked in silence through the underpass,

emerging in the day-glo of the link road. A handful of others were there already. Fran recognized old faces, said hello. Chatting, someone cracked a joke: she giggled with delight. The tension sometimes got to her that way.

A transit van came crawling past, and dropped off several coppers. She watched one cross the road to shine his torch into the woods. The others started spacing out along the nearside kerb.

'Come far?' one asked her, amiably enough.

'Oxford.'

'So when'll you be getting to bed tonight?'

She shrugged. 'God knows.' *Not much before three, if we follow it down. And I've got a* tutorial *in the morning . . .*

'This may be a silly question, right . . . but why are you wearing shades at half-past midnight?'

She reached up to adjust them with an impish little grin. 'To preserve my anonymity, of course.'

'Famous, are you?'

She shook her head. 'Notorious, more like.'

The snarl of motorbikes made her heartbeat quicken. She turned her head as the outriders reached the underpass, and paused to rev their engines. Four or five patrolmen, helmets swivelling: waiting for the signal to proceed. They had it a moment later, and peeled off past her, roaring up onto the flyover and westward.

Frivolity had fizzled out. The thump of her heart felt as heavy as lead. Dry-mouthed, she started up towards the crest. A couple of Watchers were waiting there, well-marked. Silent now, the copper matched her pace.

The police car on the flyover came suddenly to life: drove backwards, blue lights flashing, to block the access road. Fran looked beyond it – but the A34 lay empty in the darkness.

A glance back at the others: they'd stayed down in the shadow of the heavy concrete span. But then she'd always been the type to strike out on her own.

A squad car – London plates – came cruising past.

'Here they come,' called someone; and turning, she saw the line of lights come streaming down the hill. It nosed into the far side of the system, and came snaking slowly through it: the vehicles still hidden by the roundabout mound, but their noise now rising clearly to her ears.

She'd never forget the noise they made. Above the growl of engines, a clatter and squeak that made her hairs stand up.

Transits and patrol cars rumbled past her, driving steadily upslope onto the flyover – and then the first military vehicle came off the roundabout. A camouflaged command car, riding high on its wheels – a mottled, muddy shape behind the sleek white escorts. Whistles blew; a football rattle whirred. The turnout was too small to do much shouting. But Fran's voice would have failed her if she'd been among a crowd. All she could do was stare, and search their faces: those bleak, unsmiling faces, staring back.

Pursing her lips, she stepped up to the verge and held her hand up, proffering a silent V for peace. The copper tensed, expecting her to lunge. The first Control was following already – a clanking monster, flexing like a serpent for the turn. She challenged the gaze of its armoured cab: a skull with a sarcophagus in tow. The second rumbled after it – and then the missile launchers, in a sinister cortege, their long, low backs enshrouded with tarpaulins. Engines roared at her, and axles squealed. As each one passed, she saw the double blast-ports at the rear; the missiles resting snugly in their tubes.

Four Cruise launchers: one full flight: the standard monthly exercise deployment. The wrecker came behind them, like an iron scorpion rattling with chains. A rearguard of police vans straggled after; and then the first pursuers came in sight. Used-looking cars, bedecked with CB aerials. Merlin passed, then Elderflower. And here came Torquemada too – a Dominican priest and friars in full regalia.

Everyone on foot was running now: the police for their

parked transit, the Watchers for their cars. Fran wavered for a moment – watching the tail-lights fading in the darkness; almost shaking with the force of her reaction. Then she was off and pelting down the hill.

Reaching the car, she scrambled in. The others were all aboard, the engine running. She was still fastening her seatbelt as Paul took off – back through the underpass and onto the convoy's route. Less than five minutes after its passing, the roads were clear again, the junction silent.

It didn't take long to catch the convoy up again. They breasted a rise, and the snake of crimson lights was there ahead of them, sharp pulses of blue along its winding length. Soon they were up with the leading Cruisewatch cars. Fran could make out the control trucks at the front of the column, their high sides marked by orange running-lights.

She sat back in her seat, and braced one boot against the dash. Kate and Marie were motionless behind her; Paul's grim stare was focused on the road.

'*. . . convoy approaching first Andover bridge . . .*' someone said on the CB.

Getting on for 1 a.m., and all the world seemed dead. The chase filled her with nightmarish excitement. As they sped on through the night, she thought of all the unseen eyes that watched them: owls and foxes staring from the copses and fields. But what else might be peering through the hedgerows; what faces in the long pale grass the headlights played across? She couldn't help but think of ghostly figures, creeping up, to watch this roaring cavalcade go past.

Past Andover, and Thruxton Hill, they reached the long steep incline into Amesbury. Salisbury Plain was spreading to the north: a sea of pitch.

'I'm going to try and get ahead of it,' Paul said.

They broke off the pursuit at Amesbury Roundabout – the convoy grinding on towards Stonehenge. Paul put his foot down, speeding up the empty lamp-lit road. At Durrington he spun the wheel: they turned onto the Packway and raced west.

Parallel to the convoy's route; Fran looked and glimpsed its winking lights, a mile to the south.

Behind her, Kate was studying the map. 'They'll road-block us at Shrewton, sure as hell.'

'Any way round?' Paul called over his shoulder.

'The road from the Bustard to Westdown Camp. They won't have covered that.'

'Right. They might have closed it, though.'

'It's worth a try.'

'Fran?'

'Go for it,' Fran said.

They came to Rollestone Crossroads and went tearing north again. The road rose up, and let them see for miles; then dipped again. Darkness stretched away in all directions, but strange red lights were glowing here and there. The fringes of the firing range were coming up ahead.

Fran hung on, and braced herself. The Bustard vedette showed up in the headlamps as Paul swerved onto the narrow westbound road. No one was there to see them pass. The lonely sentry hut was locked and dark.

The unlit military road led up towards West Down. It might have been a country lane; Paul took it at exhilarating speed. The murk out here was dense and overwhelming: trapped beneath the starlight like a layer of London smog. Fran straightened up, and peered through her window, still searching for the string of phantom lights.

Then Paul yelled: 'Jesus, *SHIT!*'

She swung around, and saw it in the headlights: a figure in the middle of the road. A featureless, inhuman face, with gaping holes for eyes.

Paul wrenched the wheel, and lost control.

The car went slewing off the road and plunged into a ditch. The bonnet crumpled up, the windscreen shattered. Fran was thrown against her belt: the impact mashed the breath from her lungs. Her head struck something hard and bounded off. Stunned, she felt herself flop back.

The world had just stopped dead.

She lolled there for a moment, sick and winded. Her whole head had gone numb – as if a piece of it was missing. Cold night air blew softly on her face.

Something started fizzing by her knees. *Sparks*, she thought, *oh Jesus, we'll catch fire*. Galvanized, she struggled with her belt – and glanced at Paul. He was slumped against the wheel, head down. 'Paul . . . ?' she quavered, reaching out to take hold of his shoulder. She shook him, hard. He made no sound.

The muffled sizzling came again. She cringed away – then realized it was just the CB set: skew-whiff on its rack, but still lit up. She peered at it stupidly. Someone whimpered softly from behind her.

'. . . *convoy coming into Tilshead* now . . .'

Help, she thought, and groped round for the handset. She found it dangling; scooped it up.

The radio *hissed* at her.

Fran recoiled again, as if she'd just picked up a snake. The hiss broke into eerie gibberish: almost like another voice, but mangled and tormented. Fear lanced through her. She dropped the handset, fought against her door and felt it give. She slithered out, and rolled onto the grass.

The headlamps were still on: staring and blind, like a dead thing's eyes. The tail-lights left a bloody trail that almost reached the road.

They tinged the silhouette that waited there.

Someone in the car was weeping quietly. Ignoring them, she peered towards the road. Her mind flashed up the face she'd glimpsed. She thought its horrid gauntness had been muffled by a hood.

A soldier. In a gas mask?

But then the figure started coming forward. Something about its shambling gait made her struggle to her feet. Then the scarlet glow lit up the face beneath the cowl.

Oh Jesus Christ.

A metal mask stared back at her: brow and cheekbones

setting off the tar-pits of the eyes. The lower face remained scarfed up in shadow. The sight was almost toad-like – and revolting. She stumbled back – then swung around and fled. Clear of the car, and out into the darkness of the range.

The shadow thing came striding in pursuit.

I

WATCHERS

(1993)

Beautiful city! . . . Whispering from its towers the last enchantments of the Middle Age . . . Home of lost causes and forsaken beliefs.

MATTHEW ARNOLD, ON OXFORD

CHAPTER I

Spire Dreams

I

Lynette caught sight of her from over the road, and gave a little wave. The gesture, like her smile, was almost shy; but her pretty face was bright with expectation.

Fran almost turned and walked away right then.

It had taken her so long to get this far. She hadn't even answered that first letter. But Lynette had patiently persisted: so gentle, so *committed*, that all at once, one afternoon, Fran's brittle shell had cracked. She'd wept a year's worth of tears that day; her mum had told her later what a blessed sound it was – drifting downstairs from the bedroom through the silent, sunlit hall. After all those months of torpor and withdrawal, her daughter sobbing like a little girl.

More letters; then a phone call. *We have to meet*, Lynette had said. And Fran was feeling better, but still delicate and drained – as if she'd just brought up the poison of the world's worst tummy ache. She'd hesitated; hummed and hawed. The soft voice on the phone was a voice from the past. And the past was forbidden ground.

Yet here she was, right now, in sunny Oxford, nervously waiting while Lynette crossed the street. As ever, Lyn looked gorgeous – a picture of elegance in her smart black trouser suit and snowy blouse. Fran suddenly felt dowdy in her cardigan and leggings.

Lyn hesitated for a moment, then gently touched her shoulders – kissed her cheek. When she drew back, her smile looked stretched; her eyes were bright and wet.

Fran felt her own eyes prickling behind the shades she wore. Her throat had tightened up, she couldn't speak. That smile was from the Old Days: from *Before*. She'd almost forgotten what the sunshine looked like – the nuclear winter in her head had blotted it all out. But now, at last, the cold, black smoke was lifting. A glimpse of light again. A breath of spring.

And more than that: her friend was here, and beaming her delight. It made Fran warm inside, to see her pleasure. It made her feel so happy she could cry.

Lyn had worked so *hard* for this. She'd earned it. Fran wanted just to hug her, and hold tight.

'Oh, God . . . Sorry . . .' Lyn blinked and sniffed, still smiling. People kept on passing, heedless of the reunion in their midst. 'I've missed you,' she said simply.

Fran swallowed. 'Thanks for waiting.' An even bigger understatement, but she couldn't find a better way to say it. And had it only been four years? She felt like Rip van Winkle (Sleeping Beauty was too flattering a parallel): waking up to find the world had changed, and all her friends were dust . . .

Except for one. And who'd have guessed it, back when they were freshers?

'Come on,' Lyn said, and took her elbow. 'Remember *Heroes*? It's still there. Let's have coffee.'

2

She'd been down for her interview, and seen its winter colours; but it had taken that golden first weekend to really bring her under Oxford's spell.

Michaelmas Term: even the name was strange and rich somehow. The city in the autumn sunlight had seemed part of a whole new world. After the rugged countryside of home, it might have been a magical realm. She could feel the *age* of things down here: the buildings, and the books. And though she'd grown up close to ancient places, they'd never had a hold on her like this.

The place was beautiful enough; she had watched the stonework glowing in the amber setting sun. But for her, the fascination was its treasury of thought. That was why she'd worked to come to Oxford: to study there, and somehow soak it up. Those hoards of books; those centuries of learning. It wasn't the prestige: that didn't matter.

Well, not much.

She'd signed herself in at Christ Church, unable to stop smiling. The college had entranced her from the start: a citadel of honey-coloured stone. Exploring, she'd found shady cloisters, quiet little nooks. A maze of spires and ivy. It was like an old-world castle in some fantasy she'd read. But this time it was real, and she was here. Little Frannie Bennett, from *Up North*. Her accent was soft, but she'd broadened it when posher ones cropped up. *I went to a comprehensive, but I'm just as good as you.*

Her spacious study bedroom overlooked an inner quad. Halfway through unpacking, she'd sat on the bed, and started taking stock. Still high on her excitement, she felt a little awed as well: belittled by the splendour of the place. She was suddenly grown up, and on her own. In Oxford – *hours* from home. No turning back now. The thought upset her buoyancy somewhat.

The first thing you should unpack is your kettle, Mum had said. Fran did so – and her mug and coffee too.

Lynette, meanwhile, was moving in next door.

Fran's mum and dad had seen her off at the station, but Lyn's had driven down here. There was lots of to-ing and fro-ing; the mother sounding anxious, the father more laid-back. Fran had the impression they were pretty well-to-do.

'Oh Mummy, please don't fuss,' was Lyn's first plaintive contribution.

She was hovering in the corridor when Fran peered out: awkwardly aloof, as if watching someone else's room being furnished. She looked tired and rather miserable already. Someone else whose heady day might yet end in tears.

'Can I offer you a coffee?' Fran asked.

The girl's smile was so grateful that it forged a bond at once. Posh though she was, her face was naturally friendly; her toffee-coloured eyes were warm and soft. Fran beckoned her in, and made another mug.

They swapped details like the schoolgirls they'd so recently been: Fran sitting cross-legged on her strange new bed; her first guest perched politely on the chair. Lyn was from Coventry, and had come here to read History; her father was a professor in the subject. Fran, who lived in Derbyshire, was doing French and German. Listening to Lyn talk – each consonant impeccably pronounced – she couldn't help but feel a little distanced. Yet the other's well-bred poise offset a shyness that she warmed to; a *niceness* that she couldn't help but like.

'You're sure you'll be all right, Lyn, darling?' her mother asked from the doorway. The smile she offered Fran was gracious enough, but Fran had felt herself assessed, the woman clearly wondering who her daughter would fall in with, once free of the parental gaze.

'Quite sure, Mummy. Thanks ever so much for everything . . .' On which sweet note she saw them firmly to the car.

'Fancy a wander?' Fran asked, when she came back; and out they'd gone together, looking round the mellow college buildings, before meandering down onto Christ Church Meadow. Back to the Hall for a welcoming communal dinner; then coffee in Lyn's room, the window open wide on the Oxfordshire dusk. Their friendship put its roots into that balmy autumn evening, and blossomed through the busy weeks ahead. By the end of that first short term, they might have known each other years: sharing secrets, clothes and sound advice. Fran and Lyn, inseparable as sisters.

3

'Remember that time we hired a punt?' Lyn asked her, smiling: drawing her gently back towards the past.

'God, yes. *Frannie and Lyn Go Boating*. And wasn't *that* a bloody disaster . . . ?' But she was smiling herself, recalling how that afternoon had gone: a piece of farce so perfect that they'd ended up quite helpless with the giggles (though without a pole). And underpinning it, the river's calm, the spires that gleamed with sunlight on the skyline; a clocktower chiming three . . .

'Why don't you take those sunglasses off?' Lyn said, making a mischievous face, in case Fran took it the wrong way. 'People will think you're a spy or something . . .'

Fran stared at her for a moment; sensed a flicker of unease behind her friend's determined smile. Then, slowly, she reached up and took her shades off. They were the pair she'd always used to wear: cheap wraparound black plastic. Her mocking, mock defence against being photographed and filmed. No laughing matter now, though; she hardly ventured out without them. They filtered the day – made it colourless and safe. Their lenses were anonymous, a mask.

The coffee bar grew brighter; Lyn watched her, looking anxious. And how must *I* look? Fran thought. She knew how she felt: as if she'd pulled her knickers down in public. That helpless; that exposed.

But she placed them on the tabletop, beside her sipped-at cup, and clasped her hands upon them. She didn't need a mirror to see the paleness of her face, the vulnerable depths of her wide green eyes. She could read all that from Lyn's concerned expression.

Go on, she thought, *just tell me I've lost weight*. She'd always been a slender girl – a real Slim Susan, Mum said – but now she felt uncomfortable and scrawny. And while Lyn still wore her dark hair in a stylish, silky bob, she'd let her own grow shaggy: a malty mane that brushed against her shoulders.

But Lyn said nothing; just placed her hand on Fran's, and gently squeezed.

'You're sure you want to do this today?' she asked after a pause.

Fran nodded quickly: shaking off temptation before it really got a grip. 'Have to start somewhere.' Especially *there* . . . where it had all begun.

'There's no hurry. Plenty of time . . .' From the look on Lyn's face, she wasn't sure if it was a good idea at all.

Fran drank some more cool coffee, and changed the subject. 'How's the thesis coming on?'

Lyn wavered, then went with the flow. Smiled modestly. 'Oh . . . it's coming.'

'So, when's it going to be *Doctor* Simmons, then?'

'God, don't ask . . .' But she was beaming at the prospect, and Fran felt a little warmer, deep inside. It eased the guilt she felt for having missed Lyn's graduation; she wouldn't lose this coming second chance. Even as they chatted on, she searched Lyn's smiley face. It sounded like her future was as clear as her complexion. No storms on her horizon; not a cloud in her blue sky . . .

'You're working, then?' she asked her.

'Mm,' said Lyn, 'but not this afternoon. It's temping – just to pay the bills. I'm a bit of a church mouse at the moment . . .' She flicked at the sleeve of her well-cut suit. Fran couldn't help but smile to herself.

Lyn hadn't noticed; her own gaze lingered on her cup. Carefully she set it down, and bit her lip; then took the plunge.

'Craig's been in touch,' she said.

Fran's chest grew hot and heavy in the silence that followed. She fiddled with her rings; then swallowed. 'Is he here?'

Lyn nodded. 'Staying with friends in London.' Her eyes were down again, embarrassed. 'He . . . never forgot you, Fran. All the time you were . . .' Tailing off, she twisted round to unfasten her bag, and took an envelope out. After the briefest hesitation, she laid it on the tabletop between them.

Fran rested her mouth against her hands, staring at the neat white rectangle. No stamp on it, and no address; it had gone from hand to hand. Just one word, written with a flourish. Her own name.

'He gave me that for you,' Lyn said, unnecessarily. 'He wants to see you.'

Oh, Jesus, Fran thought numbly. She felt empty inside: unable to react.

Lyn leaned forward. 'Fran, we're *here*,' she whispered. 'You don't have to face anything alone. He really cares for you – believe me. Just . . . let us hold your hands; go through it with you.'

Fran felt a tear trickle down her cheek; like the first drop heralding a downpour. She fought to keep herself in check. Lyn took her hands and held them. The threatened cloudburst faded back to grumble gloomily on the horizon.

Fran took a shaky breath. '. . . Thanks.' She sniffed, her eyes still shining wet; then managed a damp smile. 'You're an angel, Lyn. Friend in a million . . .'

'Let's leave it for today,' suggested Lyn. 'Come on: let's just go and sit in the Meadow . . .'

'I can't,' Fran said, and shook her head. 'We'll take it slowly . . . but I have to go back. I can't go any further till I've laid the past to rest.'

CHAPTER II

Grey Ravens

I

Lyn drove out of Oxford and northward through the country-side. The world through Fran's shades had a monochrome look, but she could smell the breadth and texture of the fields: new-cut grass, and fresh manure, and fleeting wild flowers. Her heart throbbed hard, constricted. She felt a little sick.

Lunch was a welcome hiatus. Past a picturesque village, they found a shady spot above the road, and stopped to eat. Lyn had prepared a modest picnic: French bread sandwiches, fresh fruit, and cans of sparkling wine. Two glasses and a tablecloth as well: she'd always been an organized young lady.

'Found yourself a man yet?' Fran asked casually, between mouthfuls. She'd sneaked a glance at Lyn's left hand soon after they'd met, and the ring finger was bare.

Lyn gave one of her shy smiles, and shook her head. 'Not yet. Too busy. Too much work . . .' She ducked a wasp, and swatted it away. 'Besides . . . I'm not sure if I *want* a relationship right now . . .'

That last one really hurt you, didn't it? Fran thought, but didn't say so. Best to let that lie. Sitting back against the rough bark of the tree, she recalled how it had started. Lyn had been coy at first – Big Secret – but of course she'd had to share it in the end. He was from one of the other colleges: she'd met him at a lecture. The relationship had deepened during Hilary Term; Fran hardly met the bloke throughout, and saw Lyn less and less. She knew she'd been quite jealous at the time. Not that she didn't have interests of her own. The day Lyn came to tell her how their Valentine's date had gone, Fran had been prostrate with the after-effects of chasing Cruise missiles round Salisbury Plain until four in the morning. There Lyn had been, bright-faced and bursting to tell all, while her confidante was half-asleep and lolling in her chair . . .

She took another bite of bread: the taste as bland as cardboard in her mouth. She didn't feel the least bit hungry. The countryside was peaceful in the sunshine; sheep and lambs were grazing in the field. But their destination – still miles distant – had already cast its aura this far out. She felt its chill and shadow on her heart.

And then there was Craig's letter: folded and crammed, still sealed, into her bum-bag. Food for thought that overfilled her stomach.

Lyn sipped at her wine; hooked her hair behind her ear. She sensed Fran watching from behind her shades, and beamed encouragingly. Fran found the strength to smile faintly back.

'All right,' she said. 'Let's go. Let's get it done.'

2

They came to the wire. It stretched and weaved away to right and left. Reinforced mesh, with razor coils on top.

Fran stood there on the footpath, staring blankly through the fence. There was an empty road beyond it; then a vast expanse of grass. In the hazy middle distance, a scattering of buildings basked – smooth-backed, like concrete whales.

Her fingers closed on Lyn's: so tightly that she feared they might do damage. But the gesture was convulsive, and she couldn't let them go. They'd linked hands coming up the hill from Heyford – Fran had wavered to a standstill when she saw the water-tower. It rose above the skyline like a scaffold.

'Come on, now,' Lyn had whispered. 'You can do it.'

If she felt her knuckles popping now, her quiet voice didn't show it. 'Are those the hangars, then . . . ?'

Fran nodded once, like someone in a trance. The last time she'd been up here, the day had been as bright and hot as this one; but lamps had still been burning on those buildings – shimmering like day-stars through the haze. The quick reaction flight was lurking there: bombed-up, and ready to go.

Today, the lights were off again; the hangars seemed abandoned. An eerie silence hung across the base.

'Ugly-looking things . . .' Lyn murmured.

'They called them TAB-Vees,' Fran said; the term came back to her from nowhere. 'Theatre Airbase Vulnerability Shelters.' She nodded to herself; then pinched a smile. 'I used to know all the jargon, you know. Proper little trainspotter, I was.'

'But nothing's in them now?'

Fran shook her head. 'They've gone. They've all flown home . . .' The hush was huge: unnatural. Her inner ear recalled that disembodied rumbling in the air, when the hangars had been open, the aircraft on the prowl. Turning, she studied the empty sky – half-expecting to see a light in the distance: a bright, approaching star. A roaring bomber coming in to land.

A cloud obscured the sun. Its shadow slid across them, the green fields greying out – and she found herself right back where she had started.

It had been an overcast day, that Saturday in autumn '88. She could almost smell the damp October air; the thinning veil of mist along the fence-line. The bitter tang of jet-fuel as the planes came screaming in.

She watched them land, like hungry iron hawks. The camouflaged ones were bombers, she was told: F-111s that could carry nuclear loads. They were followed down by others, grey as ghosts. Those were the Ravens, someone said: the radar-jamming planes.

Ravens. It had struck her, though she couldn't quite say why; the weirdness of the choice of name, perhaps. Sinister, portentous – but a raven's coat was black. These grey things came like spirits: like pallid spectres of their former selves . . .

Her fingers loosened; Lyn's hand slipped away. And Lyn could only hover, like an anxious hanger-on. Excluded by the memories of things she hadn't shared.

'What are you seeing, Fran . . . ?' she almost whispered.

But Fran didn't answer; her mind was too full of restless ghosts.

Of *Ravens*.

3

It had still been Freshers' Week when Paul had knocked on her door; she hadn't even got her posters up. The societies were recruiting fit to bust, of course; she'd seen the cross on his lapel, and guessed what he was selling.

'Would I be right in thinking you're a Christian?' he'd said, after a brief, polite preamble.

'Well . . .' Fran said, and felt a bit evasive. It was true she'd shopped around at the Freshers' Fair. The Student Christian Movement had intrigued her; she rather liked their radical approach. But the college branch of *Greenpeace* was the only one she'd joined. She classed herself as C of E, but hadn't been to church for quite a while. A charismatic-slanted group at school had sucked her in, bolstering her final year with happy-clappy pap; but in pulling up her roots to come here, she'd set herself adrift on that score too. Simplicity had brought no satisfaction: *If God gave me brains, why won't you let me use them?* Right now, she wasn't sure what she believed.

And now this pleasant second-year was trying to tempt her back. Whichever group he spoke for, they were doubtless keen on choruses and earnest Bible study. She shifted with discomfort at the thought.

'I'm still deciding at the moment,' she said carefully.

Paul gestured, smiling. 'Fair enough. But me and some

friends are going on a sort of religious outing on Saturday, and I wondered if you'd maybe like to come . . . ?'

Fran hesitated. 'Going where?'

'To Upper Heyford airbase,' Paul said softly. 'A place that *needs* to hear the Word of Life.'

Now that, she'd told him afterwards, *was what I* call *a religious outing*.

The base had been the scene of a national demo; the Christian groups had gathered at Gate 8. Walking down the track towards it, the sight of those sombre, vaulted hangars so close to the fence had given her a chill. A brooding sense of threat hung all about them. Paul told her that the bombs were stored elsewhere, but it felt like one was ticking in each building.

The service, in their shadow, was more stirring than she'd dreamed. She'd listened to the speakers, and joined in with the songs; shared the Peace with total strangers; hugged Paul tight. As people breached the wire and got arrested, she'd clung to the fence and shouted her support.

It was a rainbow congregation, lively and colourful; but most of all she remembered the Dominicans, in their solemn cloaks, and their banner behind them: a black dog running, with a firebrand in its jaws.

Paul had led her on down the perimeter path; taught her the difference between Blazer patrol trucks and Hummvee armoured cars (while one of the latter paced them, like a hunchbacked iron toad). An impromptu Mass was being held near the Peace Camp. Paul, being a Methodist, hung back – but Fran went and knelt at the roadside, to take a torn-off piece of Tesco's Sliced, and sip from the chipped cup of wine. And all the time, beyond the fence, the planes were prowling past, their tailfin beacons pulsing bloody red.

They'd hung around in the waning afternoon, until the people who'd been arrested were finally released. Then one of the Oxford groups invited them back for a social at someone's house. It lasted late into the evening, and she'd loved it: food and drink and dry good humour, ending up with some decidedly secular songs. She sang along delightedly with those; but the melody that stayed in her buzzing head was one she'd heard at Heyford's iron gates. *The people who stumbled in darkness, their eyes have seen the light . . .*

4

And those who sit in the deepest pit: on them has the day dawned bright.

She ran the lines through her mind again – worrying each word like a Rosary bead; but the gloom was deep and glutinous inside her. There was just that pale, thin gleam on the horizon.

'How do you feel?' Lyn asked her gently.

They'd adjourned to a pub in Somerton, north of the airbase. Such a pretty little village, so close to that desolate field. Fran had made for the dimmest corner of the room, well away from the golden sunshine. And still she hadn't taken off her shades.

'Glad I came,' she murmured, staring down at her drink; fingers playing with the stem of her glass. 'Well no, not *glad* . . . but no regrets. I needed to start here.'

'You came out here with Paul before?' Lyn said after a pause. Proceeding with exquisite caution.

'Yeah,' Fran said. 'He brought me. And after what I saw that day, my perspectives were all different.'

Another silence, while she took a sip of wine, and set the glass down carefully. Then her shielded gaze rose back to Lyn.

'I'd never had such a sense of pure *evil*. You could feel it, coming at you through the wire. You could feel how close the warheads were; their power. Like sleeping suns . . .' She shook her head again; more like a shudder. 'And meanwhile, Cruise was coming out of Greenham, once a *month*.'

Lyn waited with her own glass barely touched.

'It scared me – so I had to get involved,' Fran went on

softly. 'Every time those missiles moved, I had to *witness* them . . .' Behind the shades, her eyes had lost their focus: but now she could see deep into the past. 'That night, they were headed for the Imber firing range – the most restricted part of the whole Plain. We tried to take a short cut: get ahead of them again. We cut across a corner of Larkhill range, the next one to the east. And Larkhill range was where we came to grief . . .' She bit down on the final word, and dropped her gaze once more.

Lyn shifted awkwardly. 'And they never found that person in the road?'

Fran didn't answer for a moment; then took a deep, slow breath, and shook her head.

'Did you hear from Paul again?'

'Not since he came out of hospital. He just withdrew from everything – like I did. Marie died, and Kate broke her back. He blamed himself for that.'

'And you . . . Do *you* feel guilty – for surviving?'

Fran wavered; gave a shrug of her thin shoulders. 'It was my fault, as much as his. I said to go for it.'

Lyn took her hand. 'Oh Frannie, don't you think that you've been punished enough? *You* were traumatized as well. That's why you had your . . . er . . .'

'My breakdown, Lyn. Just say it.'

'Sorry. Your breakdown.'

'I was in a psychie hospital for nearly a year,' Fran said in a grim, steady tone. 'Voluntary admission: clinically depressed. I didn't mention that, did I?'

Lyn made a hurt little face. 'Oh, Fran . . .'

'It must have been . . . the shock, or the concussion, but I had a real panic attack out there. I thought that things were chasing after me . . . And months, and *years* later, I was still convinced they'd creep into my room . . .' And as she voiced her dread at last, she felt the gooseflesh ripple up her arms. Just then, for just an instant, she was back on the Plain, and lost in its featureless dark.

'Shh,' Lyn whispered, massaging her hand. 'It's over now. You're safe.'

Fran swallowed back her tears again, and nodded. The flush of cold was fading, in the sunlight and Lyn's love. Her memories were twisted up: her illness had done that. Her mental illness. The thought of it still shamed her, but she'd shared it. Like naming a demon to gain power over it. The past was the past. And here she was, objective: looking back.

It's over now. You're safe. Oh God, she hoped so.

'Your parents must be so glad . . .' Lyn said. 'Seeing you able to come back here like this.'

Fran nodded again, and took her shades off – but only to wipe her eyes. 'Yeah. They've put up with me a lot, these past few years . . .'

'Your Geordie accent's coming back, you know,' Lyn said: a tentative attempt to tease.

'Is it?' Fran said wryly. 'I can't tell. We moved to Derbyshire ten years ago – that's practically Down South!'

Silence settled between them. The ticking of a clock was quite distinct. Lyn moistened her lips.

'Where was it you said you'd meet the man of your dreams?'

The gambit won a rueful smile. 'Heaven's Field.' Fran murmured back. 'Up north, on Hadrian's Wall.'

'So, did you ever take Craig there?'

Fran sniffed, and shook her head.

'Are you going to see him?'

Fran shook her head again. Not negative this time; nonplussed. 'I don't know,' she said softly.

And she didn't. Thinking of Craig sent a giddy ripple through her – a sense of need as physical as hunger. But this was four years later, and the world had changed around. To visit old haunts was one thing; to meet old ghosts was something else again.

The conflict of emotions filled her mind; but something more subliminal still lingered. The faintest, phantom echo of that moment on the Plain. As if those twisted memories were still alive behind her: more distant now, but following her trail. As relentless and black as a Dominican dog.

5

Lyn's flat was in a quiet, leafy street off Iffley Road: part of the first floor of a conversion. Fran wandered through, admiring, as Lyn showed her around: a cheerfully self-deprecating hostess – but Fran's small suitcase made her feel too much like what she was. A stranger, from the past, just passing through.

'This'll be yours,' Lyn told her brightly, opening the door on her spare room. A futon was spread out, all ready; the pillowcase and quilt smelt freshly washed.

'I'm not sure how long I'm staying . . .' Fran murmured.

Lyn's beaming face grew earnest. 'You're welcome for as long as you like – all right? As long as you need.'

'I'm . . . not very good company at the moment. Need a lot of time to myself . . .'

'I can understand that. You need a base, you need a bed . . . they're yours. Other than that, you can come and go as you want.' She hesitated, almost shyly. 'But I'd be glad to keep you company, whenever that's okay. I've really missed you, Fran . . .

'Now,' she went on quickly, before they both got embarrassed, 'would you like some coffee?'

'Oh, please.' Fran put her case down on the bed, and went over to the window. The evening was warm and light: the air like honey. She peered across the rooftops for a minute, listening to the distant city sounds – and those that Lyn was making in the kitchen. Peace, domestic comfort, all around.

Her heart began to race then; before she even realized that she'd just made her decision. Biting her lip, she went through towards the sounds of brewing coffee.

Lyn looked round, smiling. Wiping down her breakfast plates, and putting them away.

Fran swallowed. 'There's something else. I need to tell you.' But in the expectant pause that followed, she no longer thought she could.

'No hurry,' Lyn said gently. 'We've plenty of time . . .'

Fran glanced aside. An itemized phone bill caught her eye: stuck to the freezer door with a cat-shaped magnet. Staring at it, she said: 'When I was in hospital . . . it wasn't just depression. I was hallucinating; hearing voices.'

Silence from Lyn.

'And I never told them,' Fran went on, with just a hint of tremble in her voice. 'I never said a word. I thought that if I did, they wouldn't let me out again.'

Another pause. She risked a look. Lyn's eyes were wide, her air less certain. 'Oh God, Fran . . .'

'But I'm better now,' Fran finished quickly. 'They just went of their own accord. Not a whisper for six months . . .' She took a shaky breath. 'And I've told no one else about them. Not even Mum and Dad.'

Lyn's reassuring smile looked forced. 'It might be . . . an idea to tell *someone*, though . . .'

'I have,' Fran came back evenly. 'I've just told *you*. And believe me, it's a load off my shoulders.'

Lyn nodded, looking doubtful, mechanically polishing a bowl. 'But just to be sure . . .'

'Oh Lyn, don't worry: I'm not a bloody schizophrenic or something. It was just my mind getting straightened out. I'm all right now.'

Lyn put down the bowl, and came across and hugged her. A gesture worth a million words. *I'm not unclean*, Fran thought – and held on tight enough to hurt.

'Sorry,' Lyn said after a minute. 'I know how hard that must have been to say. I'm really, really glad you told me first . . .' When she eased away, her smile looked fresher: as if she'd shrugged a burden off as well. A weight of doubt and prudent disapproval. Fran grinned – and felt quite giddy with relief. Her leap of faith had landed on firm ground.

Oh Lyn, you angel. How ever did I find a friend like you?

With the subject safely broached, the rest came easier. She described the hospital, the staff, her fellow patients. Talking it out felt physical, a purging of her system. Like the tears that Lyn had won from her before; the rains that broke the drought of her depression . . .

'What sort of things did these voices say?' Lyn asked her after supper. Her tone still cautious, but curious too.

Fran hesitated. 'I don't know: that's the really weird thing. It was a man's voice, just a whisper . . . I'd look around, you know? – and the room would be empty. But it wasn't English; more like Dutch or something.'

'God, it must have frightened you.'

'It did. You bet it did. And yet . . . the tone, it wasn't really threatening. It sounded *urgent*. More like an appeal . . .'

She could analyse it calmly now; back then, she'd just been petrified with fear. The whispers had haunted her down the long, dingy corridors, insidious in their promise of madness. Perhaps finding a lump in your breast brought a stab of dread this sharp. Her voices seemed like symptoms of a tumour in her *mind*.

And if you ignored them, would they go away? A lump in her flesh would not. She'd heard of women losing precious time – too scared to see a doctor, till too late. And she'd been just as stymied: afraid to tell a soul about the voices in her head.

The world had closed down like a coffin-lid upon her; the voices were the hammer and the nails. Fragments of phrases, faint with distance; sometimes they'd fall silent for a week. The silences were worst of all. She'd sit and cringe for hours: just waiting for the words to come again.

But she'd kept them secret – and they'd gone away. The malignant lump had simply disappeared. A miracle cure must feel like this. She hardly dared believe it, even now.

'Shall we do the washing up?' she said, to change the subject.

'Oh, shh, don't worry about that . . .'

'Don't flatmates share their chores?' Fran asked her drily. 'I'd much prefer it that way. So come on, let's get to it. And then I think I'll have an early night. It's been a tiring day . . .'

6

Fran
So much has changed. The whole world's turned around. But I've not forgotten you. Can we meet someplace – and sometime soon? Lyn's got my number. I really hope you'll want to get in touch.
Still thinking of you
Craig

Fran read the letter through again. Much more slowly: savouring each word. Her heart beat like a slow drum in her chest.

His face was very clear now; the years between had faded like a fog. She remembered every line of his rugged good looks. The short brown hair, brushed back; the deep-set eyes. The wry mouth, sometimes smiling; sometimes grim.

Still thinking of you – even four years down the road. She felt a pang of pleasure, a twinge of helpless pride. Like someone with a treasure, hidden secretly away. *He's mine*, she thought: *he still belongs to me.*

She folded the letter carefully, and slid it back into the envelope. Laying it aside on the bookcase, she started to unpack. Nightie, towel, toilet bag . . . but then she let an impulse overcome her, and delved into a side-pocket instead. For a moment her fingers searched in vain; but then they found the badge, and drew it out.

She'd been wearing it the day they met. A rectangle of metal, with a sheen like bluish gold. The stern and haloed image of a saint. She ran her thumb across the rough, raised lettering. Cyrillic script: an alien language. Only the dates made sense.

988–1988. One thousand years. Stretching like a bridge from the Dark Age past to the year she'd come to Oxford.

She laid her head down cautiously. First night away from home for many months; her first night back in Oxford since her breakdown. For an hour or more she lingered on the very edge of sleep: afraid of what unconsciousness might bring. But the stresses of the day had worn her out. Oblivion pounced, and caught her unawares.

She didn't dream.

CHAPTER III

Cross of Iron

I

'Is this seat taken?'

Fran studied her drink for a moment longer; then slowly, almost archly raised her head. After all the keyed-up waiting, she was suddenly so cool. She'd known it was him as he'd crossed the room towards her. She'd known it when he walked through the door.

Craig stood there, looking just a little awkward. She'd sensed him hesitating on the threshold; how long had he been standing just outside? But to judge by his face, his doubts had been won over. For all that he was ten years older than her, his smile was as engaging as an eager little boy's.

She gestured. 'Be my guest.'

He pulled out the stool, and sat. Still smiling; but his pale blue eyes were watchful. Their clearness – with his slightly scrappy haircut – helped preserve his boyish aspect; but that handsome face had harshness in its lines. Fran felt herself excited by the contrast – just like she'd been before.

He'd brought his bottle with him from the bar. A Budweiser, of course. He raised it to her – 'Hi,' – and took a pull.

She raised her glass in turn; then sat back, looking smug.

Craig cocked his head, enquiring. 'What?'

'I just *love* a man out of uniform.'

He gave a snort at that, amused. His coat was brown brushed leather, well worn-in. Fran, by contrast, was wearing Lyn's best bomber jacket, complete with sheepskin lining. Which was quite ironic, really.

'How have you been?' Craig asked after a pause. His tone was quiet and calm, as always; the concern was in his eyes.

'All right,' Fran told him softly. 'Coming on.'

'You're looking well.'

She shrugged.

The lunchtime buzz and bustle of *The Grapes* drew in around them.

Her hand was on the table; so was his. She felt his need to reach across and touch her – and knew he wasn't sure how she'd react. He moistened his lips, his pale gaze still intent. 'I'm glad you called me, Fran.'

'I'm glad you waited, Craig. I *mean* that.'

He took her hand, and squeezed it. She squeezed back.

'You're sure about this afternoon?' he asked, his voice a murmur.

'Yes,' she said, still holding on. 'I'm sure.'

2

The first time she'd seen him, he was doing some repair work on a truck. Thinking back to that first moment, she knew she hadn't dreamed where it would lead. All she'd done was stand there, feeling curious: wanting contact. Above all else, she'd wanted to *get through*.

He'd realized she was watching; turned and grinned. Encouraged, she'd smiled back. He'd wavered for a moment, then wiped his hands and slowly walked across. Right up to the high mesh fence that blocked his way.

'Hello,' Fran said politely.

He nodded amiably, tweaking the brim of his cap between finger and thumb. His camouflage fatigues – green, brown and black – bore a master sergeant's stripes: she was getting good at recognizing ranks. FLAHERTY was the name stencilled over his breast pocket.

Fran hooked her fingers through the mesh, and leaned against the wire. She wondered if her shades made her look flirty. 'How are you liking England, then?' she asked.

'It's not so bad,' he murmured. 'Nice little place you've got here. Some of the natives aren't too friendly . . . but there you go.'

She took that coyly; cocked her head. 'I thought you weren't supposed to talk to us.' He'd caught sight of her Cruisewatch badge, of course.

His smile grew broader. 'I'm a great believer in freedom of speech.'

'Which is what you're here defending?'

'Surely. Yours and mine.'

'When we put all our resources into preparing for war, humanity hangs from a cross of iron. You know who said that?'

He shook his head, still smiling.

'Dwight D. Eisenhower.'

'Yeah? I never heard that.' He leaned forward for a better look at the other badge she wore. Fran eased herself away along the fence; he followed. She felt a sense of mischief, like playing hard to get. The barrier was frustrating. She clung to it, and kept him close.

'Aha,' he murmured drily, having seen the thing at last. 'I *knew* you were a commie.'

'No, I'm not,' she told him. 'That's my *icon*.'

Intrigued, he studied it more closely. 'What does it say?'

'Russia Baptized: One Thousand Years.'

He raised an eyebrow. 'You been over there?'

''Fraid not. I got it at the Orthodox church in Oxford.'

'Oxford, huh? That where you come from?'

'It's where I'm studying.'

'Always wanted to visit Oxford . . .' he said lightly, and would have said more, but a patrol truck was approaching: chugging up along the perimeter road. It came to a halt behind him, and the driver climbed out. Fran saw it was a woman, not much older than herself. Dressed in camouflage like

Flaherty, but with a black beret – and a holstered pistol at her belt. MATTHEWS said the name-strip on her blouse.

'Any problem, Sergeant?'

'No problem.' He held Fran's gaze for a moment longer; then turned away. Fran stared at his retreating back, then looked across at Matthews. The other woman was eyeing her levelly. Her fresh-complexioned face was set and grim.

Fran tipped her head back: took it on the chin. Resentment twinged inside her, mixed with something more unsettling. She'd thought there'd be some fellow-feeling somewhere – one woman to another. But there wasn't the slightest spark of it between them.

She'd shoot me, if she had to. Shoot me dead. The knowledge took the wind out of her sails.

Flaherty was back at his truck. He gave her a final, sidelong glance; no more. Matthews was still watching her. Dispirited, Fran turned and walked away.

But now she was here again, and reaching out to touch the fence. Curling her fingers round the cold green strands, and holding tight.

'Looks different,' Craig said softly; 'from the wrong side of the wire.'

She glanced over her shoulder. *He* looked different: standing there behind her.

They'd driven up the road from the A339, Craig silent at the wheel of his rented car. The tunnel of trees had closed around them, channelling them through gloom until they were almost at the fence. They'd parked there and got out; Fran pausing with her hand on the open door. It had rained that afternoon, and the wood smelled damp and green, still dripping. The song of a blackbird came from somewhere close.

Greenham Common airbase lay in silence.

They were close to the silos here. The last time she'd ventured up this way, the MoD police had chased her off. A winter's night, dark early – but the those sinister mounds had been brightly lit. They'd made her think of spiders' lairs – nestled deep in their funnels of gleaming razor wire.

A ripple of cold went through her flesh. She shivered, and hunched her shoulders.

The webs were empty now, though; their spider-holes as derelict as Heyford's silent hangars. Life had gone on while she'd lingered in the dark. The world had changed so much.

'I heard they're gonna turn it into a theme park,' Craig said, with wry amusement. 'Or something like that.'

She shook her head, bemused. The place had been an inspiration through her teens; had drawn her down from Oxford again and again. Now here it lay, forgotten. What was it they'd sung around the campfire? *And we shall build Jerusalem in England's Greenham pleasant land.* Well the missiles were gone – but no sense of peace had come to take their place. The silos had a haunted feel; like burial mounds, robbed out.

The evening sky was overcast and low. Crimson light seeped through it here and there, staining the clouds like blackberry juice.

'I didn't like it here,' Craig murmured.

Fran turned her head.

'Don't get me wrong,' he went on drily. 'I think we were right; I think we did some good. But we never fitted in. Just stuck in our own little world behind the wire. And so much hostility outside . . .'

'Was that the only reason?'

He was silent for a minute. 'I'd be lying if I said that sharing a base with ninety-six Cruise missiles didn't give me the creeps sometimes.'

'It wasn't the nukes that scared me,' Fran said slowly, looking back towards the row of gutted silos. 'It was the fact that people were actually ready to *use* the bloody things.'

'It wouldn't have happened. That was the whole point.'

'Maybe not. No, really . . . maybe not. But the *readiness* was there.'

A pause. Then he slid his arms around her waist. Fran stood

there for a moment, not reacting; then let herself relax against his body. He squeezed her gently; touched his cheek to hers.

'You know what it reminds me of?' he said after a while. 'Cape Canaveral. You go there now, there's just these burned-out shells of concrete, where the rockets blasted off. Dead silence. When the clouds are like this, and there's a wind off the desert, it's so damn' eerie. It feels like the end of the world.'

CHAPTER IV

Testament

I

Lyn tapped her pen against her teeth – and wondered if she'd found her man at last.

The library was hushed, as if expectant. The lamp above her recess cast a cosy golden glow. The cloudy afternoon had brought a premature dusk, like grey fog seeping inward through the windows. The lamps were beacons, keeping it at bay. Back down the unlit aisles and stacks, the gloom was growing thicker.

The manuscript before her was the fragment of a will. Ninth century West Saxon; the testator's name was written *aeðelgar*. She felt uncertain, rather than excited. Was it him? Perhaps – but she was never going to know. He didn't even have a face, to match the name against.

She'd been looking for him since childhood – whether consciously or not. It went back to that holiday in Norfolk. The thesis she was writing now had been conceived that summer. Not that she had known it then: she'd just been ten or twelve. They'd visited an ancient church, for Daddy to take pictures. Martin had moped around outside, as little brothers would, but she had walked on in to look around. The place still had its medieval rood screen, with painted figures dimly visible. Pictures of saints, according to the leaflet – some of them not known outside the district.

One disfigured shape had caught her eye. It had been worn to a shadow, with the face completely gone. *The presence of a raven suggests Paul of Thebes or possibly Elijah.* But maybe he was just another nameless local saint.

It seemed there were traditions of some link with nearby Ely. She'd heard how Hereward the Wake had fought the Normans there. Was this one of his warriors? Or a hermit of the fens who'd prayed for him?

She'd walked out of the church – and like a shadow, he had followed. Ever since that day, he'd been an element in her imagination. How had local glory turned to centuries of silence? What could be inferred about the medieval mind? The thought had slowly gelled into her topic for research: this interface of history and myth.

The study would be a social one; but still there was this itchy fascination. The twelve-year-old inside her kept on wondering. She couldn't help but follow up the vaguest reference; the thesis grew in tandem with her search. Here, an ancient grant of land; there, a manuscript that spoke of *scincræft*. Cryptic mentions; fleeting clues. They'd led her to this brittle testament.

She glanced at her watch – it had just gone six – and wondered how Fran and Craig were getting on. The rain had stopped some hours ago, but the sky outside was dim. They knew that she was working late tonight. They'd be eating out, Fran said – somewhere in Oxford. She was aiming to be back by nine.

But what if she'd upset herself, revisiting the past? What if the reunion wasn't working out . . . ?

Lyn realized she was doodling, and sat up straighter. She read her rough translation through again, then looked back to the text. The Old English script seemed to creep before her eyes: clinging to the page with its hooks and downward strokes. Her attention was drawn once more by the name of the testator.

aeðelgar

It was different from the wills she'd seen before. Part of it was set out like a poem.

Seek a lord *whose heart is whole*
And hold to him *until his days are done*

Written by the man himself, or by some later copyist? This version was two hundred years more recent. So no, she couldn't even answer that.

We know nothing at all about Æthelgar.

She re-read her last sentence with a real sense of loss. Whoever he'd been, the flow of time had carried him away. There was just this frozen glimpse on the horizon. Like Martin's stars – so distant that you saw them in the past. 'See that one?' he'd told her once. 'It could have died a thousand years ago. Now *that's* the kind of ghost I can believe in . . .'

Dispirited, she pushed him from her thoughts – and then felt guilty. Frustration gave the knife an extra twist. She'd better take a break, before she really got upset. Gathering her papers up, she read her glum conclusion one more time. The verdict seemed to mock her: an admission of defeat.

And yet the name was curiously familiar.

2

She was still worrying it when Fran got back; the chapter only halfway pieced together. Her neatly ordered notes were strewn all over her front room: a pile on the floor, a sheaf on the arm of the sofa. One open textbook lay upon another. But the A4 sheet in front of her stayed blank. The flow of her analysis had got itself hung up.

We know nothing at all about Æthelgar.

Perhaps she'd seen the name before in one of Daddy's books. Since childhood, she'd spent hours in the treasure-house of his study. The Old and Middle English texts had lured her with their strangeness; the manuscripts enchanted her like giant picture books. Martin had come and teased her: called her bookworm. She could hear her brother's goading voice right now . . .

Oh, where had she seen that bloody name before? It niggled, like an itch she couldn't scratch.

Lyn allowed herself another chocolate biscuit, and crunched it feeling guilty; then straightened as she heard Fran's key in the lock.

She went into the hall, trying not to look too anxious. 'How did it go?'

'Fine,' Fran told her, smiling. 'Really well.'

Lyn could see that it had. Fran had been so nervous over breakfast, just picking at her cereal; but her face looked fresher now, and more relaxed. Lyn stayed where she was, admiring. 'That jacket really suits you . . .'

'I know. So can I keep it?'

'Don't push your luck, Miss Bennett. Do you want coffee?'

'Mmm, please.' Fran followed her as far as the kitchen threshold; watched as her friend got the percolator going. Lyn glanced over her shoulder.

'You can ask him back, you know. I do quite like the man.'

'Thanks . . .' Fran murmured. She pushed her hands into the jacket pockets, and rested her shoulder up against the doorframe. Leaned her head against it too. 'We're trying to take things one step at a time.'

'Where's he staying?'

'The Randolph.'

'Expensive tastes.'

Fran grinned. 'Well he's American, isn't he?'

'Help yourself to bikkies. They're in the front room, on the table.'

Fran wandered through. The biscuit jar was doubling as paperweight for some of Lyn's notes. 'How's the thesis coming, then?' she called.

'Slowly. Too easy to get distracted – not by you, don't worry, I need the break.' Lyn joined her, took a biscuit of her own.

'I was reading someone's will today, and it sent my mind off at a tangent. I just keep wondering who he was.'

'Why, did he leave you anything?'

'Hardly, since he died about a thousand *years* ago.'

'Well, you've made a start, at least,' Fran told her drily.

Lyn pulled a rueful face. 'That's just his name. I doodled that.'

Fran craned her head. 'So how do you say that, then?'

'Athelgar. The TH sound was written like a D, it's called an *Eth* . . .'

'Lithp'd a lot, the Anglo-Saxons, did they?'

Lyn didn't deign to rise to that. '. . . And AE had an A sound – like in cat.'

'A*thel*gar . . .' Fran murmured, trying it out. 'So who was he?'

'I don't know. No one does. He died in Wessex, but he might have been in East Anglia at one time. Maybe he's a saint I saw a painting of once. Then again, I dug up something about *shine-craft* – meaning phantom-art, or magic . . .' Lyn shrugged. 'According to the will, he was an *eorl*.'

'Meaning an earl, presumably?'

'No, not then. It was more of a warrior's term.' She gestured. 'A man of high degree. A man of *honour*.'

'Sounds just my type,' murmured Fran with a mischievous smile, and pinched another biscuit.

3

Both of them had dreams that night, as the slow stars turned above the silent house.

Fran took ages getting off to sleep. The barrow-mounds of Greenham were still looming in her head. Rusty iron, and crumbling concrete; cavernous black gateways. The watch-tower like a giant alien robot in the midst.

The futon creaked beneath her as she turned, and turned again. A nauseous chill had wormed into her stomach. Those silos would stand open until doomsday; she'd felt the drip . . . drip . . . drip of their decay. But what might still be lurking in their shadows; in the labyrinth of tunnels underneath?

Something could have seen her from that long-deserted watchtower. Something could have crept out of its lair, and followed them. All the way back here, to sleeping Oxford.

Fear embraced her like a ghost; she wriggled to get free. The past was in the room with her – a shadow at the foot of the bed. The part she hadn't shared with Lyn. The part she couldn't bear to think about.

Her fingers found the cross around her neck. A Coventry cross, of silver nails: a Christmas present from Lyn. She turned and tweaked it, listening to the hush.

But even Lyn was sleeping, in her tidy bed next door. Fran could almost hear her gentle breathing. Like a soft, recorded message. *Lyn's not home right now. You're on your own.*

The house was quiet around her. The night outside was soundless – undisturbed. She pulled the pillow close, and closed her eyes. Her mind cast round for brighter thoughts, to keep the dark at bay.

Where was it you said you'd meet the man of your dreams . . . ?

Wistfully she huddled up, and thought of Heaven's Field. She'd been about thirteen when she had gone there with her parents – their final summer in Northumberland. The sky had been like heaven all right, above the gaunt black cross. She summoned back its pinkish glow – the tufts of golden cloud. There'd been a famous battle here, in Anglo-Saxon times. Northumbria freed from tyranny, and won back to the faith.

She'd wandered round the empty field, enchanted by the twilight. And over by the church, she'd had the strangest rush of feeling: a rich, exciting glow from deep inside. It was over in a moment, but had left her flushed and giddy. A sense of being *needed* – and adored.

Even then, she'd realized that it hadn't been religious. The thrill was much too physical for that – tugging at the instincts that were stirred by boys and babies. She'd told Lyn so, years later, in an earnest heart-to-heart. It had felt more like the shadow of a lover; a presence in the marriage bed she hadn't dreamed of yet. A closeness that was soul to soul, as well as skin to skin.

She'd hoped it was a foretaste of her knight in shining armour – something for the boys at school to match themselves against. But that was just an old, romantic notion; Craig was real.

And what she'd felt this afternoon was pretty much the same.

The sun was going down on Heaven's Field. Bathing in the memory – its warmth, and rosy light – she let herself relax into oblivion.

By rights, she should have taken that bright image to her dreams. Yet what her mind threw up was something different. She found herself, in spirit, at an isolated junction, along a road she hadn't walked for years. Not Heaven's Field, but Salisbury Plain; a place where nothing moved. The bleak, deserted grassland of the Imber firing range.

Danger Area.

Nervously she looked around. Sullen hills rose up to left and right, cutting off the outside world. The public roads were miles away; no passer-by could see her. She was stuck here, in the middle, all alone.

The junction was smeared by tank-tracks, its approaches hedged with posts to shore it up. Set against the gloomy slopes, they made her think of First World War defences: the barbed wire stripped away to leave the pickets standing bare.

There were insects buzzing faintly in the grass – but the silence overwhelmed them. That huge, unnatural firing range silence: as pregnant with threat as the grey clouds overhead.

A wrecked tank sat atop the nearest hill: its turret painted orange, for the guns of other tanks to zero in on. She studied it uneasily; then looked away, along the eastbound road. Imber village lay in that direction – out of sight, but close enough to fill her with foreboding.

She glimpsed a moving figure then – away to the left, where the ground began to rise. It was casting round, as if in search of something. She saw that he was dressed in black. A long coat or a cloak flapped out around him.

The icy surge of panic should have shocked her awake. But something deep inside her was determined to hang on. Fascinated, petrified, she watched him scour the heath. He waded through the knee-high grass – then crouched to root around. His face was turned away from her. Despite the muffling garment, she could see his short fair hair.

He seemed to sense her presence, then – and swung around to look. He didn't have a metal face. He had no face at all. There was just a patch of shadow, framed with gold. Fran recoiled in horror, still suspended in the dream. And then the mouthless figure spoke to her.

She didn't understand a word – but recognized the voice. With a wail of fright, she came flailing to the surface, kicking back the duvet to sit upright on the bed. Her nightie and her briefs were damp; she was suddenly and wretchedly convinced she'd wet herself. Then realized it was only sticky sweat.

Oh God. She cupped her hands against her face.

It was the voice she'd heard in hospital; the harsh, corrupted language was the same. And so was its appealing tone: the note of desperation. She felt he'd meant to snatch at her, and drag her down with him.

But the room was silent now. She strained her ears against the hissing hush. It hadn't really been the voice; just memory. An echo. Now that she had woken up, it wouldn't come again. Not even if she waited until dawn.

Full of her fear, she hugged herself, and started counting minutes, one by one.

Lyn dreamed of Martin. He was waiting in the hall as she came downstairs. *You look great*, he said, and she could see how much he meant it in his face. The spiteful fights of growing-up were all forgotten now. Still fiddling with an earring, she let her smile grow wider. As she gave him a twirl to show off her dress, the house was spun away into oblivion.

She woke up awkwardly; her room felt unfamiliar and distorted in the dark. A piece of dream went scuttling away. Lyn recoiled, and shrank against the headboard. She felt a rush of dread from out of childhood – back in her old bedroom, with its imps and demons scurrying around. And the pale, grinning skeleton of Death behind the door.

Instinctively she turned her head – then sighed, and let her shoulders slump again. The door was safely closed, of course, her dressing gown a silky wraith against it. The demons melted back into the picture that they'd come from: the print in Daddy's study that had scared her as a girl. *Death of the Miser*, by Hieronymus Bosch. It had figured in her nightmares more than once. But not for years . . .

Athelgar.

Sitting there, she realized where she'd seen the name before. She'd picked at it all evening, like a scab. Now, with the top knocked off at last, she was suddenly bled dry. She curled up, feeling miserable, and didn't sleep again.

CHAPTER V

Heaven and Hell

I

Lyn had lent her a bathrobe, but Fran was dressed when she came on through for breakfast. Mucking in like a flatmate was all very well – but she still ventured round with a visitor's reserve. Finding Lyn at the table in her dressing gown was vaguely embarrassing: like having her friend at some kind of disadvantage. But Lyn looked preoccupied, and pale: chewing mechanically on her toast. Her normally bright greeting was a wan, subdued hello. Being seen half-dressed was obviously the last thing on her mind.

Fran moved past her to the coffee pot and toaster, surreptitiously glancing at the tabletop. The paper was still folded; a couple of brown envelopes lay unopened. So what was up, she wondered?

Sitting down, she saw the shadows round Lyn's eyes; the pinched look to her mouth. 'Did you sleep all right?' she asked.

Lyn shrugged, and shook her head. 'Not really. Woke up about three, and couldn't get off again. You know what it's like.'

Fran knew, all right. She'd lain awake for ages, before snatching back a couple of hours' sleep. She was just about to say so when Lyn breathed out and went on.

'I was dreaming about Martin.'

There was a wistfulness in her voice that made Fran feel a little wary. She didn't know much about Lyn's brother; had only met him once, when he'd come visiting at Oxford. He had his sister's dark, straight hair; her brown, expressive eyes.

Caught unawares, his clean-cut face was serious, almost solemn. Then Lyn had introduced him, rather proudly, and he'd charmed her with a warm, engaging smile.

'Oh,' Fran said. Then: 'What's he doing now?'

A moment's pause, Lyn staring at the table. Then she shook her head again. Said softly: 'I don't know.'

Fran put her coffee down, and waited.

'He left home two years ago. Just chucked everything and went. I got a card from him at Christmas . . . but Mum and Dad heard nothing. Not a word. It worries them so much.'

'Where is he?'

'Don't know. He didn't say. I couldn't even read the bloody *postmark*.'

Fran bit her lip. 'God, Lyn. I didn't know.' She felt a stab of guilt. 'You don't need my troubles on top of yours . . .'

Lyn waved that off. 'Don't worry. Please don't think that. He's twenty, he can look after himself . . .' She ran her hand back through her hair. 'We were happy at home, the two of us. Really happy. But it was getting so that he felt cooped up there – always under our parents' feet. He mucked his A-Levels up, you see. He couldn't get a job.'

'I remember him visiting you,' Fran said carefully. 'You got on well together, didn't you.'

'I think about him every day. I mean, I don't just sit there moping, but . . . he'll get into my head at some point. Just for a minute, maybe; but he's there.'

Fran thought of them together, in the Christ Church staircase. No shadows there, no worries; just a handsome teenage boy with his big sister. The thought of that lost happiness made her ache on Lyn's behalf. And how must their parents feel?

Maybe just the same as *hers* had, when their daughter withdrew into a world of her own: slamming the gates behind her.

'Anyway . . .' Lyn sighed, 'there's no point brooding. He'll get in touch when he's good and ready.' She straightened her back, and summoned up a smile. 'What are your plans for today? You're seeing Craig again?'

Fran nodded. 'I'm meeting him for lunch; and then we'll go . . . wherever.'

'Remember what I said about bringing him back. He's welcome. I'll cook you dinner, if you like.'

'That's an idea. That would be great, actually. When would be a good time?'

'Well . . . Not tonight, I want to stay late at the library. How about tomorrow? Ask him.'

'I will,' Fran murmured, 'thanks.' And even as she smiled, an idea slipped into her head. A sudden thought that left her short of breath. She could bring him home this afternoon, if Lyn was working late. She could shag him on the futon, and her friend would never know.

She glanced down quickly; raised her mug and drank. Surely her guilt was showing on her face. But if it was, Lyn clearly hadn't noticed. She was opening the paper in a listless sort of way.

Fran let her gaze drift off around the kitchen: a show of calm disinterest while she weighed the options up. She *couldn't* take advantage, not like that. But then again . . . where was the harm? It wasn't as if she'd lied to Lyn. She could just neglect to mention that she'd brought Craig back for tea. And let him screw her.

The prospect was as thrilling as their very first weekend. He'd taken some leave, collected her at Oxford, and driven them out to that posh country hotel. This wasn't the place to think of that (though she wanted to, right now). But her appetite was back, and undiminished. Her feelings had lain dormant, like a seed in frozen ground; but now, at last, the thaw was setting in.

Love is come again, like wheat that springeth green.

God, it was years since she'd sung that hymn. It made her think of Easter at Aldermaston. She felt a bit abashed about misusing it like that. But only a bit.

'Any shopping you'd like some help with?' she asked, as a salve for her conscience.

'It's all right, thanks. I'm going to take things easy this morning. You have a really good day.'

The churning in Fran's belly quite belied her modest smile. *I'm going to*, she thought. She couldn't wait.

2

When Fran had gone, Lyn dumped the breakfast dishes in the sink and let them soak. It normally went against the grain, to leave a chore for later; but this morning she just couldn't be bothered. The apathy extended to her morning ablutions; she hadn't had her shower yet, nor even cleaned her teeth. She was running on flat batteries – but going back to bed would do no good. It was more than simple lack of sleep that had left her feeling drained.

She walked through the flat, and found it looking duller. The carpet felt rough and fluffy under her bare feet. Bits of her thesis were still scattered round the living room. She went round picking them up, and took them over to the table.

Æthelgar. The name that had burned in her head last night seemed cold and lifeless now: like ashes in a grate. She gazed at the word with a vague sense of resentment – then dumped her notes on top, and crushed it flat.

She could remember the book quite clearly – tucked away at the end of a shelf. *Myth and Magic in Medieval Europe*. One of Daddy's expensive books. One of the ones he'd told her not to touch.

She'd kept away at first, like a good little girl. But curiosity had got the better of her in the end. She could see herself now, nine or ten years old and sitting on the carpeted floorboards with an open book before her, the summer evening sunlight spread like syrup on the wall.

The first book was huge, too big for her to hold. Most of the pages were grey, and rough: a bit like paper towels. But some were smooth and shiny, with black and white photos – or paintings in glorious colour, like the sun breaking through clouds.

It was called *The Flowering of the Middle Ages*. She'd often seen Daddy browsing through it, sitting in his easy chair beside the window. There was a painting of a knight on the cover – a horseman with a dark, mysterious face. So this evening she'd come in, and hauled it down off its shelf, and slowly started leafing through the pages. The words were dull and difficult, but the pictures held her spellbound.

The second book had caught her eye as she'd put the first away. *Magic* was the word that had intrigued her. At her age, it meant mystery, romance – and something more: a *cleverness* she envied. She wasn't quite sure what *Medieval* meant, but knew it was to do with the Middle Ages. 'Evil' was clearly a part of it, though. Perhaps it was because they'd been wickeder times . . .

She'd pulled the book out carefully. It was smaller than the other one, but thicker; it felt almost as heavy. Sitting herself down again, she started going through it. But this book, it turned out, was mostly words: page after page of them, densely packed. Only a handful of photos, and those were black and white. One shiny-looking page was folded over. She opened it out, and found the photo of an odd-looking drawing, covering both pages: a circle filled with scribbling and stars. She could see no pattern to them, but guessed they were arranged in constellations. Martin would know about those, of course. She wondered if he'd seen it.

The writing was difficult to read, like the place names on their shire-map in the hall. She looked for a caption. It was there at the foot of the facing page.

The enigmatic Malmesbury Star-Chart. Fourteenth century.

Enigmatic was a word she had recently learned. It meant 'mysterious', Mummy said. But surely the man who had written this book knew what constellations were. A map of the stars, with the names written in. So what made it mysterious?

Even as she frowned over the word, she felt a sort of shadow in the room. Not from the window, where the syrup of sunlight had turned into marmalade now. Nor from the open doorway, with the rattle of pans coming through it from downstairs. It came from the thought of the *unknown* in this picture. Something was here that even grown-ups didn't understand. Something to do with magic, she supposed. If this had been a story, she would doubtless be the one to find its secret. But this was Daddy's study, and she didn't feel excited, but uneasy.

The *enigmatic* stars were like a hundred open eyes.

'Lyn!'

She jumped, and twisted round: flushing with guilt as Daddy came in through the door. He crossed the room, snatched the book up from the carpet and folded the map away – so quickly that he creased it. Closing the book, he took it back to its shelf, while Lyn just sat and watched him, feeling very cold and small.

'How many times?' he snapped. 'You're not to touch these books. They're very valuable, some of them, very expensive. I don't want your sticky fingermarks all over them.'

Lyn felt her sobs come rising to the surface. She pinched her lips tight shut to keep them back, but they tried to get out through her eyes instead, and squeezed them full of tears.

'Oh, don't start crying,' Daddy said, still looking tired and cross. But when Lyn couldn't keep the flow in check, he sat down in his chair, and beckoned her over, and heaved her up to huddle on his knee.

'Shh, now,' he murmured, as she sniffled against his worn tweed jacket. 'Shhh . . .' He stroked her hair. 'I'm sorry I was cross, all right? It's just that I don't like you looking at some of those books.'

'I washed my hands,' she whimpered. 'Promise.'

'It's not just that. Shhh. Be a brave girl, now, and listen to me. Some of those books, you see, are about things you don't need to know about, not yet. That one you were looking at . . . You know what magic is, don't you?'

She nodded.

'Well people used to believe there were different kinds of magic – good and bad magic. That book talks a lot about bad magic. You can read it when you're older, but if you read it now you might get upset and have bad dreams. You don't want to have bad dreams, now do you?'

Lyn shook her head in tearful mute agreement.

'There's a good girl . . .' He fingered her fringe; then smiled at her. The fond, familiar smile she knew of old. 'You really like reading, don't you? Like to find things out. That's good, Lyn. Very good. I shouldn't blame you.'

'Martin calls me Bookworm,' she mumbled.

'Never you mind what Martin says. You keep on reading. But remember that some things aren't for you yet. Until I think you're old enough, all right?'

She nodded again; then hesitated. 'Daddy . . . will I need glasses?'

He gave a quizzical frown. 'What makes you think you do?'

'Martin says I'll need glasses, 'cos I read too much.'

'Does he, indeed? Well *I* don't need them, and look how much *I've* read. Don't worry about your brother, he's just a jealous little rascal.' He jogged her on his knee. 'What is he?'

She smiled tremulously. 'A jealous little rascal.'

'That's more like it. Come on, now. Let's see if Mummy wants some help with supper . . .'

Or something. He'd said something like that. It was curious how clearly she remembered. Most of the words had faded, but the pictures were still clear. Daddy's hair had been mostly black – not silver-grey like now. And there she'd been, still small enough to sit on his knee. So different from her tall, slim self today.

Daddy's grown-up daughter now; the clever girl he'd always been so proud of.

Lyn sat down on the sofa, and tucked her legs up under

her. A dull weight of nostalgia filled her chest. She'd already written home this week – but when she got back tonight, she'd phone as well.

After more than a decade, she could still feel a twinge of guilt. He hadn't made her *promise* not to read those books again – and so, one afternoon, she'd gone and done so.

It had taken her a while to work up the nerve. He'd told her not to do it, and by and large she did what she was told. But a strange, perverse attraction won her over in the end. The lure of the forbidden: sickly-sweet. An urge to peep at things that might *upset* her.

She remembered how her heart had thudded as she'd taken down the heavy book, and turned its dusty pages. The picture of the star-chart had stayed in her head; a shadow at the back of her mind. *Enigmatic*. Secret. Her lips felt as dry as the leaves of the book as she unfolded it again.

Memory had built it up; spread out, it looked much smaller. The words still made no sense. Not even the ones around the rim, which – though clearer – had been printed in some foreign-looking language.

She'd turned to the text: there had to be a reference in the chapter. Something to explain that troubling description. She'd found the passage, but could only remember fragments of it now. *Fourteenth-century copy of an earlier work, now lost.* The word had struck her, even as she kept on reading. With all these books around her, how could anything be *lost*? Surely it was hidden somewhere; forgotten, in an attic or a cellar. It bothered her to think that it had ceased to exist. If there hadn't been a copy, all that work would just have vanished. As if it had never been.

The writing (she discovered) was Medieval Latin, with the constellations labelled in Old English. Hebrew characters as well. No wonder that she couldn't understand it.

. . . Ursa Major is marked as 'æðelgar' (a personal name), while 'fluðar' (meaning unclear) denotes the constellation Draco . . .

There was more on the way the star-chart was set out; but

though she strained her mind now, only those two names had stuck. She'd taken them phonetically back then: Edelgar, of course, not . . .

Athelgar.

She knew it was coincidence, the testament she'd found. So that was enigmatic, too. So what?

Fluthar was a nonsense-name. She couldn't work it out. Scribal error, probably. The earlier work already being corrupted.

She lay there on the sofa, feeling listless. It must be the link with Martin that had got her down like this. Her jealous little rascal of a brother. She sniffed, and was surprised to find how close she was to tears.

She'd got what she deserved, that day; the thought was almost satisfying now. Growing bored with the so-called *Magic* book, she'd put it away, and returned to the big volume on the Middle Ages. One of the chapters was called *King Death*. Something had made her hesitate; and then she'd turned the page – and kept on turning.

Horrors swarmed towards her, almost boiling from the book. A painting from a manuscript showed knights being hacked to pieces, limb from limb. Statues carved on tombs were split and rotting, full of worms. A skeleton was riding down his victims, his eyeless horse as ghostly as an X-ray. And there he was, King Death himself: a gutted, grinning figure with a gold crown on his skull.

She'd wanted to stop looking, but she couldn't. As if she had to know the very worst. She'd come to another fold-out page – and opened up the gateway into Hell.

A panoramic painting, full of horrid, screaming detail. A tide of naked people, flowing down into the Pit. Hideous monsters clutched at them, and beat them with spiked clubs. Real, despairing faces cried for help – but the devils overwhelmed them. They seemed to spring up everywhere, alive on the page: shaggy, scaly, horned and fanged. She'd sat there with wide eyes and soaked it up.

It had taken quite an effort to close the book again. The images stayed crowding in her head. Subdued, she'd put the book away, and crept out of the room. And Daddy had been right, of course. That night she'd had bad dreams.

CHAPTER VI

No Man's Land

I

They'd walked for a while in Christ Church Meadow, then meandered into Oxford through the backstreets and the lanes. Sitting on the steps of the Martyrs' Memorial, Fran reckoned she must still look like a student. Same gypsy clothes, same sturdy boots. Same undernourished look.

Craig's arm was resting gently round her shoulders. He'd held on a little tighter as they'd walked past Christ Church College, as if afraid she'd break away and run towards the walls. But all she could do was turn her head, and watch it passing by. The citadel from which she'd been excluded.

The pavements here in front of her were thronged with real students. She wished she could slip through time again, and fall into step beside them. Being twenty-three had never felt so old. She rested her head against Craig's shoulder, and smelled the musty leather of his coat.

'You sure about this evening?' he asked quietly.

She raised her head again. 'Would I have asked you if I wasn't?'

He conceded the point with an amiable shrug. 'I wanted to be sure I wasn't . . . rushing you too much.'

'Don't worry. If you do, I'll let you know.'

She remembered the doubts she'd had, before the first time. They came from every side. She'd lost her virginity while still at school, but still felt inexperienced. Her religious instincts were none too keen on sex outside of marriage. And besides – above all else, in fact – the man was one of *them*.

Did that make her a hypocrite? A *quisling*? She'd agonized for hours, without an answer. She looked for deeper motives: was she trying to win him over? And was he trying to do the same to her?

Maybe all he wanted was her body. She wasn't twenty yet, of course. Still a rather wide-eyed student, once the shades were taken off.

He hadn't rushed her, though. He'd let her pick the pace. He fancied her a lot, that much was clear – but took each step as cautiously as she did. Two lovers, separated by a fence. Fumbling along till they came to the end of the wire.

'Where will you be going next?' Craig asked. He couldn't cope with silences like she could.

'Back to the Plain,' she said, after a pause. 'To see the place we crashed. Then I can get on with the rest of my life.'

Silence again; but she could tell what he was thinking. Was he included in that brave new future? She took his hand and squeezed it, just to tell him that he would be. But whether as a lover or a friend, she wasn't sure.

'You want to put some flowers where it happened?' Craig asked gently.

She shrugged against him. 'Maybe.' And it seemed a good idea. But what she needed most of all was to go back there in daylight, and *know* what had been real, and what had not.

She thought about her dream last night. The faceless man on Imber – and the voice. The recollection filled her with a conflict of emotions, unsettling her, but haunting her as well. She knew it was a throwback to that night on Larkhill range. But his pleading tone still echoed in her head.

Perhaps she'd dream of him again – unless she went to Imber range as well. And walked along that empty road, to exorcize his ghost.

Anyway, with Imber, there were other factors counting. Another memory to draw her back.

2

MOD RANGES
This is a live firing area
and is closed to the public
KEEP OUT

Sod off, she'd thought, and kept on walking. Past the weathered crimson sign that marked the limit of the range, and down the grassy slope into the valley.

It took nerve to do a walk-on in broad daylight. An element of recklessness as well. She could feel the tension fizzing in her stomach – threatening to erupt into a fit of nervous giggles. She was committed now, no turning back; exhilaration lengthening her strides. Her long coat flapped and fluttered in the breeze. The heady sense of *trespass* made her giddy.

They'd catch her in the end, of course – and that was the whole point. The worry was, they'd cut her off before she reached the village. She *needed* to meet those airmen, face to face. Her one chance to appeal to them directly.

She knew she'd get arrested, and would probably be charged – which might cause complications back at College. She'd thought long and hard about crossing the line. It wasn't really something she could talk about with Lyn; her friend regarded *protest* with suspicion. Two things had tipped the balance in the end. The urge to bridge the gulf between the missile crews and her; and a compulsion to confront her fear of Cruise.

The range was silent: brooding under clouds. Empty slopes, and straggling dark copses. On the dry floor of the valley, she felt hemmed in: overshadowed. Even with the sun still up, the place gave her the creeps. A void at night; a wilderness by day.

Two flights were out on exercise this month: four launchers up at Imber Firs, and four down in the village. Their presence only added to the ominous silence.

She came to the single metalled road, just east of Imber village. Pausing, she looked both ways; then ventured out. Across the road, a pillbox seemed to watch her. Overgrown and derelict; as empty as a skull.

Getting close, now. Very close. She cut away from the road again, and slipped into the undergrowth. There'd be sentries on patrol from here on in. She hesitated, listening. The distant whirr of a generator reached her ears, but nothing more. She could see the old church tower, rising up behind the trees.

She decided to skirt around to the north of the village: come down past Imber Court, and try and get among the vehicles. It was the first time she'd approached Cruise on deployment, but she knew there were two levels of defences. The outer and inner rings. Neither was apparent at the moment.

She was feeling quite keyed-up now; quite excited. Creeping through the wood, she got a glimpse of the first building: a weed-infested shell across the road. And still the ruined village kept its peace.

Again she stopped to listen, easing down on hands and knees – and heard a brittle twig snap right behind her.

Galvanized by shock, she twisted round. A bloke in US camouflage was standing there, half-smiling. His face looked quite familiar; she placed it just before she read the name-strip on his blouse. Master Sergeant FLAHERTY, again.

'A man can't even go for a *pee* these days without tripping over you guys.'

Fran let herself relax a bit: her heart still beating hard. 'Your security is crap, I hope you know.'

He snorted. 'Tell me about it.'

They looked each other over for a moment. He was wearing his cap, rather than the sinister 'Fritz' helmet of a trooper on patrol. She was relieved to see he didn't have a gun.

Perhaps he drives a launcher, then. This amiable man.

'You been down here all week?' she asked.

He shook his head. 'We came in last night . . . got *porridge* thrown all over us. And paint.'

Fran couldn't help grinning. 'Are you QRMT, then?'

'Quick Response Maintenance, yeah . . .' He raised an eyebrow. 'You're pretty well clued-up, ain't you?'

'Oh, we are, we are.' She let her grin grow teasing. 'Know how we can tell a Convoy vehicle? It's got no number plates, and it's going the *wrong way*.'

He chuckled at that; then squinted at the sky. 'Gonna rain soon. You want to stay out here and get wet, or are you coming in with me?'

Fran wavered for a moment; then shrugged. 'Might as well get it over with.'

'My name's Craig,' he said, as she got to her feet.

She nodded back. 'I'm Frances.'

They started down the slope, between the trees. The contact that she'd come here for – and now her mind was blank. She couldn't think of anything to say.

'I kind of get the feeling we're not welcome here,' Craig said.

She gestured rather sullenly. 'I'd rather you went home.'

'Don't like Yanks, huh?'

She stopped. 'That isn't true. Believe me it's not. I think you're quite nice people, actually. It's your missiles I don't want.'

'Just keeping the peace – that's all we do.'

'I thought it was called Cold *War*.'

'Making the world safe for McDonald's, then.'

She gave him a half-suspicious glance. 'You can't be American . . . you've got a sense of irony.'

'Oho,' he grinned. 'Unfair!'

'No, but listen . . .' They were nearly at the road, now, she had just a moment left. 'I'll be honest, I despair of you lot sometimes. Then I think of the Gettysburg Address, and Henry Fonda in *Twelve Angry Men*, and I feel a bit more hopeful.'

'I like Fonda, too,' he said.

'But when you aim your missiles at civilians, you're selling it all out. You shame your *country*, Craig.'

He looked at her more soberly. 'I guess we're not going to see eye to eye on this one.'

She shrugged. 'Well, thanks for listening, anyway.'

'Maybe we should talk some more.'

Fran hesitated: not sure what he meant. He'd dropped his gaze, eyes shadowed by the peak of his cap.

'You're studying in Oxford, aren't you?'

She nodded.

'Maybe I could meet you there sometime.'

A heartbeat's pause. 'You serious?'

'Yeah,' he said, and looked at her. 'I am.'

Fran stared back for a moment. Then: 'Christ Church College. Write to me.'

She sensed his relief, though he masked it with a faint, ironic grin. 'You won't get tarred and feathered just for talking to me, will you?'

'I shouldn't think so. Why, will you get shot?'

Touché. He let her go ahead of him, and out onto the road; falling behind as she walked into the village. She felt him in her footsteps, but she didn't look back once.

A control vehicle was lurking at the roadside up ahead, its bulk draped in camouflage netting. The tactical ops truck was parked nearby; she could see the maps and clutter in the back. A burly, crop-haired officer was staring out at her, a white enamel mug still in his hand. His face was a sight: slack-jawed with disbelief. The flight commander, surely. She put on her sweetest smile, and walked towards him.

'Hey! We've got another peacenik walking round out here!'

Some MoD police appeared from nowhere, and rushed across the road to intercept her. She recognized the bloke who took her elbow; she knew most of the Support Unit now, at least by sight. And they knew her, as well.

'Gawd, Frances: you again? Come on . . .'

As they led her towards the transit van, she twisted round

to look behind her. Craig Flaherty was standing by the TO truck. He waited till their eyes met; then dropped his gaze again, and turned away.

3

Fran opened Lyn's front door a little warily – still composing an excuse inside her head. Lyn hadn't looked too great this morning. Perhaps she'd stayed at home.

On up the stairs. She felt Craig's presence climbing them behind her, his footsteps slow and patient on the treads. She gave him a nervous smile – he grinned easily back – and fumbled the key into the door of the flat.

Hush and stillness greeted them: each dust-mote hung suspended. Fran almost tiptoed through to check Lyn's bedroom; then breathed a sigh, and shrugged out of her jacket.

'What time will she be back?' Craig asked her calmly.

'Sometime after seven.' Her mouth was dry.

They stood together awkwardly: like two kids not quite sure who should be making the first move. Then Craig sat on the sofa, and beckoned her to join him. She did so, snuggling close. They started kissing.

She hadn't snogged like this for four whole years. Excitement surged inside her, sending thrills along her nerves. But when his hand began to fumble with the buttons of her top, she felt a plunge of doubt, and pulled away.

He managed a smile, and gently stroked her shoulder. 'Second thoughts?'

She swallowed. 'I'm not sure if we should. Behind Lyn's back, I mean . . .'

'I can wait for as long as you want, you know.' His voice was slightly hoarse, but she believed him.

'Can we . . . just sit for a bit?'

'Sure.'

'Sorry . . .'

'Shh. No problem.'

Curling up, she let herself be cuddled. This was enough: to feel him there beside her. She couldn't take it further, not right now.

They watched the room turn greyer as the dusk came creeping in. As if each mote of dust had multiplied a million times. From time to time he kissed her, very softly. She nuzzled him back, feeling cosseted and safe. No worries in the world, so long as they were here together.

At last she let him go, and straightened up. 'Would you like a glass of wine, at least? Lyn's got some in the fridge.'

'Sure. I'd like that.' She heard him settling back again as she went into the kitchen. A paranoid twinge made her wonder what expression he was wearing. Exasperation, maybe? Or resentment? She flicked the radio on, as if that would tame the situation. Make the place more like a flat just being visited by a friend.

Lyn usually had it tuned to Classic FM – but maybe she'd brushed the dial while she'd been dusting. All that came out was the empty, crackling ether. Fran thought she heard a burbling in the distance; but the voice, if voice it was, was too distorted to make sense. Ignoring it, she opened the fridge, letting yellow light spill out into the dimness. The wine-box was on the bottom shelf. She brought it out, and shut the glow away.

The tuned-out radio fizzed and crackled sharply. She guessed that meant a thunderstorm was close. Turning towards the cupboard where the glasses were kept, she glanced out of the window. Heavy cloud had crept across the city – but a stripe of crimson twilight formed a backdrop to the spires.

A corrupted voice behind her said: '. . . *they're coming* . . .'

Her head snapped round. The words had come from the radio, suddenly clear; but now it was just hissing to itself. The noise jogged her memory – then jolted it. She could smell the stuffy confines of Paul's car; feel the air of tense expectancy that filled it. Hear the CB radio hissing like a snake.

'I see their lights . . .' the kitchen radio said.

Then silence for a minute – maybe two. Fran stood there like a statue, her spine against the hard edge of the sink. Listening with her hand over her mouth. Her heart had started beating very fast.

Just isolated crackles, now; the sharper pops of static made her jump. She was just about to cross the room, and switch the damn thing off, when the voice, now more contorted, came again.

'Elderflower, to Watchers at Gore Cross. First Dodge is now approaching the vedette . . .'

Oh no, Fran thought. Oh please.

She knew the words, she'd heard them all before. They dragged her back four years, to a night on the Plain. The scene was there before her; she could feel the winter chill. An unlit country crossroads, at the exit to the range. She was waiting with the others: the protestors, the police. Under a cloud-fogged moon.

One of the cars had driven up as far as the vedette. He was out of their sight up there, cut off – but still in touch by radio. How must it feel, she'd wondered, to be sitting there alone? As the snake of lights came creeping up towards him . . .

She remembered every detail, as fresh as if she'd been there yesterday. The convoy's escort, parked along the farm-track: dim shapes of transit vans with engines running. Two Land-Rovers were sitting on their sidelights, up the hill. But the road to Imber village was still dark.

'All vehicles now on the vedette . . .'

Fran felt herself go cold and faint. She slumped onto her haunches, sliding down. Still staring at the radio; but her eyes saw other things.

'Eight launchers, four controls, two Rams, two wreckers. They're coming through. They're coming.'

And over the hill they came, in a serpent of slow headlights. From the black heart of the Plain; the ghostly wreck of Imber village. Fran cringed against the cupboard – gripped her head between her hands. The voice had fallen silent, but her mind filled in the rest. The whistles and shouts as the convoy came off, its escorts slotting in between the flights; then the scramble for the cars, and the pursuit into the night. The terrifying chase to Greenham Common . . .

She was still huddled there when Craig came through to see where she had got to. Jerkily she raised her face; he saw her tears glistening in the gloom. He knelt beside her, hugged her: held her close. Fran hung on tight for dear life – and sanity as well. But she couldn't shake off that eerie voice. Those sombre words.

They're coming.

CHAPTER VII

Running Blind

I

They sat in silence, round the kitchen table. Fran was halfway through another cigarette, eyes fixed on its smouldering tip. Lyn wasn't a smoker, and clearly didn't like it in the flat, but had made allowances tonight. Fran sensed her watching anxiously, hands clasped beneath her chin. A lukewarm pulse of sympathy went through her, just tingeing her self-pity. Poor Lyn had come in late, and looking knackered (*not* a word she'd use) – to find Fran on the sofa, as white as a sheet, and Craig with his arm around her. And now here they were, much later, with the second round of coffees still half-drunk. Just like bloody student days again.

'I still think you'd be crazy to go back,' Craig told her quietly.

Fran looked at him with narrowed eyes. The bright glare of the strip-light didn't do him many favours: lining his face, and picking out grey hairs. What was he, thirty-five? Weathered and worn by the gap of years between them. His earnest, grim expression didn't help; but those pale blue eyes of his were clean and sharp.

She hadn't believed he'd wanted to pursue her. Too challenging; too risky. Waiting to be charged at West Down camp, she'd realized that he didn't know her surname. Well, there was a test of his commitment – and he'd passed it. Made a few discreet enquiries of the MDP who'd nicked her . . .

'I have to,' she said flatly – taking a drag as if to set her seal on the matter. The ash flared: hot, defiant. She got a glimpse of Lyn's discomfort from the corner of her eye, and turned her head aside to breathe the smoke.

'Look at the effect it's having,' he persisted. 'Even now. You go back there again, you're gonna screw yourself *up*, Fran. Back into therapy. Is that what you *want*?'

'Of course I bloody don't. And I'm not *going to*. I had a real shock down there: it screwed me up for years. I need to get my head round it. I'll be all right then.'

'So what about what happened here tonight?' Lyn said – jumping quickly in between them, but the question was pertinent enough. 'Was that just in your head?'

Fran sat back, glowering at Craig. 'Of course it was.'

'You were hearing voices again.'

Fran turned her head, and saw how pale Lyn looked. Not just from fatigue; her eyes were big with worry. With her hair tied back, not her usual style, she seemed younger and more vulnerable somehow.

Fran swallowed. 'Not like before. No, really. This was just a memory. A flashback.'

Lyn moistened her lips. 'Oh, Fran. Don't you think it might be better if you saw someone?'

'No, I *don't*. I'm finished with that, all right? Going to Heyford and Greenham *helped*. I'm getting it all back into perspective now. And I know I can face up to the Plain. If I don't, then those flashbacks, those whatever, will just keep coming.'

There was a pause. Fran drew determinedly on her cigarette. Craig tapped his fingers thoughtfully on the table, watching her from under his brows.

'Would it help,' Lyn ventured slowly, 'if you told us what you thought you saw, that night?'

Fran focused again on the shrivelling ash, and felt her skin becoming cold and tight. A vacuum seemed to form inside her belly.

'It might be an idea . . .' Lyn faltered on. 'You talked about . . . these things you thought were coming after you.'

Fran breathed slowly in; then out. She shook her head.

'Oh, Frannie,' whispered Lyn. 'Please let us *help*.'

For a moment more she wavered. The memory was there at the back of her mind: a dense, amorphous shadow. To speak of it would give it shape – in all its ghastly detail. But the prospect before her was more frightening still: that her friends would take her at her word, and leave her to resist the thing alone.

Fran crushed her cigarette against the saucer, and looked up. Her expression made Craig reach across and take hold of her hand. Lyn followed suit: grasped Fran's left hand in both her own and squeezed.

Just like a séance, Fran thought dimly. And that's what they were doing, in the end. Summoning spirits. Raising ghosts.

She opened her mouth, and realized she was on the verge of tears. She sniffed, and swallowed thickly. Then looked from Craig's set face to Lyn's – and started talking.

2

She'd got as far as Greenlands camp before she paused for breath.

Her limbs were numb with shock, but they'd kept moving. Adrenaline sang madly through her veins. Her three friends were forgotten; the crash was like the fragment of a dream. The only thing that mattered was the shadow at her heels.

Glancing back, she'd glimpsed it moving – indistinct and blurred. It had left the road already, and was following her trail onto the range. She'd lost it for a moment, and looked round in utter panic. But then it passed in front of the car headlamps, quenching them like a cloud across the moon.

Oh God, oh God, oh God.

The unseen ground was rough and treacherous. Brambles

vied with thatchy tufts of grass to bring her down. A tank trail almost tripped her up: as lumpy as a ploughed field in the dark. Whimpering, she picked her way along it – then looked again, and found him gaining ground. Lurching but relentless, like a scarecrow in the starlight. She flailed back onto grass, and kept on running.

A red light glowed above the nearest trees – a warning beacon, mounted on a flagpole. She'd made for it instinctively, and stumbled on a narrow, northbound lane. Gasping, she had followed that, uphill and round a bend. And Greenlands had been waiting there: as silent as a village of the dead.

The old camp was disused, its buildings derelict and empty. The road led through the middle, and on up towards East Down. The night was brighter up ahead: the stars like waiting gems above the black lip of the earth. But safety seemed as far away as they did.

Breathless now, she came up short and forced herself to listen. There was no sound of her pursuer. She could just hear the range flagpole in the distance: its cable striking metal in the cool night breeze. *Clink . . . clink . . . clink . . .*

The ground rose up to left and right, and murk had settled thickly in the fold. The way she'd come was as black as the mouth of a tunnel.

She tried to fill her aching lungs; fighting back the sobs that would have emptied them again. Now that she'd stopped moving, a dozen cuts and bruises were competing for attention – engulfing her in pain and nausea. Her head had started throbbing; it felt like a drill-bit slowly grinding on the bone.

Her face was warm and sticky. Reaching up, she touched her cheek, and felt the slime of blood.

She wavered, shivering with shock – and heard the whine of engines. Something moving slowly through the night. Distance and direction were impossible to judge. She looked ahead, along the road: hoping for the blessed flash of headlights. But the darkness of the skyline didn't change.

Then she heard the scuff of footfalls, coming up the lane.

For a moment she stood petrified; then dodged towards the nearest gutted building. The way ahead was too exposed, wide open – he would catch her. She had to hide, and wait for him to pass.

Despite its gaping window holes, the hulk was dank and smelly. Animals had pissed in here – and maybe died, as well. She ducked into the doorway, and put her back against the crumbled bricks. Litter rustled underfoot. The grainy dimness clung to her like glue.

She froze, and strained her ears. The camp was silent.

Then she heard a scraping noise that made her hairs stand up.

A rusty and abrasive sound, from somewhere very close; perhaps the nearest empty house but one. She visualized an iron bar, being drawn along the brickwork. A hunter trying to winkle out his prey.

Oh God, help meeeeee! Oh God!

The silence settled down again. She swallowed, like a spasm. The pause went on for minutes. He must have gone inside the house, to search its filthy shadows. Gritting her teeth, she forced herself to move: across the darkened shell, towards the window. Reaching it, she peered carefully out.

Nothing for a moment; then she glimpsed him – a blob of deeper darkness, moving back into the road. His shadow flickered on the barracks block – then peeled away, and struck off on its own.

It took another moment just to realize what she'd seen. A power-surge of fright blazed through her nerves. *Two* of them were searching for her now.

The first one started up the road. She recognized his shabby, muffled outline. The cowled head turned from side to side; the starlight winked off metal. It glinted on the bar or *implement* that he was holding. Fran just stared – then clasped her mouth, and slowly backed away. Oh Jesus, he was carrying a *sword*.

He struck the blade against the road: it rasped, and scattered sparks. The other shape was rooting through the long grass by the barracks. The stars reflected dully off a helmet of some kind. Fran was seized with disbelieving horror. They might have been two phantoms, from the ancient earthworks all around this place.

Except that they were real, and closing in. She dragged her gaze away, and tiptoed back towards the doorway.

Something furtive shifted in the corner.

It might have been a rat, but she just bolted anyway. Or tried to – but her joints had stiffened up. The minutes she'd spent standing still had almost crippled her. She pitched out through the doorway – then caught herself, and fled across the road. Trying to get clear of them, before they could react – but then *another* shape emerged, from one of the outbuildings. Squealing now, she veered around it, ducking as it aimed some kind of club. She heard it snarl behind her – and then her ears were full of her own heartbeat, as she struggled up the slope towards the crest.

She felt them scrambling after her, and whimpered with despair. The night ahead had neither depth nor distance. She staggered on, and seemed to make no progress.

Then she saw the vehicles – three moving sets of lights. They looked to be heading for Half-Moon Copse. She put on a spurt. All three were towing trailers, and their sidelights were bright orange. Cruise support – an ADVON unit, maybe. She never thought she'd look on them as saviours.

As she panted to catch up, they seemed to sink into the ground and vanish. Within moments she had lost her way – the darkness looked the same in all directions. But there was the Plough, rising clear of the gloom – so that way must be north . . .

Even as she wavered, she felt the shadows coming at her back.

She swung around and saw one: heading straight towards her, in a grim, relentless line. She turned to run – and heard a knocking sound, insistent as a knuckle on a buried coffin lid. A string of tracer bullets seemed to float across the range. And then they speeded up and hurtled past her, cracking and wailing blindly through the night. She threw herself forward, sobbing: hitting the dirt before she even saw it.

The shooting stopped abruptly, its echoes fading off towards the stars. The hiss of her ears filled the silence that followed. Until the blackness stirred again, just twenty yards away. Stirred – and then came scurrying towards her.

She gave a little shriek, and scrambled upright. Escape was all that mattered now – the live rounds as irrelevant as raindrops. Sobbing for breath, she kept on fleeing. *Oh please*, she thought, beside herself. *Oh please* . . .

The stutter of machine guns came again. Globules of coloured light went streaming through the darkness. Instinct tried – and failed – to change her course. Then she tripped, and plunged into the grass.

A burst of shots stitched up the ground behind her. She heard a pig-like grunt and squeal. Squirming round, she realized her pursuer had been hit. He kicked and rolled; then started crawling forward. Relentless as a crippled dog. She hauled herself away on hands and knees.

The rounds were coming single-shot now. She recognized the *crack* of Armalites. Another vague shape foundered in the darkness.

And then the glare of headlights, right ahead.

'Cease *firing*!' someone yelled.

She risked another glance – still scrabbling forward. Beyond the spreading halo, the darkness of the range lay undisturbed. The shadows were still out there, she could sense them. But hanging back, now. Lurking in the gloom.

The vehicle's lights approached her like two glowing pairs of eyes – the amber sidelights well outside the headlamps. Its width gave it away at once: a Hummvee armoured car. She watched it taking solid, crouching shape behind its stare. The gunner was a looming silhouette against the stars.

Running out of strength at last, she cowered like a rabbit in the lights. The Hummvee stopped, and men came stalking up on either side. She recognized their camouflage and German-looking helments, and almost started weeping with relief.

'Jesus, it's another goddamn peacenik,' someone said.

'Help me . . . *please*.' She struggled to sit upright.

'Back off. Get the cops to deal with her.'

'Stupid bitch. You coulda got your stupid *head* blowed off.'

'Hold it. Jesus, hold it. She's been hurt.'

The man who'd spoken slung his Armalite and started forward. The others stood around her in the stagnant lake of light. A couple had their rifles still half-aimed.

'*Watch yourself*.'

Ignoring that, he hunkered down and tried to check her head-wound. Despite herself, she wrapped her arms around him. He stiffened for a moment; then relaxed and hugged her back.

'Shh, girl. It's okay. Did you get hit?'

'Someone *chasing* me . . .' she sobbed.

'Where? Back there?' He looked over her shoulder. One of the others raised a torch, and shone it further out into the dark.

The American smelt earthy. The cowling of his gun was hair-dryer hot. Easing back, he tried a winning smile. 'Target dummies – that was all you saw.'

'Dummies? They were *moving*.'

'Uh-uh,' said another Yank, 'there's no one else out there.'

Fran looked round. The man was peering through binoculars of some kind.

'That's a thermal night-sight, hon,' the first man told her wryly. 'Sees body heat. Ain't nobody can hide from one of those.'

Unless they're dead already. Dead and cold . . .

'You crazy, girl?' a third man said. 'This here's a *firing range*.'

'Our car crashed,' she said brokenly. 'Back down by

Greenlands camp. My three friends need an ambulance . . . right now.'

They helped her to her feet, and led her past the ugly armoured car. The 'Whiskers' Blazer squatted there behind it, its pair of aerials bending like antennae in the breeze.

One of the riflemen glanced back. Fran twisted round as well – but everything behind them was a void. Black emptiness. And nothing to hear but the night wind hissing through acres of unseen grass.

The shakes had really started as the Whiskers drove her back to Westdown camp. She'd been sick soon after they arrived there: hunched miserably over the toilet bowl, while an MoD policewoman stood watching from the doorway. An army medic checked her up; and then she got to see the duty sergeant.

'Your friends have been taken to Salisbury General,' he told her as she sipped some tasteless tea. 'We'll get an army ambulance to take you down there too.'

She realized that she'd left them at the mercy of those *things*. 'Are they all right?' she mumbled guiltily.

He seemed to hesitate. 'They're in good hands. The medics over there can tell you more. You've been a very lucky girl. We won't be charging you.'

Dawn was almost up by the time the ambulance arrived. Pallid light had bleached away the blackness, and the Plain looked dour and barren. A Hummvee was sitting just inside the Danger Area, its lights still on. The machine gunner slouched on his open hatch, watching her and chewing thoughtfully.

The camp lay in misty silence. She walked forlornly down between the rows of unlit huts, escorted by the WPC. Two of the troopers tagged along. The one who'd helped her still looked quite concerned. She felt a spark of gratitude – but one that grew no brighter than a glimmer. And nausea yawned beneath it like a bottomless pit.

By the time she reached the ambulance, the tears were running freely down her face.

3

And her cheeks were dripping now – but she was safe here in the kitchen, holding on tight to her two friends' hands. Craig hadn't dropped his gaze for a moment; willing her on whenever she had stumbled. Towards the end, the room was losing focus: the past becoming solid in its place. The bare skin of her arms began to pimple with the chill. But Craig was always there, and hanging on. His eyes were mild blue steel, his face as steady as a rock.

Lyn was leaning close: she pressed Fran's limp hand against her cheek. 'Oh, Fran,' she almost breathed. 'You poor thing.'

Fran sniffed and swallowed. Lyn let her have her hand back, and she wiped her swollen eyes.

'Jesus,' Craig said softly. 'No wonder you needed therapy. No wonder.'

She tried to smile, but the muscles wouldn't work. All she could do was stare, and hope her eyes would say it for her. How much she'd needed him to hear that. How very glad she was that he was here.

Back then, there'd been no time for explanations. Numb with shock, she'd sunk into depression – the depths of bleak midwinter, while the autumn still blazed golden in the trees. She'd bitched at Lyn with real spite, and snapped at her concern. Craig she'd just ignored – until he'd driven up to see her. The row they'd had that afternoon had almost made her puke: but all her bitter prejudice came spewing up instead. *Just doing your job, of course you are – just like the bloody SS.* And Craig, being Craig, gave as good as he'd got. *Grow up and get a life, you stupid bitch.*

They'd parted on those hateful terms; she'd dropped out of

college soon after. Crawled back home to Mum and Dad, and let the darkness take her. Just as it had almost managed on the Plain.

But Lyn, on top of all her work, had done her best to keep the flame alive. Keeping them linked up across the distance and the years – even when Craig's tour ended and he flew back to the States. Lyn, whom she'd called a stuck-up cow, and told to go away . . .

'Sorry,' Fran said lamely, looking down at the tabletop; addressing them both.

Craig squeezed her hand. '*I'm* sorry, Fran. I didn't *know*.'

She raised her eyes. His face looked almost haunted with concern.

Were you on Larkhill range that night? She'd never dared to ask him, and couldn't now. Because the answer yes would beg the question: *Did you see them too?* And he couldn't have, of course – because it had all been in her mind.

'Another cup of coffee?' Lyn asked gently. There was a hint of relief in her calming smile. Fran guessed she'd worked it out from her reserve of common sense: the obsession with Cruise had somehow caused a post-traumatic backlash. Craig had doubtless reached the same conclusion. They were probably right, as well; and yet . . .

Fran realized she was frowning very slightly.

'So what happens now?' Craig wondered, as Lyn got the kettle going.

'Now I have to go back,' Fran said. 'You see why, don't you?'

He didn't look entirely convinced. 'And what, retrace your steps?'

She nodded. 'Right through Greenlands camp.' A pause. 'And I think I'll take in Imber village, too – for old times' sake.'

He acknowledged that with a wry smile of his own. 'So when d'you want to go?'

'Spring Bank Holiday's coming up. The roads are open then.'

She hesitated. 'But I want to go alone this time. You've had to carry me for long enough.'

'It's no problem–' Craig began, and Lyn was turning round to say the same. Fran cut back in, eyes wide and earnest. 'I mean it, Craig. It's got to be that way. I was on my own the first time, after all.'

He shook his head, unhappy. 'And what if you have a problem?'

'I don't think I will. Not in broad daylight. Just a stretch of open country, that's all it'll be . . .'

The kettle boiled in the background, and switched itself off. Craig looked at Lyn. She shrugged.

'I'll be all right,' Fran murmured. 'Really.' A pause; and then she glanced at Lyn, and smiled a little wanly. 'Would you mind if I have another cigarette?'

'He's quite a catch,' Lyn said, when Craig had gone.

'I know,' Fran said. 'I'm glad you like him too.'

She'd started going with Craig just as Lyn was breaking up with her new boyfriend. She remembered the heart-to-heart they'd had, one afternoon together: Lyn very delicate and weepy, while she herself was glowing with excitement. And marvelling at the irony, as well. A Yank from Greenham Common – of all people. Even Lyn had giggled tearfully at that.

And Lyn, despite her tiredness, was smiling, teasing now. 'You won't let him get away this time?'

Fran shook her head. 'Not on your life. Not this time.' Once she'd put her past in order, she could think about the future; but the horizon was already looking bright.

But now it was well past bedtime. She gave the washed-up mugs a wipe, while Lyn went round locking up. Finished, she switched the light off and headed for the bathroom. Lyn passed her in the doorway, touched her arm. Her soft brown eyes were serious now. 'You're sure you'll be all right?'

Fran hugged her: held her close. 'Oh, yes. I'm sure.'

Climbing into bed, she realized just how tired she was. The drain on her emotions had sapped her strength. But talking out her memories had purged her; she felt lighter than she had for many weeks.

Or months, perhaps. Or years.

The long dark was nearly over now. Just one more place to go. The night outside felt safe – its demons caged. She laid down her head, and realized she was smiling very faintly. Then closed her eyes, and slept.

'This is Woodbine at Greenham . . . all vehicles now inside the gate.'

'Thank you, Woodbine . . . Thanks to all Watchers along on this one . . . Goodnight . . .'

CHAPTER VIII

The Waste Down

I

She lingered for a long while in Edington church.

Weeks had passed. She'd nursed her sickly courage: felt it grow. But here, in the shadow of the Plain's northern edge, she knew her nerve might fail her even now.

She'd got off the train at Westbury and walked – heading east out of town towards Bratton and White Horse Hill. The country road meandered round the foot of the scarp, with flat fields spread and drowsing to her left. The day had started sunnily enough; but now the wind had freshened, bringing clouds. Stray sheep across the field of blue at first; then slower, grazing groups with dirty fleeces. The warm air felt diluted as each shadow passed across. She had her sleeveless top and flowing skirt on. When the coolness started lingering, she slung her jacket loosely round her shoulders.

Not Lyn's big comfy jacket, sad to say. This was an old denim one from home. She'd been back to see her parents; they were so pleased with her progress. Some doubts about the wisdom of what she'd wanted to do next – but her rising confidence had won them over. She'd bloomed in sunny Oxford; Lyn had fed her up a bit, and made her get her hair done. She liked the cut: it framed her pale complexion like a cowl. Her eyes seemed greener: fresh as spring. She'd left her shades behind.

It felt as if she'd been away from home for years, not two short weeks. She'd had to rediscover her own bedroom. Her books had still been there where she had left them. Old favourites like *Rebecca* and *Jane Eyre*, alongside *Einstein's Monsters* and *The Fate of the Earth*. Stuff she'd read at school, as well. She'd fingered her way along the row: from Shakespeare to Milton and *Paradise Lost*.

> *Long is the road, and hard* (she thought)
> *That out of Hell leads up to light* . . .

Her mum had found her mulling that one over. Unable to contain herself, she'd hugged and kissed her daughter. 'You're looking so well, Fran. Pretty as a pixie – like I always used to say.'

'*Mum!*' she'd said, embarrassed and delighted. That was when she'd realized she was going to be all right.

Her confidence had faltered as she came to Bratton village, and reached the turning off that led to Imber. At this point it was nothing but a quiet country lane, curving off around the hill and out of sight. Yet it ended at that junction in the middle of the range. The fields in which the faceless man was searching.

Despite her resolve, she'd wavered at the prospect; stood staring up the lane – then walked on by. Oh, she was going back to Imber, right enough – and on to Larkhill range and Greenlands camp. This very afternoon. But not quite yet.

Edington was tiny; picture-pretty. She let its stillness soothe her. A glance at her watch gave her plenty of time. Lyn wasn't expecting her back in Oxford until mid-evening. Exploring, in an aimless sort of way (distraction from the uplands right behind her), she found the church at the bottom of a lane. *St Mary, St Katharine & All Saints*. The place was surprisingly big – a priory church, built with medieval grandeur. Intrigued, she wandered down to take a look.

The interior was cool and dim; she kept her jacket slung around her shoulders. A woman was busy cleaning near the back. She looked up with a smile. Fran smiled shyly back, and hoped she wouldn't want to talk.

The flagstones clicked beneath her boots as she slowly paced around. Down the high, vaulted nave, and back along the aisles. Stone figures lay on recessed slabs, disfigured by the years. She picked up a guide from the table by the door; flicked casually through it. The date of consecration was 1361. She felt a haunting sense of *age* – a link with the past. As if long-dead congregations might still linger here in spirit.

Those sleeping statues: all unknown. That faceless knight had come from Imber church. Was thought to be a *Lord* of Imber . . . She gave it a slightly wary glance; tried superimposing a fourteenth-century village on the ruined one today. The effect was disconcerting. She put the leaflet down again.

The sun emerged outside, spilling blocks of dusty light down through the windows: a sandstorm in suspended animation. Undaunted, the woman in the housecoat kept on polishing the woodwork. The sun went in again.

Fran sat herself in one of the pews, and waited while her instincts fought it out. She knew she couldn't turn back now; but a part of her still dragged its feet, and looked for an excuse.

A gentle footfall in the aisle behind her. 'Anything I can help with, dear?' the woman asked.

Fran glanced back with a smile. 'I'm all right, thanks. Just savouring the atmosphere.'

'It's peaceful, isn't it? Very calming.'

Fran hesitated, hoping that she'd leave it at that. But the pause made her uncomfortable: aware that there was more she ought to say. The woman had a friendly face; it seemed unfair to turn her own away.

'Do you get many visitors here?'

'A few. There was someone here earlier, came for the quiet like you did. Young man; I think he was one of those travellers or some such. But he sat here for a long while.'

She nodded, half to herself; then smiled and moved away, clearly sensing that this visitor preferred to be alone. Fran glanced gratefully after her; then settled back again, and thought of Greenlands.

It had to be faced: got over with. Like a smear test, or a visit to the dentist. And once it was done, the way ahead would be clear for her and Craig.

She couldn't help but smile as she remembered their first date: the terms that she'd laid down, across the table. *Call me 'honey' and I'll clobber you, all right?*

'Okay.'

Or 'Sugar' . . .

She'd been there for a drink, and that was all. Still wary; still confused. But as they'd talked, her sense of guilt had slowly started fading. She liked him – he was honest and direct (good-looking, too, she'd add, if *she* were honest). They'd agreed to meet again. And from such small beginnings . . .

'Well, what do you make of this?' the woman said.

She'd just unlocked the collection box to empty it, and was peering at a small coin in her palm. Fran could see from where she sat that it was badly discoloured; but a muted gleam of silver caught the light. Probably an old two-shilling piece – a change, at least, from bus tokens and coppers.

It was time to move on. She got to her feet.

The woman gave her a glance. 'That young man must have left it, he put something in the box. It can't be real, can it?'

Fran joined her on the way to the door, and saw for herself. The rough-edged coin was tarnished, almost black, but she could make out the small cross stamped into the metal. The woman turned it over, and they saw it had a bird on the back: one with a curved and cruel-looking beak. A circle of crude lettering surrounded it.

The woman shook her head. 'I've not seen anything like that before, I must say.'

Fran was picking out the letters, but they didn't make a word. Hard enough to tell where the sequence began, apart from a cramped initial cross – and the bird's malicious beak that broke the circle.

✠ A N L A F C V N V N C

A scavenger's beak, Fran thought – and frowned. A carrion bird. A raven.

2

Up on the hill, she turned around, and saw the country spread out like a quilt.

The patchwork was uneven, mixing greens and browns and yellows; its hedgerows like rough stitching in between. Isolated farms stood out in tiny detail. And over it all, the shadows of clouds came creeping: as shapeless as amoebas, vast and dim.

Wiltshire, stretching off into the distance. She'd originally thought of the *Plain* as flat, but here it rose much higher: thrust upward from the lowland like a cliff. Edington was down there, to the right: the church peeping out between trees. It looked like a toy village from up here.

She'd taken the footpath up Edington Hill. The way was steep and hollow, worn into the chalky ground. Clearing the trees on the lower slopes, it rose towards the crest – then skirted round it. She'd cut away, and climbed up to the top. The breeze grew fresher, plucking at her jacket; she shrugged into its sleeves. Her icon badge was pinned to the lapel.

Gazing out across the landscape, she remembered her walk with Dad the other week. Up the path behind the houses to the high ground overlooking Hathersage. They'd watched the evening settle on the village. The lights had come on one by one: a colony of fireflies waking up to greet the dusk. Dad had put his arm around her – drawn her close against his side. Content, she'd leaned her head against his shoulder.

'You're serious about him then: this lad?'

'He's really nice, Dad. You'd like him.'

They'd always been close: she didn't need to see his face to know what he was thinking. He'd got his daughter back, to see her snatched away again. Every instinct said to hang on tight.

When he let go, she heard it in the wryness of his voice.

'You'd best bring him up here, then. Let your mother have a look at him. And I can see what he thinks of Real Ale.'

Love you, Dad, she'd thought, and slid her arm across his back. Aloud she said: 'He won't drink pints, you know. Has to be the bottled stuff. And cold.'

He snorted. 'Typical Yank, eh.'

'That doesn't bother you, does it?' she'd asked, after a slightly anxious pause.

'If he makes you happy, girl, he won't bother me at all. Just don't let him take you for a ride, all right?'

'*Dad*. I'm twenty-three now.'

'You're still my daughter, Frannie. My little lass. That's never going to change.'

She didn't doubt it, either. Though they'd just been to see the local team, and Fran had shouted louder than the blokes, she was always going to be his little girl.

But even as they spoke, she'd felt the gloomy heights behind them: the tors like tumbled fortresses, and then the open moor. They were right out on the edge here, and dusk was coming quicker than a tide.

A wind had risen out of the distance. She'd felt it on her spine, and snuggled closer to Dad's coat. But when she turned her head, she saw the yellow moon was up: its outline smudged and swollen, but the glow was like a lamp's. The lantern of a friend, to light them home. The barren moor seemed thwarted – almost sullen.

The rustling breeze brought her back to the present. No wind from the back of beyond this time; just a whisper through the thistley grass. A snuffling round the dandelions and daisies. She breathed it in, and knew that she was ready.

Turning to come down off the crest – her face set firmly south, towards the range – she saw the black-clad figure in the hollow of the hill.

* * *

She ventured further down, and reached the track; then stopped again. The man was crouching on the slope a dozen yards below. He was head-down over something, unaware of her approach.

The falling contours made a basin here. The pathway curved around it, like a gouge along the rim. The ground was steep and strangely crimped: old terraces, she guessed. But grass this rough was just for grazing now. Tufty bushes sprouted up, like fungus on old bread.

The man had a tattered coat around his shoulders. Trailing in the dirt with the sleeves hanging loose, it gave him the look of a large, bedraggled bird. She thought of a rook in a fresh-ploughed field: rooting through the soil in search of grubs.

In the lee of the hill, the breeze had dropped completely. Fran stood there, scarcely breathing, her eyes fixed on his back. Her confidence had come crashing down; the world was huge and hostile once again.

The man was wearing black, just like the figure in her dream. He had the same fair hair. She was suddenly sure that his unseen face was featureless: a hole. Empty – and about to turn towards her.

Cold beads of sweat popped out across her shoulders. She forced her gaze away, along the path. It led over the rise and out of sight. Or should she just go back around the hill? Retrace her steps to Westbury; pretend she'd never come.

She knew she couldn't. It was clear as the air, and the sudden, splashing sunlight. If she ran away from this, her mind would never rest.

It wasn't a dream – not this time. It might be a coincidence, of course . . .

Oh, yeah, she thought, with fatalistic scorn. *Oh, sure*.

Perhaps a premonition, then. Perhaps it was her fate, to meet this man. She'd never sniffed at things like that: second sight and such. But when she met him – what would happen then? The thought compressed her stomach. A chill of nausea rose towards her throat.

What was he doing? Writing with his finger in the dirt? Whatever, he was too engrossed to see her. She recalled what that woman had said in the church: about the man who'd visited before her. *One of those travellers*, she'd thought – and this man looked the part, at least. She tried to squeeze relief from the conclusion. A few diluted drops. They didn't soothe the churning in her belly.

The air grew briefly darker as a cloud cruised overhead. She glanced up, feeling trapped, as if a lid had just come down upon the bowl. The man kept working, head still bowed. Still tracing random patterns through the short-cropped grass.

The trackside fence was there between them. Barbed wire and iron pickets brown with rust. But the strands were wide apart here, and almost before she'd realized it, she had ducked her head between them, climbing awkwardly through. Something snagged at her jacket, drew it tight – and lost its grip. Setting foot in the field, she straightened up, and pulled the denim round her. Though she'd barely closed the distance by a yard, the hunched man was immediately more relevant. More real.

She saw him sense her presence. His loose, unwary posture grew suddenly stiff – as if he'd turned to stone beneath his coat. Like an animal's reaction: scenting danger. Adrenaline blazed through her, but she couldn't back off now. Too late, and much too close. She was committed.

His head, still turned away, came slowly up. A faint breeze touched his short, fair hair. Fran felt a leaden pressure in her chest.

He twisted round, still crouching, like a statue coming suddenly to life. Full of her fears, Fran started back; then saw his face, and froze.

It was just a man, of course: as real as his rags. His face was lean, unsmiling; thinly bearded with a stubble that looked darker than his hair. A thirtyish face, with a calmness that transfixed her. Some of its lines looked capable of laughter; but there was hard, unflinching bleakness in the bones. Both aspects came together in his gaze: eyes that were clear and choirboy-blue – but cold. As chilly as a frosty morning sky.

He watched her for a moment, still hunkering down. Dismayed though she was, she glimpsed a flicker of reaction on his face. Then he dropped his gaze once more, and rubbed his index finger in the soil.

She breathed again . . . and felt a twinge of pique. Absurdly, after what she'd feared, the anticlimax threw her. As the seconds passed, and he continued to ignore her, she felt her courage gathering afresh. Taking a breath, she risked a slow step forward. He didn't raise his head. But it was clear that he was watching from the corner of his eye.

'What are you doing?' she asked. Her voice seemed very small amid the stillness.

'Praying,' he replied, not looking up. 'I have many friends here.' His tone was low and thoughtful, made rougher by an unfamiliar accent. No time to try and place it. Fran hesitated; looked around. There was nothing to see. Just the slope of a depression; a grassy bowl of leached, infertile soil. A cluster of cows were grazing at the bottom.

Perplexed, she edged in closer. He glanced at her sidelong; did that nonchalance seem forced? For a moment he stayed motionless, as if in meditation. Then, bending forward, he resumed his finger-writing. She saw a ring gleam dully on his dirt-discoloured skin.

Some sort of New Age priest, or what? The landscape was peppered with earthworks, after all. And him wearing black like that . . . The breeze caught the sleeves of his sombre coat, and stirred them like vestigial wings.

Rook, she thought again. Then: *Raven*. Remembering the coin in the Edington poor box. It had looked like an antique, from a museum or a dig. Was he the one who'd left it?

She came to a halt: unwilling to go nearer, or retreat. The turn of events had left her quite bewildered. Her mind, not sick at all, had *shown* her this – but making contact with the man had settled nothing. What was he but a traveller, chasing visions of his own? She felt herself deflating: the upsurge of excitement plunging headlong back to earth. She was opening her mouth in helpless protest when something in the short grass caught her eye.

Even from a yard away, she thought it was a stone. A piece of flint, half-sunk into the soil. Then the sunlight shifted – and like a double-image drawing, it was suddenly quite different. She realized she was looking at the fragment of a skull.

It had barely been unearthed; just one socket, with its cheekbone and the curve of the temple. The bone was brown and flaky like blistered paint. Fran stepped around it, staring – and saw another one. There, where the soil crumbled, as if a molehill had caved in. No feature was distinctive; but the brittle, bony texture was the same.

Her skin, still damp with sweat, grew prickly-cold. She gave the man a nervous glance – and saw that he was watching. There was distant, grim amusement on his face. Then he signed the ground again; and the grass began to stir.

Fran felt a rush of disbelief: a giddiness that said *This isn't true*. The topsoil was decaying, breaking up before her eyes. A faint dust rose, and scattered on the breeze. The man had sat back on his bootheels, unperturbed. He gave her a fleeting glance, face solemn now. She saw a depthless satisfaction there.

The ribs came poking upward first: broken and bent, like trampled stalks. The sight was clear; her brain could not deny it. Then the jaw, still choked with dirt and full of rotten teeth. The sockets of the skull were blocked as well. They came up gazing blindly at the sky.

Fran's own eyes were just as round. She'd heard of the grim harvest in the battlefields of France: bullets and bones working upward to the surface. But this was like a time-lapse film: that creeping process crammed into a minute.

The earth grew quiet again. The skeletal remains were still half-buried. The man reached down, and gently touched the skull: tracing the sign of a cross on its fragile forehead. Then he straightened up, and turned towards her.

Fran took a small step back, still fingering her mouth.

The shabby coat hung on him like a cloak, reaching down to his knees; a straggle of dark fur around the collar. His trousers and shirt were black as well; the latter a granddad-type, its buttons gone. It revealed a vee of wind-burned skin, stretched shiny by the collarbone beneath it. A cross on a thong hung round his neck; a leather pouch as well.

A part of her, trapped deep inside, was urging her to run. But she felt as if she'd waded into glue. He began to move again, and so did she – trying to match his steps and keep her distance. Step by step, avoiding bones, they turned around each other. A slow, unnerving ballet. *Danse Macabre*.

His eyes on hers, he gestured – and she heard a scrapy rustling sound behind her. She craned her head around, and almost squealed. The crown of a skull had pushed up through the soil, as if to block her way.

When she turned again, the man was very close. The look on his face seemed darker than his weathered, grimy skin.

'These were my brothers once,' he said. 'They died their second death on Waste-Down. I come to set their souls to rest at last.'

He gazed at her in silence for a moment. From this close, only feet away, she thought that he seemed *wary*. Then, without warning, he spat into her face.

Fran stumbled back from that, as if he'd slapped her. Wide-eyed, she raised her fingers to her cheek. Anger sparked, but failed to ignite. Instead, she felt a stupefied despair.

He closed with her, grim-faced. She cowered back, still mired in glue: so shocked, she felt her balance start to go. Her arm flailed up; he caught and held it – grasped her slim wrist tight. Before she could get her free hand in, he was reaching for her face.

Don't let him, God, she thought, too late. Rough skin and calloused leather touched the smoothness of her cheek. She tried to twist her head away, her mind a blur of panic. The dark thing on her face began to move, its fingers creeping . . . but gently, almost tentatively now. Gasping for breath, she realized he was wiping off his spit.

She gawped at him; he stared right back. Eyes lurking in the dark between his brow and slim, straight nose.

'If the Virgin appeareth in a vision,' he said, like someone quoting, 'then spit thou in her *face*. Thou shalt presently know if she cometh from the Devil.'

He let go of her wrist, and fell to his knees, head bowed. 'Forgive me.'

Fran stood there, swaying: staring down at the breeze in his hair. *What?* she thought, quite flabbergasted. *What?* And now the anger came, so that she very nearly hit him. The anger and the fright.

He rose to his feet again. They faced each other. Her cheek felt raw and tingling from his touch. But she didn't, couldn't, flinch away as he reached for her again – and took her Cross of Nails between his fingers. Heart pumping hard, she watched his face. There was a hint of wonder on it now.

'You *are* she, then . . .'

The Virgin? Bloody Hell . . . 'I'm not,' Fran mumbled, shaking her head. 'Of course I'm not . . .'

His hooded eyes came up. 'I know. You are My Lady.' His fingers left the silver cross, and moved to her lapel. Shuddering, she watched them trace the contours of her icon.

'I have prayed to you long,' he murmured. 'For I knew that you would answer.'

Fran stared at him. It wasn't true, of course. It couldn't be. But neither could those skeletons have risen while she watched . . .

'Lady . . . may I know your name?' he asked.

She swallowed, once. 'I'm Frances.'

Something flared in those pale eyes. He took a step away, and crossed himself. Then nodded with a sombre, slow acceptance.

'So,' he said. 'You come from her? She has . . . forgiven me?'

Fran just nodded woodenly, not knowing what he meant.

'I know it is a sign, that you are come to me like this. What befalls? You must tell me. You must remember who I am.'

'I've . . . seen you in my dreams,' she said.

He nodded heavily. 'I pray I did not soil them. Our work was red and filthy, was it not? And now the call has come again, and we must answer.' His tone was almost weary – yet resigned. Like a soldier sick of war, she thought. A prisoner of his duty.

Then he said: 'Come with me.'

The whole world seemed to wait for her to answer. She was aware of every detail: the shifting clouds and shadows, and the breeze across the grass. Only the distant cattle stayed aloof.

'Who are you?' she whispered.

He gave his head the smallest shake. 'You do not know me, Frances?'

'Oh, please . . .' she said. 'I just don't know your *name*.'

'I am Athelgar,' he said, 'of Meone. Lord of the Ravens now.'

She remembered the testament at once – the will that Lyn had studied. Athelgar, *eorl*: a saint, or a magician. A man of high degree.

And here he stood before her now. She hadn't any doubt that it was him.

He was on the move already, walking off across the field. But his eyes were still on her, his hand held out. Invitation, and entreaty. Fran teetered on the brink – and then stepped forward. With a sense of plummeting through space, she followed in his wake.

From the top of the rise, the chalky track led down towards the range. There were fields to either side of it; farm buildings up ahead. The vedette post lay beyond them, cutting off a country lane: looking like a toytown sentry-box, from this far out.

Athelgar strode forward; Fran hurried to catch up. She felt a crazy confidence, as if nothing else could matter in the world. Maybe madness felt like this. But now, at last, she knew that she was sane.

'Why are you here?' she asked the man beside her.

He gave her a searching glance, as if expecting her to know. 'Here was that first battle when the Raven flew for us. And thus did Alfred hold the slaughter-field.' Again his accent puzzled her; that *gh* had a harsh, Germanic sound.

He didn't break his stride; the pale dirt crunched beneath their boots. She thought about those crumbled bones. 'You fought here, then?' she said.

A nod. 'We came, and fought, and many of us died. I have not passed this way again since then.'

'So, why come back?'

'I seek to know the reason we are called. We slept amid the houses of the stars, and someone roused us. But the summoning was all awry.'

She stared at him, still stumbling to keep up.

He seemed to sense her bafflement; indulged it. 'We are not many, now – but still enough to answer a petition. Yet no trysting-place was told this time. The Ravens have been scattered. I have wandered many months, and have not found them.'

They came to the farm, and crossed its stony yard. The sheds and silos looked deserted; but then a dog began to bark, a fierce and frantic sound. Fran's stomach jumped instinctively, but the animal stayed out of sight. Athelgar seemed unperturbed; she sidled close, and stuck to him like glue. As they left the farm behind, she risked a glance. Still no sign of the dog; but its disembodied barks went on and on. The thing was afraid, she realized then. Was frightened of the presence on its ground.

She looked at Athelgar; but Athelgar was staring up the road. They'd joined the lane from Bratton here, just short of the vedette. The way ahead to Imber was wide open.

'What are you doing here?' she asked again.

'This is my pilgrimage,' he said. 'To all the fields of mystery and slaughter. If I pass this way again, I may be shown the road I need.' He looked at her then: gazed right into her eyes. 'And did I not find *you*, my Lady Frances?'

Before she could respond, he'd started walking. Fran lingered on the spot for just a moment; then scurried up behind him as he crossed onto the range.

The ground was waste, all right. Churned-up earth, and barren heath, and shrapnel-peppered trees. Hunks of rusty wreckage lay beside the narrow road. Here and there, across their path, the tanks had gouged out trails of their own. Athelgar's gaze kept straying off along them. She wondered how she might explain: would *giant armoured wagons* fit the bill? Perhaps he thought they were the tracks of monsters.

A deathly silence hung across the land. They might have been the last two people living. Athelgar set the pace, and it was steady, unrelenting. Fran had to pant for breath before she got the question out.

'You said you'd not been back since . . . Waste-Down?' He nodded. 'But listen. Four years ago, not far from here, I ran into some *things* that looked like men. They chased me – almost caught me.' She shuddered at the memory; then gazed at him, wide-eyed. 'I thought they were a . . . vision, like. But now I know they weren't.'

He looked at her gravely. 'Even one like you should not go down these roads alone. This is dead, forgotten ground. Wolves and warlocks may walk freely here.'

'I had to come,' she muttered.

'I felt you near to me,' he said. 'That day at Heofonfeld.'

Heofonfeld, she thought. Then: *Heaven's Field*. Despite herself, she grasped his coat and brought him to a standstill. 'Who do you think I *am*?'

'A lady of the Northern saints,' he answered, vary calmly. 'At Heofonfeld, I opened up my heart and felt your light. From that day on – through all the blood – I have blessed your memory. Yet I never knew the name you bore, till now.'

Fran recalled what *she* had felt: that weird euphoria. 'When was this?' she whispered.

'The year nine hundred, four and thirty. When we brought the Scottish oath-breakers to heel.'

Fran just stared at him, open-mouthed. She loosened her grip; but he didn't move until she'd dropped her hands completely.

'Come,' he said, and touched her arm. 'We have many miles to go.'

They came down towards the junction where she'd dreamed of him before. The east-west road was empty, stretching out in both directions. Athelgar slowed his pace at last, scanning the barren slopes across the valley.

'Know you of the dragons?' he asked softly.

For a moment Fran was quite unnerved – then realized what he meant. She could picture them herself, as well: green monsters creeping west along the road. Clanking and roaring and coughing out fumes. She nodded once, unsmiling.

'I came this far two days ago,' he murmured, eyes still searching. 'One was abroad: I watched it for a long while. Others I heard, which were prowling in the hills. And a thunder like the ending of the world . . .'

'They're . . . back in their lair today,' Fran said: thinking of them in rows at the Warminster tank wash.

They reached the Imber road, and halted there. She glanced around at Athelgar, and saw he had a coin between his fingers. An ancient-looking silver piece – like the one back in the church. The silent pilgrim's parting gift. Of course it had been him.

'What say you, my Lady?'

'Oh, call me Fran,' she muttered.

He looked at her with narrowed eyes: as if the more familiar form had struck some deeper chord. Then he shrugged, and gestured with the coin. 'Crowns or Crosses, then. The left hand, or the right . . .' He flipped the coin up, caught it and displayed it on his palm. Fran stepped in close to see.

The design on this was different: just an Alpha in the middle. EADMUND REX the script around it said.

'It comes down Crowns,' said Athelgar, and closed his grimy fist around the coin.

They stepped onto the road, and started eastward away from the great bleakness of the Warminster downs. Even heading for the village, with its skull-eyed empty buildings, Fran felt a tiny flicker of relief.

They were just short of the village when Athelgar stopped – so abruptly that Fran went another yard before she realized. Looking back, she saw him tensing up.

She waited, frowning; suddenly uneasy. His dragons weren't around today – so what had he sensed?

'There are phantoms here,' he said.

Fran turned again, and looked along the road. The first building was just visible: a hulk of crumbled brick, behind the trees. Out of Bounds, as she recalled. Too dangerous for soldiers.

'This place is changed,' said Athelgar.

She prudently retreated to his side. 'You know it, then?'

'Immerie . . . not so?'

She hesitated. 'They call it Imber, now.'

'What befell it?'

'The soldiers came,' she murmured flatly. 'Nobody lives here now.'

'There are phantoms in our way. I will not go there.' He nodded to the grassland on the right, and crossed the road.

'Hang on!' Fran protested, as his meaning became clear. 'We're not allowed to leave the road . . .' She tailed off then: who gave a shit for by-laws on a day like this? And as for safety reasons – the risk of unexploded shells – she felt beyond reality right now. Able to walk on water, or through minefields.

With a quick glance back the way they'd come, she followed where he led.

The range wardens were doubtless on patrol, but they saw no one as they skirted round the ruined village. Fran had the same giddy feeling she remembered from her first walk-on: stumbling through the wind-bent grass, across forbidden ground. And nobody could touch her – not while she was walking with the man of her dreams . . .

(or nightmares)

Looking down at Imber from the hill above it, she was glad they'd given it a miss. The place still held memories of Craig, of course, but not enough to lighten its grim silence. The few surviving buildings were outnumbered by mock houses: just blackened concrete shells beneath the church. Like a pile of broken skulls, she thought. The harvest of the killing fields around it.

The ruins slipped away, into a fold of the valley. By the time they joined the road again, only the church tower was visible. Athelgar stared back towards it.

'How can there be a church without a flock?' he asked.

Fran shrugged. 'We had a war. Fifty years ago . . . They used it to train soldiers, and destroyed it. Then broke their word. They never gave it back.'

He frowned. 'Small wonder that the place is not at peace. Were they hirelings from across the sea who did this?'

Fran gave a small, bitter smile. 'No. They tried blaming the Americans . . . but it was British troops destroyed the place. On purpose. Their own people.'

'The warriors of the King?'

She thought about it. 'Yeah.'

He walked a little way along the road, then turned again. His face was difficult to read. Was it anger glinting in his eyes – or pain? 'I came back with the hope the land had changed,' he said. 'At last.'

'Oh no,' said Fran, and shook her head. 'It hasn't changed at all.'

The road led south and west, across the uplands of the range. The clouds had massed above it, like great heaps of slate and slag; but a buttermilk sky still showed on the horizon.

Fran plodded onward, lost in thought: the ache of her feet was scarcely getting through. The road stretched out ahead of them – so long, and still no turning. The empty heathland rustled in the wind, made bleaker by the shadows of the clouds.

Athelgar touched her shoulder, and she stopped. 'See,' he said. 'That dragon is still hunting.' His voice was low – but calm enough, considering.

She looked, and saw a helicopter, perhaps two miles away. A double-engined Chinook, quite familiar. She followed its course, and realized it was circling.

His touch became a grip. 'We must find shelter.'

'No, it's all right. Um . . . It's sort of a ship that flies. Those things going round, like windmill sails . . . they lift it through the air.'

He nodded gravely, staring at the thing. The chopper dipped into the valley, where its clatter was redoubled; then rose back into view again and curved towards the south. It felt like they were standing at the centre of its orbit. The clear sky silhouetted it; then murk became the backdrop once again. A crimson light was flashing, on and off.

Athelgar watched, fascinated. 'It makes signals.'

'Not to us.'

They tracked it over Imber Firs, where Cruise had lurked before; past Strip Wood, like a dark Mohican haircut on its hill; and finally it veered away, and faded in the grey haze to the north.

'Men have grown wise,' said Athelgar softly.

Fran let that pass without comment.

* * *

The end of the hike came suddenly, and caught her by surprise. The road began descending, turned a corner – and the Heytesbury vedette was up ahead. The walk had been interminable, yet now it seemed cut short. Fran stopped beside the barrier; the dull green sentry hut was locked and empty. Beyond, the road ran down to meet a farmer's sloping fields, and turned into another country lane.

As soon as she stopped moving, the weariness caught up. She felt her legs solidify like lead. She leaned against the grassy bank, and looked at Athelgar.

'How far are you going?'

'No further. I will turn again. No hand shall be against you from here on.'

She blinked at him; then looked back up the road. The thought of all that emptiness they'd come through . . . She swallowed, looked away again. Maybe not so empty, after all.

'What about me?' she murmured.

He gave her a sidelong glance. 'The road is hard and grievous, Lady Frances; and many lifetimes longer than today's.'

'Meaning what?' she asked. 'That I should go home and forget it?'

He looked at her full on, and then spoke grimly. 'You know the Ravens' calling: death and terror. Our way is paved with corpses. It is *no road* for one like you to walk.'

Chastened, she moved back a step – but couldn't keep from staring. 'You think I can run into *you*, and then just walk away?'

'Always shall we need your prayers. Watch over us in spirit. But with us, in the flesh, you may be *harmed*.'

But even as he spoke the words, his eyes were full of need – like somebody who'd had his fill of wandering alone. She stood there, gazing up at him, and felt a rush of feeling: delayed reaction, bursting through at last. Not disbelief, or even fear, but sheer exhilaration – the like of which she hadn't felt since roaring down the highway after Cruise.

But even more exciting was the sense of being called. The heady thrill of Heaven's Field. *My Lady. Come with me.*

She'd never felt so honoured – or protected. The violence that he'd talked about seemed mythic and unreal. Whatever journey he was on, it led to magic places. If the shadows were still out there, she could face them at his side.

She raised herself, and took hold of his coat. 'I want to come.'

'So let it be,' he said after a pause. 'There are things which I must seek amid the downland. Give me leave to see the way is clear, then come to me again.'

Swallowing, she eased away. 'When?'

'When the moon is round.'

Her heart was really thumping now. 'And . . . where do I find you?'

'There is a hamlet I have passed through, called Tils-Head. The downs are all around it. Seek me there.'

Fran nodded, knowing Tilshead well. She hadn't a clue when the next full moon was. Perhaps Lyn had an almanac or something.

A silence fell between them, almost awkward. *The parting of the ways*, she thought – and felt it like a wrench.

'Going to see me to the road?' she asked.

He nodded, and they crossed the line together: followed the leafy lane towards the grumbling main road. The windswept downland fell behind, and neither of them looked back. Though every instinct warned her that she should.

3

'I'm going to be quite late,' she said to Lyn. 'Expect me when you see me, I should think.'

'Oh Fran . . . Are you all right?'

'Yeah,' Fran said, and realized she was grinning. Euphoria fizzed inside her, like she hadn't felt for years. Top of the world

– on tiptoe. Later would be time enough to think about the drop.

'I've missed the bus from Heytesbury,' she gushed, 'that's all. I'll have to walk to Warminster, and catch the train from there.'

'Is it far?'

'Not very.' Though the way her swollen feet felt now, she'd have a job to manage half a mile.

'So how did it go?' Lyn asked, still sounding anxious.

'Really well. I think I've worked it out.' She peered out through the glass of the telephone box. Across the busy A-road, at the mouth of the lane, his figure was just visible: still watching.

'I'm so glad, Fran. I've been thinking about you lots today.' Fran could hear the relief in her friend's soft voice, and picture it on her face. Her love for Lyn just added to the inner glow she felt. But her stare remained fixed on the dark shape in the lane.

'I'll tell you more about it when I get back,' she promised. Though not everything, of course. Least of all the part that would make Lyn think she'd flipped her lid completely.

She talked, and gazed at Athelgar – until he turned away. Back towards the range, and all its ghosts. With clouds now over everything, the evening had come early. The lane was full of shadows, and they sucked him in at once.

II

SLEEPERS

Do your nightmares tear you apart?
Do you wake up screaming, shouting in the dark?
Do the demons keep you awake?
Does the clock tick more slowly with every breath you take?

THE LEVELLERS

Dear Craig

Hellooooo, gorgeous! Sorry that I haven't been in touch. I hope you had a good flight back. I'm really missing you.

I know you're wondering how things went, down on the Plain. Well, I walked across the Imber range, from Bratton down to Heytesbury. I took the 'American Road' (of course!) – right past the place where D-Flight got ambushed by their own blokes *back in February '89. The mission when you asked me out, in case you don't remember.*

I'm on a bit of a high at the moment (have you noticed?!). I've got things sorted out at last – more than I dared hope. Have you ever felt there's more to life than any of us dreamed? I won't go on about it, though. You'd really think I'd lost it if I did.

Lynnie sends her love. She's thinking a lot about her brother Martin at the moment. The family's lost touch with him, and she just got a card at Christmas time. He didn't give his address – nor a reason why he simply upped and went. The silence is the worst bit: the not knowing. I hope that I can cheer her up. She's done so much for me.

Write soon!

Love,
Your pinko commie peacenik girlfriend
Frannie

PS. What do you mean, the Air Force checks your mail??

CHAPTER I

Fiends and Ashes

I

Martin woke abruptly, with the dusk.

The gloom had seeped in silently, and caught him unawares. The bedroom was engulfed in it, the furniture submerged. The double bed, his life raft, was awash.

Panic clenched his muscles; he almost struggled upright straight away. Then slumped, as he remembered where he was. The dull, familiar room took shape again. Gloom clung to the wallpaper like filth. Only the window showed some light – a segment of colourless sky. From where he lay, the rooftops almost masked it.

Everything was in its place. The digits on the bedside clock were bright and reassuring. But the coldness in his limbs took several moments to recede. He felt as if he'd woken with a spider on his cheek.

He sat up stiffly, swinging his legs off the bed. The change in equilibrium made his empty stomach churn; he waited with his head down while it settled. Muzzily he rubbed his face; felt bristles rasp and chafe against his palms.

The flat was very quiet. The dusk had flowed right through it, soaking in. A couple more hours before Claire got back: sighing her way through the door and switching lights on. She'd find the place deserted, yet again. It would be full dark by then – and he'd be out there, in it.

Martin stretched inside his slept-in clothes; then got to his feet, and walked through to the bathroom. The cold tap knocked and shuddered as he filled a glass and drank, rinsing out the fetid taste of sleep.

A dim shape peered towards him from the mirror. He switched on the light and met it face to face. He was looking pale, his eyes half-sunk in shadow. They had a slightly mournful cast: it made his grin engaging, in a way that women liked. But when he was expressionless, like now, his stare was sombre.

The beard was five days old. His fingers reached above it, brushed the small scar on his cheek. A tiny nick of callused skin. He realized it was itching.

Still healing, after all these years.

Lyn had done that. He'd just turned five, but remembered every detail. At seven she'd been insufferable, a spoilt little brat: always bossing him around, as if two years made any difference. They'd been fighting in the playroom and she'd thrown a building block. The gashing pain had made him cry; the blood had made him bawl. But even through his tears, he'd seen her horrified white face, and known he was the winner after all.

He'd had to have a stitch, and been the centre of attention. Mum had fussed and held his hand, while Dad waited in the corridor with Lyn. She was going to get *what for* when they got home: that spiteful hope had kept his tears in check. But Dad had seemed to think that she'd already learned her lesson. And when Martin had emerged and seen her waiting – all big, scared eyes and tear-stained cheeks – he'd realized that he didn't *want* to see her this upset. Her fear was there for him, he sensed, as much as for herself.

Naturally, they'd fought again – but never quite as fiercely. From that day on, it sometimes seemed, they'd started drawing closer.

Lyn.

He savoured her name in silence – then swallowed it. A lump in his throat, then a dull ache in his stomach. But there was no point wondering what Lyn was doing now. Tonight, of all nights, he could do without the niggling dilemma: whether to get in touch, or keep his distance.

He killed the light again. The dusk, already thicker, closed around him. He went back to the bedroom, and walked over to the window. His heart began to thud against his ribs.

The sky was pale and clear outside. There would be stars tonight.

2

The house was on the corner, just down from the junior school. The orange streetlight bathed its bricks, which made it seem less menacing – at first. But even from across the road, he could see where smoke had blackened it: freakish shadows underneath the lamp. The chipboard in the windows stood out clearly.

The Burnt House – that's what everybody called it. The kids had told him so. On winter nights they hurried past it, straggling in groups. A ghost was boarded up inside, and that was gospel. A little boy's ghost – burned black.

Martin looked both ways. Nothing was coming; but still he hesitated.

He'd been working as a cleaner when he picked the story up. Some of the kids had been talking in the corridor: clearly trying to dare – and scare – each other. Intrigued, he'd slowly mopped his way towards them, feeling his breathing tighten as the pieces made a whole.

'Someone went in there, right? Went in there, and they found him, and he'd been trying to crawl under a door. Something in the room had scared him so much . . . he was trying to crawl under the door.'

He'd ventured to intrude, and they'd been happy to include him. 'Do you believe in ghosts at all?' a fair-haired boy had asked him.

'Yes,' he'd told them solemnly. 'I do.'

Or something like them.

So they'd told him what they knew about the Burnt House. Different people had subtly different versions; there were elements of urban myth developing already. But he didn't doubt the truth behind it all. The knowledge seemed to suck his stomach dry.

He'd wondered if the tale they told was giving them bad dreams. Perhaps, with some of them, it was – but they kept on coming back to it. Their growing minds could stretch to fit. But Martin had felt nauseous for hours.

The house looked unassuming in the daytime, despite the sooty marks around its windows. The sheets of board were blank and bland – screening off the gutted depths within. But the first time he'd walked past it, he had sensed the void inside. The place was light-proof: sealed against the day. Tonight, by sallow streetlight, it seemed so full of darkness it might burst.

The sound of footsteps reached him, coming up towards the corner from the south. The railway arch was back that way, an unlit lane beyond it. He turned his head uneasily – then breathed out as he recognized her shape.

She paused at the junction, spotted him, and crossed: relief had put a spring into her step. He didn't blame her. The Burnt House was the last place you would want to get stood up.

'Hello,' said Martin drily.

Lucy smiled. 'All ready, then?' Now that they'd met up, she seemed quite perky.

'Yeah,' he said, encouraged. 'Thanks for coming.' He glanced towards the house again. 'Romantic, isn't it?'

Looking, she laughed softly. Eighteen now, with college in the autumn. She had a pleasant, snub-nosed face and short dark hair. Claire – who didn't know – would be suspicious: naturally. But Lucy was a friend, and nothing less.

He'd met her at a vigil in a local, 'haunted' church: the sort of thing he would have jeered at once. Like many of the ghost-watchers, she had a sceptic's mind: always on the lookout for an easy explanation. And yet she felt the *mystery*, like he did. She had a real scientist's awe for that.

He felt he could see eye-to-eye with someone who'd enjoyed *The Selfish Gene*. He'd heard about the Burnt House and had called her. He didn't want the group along, with all their paraphernalia. Their vigils were too organized. They made the dark too safe.

'So what are you expecting?' she had asked him.

'To see if something's in there. To get close.'

She'd hesitated. 'We've nothing to record it with.'

'Maybe not,' he'd murmured. 'But we'll *know*.'

They went in round the back way, under cover of the overgrown garden. The back door had been forced before, presumably by squatters. It occurred to him to wonder just how long they'd stuck it out. A night, perhaps. Or maybe less than that.

The dark inside was choking – like a foretaste of extinction. He flicked his torch on quickly and played it around. The kitchen was bare, its walls begrimed, but the damage here was minimal. The seat of the fire, for once, had been elsewhere.

A foul smell still lingered in the air. The stench of stuff corrupted by the flames.

Grimacing, he looked up towards the ceiling. The plaster and paint had cracked like a drought-ravaged field. The light-fixing was gone, the flex protruding. It hung in the penumbra of the beam. He moved the light away, and glanced at Lucy.

'Okay?'

'I'm fine,' she murmured calmly.

He led the way in deeper, hearing brittle cinders crunch beneath their boots. The fire had swept the front room and the hall. The walls looked black and oily in the beam; there were traces of a pattern in the rags of wallpaper. The ceiling had collapsed, exposing skeletal charred wood. The ruin of an easy chair still squatted in the corner.

Lucy had her own torch out: she shone it up the stairs. The gloom up there absorbed the light completely.

'It started up there?' she asked – almost whispering now.

He wet his lips and nodded. 'In the bedroom.'

The glow of her torch slid down onto the staircase. 'Reckon it's safe?'

The stairs looked fairly dodgy, but he wasn't sure she'd meant them. 'Let's . . . just wait for a bit.'

'And see what happens?'

He waited for her to turn her head; then nodded grimly. 'Yeah.'

She shrugged. 'Is it all hearsay, then? Or has anyone actually seen it . . . heard it?'

'Well, one of the girls *claimed* she heard something knocking on one of the window boards, when she was running past one night. She always runs past the place, she says.'

'Could have been anything, then. Or any*one*.'

'That's what I thought. But one thing's for sure, she's scared of something. They all were, underneath their smiles.'

'And one child was killed in the fire here, right?'

'Right. About a year ago, I think. But there's more to it than that . . . or so they said.'

She clicked her torch off and came back into the shell of the front room. 'Oh yes? You didn't tell me that.'

'It isn't nice,' he muttered flatly.

'No . . .' she said. 'I don't suppose it is. Well, you've obviously been saving it, so better tell me now.'

He let the torch beam sink, and pool between them.

'This is what they said, all right? The little boy who lived here kept having bad dreams. Someone was coming to get him, you know the kind of thing. Anyway, one night he wakes up screaming: says that someone's in the bedroom, running fingers through his hair. So his mother comes, and gets him settled down. Then half an hour later, he's screaming again. So she goes to him again. And it's a demon, apparently. A demon keeps appearing in the room. She gets him off again. And then, on her way to bed, she decides to look in on him . . . and when she gets to the door, and touches it, it's *hot*.'

'Oh, Jesus,' Lucy whispered.

'So she opened it, of course she did, and the fire was just let loose. She and her husband got out with severe burns. The boy died in his room.'

She stared at him; then brushed her mouth, as if to wipe a sour taste away. 'Bloody hell.'

'Yeah.'

'Any . . . cause for the fire, do they know?'

'Not that I've heard. Could have been an electrical fault . . . or something.'

'Or something. Yeah.' She looked up at the ceiling. 'So what do they reckon is haunting here? *His* ghost? Or . . . whatever might have killed him?'

'Maybe both.' He paced around; then looked at her again. 'My dad told me a story once. A legend of King Arthur, 'cause he's into all that stuff. They were caught in some place, his knights and him – besieged by burning ghosts. And when the ghosts were stabbed, they lost their shape, *becoming fiends and ashes*.'

Lucy's smile was wry enough; but her shudder didn't look entirely faked. She watched as he unstuffed his bag and spread a tattered blanket on the floor. They both sat down. She'd brought her Thermos flask. Pouring a cup, she paused and glanced around.

'You can't feel anything, can you?'

He hesitated. The house itself felt looming, ghastly, steeped in its despair. But nothing seemed to move within its walls. He shook his head.

'Neither can I,' she said, and gave a wan little smile. The perkiness had died away long since.

By midnight, he'd worked up the nerve to try and broach the subject.

The Burnt House was still dormant, but its aura felt increasingly oppressive. A claustrophobic itch had started nagging: as if the place was sealed again, and they were trapped inside.

He glanced more than once at his propped-up torch, almost willing himself to see it flicker.

The past – his past – was creeping up: the atmosphere congealed to give it shape. He knew he'd talk before the night was out. Like the onset of a stomach ache that has to end in sickness. And this would be a purging, too – and maybe a relief.

He glanced at Lucy. Their small talk had subsided, but the silence was companionable enough. He'd never breathed a word of this to anyone before; he wasn't sure how even she'd react.

So begin at the beginning. Building-blocks.

'What's your theory, then: on ghosts?'

She looked at him over the plastic mug. 'I thought you knew.'

'After-images and such?'

She shrugged. 'Or psychic echoes. Call them what you like. I think they're just a way of seeing into the past. Not sentient at all.'

'And not things that can hurt you.'

She shook her head.

'So what about demons, then?'

'Doesn't that imply a Christian view?'

'Other religions have them. Evil spirits.'

'Active agents, you mean; rather than passive images?'

He nodded slowly, thinking of the burning room upstairs. The house had always felt unsafe, but now the air of dull threat seemed to grow.

'Maybe,' she conceded – and looked at him quizzically. 'Why?'

He glanced around; then back at her. 'I think I might have called one up, one time.'

Lucy straightened up. 'What, in a seance or something?'

'No, I was at home and it was the last thing on my mind. I never believed in things like that.' Restless now, he clambered up as if relieving cramp.

'But now you do?' she murmured.

He looked around, and nodded.

'So what happened?'

'I don't *know*. I was looking at something in one of my dad's old books; just stringing names together in my mind . . .' He wet his lips. '*Dubhe* and *Merak*; *Alioth*. Mean anything to you?'

'No, but they sound like mythical names. Forgotten gods, or something?'

He gave a small, tight smile and shook his head. 'They're the names of *stars*, that's all: the stars in the Plough. This was just a picture of a medieval star-chart. One that was used for magic of some kind.'

She frowned at that. 'So . . . what was it like? This thing that came.'

'There were more than one,' he said.

'You saw them?'

'I just heard them. That was worse. It was like I'd been struck blind – I couldn't see. But in my head, I saw these *images*.'

Lucy was absorbed by now. '*Martin*. How come you've never mentioned this before?'

'Because I couldn't fucking cope with it. I've not told *anyone* before – not even my own sister. I'd trust her with anything, but not this. I can't lump her with *this*.'

Her bright eyes didn't blink. 'What happened then?'

'Nothing. I just waited. I was too afraid to move. And *Christ*, I thought the dawn would never come.' He breathed in deeply. 'When it did, I found that I could see.' Another pause. He shrugged. 'The house was empty.'

'And nothing since?'

'Not a whisper. Nothing for two years. That's why I've kept searching. I need to look them in the face again.'

Lucy sat there, watching, with her back against the wall. 'You sound like my old boyfriend,' she said drily. 'He backed down from a fight one time, then kept on reliving it, and winning. It wasn't as if I minded. Stupid git.' Her tone was shrewd but amiable enough. He smiled thinly, scuffing at the cinders.

'Believe me, girl, I'd run a *mile* from this lot.'

Her expression grew more pensive. 'You've considered –'

'That it might be something psychiatric?' He shoved his hands into his pockets; took a breath. 'Jesus, Luce: of course I have. That's another reason why I have to keep on looking. I know what I saw. It's just, I need to *prove* it to myself.

'There's something else. I'm sure that what I saw that night was something from *outside*. Something science doesn't understand – not yet. And if it's there, I want another look.' He crossed the room abruptly, startling her. 'I'm going upstairs now.'

She stared up at him. 'Hey, listen . . .'

'There might be something up there. If there is, I have to see it. Are you coming?'

She hesitated. He saw how much her confidence had dwindled; she was looking very young now. 'No,' she said, and shook her head. 'I'm not.'

'I don't blame you. I really don't. But don't go away, all right?' He turned towards the stairs.

'What images?' she asked, belatedly.

Looking back, he hesitated: trying to find the words.

'Like predators with human skins,' he said.

The house, of course, was empty. Though its past was real and horrible enough, he sensed no echoes from it. The upper floor was desolate: just empty, mournful darkness. If something evil had been here, it had gone its way long since.

His reaction was the same as always: frustration and relief in equal measure. They wiped each other out, and he was left there feeling nothing.

Lucy ventured up a short while later, not wanting to be left alone downstairs. He saw her torchlight flashing from the corner of his eye, but stayed where he was: letting her track him to the scorched shell of the bathroom. One of the window-boards was missing here. He'd switched his own torch off so that his eyesight could adjust.

'What . . . ?' she asked, still waiting on the threshold.

'It's all right. Put the light out. Come and see.'

She joined him cautiously. In the black frame of the window, the stars were very bright: scores of them compressed in that small gap.

'There's the Plough,' he told her, peering out. 'Up overhead . . . you see?' The names began to form again, like whispers in his head. *Dubhe. Merak. Phecda. Megrez* . . . He forced them out of focus, and tried to fix his thoughts on something else. Like chasing Vicki round the field, beneath those same bright stars.

'I had this girlfriend, back in school. I used to try and teach her constellations.'

'And was she interested?' asked Lucy wryly.

Martin's smile came easier. 'Only in the mnemonic for classifying stars. *Wow, Oh Be A Fine Girl and Kiss Me Right Now – Smack.*'

She giggled. 'Snog or slap?'

He shared her grin, relieved at last. However briefly.

'Now *that* would be telling.'

They left the house, and lingered in the road. Martin adjusted his rucksack, looking round. The junction was deserted. The Burnt House seemed to hold it like a strongpoint.

'Want me to walk you home? I will.'

'Just to the bus stop, Martin, thanks.' They turned towards the railway arch. After a pause, she glanced at him. 'You're going to keep on looking?'

'Yeah.'

'I'm going off to Uni in October; but anything before that, let me know . . .'

He nodded wordlessly, and then looked back. The instinct was a primal one: alertness to some danger. Nobody was following, and yet the itch persisted: a nervous urge to grasp her hand and run. To flee, and keep on fleeing down these endless lamplit corridors of night.

3

It was one o'clock when he slipped into the flat. Locking the door, he tiptoed through the dark. Every sound seemed magnified; but Claire didn't wake. Not even when he slithered into bed.

He settled down beside her, and listened to her breathe; trying not to think of how she must have spent her evening. Coming back from her shift to an empty house and a scrawled note on the table. Perhaps she'd cried a little, as she sat and watched TV. A pang of guilt transfixed him – but it faded soon enough.

Perhaps he'd feel the same with a more everyday addiction: alcohol, or gambling, or drugs. Hurting somebody he loved – and yet not sparing her. Watching while things went to hell, unable to let up.

CHAPTER II

Out of the Deep

I

If you fancy her, she's got a boyfriend. Since leaving school, he'd found it was a universal rule: like the second law of thermodynamics, only stricter. But then he'd met Claire – attractive, unattached. *If she goes out with me,* he'd thought, *the universe collapses.* And yet, despite his disbelief, they'd somehow got this far.

He'd been portering at the hospital – the latest in a string of low-paid jobs – and met her when he'd come to fetch a body, of all things. Claire had been the nurse in charge: confident and friendly as she took things in her stride. Heartened, he had noticed she was rather pretty too, with her gilded, gamine haircut and clear blue eyes. He'd asked her out (not then, of course), already gearing up for a rebuttal. But she'd said yes. The universe continued to exist. And six months later, here he was: sharing her flat like a *partner*, not a boyfriend.

He stirred in the bed, still half-asleep. A shape of warmth was dwindling beside him – as if she'd left her shadow on the sheet. Claire was in the kitchen now; he could hear the kettle boiling in the background. He tried to gauge her mood by her movements. Sloppy and resigned – or brisk and angry? Sitting up, he listened like a guilty little boy.

She hadn't dumped her sleepshirt, but her dressing gown was missing from its hook. Gone were the days when she'd bring him tea, wearing nothing but her briefs. He pictured her, still pasty and dishevelled – and felt a surge of longing. So maybe it was really love this time.

And he looked set to let it go to waste.

She'd seen behind his mask by now: she knew he'd been disturbed by things he wouldn't talk about. When she'd failed to coax them out, she'd given him some room: putting up with his moods and his late-night walks. She knew he was in with the ghost-hunting group – though not that he would sometimes watch alone.

He'd moved on from the hospital: he found it too unsettling. It was the district's psychiatric unit – a grim Victorian barracks on the outer edge of town. Moving through its garrison of patients, he kept on getting glimpses of himself. Hunted faces, haunted eyes. Perhaps he really was as mad as they were.

Claire would call them *ill*, of course, and talk with them for hours. Perhaps she saw him as a patient too. Perhaps she only kept him on to pity. Or observe.

Shaking off that paranoid thought, he got up, pulled his boxers on, and went into the kitchen. Claire was sitting at the table, glancing listlessly through the paper. Her legs were crossed, and naked to the thigh – but her glance was guaranteed to kill all passion.

'So when did *you* get in last night?'

He winced. 'About one-ish . . .'

Her baby blues were hard today. 'Don't take me for granted, Martin. I know you need your space – but *I* need to be treated like a girl you care about.'

'I'm sorry, right?' He turned away, towards the cafetiere.

'I suppose something for the rent would be out of the question?' she went on flatly.

'Can it wait to the end of the week?'

He sensed her glower at his back, then look down at the paper. Here, in this cramped kitchen, he could feel the gulf between them. But how could he begin to build across it?

The cracks were showing up at last. The universe was crumbling. You couldn't break a cosmic law and hope to walk away.

2

It was Lyn, in all her innocence, who'd told him of the star-chart.

They'd been wheeling their bikes along the lane: the end of a hot day's cycling in the country. The sky was beaten gold behind the gables of the cottage, but the air still held a pleasant glow of warmth. Lyn looked sleek and trim in shorts and T-shirt. His mates all called her *Martin's snooty sister*, but he knew how envious they were of him. Here she was, this gorgeous girl, and he was living under the same roof. And Martin would smile, content to let them stew. *They* never saw her loll around, or cut her nails, or sulk. Or come round very timidly to ask if he could help unblock the loo . . .

Tick-tick-tick said the turning wheels beside them.

'Is that a star?' she asked him, looking back towards the east.

He turned, and saw a point of light, pricked out through the deepening blue.

'Not that bright, this early . . . It's Jupiter, I think.'

She shook her head, still staring. 'I think it's great, that you can *see* the planets.'

'You should look at it through the telescope. See the moons and everything.'

'I'd like to,' she said softly. 'After supper. Give me a knock, I'll just be reading.'

'Book*worm*!' he teased delightedly; she giggled, made to swipe at him. But he was pleased beyond measure by her interest. She was going back to college next weekend. He missed her very much when she was gone.

They came up past the orchard. The countryside was quiet, bathed in amber; but some swallows were still spiralling around. The west face of the cottage would be glowing, but the walls this side were dark with dusk and ivy. The place had been a rectory once: a rambling old building which their parents had restored over the years. *Cottage* was hardly the word for such a warren of rooms. But for children growing up it was a fairytale house: a castle of their dreams.

'Have you seen that map in Daddy's book?' Lyn asked him at the gate.

'Which one?'

'There's a medieval star-map. I found it years ago . . .' She let him wheel his bike into the shed.

'What, a zodiac or something?'

She shrugged, and pushed her own bike in. 'I don't know. It's got all the constellations on it. Used for magic spells, apparently.'

'Yeah?' He finished locking his bike, and straightened up. 'Sounds interesting. Which book?'

'*Magic in the Middle Ages*, or something like that. One of the ones we weren't allowed to touch.'

He grinned. 'But you did?'

'Mm. I got a real telling-off, as well.'

'Well, serves you right for being a naughty girl. But thanks,' he added quickly, both hands raised to fend her off. 'Seriously . . . I'd like to have a look.'

'Come on, you,' she grinned, and turned away. 'We're just in time. Let's see what's on the menu.'

He hadn't given it much thought, until a few weeks later. Autumn was advancing, and the nights were drawing in. He'd failed his driving test again, so couldn't use the car: it felt like being stranded in the sticks. The cottage was still home to him – still big enough to lose himself inside. But relations with his parents were beginning to grow strained.

Mum was patient, like she'd always been: soaking up his selfishness, his adolescent moods. She knew that he was raring for the off – to follow Lyn. *Not long now*, she'd told him once, *it's just around the corner*. So long as he kept studying. He had to get his grades.

His father was more distanced, as if unsure what to say. He rarely ventured up to Martin's room. And that was just as well, from Martin's viewpoint. He'd probably feel bound to pass some comment on the pin-ups. At least Mum turned a blind eye to those.

Now and again, there'd be a spark between them. Dad listened to the radio in the evening as he worked: Radio 3, on quietly in the background. But sometimes, like the other night, he'd switch to Radio 4. And Martin had stood listening on the landing – hearing the twangy, ethereal opening bars of *The Hitch-Hiker's Guide to the Galaxy* come drifting through the open study doorway. He could have gone in then, and shared his interest. But their talk might have turned to other things – like study and exams.

To some extent, he'd grown up in Lyn's shadow. She'd won all the prizes – and got the marks that he would have to match. The challenge was unspoken, and it didn't come from her. His parents hadn't pushed it, not overtly. And yet he seemed to feel it every day.

He'd countered it by digging in his heels. Lyn had gone to private school, but he'd refused point-blank. Dad had nudged him on towards an Oxbridge application, but Martin was content to go for London. *And yes*, he thought, *I'll sit down and revise*. But not tonight.

At least the unlit fields round here gave clear sight of the stars. He'd got the timer working on the telescope, and was planning to take some photos of the sky. His parents were away tonight, and Lyn was back at Oxford. As he ate his supper, he recalled what she had said.

An antique star-map. Interesting. Worth looking at, before Orion rise.

He loaded the dishwasher, then went up to the study. No prohibition now, of course; though Lyn was the one who'd always been attracted. He tracked his gaze along the shelves, and found the likely volume soon enough. *Myth and Magic in Medieval Europe*. He took it to the desk, sat down and started flicking through. Finding the chart, he unfolded it with care. Something about it made him catch his breath.

The map showed all the seasons of the stars. He sat there, poring over them, as if this were some kind of mythic realm. That was how they would have seemed, six hundred years ago. Part of him still felt that he could lose himself amongst them.

Yet each star was a thermonuclear furnace, breaking down the fabric of the Cosmos to keep running. That was more miraculous, to him, than any myth.

Nonetheless, intrigued, he kept on looking. Clustered in the centre were the signs that never set – the Little Bear, the Dragon and the Plough or Greater Bear. Each one bore an unfamiliar name.

branpen. fluðar. aeðelgar.

He didn't recognize those words – nor many of the others. Some were too obscure to be deciphered. The outer ring was full of weird scribbling, with gothic crosses used like punctuation. He made out the word *Agla*, which he'd noticed in the text. Leafing back, he found it was a Hebrew acronym, often used in medieval magic.

Ata Gibor Leolam Adonai. Thou art mighty for ever, O Lord.

Returning to the chart, he started checking constellations – tracking down his favourite ones like close friends in a crowd. The detailing was exquisite. Most of the stars bore their Arabic names, evocative and strange. Sheratan and Sadalsud; Aldèbaran; Al Nath. Antares, at the Scorpion's heart, was inked with murky red.

The stars of the Plough had their own peculiar rhythm: from Dubhe and Merak, pointers to the Pole, to Benetnasch, the last star in the tail. He knew those well, and mouthed them one by one.

His finger traced the patterns: following the lines from star to star. Boötes, the great Herdsmen, had been dubbed *leofric* here; the crooked kite of Auriga was *ealdred*. The Great Dog – Canis Major – had *dominicain* beside it. He guessed that these were magic words – the constellations being used as symbols. Or sigils, or whatever they were called.

Dubhe. Merak. Phecda . . .

Suddenly he realized it was getting hard to see. The desk lamp was beginning to go out. He looked up quickly – startled by a sense of someone with him in the room. Nobody was there, of course; but the lamp continued dying. Its yellow light turned reddish as the power was sucked out, to disappear like blood into the dark. The filament remained, a burning thread – then that faded, too. Darkness swallowed up the desk.

He saw the stars were glowing.

The first thing that he felt was awe: they had a spectral beauty. Charted with luminous paint, he thought . . . then realized this was just a photograph. And the pinpoints were too bright for that – bright enough to shed a cold light of their own. Then the stars went out: became black holes. He felt the sight being sucked out of his eyes. The last faint tinge of bluish light was swallowed by the book.

Martin sat there, stupefied – and suddenly the universe burst open all around him. It felt as if his thinking mind had risen from his body, straight up through the ceiling and the roof. The rectory just vanished, and the stars were everywhere: ones that hadn't risen yet, and some he wouldn't see until next spring. His nostrils were filled with the night's distinctive smell – a fresh aroma, strangely sweet, and *dark* inside his head.

Then he tumbled back to earth. The starlight followed, piercing the study – as if the house was riddled full of worm-holes. Something brighter than the sun came blazing through each one. The sight lasted a fraction of a second. Then darkness; and he realized he was blind. Panicking, he clawed his face, his eyes. He couldn't see.

He could still feel empty countryside; the vaulted sky above. The night was somehow with him in the room.

Reaching out, he found and grasped the book. Visions came unbidden to his disbelieving mind. Far horizons opened in his head.

He saw a landscape torn apart by war: trampled roads, and gutted towns, and fields of mud and bodies. It made him think of Bosnia, in all its eastern bleakness. But then he noticed medieval details; the corpses lashed to wheels on top of poles. They stood in silhouette against a strangely glowing sky. The night was lit, as if by fires just over the horizon. The colours were stupendous; majestic clouds reflected in the pools of stagnant mud.

With a sudden plunge of vertigo, he realized what they were. Nebulae in deepest space: the wombs of dust and gas that formed the stars. Towering above the earth, and drifting on the wind.

Voices rose around him in a babble: snatches of speech from many mouths, like samplings on a record. The language was unearthly and corrupted – but then he caught a snatch of words he recognized.

'*He hath made me dwell in darkness like those long dead . . .*'

A different smell engulfed him, and he gagged and almost retched. Like mushroom-mouldy earth and shit, stuffed deep into his nose. The dreadful stench had other flavours too: of mildewed cloth, and rotting wood, and reams of musty paper. The smell of age, and all it had corrupted.

'*My soul waits for the Lord,*' said a sonorous voice, '*more than watchmen wait for morning . . .*'

The landscape was changing, like decomposing tissue seen in time-lapse. The nebulae were different, too. He glimpsed the dark, contorted Horse's Head.

'*. . . but my face shall not be seen.*'

He turned around inside his skull, but couldn't find the speaker. Instead there was just a field of crosses. Shapes were walking past him now, and weaving through the markers. He watched them go – powerless to follow, even if he'd wanted to.

'*. . . but my face shall not be seen,*' the grim voice said.

The figures kept on trudging past, towards the haunting flares along the skyline; but one of them looked back over his shoulder. His face was gaunt, like something starved. His eyes bored into Martin's.

Terror leaped up, like a flame – but the phantom didn't

pause. The shadow-army carried him away. His pale face faded in the burning gloom. And Martin was still rooted by that glance of accusation.

'. . . *watchmen wait for morning* . . .'

He was still inside his body. His hands felt warm and slimy on the book. *Blood*, he realized, horrified. The visions melted, folding into blackness. He sensed the study closing up, encasing him in silence. It was colder than an empty grate in winter.

A scuttling movement crossed the room. The sound a rat might make – but much too loud. Martin yelped with fright, and drew his legs up. He remembered the picture on the wall: the one that used to give Lyn nightmares. It felt like he'd been swallowed up inside it.

But there was just that one swift movement; nothing more. Huddled on the chair, he hugged his knees and started shaking. His eyes were useless: dead as failed lightbulbs.

'I'm not blind,' he kept murmuring. 'It's something in my head.'

Oh Jesus, let me see the stars again.

His skin was bathed in sweat, like icy water. Slowly, as the hours passed, he felt it start to dry. And all the while he listened to the house. Now and again it creaked somewhere, and all his nerves caught fire. But nothing came towards him through the void.

He didn't dare to trust that first pale glimmering of light. He blinked, and screwed his eyes tight shut – then opened them again. A gluey smudge was growing in the darkness. Slowly it congealed, becoming furniture and shelves. The room took shape around him, still muted in the greyish light of dawn.

It was deserted.

Martin sat there stiffly for a few minutes more; then carefully prised his knotted limbs apart. His muscles cramped in protest, and his bladder started aching. Ignoring it, he clambered up and leaned against the desk.

The air smelt as it always had: a subtle, bookish, papery

aroma. He sniffed, but found no trace of fouler odours. His hands were clean and dry: no trace of blood. The desktop showed its weathered grain. The paper was unstained.

The house felt hushed and empty. He listened, breathing shallowly, then ventured to the door. The living room was spun with twilight cobwebs. The stairwell door to Lyn's room hung ajar.

Attic, he thought, and gazed at it: unwilling to go up. After a pause, he went back to the study. The star-chart was unfurled across the desk. He felt a pang of stomach cramp, but crossed the room towards it.

A photo of a drawing – that was all it bloody was. But panic kept on simmering inside him. The evidence had disappeared; the memory remained. Staring at the chart, he felt a groundswell of revulsion. For a moment he hesitated; then took one corner between finger and thumb, and folded it again. Then closed the book and crushed it. Heart spasming, he carried the volume back, and shoved it into place upon its shelf.

Even Lyn had been a stranger after that.

Her bright and newsy letters home seemed suddenly banal. He'd looked forward to her phone-calls once, but now their Sunday chats were full of small talk. Before, he'd been so envious – watching her leave home to make her fortune. Now her student life was insignificant to him: completely overshadowed by the wonders that he'd seen. Now *he* was the experienced one, and she was just an innocent abroad.

He'd wanted to share it, but he couldn't find the words. Perhaps he'd been afraid that she would laugh it off and tease him. More likely, he was scared that she'd *believe*. His turn to feel protective now. He couldn't drag her into this, and cloud her sunny sky.

The shadow didn't go away. It lingered in the corners of his heart, like winter mould. The brightest sunlight couldn't clean it out. Gradually the fungus spread: through dank and stifled places, deep inside. Everything was different now. Things like grades and college didn't matter any more.

Something science doesn't understand. The laws in which he'd put his trust were teetering – about to tumble down. He had to find the real ones, and see the Universe come back together. Above all else, he had to know the truth.

But how could he explain all that to Claire?

He sat down with his cereal now; she stood up with a see-saw huffiness. As she passed, he tried to stroke her thigh. She slapped him off.

'Fuck off, Martin. Let me be, all right?' Biting her lip, she went back to the bedroom.

Chastened, Martin watched her go; then started on his breakfast. The cornflakes tasted sodden, like wet cardboard in his mouth.

CHAPTER III

Predicator

I

Through the toughened day-room glass, the grounds looked insubstantial: receding in the mist and fading light. The afternoon was gloomy; the buzzing glare of strip-lights served to darken it still further. A thick haze had engulfed the fields and wood.

Here inside, the air seemed just as dense.

The man they knew as John was at the window – gazing out into the murk, as if entranced. There were other people in here too; but to Claire it seemed as if the man in white had brewed this up himself. He was drawing on a cigarette, detached and calm as ever; the smoke hung all about him like a wreath. The fags were second nature now: he smoked them almost absently – mechanical as an iron lung. The ash flared with the slow pulse of a lighthouse. A dozen chain-smoked butts were in the ashtray on the table, the last of them still adding to the grey haze in the room.

The air was acrid in Claire's throat; she didn't need to fake a cough. A couple of the others turned to look. But John kept his eyes on the ghostly world outside.

'All right now, John . . .'

The ash glowed fiery orange; died again. John loosed a last grey breath of smoke, and slowly turned his head. She felt an apprehensive prickle touch her neck.

A fierce face: she'd thought so from the start. The bones of a handsome man were there; the dark eyes of a wise one. But the unkempt hair and scrubby beard gave him a wild appearance. Both hair and beard were grizzled, though he looked to be mid-thirties; his skin was tanned and toughened, deeply lined. A scowl sat best upon that face – anchored firmly in the glower of the eyes.

'They're ready for you now,' Claire told him firmly. She stood aside, inviting him to come.

And John the smoker nodded, glancing down. Focusing once more on the word he'd scratched, in the paint beside the window. Spider letters, thumbnail-etched. No one else had noticed, and he knew it. But now he had it captured. He would not forget again.

More than just a word, of course; a *Name*. It had come again last night, still fresh, from out of desert places in his mind. The rest would surely follow in its tracks.

Murzim. The Announcer.

A faint smile twitched his mouth like a galvanized muscle: briefly alive, then lifeless as before. Straightening up, he walked towards the keeper of the door.

'Thank you for seeing us, John,' said Dr Lawrence.

The other's cold eyes didn't blink. He'd nursed his cigarette almost down to the butt: each puff drawn in, and lazily expelled. Like the slow, unconscious breathing of a thing in hibernation. But the mind behind those eyes was wide awake.

It seemed he'd never smoked before he came here. The case notes mentioned wariness, and blank incomprehension. But then he'd had a go, and grown voraciously addicted. Watching him, in search of a response, Lawrence noted again how he held his cigarette: between the second and third fingers, so that each drag masked half his face. Like somebody still learning the technique.

The other clients kept him well-supplied; gathering round to hear him speak. Something about his ramblings seemed to reach their deeper selves. *Bible John*, they called him; a name with sombre echoes of some half-forgotten crime.

'We're here to review the progress of your case,' Lawrence

went on. 'Dr Andrews here is on my team . . .' An affable nod from the younger man. 'And Miss Johnston is your designated social worker.' The woman smiled politely. 'I wonder, could you tell us how *you* feel you're progressing?'

John snorted, very faintly. 'There is no change in the truth.'

His tone was low and surly – made more so by the European accent. *Speaks English well, but not as a first language*, was the comment in the file. Lawrence's mind flashed forward through his questions, resetting them to iron out confusions.

'What truth is that?' he came back calmly.

'I come from the stars – to bring Good News to the poor.'

Lawrence nodded, poker-faced; then probed again. 'When you say from the stars . . . what do you mean by that?'

A fleeting smile lit John's dark face: contemptuous, and cunning. 'You have not heard; why should I tell?'

'I should like to understand.'

'Who are you, then, who asks?'

'A doctor.'

'A learned man. Why then have you not heard?' John sat back, grimly satisfied with that.

Dr Andrews rubbed his jaw; eyes shrewd behind his glasses.

Lawrence was warming to the game, but didn't let it show. 'Do you believe that you have come from another world?'

John shook his head. 'I *go* to one – which is to come.'

'But you came here from another country? Another land?'

A pause. John's stare had grown suspicious. 'I have told you this before.'

'Forgive me. Indulge me, if you would.'

John gazed at him with hooded eyes; head resting on the chairback. Then: 'I was born in the city of Siena.'

'In Italy?'

'As you call it.'

Miss Johnston's eyes flicked down towards the folder on her lap; then up again.

'And when did you come here?' asked Lawrence.

John stared at him; then shrugged. 'After the Death. I do not know the year.'

'By the Death ... you mean the Black Death, is that right?'

'The Pestilence. Indeed.'

'That was in the fourteenth century. Do you know what century you are living in now?'

'You have told me the twentieth.'

'So you believe you have lived before?'

That grim, spasmodic smile again. 'The thread has not been cut.'

Lawrence spread his hands, his smile a study in bemusement. 'But nobody can live that long. Do you see my problem?'

'No, *dottore*. I see your *unbelief*.' And as he spoke, he stirred himself, sat forward – so abruptly that the others almost flinched. Yet before they could react he was slouching back again: drawing deep upon the ember of his dying cigarette.

Silence in the room. The smoke had spread like fusty wings, brooding over the four chairs. Lawrence leaned forward, resting his elbows on his knees, his chin against his interlocking hands.

'You still maintain that you're a priest?'

'I am ordained in Holy Church,' John said: matter-of-fact, monotonous again.

'Do you belong to any order?'

'*Ordo Praedicatorum*.'

The Order of Preachers, as one contributor to the case notes had helpfully explained. Better known as the Dominicans. Black Friars. Black for their cloaks, so Lawrence recalled. The friar's habit would be white; and sure enough, John wore no other shade. Hence the institutional pyjamas, which Lawrence cordially disliked. The clients wore their own clothes here: the clinical environment was consciously played down. But John had been found wandering, a tramp in filthy rags, and refused to wear the clothes that he'd been offered. The starch-white shirt and trousers were an interim resort – but had now become his permanent attire. He still rejected shoes and socks; his bare feet brown and callused, tough as hide.

Lawrence sat up straighter; gave an understanding nod.

'The reason you're here, John . . . as I've explained before . . . is that *we* believe that you suffer from delusions. That you can see this past, quite clearly, in your head – but it's something your mind has created.'

John didn't rise to that. He sucked on the last spark, his eyes reptilian.

Lawrence glanced down at the file. 'Are you taking your medication? Your drugs?'

A sneer convulsed the other's lips. 'So am I free to choose?'

'Don't fight against them, John. They'll help you *see*.'

John slowly shook his head. 'They make me *blind*. I must be wakeful.'

'What for?'

'That Day. The Day of Anger. It comes soon.'

Andrews made a dutiful note.

Lawrence regarded his client thoughtfully; then tried one final tack.

'You let us call you John. Wouldn't you prefer it if we called you by your own name?'

John met his gaze full on for several seconds. 'I do not remember it.'

The same response as usual. 'So what do you call yourself?'

Normally John stonewalled that; but not this time. Though his face remained defiant, a shadow seemed to cross it: a tremor raised by turbulence deep down. He wavered for a moment . . . then let his last lungful of smoke stream out, like a dead man's final breath.

'Dominicain,' he said.

Cain was the bit that Lawrence's mind latched onto. Intrigued, concealing his excitement, he leaned forward.

'That's interesting. Because you're a Dominican?'

Once more the other shook his head. His look was almost pitying.

'Because I have done murder, *dottore*. Because I am a murderer for Christ.'

CHAPTER IV

Mind and Memory

I

'Come,' said the voice, 'let us bury our dead.'

Dominicain's eyes snapped open. A group of men were towering above him, like silhouettes against the milky sky. All of them were cloaked in black, with black scarves round their faces. He recognized their kind at once: he'd watched them carry coffins to the death-pits. The only figures moving in a landscape of decay. The sight awoke a long-forgotten dread.

Becchini . . .

He tried to rise; his limbs would not obey him. Numbness soaked through every muscle. He was dimly aware of lying on his bed – but the bed itself had sunk into the ground. Walls of dark earth hemmed him in. He realized he was waiting in his grave.

'No!' he gasped, and fought to raise an arm. Anything to show them he was still alive. But his own flesh had disowned him. His mind felt like a broken egg: a sticky, mingled pulp of white and yolk. The worst thing was, he was *aware* of it.

The sinister *becchini* showed no interest in his struggles. Their eyes were blank above their muffling scarves. But as he tried to lift his head, he glimpsed another figure, further back. A young girl, wrapped in black as well – but her face was bare, her head uncovered. She had blue eyes, and hair like golden corn. He recognized the woman who'd been given charge of him. He tried to reach her with his stare; but she just dropped her gaze, and turned away.

A shovelful of earth was thrown on him. It lay there, cold

and heavy on his chest. He couldn't even roll to shake it off. Then the rasp of shovels really started; an avalanche of dirt came pouring down. The *becchini* worked in grim, relentless silence, blocking out the sky like carrion birds. He made to scream – and soil filled his mouth. He choked in helpless horror, and the world was blotted out.

'What did he say?' Claire frowned.

'Sounded like *bikini*,' murmured Richard with a grin. 'They're all the same, these fundy types. All bloody hypocrites.'

She glanced at him, then back towards the bed. John lay prostrate, fully clothed; still mumbling to himself. Slipping in, she checked his chart to see what was prescribed. The dose had clearly laid him out. *Chemical cosh*, she thought, and pursed her lips. She looked at Jan the cleaner, who had kept on working calmly by the window; then hung the chart, and straightened up again. Peering down at John. His face was sweaty.

'Coming?' Richard asked her from the doorway. Their break was ticking by, of course. She'd asked to just look in on John, on their way to the canteen. Pulling her cardigan closer, she turned to the door – then looked at Jan.

'It sounded like Italian. Was it?'

Jan – Gianna – shrugged. Her face was thoughtful. 'I think he say *becchini*. Many times.'

'And what's that mean?'

'The gravediggers,' said Jan; then shrugged again, and went on with her mopping.

2

How can I escape Thee? I go down to the grave, and Thou art there. And now he'd risen up again: still trapped within the tenements of Dis.

He'd read the works of Dante, but even Dante hadn't

dreamed of this. The great Infernal cities had their colonies on earth. This was one – a fortress of the damned. Men possessed by devils raved around him, while lost souls walked the corridors like corpses. And this must be his punishment: to be imprisoned here while still alive.

'What're you thinking, John?' Claire murmured gently, sitting down to join him at the table.

He turned his head to look at her. Could somebody so beautiful be damned? Or did she have a demon's grin, behind that sweet, false face? An instinct said to strike at her – to claw her flesh, and see. His fingers twitched; then lay still on the tabletop again.

'*Il mio nome è Legione*,' he said softly. She didn't understand – or didn't seem to. Dirty sunlight bathed them both. The Lost Ones shuffled back and forth, like guards.

Claire sensed someone moving up behind her. She kept her eyes on John's for just a moment, then looked round. Prentice stood there, looking jittery. She smiled at him. 'Okay?'

He nodded jerkily. 'Wanna see John.'

'Fine. I'll leave you to it, then.' Getting up, she glanced at John; still looking for a spark of empathy. But he'd gone back to studying the Bible on the tabletop before him.

She moved away, still watching. Prentice sidled up towards the table, as gingerly as someone paying homage to his lord. He'd been here for a fortnight – a schizophrenic, suffering from paranoid delusions. Among other things, he'd claimed that his landlord had tried to kill him – by injecting spiders with petrol, and sending them along the pipes like tiny firebombs. Prentice had related this with unblinking conviction: enough to send imaginary spiders up *her* spine.

He rummaged in his pocket now, and brought three cigarettes out. With deference he laid them on the table. John looked up solemnly . . .

'How do, Sister.'

'Mike.' She knew his jovial voice before she even turned. 'And how're you today?'

He was sitting in an armchair, looking smug. 'Cooking on gas, Sister. Feeling fine. Living life on the line.'

'I'm not a Sister, Mike, I'm just a poor downtrodden staff nurse.' She went across to join him. 'You're feeling good today, then?'

'Cooking on *gas* . . .' He nodded vigorously. 'Soon be out of here, yes.'

Still wearing a reflexive smile, she glanced back towards the table. John had claimed his gift of cigarettes. He was murmuring to Prentice, who looked spellbound. She felt the faintest twinge of apprehension – as if watching a child making friends with a stray, grizzled dog.

'Care to join me in a game of draughts?' asked Mike.

'Can't today,' she said. 'I'm going early.'

He nodded. 'Fair enough . . . Cooking on *gas*, feeling fine, living life on the line.'

I'll give you bloody gas, she thought. It made her realize just how stressed she was, behind her smile.

Prentice left the day-room, with a covert glance at her. Perhaps he thought she had a spider up her sleeve. Or maybe John had warned him to watch out . . .

Now who's getting paranoid, my girl? She walked back over. John's eyes came up warily. His hand closed round the cigarettes, as if he thought she'd take them.

'It's all right, you can keep them.' She hesitated. 'Just take care not to frighten him, he's younger than he looks.'

Sitting back, he searched her face: like someone trying to see behind her eyes. She felt an inner tingle of discomfort. Her tiredness welled up, and almost peeled her smile away. The worry that had nagged throughout the shift began to bite.

'What do you tell them, John? Why do they come?'

He didn't blink; just answered in an almost wary tone. 'They think that I can save them from this place.'

'Oh, John. We're trying to help you all, you *know* that.'

He rested his chin on one hand, and returned his attention to the book.

'Remember it's no smoking on the ward,' she said, a little stiffly. 'We don't want you starting a fire.'

He looked up again, from under his brows. She glimpsed a strange, sharp glimmer in his eyes. Then the shutters rattled down again.

Claire gave a sigh, and turned away. She needed to be off in any case, her appointment was at four. Now that it was getting close, she found her mouth was dry. She thought he might be watching as she walked back down the ward, but she didn't bother looking round to see. Right now her mind was otherwise engaged.

Perhaps some holy people were allowed into this place. Perhaps the demons couldn't keep them out. He thought she might be one such: curiously attired, but still a Sister. One of the Franciscan Clares, perhaps – she'd claimed that she was poor. He closed his twitchy fingers to a fist.

We don't want you starting a fire, she'd said. He realized that she knew about his sins. He looked back to the Bible; but his mind broke free, and plunged into the past.

3

The village looked like Hell had ridden through it.

Everything had been laid waste – the place and all its people. Houses had collapsed like burnt-out bonfires. Vivid flames still licked amid the heaps of blackened timber, but mostly there was just the smoke and stench. The sewer stench of battle, like a cesspit full of blood.

Appalled, he stumbled closer. His sandals squelched through the yellow mud. Everywhere he looked, he saw destruction. People had been hacked and burned to death. There were no bodies here, just *lumps* of bodies. Skinny dogs were scavenging along the littered road.

A dusty-looking group of men had gathered in the square.

Lean and vicious as the dogs, and scavengers like them. *Routiers*, the Frenchmen called them. Restless thieves and killers on the road.

'In Christ's name, what is this?' the Preacher said – so horrified, he spoke in his own language.

One of them was an Italian, too: a smiler in a grimy leather coat. He looked towards the newcomer, and shrugged. 'The will of Holy Church. An *end* to heresy.'

His voice was harsh – the smile, a scar. As if the man was maimed inside; disfigured by the things which he had done.

The Preacher looked from face to face, in anger and dismay. The youngest were like old men now, their features smoked and callused. Souls had withered; eyes had lost their colour. Two or three of them were drunk, and glowered stupidly. The rest just stared in unrepentant silence.

And how did he appear to them? A poor friar, made sterner by his eyes and greying hair. Presence enough to give them pause? Or was he just a beggar among wolves?

The silence grew around them, except where flames still crackled in the background.

'You can't speak for Holy Church, and murder men like this.'

The other's smile became a sneer. 'It's *you* who preached the judgment, friend – you dogs of Dominic.'

They knew him by his clothes, of course. The travel-stained white habit and black cloak. A Friar Preacher on the road – as rootless as themselves. He'd railed against the heretics at every market cross. But how could he have driven men to *this*?

'Dominic came to *reason* with these people – not to burn them.'

'How can someone reason with the enemies of God? Kill 'em all, says Holy Church: the Lord will know His own.'

The Preacher braced his staff against the ground: the gesture like a challenge to their daggers and their swords.

'The *poor* are His own people. You kill them, and they cry out for revenge.'

The smiler's eyes grew narrower. 'Spare us the sermon, brother dog. You'd better get along – or stay and join them.'

Mirthless chuckles drifted round the square. The Preacher closed his fist around the staff. He gave each *routier* a last, accusing glance; then strode on through them, following the road.

One of the men called out in French: his tone was coarse and taunting. The last words made the Preacher turn his head.

Chevaliers de charogne.

'What did he say?'

The smiler shrugged. 'There are mercenaries fighting for the heretics. Carrion Knights. Black English.' His smile didn't flicker, but he quickly crossed himself. 'Try preaching *them* your sermon . . . *Domini Canis*.'

The Preacher didn't rise to that last insult. He turned, and tracked his gaze across the hills. A sombre stillness lay upon the landscape. But after the briefest pause, he kept on walking.

The whispers of the murdered followed him.

He heard them now, like dying breaths: still murmuring against him. Eight centuries had passed, but they would let him have no peace. The prison-house still echoed with their sighs.

Dominicain's eyes grew focused once again. The crawling shadows on the page congealed into words.

I have come to set fire upon the earth, and how I wish it were already kindled.

He let the sentence sink into his heart. Then he took a cigarette, and put it in his mouth.

Someone came and lit it without waiting to be told.

4

Claire found Martin lying on the sofa: slouched there with his feet drawn up, the TV handset busy in his hand. Cricket flickered on, and off; now *Neighbours*; now a game-show – each fleeting image zapped into oblivion.

She watched the jerky montage, feeling sick. 'Hi,' she said. He barely glanced around.

A solid lump had grown inside her stomach. 'Had a good day?'

He stretched his arm out – 'Nope' – and brought the cricket back again. He had his jeans and T-shirt on. She watched his biceps flexing, tanned and smooth.

How long since he had given her a squeeze?

She moistened her lips and waited, but he showed no further interest. After a minute, she glanced round at the wall. 'Hello, wall. Would you like to hear my news?'

Martin didn't bother to respond. She stared at the screen; then walked around in front of it, and switched the TV off. 'Hey!' he snapped. She turned, to find him scowling up at her.

'I was watching . . .'

'No, you weren't.' She gazed into his sullen face – the face she thought she loved. Clean-cut features, deep, dark eyes; high cheekbones, chiselled nose. A face for magazines and films . . . except he looked too boyish. Too cheeky when he smiled, perhaps. Too moody when he didn't.

She felt a sudden rush of fear. He seemed unreal, too far away to touch.

He settled back. 'Okay, so what's your news, then?'

She came and knelt in front of him. He was still pointing the handset at the TV; she took his wrist, and aimed it at her midriff.

'I'm pregnant, Martin. *Here*. Try zapping that.'

CHAPTER V

Dreams and Decay

I

Again they'd clubbed him down with their narcotics; but in his dreams he rose again, and wandered through the corridors of Hell. The colony appeared in ruins, its gateways overgrown. Owls were hooting from the chimney-tower. The shadows were unquiet, full of whispering and sobs.

Dominicain advanced into the labyrinth. A creeping fear came over him – as if this were some giant spider's lair. But something brushed his face, and drew him onward: a summons as elusive as a sigh.

He saw a light ahead of him – unfolding in the darkness like a flower. The glow was pale, unhealthy, and he wavered for a moment; then started down the passageway towards it. As he glided closer, it resolved into a face: a deathly visage, hanging in the gloom. The eyes were like two windows on the inky dark beyond.

They watched him come, those empty eyes. And then the phantom spoke.

Be patient in your cell, devoted friend.
The term of thy imprisonment is done.
Await the man of power whom I shall send.

The language was Italian – the Tuscan dialect he spoke himself. He didn't recognize the lines, and yet they were familiar. Their richness and arrangement made him think of Dante's work.

Not quoted this time, though. They spoke to *him*.

'Who are you?' he demanded hoarsely.

The white face didn't answer that; instead it threw the focus back on him.

> You *shall become that Hound the poet saw,*
> *Who drives the hungry She-Wolf back to Hell,*
> *And brings the rule of justice to the poor.*

Dominicain was dumbstruck. He recognized that image from the Comedy of Dante: his Inferno. He stared in disbelief – then shook his head.

'But how can it be me? I am *condemned*.'

The other stayed inscrutable. He had to be a Messenger, Dominicain thought wildly. A being of light, beneath his cloak of darkness.

So who had pleaded for his soul, to win him this remission?

'The lady who has charge of me . . .' He hesitated. 'Is she one of the blessed?'

The other seemed to ponder that; then moved his solemn head from side to side.

> *She owes allegiance to a darker power.*
> *It may be she will seek to hinder you.*
> *So you must show* no pity *in that hour.*

Dominicain absorbed that wisdom grimly. He was just about to speak again when everything dissolved. His soul came winging back along the darkened corridors, returning to his body like a sparrow to its nest.

His dull, unfocused eyes slid halfway open, but he lay there like a dead man until morning. The apparition's rhythmic words still throbbed in his head.

2

Martin's breathing body stirred beside her, but it felt as if she was lying here alone. Nestled against his naked back, Claire tried to warm herself – but the lump of ice inside her didn't melt. His heartbeat pulsed in time with hers; but his mind was silent, locked inside his skull.

The bedside clock said two a.m.; it might as well be lunch-time. She didn't think she'd ever get to sleep.

If only she could tell what he was thinking. If only she could see into his dreams. Maybe then she'd understand the welter of emotions he had shown. There'd been a spark of wonder, to be sure. She'd snatched at it, ignoring the dismay. Then he'd lost his rag, and started shouting. All her fault: she'd done it just to trap him. *How dare you even* think *that?* she'd yelled back. As the fight raged round the flat, she'd realized he was scared. Frightened of commitment in itself – or by their prospects? She wouldn't blame him, if it was the latter. She was bloody terrified as well.

But later, when he'd quietened down, the fear had still been there. She'd peeped into the living room, and seen him trying to read. His skin looked cold and milky pale; his eyes like haunted wells.

She'd had a horrid notion then. He looked like someone diagnosed with cancer – frightened for the people whom his illness would drag down. The family who didn't even know . . . It couldn't be. She'd crushed the inkling out. But two nights later, here it was – still smouldering.

For God's sake, don't be stupid. He wouldn't keep a thing like that from me.

At least he hadn't packed his bags. At least she had his body in her arms. She sniffed, and laid her cheek against his shoulder. A single tear ran down onto his skin. She'd cried at work today, as well – in front of John, who'd watched with solemn eyes. She wondered what *he'd* made of it. His cryptic mind was just as hard to read.

Subsiding into sleep at last, she dreamed of spiders creeping up the bed: dozens of them, all spindly legs and petrol-bloated bodies. Catching fire, they scuttled blindly forward. She felt them on her naked skin. Paralysed, she smelt the duvet burning. More of them were crawling on the ceiling: they dropped towards her face like falling stars. Her scream was just a whimper in the stillness of the room. She curled into a ball, and didn't wake.

3

The sound was just a rustling at first: like rain against the flat roof overhead. Martin lay there, semi-conscious, trying to ignore it. But slowly it grew louder: a crackling noise that seemed to fill the room. *Like burning wood.* He sat up with a start.

The bedroom was in darkness – he could see no sign of flames. And yet there was a bluish gleam, infusing the dense air. He sat and squinted, baffled – then looked down.

His hands were glowing.

He raised his palms, and stared at them in frozen disbelief. His skin was radiating cold blue light. The frosty crackle sounded like a Geiger counter now. He rubbed his hands together – no effect. The light was welling up from every pore.

Springing out of bed, he stumbled over to the mirror. His face was luminous as well, a disembodied mask. The snap and sizzle of decay was growing all the time. Yet Claire was still asleep – she hadn't heard it. She couldn't feel the particles that soaked into her skin.

I've touched her with these hands; she's kissed my face. So she must be contaminated too. Together with what was growing in her womb.

Did magic have a lethal dose? A power to *deform*?

The crackling reached a peak – and then cut off. The ghostly blue plutonium-glow went out. He thought he'd been struck blind again, and felt his heart freeze up; then realized he was buried in the bedclothes. The bed was hot, and stank of sweat. Claire lay snug against him, moaning softly.

He shrank away from her, got up, and blundered to the bathroom.

Waking up, Claire clutched herself; revulsion made her squirm against the headboard. Her skin was slick, her nerves still itching madly. The dream itself was like a web. It took her several moments to break free.

She slumped against the headboard with her arms around her legs. Her fringe was matted, hanging in her eyes. *Shower*, she thought – and realized there was nobody beside her. A fleeting twinge of dread, and then she heard water splashing. Light reflected through the open doorway. *Shit, he beat me to it*, she thought wryly.

Better join him.

Going through, she found him there, beneath the steaming blast – still scrubbing at his raw, abraded skin.

CHAPTER VI

Grief Riders

I

Daylight made the Burnt House seem much smaller.

Martin stood and watched it from across the busy road. Lunchtime traffic put it in perspective – a backdrop to the modern urban grind. The sunshine showed its cracks and crumbled brickwork; the window-boards were brittle cataracts. A blind, decrepit visage that the passing world ignored.

He'd heard that it was down for demolition. A Planning Application had been fastened to a telephone pole nearby. Soon the JCBs would come, and smash the building open like a skull. Myths matured in darkness would shrivel in the light. Emptiness would gawp from every window.

I wonder what they'd find inside my *head?*

He looked both ways, and crossed the road towards it. Today, there was no sense of being watched. He could picture the place as a dusty heap of rubble, perhaps with one wall standing, and a window framing sky. Its ghosts were shadows: primal fears. The only exorcists were light and thought.

Walking slowly round the house, he forced himself to think of last night's dream. It seemed to say so much – if he would listen. His experience in Dad's study was still damaging him now. Vibrations from the past were finding flaws inside his mind. In time, they would develop into fissures. Unless he took some action, he'd crack up.

He'd put this off for long enough: casting round for evidence of ghosts, where none existed. Trying to tell himself it was a scientific quest. Avoiding the truth like a credulous child.

He'd had some kind of *episode*, that night two years ago. Paralysis, a fit, hallucinations. No wonder that he'd looked for other answers. It could have been a one-off, and the lapse of time suggested that it was. But what if it recurred, from out of nowhere?

It wasn't just his problem any longer; there was Claire. *And someone else*, he thought. *And someone else*.

He'd watched her sleep this morning, in the clear light of day. Her belly was still flat and slim, despite the hidden wonder it contained. Martin had reached out, and very gently touched her skin, stroking in a circle round her navel. He had a life ahead of him – if he could face the past. And that meant telling all, and trusting her.

Resolved, he turned and started back. The empty house receded in his wake. An outpost of his fears, destroyed by reason – like a sandcastle demolished by the sea.

Coming home, he knew he was committed. A sobering prospect – yet he welcomed it. A bridge out of the haunted past; a road towards the future. Perhaps it meant he'd finally grown up.

He hadn't seen this far ahead two years ago, at school. Back then there'd been no call to settle down. He liked girls who were clever, but they had to have nice tits – the impossible perfectionism of *Playboy* and Page 3. He'd only slept with Vicki twice before they'd broken up. Other girls had come and gone (Nadine had been quite noisy on both counts). He'd never really thought of growing old with one of them.

Lyn, meanwhile, was always being asked out. He could see her now, in slinky black and made up to the eyebrows (he thought she put too much powder on, but what did he know?). He'd tease her as she waited in the hallway for a date – and feel like swearing vengeance if a boyfriend made her cry. But that was different: she was his own sister.

It had taken Claire to match the angles up. She made beauty everyday, and sex a part of something so much greater. He'd never lived so close to someone else, or shared so much.

So grab her with both hands, and hold on tight.

The flat was quiet, full of stagnant sun. Today was her day off: she might be spending it elsewhere. He'd been morose this morning – still shaken by the dream and his reaction. Perhaps she'd gone round to a girlfriend's, for a moan.

But no: he found her curled up on the sofa, catching up on lost sleep from last night. An open book still rested in her lap. She had her faded jeans on, and an England rugby shirt. Kneeling down, he leaned across, and blew the wispy fringe back off her forehead. She frowned to herself, and opened bleary eyes. A pause – and then she smiled at him. 'Hiya . . .'

'Sorry about this morning,' he said softly.

She stretched, and shook her head. ''S . . . all right.'

'And last night,' he insisted. 'And the past however many weeks it's been.'

She looked at him more shrewdly. 'It's okay, Martin. Really. I just wish you could *talk* about whatever's on your mind.'

'I'm going to,' he said.

She frowned again, and raised herself. Still kneeling there, he took her hands and gripped them.

'I know you're going to take this like a psychie nurse,' he muttered.

'Take what?'

Martin swallowed, staring at their hands. 'Two years ago . . . I had some kind of fit. I couldn't see, or move . . . it lasted hours. I thought I heard and smelled things in the house – but it was empty. And I had a sort of vision, in my head.'

'What of?' she prompted quietly.

'A wasteland of some kind. A haunted place.'

'How often has this happened?'

'Just the once. It screwed me up completely, I left home because of it.' He managed a wry smile. 'It's why I'm *here*.'

'Was it voices that you heard?'

'Lots of them – a real psychobabble. I've tried to tell myself that it was something paranormal: as if that sort of crap was really true. But now I want to face the truth. I reckon that I owe it to you both.'

That last inclusion wasn't lost on her. She nodded, looking thoughtful.

'So – what?' he said, and forced a laugh. 'You think I'm going nuts?'

'Oh, Martin: no I don't. You've got your moods and hang-ups – so have I. But I've known your for six months now, and I think you're very normal.' She smiled, a little slyly. 'And quite gorgeous.'

'I was dreaming of it last night. I was scared that I'd contaminate you somehow . . .'

Her hands were still clasped tight in his; but now she squeezed him back. 'You know I've seen a lot of psychie cases. I don't think you're one of them at all. Lots of people have hallucinations. The mind's a weird thing, you know, even when it's healthy.' The briefest pause. 'It did just happen once?'

'Yeah. But can you trust me?'

'I trust you, Martin. Want to know how much?' Leaning down, she kissed him. 'Come to bed.'

'Now, wasn't *that* a waking dream?' she asked him afterwards.

Martin grinned, still short of breath, and let her snuggle closer. She laid her cheek against his chest; her smile was warm and smug. But after a pause, her soft eyes grew more thoughtful.

'This is how a doctor once described hallucinations. It's like you're in a fire-lit room, and looking through the window. While it's light outside, you see the garden and the sky. But as it gets dark, you start to see reflections of what's with you in the room. The furniture you've got inside your head. Your mind's the fire – and sometimes it flares up.'

'And that's quite normal?'

'For lots of us, at some point in our lives. Visions, voices, even smells . . .'

He smiled at her, and stroked her hair. She purred, and closed her eyes. The light was evening-golden now, like syrup on her skin. He felt a deep, delicious calm – much more than just the afterglow of sex.

At last he glanced towards the clock. 'Listen . . . That's twice I've spoiled your beauty sleep, so let me make us supper. What'd you like?'

'Just salad would be fine . . .' she murmured.

'Reckon I can manage that.' He slithered out of bed and dressed, and went into the kitchen. The lettuce in the fridge didn't look too wilted. He found a tin of anchovies; a jar of pitted olives. And something he could spoil her with: a chocolate Viennetta for dessert.

He was chopping up ingredients when a knock came at the door. The wood resounded, hollow in the hallway. Martin glanced round irritably, and almost kept on working. But the blows had been insistent, and the silence was too pregnant to ignore. Somebody was waiting for an answer. And maybe they would go away – but then he'd be no wiser.

Might be something interesting. Just might. Tucking in his granddad shirt, he ambled through to see. The door loomed up, he opened it – and felt a punch of shock: so brutal and abrupt it left him winded.

He saw a face as rugged as a crumbled granite cliff: all bony cheeks, and jutting brows and lichen-bearded jaw. The eyes were narrow, deeply-set: a clear, ferocious blue. One of the cheeks was scarred beneath its thatch of dirty gold. It turned the baleful stare into a sneer.

Cutthroat said a cold voice in his mind.

He'd never seen that face before – and yet his heart leaped up in recognition. The man was dressed in brown and black: clothes for the road, from his army boots to his greasy drover's coat. But Martin knew at once where he had come from: those medieval battlefields he'd seen. The visions Claire had said were from *inside*.

And Claire was lying naked in the bedroom, unsuspecting.

A gout of fear went through him, and he tried to block the doorway. The other's gaunt expression didn't change.

'What do you want?' hissed Martin frantically.

The watcher flicked his coat-tail back, and Martin glimpsed a *sword.* It seemed more like an answer than a threat.

'*Follow*,' growled the man, and stepped away.

Martin stumbled forward, off the threshold. Rational objections burst like bubbles. Past and present melted into one. The street was full of shadows; the evening hush polluted by their prayers and lamentations. Suddenly he was a stranger here.

No time to say goodbye to Claire. He didn't even pause to shut the door. By opening it, he'd wrenched his life completely out of joint. Claire was disconnected now. She might as well have been another pin-up on his wall.

The swordsman led him off down greying streets, past lamps that sputtered on in ones and twos. Martin's chest was breathless, but he matched the other's pace. It felt as if he'd joined some kind of underground resistance. The people they passed were refugees; non-combatants who hadn't heard the curfew.

Three streets away, he knew where they were going.

With the sun now gone, the Burnt House looked totally charred: a stark, black wreck against the fading sky. The swordsman crossed towards it, with Martin at his heels like a dog.

They slipped in through the back way, like before – and Martin froze. An eerie phosphorescence tinged the kitchen, as if some glowing entity was waiting in the passageway beyond. He remembered that same aura from the decomposing Chart. But scar-face was behind him now, he had to keep on going. Onward and inward: through into the hall.

A new constellation had been born in this dead house. Flames glowed in the cinders, like small ghosts of the roaring beast that had devoured the place. Night-lights lined the blackened stairs, ascending like the stairway to a shrine. Another man was waiting at the bottom: crouched there like a hunter, with his back against the wall. His figure seemed unearthly in the half-dark. The light showed up an atavistic face.

Martin came up short again; the swordsman nudged him forward. With nauseous reluctance he went over to the staircase. The second man stayed motionless, enjoying his discomfort. His nose was broken, scarred across the bridge. It gave his grin a stupid, sneering cast.

Martin tested the first step. The brittle wood creaked dully. A voice upstairs was speaking into silence. Murmuring, monotonous: a language that he couldn't understand.

He started up. The swordsman followed. He heard the hunter climbing to his feet. The disembodied voice kept up its dirge. Two more men were waiting on the landing. They moved aside to let him pass; he did so with his heartbeat in his throat. It felt like he was stuck inside the hospital again – beset by human faces, alien minds.

The voice had died away. He heard them breathing.

A gaping doorway loomed ahead. The darkness had the pull of an abyss. He knew it was the black heart of the house – its crematorium. The thought brought bile seeping up; he swallowed it back down.

The furnace was as cold as ashes now. The murk was thick and soupy, like a sewer. But as he reached the threshold, a rustling movement came from just ahead. The dank air shifted faintly. Somebody was waiting in the room.

Martin tried to back away – and found the other men were all behind him. Their clothes smelled ages old. He looked from face to stony face – then quickly turned his head.

The shape inside the room was coming forward.

A mane of pale hair grew clear; the highlights of the face. The mask of shadow peeled away, revealing pallid skin; but pools of darkness lingered in the sockets of his eyes.

It was the face he'd seen before, of course: the figure who'd looked back. The one with eyes like somebody insane.

'So,' he said, 'the Summoner, at last.' The voice was harsh, but there was humour in it. A grim amusement, bleak as bone. He reached out with one finger, prodding Martin in the chest. The shock of contact gave the touch the impact of a blow: a hammer-stroke against his pounding heart. Martin had to gulp for breath. The other merely smiled.

'You woke us, and we came. We always answer. Has it seemed long, the waiting for the Ravens to return?'

III

SHADOWS

Do I belong to some ancient race?
I like to walk in ancient places:
These are things that I can understand.

THE LEVELLERS

Dear Craig

Hi there, how's it going? I'm still waiting for that airmail envelope to come plopping through the letterbox, but I expect you've got your work cut out upholding the New World Order. If you get a moment free, I'd appreciate it if you'd let me know.

Look, new pen now: different day. I don't mean to sound snotty; I'm just missing you, that's all. I've got a lot on my mind right now, and I'd love to hear your voice. I'm still at Lyn's. Please ring me.

Love you
Frannie
x

CHAPTER I

Green Blades Rising

I

Sitting on the sofa, listening to Lyn gushing on the phone, Fran felt a strange, resentful little twinge. Was that a man at the other end? She rather thought it was. Leaning back, she peered into the hallway. Lyn stood there, sideways on to her, head nodding as she listened. Her sunny smile was private, like a dreamer's. It soured Fran's mood to know she couldn't share it.

The twinge became a pang of guilt. She shifted with discomfort and sat forward. After all that Lyn had done for her, she still begrudged her friend her separate pleasures. *You selfish cow*, she told herself; went glumly back to towelling her hair.

She was fresh from the bath, still flushed with warmth; wrapped up in Lyn's spare bathrobe. She rubbed her damp hair harder as if jealousy was something she could simply scrub away. And how might Lyn be feeling, when she thought of Fran and Craig? Having brought them back together, she could only stand and watch. *She* knew how it felt, to see a friend enticed away . . .

Reality engulfed her then. The whole room seemed to change, as if the sun had shifted round. Her mundane instincts fell away; Craig's smile was just a picture in her head. The cold blue gaze of Athelgar dispersed it like a mist.

'Oh, *no*!' said Lyn delightedly, still giggling.

Fran sat there, very still: the towel's dampness clutched against her chest. She'd spoken with a *ghost*, the other week. A solid phantom, trapped in time; still wandering those half-forgotten roads. He'd called on her to follow him – and she had said she'd come.

Jesus, Fran: what were you thinking *of?*

So what if Lyn had just acquired a boyfriend? So what, if it was Fran's turn to be eased politely out? Such things seemed almost trifling now. The world through which she walked had been upturned.

How could he have reached her from a thousand years ago, to warm her carefree heart on Heaven's Field?

Swallowing, she stood and padded through into the kitchen. Her mouth was very dry, she needed something to drink. She poured herself some fruit juice from the fridge, still listening to Lyn with half an ear. Her jealousy, still vague, was of a different order now. An *envy* of her friend's unclouded sky.

Turning round, she took a sip. The Tropical Mix was cool and sweet; but it went down quickly, leaving her still dry. Moodily, she wiped her mouth; then stiffened. The calendar had caught her eye, hung up beside the pinboard. She stared at it for a moment, then slowly crossed the room. The lino seemed to cling to her bare feet.

There were neatly written notes beside some of the dates. *Dentist 9:15 . . . Piano recital . . . Mummy (49)*. The memos barely registered. She craned in closer, looking for some printed information. Some indication of the next full moon.

But there was nothing.

She straightened up, and felt her heartbeat throbbing. She'd put this off for long enough, but still she wasn't sure if she was ready. There'd be no turning back, she knew that. As soon as she learned the date, she'd be committed. Back on the road to meet her ghost again.

Athelgar. A man long lost. She felt her fine hairs rising.

It had taken her until yesterday to start some cautious digging. She'd waited for Lyn to take a break from her books, then idly broached the subject: hoping it sounded casual enough.

'Do you know of any battles fought on Salisbury Plain?' she'd asked.

Lyn finished stretching. 'What, in Roman times, or . . . ?'

'Whenever.'

Lyn had thought it over. 'Edington's the only really famous one, I think. That was in 878. There are legends about others. There's even something in Malory about King Arthur's final battle being fought there.'

'But Edington was King Alfred?'

'Mm. They're not *exactly* sure where it took place, but Edington's the likeliest contender. The Chronicle calls it *Ethandun* – the Waste Down.'

Fran blinked as she absorbed the blow, but kept her pale face straight. Lyn hadn't noticed. The topic dropped, and Fran had let it lie. But now it had started nagging her again. Still nursing her cold glass, she went back into the living room. Lyn caught her eye, and waved, as if to say *I won't be long*. Fran grinned and gestured back at her. *No hurry* . . .

Out of sight of the doorway, her bright face faded; she went quickly to Lyn's desk. The top was strewn with papers, books lined up against the wall. There was a photo of her parents in a polished silver frame; a snapshot of her brother, too, propped up against the lamp. And a compact desktop calendar.

Still nothing on the phases of the moon.

Not sure if she should feel relieved, she drifted back, and over to the bookcase; too restive to sit down again and wait. Lyn had mentioned a reference in 'the Chronicle'; and there was the *The Anglo-Saxon Chronicle*, just waiting to be read. She set her glass aside, and pulled it out: a dog-eared paperback. Flicking slowly through, she found the entry dated 878. Edington was over in a sentence.

Our work was red and filthy: that's what Athelgar had said. A voice from the past, addressed to her alone. The memory of someone who had fought there. Fran shook her head, quite giddy with the thought. Nobody on earth had heard what she had.

So what had it been like? Not bloodless like this dry account, she guessed that much. The fight would have been savage –

full of swords and spears and axes. Medieval warfare; mud and guts.

It is no road *for one like you to walk.*

She gave a faint grimace, and tracked her gaze along the books. There was another, hardback version, with a musty-looking spine. Curious to compare the two, she took that down as well – and found that this one wasn't a translation.

Typeset though it was, the text was meaningless to her. Weird, distorted letters mixed with modern ones throughout. The words were like a thorny hedge: impassable, entangling. But she picked her way through them to 878, and found what she was looking for again.

Eþandune

Studying the word, she sensed the distant past draw nearer. The man she'd met would write the name like that. This was his dead language, still alive inside his head. Still roughening the form of modern English that he'd learned.

She was just about to close the book when her grazing eye was snagged by something else.

ræfen

She felt her heart leap up. Her mouth was powder-dry again, but the drink she'd set aside was quite forgotten. She focused on the sentence (elusive as a snake amid the brambles), and mouthed the alien words as she read through them.

Dar wæs se gudfana genumen de hi ræfen heton

Heart thudding, she turned back to the translation. It touched upon another, unnamed battle: still months before that victory of Alfred's in the spring. The English were outnumbered, with their backs against the wall – yet suddenly the war was turned around. A force of the invaders had been set upon and killed.

And there was captured the banner which men call Raven

'I never knew you were so interested,' Lyn said brightly from the doorway.

Fran almost jumped; then glanced at her, and shrugged. 'Something about the Plain, I think. It brings the past much closer . . .' She hesitated. 'Do you know what this bit means . . . about the banner called Raven?'

'It was an emblem that the Vikings had; it led them into battle.' Coming across, she leaned in close and nodded. 'Yeah . . . It was one of the things that damaged their morale, the English capturing it. Hang on, there might be something in Brewer's about it.'

She selected a fat paperback, and started leafing through it. *The Dictionary of Phrase & Fable*, according to the cover. Fran stood beside her, waiting; feeling hollow.

'You can browse through this for hours,' Lyn said; 'dig up all sorts of gems. *Raven*, here we are . . . yes, look.' She passed it across. Fran looked, and read.

> *The fatal raven, consecrated to Odin the Danish war-god, was the emblem of the Danish standard. This raven was said to be possessed of necromantic power. The standard was termed* Landeyda *(the desolation of the country)* . . .

She pursed her lips and nodded once – as if to say, *Well, fancy that* – and handed back the book.

Lyn's eyes strayed down towards her Cross of Nails. 'Still wearing it, then?' she asked, in a casual way that couldn't hide her pleasure.

Fran glanced down, and touched the pendant; let it turn between her fingers. 'A very special present,' she said softly. 'Thanks again.'

Lyn glowed at that. 'You're welcome.' Replacing the book, she went off towards the kitchen. Fran stayed where she was, still worrying the pendant. To Athelgar, the thing had been a relic: the sign of a saint. Perhaps he even thought that she'd been martyred.

Nailed to a cross with those medieval spikes. She felt the notion tightening her stomach. To his mind, he was still alive, and *she* must be the ghost . . .

But Craig had seen it too, of course. She jumped at the

distraction – fixed her memory on that. The first time that she'd slept with him; that posh country hotel. They'd helped undress each other (*How do I look?* her nervous mind kept asking); she'd left the cross around her neck till last. Drawing back – 'Hang on,' she husked – she'd fumbled for the clasp.

He touched her arm. 'Why take that off?'

Fran hesitated, ashen-mouthed. 'I . . . think I should.'

'You think we're doing something wrong?' He searched her face with serious eyes. 'If you do, we can stop right now.'

She'd stared at him, her hands behind her neck; her breasts unguarded. But Craig reached up to stroke her cheek instead.

'You think this is a one-night stand?' he asked.

Fran sighed, and swallowed. Shook her head.

'We've waited long enough,' he went on softly; fingering a strand of her dark hair. 'I want to be a *part* of you, Frannie. I want to be a part of your life. Is that what you want too?'

Fran moistened her lips. 'It's like I want to climb inside you.'

'So how can it be wrong?' he asked her mildly.

She'd wrestled with her conscience for a silent moment longer; then let the clasp alone, and reached for him. And Craig had leaned forward to kiss the cross, where it nestled in her cleavage; a gesture full of reverence and awe. She'd hugged him to her, closed her eyes; and felt his loving mouth begin to rove . . .

'You sure you don't mind cooking supper?' Lyn called from the kitchen.

Fran came to herself with a rueful little smile. ''Course I'm sure.'

'Shall we have some wine with it?'

'Why not?' Fran said. Retrieving her glass, she wandered through; found Lyn comparing labels.

'Any preference?'

Fran's smile grew wider, mischievous. 'What the hell, it all tastes the same, anyway.'

'You are a *philistine*, Fran Bennett. I hope you know that.'

Lyn gave her a mock-snooty look, then glanced at the clock. 'I'm just popping down to the corner shop; we're getting short of milk.'

Fran finished her drink and rinsed the glass out; listening while the front door opened and shut. She waited for the fading sound of footsteps on the pavement – then wiped her hands and went quickly through the flat towards Lyn's bedroom. She lingered on the threshold, almost guiltily; then darted in, and started looking round.

The room was neat, but comfortable and lived-in. A musky pot-pourri infused the air. She found the diary lying on the dressing table.

No way could Lyn have come back in; but Fran still glanced behind her before picking it up. The temptation to start reading came on strongly. Lyn's private thoughts were hidden here. The secrets of her heart she hadn't shared.

With an effort of will, she focused on the dates: ignored the tidy writing, till she reached today's blank page. Then on, until she found it marked. The next full moon.

A woozy calm came over her, and muffled the slow drumbeat of her heart.

She could always stay up here, of course – in safe, secluded Oxford. Just wait, until the moon was on the wane. His influence would surely dwindle with it. He'd fade out of her life again, as quietly as he'd come.

She toyed with the temptation – then flicked it away. Its bright spark flared and died in smoke and ash. She really didn't have a choice: the dream had told her that. She had to meet this ghost again – and somehow lay his troubled soul to rest. If she turned her back, and left the thing unfinished, she knew she wouldn't rest herself; would still be sleepless twenty years from now.

Laying down the diary, she went back towards the kitchen. As if all that were not enough, she also had a casserole to cook.

2

'Who was it, then?' she asked Lyn after supper.

'Who was who?'

'That *person* on the phone.'

'Oh,' Lyn said, and shifted; then settled back and let her face light up. 'That was Simon, actually.'

A pause. Fran prodded her. 'Well, don't go all coy on me. Who's he?'

'Someone I met at work. The temping side of things, I mean.'

Fran offered up a smile as bait for more. They were curled up on the sofa, feeling comfortable and full; a CD playing softly in the background.

'He's nice,' Lyn went on dreamily; 'quite shy.' That conspiratorial grin again. 'He still calls me Lynette.'

'And a very nice name it is, too. Shame to shorten it, really.'

'He thought I was *French*, first off!'

'Well, you look French. Sort of.'

Lyn tittered. 'You know my middle name's Isabella? Well, my Dad chose that, after Princess Isabelle, who was married to Edward II. They called *her* the She-Wolf of France.'

Fran shrugged. 'Well, *my* middle name's Elizabeth because my Mum was really into *Pride & Prejudice* and stuff.' Leaning back, she looked at Lyn again. 'You think it's getting serious?'

Lyn smiled again, with lowered eyes. 'It might be.'

Now that they were discussing it, the jealousy was gone. Just as her decision to return to the Plain had brought an inner peace, so acceptance of Lyn's separate life had left her satisfied. She felt a glow of pleasure for her friend.

3

Lyn had more work to do that evening. She was still slogging away in the glow of her desk lamp when Fran came back from the bathroom to say good night.

'Don't work too late.'

'I won't,' Lyn smiled, and nodded at the jar at her elbow. 'There aren't many biscuits left.'

Fran grinned at that, and gently closed the door. Lyn heard her moving round, then settle down. The flat grew quiet again: a cosy, womb-like hush beyond the lamplight.

She usually worked best in an environment like this; but tonight her mind felt fidgety – distracted. Instead of ploughing a proper furrow through some untranslated texts, she knew that she was grazing: wasting time on fallow land. There was nothing that she needed from the *Chronicle* right now. But Fran had picked it up today, and now Lyn found she couldn't put it down.

The text was full of haunting gaps: so much had been forgotten. AD 904. *The moon darkened.* That was *all.* Whatever else had happened had been literally eclipsed. They must have thought their world was going to end.

Her eyes flicked to the Riddle, as if seeking reassurance.

It was pinned there on the wall, so she could see it while she worked. It had lived above her desk in Christ Church, too. A teasing gift from Martin, copied out with loving care. He'd never done Old English, but he'd formed each word just right.

Moððe word fræt . . .

She rather thought that Daddy had conspired with him on that. An Anglo-Saxon riddle from the Exeter Book: the subject was a moth, devouring words. And though it chewed and swallowed them, it never took them in.

The answer was a Bookworm, of course. *Oh, very droll,* she'd told him; and kept it very carefully ever since.

Beside it was a colour print of *Beowulf*'s first line, the H illuminated like a manuscript. *Hwæt!* the long-dead poet called to her. In the context it meant, *Listen!* As she'd once explained to Fran, it summed things up for her. History demanded her attention just like that.

Returning to the *Chronicle*, she browsed on through the entries, and came to the Brunanburh poem. A famous English victory of 937, and the chronicler had really pulled the stops out, painting an epic scene of strife and carnage. Yet no one knew the site of it today.

The march of time. So much fell by the wayside. She felt that old, nostalgic twinge again.

It was doubtless Fran's enquiry about the Raven banner that focused her attention on the grisly reference here. A real raven this time, though – and written in the common English form. More familiar; harsher-sounding. *Hræfn.*

> *Behind them, to divide the carrion meat,*
> *They left the raven, dark and shadow-clad . . .*

She thought of Simon suddenly, and couldn't keep a wry smile from her lips. He failed to see how she could find this stuff so *interesting*. Give him football any day. Or tinkering with cars.

They had some common interests though – like good Italian food and conversation. He'd booked them a table for Saturday night. The prospect was a pleasing inner glow.

> *. . . and þæt græg deor,*
> *Wulf on wealde.*

Time for bed. She yawned into her hand, and closed the book. No wiser for the words she had consumed.

CHAPTER II

On Earth as It Is in Hell

I

Tilshead Tea-Rooms hadn't changed a bit.

Sitting by the window, gazing out into the sunny village street, Fran felt her instincts fusing with the past. She might have come here last weekend, not four long years ago. She couldn't help but straighten, every time she heard an engine – a hollow feeling growing in her stomach. A farmer's truck would clatter by; the void would fill again. But she'd keep her hearing focused on the noise, until it faded: dispersed across the still air of the Plain.

The room was dark with polished wood: a refuge from the sunlight. Silence filled it, seeping from the panelling and beams. An antique clock ticked drily in the background. It seemed she had the whole place to herself.

She glanced down at her untouched plate. Her mouth felt dry, too dry for scones; her stomach much too sour for jam and cream. She poured herself a splash more tea, and turned her gaze towards the road again.

The proprietress had welcomed her with friendly, searching eyes. Fran sensed that she'd been recognized, but guessed the woman couldn't place her face. That suited her just fine, of course: she didn't want to talk. Just sitting at this window brought back memories enough.

Didn't you use to come down with Indra and the others? The unasked question hovered as the cream tea was brought through. But Fran's smile had been fleeting, and the other woman hadn't pushed her luck.

The old clock kept on ticking in the corner.

An army Land-Rover bowled past; Fran's pulse-rate leaped again. She thought about the last time she'd had tea here, along with Paul and several other Watchers. They'd just been starting on the scones when a packet of Hummvees rattled past outside. A moment's startled silence; then *Crash, thud, Bloody hell!* and they'd all been piling out onto the pavement. She remembered that last glimpse she'd got: the mottled iron cockroach-shells, and lights like dim red eyes. But the vehicles were clear, and heading north towards Gore Cross: their dismal, diesel clatter fading slowly in the fields.

The Tea-Rooms had grown used to scenes like that.

She felt a quirky glimmer of nostalgia. Memory was a comforter, especially when it drew old friends around her. But as she sat, and watched the road, their grinning faces dimmed, the banter dwindled – leaving her among the empty chairs.

The shadow of the Hummvees seemed to linger, like a stain. Part of the bleak atmosphere that overhung the land. As if those evil armoured bugs had gone to ground somewhere.

She tipped her face into the light; it warmed her skin, but couldn't reach her heart. Because now, of course, she knew what really lurked out there. Waiting for the dusk, perhaps. The rising of the moon.

She lowered her gaze, and sipped her tea . . . and wondered, very calmly, when he'd deign to show his face.

2

With afternoon now wearing on, she thought about some old haunts of her own. Points around the range where she had watched from. Places that still called to her, their voices zephyr-faint.

Other ghosts were waiting there. The shadows of her past. To stir them up would pass a little time.

Finishing her tea, she pulled Lyn's jacket off the chairback.

She hoped the lady wouldn't mind about the untouched scones. Pausing at the door, she looked around the empty room. The ghosts were here as well, amid the dimness and the dust-motes. She tarried, as if waiting to be noticed. Then turned away, and left them to their unheard conversations.

Outside, the day was bright but fresh; she shrugged into the jacket's fleecy warmth. The Black Horse down the street was where she'd booked in for the night. Perhaps she'd still be waiting here tomorrow. She had no way of knowing when he'd put in an appearance.

Perhaps he wasn't coming back at all.

She glanced up and down the street, but Tilshead seemed deserted. Empty country slumbered all around it. Would she be relieved, if she had come down here for nothing? She almost dared to hope for such an outcome; then realized it would bring no hope at all. Tense though she was – not butterflies but hornets in her stomach – she knew she had to raise this ghost again.

She walked past Lyn's parked car (blessing her again for the loan of it) and strolled on out of the village. The convoy route curved northward, but she took the westbound fork, towards Breach Hill. A lesser road, and quieter still, with hedgerows blocking off the Plain's expanse. She passed the old brick water-tower, set back among the trees; a bird sang out in solitary vigil. But trees and bushes petered out before she reached the crest.

The place was as exposed as she remembered: just barren, windswept heath on either side. Cruisewatch cars would park here at the roadside, looking north across the dreary slopes of Imber. She halted with her hands deep in her pockets: gazing off towards Fore Down and Imber Firs. The breeze was stronger here, stirring her hair like unseen fingers.

She stood there for a while, but saw no movement. Nothing walked amid those miles of grassland. The dark, contorted copses kept their secrets. At length she turned, and started slowly back.

A sombre shape was waiting by the roadside: in the shadow of the trees, beside the tower. Fran saw him, and stopped dead. The hornets in her stomach bared their stings.

He watched her for a moment; then came forward. Her nerve-ends quivered briefly with the impulse to retreat. She overcame the instinct and stood her ground. And Athelgar himself seemed almost wary: approaching her with reverential steps.

He wore his grimy coat more strangely now: hitched up and wrapped around him like a shawl. More comfortable like that, she guessed. A closer imitation of the medieval cloak.

How weird this modern world must seem to him.

He dipped his head in greeting, but his eyes remained on hers. He had his warrior's pride, she thought – whatever awe he felt.

'Well met, my lady Frances.'

'Fran,' she said, as drily as her dry mouth would permit.

He nodded slowly. '*Vrahn*,' he said: a soft, distorted echo. His rough and rustic accent was becoming more familiar – enough for her to register an *oddness* to the sound. As if it were a foreign word for him.

He paced around her thoughtfully. 'I see that *you* are now dressed for the road.' He sounded quite impressed as well as awed. She guessed he wasn't used to girls in trousers.

His own dark clothes were dustier than when she'd seen him last: the chalkiness suggestive of much tramping round the Plain. 'Have you found what you were looking for?' she asked.

'Perhaps.' He turned away, looked back towards West Down. 'The troops who muster round this place: more warriors of the king?'

'Yeah.' She tried to see them through his ancient eyes: their helms, and muddy livery, and horseless iron carts. 'So what did they make of *you*?' she went on curiously.

A faint smile touched his lips. 'They have not seen me.'

The dust was in his hair as well; or was he turning grey

before his time? The light found paler bristles in the shadow of his beard.

'There is something in the wastes,' he said. 'The call is growing stronger.' He fumbled in the pouch around his neck, and came up with a coin: the antique one he'd tossed, back at the crossroads. 'I think that it is metal kin to this.'

Fran looked at it again, and saw how thin it had been worn: as if by years of slow, obsessive rubbing. He turned it in his fingers even now.

'You haven't been to get it then?' she prompted.

'I . . . will not go alone,' he said – and glanced towards her.

She wondered what it cost him to admit that. A warrior's pride would only go so far. For a moment she felt flattered; then second thoughts took hold, and gripped her hard. If he needed her along – a saint, as he supposed – what kind of evil powers did he need protecting from?

'Where?' she asked, her heart already thudding.

He turned away and pointed: at West Down, and the slopes that rose beyond it.

She felt a thrill of icy pins and needles. 'Not in the dark . . . ?' she ventured, trying not to sound appalled. *I can't do that*, she thought at him. *I won't.*

He shook his head. 'The downs are sleepless, once the sun is set. I have crossed the tracks of things that walk in darkness. We must claim the thing we seek before the nightfall.'

The glimmer of relief was cold and faint. His words awoke the memory of shadows at her heels. She swallowed, wiped her mouth. 'We can't go on yet. Not until the flags come down. The soldiers will be moving round till then . . .' Her mind raced onward, mapping out their course. The range was closed till five or so. How many hours of daylight would that leave . . . ?

'Whose is the scarlet banner on the roads?' he wondered.

'It's no one's . . . Just a warning.' She hesitated. '*Your* banner was the black one . . . wasn't it?'

He looked at her, and nodded.

'Rafen . . . ?' she asked cautiously.

He searched her face. 'I know we are unworthy. I ask that you will pray for our redemption.'

She hesitated, staring back. His grim expression tightened at the pause. But then he let it twist into a wry, self-mocking smile.

'Nor would the Bishop do so.' He turned away; then wheeled again towards her. His voice had been resigned and low, but now it rose in tone, and grew more bitter.

'"What would your petition be?" he asked me. "*Pray to kill and return alive.* I cannot intercede for that. I will not pray for you."' He pointed as he said it; but Fran sensed he was mimicking this Bishop, and pointing at the shadow of himself.

She moved without thinking: grasped his sleeve. He looked at her askance, arm still extended.

'What's to forgive?' she whispered.

'Shinecraft. Murder. Treachery. You *know* what we have done.' Gently now, he disengaged himself. 'Our chronicle is ashes now, and we shall soon be dust.'

Again she felt those pricking pins and needles, but was afraid to ask him more. If she showed her ignorance too much, she'd give herself away. He might begin to think that she'd deceived him.

She'd never claimed to be a saint. But nor had she denied it.

A breeze crept through the summer leaves above them. The real world fell back into its place. Fran swallowed down the lump in her throat, and made a show of looking at her watch. Nearly quarter to five already.

By the time they'd got to Westdown Camp, the trackways onto Larkhill would be open.

3

They'd walked as far as East Down Wood before she tried again.

They were following a gritty road that cut across the contours to the north. The sinister plantation was a sunken field away – as hostile as a square of troops deployed on open ground. Shadows filled it, guarded from the sun. The croak of rooks came drifting from the trees.

Beyond, the empty grassland looked innocuous enough. She could see the distant copses to the south, where Greenlands was. So different to the gulf of night she'd fled across before, and yet the view still made her tense and clammy. Greenlands, though unseen, was an ominous presence: as repellent as some village with the Plague. No way could she go nearer, she might catch it . . .

(Or be caught)

More cawing from the rooky wood, as if to spread the word.

Light thickens . . . said a dry voice in her head: a trigger-phrase that brought the whole quote with it. Lines she'd learned while studying *Macbeth*, way back in blissful ignorance at school.

> *Good things of day begin to droop and drowse,*
> *While night's black agents to their preys do rouse.*

Swallowing, she glanced towards the sun. The south-west sky was flushed with marigold. They had perhaps two hours.

Athelgar walked just ahead; his pace was slow but steady. Whatever he was searching for, he hadn't got a fix on it as yet. At least there was a method to his mode of navigation – but it didn't make her feel too confident. Whenever they'd come to a parting of ways, he'd simply flipped his coin to choose between them.

This way would take them east, to Prospect Clump: a high point on the road to Redhorn Hill. Fran turned to look the way they'd come; the dusty track smoked palely in the sunlight, quite deserted. She looked towards the wood again. The rooks were growing fainter, as the ragged block of shadow slid away.

'Was it you who took the Raven, then?' she asked – so suddenly, she caught herself off guard.

Athelgar glanced back at her, and nodded.

Necromantic power: that's what Lyn's book had said about it. Fran shoved her hands down deeper in her pockets – as if to brace herself against the throbbing in her belly.

'And is that why you can't rest?'

Again his pensive face came round. A shadow of perplexity had crossed it.

Fran gestured quickly, caught him up. 'Please. I . . . just don't know the whole of it. We don't see everything.'

Ooh!, her conscience squealed at her. *You fibber!*

'You know the power the Raven has,' he said.

Instinctively she nodded, and he offered nothing further. On they trudged, uphill. The silence of the Plain closed in: immersed them like an ocean. At length she had to break it, like she simply had to breathe.

'How did you come to capture it?' she said. Then: 'Sorry . . .' as she saw his sombre look.

But Athelgar just raised his hand. 'Of course you do not know these things. I *envy* you that blessing.'

They kept on walking; he with his head bowed. She sensed him calling memories back up towards the surface: awaiting them like vomit from a sourness deep inside. Fran waited too, her own mouth dry and bitter.

'You know I am from Wessexena Land,' he said at last. 'But in those days I bore arms for Holy Edmund, in the east. Edmund, king, as he was then. The Danes had taken York, and festered there. Edmund raised our sword-force to resist them. We heard tell of the Raven, and his black and evil power. Land-Waster, they called it. But we had faith in Christ, and this was stronger . . . we supposed.

'Then the Raven came south. It over-shadowed all the Eastern English. Holy Edmund fell, and all his kingdom was laid waste. I wished to die beside him there, I had no use for life. But something in my dreaming called me back to my old country. It told me that our war was not yet done.'

Fran glanced at him; then looked ahead. The ragged shape of Prospect Clump loomed closer by the minute.

'Our sword-force was the last one to escape. We fought for every place along the road: field and weald. They lost us at the last – and many men we cost them in the losing. But night was falling all across the land . . .'

She listened, fascinated. The Chronicle she'd read was a voice from the past; but Athelgar's was speaking in the present – here and *now*. She almost smelled the mud and sweat. Her mind's eye saw his shouting face, bespattered with bright scarlet.

'The shadow spread like blood upon a cloth,' he went on slowly. 'Now only Alfred, king, held out against them. The Danes came from the west, and thought to trap him. But we were waiting there for our revenge.

'We met with Edmund's murderer, and killed him in his turn. We took the witching-Raven, and we used it. It flew for us at Waste-Down, and we held the slaughter-field. It has led us in our war-play ever since. And that is why men call us *Ravensbreed*.'

She was still chewing all that over when they reached the lonely junction. The single metalled carriageway stretched out in both directions. Southward, sloping down towards the Bustard vedette; and north, across the wilderness of heath.

Athelgar's coin spun up again, and dropped into his palm. Fran quickly checked her watch. The Bustard was two miles away, at least. It was almost time to think about heading back. They'd be off-range before dusk, of course they would; but her skin had started crawling, and she knew it wouldn't stop until they were well on their way.

'*This* way,' said Athelgar – and started northward.

She felt her stomach lurch. 'We . . . need to be turning back soon,' she said, as calmly as she could.

He glanced at the sun. 'We have daylight enough.'

'It'll take us a while to get back, though . . .'

He turned, came back to join her. 'We *must* find what is calling us. I think a brother-Raven has concealed it. Disclosing it, we may find him as well – and then the rest.' He stared into her apprehensive face. 'Five hundred *years* have passed since we were woken last from sleep. What danger is abroad, that we be summoned back here now?'

She hesitated; swallowed. 'I don't know.'

'Nor I. So we must both be ready – lest it take us unawares.'

Adjusting his furled coat, he set off along the gently sloping road. Fran followed, with a last glance at the safe, familiar country to the south. Distant buildings slumbered in the sunny evening haze. Too far away already. Getting further.

The way ahead was desolate, a wasteland. Just north of the bedraggled clump, the route forked left and right. Each way looked as barren as the other. Fran stared up at the weathered fingerpost, as stark as an old gibbet. West to Market Lavington. Due north, across the heights, to Redhorn Hill.

Athelgar's fingers turned the coin. Its silver glinted flatly, like his rings. He tossed and caught it; nodded to the right. The bleaker choice (*of course*, she thought). It seemed a road to nowhere.

They reached an open barrier, with a warning sign beside it. She paused to stare at it; then kept on walking.

DO NOT LEAVE THIS ROAD
DO NOT TOUCH ANYTHING
IT MAY EXPLODE AND KILL YOU.

Unexploded Military Debris said a notice on the verge. Another showed beyond it, then another. Every fifty yards there was one waiting at the roadside. The effect as they trudged onward was progressively unnerving. Fran felt herself hemmed in and driven forward – as if this was a path through a minefield. The grim, forbidding aspect of the grassland was redoubled. She turned and looked behind them. The isolated signpost seemed as tiny as a matchstick.

Athelgar was flipping his coin repeatedly now: he seemed absorbed with it. She let him catch it one more time, then quickly touched his arm.

'Listen . . . We have to turn back now. It's *miles* to Redhorn Hill.' And pretty soon, she knew, they'd reach the point of no return. No way from that but forward – through the wildest, deadest area of the range.

He offered her the coin, as if in answer. It gleamed in his half-gloved palm. She stared at it uncertainly.

'It has come down crosses eight times out of ten,' he said. 'We must be close now.'

The sun was still a yellow ball; the western sky engorged with blazing light. How long before it started turning orange? *We're really going to cut it fine*, she thought.

'*See*,' said Athelgar, and pointed. Startled by the sudden word, she looked along the road – and saw them waiting. Hulks of mangled metal, lying close to the verge: like the carcasses of monsters that had crawled out here to die.

Just three wrecked tanks, she realized. Used for target practice now.

Athelgar had stopped, and stood there, staring. 'It is like the tale of Beowulf,' he murmured.

She had an idea what he meant: it was getting easier to see things through his eyes. The bones of three dead dragons by the road. So what about the treasure they had guarded?

'Men made those,' she told him quickly, anxious to get going. 'Just siege-engines . . . you see?' Her turn to lead the way along the road. He came behind her, pensive now. Still dowsing with his coin.

'Crosses . . . crosses . . . and again.' He reached the tanks and halted. 'It is *here*.'

Fran turned in a full circle. Dead ground in all directions. 'Where?'

He closed his fist around the coin, and raised it to his chin. She waited: felt her nerves begin to twitch. The silence of the shattered tanks hung heavy in the air. She glanced at them, just yards away. Dead things. Gutted things. The nearest turret looming black against the golden sky. Their spreading shadows almost reached the road.

She looked at Athelgar again. His eyes on her were thoughtful.

'Perhaps your blessed relic can disclose it.'

My *what?* she almost said – then realized what he meant. Or thought she did. Frowning, she fished up the Coventry Cross. It caught the sunlight: silver-gilt. And suddenly she seemed to feel it twitch – as if, for just an instant, something tugged it.

She glanced at Athelgar, wide-eyed.

'Let it have his way,' he breathed.

Cautiously she took it in her finger and thumb, the cross-piece braced between them like an axis. The fine chain slackened round her neck. The upright nail hung motionless, suspended. Part of her was sure she hadn't really felt it move. The rest of her was clenched in expectation – as if the thing was live, about to shock her.

And then, although she never moved, the nail began to lift.

She stared in disbelief. It was like watching someone dowse for water. She'd seen that done before – when she was little. The dowsing-rod had seemed to come to life. Her childish awe returned with all its force.

The cross swung up and dipped again, as if pointing her ahead.

Slowly she stepped forward, off the road. The turf was tough and springy underfoot. A sidelong glance at Athelgar; he was watching her, entranced. She felt a sense of *power* then, so heady that it almost made her laugh.

The cross twitched again. It was taking her towards the gap between the first two wrecks. Step by step she went in that direction. The risk of unexploded shells was quite forgotten now.

Athelgar was on the grass as well: circling round to her right. A respectful distance from her divinations. She let her glance stray past him, to the road, but it was empty.

The breeze picked up, and rustled drily round them. She heard it moaning faintly in the turret of the tank. The jagged shadow chilled her as she baby-stepped across it. The sun was getting very low, but now she didn't care.

She reached an unmarked piece of ground. The nail swung down and stayed there.

'Here,' she called, a little breathless now. 'I think it's here.'

He came across, and knelt, and started tearing at the turf: translating the momentum of her thoughts. She gave him room and waited, fairly buzzing with excitement. The cross had turned inert again; she fiddled with it, pressing at its points . . .

Athelgar said '*Jesu,*' then: still digging like a dog. She edged a little closer and saw him scratching something up. A clod of earth, it looked like; but then it started crumbling as he turned it in his grasp. A dull, metallic glint showed through the dirt.

A cross of tarnished gold took shape as the soil came sloughing off. It was a Canterbury type, the size of his palm. He studied it a moment; then twisted round, still kneeling, and extended it towards her. She saw his exultation, on his face and in his eyes: so strong that he relapsed into Old English.

'*On eorthan swa, swa in heofonum!*'

The battered, almost bony cross was curiously familiar. Flecks of dirt still clung to it, half-blending with its dark, encrusted stones. And then it clicked. St Cuthbert's Cross. She'd seen it once in Durham. A glowing holy relic in the dim cathedral hush. So this must be a copy, but it still looked just as old.

Athelgar was watching her, expectant – to see how she'd react, she realized then. The cross was still extended: the relic of one northern saint, presented to another. She took it carefully, weighed it in her hand. Dead metal, that was all it was. But her nerves began to tingle with its sense of latent *age*.

Athelgar seemed satisfied: he went back to his digging. A blackened lump of something came up next. A larger object, sunk into the ground. He scraped more soil away. Fran looked on, still fingering the cross.

The thing had the look of cracked and hardened leather. Athelgar kept at it, and abruptly dragged it free. She saw that it *was* leather then: a shapeless bag, compressed round something solid. Sitting back, he reached behind himself – and produced an ugly knife as if from nowhere. Instinct sent Fran back a wary step. The eight-inch blade had lost its sheen, but still looked razor sharp. She'd known he was a warrior, yes – but now she saw as much. All this time he'd carried *that* beneath his scruffy coat.

He didn't even glance at her; just hacked into the bag, and sliced it open. A thick, metallic clinking sound – and then the coins spilled out.

Wonder overcame her trepidation. She craned her head to look. The pouch was crammed with antique silver pennies. Kin to his old coin, just as he'd said. Only a few lay scattered on the soil: the rest were still tight-packed. Time and dirt had fused them all together.

Athelgar scooped a handful up; let them chink in his cupped palm. They glittered in the westering sun. She saw that he was smiling very faintly.

'*Rathulf*,' he said softly, as if putting a name to a half-forgotten friend.

Fran waited. The breeze renewed its purchase, and she shivered, shook it off.

'Rathulf has been this way,' he said.

'Who's he?' she asked. The name was a forbidding one, somehow.

'The keeper of our purse.'

'And this was after Waste-Down?' She wondered when those coins had last seen the light of day. How many murky centuries ago . . .

'This is our hrafngeld. It has not lain for long. Perhaps a year, or two.'

There's another of them out there. The thought became a shiver down her spine. *Another of these warriors, walking round* . . . She turned to scan the empty heath. The windswept land was desolate, their solitude still total.

The sun was sinking close to the horizon.

A wave of gooseflesh surged beneath her clothes. 'Come on, we've got to get back.'

He glanced at her: hearing the nervous rising of her voice; surprised by it, perhaps. 'We will be safe on the road until full dark.'

Oh, will we? She couldn't keep from glaring – with a vague sense of betrayal. She'd only ventured out here on condition they'd be off the range by nightfall. Athelgar turned back towards the coin-hoard, unperturbed. She watched him start to sort through the loose pennies.

'What do you want with those, then?' she asked.

'I told you, they are hrafngeld,' he said thoughtfully: still counting. 'The wages of war. Perhaps their shine will draw my brothers back . . .'

Again she looked towards the west. The sun was tinged with vivid orange now. Jittery, she started pacing round him – then wandered over to the nearest tank. Its brooding, burnt-out silence seemed to focus all the stillness of the Plain. The tracks were gone, it sat on naked wheels. The open hatches added to its lost, abandoned feel.

The three wrecks cast long shadows now. Like tracts of swamp, untainted by the last warmth of the day. She waded clear, around the hull, and gazed into the golden-orange sun-set. She felt it light her face and lift her spirits; but her belly was still tight with apprehension.

She looked down at the grimy cross, and angled it to catch

the flaring light. Wishing she could feel some kind of power.

'It is almost done,' said Athelgar behind her. She turned her head; he was pressing the last few coins into the bag. A flicker of faint movement caught the corner of her eye. She looked beyond him, back the way they'd come.

Someone else, a mile behind, was with them on the road. A single, lonely shape amid the heath. Distance shrank it; slowed it to a crawl. Not a man on foot, she saw: too tall and gaunt for that. She realized it was someone on a horse.

'Athelgar,' she murmured. 'Look.'

Still on one knee, he turned; went very still.

'One of your men?' she asked him; and felt her heart beat faster as she waited. Though even if it wasn't, that was no cause for alarm. People from the local farms could ride their horses here . . .

Athelgar kept looking; still not speaking.

The glowing grass was turning now. The light grew rancid: reddened as she watched. Fran took a slow step backwards and heard a creak of movement from behind her. The furtive sort an animal might make. With prickling nerves, she glanced around – and *screamed*.

Grown woman though she was, the sight demanded that response; the only other option was to faint. She knew she'd seen the face before – the ghastly thing emerging from the tank. That photo from the Gulf War, of the burned Iraqi soldier. The figure in the driver's hatch had just the same expression, all socket eyes and bared, grimacing teeth. It craned towards her, glaring down: still climbing stiffly out. And no, she wasn't seeing things – the hideous thing was *here*.

She staggered backwards, horrified. The creature's skin was black, its dark fur peeling. Then her mind refocused, and the battered hairless skull became a helmet. A visor masked the upper face. The staring eyeholes followed her retreat.

Athelgar yelled something, but the words were harsh and foreign in her ears. Defiance or alarm, she couldn't tell. He seized her trailing arm and hauled her back towards the road.

She came without resistance, her eyes still fixed and staring at the thing's disfigured face. And then another movement drew her gaze, a second figure, prowling from behind the middle tank. Her bulging heart bounced up into her throat. This one too was wrapped in rags and draped with matted fur. A rusty axe was raised in one gloved hand.

They gained the tarmac: its firmness made her whimper with relief, as if they'd found a causeway through a swamp. They halted there, both breathing hard. Athelgar still held her sleeve, the knife in his free hand.

The first grim figure cleared the hatch, and dropped into the grass: coming to rest in a stiff, arachnoid crouch. It stared towards them, motionless, its rictus-grin a parody of mirth. Her mind threw up the image of a giant trap-door spider – and matched it to that night at Greenlands camp. The things with metal faces that had *scuttled* at her heels. Her fine hairs rose like needles, cold and sharp.

The other figure, too, had ceased to move. But then she heard more stirrings, from the carcass in the middle. A dull, metallic booming noise like rumblings of hunger in the belly of the tank. The turret was gone on this one; there was just an empty socket, full of shadow.

She looked away, along the road. The mounted man was drawing slowly nearer. And out in the surrounding grass, she glimpsed more helmets raised, and figures rising. Emerging from the empty heath, like drowned men from a marsh. Even from this distance, she could see their eyeless masks.

Instinct begged to break and run, but her legs were like a foal's. They threatened to give way if she so much as took a step.

'Beata Francesca, ora pro me . . .'

The words seemed to come from a dying man's throat – but it was Athelgar who spoke them. He didn't turn; his narrowed eyes stayed focused on the wreckage. She realized he'd addressed his prayer to *her*.

She glanced back at the decapitated tank – just in time to

see a pair of arms grope blindly into view. Lean and stiff, like bony cranes, they braced themselves against the turret-ring, and levered up another iron head.

Fran grasped Athelgar's shoulder, squeezing hard enough to hurt. 'Oh God,' she hissed, '*what are they?*'

'Ashmen,' he said tightly – then twisted clear, and jumped back off the road. She felt a plunge of panic; then realized he was trying for the coins. The crouching figure came to life, and quickly stalked towards him. The axe swung up and scythed across. Athelgar ducked the backhand slash, rolled clear and finished up beside the purse. Snatching it, he scrambled back. The thing he'd called an Ashman followed through, and swung again. But Athelgar was quicker: he rolled once more, and found his feet. Hugging the bag against his chest, still brandishing his knife, he retreated to the safety of the road. The grisly figure halted, leering blackly at them both.

Fran felt her fingers aching, and had to turn her head to find the cause. Her hand was tightly wrapped around the skeletal gold cross. She watched it like a stranger's: saw it shaking with the strain. The relic seemed about to snap in two.

'They cannot take us on the road,' breathed Athelgar beside her. 'It is a way for *living* men till nightfall.'

Fran looked around. The horseman was approaching at a walk. Like the others, he was helmeted: the visor covered all his face. He reined in twenty yards away; sat watching like a statue. The mask made her think of the Sutton Hoo Man. Its lips were sealed; its stare was cavernous.

'What about *him?*' she whispered. The horse's skinny flanks were panting faintly, but the rider sat as motionless as stone. No living man: she could tell that much from here. Another of these creatures. *On the road.*

'He keeps his distance too,' said Athelgar.

But he had cut off their retreat. Even as she watched, the rider nudged his mount towards them: came forward at a slow, relentless walk. She knew he meant to herd them on before him; to drive them ever deeper into Larkhill's barren wastes.

The figures in the open started moving in as well. The fading day gleamed dully on their helmets.

'They cannot reach us,' Athelgar insisted. 'Not until the shadows come together on the road . . .'

Four miles to Redhorn Hill at least; how long until full dark? The sun was gone: just gold sky in the west, and bars of salmon-coloured cloud. They were stuck in the middle of nowhere here, and dusk was coming down. But Athelgar still thought that she could save him.

Blessed Frances, pray for me . . .

She felt his faith like energy inside her. Brandishing the northern cross, as he had held his knife, she turned and led him on along the road.

The light was turning greyer, as though thickening with dust. They crested a rise – and another evil Ashman shape was crouching at the roadside, its helmet's gaping sockets turned towards them. Horrified, she veered around it – holding out the cross. It grovelled like some medieval leper as they passed: she sensed its desperation to crawl up onto the road.

They quickened their pace; the sombre horseman matched it. Fran looked back, and almost started running. The mask was still impassive, and more frightening for that; but its lips had the beginnings of an enigmatic smile. It had to be a trick of the failing light: the dusk that lay like silt upon the road.

She was panting with exertion: enough to make her sweat inside the sheepskin. On and on they hiked, but made no headway. The lonely road stretched out ahead; the desolated landscape never changed. The salmon clouds above the west had changed to mackerel grey. And shadows were converging from the countryside around.

She heard a tinny rattle: coins on tarmac. Glancing back, she saw that Athelgar had stopped. He was struggling with the purse – still trying to hold its growing split together.

'Come *on*!' she hissed. 'Just leave it!'

He shook his head. 'This hoard will bring the Ravens home.'

Staring back at him, she was horribly reminded of a tale

her mum had told her. A certain man made a deal with the Devil, to own all the land he could walk round in a day. But the man was too greedy, and walked too far – and in his haste to get back before nightfall, he gave himself a heart attack, and died.

How much land did that man need? Just six feet, from his head to his heels . . .

The grassland had become a gloomy fen. The Ashmen waded through it, ever closer to the verge. But Athelgar's treasure was slowing him down. Unless he ditched it, they would both be lost.

How much wealth does a man need? Just two pennies, to be placed upon his eyes . . .

Oh, Mum, please help me. Please.

The hunters, left and right, were closing in. She could hear the snorting horse; its measured hoofbeats.

Athelgar got a tight grip on the bag, and started forward. Fran strode beside him, gasping. Night was coming quickly now, like coal-dust on the breeze. The road beneath their feet was indistinct.

She stumbled, fell on hands on knees. The cross went skittering away; the tarmac raked her palms. She scrabbled forward; grasped the gold again. It seemed to burn against her ravaged skin. Athelgar seized her collar, hauled her up with his free hand. Faces flashed like ghosts before her eyes. Mum and Dad, and Lyn, and Craig. People from another life: a world beyond the grey rim of the Plain . . .

'Up, my Lady. *Onward.* We are nearly at the hill.'

She raised her face and saw the tower ahead. The watchtower, on the ridge by the vedette. The gradient rose towards it, but her strength came in a spurt. Stumbling into step again, she headed for the crest – quite heedless of the stinging in her hands. Athelgar was at her side, still clutching at her jacket; looking back to check on their pursuers.

The tower wobbled closer; she could see the sentry hut. Fran ducked her head with effort; just a hundred yards to go.

She sensed the Ashmen pacing them. The horse's hoofbeats clattered on the tarmac. But dusk was almost darkness now, covering the road like rising tides across a causeway.

The hoofbeats were approaching, getting faster.

'*Fly*,' said Athelgar – and shoved her forward. Despite herself, she twisted round to look. The rider loomed behind them, indistinct against the sky. He was coming at a canter. He was going to catch them up.

But Athelgar was moving back to meet him. A thrill of horror froze her to the spot. Her instincts balked at leaving him – but then he turned and gestured, waved her back from him, *away*.

'Come on!' she shouted. '*Run*!'

'Save yourself,' he shouted back – and then the horse was on him.

The sooty air absorbed them: two ghostly shadows clashing in the murk. Athelgar was knocked aside; the dark horse skittered round. She heard its whinny, pitched with pain. Perhaps he'd got his knife into its flank.

Sobbing for breath, she turned and pelted onwards. The effort scorched her lungs and filled her throat with scalding bile. The Ashmen were behind her, she could feel them at her heels. And then she reached the sentry-hut, and passed it. A gravel parking-apron crunched and turned beneath her boots.

Off-range, she felt no safer: the ground ahead slipped down into a gulf of unlit country. Staggering, she came up short, and spun to look behind her.

And Athelgar was coming, like a raven on the road; his coat flared out around him as he ran. There was just enough light to glimpse the paleness of his hair. He crossed the line, and slowed at once – came stumbling towards her. She fell upon him: hugged him tight. He let his burden fall to earth and clutched her in return.

'Oh, God . . .' she gasped, and peered over his shoulder – but the countryside lay empty in the last gasp of the twilight.

There was just the lonely tower, rising gaunt against the sky. Nothing had pursued them to the barrier.

Still staring, she began to shake. Athelgar held her tighter. She had the dim impression that he was seeking reassurance, as much as giving it.

'Where have they gone?' she whispered.

'Back into deeper dark.' He paused for breath, then turned his head, as if to make quite sure. 'That ground is lost . . . and they can walk it freely . . . but they must gather strength before they follow.'

She nodded dumbly, took him at his word. Slowly she released him and stepped back. Her skinned palms burned and tingled now. She held them out, as if the breeze could cool them. Her fingers were still knotted round the cross.

One of her knees was aching, too; she really hoped she hadn't scuffed her jeans. With the dreadful threat removed, such things were suddenly important. Adrenaline had taken her as high as a kite, but now she felt her heart begin to drop.

Athelgar was kneeling, scooping coins into the purse. She glimpsed a wincing stiffness in his movements, more obvious as he straightened up. He looked back once again – then turned towards her.

'Blessed may you be, my Lady Frances.'

The words were quiet and simple; she was touched. No point in trying to argue. Instead she said: 'I don't know who they were.'

'*Asherra*,' was his grim response. 'The wolves are loose again.'

Which didn't shed much light on things, but summed the horror up. She could sense them slinking round out there, frustrated.

Warily he touched her arm. 'We must go forward and leave this place behind us.'

There was a trackway leading off along the edge of the range: heading west into the dark, towards Gore Cross. She hoped to God he didn't mean to take it. They'd be walking blind, along the very brink – and if they missed their way . . .

'That is an ancient path,' he murmured, following her gaze. 'We might walk safely on it. But I fear it is too close to them. So come, we go this way.'

Drained, she looked ahead of her. The road ran down off Redhorn Hill, and vanished in the night. The lowlands had been drowned in murk already. The lights of lonely houses glimmered faintly in the distance, like ships on a deep black sea.

But the Devil was behind them, so they didn't have much choice. Clinging to each other, they started slowly downward. The lane was gloomy, overgrown with trees. Fran began shivering again; he shed his coat, and draped it round them both. Nursing her against him; speaking softly in her ear.

By the time they'd got to level ground, the moon was up and glowing: suspended like a frozen pearl above the dark horizon.

CHAPTER III

Wessexena Sky

I

'I hope I didn't get you up,' Fran said.

'No, no,' Lyn told her hastily, 'you didn't.' Tucking the phone under her chin, she tightened the belt of her dressing-gown, before it came adrift. She'd thought it was her mum, in fact. The warm glow was still fading from her cheeks.

Mid-morning, and the flat was full of sunlight. She stroked away a fall of unbrushed hair.

'Just ringing to say I'll be staying down here another night . . .'

'How's it going?' Lyn asked. Her friend's voice sounded bright enough – but somehow it was different. Nothing she could put her finger on; like the time she'd rearranged her hi-fi speakers, and favourite albums hadn't been the *same*. But that had just been pickiness on her part; her ears had readjusted soon enough. This was something deeper. Intuition. Empathy.

She didn't stop to wonder; more concerned that Fran might think *she* sounded different too.

'Fine,' Fran said. 'It's strange, the Plain. A really . . . weird place.'

That oddness in her tone again: a softly haunted note. But Lyn just smiled, and shrugged the feeling off. 'I'll have to check it out some time,' she said, politely vague.

Silence, then. A sense of empty space at the end of the line. She listened to it, waiting; swinging her hips in a restless sort of way.

Fran seemed to swallow. 'Lyn . . .'

'Mm?'

Another pause. 'No, it's all right. Nothing.'

Impatience started niggling inside her. She wrapped her free arm round herself, as if to hold it in.

'Anyway . . .' Fran said. 'I'll see you tomorrow, sometime. Take care. 'Bye . . .'

Lyn echoed that, and waited till she heard the contact break. It felt like losing something – opportunity, perhaps. *Sorry, Fran*, she thought, *I should have listened*. Hanging up, she stood there for a moment; then shrugged again, inside herself, and went back to her room.

Fran stepped out of the phone box, and crossed the road to where Athelgar was waiting.

She hadn't slept at all last night; fatigue was like a buzz behind her eyes. They'd sheltered in an open-sided barn until daybreak: listening to each furtive noise, each rustling in the fields. The countryside looked spectral in the moonlight; the high scarp loomed beyond it, like a sinister black cliff. Though Athelgar had held her close, she'd still felt icy cold.

At first light, they'd moved west, onto the old Devizes road, and followed it back south to Tilshead village. The rosy-golden sunrise tinged the slopes to left and right. The farmland and the ranges seemed deserted: green and fresh. But the long walk down between them still felt like the Valley of Death.

'You have spoken with your friend?' said Athelgar. His tone was wary; muted with respect. She noticed he was fingering the cross around his neck.

She wondered what the phone box meant to him. A road-side shrine, perhaps, where she communed with unseen spirits.

God knew how she was going to explain about the car.

Lyn slipped out of her dressing gown, and climbed back into bed.

'No coffee?' murmured Simon, with a sly and sleepy grin.

'Get it yourself,' she giggled, curling up with him again. Sated and smug, like a cat with the cream; the phone-call was forgotten. No shyness now, why should there be? Her sylph-like figure (Mummy's term) was there for showing off.

'Was it your mum, then?'

'No. That was Fran. My friend who's staying here. Just letting me know . . .' she kissed him '. . . that she won't be back tonight.'

'So – we can stay here all day?'

She propped herself up on one elbow, pouting. 'I thought you said that *you* were making breakfast.'

'Damn,' he said, and gently stroked her breast. Lyn simpered and relented. The warmth began to build in her again.

'She staying long?' he asked. 'This friend of yours?'

Lyn flicked her hair back, serious for a moment. 'I don't know. She's had a lot of problems, poor girl.' Then she smiled, and nuzzled at his chest. 'But I think she's got them sorted out. I think it's all right now.'

2

Athelgar knelt, and scooped up a handful of soil. He raised it to his mouth; then let it trickle through his fingers. The look on his face was rapt and far-away.

Fran stood back and watched him, frowning slightly. The gesture seemed to link him with the *oldness* of the earth: the loam beneath these sunny Hampshire fields. A wanderer returning to his time as well as place. The hunter home from the hill.

He turned his head towards her.

'The ground is bitter, but it is my land.' Still hunkered down, he wiped his lips, and very slowly dusted off his hands.

They were just outside the village. West Meon, on the Alton road. The countryside was hazy-still around them.

'When did you come here last?' she wondered softly.

He seemed to think about it, glancing round. Studying the copses and the fields. *It can't have changed too much*, she thought, *these past one thousand years . . .*

'When Athelstan was king at Wintanchestre,' he said. 'This place he granted me as my estate. I thought that I could stay here, make a place for hearth and hoard. Grow old with the land. Find peace. It was not so.'

She heard his tone get harder. Bitterness, perhaps; or just regret. He'd never come back since – that much was clear. Perhaps he'd felt the pull, and fought against it: just as she had with Oxford and the Plain.

Today, though, he'd insisted that they come here. To *Meone*, as he called it. She'd finally located it in Lyn's road atlas, while Athelgar sat silently beside her – reduced to wary stillness by this glass and metal shell. He'd go rigid when the vehicle was moving: enough to make her tense in sympathy.

She'd stopped to get her bearings in a quiet country lane. 'There's two of them,' she'd told him. 'East and West.'

'There was a church,' he'd murmured. 'Two mills, and a meadow. The burn turned southward there.'

The western village seemed to fit the bill. 'And . . . what will we be looking for?'

'Sky-Edge,' was his grim reply. 'I must reclaim my sword.' He said that with the 'w' pronounced.

And what if the Ashmen were waiting at the end of the road? The very thought suffused her in another pulse of sweat; she sat and felt it soaking through her blouse. Things were out of her control, and happening too fast.

'Listen . . . Can't we wait a while?'

He shook his head. 'There is no time. Perhaps the wolves are following our path.'

She felt a pang of cold, and checked the mirror.

'And the sword will be concealed with craft,' he went on calmly. 'It will not be found, unless the moon is full.'

The sunlit lane behind them had been empty. But the chilly sense of being pursued had lingered. All the way to Meon, like a cold-spot in the car. She could feel it here, beneath this vacant sky.

Athelgar had straightened up.

'So when did you leave your sword here, then?' she asked.

'When the Ravens were scattered. The fourteen-hundredth Year of Grace, or near enough to that.'

Her history was sketchy; but 1400 was getting on for Tudor times, if she remembered right. She'd studied those at school, which made them slightly more immediate. The Middle Ages drawing to a close.

They must have felt so out of place by then, these Saxon Ravens. An ancient race. No wonder they'd been shunned.

'We must follow the bounds of the estate,' he said. 'The sword will lie along that path.'

Concealed with craft. She frowned. 'You didn't bring it here yourself?'

He shook his head. 'It was entrusted to another.'

'One of your brothers?'

Sombrely he shook his head. 'No brother.'

Fran raised her eyebrows, curious; but he took that as a query on the hiding of the sword. Or chose to take it so, she thought. His face had grown as guarded as his words.

'It is the way of Stranger-craft. The blade is in the circle, but it overlies the ring.'

Whatever that meant. She turned away and stared out across the farmland. Sleepy silence. Nothing moved. But woods and hedgerows everywhere. Who knew what lurked inside, awaiting nightfall?

Stranger-craft. . . .

'Here it begins,' said Athelgar, at the edge of the road. An overgrown track led off through trees and brambles. He looked back once, then waded in. Fran gave Lyn's car a yearning glance, as if it were a lifeboat anchored there. Then turned away and plunged into the green depths of the past.

Athelgar was waiting, just a few yards further in. He'd clambered up a slope beside the path. She picked her way towards him, unsnagging thorns and briars from her jacket. The earth rose in a lumpy mound, its aspect oddly sinister. She stopped.

'This is the Giant's Grave,' he said, still glancing round. 'This was their land, in olden days . . .' He was back in his element now, she saw: once more the lord of all that he surveyed.

It looked more like a giant's skull – split open and scooped out. Trees rose up like antlers from the earth. A barrow-mound, she realized, as he scrambled down again. Even to him, this was an ancient place. So might the sword be hidden underneath? Birds were singing in the wood, but she felt a nervous chill.

But Athelgar turned his back on the misshapen lump. 'Now we follow the *herepath*, southward.'

She hesitated. 'Harrow path?'

'*Herepath*,' he said again. 'A road for muster-men.'

It clicked after a moment. 'What . . . like Hereford?'

'It is the same,' he said.

The forgotten track took them down to a disused railway: the cutting lined with trees and filled with bushes. They paused there in the filtered sunlight, listening to the birds.

'Toller's Dene,' he said. 'But this was not a road before.'

She imagined his reaction if the trains had still been running. Steam trains, in all likelihood – puffing and clanking through this shady place. Dragons on the prowl again. But all was silent now.

Athelgar looked pensively towards her.

'The giants have returned, is this not so? I have seen their buildings everywhere; their roads across the land. The greenwoods and the grass are eaten up.'

She took his point; it pricked her with a twinge of his nostalgia. Yet here the modern world had fallen silent once again with nature slowly claiming back its own.

They climbed up from the cutting, and continued on their way. The *harrow-path* had turned into a lane. Looking ahead, she saw a hill fort in the distance, rugged and dark against the afternoon sky.

Ancient places everywhere; and Athelgar was bringing them to life. Instinctively she groped into her pocket, and felt the brittle hardness of the cross. Still clutching it, she turned and checked behind them – but nothing was following. She saw a tractor cross a field; a grazing flock of sheep. Apart from that, the countryside was empty.

'Athelgar . . .' she murmured. 'Could you tell me what you know about the Ashmen?'

Not that she wanted to hear it; she didn't want to *think* about last night. But mystery just made them seem more frightening.

He paused and glanced behind him, following her gaze. 'What would you learn of them?'

'What are they?'

'They are slaughter-wolves,' he said.

She thought about the ragged cloaks that some of them had worn. Grey as wolf-skin, right enough. And greyish powder coating them like dust.

'Why do you call them Ashmen, though?' she asked, already guessing. Imagining the fallout of great fires.

But the answer wasn't what she had expected. 'The wordsmiths had that name for them,' he said. '*Ash-army* – for the grey wood of their ships.'

She blinked at him. 'What ships?'

'The dragon ships. They are a witching-force.'

'But we're *miles* from the sea.'

'The wolves will venture deep inland. You saw how they were salted? Enough to keep their carrion-meat from rotting.' He shook his head. 'Who can say how long have they been sailing? How far along the ship-roads of the north?'

Thinking back, she realized he was right. She'd seen those grey deposits on the cooker back at home – when a pan of salted water had been boiling.

The black, grimacing face came back to haunt her. The

skin like toughened leather, tight enough to bare the teeth. A corpse preserved by centuries at sea. And *still* the thing was able to pursue them.

She felt a queasy vertigo. The empty lane did little to abate it.

'I heard this tale before,' he went on grimly. 'The watchers on the longships – condemned to roam the wave-wastes to the ending of the world. But something has called them back.'

She swallowed. 'To find you?'

He nodded. 'Why else would they have lurked round Rathulf's hoard? I think they mean to slay us all; perhaps to claim their Land-Waster again. So we *must* find my sword – and raise the Raven.'

On they walked, up rising ground; still following the landmarks he remembered. An ancient copse; a quarry pit; a hedgerow on the skyline. The *herepath* led on towards the hill fort. Summer had reclaimed its slopes; she glimpsed the pink of orchids, and the dancing blue and white of butterflies. But the sunlight failed to warm her now. The country seemed less peaceful.

Naked thorn trees grovelled on the ramparts of the fort.

Close by, they reached a pond or flooded pit. Trees had gathered round it, and the surface lay in shadow. 'The mere,' he muttered, 'just as I recall it.' He looked about to carry on, towards the fort itself; but something made him stop, then venture closer to the pool.

'What?' Fran asked him, panting up. She'd lagged behind, legs aching. Her lost sleep weighed more heavily with every step she took.

'Some thing is here . . .' he said.

She joined him as he knelt beside the water. The pool looked cold and very still, the muddy bottom fading into darkness. Athelgar dipped his fingers in, and flexed them.

'Of course,' he murmured. '*Sea-born* one; where else would you have left it?'

Puzzled, Fran craned forward, staring down into the glacial

murk. Despite the sun above the trees, a chill was rising off it.

'Is it there?' she whispered.

'I think it is.'

'Won't it have gone rusty?'

He shook his head. 'The craft that keeps it secret will preserve it.'

She couldn't tell how deep the water was. 'So . . . how do we get it out?'

Athelgar sat back on his heels. 'This is Stranger-craft, as I have said. I know such charms as this. The only time the thing can be reclaimed is when the full moon shines upon the hiding place.'

Fran felt protest rising up inside her. She tasted panic in it – as bitter as a half-digested meal. 'You mean we've got to come back here after *dark*?'

'Yes,' he said. 'The sword is in the moon. Someone must go down into the world beneath the water. Reach out in faith, and they shall find the sword.'

There was a pause. She looked at him. He turned to look at her.

'I know not how to swim,' he added drily.

CHAPTER IV

Moonblade

I

'Touring are you, love?' the landlord asked.

Fran nodded glumly, fiddling with her purse; watching while he pulled a pint of Real Ale. Would Athelgar find the taste at all familiar? She had the briefest picture of him spitting it back out.

The glass was filling slowly; the brew looked chocolate-dark. She glanced down at her G&T. By God, she needed that.

'We get a fair few people passing through,' the landlord said. 'But Meon's still a quiet place, and that's the beauty of it.' His eyes flicked up; surveyed her. 'We're lucky there's not many want to spoil things.'

Instinctively she reached up, smoothed her hair. She knew it was a mess, in need of brushing. Lyn's jacket still had burrs attached; and did she smell as clammy as she felt? And as for Athelgar . . .

He was sitting at a table in the corner: his back against the whitewashed wall, so he could watch the room. His coat was still wrapped round him in that old, peculiar way. He was pushing beer mats round like playing cards.

The landlord set the glass down on the bar-towel. 'East Meon church is worth a look, as well . . .'

Fran smiled politely, and handed him a fiver. He made a point of checking it before turning to the till.

'We were looking round the old estate,' she told him, slightly miffed. 'The Anglo-Saxon one. The boundary's still there.'

He glanced at her, more affably. 'Following the charter,

you mean? Yes, we've had a few here doing that. Brings the countryside to life, doesn't it?'

Fran hesitated. 'That pond, up near the hill fort. We . . . thought it looked quite dangerous like that.'

'Aye, well,' he said, and shrugged. 'I think it's claimed two children in the twenty years I've lived here. There was talk of it being filled in, but nothing happened.' He paused again. 'I've heard it said their ghosts still go to play there after dark.'

His smile seemed warm enough, but she could read the mischief in it; his shrewd eyes watched to see how she'd react. Something for these passers-through to take away with them. She pinched a faint smile of her own, and picked the glasses up.

Thanks a bunch, mate. Keep the bloody change.

Walking back over, she sat across from Athelgar, and set his pint before him. His eyes came up; she thought he looked bemused. Perhaps because his saint had bought the drinks.

She looked at him morosely, and took a sulky sip. The pool had been cold enough in daylight. Tonight, that murky water would be freezing. And pitch-black. She felt her skin begin to shrink – anticipating the icy thrill of contact.

And would those children's ghosts come out to play? Up across the meadow in the stillness of the dusk, to frolic round the bottomless black pool? Her shrinking skin drew tighter, and she made a conscious effort to relax. It had to be a rural myth: one the locals put about to titillate outsiders. And to scare them.

But even if the ghosts were just a whisper, the accidents had probably been real. The drownings in those chilly depths. Her mind's eye glimpsed the splashing and the panic. Her inner ear just caught the distant screams . . .

'Talk about yourself,' she blurted quickly. 'Anything. Your past, your life . . . I *need* to know you better.'

He was silent for a moment: gazing down into his glass. She watched the bubbles rising to the surface.

'I had a farm,' he said at length. 'At Freefolc. And some land. Rich pasture that rolled out to meet the sky. I was young, and thought that I had everything I needed. But when I left my hearth, and travelled eastward, I saw the road had only just begun . . .'

His voice had grown more wistful; his pale eyes, when he raised them, were less focused.

'I followed the wanderer's way,' he said. 'No land, save the six feet we receive at burial. No roof, save a skyful of stars. My sword was pledged to Edmund; then to Alfred. I have answered to the summons of a dozen lords since then. Yet at the last, I sometimes think we only serve the Raven.' He hesitated: stared at her. His eyes were haunted now. 'Do *you* believe this, Frances?'

'*No*,' she said instinctively, and leaned across the table, taking his free hand in both her own. 'Talk to me about it. Tell it out . . .' Saying that, she felt like a confessor. It seemed that he had plenty to confess.

He took a breath – and began to shed his burden.

'The Raven has the power to lengthen life. It can take us from the world, so we are not aged by her turning. It is how we fought with Alfred, and with Athelstan, his grandson. I knew them both. I see their faces now.'

'How do people summon you?' she asked.

'There is a map to show the way,' he said. 'A chart of stars. After our victory at Waste-Down, we brought the Raven south, to the holy hill of Glastingabury. You surely know of it.'

She stared at him. Then: '*Glastonbury*, we call it now,' she said.

'Certain of the brethren knew of wisecraft in those days. They wove this chart around the signs which men see in the sky, and bound the Raven's power within the ring. And we, the Raven's Breed, could sleep around it – to wake when we were summoned by the king.

'Athelstan convoked us next, when fifty years had passed. We rode with his great army – leading the attack, as he subdued the west and north. For he was like a thunderbolt – like *lightning* to his foes.'

Fran just nodded, spellbound now. Despite herself, she tasted his excitement. It sounded like some medieval blitzkrieg.

'At Brunanburh, I saved his life – for which he granted me this place, as I have said. He said that I had earned my rest; that I could cease my wanderings. I tried . . . but it was all to no avail. We have our curse of duty. It lies upon us still.'

She couldn't help but glance towards the landlord. He'd given this unshaven man a supercilious look, not knowing – never dreaming – who he was.

The owner has returned, and at an hour you do not expect.

'The sky-chart binds us,' Athelgar went on. 'Each warrior has his sign. Mine is the Bear that never rests. The Latin name for this is *Ursa Major*.' He pronounced the last word *meior*, like a German.

'Rathulf had the dragon-sign, called *Draco*. Dragons in the elder tales are guardians of gold. Thus he left the purse amid those dragon bones near Waste-Down – as a sign to any Raven who might follow.'

'And the cross?'

'Rathulf is of the north. As you are.'

'I don't know him,' she admitted, after a moment's awkward pause.

The look he gave her then was veiled. 'No,' he said. 'I fear that you do not.'

'Not a lot of people know of *Athelstan* today,' she prompted carefully. At any rate, *she* didn't.

Athelgar just nodded, looking grimly unsurprised. 'He was the first king of all England,' he said softly. 'His laws drew us together – made us one. English and Danes, and Strangers too.'

What did *Strangers* mean to him? She thought of faceless figures, casting spells. Like fallen angels, come to teach men magic.

'The Strangers . . . who were they?'

He gestured. 'The foreign peoples, dwelling on the edges of our land. *Wealas* was the word we had for them.'

It took her several seconds to work out that he meant *Wales*.

Then: *Stranger-craft*, she thought again. Welsh magic, in these oh-so-English fields.

'So it was one of them, who hid your sword?'

He glanced down at his untouched drink, then raised his eyes again.

'My brothers said she brought the Raven down. But is the blame not mine,' he sneered, 'for fighting in the service of a *witch*?'

She, thought Fran, and stared at him. 'And she's still out here somewhere?'

Athelgar sat back and shook his head. When he spoke, his voice had lost its sarcasm. Now it was as solemn as his face.

'God forbid it, Frances,' he said quietly. 'Every dawn, I pray that she is dead.'

2

The moon was high above the trees and shining on the pool, like a polished silver coin on cold black glass. The dusky air was motionless around them. Not a breath of wind to stir the water.

Oh God, I can't do this, she thought, and felt her stomach churn.

Athelgar crouched at the water's edge. His head was up, like a night creature sniffing the breeze. Fran sidled up behind him, her arms wrapped round herself. Even through the jacket, she could feel the growing chill.

From up here they could see for miles; but everywhere was black, submerged in ink. Isolated lights picked out the farms. Villages were glow-worm nests along the unlit road. West Meon lay ahead of them, perhaps a mile away.

She took a breath, and swallowed. 'Athelgar . . . ?'

He turned his head.

'How do you know the Ashmen haven't got here?'

'I trust we are ahead of them,' he said.

Well that's not good enough, she thought, with nervous pique; but knew it was the best they had to go on.

Twisting round, she peered up at the moon. It hung there like a blank white face, a watcher in the night. The cold she felt was radiating from it. She looked back to its floating ghost: an eerie light amid the clump of shadows. A sudden shudder racked her then – so violent that it felt more like a spasm.

She glanced across the field, towards the car. She'd driven up as close as she could, and left it in the lane that was a *herepath* before. After her dip, she'd grab her towel, then run back there and turn the heater on . . .

The hush was like a wall, it hemmed them in. Just the sound of a car on a distant road. The solitary barking of a dog.

She realized she could put this off no longer. Every instinct still rebelled against it: taking off her clothes out here, beneath that gloating moon. The sense of sheer exposure was unnerving; the prospect of the water was enough to make her cringe. Like bedtime, long ago, before her bedroom had a heater – she'd hesitate for ages before undoing the first button . . .

But now, as then, she couldn't wait for ever.

Retreating half a dozen steps, she started to undress. His raised head kept on turning, but he didn't look around. Sitting down to pull her boots off, she could see his silhouette against the dead light of the sky. Only the brightest stars showed up. They seemed to swarm around his head, like spectral fireflies.

Once she'd started stripping, it was much too cold to stop. Jacket, blouse and jeans came off; the moonlit air soaked in. She kept her bra and knickers on – silently thankful that she had a change of undies. She'd worn these for two days and nights already: the bloody things were *ready* for a wash . . .

Her bare skin pimpled painfully: it felt as if her fine hairs were being plucked out by the roots. Shivering, she picked the jacket up again, and draped it round her shoulders. Then tiptoed forward through the grass to join him.

Athelgar glanced round at her, and back towards the water. Too quickly – as if he didn't want to see. In deference to her modesty, no doubt. She sensed he was abashed to see his blessed saint like this.

Perhaps he was afraid he'd be aroused.

The moon's reflection rose above the lip of the pool. Its cold light seemed to draw her, with a mesmerizing power. She came to the edge, and almost teetered there. Her fingers found her cross of nails, and tugged it on its chain.

'How will I find it?' she whispered.

'Reach out with faith,' he said again – still staring at the water. 'For you it shall be easy.'

No, it won't, her frantic mind protested. She wasn't a saint, she was a frightened little girl. In too deep already. In over her head . . . The ring of black water seemed to gape like a grave: a watery grave that went down and down forever. She thought of the burial mound they'd passed. Did that conceal a void as deep as this one?

And if a *faithless* person ventured down? Someone masquerading as a saint? At best, she'd splash around and fail to find it; dash his hopes, and leave him with his doubts. At worst . . . there might be power beneath the water. A net to catch her, woven by a witch.

An owl hooted softly in the branches overhead. Curiously enough, it spurred her on. She had to get this over with, right now.

Please come with me, God, she thought, and pulled the jacket off. With a last scared glance around them, she braced herself and slowly waded in.

The water was so cold, it *bit*: a gin-trap springing up to seize her legs. She felt her muscles clench, her nipples harden. Gritting her teeth, she waded deeper, right towards the floating, phantom moon. Ripples spread around her. The brightest stars, reflected, swam and shimmered – like phosphorescent sparks beneath the surface.

Carefully she hunkered down; the water rose, engulfed her breasts, and lapped against her shoulders. She groped around, but found only muddiness and weeds.

Deeper. She would have to go in deeper.

Her body was becoming numb. Her breaths were tight and shaky. She straightened up, looked back again. Athelgar was just a black shape at the water's edge, the moon above him silvering his hair. He watched, but made no gesture, gave no sound.

Fran let herself subside into the cold bath of the water, and swam towards the centre of the pool; then took a gulp of air, and dived. Through the glowing scum of moonlight, and into the black and liquid night beneath.

At once she felt a suffocating dread. The water was like pitch. There was just the faintest, ghostly tinge above her head; the rest was blindness. Heart bulging with each stifled beat, she swam down and touched bottom. The pool *was* deep – much deeper than it should be; she tried in vain to tell herself she'd simply lost her bearings. Again she felt around her. Something gluey; furry growth; a single, greasy stone. The dull ache in her chest grew hot and painful. It forced her to the surface, and she gasped to fill her lungs. Treading water – the bottom out of reach – she ploughed the wet hair from her eyes, and looked towards the bank.

Athelgar's dark outline hadn't moved.

She shook her head at him; then took another breath, and dived again. Fear reclaimed her, colder than the cold. She knew it would be panic before long. Her blind hands touched the bottom, and groped forward. Reach out in faith. Reach out . . .

And then she sensed the presence, just ahead. A mass of some sort: denser than the water. Floating in the dark before her face. She stared at it with sightless eyes. Her hypothermic skin had lost its feeling, but a frosty prickling swarmed across it now.

The glacial darkness didn't stir; but something there was waiting, very close. Fran felt her body drifting, but was too afraid to move. Her heart was booming, giving her away: each beat was like a depth-charge going off. Her senses couldn't find a solid object; but her spooked imagination saw a drowned and bloated ghost. Still waiting for a rescuer – or playmate.

Frances . . .

She started, as if galvanized; her own name in her mind, as if she'd heard it. For a moment she was sure it must be Athelgar who'd called; but no, she'd never hear him through the water. Down here she was deaf to the world. The speaker was a voice inside her head. Not Athelgar this time, but someone else.

Fraaaaances . . .

She couldn't help but glance around again. If the voice was in her mind, why was it full of water? Muffled and misshapen like the voice a ghost might make.

Panicked now, she struck towards the surface – and realized that her ankles had been caught. Something slimy wrapped around her calves. *Weeds*, she thought, and wriggled to get free. The sticky, cold, entangling fronds drew tighter.

Oh, God, she thought. *Oh, no.* Still believing she'd pull free, of course – but the pressure in her chest was growing now. Her heart seemed loud enough to cause concussion.

Beware the Raven, Frances.

Still she kicked and squirmed in vain; not knowing who was calling her, nor caring. Her mind was white and bubbling now. Those children who had drowned up here: they'd felt this terror too. Some part of her had given up already, and was urging submission and acceptance. If she let herself go, it would be over in a moment and then she could relax . . . and drift . . . and float . . .

She threshed again; the weeds were getting looser. Doubling forward, she scratched and scrabbled at them. *Please, God, please*, she thought – and felt them peeling back. A final, frantic kick, and she was free. Up she rose, broke surface, and whooped to fill her aching lungs.

She heard the voice one final time, before she reached the realm of air and moonlight. It faded in the depths, like the call of a drowning man.

Beware . . .

Hair in her eyes, she flailed around; fairly sobbing for breath. It took her several moments to reorient herself again. The black pool was a gulf beneath her – and something might rise up from it to snatch her trailing legs. Still sobbing, though her lungs were full, she swam towards the bank. Her feet touched muddy bottom, and she floundered to the edge.

Athelgar was there to meet her: a murky shape against the scattered stars. She glimpsed him reaching out and felt another jolt of panic. The echo of that drowned voice was still with her.

She forced it from her mind, and let him haul her in to safety. Clear of the black water, she collapsed onto all fours – shivering with reaction and the cold. He crouched before her, clutched her shoulders; raised her face to his. The moonlight showed a grey mask of concern.

'Frances . . .'

It *must* have been his voice she'd heard. Her memory was muddied and confused.

She panted: 'Couldn't find it . . . sorry . . .'

'Look,' he said.

Unwillingly, she turned her head – and felt her heart contract.

Something had floated to the surface in her wake. It drifted there, a dozen yards away, like a splinter in the moon's eye. The reflection had been marred now – that perfect glowing disc was smeared and bleary. She frowned, and tried to focus. The floating thing was long and strangely lumpy, like a bone distorted by calcinous growths. A slender object, wrapped in sodden cloth. The shroud was bulging with trapped air. She thought of tumours, swelling fit to burst.

Athelgar squeezed her shoulders. 'You have freed the thing,' he said. Somehow, her threshings had disturbed its resting place. It had risen back to light like a long-lost corpse.

He let her go, and waded out to fetch it. Fran watched, still sitting on the grass; hugging herself tight. She waited till he'd snared the thing, and was sloshing back towards her; then scrambled over to where she'd left her towel. Glancing down, she realized that her briefs had turned transparent; but modesty was the least of her concerns. She began to rub her soaking hair; her numb and icy skin. Friction brought sensation back: the first faint tinge of warmth. Her teeth still clicked and chattered in her head.

Athelgar was down on one knee, examining the bundle. He didn't unwrap it – but its long, malignant gauntness made it clear what it was. Fran stared at it – then back towards the pool. The deep was calm and soundless once again. The moon-glow on the water was dimmer now, diffuse; she realized that the night was clouding over. Back here on dry land, it was easier to believe that her own scared mind had conjured up that ghost, that eerie voice.

For sure, her head was silent now.

'This is Sky-Edge,' said Athelgar softly – as a man might introduce his oldest friend. Fran almost started shivering again. Wrapping the towel round her shoulders, she gathered up her clothes and headed quickly for the car. She gave the moon a final glance, but its disc was lost in cloud. Just whorls of luminescence now, spread out across the churned murk of the sky. As if the moon were soluble: dissolving like an aspirin in the dark.

CHAPTER V
Harrow Path

I

She woke with a start, to find Athelgar's hand on her sleeve. He was leaning in, his calm face very close.

'Frances – will you come?'

She blinked at him, her eyes as bleary as her mind. Her mouth was dry and sour. She'd slept perhaps two hours, all told – curled up here on the back seat of the car. Now it was light outside, the birds were singing. Early, maybe six a.m., but she knew she wouldn't get to sleep again.

She straightened stiffly up – her muscles cramped, complaining. Still dressed, apart from her boots, and the jacket, which had served her as a blanket. 'What is it?' she mumbled.

'Someone comes,' he said.

Which shocked her awake like a bucket of cold water. She felt her heart speed up. 'What, the Ashmen . . . ?'

He shook his head. She saw suppressed excitement in his face.

'I think it is a Raven. One of my brothers, here.'

Abruptly she recalled the voice she'd heard beneath the pool. The voice she *thought* she'd heard. *Beware the Raven, Frances.* For one unnerving moment, she felt her situation with full force: stranded in the sticks out here, with two survivors from another time. Men inured to sorcery and slaughter. Men who'd judge her worth with ancient minds. The future in that moment seemed precarious as a tightrope.

Huddled on the seat last night, she'd listened to him working with the sword. The intermittent sounds had made her shrink into the corner, a refuge from the darkness of the field. She'd heard that grisly bundle being carefully unwrapped; the faint but steady squeaking of a rag along the blade. And then, as night crawled slowly by, the *swoosh* of polished metal cleaving air. Eyes closed, she'd sensed him ranging round – slashing at phantoms; parrying their thrusts. Once more becoming used to weight and balance. No wonder that the sleep she'd had was shallow and unsettled . . .

Athelgar was waiting. Fran rubbed her pasty face, and tried to stretch. The sword was slung across his back; the hilt poked up behind one shrouded shoulder. The grip, she saw, was leather-bound. A milky pearl was set into the pommel. She couldn't help but think of a blind, boiled eyeball.

The ancient sword repelled her – its aura medieval and macabre. It might have been a relic from a grave.

She pulled her boots on; shrugged into her jacket. Athelgar had turned away and was staring past the fence into the field. Doing up her laces, she wondered how much longer they'd be wandering around. She had to get back to Oxford by this evening. Poor Lyn would be rending her garments soon. *My car. What has she done with my car?* The image brought a thin smile to her mouth.

Sanity; the real world. But so, of course, was this.

Athelgar looked back at her; then climbed over the fence – a sombre silhouette against the rosy-golden sky. Fran bit her lip; then clambered out and followed.

The ground beyond the fence was bleached and stony: a harrowed field that slipped into the valley. Morning mist still clung to it, but couldn't blur its bleakness. Chalky rubble stretched away, and crumbled underfoot. Glancing down, she realized that the ruts were full of weeds.

Athelgar had squatted, and was fingering the soil. But not to kiss it this time. He gave her a pensive sidelong look; then turned his face towards the middle distance.

'Your farmers plough too deep these days. The land has lost her skin.'

She scrunched across to join him as he straightened up again. The hush was deep, uncanny – the more so with the sky now light. The world still hadn't woken. His head turned as he scanned the empty field.

'There,' he said – so suddenly he made her heart leap up.

Someone *was* there, on the far side of the field. A black shape in the fading mist. She watched him move along the smudgy hedgeline: slow, and almost furtive. As eerie as a scarecrow who'd been wandering all night, now slipping back to hang upon its stake.

Then she saw the horse that walked behind him: its grey becoming solid through the haze. She swore, and started back.

Athelgar reached quickly out, and caught her sleeve; then remembered himself, and let her go again. 'Be not afraid,' he said, 'this is a friend.'

She envied him his confidence, especially this far off; but stood her ground and waited at his side. Her heart was beating fast again, she felt a little breathless. Her fingers tweaked and fiddled with her cross.

The man in black was ambling uphill. As he drew closer, she saw he was wearing a knee-length coat; dusty and unbuttoned, though *his* arms were in the sleeves. His hair was flaxen-yellow, hanging almost to his shoulders. The grey horse trailed behind him; he held its long rein loosely at his side.

A dozen yards away, he stopped; braced his boots, and stared towards them both. For a moment there was stillness; just the faintest breezy stirring of his coat-tails and his hair. Then Athelgar went forward. His steps became strides. The two men came together and embraced.

Fran stood and watched them, hesitant; then ventured forward too. Athelgar turned, his hand still on the other's shoulder. His face was almost fierce with satisfaction.

'This is *Leofric*, of Mercia. My sworn brother.'

'*Lay*-off-rich,' Fran said carefully. She nodded once in greeting, like an earnest little girl.

The other nodded back. His rugged face, clean-shaven, looked quite amiable to her. The bright blue eyes and slightly crooked smile seemed to give it a mischievous cast.

Athelgar's fingers tightened on his shoulder.

'This is blessed Frances, brother. *Lady* of the Ravens.'

Leofric's face grew serious then. He crossed himself – his frank gaze almost wary. Fran felt the distance grow between them, and shifted with discomfort. She'd never thought that sainthood would have made her such an outcast.

But Athelgar was speaking now in his old, harsh language. Leofric answered him in kind; Fran felt even more left out. She stood there with her hands deep in her pockets; shoulders hunched against the daybreak chill. Waiting on the margins there, she looked Leofric over. His scuffed and grimy frock-coat had a solemn, gothic look; she wondered where he'd scavenged that from. The cords he wore were dark as well; but his shirt was white, his waistcoat charcoal-grey. When he raised one hand to wipe his mouth, she saw the silver rings on every finger.

He had a sword with him as well. It dangled from the saddle-horn behind him.

Athelgar glanced round the field, and grimly spoke again. She heard the *witching* word he'd used before.

(Witching-raven. Witching-force.)

Nervously, she looked around as well. The countryside was still asleep; the field and fence deserted.

'Where came you by that horse?' said Athelgar beside her. She turned back with a start. He'd clearly just remembered that she didn't speak Old English.

Leofric smiled thinly. The rough burr of his accent couldn't hide his wry amusement. 'There are horses to be had across the land.'

Which doubtless meant he'd stolen it from somewhere. The saddle looked well-oiled and new; a contrast to the scabbard hanging from it.

'What news of the Ravens?' Athelgar asked.

'Edgar I have seen. He waits near Wintanchestre; the giants dwell there now. He has met with Athelwulf and Eldred.'

'The Land-Waster?'

'He holds it still.'

Athelgar nodded. 'We have found the purse, which Rathulf left.'

A flicker crossed the other's face. It looked like faint unease. 'Rathulf walks alone?' He dropped his gaze, and scuffed the soil; then raised his eyes again. 'I do not like this, brother.'

Athelgar's gaze remained steady. 'He will answer to our muster soon enough. The time is ripe to gather in our swords – and swiftly.'

Leofric glanced towards his horse. Ironic humour stirred his mouth again. 'Behold, there are two swords here.'

'It is enough,' said Athelgar, with a faint smile of his own; as though some private joke had passed between them.

Fran forced a cough, and cleared her throat. Like a guest about to leave a social gathering. The notion, in this barren field, was very nearly funny.

'Athelgar,' she said. 'I have to go back.'

He nodded. 'I know that you have many cares. But heed us when our war begins again.'

She hesitated, feeling almost guilty. 'I . . . can't always come, when you pray.'

His grave face seemed to fall at that: a shadow of dismay she barely glimpsed. But then acceptance masked it. 'Be there in spirit, then.'

'Find me,' she said quickly. 'When you need me . . . say you'll come and fetch me. Please? I . . . want to go along this road. I want to see this through.'

He stared at her with narrowed eyes: debating with himself. Then dug into his neck-pouch, and produced a small gold object. It glittered like a nugget in his palm. He held it out to her; she frowned, and took it – then drew a breath, delighted by its beauty.

He'd given her a *jewel*: no other word would do for it. Oval as a teardrop; no larger than a walnut. A piece of amber, set in gold, with words engraved around it.

'This is my lodestone,' Athelgar said. 'I cannot leave this world again without it. I would trust it to no other.'

Her impulse was to give it back: she didn't trust herself. Didn't *want* to be responsible for this. But the jewel was enchanting; his confidence more so. In that moment's indecision, as she gazed at the gilded piece, he took her hand and closed her fingers round it.

'Keep it with you always,' he said softly. 'We will find you. Every one of us has his own lodestone. One shall call another, as the Raven gathers strength.'

Fran just nodded dumbly, lost for words.

'It will be soon,' he said, and held her hand a moment longer before letting go.

She watched the two men start across the field, the horse's slow hoofs muffled by the soil. Athelgar looked back, and raised his palm; she lifted hers in turn. Then, as the pale mist smeared them into shadows, she turned away, and trudged towards the fence.

It seemed as if she'd never felt so hungry or so tired.

CHAPTER VI

Home from the Hill

I

Somehow, subtly, Fran had changed; Lyn couldn't quite say how. Outwardly, of course, she was the same: her wide eyes just as soulful, her face still peaky-pale. But the waifish air was now completely gone. She'd come back full of confidence the first time. Now, in some elusive way, she seemed more grown-up too.

Lyn welcomed the development, delighted for her friend. A part of her would miss the chance to spoil and cosset Frannie; she rather liked this role she'd come to play. It made *her* feel more grown-up, too: maternal and protective. Perhaps a bit superior, in the nicest kind of way.

Of course, there was Simon to think of now; a very different slant on growing up. He'd soon be taking much more of her time. So was it a relief, as well, that Fran was back on form?

Perhaps: although it wasn't quite that simple. Fran would be off home before much longer – but they hadn't come together just to drift apart again. They belonged to one another: always would, to some degree. If Fran withdrew from time to time, so Simon must as well.

She nodded to herself, and settled back; the sudsy water closed over her breasts. The bathroom, full of steam, was hushed around her: the snoozy calm of Sunday afternoon. She felt that she could lie here until teatime.

Things were going nicely, all in all. Her thesis was in good shape now. She thought back to her tutorial on Friday; the discussion had been helpful and encouraging. Dr Walker clearly felt that she was on the right lines. He'd offered her a sherry, and she'd sipped it in the honey-coloured sunlight from the window, surrounded by his laden shelves of books.

'It's coming really well, Lyn. Fascinating stuff. It's high time someone made a study like this.'

She'd smiled modestly, and glowed inside. Walker was in his thirties, with bouffant hair and boyish good looks that went oddly with his shrewd historian's mind. Sat there in his shirtsleeves, with his back against the sunlight, he came across as really rather dishy. Pity she was spoken for, in fact . . .

He was leafing through the pages of the chapter once again. 'Did you find out any more about that local Norfolk saint? Athelgar, wasn't it?'

'No, not much, but I think that section will have to go. Obviously he fell from grace before the Reformation . . . but most likely he was legendary to start with.'

'No independent evidence?'

'Not that I could find. Nothing really links him to that testament I found. I did find a reference to an Athelgar who was indicted as a sorceror or something: betrayed the church, killed for money, and generally blotted his copybook. According to that, he was seduced by a witch, who stole away his sword, and drowned herself.'

He glanced up, eyebrows lifting. 'I see what you mean . . .'

'All sounds very mythic, doesn't it? And the witch is named as *Morcant*. I checked that out, and it's the Old Welsh form of *Morgan*. So it's probably just some local legend that got mixed in with the Arthurian strand . . .'

'Perhaps you *should* make mention of it, then. An example of how a cult can be distorted. It's nuggets of detail like this, you see, that bring the whole subject to life.'

She'd said she would consider it; but really she'd be glad to put this *Athelgar* behind her. Exciting though it was to trace a reference to its roots, it wasn't one she wanted in this study. The half-remembered saint was just a phantasm; what clues she'd found all pointed to a dark and ruthless man. Nothing to do with Daddy's chart, of course; but the name had lingered with her for that reason. It was time to close the book on it at last. Return him to the murk from which he'd come.

Her pinned-up hair had started wisping loose. She pouted, blew a strand back up her forehead; then closed her eyes, and settled down again.

2

Somehow, subtly, Lyn had changed; Fran couldn't quite say how. Demure and rather delicate, as always – but now she seemed more self-assured, less shy. *It must be love*, Fran mused, and felt a distant sense of loss. She thought of how relieved she'd been, the day of their reunion – finding Lyn the same as when they'd parted. More mature, of course, and proud of it; but coy beneath her elegance and grace. Her voice still modest, gentle; soft as breath. Now – within the space of days – her friend had reached full bloom: a new assurance glowing in her smile. From girl to grown young woman – here and now. Their shared first year at Oxford seemed to fade into the past.

Fran thought of happy highways that she'd never walk again.

At first, it had upset her: she'd come back from another world, to find her own had changed. But nothing, after all, could stay the same. Not now.

She paused again to listen; heard soft splashings from the bathroom. Then returned her attention to the book. Another of Lyn's reference works: an Old English dictionary and thesaurus. Somewhere she could look up the words that throbbed and ached like symptoms in her head.

Æschere was the eerie term that Athelgar had used (*Asherra*, as she'd heard it). The army from the ash-ships. The image might refer to wood, but the other meaning loomed up just as strongly. Like funeral barges, drifting back to land: returning with their grey, cremated crews.

She thought of that charred soldier once again.

Wælwulf was a synonym. Slaughter-wolf, that meant. And *wicing* was a raider from the sea. She read the word again, and felt her comprehension click. Athelgar still used it – and he still pronounced it *witching*.

Wicinga werod. Viking-force.

The slaughter-wolves had come so very close. She felt a chill go creeping up her arms. They'd left them well behind – but had the grisly creatures followed? Where were they lurking now, this very minute? Sheltering from daylight; but come dark . . .

She told herself that Athelgar would stop them. He and his men. Which battle had he said that he had fought in? Still clammy-skinned, she went back to the Chronicle, and searched until she recognized the word.

Brunanburh.

937. The entry was extravagant, a poem: heroic language glossing over savagery and squalor. But there, amid the carnage of the aftermath, she came upon the *shadow-feathered one*. The Raven.

It seemed her skin grew colder as she read around the word. Ostensibly the poet was just glorying in the slaughter: evoking all the carrion beasts that had come to claim the field. But her knowing what she did gave the lines a more sinister ring. As if the wolf and raven here were only meant as symbols: an esoteric reference to some darker, secret truth.

Beware the Raven, Frances . . . The words still echoed dimly in her mind.

Pensive, she replaced the books, and went back to her room. Even though she knew that Lyn was still there in the bathroom, she closed the door behind her before digging in her jeans for the jewel.

With the sunlight on the far side of the house, the thing was dull and cool – its presence oddly heavy in her palm. The lettering was cryptic. Words like *DVBHE* meant nothing. So did the stone have magic powers? Some latent energy, like radiation?

We will find you, Athelgar had promised. Suddenly – against all expectations – she wasn't quite convinced that was such a good idea.

Uneasy now, still fingering the stone, she curled up on the futon, and studied it with solemn, anxious eyes.

3

The phone began to ring as she was laying the table for supper. Lyn went through – rather hurriedly – to answer it; disguised her disappointment with a cheerful hello. Then called for Fran to take it. It was Craig.

'Hi, Frannie,' he said drily: his warm voice undiminished by four thousand miles between them. 'How're things?'

Fran thought of what had happened since she'd seen him last. The memories went through her like a deep, cold current. She shrugged and said: 'I'm fine.'

'Hope I'm not interrupting anything; never did get the hang of these time zones. What time is it with you?'

'Nearly seven.'

'It's still mid-morning here. Blazing hot, sun's high, you can see the hills so clear . . .' She sensed him leaning comfortably back; she heard his lazy smile. 'Just had breakfast, cereal with fresh strawberries, iced milk then bacon, eggs, hash browns . . .'

Fran grinned into the phone. 'Oh, don't, you'll make me jealous.'

'Well, you'll just have to come over, girl, and try it for yourself.' A pause, and then he said: 'I'm paying.'

Fran hesitated, her smile uncertain. 'I'd love to come over there someday, but . . .'

'I'd pay your air fare, Fran, no problem. Why not come and meet my folks? Mom reckons she half-knows you already, I've talked so much about you. Her great-granddaddy came from Durham . . .'

'Craig . . .'

'It's just what you need, girl. Can't you just see yourself? Sitting in a rocker on the porch, with a view of the mountains, and as much iced Coke as you can drink. I'll take you down to the river, and up the forest trail. Shorts and T-shirt every day. No more grey skies. No need for you to worry anymore.'

Fran stood and listened to her heartbeat. The picture was enchanting. All that, and him as well. She could dump her dismal baggage at the roadside; fly west, into the promised land. Escape from the past, and all its living ghosts. She'd be safe in a wholly modern world while they fought their ancient war.

'Sound good?' Craig persisted.

'Shush,' she said, as brightly as she could. 'I'm thinking about it . . .'

'What's there to think about?'

She felt a bitter smile twist her mouth. *Oh, Craig. If only you knew.*

Athelgar would call her – and she would be a *continent* away. Too far away to hear him, or to help.

'I'd like to come. I'd *love* to, Craig.' She swallowed. 'But not yet.'

'So when?' he pressed her calmly.

She could almost feel the sunny day that underpinned his voice. It felt like she was clinging to a life-line, four thousand miles long; a life-line that could pull her from the darkness into light.

Long is the road. And hard . . .

'Okay, listen . . . I'm coming back over towards the end of the year. When I fly back, I'd like you to come with me.'

'You make me sound like a GI bride,' she said.

Silence from the far end of the line.

Jesus, she thought, and felt a thrill go through her.

'No need to make your mind up now,' he blurted quickly. 'I'll talk to you nearer the time. You can come over for a month, or . . . even longer. Think about it.' She was dimly aware of his discomfort: that he'd given himself away too soon – or thought he had. Or had he?

Jesus.

'Talk to you soon, Frannie. I think about you every day, you know that.'

'Take care, Craig,' she murmured. The past few day's events had dimmed his face into the background – yet she knew how she had felt on Larkhill Range, when the Ashmen were upon them and it seemed she'd never see his smile again.

'I love you,' he said quietly.

'Love you back,' she breathed.

He put his phone down gently. The click became an empty transatlantic hum. Fran kept on listening for a moment; then sighed and hung up too.

4

'How is he?' Lyn asked brightly over supper.

Fran smiled, but didn't raise her eyes. 'Oh, he's fine. Wants me to go over there and see him.'

'Oh, Fran, why don't you? A holiday in America would do you so much good.'

Fran chased a twist of pasta round her plate; then let it go, and sat back in her chair.

'Lyn . . . I think he wants me to stay.'

Lyn paused, her fork half-lifted. 'What . . . you mean . . . ?'

'Yeah.'

'*Frannie.*' Lyn beamed at her, eyes shining; then adopted a more quizzical look. 'So, what do you think?'

Fran gave her head a helpless shake. 'I don't know, that's the problem. I love him, Lyn, I really do. But to pull up my roots and *go*.'

'He hasn't actually asked you, then?'

'Not yet. But I think he might be getting round to it.'

'Any time you want to talk it through,' Lyn offered softly.

'Thanks. Not now, though. I think I'll chew it over for a bit.'

A pause while they finished eating. Lyn put her fork down, dabbed her mouth; then looked at her again.

'You know my birthday's coming up.'

Fran nodded, smiling. She'd already bought Lyn's present, a camisole from M&S. It was hidden at the bottom of her suitcase.

'I'm spending it with Mum and Dad, and I wondered, would you maybe like to come?'

'What, you're having a party, or . . . ?'

'No, just a quiet dinner at home. But I'd like you to be there.'

Fran felt a glow of pleasure, deep inside. A faint anxiety crept through it. 'Won't they mind – your parents?'

'No, they won't, I've asked them. They'd like to see you again.'

'What about Simon?'

'Simon,' Lyn said quietly. 'Yes.' She smiled and dropped her gaze, resting her chin on her clasped white hands. Her rings and wristlet glittered in the light.

'I think he's the real thing, Frannie. I think I've found the man I'm going to spend my life with. Mum and Dad both like him . . . but he's going to take their little girl away. This might be the last time we can really be together.'

'Oh, Lyn,' Fran said. 'I'm really glad for you.' After a pause, she had to ask. 'You're sure you want me there, then?'

'Of course I am. You're like a sister to me, you know that.'

Fran thought of Martin then: Lyn's brother. Would he be there as well? Or just in spirit? A spectre at the feast, an empty chair . . .

She felt a sudden, urgent need to blot that image out. Summoning a grin, she shook her head.

'Well, here we are. The blokes are getting serious. And did we *dream* of this in '88?'

The melancholy swamped her without warning: nostalgia

for those first ebullient months. The shining city; dream-spires on the skyline. The rich and folky fellowship of protest – and then the aching solitude of love. She'd had it all ahead of her, like sunlight on her face. Then black and chilling night had come from nowhere.

Her eyes began to sting, then overflow. She tried to stem the flood, but it was hopeless. Lyn reached across and took her hands; then squeezed them. 'Oh, Frannie, shhh. We're all right now. We're going to be all right.'

Fran nodded; freed one hand, and wiped her cheeks. The world had turned, that much was true. The dawn had touched her face. But sombre clouds were massed on the horizon.

Whatever storm they promised, she would face it. She would have to. Her past life seemed as golden as a sunset; but night had come, and now another morning – cold and clear.

Lyn leaned forward, filled her glass, and topped her own up too. She lifted it; the pale wine caught the light.

'High hopes, Frannie.'

'Yeah,' said Fran. She raised her glass, her smile still full of tears. 'High hopes.'

CHAPTER VII

Our Summer

I

Fran turned around, and looked towards the house. It basked there in benign repose, its stonework painted yellow by the afternoon light. The attic windows peered back, inquisitive but friendly. Birds flitted to and fro around the chimney.

'Oh Lyn, it's beautiful,' she said. 'You must have loved it, growing up here . . .'

'Yes,' Lyn murmured wistfully. 'We did.'

They were down in the small orchard, at the bottom of the garden; the ground descending gently from the back door of the house. Beyond the hedge, it rose again as farmland. A warm breeze wove and whispered through the branches.

Blossom drifted downward, like snow under sun.

Fran was still enchanted: she had only just arrived. Lyn had met her off the train, and driven them back out here. 'Happy birthday,' Fran had said, and kissed her beaming cheek. And yet, despite her pleasure, Lyn had seemed distracted somehow.

Carrying her bags upstairs, and leaving them beside the turned-down bed, she'd had an inkling why. The attic room, next door to Lyn's, was Martin's; the walls still bore his posters and his pin-ups. The paperbacks and textbooks must be his.

'Sorry about his females,' Lyn had said. 'Perhaps I should have taken them down, but . . . they're part of the room, you know? And this is all we've got.'

Fran smiled faintly. 'I don't mind.' It tickled her, the sniffy way that Lyn described the pin-ups. She glanced at one, a doe-eyed *Playboy* centrefold. 'Wish I had a figure like that, though . . .'

Lyn tittered; tossed her head. 'Come on and see the garden.'

'Yeah,' Fran said, but didn't move. 'You're sure it's all right, me sleeping here?'

''Course it is. Really, Fran. Mum says it's only right to share it. It's not a shrine, after all. He isn't dead, or anything . . .'

Fran heard the heartbeat's pause in that; the unborn thought Lyn couldn't countenance.

. . . as far as we know.

But that was doubtless why she wasn't quite her sunny self. Fran breathed the scent of apples now, and wondered if she ought to steer well clear. But maybe Lyn would rather get it all out of her system.

'You're not expecting Martin back for this?' she asked.

Lyn shook her head. 'No reason why he'd come.' She hesitated. 'Usually, you know, he sends a card . . . but this time there's been nothing. Perhaps he's just forgotten, though, he's done *that* before . . .'

'I wouldn't be surprised,' said Fran. 'You wait, you'll get one in the post next week. They make a whole range of grovelly late birthday cards for people like him . . .' She put an arm round Lyn, and hugged her. 'I know you still worry about him; but this is *your* day, Lynnie. He wouldn't want to spoil it.'

Lyn sniffed, and wiped her glistening cheek. Fran held her closer, whispering encouragement. Lyn sniffed again and looked at her, a little sheepish now.

'Sorry.'

'Shh, don't worry. You've let me cry on *your* shoulder often enough.' She gently picked some petals from the dark silk of Lyn's hair. 'Feeling better?'

Lyn nodded. Her smile looked fresher now: washed clean by tears.

Fran squeezed her. 'So what presents did you get, then? Can I see?'

They started back towards the house. 'It's not just Martin,

though,' Lyn said – then lapsed back into silence. Fran tried to coax her further; but Lyn just shrugged, refusing to be drawn. Up in her room, she showed off her new jacket with genuine pleasure. But even then Fran sensed a shadow, deep beneath the surface. Something had upset her, that was clear. Something dark was preying on Lyn's mind.

2

The day had started off so well. Mummy had brought a wake-up cup of tea, and wished her happy birthday. She'd come down in her dressing gown for breakfast; opening her cards on the stripped-pine kitchen table, while her parents looked on fondly and the smell of toasting bread came from the Aga. 'Feel any older?' Daddy asked, as she pulled apart her parcels. She'd glanced up grinning. 'Not a day.' Younger, even: she might have been a little girl again.

It was nice to be spoiled; but Lyn found time to be glad for Mummy too. She looked relaxed today, in better spirits, where yesterday she'd been distressed and fretful. Lyn had found her sitting in the lounge, trying to read, but on the verge of tears.

'Oh, Mummy . . .' She'd knelt down before the chair. 'It's Martin, isn't it?'

Her mother's smile was strained. 'Have you heard from him at all?'

'Yes,' she'd lied, with earnest eyes. 'I had a card from him. No message.'

'I still keep seeing him, Lyn. Boys who look just like him from the back. There was someone this morning, down by the road, and for a moment I just thought . . .'

'Oh shhh,' Lyn had said, and hugged her. 'He'll be all right, you'll see.' Mother and daughter, roles reversed. *That* was when she'd started feeling older.

So Mummy's face was brighter now – but Lyn had started brooding in her place. Left to herself, she'd flopped around and felt her mood deflating. No cause that she could really put a name to; but when the knock came at the door that afternoon, she'd swung around and felt her heartbeat skip.

It was almost time to meet Fran's train. She was in the kitchen, reaching for her car-keys. Then that muffled rapping on the wood. The back door: no one called round there. She hesitated – then came back through the kitchen, walking slowly to the door. The house was silent, both her parents out. Perhaps he'd lain in wait till they were gone. Reaching up to turn the latch, a part of her was *sure* that it was Martin.

But no. A dark-haired gypsy girl was waiting on the doorstep.

Lyn guessed her background straightaway. The hair was short, a boyish cut, and very much in need of a good wash. The face that turned to greet her looked as grubby as a toddler's. Her clothes were jumble-scruffy, mixed and matched. *Mis*matched, when it came to style – but clearly they'd been chosen for their colour. Skirt and jersey, leggings, boots; the threadbare shawl she'd wrapped around herself. All were dirty black or sombre grey.

'Hello,' Lyn said, with cold politeness. 'Can I help you?'

The girl said nothing; just gazed at her with strangely searching eyes. They were beautiful eyes, Lyn couldn't help but see that; unsullied by the grime on cheeks and forehead. Hazel, flecked with faint, elusive gold. Perhaps, with all that dirt washed off, her face would be attractive; but now it had a hungry, haunted look. Her body was petite and slim. She didn't look much older than sixteen.

Her scrutiny unsettled Lyn, who tried to hide discomfort with impatience. 'We don't want any lucky heather, thank you. We've nothing to sell. And round here's our back garden: private property, all right . . . ?'

'Have you food that I can eat?' the girl asked slowly. Her accent sounded Welsh, but very strong – as if she wasn't used to speaking English.

Lyn shook her head. 'I'm sorry.'

The girl absorbed that, silent; then suddenly reached out and gripped her hand. Lyn flinched, and gave a startled little gasp. The girl's cold fingers squeezed, and then relaxed.

'God does not want you yet,' she murmured softly.

Lyn just stood there, open-mouthed. Those gilded eyes kept staring for a long, unnerving moment; and then the girl let go and walked away.

Lyn was left there, shaken, caught off balance: as if this was a cliff-edge, and a rescuer had snatched away her hand. Perspiration bubbled up, and cooled her crawling skin. She steadied herself, one hand against the door-frame; then nervously leaned forward, peering out. The girl was out in the lane already, walking briskly down towards the fields. Her dark head disappeared behind the hedgerow.

Stillness then. Piping birds, and reassuring sunshine. Lyn moistened her lips, drew back and shut the door. Weird woman. Strange encounter. No wonder people grumbled about gypsies. She twitched and wriggled briefly, as if the strangeness was something she could physically shake off.

Fran. It was time to go and meet her. She focused on the prospect with relief. But first things first – she went straight to the sink, and gave her hands a scrub: still soaping when the film of grime was gone. Still frowning.

It felt as if someone had just walked over her grave.

3

Fran's favourite summer dress was folded neatly in her case. She hadn't worn the thing for years. But back at home last week, she'd tentatively tried it on – and glowed to see it fit and flatter her. Mum had given it a wash, and now it smelled as fresh as when she'd bought it.

She changed in the daunting company of Lisa Matthews (Miss April) and Brittany York (Miss October). Brittany – *you poor girl* – had eyes that matched her own. Deep and greenish:

vulnerable somehow. No sulky pout or silly smile; her face was almost anxious.

Fran searched it for a moment; then let her gaze drift off around the room. Clearly Martin's interests extended to other kinds of heavenly bodies. There were pictures of the night sky on every wall. Stars that hung together in a spectral bluish haze; a galaxy on edge, like a whirlpool of light. All photographed with a luminous beauty that stood out in the gathering dusk. A large celestial wallchart was pinned up behind the bed.

Athelgar had spoken of a star-map. Intrigued, Fran wandered over, had a look. Unfamiliar as she was with constellations, the patterns were a labyrinth to her; but then she found the old, familiar Plough. *Ursa Major*. His summoning sign.

Some of the stars were named as well. The one shown as the brightest was called *Dubhe*. Frowning, she picked up her bag from the bedside table, and brought the jewel out.

DVBHE. Of course. Pleased with herself, she put the lodestone down beside the bag.

It had given her the jitters at first: made her feel shadowed and spied-on, like someone with an electronic tag. Athelgar's words – *it will be soon* – had an apocalyptic ring. But gradually, these past two weeks, she'd let herself relax. Sometimes she'd forget she even had it.

She moved to the window, gazing out across the farmland to the east. The view was perfect, the hazy fields still tinged with fading light. The English countryside.

She knew that they were out there: as ancient as the landscape. Crossing it like shadows under clouds. Knew – but couldn't feel them. The fields were warm as honey, and at peace. Athelgar was far away; the Ashmen even further. Tonight, at least, she could pretend she'd never known them.

A last glance in the mirror – her face looked so relieved – and then she went to tap on Lyn's door, and they went downstairs together.

* * *

Lyn's parents made a fuss of her, and put her at her ease. Reclining on the sofa, with a glass of crisp white wine, she felt preoccupations slip away. Her life was firmly back in her control. At one point, as she chatted with Lyn's father, she even considered showing him the jewel. He was a history professor, after all. She could casually produce it, say she'd bought it in a heritage shop or somewhere (a reproduction, naturally) – then sit back and see what *he* made of it.

The impulse came and went again. Her secret, not for sharing. Instead she said how much she liked the music.

'Vaughan Williams, yes,' Lyn's father said, obviously approving of her taste. 'It seems to go so well with the countryside round here.' Pause. 'Are you familiar with his other pieces . . . ?'

God, she thought. 'Not really, no . . .' She wasn't really into classics. But Mum had had a record of *The Wasps* by this composer: it made her picture hazy days, and sunny summer country.

She smiled, and took another sip of wine.

Lyn had clearly ditched her worries, too. She looked sexy and smart in her little black dress, but pleasure made her radiant as well. The dinner was delicious, with no apparent limits on the wine. By the time they'd reached the coffee stage, she and Fran were both like giggly schoolgirls.

'Thanks ever so much for coming,' Lyn said, as they finally went upstairs. Her voice was husky, more subdued – the inevitable descent from giddy heights. Fran sensed the tang of tears before bedtime.

'My pleasure, Lyn. It really was.' She turned around and hugged her on the landing. Lyn sniffled, and clung on for quite a while.

The sounds of late night washing-up came drifting from the kitchen.

At length they kissed and went their separate ways. Fran slipped into Martin's room, her head now numb and singing from the wine. She went to the window, opened it, and breathed the warm night air. It smelled of hay and honeysuckle. The fields were hushed, the sky deep velvet blue. A few bright stars hung over the horizon.

She felt too flushed to bother with her nightie. Undressing, she turned off the light – *'Night, Brittany* – and was just climbing into bed when the star-chart on the wall caught her attention. The panoramic stars were glowing faintly.

Luminous paint, she realized, as the pulse of shock subsided. The thing was designed to glow in the dark. A sickly phosphorescence, green and ghostly. The effect was quite unsettling. She hoped that it would fade before too long.

Shifting to get comfortable, she glanced towards the bedside table – and went completely still.

The jewel was glowing softly too: a tiny orange smudge-fire in the gloom.

Fran gazed at it for a moment; then shook her head, rolled over, turned her back. Too much wine, she muzzily supposed. Even if the thing *had* a magical charge, she'd never seen it glimmering before. Time to get some sleep. She couldn't cope with things like this right now.

After a minute, she pulled the bedclothes up over her head.

She dreamed, of course; the dream was very simple. She was standing there in Martin's room, the jewel in her hand. Although it was now daylight, the amber stone still glowed against her palm: but dimly, like a dying coal.

She saw no more than that. But her sleeping mind was spinning, throwing out all kinds of echoes and impressions. The stone was like a radiation warning; there must have been an accident, a leak. As if the house were built on a sarcophagus of waste. But the sense was worse than that, more catastrophic. Some energy had been released. A nuclear explosion, somewhere close. The radioactive residue still throbbing in these walls.

Something happened here.

It was curious how the next impression came. She knew next to nothing about astronomy or physics. But this was Martin's room, his private space – and in the dream she felt his presence strongly. It seemed that *his* ideas came together in her head. How else could she have thought of *pulsars*; the crackling radio sources left by long-exploded stars?

Something. Happened. Here.

She woke without warning. The sky was light, the day already warm. Rolling over, she fumbled for her watch: squinting through her fringe with sleepy eyes. Just gone six. She peered towards the jewel, lying just out of reach. The stone was dull, inert again – a piece of coloured glass. Perhaps she'd dreamed that, too. Slumping back, she snuggled up, and drifted off again within a minute.

4

Lyn put the coffee on, and yawned, and stretched. Pomfret, her parents' ginger tom, came prowling round to rub against her legs. 'Shoo,' she chided sleepily. 'Greedy guts, you've had your milk already.'

Pomfret padded lightly back across the kitchen. He was old for a cat, but still in haughtily good health. The name was Daddy's choice, of course: the Norman form of Pontefract. For ages, with her schoolgirl French, she'd thought it was some ancient word for *chips*.

The Rectory was quiet. Daddy was at work today, and Mummy was round at coffee with some friends. And Frannie was still dead to the world. Lyn paused to listen, making sure; then smiled, and got the muesli from the cupboard. She'd lain-in long enough herself – a teensy bit hung over from last night.

Pomfret was curled up in the corner, washing himself and watching her. Ignoring him, she walked back to the table. The floor felt cool and dusty underfoot, like a bottle freshly brought up from the cellar. The coffee percolator glugged and snorted. The phone rang as she poured herself a cup.

She sighed and went to answer it. Hooked back her hair. 'Hello?'

The line was live, but silent in her ear. A moment passed. She frowned.

'Hello . . . ?'

'Lyn,' a dry voice said.

She knew him with that single word: the way he said her name.

'*Martin*.'

'How are you?' Martin's voice asked.

She hugged herself with pleasure; it threatened to erupt in stinging tears. 'I'm fine,' she managed. 'What about you? How're *you*?'

'I'm making out,' he said, his tone still flat. 'Happy birthday, Lyn. Sorry I'm one day late.'

She swallowed, shook her head. 'Where are you?'

'Phone box down the road.'

Another thrill went through her, even bigger. 'Oh, *Martin*. Mum and Dad will be so *pleased* . . .'

'Lyn, they *mustn't know*. You mustn't tell them.' His voice was tight and urgent.

She stood there, blinking: disbelief now vying with dismay. 'What?'

'I know they're out,' her brother said. 'I waited. I've been watching.'

'Martin, listen . . .'

'Sorry, Lyn. I won't be stopping. Just let me in, okay? There's something in Dad's study that I have to come and get.'

IV

HUNTERS

Now the wasted brands do glow,
While the screech-owl, screeching loud,
Puts the wretch that lies in woe
In remembrance of a shroud

SHAKESPEARE

Dear Frannie

Sorry for the loooong delay: I'm terrible at letters. Guess I can only hope a peace-loving babe like you is able to forgive me!! Seriously, you're better than a guy like me deserves. There's not a day goes by when I'm not grateful.

It was great to speak with you, the other week. You sounded good, I hope you're feeling better. And I meant what I said: I want you to come over. Now you've got things straightened out, I reckon you could use a change of scenery. Put the past behind you, and get pampered for a while.

Has Lyn heard from her brother yet? He'll be fine, I'm sure he will. Tell her that I'm thinking of her too.

After all the fuss you made, I hope you ain't gone swanning off together, so that this letter gets left lying in your mailbox for days!

Love,

Craig

CHAPTER I

The Watchman's Mark

I

Two nights ago, he'd dreamed of Claire again.

The house was well behind him now, but still loomed in the background: as ghastly in its promise as some accident he'd glimpsed. Instinct said to shun it, walk away; but his mind kept breaking loose and darting back – ghoulishly resolved to see the worst. Through the open doorway, down the hall into their room – and there she'd been, still curled up on the bed. After a while, she got up and came through to see what was keeping him. His mind's eye couldn't tear itself away; her happiness had withered as he watched. The smile, bemused, had faded to a frown. Puzzlement . . . perplexity. And then – as minutes became *hours* – the nauseating onset of despair . . .

He'd sat up quickly, shuddering awake. The dampness and cold which had underpinned the dream came fully into focus. Across the yard, the scar-cheeked man had turned his face to look. *Aldhelm*, Martin thought, still shaky. Aldhelm was the name he called himself.

The pre-dawn light was thin and grey – as if polluted by the factory ruins, the stony yard around them. The others were wrapped up in their blankets: shrouded and still, like corpses at the scene of a crime. But Aldhelm was crouched, brooding, by the remnants of the fire. His head stayed cocked: his cold gaze didn't waver. The blue eyes glittered faintly in the shadow of his brows.

A sour taste filled Martin's mouth; he tried to spit it out. Despite his borrowed blanket and his clothes, the chill of night still ached in every joint. He stretched and winced; looked round. Rubble and grey stone on every side. Reluctantly his gaze came back to Aldhelm.

The other regarded him a moment longer. 'Again your sleep is troubled,' he observed.

Martin shrugged, glanced down into the ashes. The bleak-faced man still made him very nervous. And yet his solid presence was a reassurance too. His weathered features hinted at *experience*; his gaze, though unforgiving, was direct. Martin drew strange comfort from that grizzled, grim resolve.

'Someone I left behind,' he said at length.

'A woman?'

Martin nodded. Still feeling stiff and shabby, like a bundle of bones.

'And children also?'

'She's going to have a baby, yeah . . .'

At last the other dropped his stare. He picked a shrivelled stick up, and poked the lifeless ashes.

'*I* had a wife,' he said. 'And two fine sons. I left them, and our farm besides, to ride out with the Raven. The land had need of us . . .' He paused, still writing slowly in the ashes. 'I know not what became of them. Their bones have been in mother-earth one thousand years and more.' Now his eyes came up again. 'We all have left our lives behind for this.'

Martin just absorbed that, and drew his blanket tighter round his shoulders. After a minute he glanced around again. There were four more of these revenants . . . but only three were huddled in the dust. He couldn't see their faces, but he knew at once which one was up and walking. The leader, with his bony face and restless, chilly eyes.

Aldhelm made him nervous, yes. But Rathulf made him terribly afraid.

2

The first time, in that blackened room, the man's impassive stare had been enough. The candles stained his lean, gaunt cheeks, and tinged his tawny stubble: giving his face a hungry, wolfish look. But then he'd smiled, with face and eyes – and really sent a chill through Martin's blood.

'I am *Rathulf*,' he had said. 'Rathulf is my name.' There was something almost mocking in the tone: a glint of humour, like he'd heard before. But the deep-set eyes still watched him like a wolf's.

Martin had no words for this. He simply stood and stared.

The smiling apparition stepped away, back into the dark. A match rasped, and another flame was kindled. For a moment Martin thought that it was floating in mid-air; then realized it was resting on a table. The man called Rathulf craned across, and touched the match to other waiting wicks. A golden constellation was created from the gloom – but the candles were all night-lights, and the glow they cast was dim and insubstantial. Just enough for Martin to see that the table had a chair on either side. The farther one – an armchair – must have come up from the living room. With its cover burned off, it made him think of a skinned and shapeless carcasse. The nearer chair was wobbly-looking wood. The table itself didn't look too sound. The last sticks of furniture to be salvaged from this gutted house . . .

Rathulf lowered himself into the easy chair; its shrivelled cushion seemed to *squish* beneath him. The aura of the night-lights wreathed his face. The smile still lingered there.

'Be seated, Summoner,' he invited; the calm voice like a rivulet of ice down Martin's spine. 'We needs must speak.'

Martin approached with nauseous reluctance. Slowly, very carefully, he sat down. Rathulf watched him pensively, one elbow on the arm of his chair; his fingers curled, and snagging at his smile. The dim light gleamed on gold and silver rings.

Martin realized that the black thing he was wearing was a half-unbuttoned cassock. Soiled white linen showed through the open collar: slung and sagging round his neck, like folds of torn table-cloth. It gave him the look of a vagabond priest.

Rathulf dipped his head towards the table. Martin forced his own gaze down, and saw a random scattering of gems. The glowing night-lights picked them out, winking and elusive in the cinders on the tabletop. Diamonds, prised from jewellery and rings; a few small pearls as well. He stared at them, nonplussed – and saw a pattern: a stark, familiar skeleton of stars.

The constellation *Draco* was suddenly before him, with every star in place and in proportion. Coiled in the ash like a sleeping snake.

Rathulf's finger pointed to the largest of the pearls, midway along the dragon's twisted length.

'What star is this?' his dry voice asked.

Martin swallowed, raised his eyes. An icy tension gripped him: as if this were a test he mustn't fail. 'Thuban,' he croaked. '*Alpha Draconis*.' He added that instinctively: the star-watcher's tag. The first star of the Dragon.

Rathulf offered up his fist: displayed his tarnished rings. A pearl was set in one of them as well.

'Thuban,' he agreed. 'My lodestone, and my watch-word.'

Martin stared back, petrified; and realized that the other men were coming in behind him. Shadows that shuffled and creaked. He sensed them spreading round him in the murk.

'Why are we called?' asked Rathulf softly.

Martin gave a gaspy breath. It showed up like a wraith across the table.

The scar-faced man came into view, to stand at Rathulf's elbow. Rathulf, leaning back, inclined his head. 'He thinks that we are hedge-riders, perhaps.' Again the hint of mockery; but scar-face didn't share it – his brows still full of thunder: glowering down.

Rathulf's thin smile faded. He stared impassively at Martin. 'I ask, why are we called?' he said.

'Christ, I didn't mean to,' Martin blurted – and broke off. Rathulf's hand had twitched upon the table: once, like a spider in spasm.

The cold eyes probed him; didn't blink. 'Who *dares* to summon us without a cause?'

Martin's heartbeat thundered in his chest. His mind fled back across the years, to a story Dad had told them – about knights who slept beneath a hill, and their *anger* at being woken in vain. As ever, Lyn had been entranced, while he'd just shrugged it off. But now he'd found the story's heart: its core of childlike dread.

At last, and much too late.

The spider-hand sprang up, and struck his face: a backhand blow that locked his head in numbness. But the force in it was sluggish and dismissive – almost like a *show* of punishment. Martin reeled, and heavy hands came down upon his shoulders. They closed like claws. He almost yelled in panic.

Rathulf leaned forward, eyes intense.

'*Athelgar*. Where is he?'

Martin simply gaped at him – then groaned through gritted teeth as one of the men behind him yanked his head back; the lever was a fistful of his hair. He squirmed and flailed in vain: they pulled him further. The old chair teetered; something cracked. Then his head was forced forward and down, towards the table and its pointed, glowing flames.

'Where is he?' Rathulf asked again.

Held there with his face above the night-lights, so close he felt their warmth against his cheeks, Martin saw the second pattern open out before him. The clustered yellow flames marked out another constellation, entwined with the jewels of the Dragon.

'You see his sign?' came Rathulf's voice.

Martin could. The ancient Plough. The Great Bear. *Ursa Major*.

'Yes . . .'

'Where *is* he?'

Martin couldn't shake his head. He panted: 'I don't know.'

Rathulf rose abruptly. 'Bring him.'

They hauled him upright – and let him drop. The floorboards squealed beneath him: a loud, unearthly protest in the gloom. The shabby figures closed in, eclipsing the light. Martin kicked, and tried to fight them off, but it was hopeless: they engulfed him. Half a dozen bony hands competed for a purchase. Ravaged faces crowded in. A boot in the belly drove the air from his lungs. They pulled him up, and bounced him off the wall; wrenched him round, and dragged him to the door. Rathulf was already on the landing.

They hauled him down the passage, with their leader like a phantom up ahead. He reached the doorway at the end, went through, and melted into deeper dark. Martin's captors took him to the threshold, and quickly shoved him over. It felt like being pitched into a bottomless gulf; but even as his stomach started plunging, the gritty unseen floorboards broke his fall. Shaken, he sensed the others drawing back: retreating down the passage. And then the door slammed shut.

The deathly hush that followed was as frightening as the darkness – and as cold. But slowly the room took murky shape; and Martin thought he saw the stars spread out around him.

The panorama stopped his gasps for breath. Crouched on his knees, he stared at it. The whole of the northern sky had been mapped out, in intricate detail. The stars were marked by bright and shiny things, strewn out across the ash in all directions – a *colony* of jackdaws might have stolen these away. Prised-out jewels; pearls and coins. A tarnished silver thimble at the Pole. There were bones set out among them, too: the skulls of mice and birds.

He realized he was looking at an image of the star-chart. A fresh chill rippled through him. The light, though faint, was stronger than it should be. No candles here, no window – but a bluish phosphorescence tinged the walls.

Rathulf too was crouching, on the far side of the ring. The folds of white cloth round his neck were now drawn up, to muffle his head like a cowl. His face was like a doorway into darkness.

'The All-Father is here,' his disembodied voice said softly: almost awed. 'Can you not feel him?'

Martin cowered, feeling *something*. The cold had teeth, and was chewing like a dog.

Rathulf gestured then: taking in the map with a sweep of his arm.

'Athelgar we seek; and Branwen also. Discover them for us.'

What? thought Martin. *Who?* He spread his hands, despairingly. 'I don't know where they *are*.'

'You hold the Chart,' the cleft of shadow said.

He gave his head an urgent shake. '*No* . . . the one I used was just a copy, in a book.'

'It matters not. The words remain the same. Winter runes, for winter signs. For grief-riders.' The shrouded head came forward. 'We must possess the Chart again. And you will take us to it.'

3

Day had come at last, of course, but light and warmth had brought no reassurance. The nightmare lingered on, like an incurable disease: its symptoms fear and nausea. Racked with both, he'd stumbled in their wake these past three days, a sick refugee on the road. He felt his belly griping now, as he stared across the early-morning fields.

'This is your hearth?' asked Aldhelm from behind him.

Martin glanced back. 'Yeah . . . It used to be.'

Only the scar-cheeked man had come this far. The others were still waiting in the copse two miles away; the damp gloom where they'd snatched a few hours' sleep. More accustomed to his fear now, like a cancer patient getting used to pain, he'd tried to insist on going this alone. The thought of these crow-men getting close to his home was the worst one of all.

Rathulf had relented in the end – sending Aldhelm to keep watch on him. But Aldhelm was looking past him now, towards the Rectory. It drowsed there on the skyline, well-placed to catch the rising summer sun. A peach-coloured glow suffused the stonework.

The eldest Raven nodded to himself.

'It is hard for a man to come back home, when he has left that place for ever. See that it does not snare you. The past is the land of the dead.' He looked at Martin then: his face as bleak as ever, but the light of something distant in his eyes. 'I am old, I will not rise again. This will be my last war.'

Martin didn't ask which war this was: he didn't want to know. Instead he said: 'I'll be straight back,' and turned towards the lane.

Aldhelm's hand took firm hold of his collar. The eyes, when Martin twisted round, were cold as ice again.

'Do not betray us. Rathulf has power, and spirit-sight; be mindful you are marked. Thus it was we found you. Thus we will find you again.'

Martin nodded, stifling a shudder. Rathulf himself had been more forceful in his warning: searching Martin's face with fierce eyes.

You will die slowly. Slowly you will die. May Christ have mercy. I will not.

'I told you: I'll be back,' he said; shrugged free, and started off towards the house.

CHAPTER II

Odysseus

I

Lyn opened the door at once, and stood there staring, clinging to the latch as if afraid to let it go. She was wrapped up in her dressing-gown, her face still wan with sleep. Her eyes were like dark holes.

Martin found a worn-out smile from somewhere. 'Going to let me in?' he asked.

She nodded dumbly, backed away. He came through quickly, shutting the back door firmly on the fields. Aldhelm would be watching in the distance. He mustn't know that Lyn was here. He mustn't see that Martin had so beautiful a sister.

Lyn, I've missed you. Missed you lots.

She looked so vulnerable, standing there: her pretty face all doe-eyes and dismay. The beaming smile he'd pictured was completely wiped away. Back in the phone box, he'd heard her startled joy, and cringed; then reached for it along the line, and strangled it at birth. A hurtful, hateful thing to do – but what choice did he have?

He bit his lip. She'd never been so lovely. Her hair unbrushed, no make-up . . . but *now* he could perceive why men adored her.

The missing years changed Lyn's perspective too. Here he was, her little brother – draped in an old blanket like a beggar. His grim face thinly bearded, and his eyes full of foreboding. She realized with a jolt that he'd grown up. It felt as if he'd overtaken *her*.

'Martin . . .'

He shook his head – 'I'm *sorry*' – and walked past her to the stairs. His clothes looked slept-in, filthy. He smelled of earth and sweat.

His muddy boots went creaking up the staircase. '*Shhh*,' she hissed, and scurried after him. 'There's somebody upstairs.'

He swung round quickly. 'Who?'

Lyn hesitated, halfway up: his tone had made her flinch. 'One of my friends . . . she's still asleep. We put her in your room,' she added dolefully.

He glanced up at the ceiling. Lyn came towards him, cautious now. 'You're not sleeping *rough*?' she whispered. The question fairly begged the answer no.

'Don't ask.'

'Martin . . . Mummy saw you. The other day. I'm sure she did.'

He glanced at her. 'Did she? Well I'm glad she bothered looking past the dirt.'

Lyn's mouth became an O, as if he'd slapped her. Turning his back, he headed for the study. After a moment he heard her following, and rounded on her.

'*Don't* come in here.' He saw her eyes grow big with tears, and let his own concern show on his face. '*Please*, Lyn. Believe me, you don't want to know.'

She hung back, hugging herself. He watched her for a moment; then went on into the study. The room was filled with golden morning light, cleansed of all its memories and shadows. But now he'd brought them back, inside himself.

He glanced round at the doorway; he hadn't felt able to shut himself in. Lyn wasn't in sight, but he could sense her mournful presence just outside. Swallowing, he turned towards the shelves, tracking his gaze along the rows of books. And there it was, exactly where he'd left it. Perhaps Dad hadn't opened it, these past two years.

Drawing a breath, he took it down. An itchiness developed in his hands. Dust, perhaps – or gruesome paranoia. As if the thing was riddled with the eggs of flies and spiders, laid that dreadful night, and developing since then. Ready to come swarming out when he lifted up the cover . . .

He gritted his teeth, and opened the book. Nothing emerged but mustiness and dust. The pages rustled faintly as he turned them. He came to the folded chart at last, and felt his thudding heart begin to pound. Going over to the desk – its top now bathed in sterilizing sunlight – he spread the book and opened out the chart.

Instinct raised his hackles as the circle was revealed; but in truth, it seemed less frightening than the version in the Burnt House. The star-chart was inert now. The spell had been unravelled. Wherever they'd been summoned from was empty.

They, he thought. These ghosts. These demons.

He tried to focus on its tiny details. There was *Draco*, with Thuban marked, and *fluðar* written in beside its name. He frowned at the word – and cracked it with a flash of inspiration. Read backwards, that was *raðulf*. Too close to be coincidence, he thought.

The sudden flash was followed by a rumble of deep dread. He moistened his lips, kept looking.

The word *aeðelgar* was written by the Plough. Again, too close to Athelgar – one of the people that Rathulf had spoken of. Athelgar and . . . Branwen, he had said. And there was *branpen*, by the Little Bear.

He looked for *aldhelm*: found him by Orion. Hunter and warrior of winter nights.

His concentration switched to the outer circle: its signs and crosses and cryptic scribblings. The runes and words that Rathulf had demanded. If he handed this thing over, what would happen? What powers did it contain?

His mind balked at the prospect. Better to take the thing and run, get far away . . .

Rathulf has power.

He shivered in the sunlight, hearing the words as clearly as they'd come from Aldhelm's lips. He stared out of the window. The stars were still out there, behind that high blue sky. Still turning slowly: staring down. It would be the same with Rathulf, and his gaze.

Slowly you will die.

A breath of movement made him turn his head. Lyn was in the doorway, one shoulder rubbing up against the frame. A single tear had dribbled down her cheek.

What else had Aldhelm said? The land of the dead was full of snares. And Lyn was one, the sweetest of them all. He knew he had to fend her off – but suddenly he lacked the strength to do so. She stood and watched with pleading eyes. He tried to hold *his* yearning in; then gave in to temptation, and let go.

'How are you?' he asked haltingly.

She sniffed, and said. 'I'm fine.'

'Really, though.'

'Getting on. I've nearly got my thesis finished. I've got a boyfriend called Simon, and I think I'm going to marry him . . . Now what about *you*?'

He folded the map, and closed the book, and crossed the room towards her.

'Lyn, this book of Dad's . . . you have to get rid of it.'

'What?'

'Get *rid* of it. Listen . . . when I've gone, just wait for an hour, then take it out the back and burn it.'

She was gaping at him. '*Martin* . . .'

'It's *evil*, Lyn. Believe me, it is.'

'But . . . magic's not real.'

He almost sneered. 'You reckon?'

'Martin, it's one of his *books*. You can't just come barging in here and tell me to *burn* it.' Her patience was clearly fraying now. At last she was beginning to get angry.

'Lyn, for God's sake, trust me, okay?'

'So why don't *you* get rid of it?' she snapped. Fran upstairs was quite forgotten now.

'I couldn't get away with it,' he said – so simply that he made her pause. 'Believe me, Lyn. I couldn't get *away*.'

He thrust the book into her hands; she took it without thinking. They stared at one another for a moment. The scar on his cheek was slightly red; Lyn thought of how she'd thrown that brick, remembered every detail. Her tearful eyes made Martin think of toffee on the melt.

'Love you, Lyn,' he croaked, and blundered past her – striding quickly for the stairs. She dumped the book, and hurried in pursuit.

'Martin, *please* . . .' She tugged at his sleeve. 'Please wait for Mum and Dad.'

He shrugged her off. 'I can't.'

'Oh, God . . . Are you in trouble?'

'Yes,' he said. 'I am. And you can't help me.'

They reached the kitchen, heading for the door. He swung around and stopped her in her tracks.

'I'll get in touch, all right? I'll be okay. But now you've got to let me go.'

She wavered, undecided, her hair in her eyes. Martin glanced away. Their father's shabby gardening coat was hanging on its peg. He shrugged out of his blanket, walked across and put it on. The dark, rough wool was oddly comforting. A pair of sturdy leather gloves were crammed into the pockets.

'Martin . . .' whispered Lyn.

He gave her an unsmiling look, and opened the back door. The wrench was agonizing – but his parting shot was pitilessly terse.

'Remember – burn that book,' he said. 'It has to be *destroyed*.'

And with that he was gone. Lyn darted to the door, but didn't follow. All she could do was sob for breath, and watch him walk away.

Fran had lain-in for a while, feeling woozy. Another gorgeous summer day; she'd kicked the duvet off and curled up nude. It made her think of being in bed with Craig. She smiled contentedly against the pillow.

Half-asleep, she thought that she'd heard voices from downstairs: a muffled argument that came and went. But when at last she dressed and ventured down, there was only Lyn at the kitchen table, with a stone-cold cup of coffee: crying as if her heart was going to break.

2

'It isn't there,' said Martin. Light-headed now. Not caring very much.

'Do not lie to *me*,' said Rathulf calmly.

Martin felt his skin turn cold. His body cared, all right. He swallowed twice, and spread his hands. 'I looked. It's gone. I think the book's been sold.'

Silence then, apart from the breeze in the treetops. The ragged Ravens stood around. Their faces showed no pity.

Martin knew he had to seize the pause. 'So why did I come back?' he said. 'I could have got away.' He felt like Regulus right now – another of Dad's heroes. Returning to his captors, though he knew what they would do.

Aldhelm spoke morosely. 'Perhaps the book-hoard should be searched again.'

'So go and look yourself,' snapped Martin, thinking: *Jesus, don't.*

Another pause, with Rathulf deep in thought. Then he raised his eyes again. Martin almost flinched away, convinced that he would *see*. But Rathulf's gaze had focused on his men.

'The Raven has been raised again. The lodestones say the call is from the south. We needs must join our brothers; but on the road, we yet may find a trace.'

Martin prayed there'd be no trace to find; that the book was burning, ashes, even now. He itched to double back and see the smoke.

Please, Lyn. Say you have.

He was tempted to suggest that they no longer needed him. The words rose, and he gulped them back again. Once he'd outlived his usefulness, would they really let him go or simply kill him? Better to keep his peace and count the minutes.

'Cofentreium,' said Aldhelm, looking north towards its towers. 'You think that it is somewhere in the burgh?'

'Perhaps,' said Rathulf slowly; he was frowning. 'But there are other lodestones in this shire. I felt one pass us, yesternight. Another of our kind abroad . . .' He glanced round with a ugly smile. 'So which of you will wager who it is?'

'Leofric,' suggested someone drily.

'Let him cross our path, and we will leave him for the crows.'

'Eldred.'

Rathulf scuffed the woodland mulch, still nursing his amusement. 'Eldred cleaves to Athelgar as well.' He paused, and then his tone became more pensive. 'And yet he bears much anger in that *noble* heart of his. Perhaps we might speak gainfully with him.'

'Branwen,' Aldhelm said, sardonically.

Rathulf turned; his face had grown corpse-cold. 'Cut her throat, or strangle her – but be sure that she *burns*.' Still glowering, he jerked his head, and turned along the path.

'What of the Summoner?' asked Aldhelm – right at Martin's elbow. Martin winced.

'He comes with us,' said Rathulf. 'He knows of star-lore. His learning may be useful when we find the Chart again.'

Martin sighed, and felt his muscles loosen. He realized then, as Aldhelm moved away, that the Raven's hand had rested on his dagger. Reaction spasmed within him, so violently it almost made him sick. He swayed there in the clearing, cold with sweat.

'Come,' said Rathulf, turning. 'Follow me.'

Martin did so, shakily. Not sure if he should really feel relieved.

CHAPTER III

Stranger

I

Lyn sniffed and said: 'I don't know what to do.'

Fran squeezed her friend's hand tighter, oblivious to the bustle of the coffee shop around them. She'd pieced events together from Lyn's tearful account, and persuaded her to wipe her eyes, get dressed and come to town. Lyn really wasn't in the mood for shopping; but Fran had asked if they could look round the cathedral. The modern building's awesome beauty took her breath away and left Lyn with a little of its peace. They'd moved on for a coffee, and a more reflective talk.

'Are you going to tell your parents?' Fran asked gently.

'Oh Fran, I *can't*. It would hurt them even more, to know he's been.'

'Just say he phoned you, then. Let them know that he's all right.'

'But he's *not* all right, he said so.' Lyn looked at her appealingly, her eyes still dark with worry. 'He's been living in the *open*, Fran. And some of the things he said . . .'

Fran hesitated. 'This book he wanted you to burn: you said it was a book about magic?'

'Yeah.' She shook her head, bewildered. 'I mean, Martin was always the rational one . . . the *scientist*, you know? He takes after Mum like that. But the way he looked this morning, it was like he believed it all.'

He's not the only one, Fran mused; but didn't think it any further through.

2

The door creaked open slowly. A pause; then Pomfret padded through to see.

Somebody was standing in the doorway – shabby and dark against the sunlit garden. Pomfret's prying stride became a prowl. He crossed the kitchen slowly, regarding the figure with shrewd green eyes. Its shape and scent awoke no recognition.

The dark-haired girl stared back at him, unblinking as she closed the door behind her: nudging it into place with the heel of her boot. The latch – which had been locked – clicked gently to.

She raised her eyes and glanced around. The kitchen was cool and dim after the sunlight. The wealth of it would not have shamed a manor. There were wicker baskets hanging from the rafters; wooden coffers mounted round the walls. She smelled fresh bread; the tang of pine; the piquancy of herbs.

The wider house was quiet. She looked back at the cat.

'*Kath*,' she summoned softly: the vowel like a sigh. Pomfret sat up straight; came forward slowly. He liked that breathy sound, it was alluring.

The girl squatted down to greet him, and rubbed her grimy fingers through his fur. A faint, indulgent smile touched her lips, and tinged her voice.

'What is your name? You will not say?' She clucked, and smoothed his silky fur; then raised her head again. Sampling the silence of the house. 'And what of your mistress, Cat?' she said. 'Is it true she serves the Raven?'

Pomfret purred, and rubbed against her knee. The questions were just noises; their sound was unfamiliar and seductive. Yet they ended with two syllables that put him on his guard – like the brittle smell of frost on winter air.

Kicvran.

The soothing tone had hardened; the stroking fingers paused for just a moment. Then resumed. She cocked her head, indulging him once more.

'Why do you stare like this? I am *Branwen*. You must have heard of me. When I was young, my grandmother called me *queen* of the cats . . .' Her tone was softer, almost teasing now. Pomfret purred more briskly. Human speech was much the same to him; but Medieval Welsh made softer music.

Branwen stroked his eager head; then straightened up again, and looked about her. The cat slid round her legs, but she ignored him. A bowl of apples caught her eye. They were polished and smooth, like a tableau of temptation. She went across and took one. It tasted crisp and juicy, faintly sour.

Crunching it, she pondered on the maiden who lived here.

She'd had the courtly bearing of a lady; the coldness of a princess to a slave. Dressed in Raven-black – yet with her sable hair and doe-dark eyes, it was clear she was no Saxon.

But nor am I, mused Branwen. She shrugged, and flipped the core away.

She tried to get a hold on the feeling that had gone through her when she'd gripped the maid's soft hand. Through her like a lizard – squirming, swift. Gone before she'd grasped it: back into some cranny of the mind. She stood in silence, trying to coax it back. She could sense it lurking down there, but it wouldn't venture out into the light.

She leaned against the worktop, frowning now. Whatever the feeling was, it troubled her. The day outside was fresh and clear; but something was still brewing, like a storm. She'd smelled it on the wind for weeks. And then, three nights ago, she'd seen the portent.

She'd come to the course of the old Rome-Straight: the Fosse Road through the heart of Mercia. Giant creatures scuttled up and down it. After dark, their eyes would start to glow.

Branwen had seen them swarm before; she kept her wary distance. But even in the fields, she'd sensed that something else was following the road. Something that could not be seen;

and yet it chilled her soul. A cold, uncanny power was flowing northward, like the spirits of the damned upon the wind.

Near middle-night, she'd climbed a rise and seen the cloud before her, spread out across the southern sky. Crimson gloom: the heavens stained with blood. Nearer the ground, it had a brighter taint, like orange woodsmoke rising from a fire. It hung over the distant town: the towers of Cofentrium. She'd stood and stared towards it, unwilling to go further. She'd heard of signs like this before. She knew they foretold *evil*.

As dawn came up, the looming cloud had vanished; but she'd seen it forming every night since then. Something was *brewing*. Some dark and fearful storm was going to break.

How soon? She didn't know.

The cat was washing himself in a splash of sunshine. Whatever *he* had sensed, he didn't care.

Branwen folded back her shawl, took hold of the ring-brooch that was pinned to her jersey, and twisted it to see. A cross within a circle: the silver patterned, endlessly entwined. A sardonyx was set into the centre. She cupped her other hand, and shaded it. The stone was still alight.

She'd read the Raven's summons in its intermittent glow like the slow wink of the demon star, Al-Ghul. But as she'd skirted round the hostile city, some instinct had drawn her here, to this rich house. And now she was inside, the stone seemed brighter.

Polaris, Kynosura. The watch-words came unbidden to her mind.

Her pensive gaze rose up towards the ceiling.

She found the lady's bower in the garret: its atmosphere was delicate, distinct. It had the smell of petals, and an aura of contentment. Yet a melancholy shadow seemed to linger there as well.

Opening an inner door, she found a recess hung with Raven-garb.

The black attire was surely emblematic – and yet the maid

had given her no hint of fellow-feeling. She fingered the rich clothing: the long, velvet skirt; the short and shiny coat. *Raven-garb.* A slow smile crossed her face.

Impulsively, she stepped away, and started to undress. The sombre clothes she'd scavenged were threadbare and poor, as befitted her calling; but she couldn't resist the dark glamour of these garments. She'd walked too many miles already. Lived in dust and ashes for too long.

The maid was tall; her skirt brushed Branwen's ankles. The short coat smelled of leather, and reached to her thighs. She shrugged into its creaky depths, and wound the black wool muffler round her neck. A looking-glass was set into the door. Sober now, she studied her reflection. A part of her was flattered – but the overall effect was one of strength. The black clothes gave her presence, like a focus of her power. Dressed like this, she was a slave no longer.

Her former clothes lay crumpled in a heap. *Like grave-clothes in the tomb*, she thought – and felt a heady thrill at her presumption. She squatted down, unpinned her brooch, and raised it in her fingers. Her thumb caressed the stone again. Its glow was steady now.

CHAPTER IV

Wolf Hook

I

Martin knew he walked with madmen now. No matter that their mental state seemed rational enough. Their minds were from another world: they lived by different rules. Rathulf and his men were mad. But murder brought the real horror home.

It happened on a bridlepath, beside a wire fence. There were horses in the open field; two mares had sauntered up to take a look. Rathulf reached for one, and stroked its muzzle; murmuring words that Martin didn't understand. His cruel face was thoughtful. The horse just twitched and snorted, nostrils flaring.

Martin shifted restlessly. A wood stood hushed behind them, Very faintly, in the distance, he could hear the city's hum.

'We need such horses . . .' Rathulf said.

'You can't just *take* them,' Martin pointed out, like someone trying to reason with a spoilt, malicious child.

The other's sidelong glance was almost mocking. 'We are *Ravens*. Warriors of the King. Why can we not?'

They heard another horse approaching then, along the dry mud path. Martin turned to look. A man was riding up along the edge of the wood. Jeans and sweater; green waxed coat. He looked about nineteen.

'Well here's one reason . . .' Martin said.

The young man was bareheaded, his reddish curls unruly in the breeze. Out for a trot round safe, familiar ground. Martin guessed he lived round here. The horses and the field might be his father's.

He reached them and reined in: glancing round the Ravens, before focusing on Rathulf. And Rathulf stared right back at him – still fondling the muzzle of the mare.

'Help you?' asked the rider. His fresh face seemed good-natured, but his tone was cool and stiff: he'd clearly judged them all by their appearance. Lyn could sometimes be like that. Martin heard the likeness with dismay.

Rathulf didn't answer. His gaze was steady: calculating. Martin stood his ground as well, uneasy and alone. He felt like someone trapped between two worlds.

'I'd move on if I were you,' the young man said: still speaking with the confidence of horseback and home ground. He'd doubtless seen men dressed like this before. *Medieval brigands* was the term someone had used. Only this time – God above – they really *were*.

Each man had a longsword, barely hidden by his coat. Rathulf had a second blade, sheathed just behind his shoulder. To Martin it looked horribly like some kind of machete. But the rider hadn't noticed them nor sensed the air of threat.

'They don't want trouble,' Martin said. 'Just let them be, all right?' Sudden dread had squeezed his throat; his voice was hoarse and dry.

The rider glanced at him then back to Rathulf.

'Clear off, now. We've had enough of gypsies interfering with our horses.'

Rathulf's men were spreading out around him. One stepped up, and took the horse's bridle.

'Hey . . .' the man began.

Aldhelm lunged, and slashed at him: the sword had come from nowhere. The rider gave a startled yell, reared back and lost his balance. Down he went, hitting the sun-baked mud so hard that Martin winced as well. The chestnut horse moved skittishly, twisting its head against the Raven's grasp. The latter dragged the bridle back, and snatched the trailing reins. He leaned in closer, murmuring reassurance.

The stricken man was trying to sit up, his face like dirty

snow. Blood was seeping out through his ripped jacket sleeve, greasy and crimson on dark waxed green. Aldhelm ambled forward, face implacable as stone. Martin, without thinking, swung around to block his path.

'*No*,' he blurted, holding out his hands, palms spread in supplication.

The other glowered back at him: eyes narrowed, jaw set firm. His bloodied sword was still half-raised.

'Step aside,' he growled.

Martin swallowed hard, and shook his head.

One of the Ravens made a move; he saw it from the corner of his eye. The man they called Franchisca took a single, lunging step, and Martin glimpsed his arm come whipping down. A flash of something, cleaving air – and then a crunching thud.

Martin spun to see, and almost cried out in disgust. A throwing axe had split the rider's skull: was stuck there, buried deep in bone and tissue. The man was leaning back, his face tipped up towards the sky. One blue eye was round and blank, the other full of blood. He made no further sound except a damp, deflating sigh. His body toppled sideways, and was still.

Martin pressed a fist against his mouth. A few minutes ago, his stomach had been rumbling with hunger. Now it was convulsing in dry heaves.

'*Never* place yourself between the wolf and his kill,' came Rathulf's cold advice from right behind him.

Franchisca stooped, and levered out the axe. Martin watched him sickly, still rubbing his dry lips. The weapon was distinctive, with a narrow, curving blade. The Raven wiped it in the grass, as casually as someone smearing dog-shit off a shoe. He looked around at Martin then – the blue eyes sharp and vivid in his brutish, weathered face. Martin's hand stopped moving; but he held the other's stare.

Rathulf came and took the horse's reins. The animal was nervous, scenting blood. He muttered to it, stroked its neck, then turned to look at Martin. Standing there in his cassock and loose, furled hood, he looked austere and stern: like a circuit-riding preacher from two centuries ago.

'When once you have shed a man's blood, you must *spill* it . . . lest he one day spill your own.' He studied Martin's face a moment longer; then jerked his head, and tugged the horse's rein.

The man called Erik – broken nose – was crouching down to haul the corpse's boots off. Well-made, strap-top ankle boots; he turned them in his hands. Then looked round with a lazy sneer, and lobbed them towards Martin.

'Put them on,' said Rathulf. 'You have many miles to walk.'

Martin hesitated; but his battered pair of trainers were about to come apart. The dead man's boots lay waiting in the mulch. Nervously, not daring to sit down, he pulled them on. They fitted, more or less. He was vaguely surprised the others hadn't claimed them – but then, their boots were broken-in, familiar to their feet. Franchisca's were bound with strips of cloth like First World War puttees.

Straightening up again, he took a last look at the corpse; then forced his bile back down and followed them.

That night they snared some rabbits and built a hidden, smokeless fire. Martin still felt queasy, but his hunger had returned. He accepted the slices of sizzling meat, and wolfed them down. They left his chin and fingers slick with grease, as if he'd just eaten a kebab.

His captors talked together in their rough, distorted language. Martin sat apart, and hugged his knees. Now and then he recognized a word – or thought he did. Strangely drawled, but curiously familiar. Their tone was low, but amicable enough. The low fire stained their faces orange. One of them grinned at what he heard; Franchisca chuckled softly. Even Aldhelm gave a twisted smile. But Rathulf stayed expressionless and brooding, his eyes on the flurries of sparks.

Murderers, and madmen.

Rathulf turned his head and looked at him.

Martin flinched, and felt his skin grow tight. The other's face was calm, which brought no comfort. It hinted at a mind devoid of pity. Then Rathulf spoke – but in his alien language. Martin gazed back, petrified. He hadn't understood a bloody word.

Rathulf lifted his chin, as if challenging the silence. Then lapsed into more recognizable English.

'The Summoner is silent.'

Martin wiped his greasy mouth. 'I speak when I've got something to say,' he muttered.

'What, then, have you to say?' asked Rathulf. Despite the warm glow on his face, his eyes were bleak and cold. The others, too, had turned to look. Martin huddled up beneath their stares.

'Who *are* you?' he burst out after a moment. 'Listen . . . I'm sorry I called you back, all right? But I need to understand.'

'We are the Ravens,' Rathulf said. 'We are the Raven's-breed.'

Martin nodded, none the wiser. 'And why do you come?'

'To fight for the lord who calls us. To take his silver. To put *dread* into the hearts of other men.'

'And afterwards?'

'The Raven takes flight when the bones are picked clean.'

'Where?'

'Where only the dead may follow.'

Had the ghost of a smile crossed Rathulf's face? Or was it just a flicker of the firelight?

Martin swallowed. 'So if there's no lord now, no silver . . . will you go?' He tried to look and sound off-hand: like a traveller who had stopped to share their fire.

Rathulf slowly shook his head. 'Patience, Summoner. There may yet be work for us.'

Work for swords and axes. Work to split more heads – and spill the brains. Nausea swilled inside him; for a moment he was sure that he would bring his supper up. The moment passed. He settled back again, and hunched his shoulders – as if the mild night was turning bitter. As if the summer dark was full of frost.

Later, mummified in his stained and smelly blanket, he listened to the stillness, and the rustle of the flames. The others were huddled up as well. But Rathulf was still sitting with his back against a trunk; still staring at the magic, mayfly sparks. Still waiting, like a vulture, for the starving fire to die.

2

He breathed in deeply, trying to scent the sea. The wide horizon round this place; the coming of the dawn. But the stench of gore and pig-shit blocked his nose.

There were five of them, slumped down against the wall. Bloody and bedraggled now; the earl had lost an eye. The gathered townsfolk peered at them across the wicker fence. Gawping, gloating, mocking Saxon peasants. It stuck in Rathulf's craw to be a captive of these sheep. He had an urge to lunge, and claw the smugness from their faces: once more to be the wolf among the flock. But the shock of their defeat had left him drained. The sheep had always scattered or surrendered in the past – but this time they'd stood firm against the pack. The wolves were now penned up in someone's pigsty. Rathulf felt a surge of shame. His wolfskin cloak had never felt so mangy.

But the warriors in black had won this fight; the watchers who stood guard around them now. Rathulf raised his head again, still wary of their power. They carried swords, like noblemen, but wore no kind of armour. Their sombre clothes were smudged with dust and ashes. But worst of all, they held the old Land-Waster. He'd glimpsed it, like an evil shadow up against the sky.

A murmur rose, and reached his ears: a message being passed

from mouth to mouth. 'The Raven-Lord,' the whispers said. 'The Raven-Lord is here . . .'

The torchflames shivered briefly as if brushed by unseen spirits. The villagers began to move apart. All eyes, including Rathulf's, turned to look.

The man came forward slowly. The smoky torchlight spilled across his face. His features were still grimed with smoke, impassive as a mask. One of the captives cringed, and muttered something. Rathulf glowered sullenly, but felt a growing tightness round his heart.

The Saxon leader leaned against the gate. He wore his sword across his back; his cloak was wrapped around him like a shroud. He regarded the prisoners for a moment. Rathulf saw a silver penny turning in his fingers.

'What shall we do with these?' he asked.

A grey-haired townsman shouldered to the front. His eyes were narrowed, brimming with disgust.

'They're wolves, not men. So slaughter them like wolves.' The gathered people backed him with a murmur of assent.

The Raven-Lord's cold gaze came round to Rathulf. His fingers flipped the glinting coin, and caught it.

'This one showed some courage,' he said drily.

The townsman looked askance at him; then spat into the straw. 'You don't get brave wolves, Lord. Just mad ones.'

The warrior-leader shrugged, as if allowing the opinion. He closed his fingers round the coin, and raised his hand to rest against his mouth. The eyes grew hooded, lost in thought. Rathulf watched uneasily. Folk and warriors waited for his word.

'. . . he listens to his saint . . .' a hushed voice said.

The other's eyes came up again. 'He had the chance to save himself. So why did he stay?'

'Because he was too greedy,' sneered someone.

The Raven-Lord looked round the watching faces. 'Is that the truth?' he asked.

Silence. Then a woman spoke. Her face was muffled by a shawl; her eyes demurely lowered. Her quiet, halting voice was muffled too.

'A little boy was in the hut they burned. This man . . . this *wolf* . . . he stayed to rescue him.'

The Saxon looked around at her. 'Your son?'

She raised her eyes then; tightening her hold on the child clasped against her breast. 'Yes, Lord. Yes, he's mine.'

Rathulf listened sombrely; the Saxon tongue was cousin to his own. Even now, he couldn't say why instinct had betrayed him. He'd smashed a peasant's skull tonight – and slit a woman's throat. But as they'd started falling back, towards the waiting ships, he'd heard the child screaming through the flames. It seemed he heard the cry across the grey wastes of the sea – from his small farm, where wife and children waited. He'd hacked the burning wall apart, and saved the Saxon boy. Then, before he could retreat, they'd clubbed him down and caught him.

The warrior tossed his coin again; then clenched his hand around it.

'What does it say in the laws of the King?' he asked.

One of his men replied as if by rote. 'No thief shall be spared, who is caught with the spoils.'

Again the leader nodded, his eyes on Rathulf now.

'And if a man should spare him?'

'Then the blood-price must be paid.'

The Raven-Lord considered for a moment; then folded his long cloak over one shoulder, and fumbled in a pouch at his belt. He produced a sagging leather purse, and held it up for Rathulf. The clink of coins was brittle in the silence.

'Tell me something, brother wolf . . . if I were to give you your freedom, what would you do with it?'

'Kill you,' Rathulf growled.

The other nodded, smiling grimly now. He turned, and tossed the purse towards the townsman – who almost let it drop in disbelief.

Not a murmur from the people. The Ravens were impassive too. Their leader turned to Rathulf once again.

'Your price is paid. Now you will ride with us.' His gaze invited Rathulf to dispute it if he would. But Rathulf only clambered up, and met him eye to eye.

The Raven-Lord turned back towards the church. One of his men crossed stares with Rathulf. There was something like amusement in his eyes and twisted smile. It made the raider's hackles rise – alert to sudden danger. But then the Saxon moved aside, and let him leave the sty.

'What about the rest of them?' asked someone.

The leader seemed to hesitate – perhaps awaiting guidance from his saint. But this time nothing came. When he glanced over his shoulder, his face was bleak and pitiless again.

'Enough of mercy. Hang them. Hang them all.'

3

The fire had almost breathed its last. The gloom between the trees was thick as pitch. But the stars were out and gleaming overhead.

Rathulf interlocked his hands, and laid his chin against them; the gesture almost prayerful – but he didn't close his eyes. His hooded gaze stayed focused on the lodestone. The pearl was glowing faintly, like an imitation star.

A lump of shadow stirred, muttered something, then was still. The bodies of his brothers lay about like charred remains. The grainy darkness buried them like ash. Beyond the trees, the country was a void. A part of him was conscious of its ghostly respiration; its changing smells; the stirrings in its fields. But the *weirdness* of the land was cloaked in sleep.

The patch of stars above him shifted slowly: hovering like sparks above the chimney of the trees.

Whenever they came back, the land was changed – but never had it changed as much as this. The Giants had overrun the world of men. He'd seen the iron bones of some, still standing in a valley: a single file of skeletons, with cables strung between them. They must have died an age ago, to rot away like that. Now birds had made their nests amid the bones. The cables hung like grinning mouths; he'd heard them humming faintly. Rathulf, sensing magic, stayed well clear.

They'd slept too long. He remembered the church he'd come to, not long after the summoning. Its stone simplicity had drawn him: a refuge in this unfamiliar landscape. There'd been writing on the parchment by the gabled coffin-gate. The date it bore was 1991. He'd stood and stared, unable to believe it. 991 was the year he'd come west-over-sea to England. That first stroke of the quill had wiped away a thousand years . . .

Too long.

The lodestone was still flickering. Rathulf sat and stared at it: enclosed it with the fingers of his mind. Another stone was somewhere close. The one he'd sensed before. The source was moving, miles away. Still creeping slowly southward through the night.

CHAPTER V

Witch Hunt

I

Martin's mind grew brighter, like the breaking day around him. His thoughts, still grey with sleep, began to stir. An image hung before him, like a shadow in the fog. A last dream, losing focus. Or the outside world, becoming real once more.

A ragged shape was hanging from a branch across the clearing; he saw it was the body of a man. The broken way it dangled made him think back to his childhood; the shot crows on the nearby farm, strung up like an example to the rest. The body wore a long black coat that rustled in the breeze. Its lolling head was wrapped in stained white cloth.

Still half-asleep, he heard the creaking bough. The dream was breaking up like smoke but suddenly he knew that it was real.

Rathulf.

A surge of hope brought Martin to the surface. He gasped for air, then squirmed around to see. The tree was there, all right – but Rathulf, still alive, was leaning back against the trunk. His face seemed darker, almost bruised, but bleakly calm as ever. The linen hood was slung around his neck.

The others, too, were wide awake and waiting. Someone kicked him loosely in the side. Jolted, Martin winced and turned his head. Erik gave a death's head grin, and hunkered down beside him. He prodded at the dead man's boots, which lay amid the leaves.

'A man cannot run with unshod feet,' he said, unsmiling now. Martin quickly got the point, and pulled them on again.

Erik's dusty combat boots were supple-looking leather, as if he'd lived and walked in them for years. A contrast to the grey-black suit and waistcoat that he wore.

Martin started getting up. And then he saw the dogs.

They were all around the clearing: crouched there in the leaf-mulch and the grass. Wherever Martin looked, he found a hungry pair of eyes. They made him want to shrink away and hide. There were half-a-dozen different breeds, but all of them looked hostile. He moved again; a couple of them growled and bared their teeth. Martin froze, engulfed in sweat. Another twitch might set them off, leaping for his throat.

Some of them looked starved, like beggars' dogs. Others, better-fed, were bigger. They panted softly, wreathed with ghostly breath. He risked a glance at Rathulf. The latter was studying his ring.

Aldhelm muttered something: the sombre words inflected like a question.

Rathulf nodded.

'*Wahle*,' said the man to Martin's left. It sounded like some Anglo-Saxon oath. Compounding the impression, he spat into the cold ash of the fire.

Rathulf rose to his feet. Martin saw the rope then: coiled in his fists like a captured snake. It ended in a noose. A bolt of shock went through him.

'*Hwat sayst thu?*' the man who'd spat continued. He was the only one of them not cloaked in something black; instead he wore an old, unbuttoned car-coat. But his other clothes were sombre as a mourner's.

'*Utan don swa us neod is*,' said Rathulf. His voice seemed hoarser, raspier today. He glanced at Martin, then jerked his head – and tossed the rope to car-coat. The latter caught it, and wound his way along it to the noose. Martin's heart began to pound. He couldn't quite believe that this was happening.

Then the noose was on him, being pulled over his head. Too late he tried to twist away; it tightened round his neck and choked his struggles. He sensed the Raven taking up the slack – wrapping it round wrist and arm. The dogs sat watching, poised to kill. The gallows tree rose black against the dawn.

'Do not struggle,' Rathulf hissed. 'Follow. We have business to attend to.'

He walked to where the horse was waiting, and untied it. Swinging up into the saddle, he looked towards the dogs. He made no sound, no gesture – but abruptly they were gathering around him. A labrador that might have been a guide dog; a big Alsatian, prowling like a wolf. A sheepdog, and a pit-bull terrier too. Martin watched, still short of breath, amazed at their obedience. Somehow they'd been summoned here, perhaps from miles around. Rathulf had powers; he'd called them. And from farms and homes and streets, they'd come in answer.

Rathulf heeled the horse's ribs; it started forward. The dogs pressed in behind it. The motley group was now a single body. A hunting pack.

The others followed with them. Martin let himself be hauled along. Collared and leashed like a hunting dog himself.

2

She walked in an unerring line, looking neither left nor right. The long skirt swished and rustled through the grass, its hem now damp with dew. The countryside was silent, wreathed in mist; the rosy eastern light was turning gold. Birdsong carried faintly from the woodland, but nothing else gave sign of being awake. The landscape was enchanting – but Branwen bowed her head and strode on through it. Sights and sounds washed over her, like water sliding off a sea-bird's feathers. Her thoughts were fixed on other, deeper senses.

Somebody was following her trail.

She'd been walking since before first light. The Raven's call was from the south: she felt it as distinctly as she knew the wind's direction. Whatever had arisen there, it seemed they were being rallied to resist it. After all the months of wandering in this forsaken landscape, her life was given purpose once again. Encouraged, she'd rejoined the path, still waking as she walked. But even as the shadows were diluted, the lodestone in her cross had started glimmering again.

The sight had stopped her short. Standing like a statue in the dimness of a copse, she'd tried to read a message in the glow. The sardonyx grew brighter as she watched it. She almost felt it tinge her face with pale, ethereal fire.

Ravens.

Several lodestones, clustered in a group – like one of the signs now fading overhead. Brothers with whom she could share the journey south. The knowledge should have been a reassurance but it wasn't. She felt uneasy, skittish, like a horse about to bolt. No clear reason why. She'd *longed* for a familiar face – but these men were all faceless; their unseen presence ominous and threatening.

Dismayed, she'd kept on going. And now, as dawn came up, she felt them sniffing at her heels. Still miles behind her, out of sight, but obviously aware. She felt the briefest urge to turn and wait. There was safety in numbers, after all – especially in this world turned upside-down. And these men were her brothers in the Raven. Closer than her blood kin now, for all that they were Saxons.

She pictured their reunion, and her heartened onward journey. Company and comfort. No need to walk alone any more.

She hesitated, looking back. The image was beguiling. But a warning chill still clung around her heart. Swallowing, she turned and pushed ahead.

3

They crested the rise in a straggling line. The dogs prowled forward, snuffling through the grass. The Ravens strode behind them, swords in hand. Rathulf's horse was walking at the centre of the line. He sat back in his saddle, almost languid;

but Martin sensed his cold gaze sweep the landscape up ahead. There was something more than sight involved. The groundfog should have curdled at his glance.

Martin stumbled then; the noose grew tighter. His handler hauled him into step again. The man's long sword was poised in his free hand. A fleeting glimpse showed spots of rust along the dull grey blade.

Silence hung as thickly as the mist. Just the rustle of boots and hoofs through grass; the panting of the dogs. They crossed the meadow slowly, and came to a hedge. A few of the dogs went sniffing off along it; then bounded back to join them as they filtered through its gaps.

Branwen shivered, hugged herself. The sun was almost up now; the day was getting warmer by the minute. But the chill she felt inside herself was deepening apace.

She reached a stile, and climbed it. The girl's skirt was a hindrance: she should not have been so vain. Pausing astride the gate, she glanced around her. Still nothing to be seen. She dropped into the field, and kept on walking. Her breaths were short and shallow now. The Ravens were much closer.

Rathulf sensed the pack's excitement growing. It quivered back towards him like the trembling of a web; a hungry dog attached to every strand. The mist was getting paler, peeling back. He sat up straighter, scanned the ground – and saw her. A dark shape in the next field, climbing up towards the crest.

Branwen glanced behind herself – and felt her stomach fill with icy water. Two hundred yards of open ground between them, but it felt like they were standing face to face. *Rathulf*. The realization echoed and vibrated in her head – as if a bell had tolled and stopped the world.

And then the world unfroze, and she was running.

The hunting pack gave chase at once. The silence split apart in barks and snarls. Martin started, galvanized – he'd shared the rising tension, but the sudden onslaught caught him unawares. The line of dogs had broken up, was racing through the grass. Rathulf kicked his horse into a gallop in their wake. The men on foot jogged after him, with Martin keeping up as best he could.

Branwen pelted onward, her damp skirt flaring out, then trying to furl around her ankles. Gasping, she glanced back again. The dogs and horse were neck and neck, and hurtling towards her.

Another hedgerow blocked her path. She veered towards its thinnest point, and threw herself against it. The bushes gave; she squirmed and struggled through them. Thorns dug deep into the leather jerkin; they caught her skirt, and scratched her tender cheek. For an instant she felt trapped, as if a fist of spindly claws had closed around her. Then she was through, and free to run again.

The dogs were barking madly, but Branwen's thumping heart and gasping breaths blotted out the sound. A wheatfield stretched ahead of her; she plunged on in. The stalks engulfed her like a wavy green-gold sea. She floundered through them, crouching low. The dogs were out of sight, which just unnerved her even more. She had to find a still point – a place where she could call upon the saints. But things were racing by too fast. Her time was running out.

Rathulf drove his mount full-tilt towards the ragged hedge. The animal responded well, and cleared it in a bound. Touching down, he glimpsed her shape – then saw it was a scarecrow. The tattered figure spread its arms, a parody of blessing. Rathulf wheeled his horse, and raked his gaze across the wheatfield. Some of the dogs were through already, growling in her wake. He saw a patch of trampled stalks, and heeled his mount towards it.

Branwen was down, much deeper in: she'd almost reached the centre of the field. She lay there, panting, trying to get her breath. The wheat rose up around her like a forest. Clear, unblemished sky above and disembodied snarls in all directions. The dogs were prowling back and forth. She sensed their spirits, raging and inflamed. Her instinct said to make a *caim* – but shied away from rising up to do so. The circle of protection might repel them, but what if Rathulf came on her before it was completed?

The dogs were getting nearer. Another charm occurred to her – with moments left to use it. Reaching up, she bent a stalk towards her; then rubbed the ear between her palms, and stripped it of its grains. She breathed a prayer across them; then raised herself and strewed them on the breeze.

It might have seemed that nothing changed; but her mind's eye saw them scattering like fireflies in daylight. The hunting dogs smelled magic, and were thrown into confusion. The pulse was like an eldritch whine, too high for human ears. They cast around, still barking, and the black cat slipped away.

She crawled another dozen yards, then paused to raise her head. Rathulf was still coming. His hounds were now in disarray, but men were not so easily put off. She realized he was following her wake across the field. Stalks of wheat were springing up, but some were bent and broken. From high up in his saddle, he would see the trail she'd left. And Rathulf had more than just the eyes in his head.

She felt a throb of fear in her belly and clenched her teeth in anger at herself. The saints were looking down, she shouldn't doubt them. Peering through the hazy spume, she saw more figures entering the field. Too far away to recognize; but if Rathulf was their leader, then she knew she was alone.

Away to her left, the sun was rising. She felt its first ray touch her cheek, and turned her head to look. The scarecrow stood between her and the blaze of golden light. It seemed to be engulfed in blinding flame, but not consumed. It might have been an angel – or a demon from the pit. She forced her mind to focus on the image. Effort squeezed cold sweat from her, like water from a sponge. The haloed figure burst into bright flame.

Rathulf's horse shied nervously away; he jerked the reins,

and swung it back around. The scarecrow crackled audibly. The fire was pale against the dawn, but greedy and sharp-tongued. Whorls of dirty smoke began to drift across the field.

It drew them, as she'd hoped it would. Rathulf urged his mount towards the effigy of flame. The other Ravens, spreading out, began to circle round it. She glimpsed them moving warily – no doubt they took the burning as a beacon of defiance. She couldn't help but smirk with satisfaction.

The distraction might last moments, but it was all the time she needed. Scrambling up, she ran towards the field-edge and the wood beyond it.

Someone saw, and shouted out – too late. She'd reached the shadows of the trees. More stumbling than running now: her limbs felt weak and heavy and the old, familiar pain was back as well. As if the power she'd channelled through herself had sucked blood from her veins, and stripped the living marrow from her bones.

Rathulf would be rallying his dogs.

She paused to fill her aching lungs, bracing her hand against the nearest tree. The soft, protective dimness was dispersing; golden sunbeams slanting through the green. The hounds would find her scent again, follow her trail, and catch her up in minutes. No easy task to scatter them again. She had to cloak herself somehow.

Stooping, she felt along the wet hem of her skirt. Her boots were splashed and shiny. Pure dew: the land's own holy water. Hunkering down – her breaths becoming shorter by the moment – she rubbed her moistened palms together, then anointed her own forehead.

Lord of Ravens, pray for me.

The sound of barking dogs was getting closer. Murmuring a collect of protection, she began to run again.

Martin, too, was short of breath; the progress of his handler was relentless. They crossed an empty wheatfield, with the dogs now casting round as if they'd lost whatever scent they'd had. There was no sign of their quarry; but a scarecrow burned grotesquely in the middle of the wheat. The sight made Martin's stomach gripe. He wavered – then kept stumbling, as his halter was jerked tight. The sun was up, like liquid gold; their shadows, long and narrow, fled away. But a brooding, hostile aura seemed to overhang the field. Perhaps he picked it up from the Ravens. They were moving slowly now, spaced out like beaters. As if their prey was cornered and ferocious.

Then someone shouted. He turned his head, and glimpsed it: a slim black shape that darted for the wood. Like a ghost caught out by daylight; his stomach lurched again. Rathulf wheeled his horse, and sent it swimming through the wheat. The dogs, with one accord, went swarming after him – their progress like the v-wash of a ship.

The Ravens followed; Martin too. 'Who is it?' he gasped as they reached the trees.

His captor didn't answer, but his sword was up and ready. The dogs had streamed ahead of them by now; their furious barking echoed through the copse. Rathulf's horse proceeded at a walk; he ducked a bough and straightened up, eyes restless, coldly staring. Aldhelm and the others easing out to left and right.

'Who're we after?' Martin hissed, and earned himself another choking tug. But then the man said: 'Branwen.' As if – now they were isolated – he felt the need to forge a bond of sorts.

Martin risked a glance at him, but not another question. The world around was muffled by the wood. The air seemed thicker here between the trees. The snap of twigs was eerie, disembodied. Even the sound of dogs was distant now.

'She is a Stranger . . .' the swordsman went on, between his teeth. 'The *kymry*, as they call themselves . . .' His face was closed and grim.

Another twig snapped, somewhere close. Martin's handler dropped into a crouch, his sword extended. A rustling in the undergrowth made both men's hackles rise. And then a young girl stumbled into view.

In that first moment, Martin saw his sister. Lyn loved dressing up in black, and *she* had clothes like this. Long skirt and leather jacket, with a polo-neck and scarf. But no, this girl was smaller, more petite. She gave a startled gasp, and put her fingers to her mouth. Martin's tension slackened. It surely wasn't her that they were scared of.

'*Wonfax Wahle* . . .' Martin's captor breathed. He gave the words a taunting emphasis. The girl's dark eyes grew wider.

'Osric . . .' she began, her tone appealing – like her eyes.

'*Wicce*,' snarled the swordsman in response. Releasing Martin's rope, he lunged at her. The sword slashed air – she ducked beneath it. A knife appeared from nowhere in her grasp. Swift as a cat, she sprang and drove the blade into his chest. The Raven made a guttural sound, and let her bear him down into the leaves. His body spasmed and kicked, and then went limp. She crouched on him, her dark head bowed, while Martin stared in shock. In that moment she seemed utterly malignant, her girlish aspect wiped away. A black cat with a savaged mouse. A crow with a cadaver. As if she were a Raven, too . . .

The swordsman's final word had sounded very much like *witch*.

Branwen raised her eyes, and looked at him.

She was breathing very quickly now; her face was pale beneath her dark, damp fringe. Martin waited, stupefied. Time was stretching, slowing down his heart. The girl glanced down again, grimaced, and clambered to her feet. The body lay inert where she had laid it, its sombre shirt-front glistening with blood. She crossed herself left-handed, the knife still dripping crimson in her right; but the kill had been so clean, her clothes were spotless.

Slowly she brought up the blade, and pointed it at Martin like a finger. Her face came forward, watchful and suspicious. The distant sounds of searching seemed another world away.

'*Kymro?*' she asked softly.

Martin simply raised his hands; maintaining eye contact, as

his instincts said he should. Her eyes were brown, more luminous than Lyn's. He was close enough to see their flecks of gold.

Branwen stared, debating with herself. The noose around his neck bespoke a prisoner or a slave. And something was familiar in his face and wary eyes. He put her in mind of the lady at the house.

Not a Saxon, then; but nor was he a countryman of hers. She licked dry lips, and tried the common tongue.

'Who is Rathulf?'

'My enemy,' said Martin, without thinking.

She nodded. 'As he is mine. So come with me.'

Martin felt a looseness overcome him: relief so great, he almost failed to stand. He plucked at his halter, pulled it loose, and dragged it past his ears. Branwen couldn't help but glance at Osric. The man she'd killed. The man she'd once called brother.

What evil has befallen us? The question had no answer.

'What about the dogs . . . ?' asked Martin.

She knelt, and squeezed the hem of her skirt; then touched her dampened fingers to his forehead and his shoes. He stared at her. 'And that's enough?'

A thin smile touched her mouth. 'What is your name?' she asked.

He hesitated. 'Martin.'

'You disbelieve me, Martin?'

He quickly shook his head.

'That is good,' she told him. 'I am Branwen. Now stay and die, or come with me and live.'

She took his hand, and drew him after her, her knife still out and ready. They set off through the trees. Martin still felt breathless; not out of the woods in any sense. Her grip was a constraint, just as the noose had been. But her closeness was a desperate reassurance.

They crossed behind the hunters, and pushed on through the undergrowth. The dogs were ranging to and fro. He heard one panting, very close – and then a rush of paws that made his fine hairs stand on end. But whatever she'd done had masked their scent; the dog stayed out of sight. The louder crackling sounds were doubtless Rathulf on his horse. They veered away, both ducking low. The trees were thinning out.

More barking from behind them. Deep-throated: *woe-woe-woe.* And then a vicious scurry of pursuit. Martin knew at once that they'd been scented. He turned, and saw it coming, like a shadow through the trees. It barked again, exultant. *Woe! Woe! Woe!*

Branwen twisted back to see, her knife-hand flailing out. The dog was bearing down on them, devouring the distance. Everything was heightened, every detail standing out. A spot of fresh blood caught her eye – a speckle on a stone. Martin glimpsed it too. They reached the same conclusion in an instant. Time congealed for both of them, like water on the very point of freezing. Martin saw a petrol trail, and fire that raced along it – about to reach the fuel tank beside him. Then Branwen tossed the knife away: a spasmic gesture, fearful and disgusted. The dog lost track of them at once, and swerved away off course – snuffling through the undergrowth in search of the dropped blade.

They kept on going, crossed a fence and reached a narrow lane. Martin risked a last glance back. The wood still echoed faintly, but the screen of trees was sightless.

He turned to Branwen. She looked exhausted, out of breath, but satisfied as well. Staring at the trees, she let a slow smile cross her face, like a pleased little girl.

A little girl who'd ripped a grown man's heart up while he watched.

He wasn't scared, exactly: she'd saved him after all. But like Rathulf and his men, she was from another age. Surely it was her name on that evil magic map. *Branpen*, at the sign of *Ursa Minor*.

Her fleeting smile had faded. She took his hand again, and tugged.

'We cannot wait; the Ravens are still hungry. And Rathulf is a sorcerer, with eyes upon the wind.'

Martin came with halting steps. 'What does he want with you?'

But Branwen didn't answer; merely drew him down the lane. Martin didn't argue. Whatever their feud, he knew he was committed. He was part of *their* world now.

4

When it was clear that Branwen had escaped them – and the Summoner with her – Rathulf let the dogs act out his anger. The pack had been deluded twice, and was of no use now. He set them on each other, and watched them tear themselves to bloody shreds.

They followed Branwen southward, then. But now she was aware of them, and using charms to cover up her tracks. The trail petered out amid fields and hedgerows. Every house and farm they passed seemed watchful. Once upon a time he would have looked on them with relish: isolated homesteads to be terrorized and plundered. But now it was his turn to feel uneasy and hemmed-in.

Then darkness came, and he could see more clearly.

His brother-Ravens stayed apart, respectful of his powers. He heard their quiet mutters as he sought out deeper gloom between the trees. He found an oak, and threw the rope over a branch, then pulled the dangling noose around his neck. He drew it snug, and masked himself with folds of linen cloth. Blinded now, he grasped the rope, and wrapped it round his fists. Slowly he began to take the strain.

The rough noose tightened, choking him. His instinct was to panic, but he fought to keep control. A bar of red-hot iron had been looped around his throat. He buckled at the knees, and let the rope take half his weight. His blood was pounding in his head, each heartbeat like a blow. His thoughts grew thick and muddy. He felt a surge of nauseating pleasure. And then it seemed his skull-bone burst apart.

His mind sprang out, and raced across the landscape. He was a screech-owl, winging through the night. Fields rushed by beneath him, full of slinking, crawling life. Trees loomed up and groped for him, as if to pluck his soul-sight from the air. And there he was, the Summoner – ahead of them, still moving. Branwen was a wraith-like blur, elusive in the dark. But her companion's form was all aglow with cold, decaying power.

CHAPTER VI

Tare Dog

I

Damn you, Martin. Where are you now, you selfish, selfish bastard?

Please come home.

She felt the tears come welling up again: still trying to find a crack in her composure and a flaw in her resolve. Angrily she sniffed them back, and moved on from the window. The day outside was overcast; the grounds looked dull and flat. A van was coming up the road, but otherwise the afternoon was lifeless.

He *wouldn't* make her cry at work. She *wasn't* going to beg. *You're better off without him*, Gill had told her in the pub. And Claire had nodded tearfully – but something deep inside had disagreed. Something even deeper than the seed which he had sown. Even as Gill pampered her, she'd yearned to see his face. That lazy grin of his would cure all ills.

People hooked on heroin must surely feel like that.

And he had screwed her up, all right. She should have dumped him months ago; his moods had pushed her patience to the limit. But no, she'd had to cosset him – and left herself wide open. And now the shit had gone and done a runner.

Her stupid fault, about the Pill. His *fucking* fault, for ruining her life.

'All right, Claire?' someone asked.

She blinked, and flushed as if she'd sworn aloud. She didn't often use that word: the taste of it was vile.

Dr Lawrence was peering at her with a look of mild concern.

The corridor stretched out drearily beyond him, its muddy paint washed out by bright fluorescents. Like the rest of her shift. Like the rest of her life.

She nodded quickly. 'Yes, thanks.'

He took that at face value – though her face was what had given her away. 'Could you look in on John, and check he takes his medication?'

'Certainly.'

'You do look rather tired,' he went on kindly. 'I hope we're not working you too hard.'

She marshalled her professionalism, and put it in her smile. 'Good heavens, no.'

'By the way, I hear congratulations are in order.'

She stared at him; then nodded. 'Oh . . . yes. Thank you.'

'Glad to hear it, Claire. I'll see you later.' He walked on towards his office. Claire glanced after him, her bright smile dwindling. Absently she touched her tummy – just as she had with Gill amid the loud and heedless chatter of the pub. The still point at the centre would be stirring soon enough.

Martin . . .

The appeal began to bloom, but got no further. She choked it off, and headed for John's room.

2

He was sitting on his rumpled bed, and staring at the wall: glowering as if he meant to melt the plaster. His head came round as Claire appeared; his pensive, grim expression didn't change. She couldn't help but hesitate. His eyes were black as bits of coal: smouldering, but giving off no light.

'One of those days for you as well?' she asked.

He breathed out through his nostrils, as if his lungs were full of unseen smoke. Then blinked, and let his dark gaze slide away. She came on in, and looked towards the wall. He'd drawn on it again – a meaningless arrangement of circles joined by lines. She thought of school: the science teacher's blackboard. Molecular structures being mapped out, while she had drowsed in sunlight by the window. The lesson was forgotten now, but what if there was meaning in *this* pattern? The thing was vaguely T-shaped, with a drunken tilt and several mutant offshoots. Perhaps John knew some formulae. She'd better get the docs to take a look.

He'd scrawled some words as well, in his peculiar flowing hand. *Murzim* (which he'd used before), and *Wazn* and *Furud*. Chemicals and elements – or words he'd just made up? But here was one she recognized. By the largest of the circles; on the crosspiece of the T.

Sirius.

'What's that, John?' she asked.

He didn't answer.

Claire shrugged, and didn't push it. The man had grown more reticent of late, withdrawn into the shell from which he'd started to emerge. They'd thought he was improving, making progress. He'd even given them a name to conjure with. Then restlessness had gripped him; edgy days and sleepless nights, despite his medication. His mind had frozen over. Even Dr Lawrence couldn't crack it.

The link she'd forged was hanging by a thread. But to Claire that was a challenge – and a challenge now was something that she needed.

His name. They didn't use it. He'd only let it slip the once. People still felt happier with John.

'Dominicain,' she ventured.

He looked at her, impassively. She wondered what it really meant to him. He'd spoken it, so Lawrence said, *like somebody confessing to a sin*.

'You name me well,' he said.

She noticed he was wearing boots today. A tatty scarf was slung around his neck. He'd even put a pair of fraying gloves on. 'Going on a journey, then?' she asked.

Now he turned his head away. 'The time is come. I must go.'

Shit, Claire thought. She could see a spell on the locked ward looming up. Pulling a face, she came to stand beside him. 'Oh, shh. You mustn't leave us yet. It isn't safe.'

'Nowhere shall be safe,' he said, still staring at the wall.

She hesitated. 'Why do you want to go?'

'I have been summoned.'

'Who by?'

'The messenger of God. I saw him in my dreams again last night.'

Claire gave a small, defeated sigh – then jumped as someone's car backfired outside. The sound was loud and stinging. It happened again a moment later: too jarring, too *immediate* for a car. As if a crow-scarer from the surrounding farmland had been set off in the dayroom.

The third bang took a window out: she heard its jagged, crystalline collapse. And then a woman screaming. Young woman. Frightened woman. *Nurse*.

A chill soaked through her uniform. Her hand went to her lips. 'Jesus . . .'

'*Blessed* they are,' John murmured, 'who die with His name on their lips.'

She'd been staring at the doorway, but she whirled towards him now. He sat there, calm as ever, but the look in his eyes was something close to pity.

Footsteps were approaching down the ward.

They came through huge, shocked silence; she heard a distant whimpering at its edges. Her heart began to bulge with dread. She backed towards the corner; there was nowhere else to go.

John sat waiting, massaging his jaw.

They reached the doorway, filled it, came on through. Men with scruffy clothes and stony faces. Two of them had clubs that looked like sawn-off snooker cues. One wore gloves; the other's grip was tight enough to make his knuckles gleam. She cringed, and pressed her spine against the wall. Its solid bulk repulsed her, pushing back. The men just watched her, waiting for a move. She felt a spasm inside her – as if her child had sensed the dreadful threat.

The two intruders moved apart; at least three more were standing there behind them. She glimpsed a baseball bat, a pick-axe handle. But the man who crossed the threshhold had a pistol in his hand.

Claire goggled at the gun. A bitter, firework smell hung round its owner, like the stink of cigarettes round John himself. He'd *used* the thing. He'd fired it on the *ward*. Her arms slid round her belly, hugging tight.

The man's glance took her in, and then dismissed her. He stared at John, who'd turned as if to greet him. The newcomer looked stocky and aggressive, with blue metallic eyes and ginger hair.

'*Domini Canis*,' he said, like words he'd had to learn.

And John rose smoothly to his feet.

'No . . .' Claire said instinctively; then clapped her hand across her mouth. The nearest bloke looked round at her – then crossed the room, began to aim his blow. So casually, she couldn't quite believe it.

Then: 'Please,' she gasped, 'I'm pregnant . . .'

His set expression didn't change. The sawn-off cue was lifted, poised. She realized he was going to whack her right across the belly.

Then John lunged in from nowhere to grasp the man's jacket, wrench him round, and slam him hard against the wall.

'*No!*'

From him, the word had more effect: a point-blank snarl into the other's face. From where she cowered, Claire saw anger flare in the big thug's eyes. Flare – and flicker out beneath John's stare. Like a candle in a gust of icy wind.

The others waited. Claire felt sick. An alarm bell started ringing on the ward.

John released the man, who sagged a little – his expression still resentful; still unnerved. Claire watched her patient cross the room and pick his Bible up. Then he turned his solemn face towards her.

'Woe unto them who are with child,' he told her grimly, holding out the book as if the words were gripped inside it. 'Affliction there shall be, such as was not since the making of the *world*.'

She goggled at him, nauseous with shock. A flicker crossed his face, like indecision. She had a sense of vertigo, her whole life on the brink.

Then he breathed out slowly, eyes unblinking. 'Forgive me.'

He watched her for a moment, as if waiting for some sign that she had done so; then dropped his sombre gaze, and walked on out. The men who'd come to get him followed suit. The gunman paused to look at her; she glimpsed a frightful malice in his eyes. Her numb, relaxing muscles clenched again. Then he was gone, and she was left alone.

Slowly she sank down onto her haunches, curled up around her precious, precious child. Life was safe inside her; the world outside the room had ceased to matter. But she couldn't get John's face out of her head – nor the way he'd asked forgiveness. As if he'd meant, for leaving her *alive*.

They came down the long corridor, and filled it with the echo of their boots. Dominicain now set the pace; the others flanked and followed him, like bodyguards around their general. Clubs and bats were ready, raised. The man with the gun was clearly their leader, but now he seemed content to let the man in white pyjamas choose their path.

Patients wandered in their way, or stopped to watch them come. A skinny youth stood staring. He wore a reefer jacket with his jersey and his jeans. One of the escorts veered off towards him.

'Let's have your coat, mate.'

The young man blinked, befuddled; then shrugged out of the jacket. The other snatched it, speeded up, and draped it round Dominicain's broad shoulders. The latter took it as his due, and didn't break his stride. The scruffy coat hung loose, like a hussar's.

The man glanced back and gestured. 'Get out of here, don't hang around. You're *free*.'

But the youth just stood there, staring after them.

They shouldered through a pair of plastic doors, which flapped loosely closed behind them. A nurse and porter tried to block their way – were beaten back. A wooden truncheon thudded into flesh.

'Fucking thought police,' someone hissed. Another turned, saw pale, bewildered faces. 'Don't stay!' he snapped. 'Don't let them poison you . . .'

They left the building, and turned onto a covered walkway – Dominicain still following his nose. More bells were ringing now. Another, male nurse was standing prudently back; but the leader made a lunge for him, and pistol-whipped him back against the wall. The man keeled over, crumpling, his slack face doused with blood. The leader bared his teeth in rage, and kicked the huddled body. He wavered for a moment on the very edge of murder; then seemed to get a grip, and went on walking.

Through another set of plastic doors, and down another corridor, with people standing back to let them pass. Their footsteps boomed ahead of them, the noise of a phalanx. They came to an office; the door, half-open, was kicked aside. *Patient Affairs*, according to the sign. They forced the man inside to open the key press, and unlock the property safe – then beat and kicked him back into the corner. Dominicain ignored them, kneeling down before the safe. With growing, greedy eagerness, he rummaged through the contents. Stuffed manila envelopes were snatched out, weighed, and slung aside without another glance. Suddenly he drew a breath; turned the package in his hands, then roughly tore it open. A rosary spilled out into his palm. A crudely fashioned crucifix, a string of wooden beads – and a flashing diamond dangling from the end.

Sirius.

Emotion surged inside him; exultation and relief. They boiled down to *power*, in his hand. He glanced up at the gunman, nodded once, and closed his fist round beads and gem together.

CHAPTER VII

Circle of Sorrow

I

Branwen gasped aloud, as if in pain. Martin sat up quickly, half-awake. In that first dopey moment, he thought that she was screwing – or being screwed. His instincts clashed: both jealous and protective. He'd seen the way that bloke had sized her up . . .

Then he overbalanced, almost sliding off the seat. The sleeping bag was like a winding-sheet. He freed one arm, and grasped the seat-back: gripped its metal frame. The shadowy old bus took shape around him. Apart from them, the top deck was deserted. Morning light came leaking in around the makeshift curtains.

He steadied himself, and looked across the aisle. Branwen was sat upright too, her arms around her knees. She was breathing very quickly. Her face looked small and bloodless in the gloom.

She'd kicked her borrowed blankets off; her drawn-up legs were bare. She still wore that black polo-neck, the sleeves shoved to her elbows. A silver cross was showing at her throat.

Martin freed himself a little more. 'What is it?' he mumbled.

She blurted something, full of phlegm. He shook his head, not understanding. She rubbed her forehead, eyes still wide, and went on in slow English.

'I dreamed,' she said. 'I *saw*.'

'Saw what?'

She hesitated, groping for the words. 'A black dog running

through the night – a flame red in his mouth. Setting the world on fire . . .'

Martin simply stared at her. Her voice seemed to come from a distance; her haunted gaze was just as far away. After a pause, he focused on her cross. The little thing was plain and crude, enclosed within a circle. It made him think of cross-hairs in a gunsight.

He stretched himself, and scrubbed his tufty hair. Someone was moving about downstairs – the woman, or her daughter. Two men met outside, and muttered greetings. He guessed it was still early, but the encampment was already waking up.

'Only a dream,' he offered lamely. 'It's just the dogs from yesterday, that's all.'

She shook her head; he saw that she was crying. Silent teardrops glistening like dew. Martin watched uncomfortably, not knowing what to say.

'It . . . made me to think of a man I knew,' she whispered. 'Someone who spoke of this dream of the dog – and told that the flame was the light of the Gospel of Christ.' Her face grew tight, as if with pain. 'But the fire *I* saw burned all God's people up.'

Martin gave an understanding sort of nod, and settled back. Branwen wiped her dripping cheek, still staring through the dimness. The confines of the bus closed in around her; but centuries of distance opened out behind her eyes.

2

She saw the ruined face again; her own hand gently stroking. The maiden had been comely once, but now her face was masked with dust and blood. One of her cheeks was blackened to the bone. The body lay half-buried by a spill of tiles and timber. The debris was still smouldering: still hot beneath the soles of Branwen's shoes.

Other fires were crackling in the background. A horse grew

restive, snorting. Metal clinked. The air was foul and heavy with the rotten smell of death. Bowels, and their contents. Blood and brains.

She felt a sick nostalgia for her country: its hills and deep green hollows, and the salt-breath of the sea. In vain she tried to flee there in the spirit. The stench was too insistent in her nostrils – polluting any thought of grass and rain. The landscape here was grey; the skies were leaden. She tasted dust and ashes on her tongue.

Smoothing dirty hair aside, she placed her hand against the dead girl's forehead. Her heart swelled tight with pity. The maiden looked the same age as herself.

Neither of them would be growing older now.

'Mercy . . .' said a strained voice from behind her.

She turned her head. The captain of the plunderers had struggled to his feet: in the middle of the square, beside the bone-fire. Athelgar was facing him, his bloody sword turned downwards at his side. The other Ravens stood around, and watched.

Athelgar's eyes were cold with rage. He raised his silver coin between two fingers; flipped and caught it. Then read the other's sentence in his palm.

'Crosses it falls . . . Go on, pick up your sword.'

The man spread out his empty hands. 'I surrender myself.'

'It is too late for that.'

Blood had spattered everywhere, like mud from wagon-wheels. The *routiers* had made their stand, and been cut down like corn. Limbs were off, and entrails out. A severed, half-scalped head was lying close to Rathulf's boots.

Athelgar gestured to the longsword in the ashes.

'Pick it up and fight – or stand and die.'

The trapped commander licked his lips, and glanced from side to side. 'What if I win? Will your brothers let me turn and walk away?'

'They'll only come against you one by one.'

'I must defeat you *all*? Is this your mercy?'

'What more did you expect?' said Athelgar.

Silence, barely broken by the snap and pop of flames. Branwen's fingers moved without her knowing, stroking the dead girl's forehead as if comforting a child.

The plunderer looked round again, with growing desperation. His eyes came back to Athelgar. Still watching him, he stooped and grasped the handle of his sword.

Branwen's heartbeat seemed to skip and stumble. Fear for her lord, in case he lost – and fear in case he *won*.

Eldred rubbed his stubbled jaw, impassive.

The captain lunged, but Athelgar was ready. He ducked the other's blow, and chopped him down. Blood sprayed up and outward in a cloud. The *routier* collapsed like an old scarecrow, and was still.

Branwen didn't even blink: she'd seen the like too often. Enough to soak her memories of green with filthy red. And what was one more killing, when the balance was already teetering with corpses?

She straightened up and crossed the square, its brittle cinders crunching underfoot. Athelgar looked round at her. 'No one left for you?' he asked her grimly.

Shaking her head, she walked towards the horses. The healing art was in her hands; the power that came from God. But none of it could help the people here. Poking through the wreckage, she had found some people crouching in a cellar – as motionless and black as bits of bog-oak. The zealots hadn't bothered to drag them out. Instead they'd shoved in wood and straw, and burned them in their hole.

And men called this a Cross-war: a *croisade* . . .

She gripped her palfrey's bridle, and just stood there for a moment, holding on. The Ravens were withdrawing too, surrendering the ruins to the dogs. Grey smoke eddied on the grimy air. Athelgar moved up to stand behind her. She took a breath, but didn't raise her head.

'What hope have we left,' she murmured hoarsely, 'when Christians do the Devil's work for him?'

His hand reached out and rested on her shoulder. 'We have to go on fighting – for our faith. Even if we perish here, we *have* to stand against this.'

She realized he was right, of course – and felt her spirits sinking like a millstone. They were outcasts in a world possessed by evil. Even as it closed the net, they'd keep on striking back. The ambushes and massacres would just go on and on. Labour with no hope of rest: like trying to dig a trench to catch the sea.

3

Footsteps, slow and clanking on the stairs. They both turned round to look. The woman's face rose into view, its contours tinged by bright light from below.

'Morning, you two. Sleep well?'

Martin nodded quickly. 'Thank you, yeah . . .'

'We've coffee, bread and griddle cakes. You're welcome if you want some.'

'That's good of you,' said Martin. 'We'll be down.'

He drew his legs out of the bag, and glanced around at Branwen. She'd come back to herself again, but still looked tense and watchful. Muscles bunched, and fine hairs bristling: like a cat about to bare her claws and spring.

'Want to eat?' he asked, placatingly. She gazed at him, then nodded once, and wiped the drying tears off her cheeks.

They'd reached the travellers' camp soon after dusk. The smell of drifting woodsmoke had enticed them through the trees, towards a glimpse of orange flame – a chink in the grey curtain. The vehicles were gathered in the corner of a field, with a wood fire going nicely in their midst. Two beat-up vans, an ambulance, and a brightly painted double-decker bus.

Dogs as lean as whippets came to sniff, and bring them in. The people had been wary; but their attitude had softened soon enough. Martin's shabby coat was like a passport to the fireside, but though Branwen's clothes were richer, they had made her welcome too. In fact, they'd seemed to treat her with a curious respect.

So the two of them had shared a meal, and spent the night upstairs. Dressing now, they came on down. Martin put his head around the curtain that gave access to the lower deck. The woman who owned the bus was busy in its makeshift kitchen. Her teenage daughter was sitting on one of the beds; he sensed her look him over with some interest.

'Help yourself to coffee,' the woman smiled. Martin ventured in and did so, spooning the granules from re-used jar to well-used mug. The girl – who looked about fifteen – drew up her knees and hugged them. Early-morning light was streaming in across the worktop. The woods looked very dark at the edge of the field.

'Something spooked the dogs last night . . .' the woman said. 'Did you hear them barking?'

Martin nodded. He'd lain awake and listened for most of the short night. At first he'd thought that Rathulf's pack had caught them up again; then realized that these dogs were tethered close. The barks and growls had come in fits, as if something had been probing round the edges of the camp. Drawing near, then fading back again.

'Probably a fox or summat,' the daughter said. Martin caught her eye, and looked away.

'Moving on today?' her mother asked.

Martin hesitated. 'I'm not sure. We don't want to impose on you, but . . .' *There's safety in numbers, isn't there?*

He sipped at his coffee. She gave him a shrewd look. 'You're new to the travelling life, aren't you?'

He smiled a little sheepishly. The sweaty shirt and scruffy coat were easy to see through. 'Yeah – though I've been . . . restless for a while. But yes, I am.'

'Your friend's not, though, is she?'

'Branwen. Can you tell?'

The woman nodded. 'She's got a wandering streak, all right. She's got the Goddess in her.'

He pondered that; then glanced around the bus. 'Maybe I'd get used to it.'

'It's not New Age, you know. Not really. It's as old as the earth. The Native Americans sum it up, for me. "The life my people want is a life of freedom. I have seen nothing the white man has, that is as good as the right to move in the open country and live in our fashion." '

'Chief Sitting Bull,' her daughter said, as if she'd often heard the quote before.

'You know my problem?' Martin grinned. 'I always wanted the Cavalry to win . . .'

Branwen had gone outside. He found her kneeling in the grass, her face raised to the sunlight like a flower. Her eyes were closed; he guessed that she was praying. But prayer, it seemed, more pleasurable than any he could picture in a church. He thought that she was bathing in the morning: letting it wash all the dark away.

He'd never seen her so serene – or looking so attractive. He felt a twinge of voyeuristic guilt, and glanced aside. Towards the trees. The lightless trees. 'You heard the dogs?' he asked.

She opened her eyes and looked at him. 'That was his spirit-sight, reaching out. We cannot hide from Rathulf, but he has not caught us yet.'

Her voice was quiet, but failed to reassure him. He scanned the shadows anyway, but saw no trace of movement.

'These people – are they exiles?' Branwen asked.

'Not really.' He scuffed at the grass. 'It's just, they like to keep on moving. Not wanting to put roots down anywhere.'

'I wish *I* had a place to rest,' she murmured. 'It was not granted us. The dead sleep in the earth, but we keep travelling. Following their shadows on the wind.'

She crossed herself, and clambered up. 'We must not stay,' she said.

He frowned at her. 'We're safer with these people. On our own . . .'

'Rathulf will *kill* these people if we stay. Not even the children will be spared. This wheel-house and the others, he will burn.'

'*Branwen*. There's only four of them. There's half-a-dozen hefty blokes round here.'

She grimly raised a hand with fingers splayed. 'I have seen *this many* Ravens take a warband of the wolf-coats, and lay them in the dirt without a loss. We must lead him *away*.'

Martin scanned the site uneasily. The vehicles were battered, with belongings strewn around. He found himself reminded of the Gulf War: the carnage of the Basra road. It didn't take much effort to imagine burnt-out hulks instead of vans.

'Who's Athelgar?' he asked her suddenly.

She turned her head, eyes narrowed. 'Why ask this?'

'Rathulf's after *Athelgar* as well.'

'Athelgar is dead,' said Branwen flatly.

'Who was he?'

'He was my lord,' she said after a pause. 'The only Saxon worthy to be followed. He took the side of common men, and fought to bring them justice. The people prayed to him, as to a saint. But do you still petition him today?'

Martin shrugged. She didn't seem surprised.

'He had no wish to cling to life – unlike we lesser blest. And though he was of Saxon blood, he turned again to face an English *army*.' She flashed him a defiant look; then glanced away again. '*I* still make my prayers to him. Although he is in Hell.'

4

Travellers themselves, they moved on shortly after breakfast. Martin still felt curiously detached. He felt as though he'd slipped from one dream into another but he knew the camp was real, and still behind them. The grittiness had registered; the smoky smell still lingered in his coat. A little enclave, clinging to their future – or the past.

He hoped the modern cavalry would leave them well alone. And Rathulf's vicious renegades, as well.

They reached a quiet B-road; it stretched off, arrow-straight, between the fields. 'This is the Fosse-road,' Branwen said. 'My mother said it used to lead to Rome . . .'

Her tone was thoughtful, almost apprehensive. Staring south, she hugged herself, as if against a chilly gust of wind.

The air was still.

Martin followed her gaze, then looked around. A trunk road was grumbling across country to their right. He guessed the two converged at the next town.

'Where *does* it lead?' he asked.

'Ynys Avallach,' Branwen said. She glanced at him, and saw his frown. 'Glasynbri. *Glastingabury*, you name it. The Ravensbreed, my brothers, had their consecration there. And now some power is flowing from that place. Be still a moment . . . *There*. You cannot feel it?'

He was aware of nothing but the stillness of the fields. They smelled of mud, and fresh manure . . . and something else as well. The stink of carrion, rotting in the dirty roadside grass.

'We must retrace it to its source,' said Branwen at his side. 'Our oldest house is threatened – and the Raven will be there.'

'Won't we be following *ley-lines*, then?' asked Martin drily.

She glanced at him. 'What are these?'

'Ancient trackways, so they say. Or power lines. Or something.'

Branwen only frowned; then shrugged. 'I do not claim to know about such lines. We take the Rome-Straight, into Wessexena.'

She started down the verge but Martin waited where he was. 'You know I used the chart to call you up?'

She stopped and turned to him, surprised. 'So why have you kept silent?'

'Because it was an *accident*. I never meant to do it. I never even realized what it was!'

Her frown was back, more curious now. 'So how could it have come into your hands?'

'We only had a copy of the thing. I'm interested in stars, and I was reading it one night . . .' She nodded then; but he remained perplexed. 'So how can someone call you without knowing?'

'The signs upon the Chart must be invoked in special order. Yet once enough of them are named, the wheel begins to turn. As weighty as the year: one cannot stay it.' She stared at him; then shook her head. 'Because the thing was not brought to fruition, our spirits were sown widely on the wind.'

'But how does it *work*?' he wondered – as if she could explain the thing in scientific terms.

'It is a sacred ring,' was all her answer. 'A seal to bind the shinecraft of the Norse. The brethren of Glasynbri created it for us – so we could sleep until the land had need of raven-blades.' She proffered her brooch. 'My sigil is the sign of Ursa Minor. This is sardonyx, my lodestone – see you? *Stella Maris*, the Star of the Sea.'

He guessed she meant Polaris, the North Star. The stone in her brooch was a yellowish-white. He remembered the pearl in Rathulf's ring – and realized how these *lodestones* had been chosen. Polaris was a class F star (the only one whose grade he could remember). The Fs were yellow-white, and not much different from the Sun. But Thuban's light was colder: of a different spectral class.

'Why that constellation?' he asked curiously.

'My father's name was Morcant, which means *Sea-born* in your tongue. And you have seen the Lesser Bear: it is the Greater's image. I was as a sister to Athelgar.'

'So he was Ursa Major, then?' It sounded like some kind of rank: a sinister commander.

'The Bear,' said Branwen, nodding. 'Because it prowls the

night and never sleeps. In Araby, this sign is called the Mourners and the Bier.'

She paused. He searched her face. 'And Rathulf?'

'Rathulf received the dragon-sign. Because he came with the dragon ships. Because he held our purse. The Old Ones say that dragons guarded treasure.'

'So how can he be one of you?'

'Rathulf was a sea-thief, and an enemy of God – but Athelgar saw courage in his heart. Courage, and a kind of purity. And what better way to trust a thief than to let him keep our gold?'

'And did he?'

Branwen nodded slowly. 'He had respect for Athelgar – but in his heart he held to Odin still. And Odin is a faithless god, as sly as he is wise. It is a Northman's *honour* to betray.'

'And no one realized that?'

'Athelgar knew. When Rathulf received baptism, he went down into the water – but he kept his fist upraised and dry, like so.' She brought her own fist up, like a salute. 'He freely gave his soul to Christ – but not his battle-hand. That belongs to Odin still. And like a crippled hand that rots, the blackness has spread back into his soul.

'Thus it was agreed that he be bound within the circle. His name was written backwards – *Fluthar*, so. He could not rise again without the others.'

'He's managed to get loose, though. Hasn't he?'

Again she nodded, sombre now. 'You say you used a copy to convoke us. The chart was copied more than once, as centuries went by. From time to time a scribe might err, and so corrupt its craft . . .' Her dark eyes showed reluctant comprehension. 'Perhaps what you have set in train went doubly awry. The Raven spread his wings unchecked; all bonds were put asunder.'

Still pondering, she looked ahead – and stiffened, like a cat alert to danger. Martin swung around, and saw a horseman in the road. Not Rathulf, but another of his Ravens.

Oh my God.

A stile lay on their left. 'Quickly,' Branwen said, and walked towards it.

'What?'

'We need to have the earth beneath our feet.'

The watching rider didn't move; but as Martin climbed the stile, he saw three more of them appear along the skyline. All of them were mounted now; they'd clearly spent the past night rustling horses. They lingered, silhouetted, almost brooding; then started down the sloping field towards them.

Undaunted, Branwen strode ahead and stopped a dozen yards beyond the hedge. She waited for Martin to catch her up, then slowly started turning on the spot, her finger pointing down towards the ground – as if to etch a circle on the grass. The riders came on quickly, but her motion was unbearably deliberate, like the second hand sweep of a watch. Her face was tightly masked with concentration. Martin, there beside her, had the feeling she was marking every blade.

He looked along the road again. The horseman in their way had remained where he was. But the others were approaching now, across the fallow field. Close enough for him to see their hoofs raise clods of earth – and hear the eager snorting of each horse.

Anticipation curdled in his stomach. It was like some desperate race against a stopwatch. And Rathulf and his men were going to win.

Branwen spoke a line of Welsh; her voice was low and urgent. Her eyes came up, and saw their closeness. Her next words had the tone of an appeal.

'Dewi, *sant* . . . Illtyd, *sant* . . . Athelgar, *sant*.' And with that she closed the circle round them both.

The horses sheered off and surged around it, like a current split and flowing round a rock. Rathulf checked his mount, and sat there towering above them. Aldhelm and Franchisca glowered down from left and right.

'I see you still have power,' said Rathulf drily. His mocking smile was tinged with some respect.

'Enough to keep the wolves at bay,' she answered – and glanced at Aldhelm, who was fingering the handle of his sword. 'Do not waste your effort, brother. You know that iron cannot breach the ring.'

Her tone was cool, contemptuous: a challenge. Aldhelm seemed about to rise to it. Then Rathulf raised a hand between them both. 'Enough of this. The gods have matched us well. Perhaps we should be making common cause.'

'To do what?' Branwen asked him. Her brown eyes had grown bitter-black, like frozen winter mud.

Rathulf nodded casually at Martin, who flinched at the inclusion. 'The Summoner can help us find the Sky-Chart.'

'And what will *you* be wanting with it, Rathulf?'

'It is time to choose our own road now. We have fought for others long enough – a thousand years and more. Once we hold the Chart, we can ride freely through the world, and have its gold and glory for *ourselves*.'

'So,' she said. 'And what about the oath which you have sworn?'

Rathulf shrugged, and nudged his mount towards them. It came up to the circle, and began to pace around it; Martin could have touched the horse's flank. Rathulf's gaze was gloating now. The others followed suit, and hemmed them in.

'An oath should last a lifetime, yes . . .' said Rathulf. 'But we have lived for many lifetimes now.'

The wall of horseflesh forced the circle inward, so it seemed. The animals kept plodding, nose to tail. Rathulf's face came round again, and Aldhelm's, and Franchisca's.

Branwen hugged her elbows, as if focusing her strength. 'You would profane the memory of Athelgar himself.' She turned and glared at Rathulf. 'Your lord; the man who spared your life. We see your Northman's honour.'

Her tone was bitter, sneering; it got through. Martin

glimpsed a shadow crossing Rathulf's stony face. 'You know I saved him in my turn. The *wergild* was repaid.'

She shook her head. 'You rode with us in fellowship. The thing is more than bond and debt and payment.'

'The Hooded One has counselled otherwise.'

'Only a fool trusts the Father of Lies.'

Rathulf lunged, and seized her by the hair. Branwen gasped, grimacing. He bent her like a reed towards the edge of the ring, while her arms flailed out for balance. For a moment Martin froze; then caught her round the waist, and dragged her back. Rathulf lost his grip, and his mount side-stepped away.

Branwen stared towards him, breathing hard. Martin drew her back against his chest, holding her so close that he could feel her thudding heart. Anything to stop her being pulled out of the circle. But clear ground had opened up around them. The horses were retreating, spooked and skittish. Rathulf tried to master his – then gave the nervous animal its head. His glance was venomous. Martin saw them driven back, and realized that the circle was expanding. The ring of power was spreading, like a ripple on a pond.

'Your wisecraft will not last the course,' snarled Rathulf.

Branwen shook her head. 'Athelgar of the Ravens holds this circle.'

'Your prayers to him are wasted, bitch. He cannot save you now.'

But the horsemen kept on falling back. Branwen gently freed herself, and she and Martin watched them growing smaller. He turned to check the road again. The junction up ahead was now deserted; the fourth man was still visible, but seeking higher ground.

'The circle will spread,' said Branwen, 'and push them back over the skyline.'

'How long for?'

'For long enough,' she said. 'Now let us go.'

5

Crossing the fields, they reached the noisy road. A steady flow of traffic headed south. Watching lorries sweeping past, he clutched at Branwen's sleeve.

'That's it! We can hitch a lift. Let's see Rathulf chasing one of *those* . . .'

Branwen stood and stared, wide-eyed. She'd frozen like a rabbit. Belatedly he realized why – those trucks must seem like monsters. He flexed his mind, and saw them through her eyes: stampeding beasts in armour, with their staring eyes and grinning grilles of teeth. The surf-on-shingle roar was overwhelming.

Still holding her coat, he turned to check behind them. No sign of their pursuers yet. He took hold of her other arm, and pulled her round to face him. Her expression was controlled and tight, but her eyes were deeply anxious.

'We're not in danger here,' he said. 'These things . . . they're just like wagons, there are people safe inside them. Look.'

Her wide eyes shifted nervously to see.

He squeezed her arms, encouraging. 'I'll see if I can make one stop. We can travel *fast* in one of those.' Letting go, he moved up to the verge. Another glance across the field; then he raised his hand and thumbed the air.

The river kept on flowing. Minutes passed. Martin stood and waited, with his heartbeat getting louder. It might be an advantage, to hitch-hike with a pretty girl in tow. But Branwen was still hanging back, a wary shadow up against the hedge.

Looking round again, he saw a horseman on the skyline. The figure sat there, motionless – perhaps a mile away. Too far to make out any kind of detail. But Martin could feel the watchful eyes on him.

He came right to the kerb, and did his best to look appealing. Branwen ventured forward a few steps. She sensed the rider too, and turned to look.

Half a minute later, a truck came pulling in. He scarcely dared believe it for a moment – then stepped back as it rumbled past and stopped. The indicator light was winking warmly. *This is it.* He looked around. 'Come on!'

Branwen didn't look at all convinced.

Leaving her, he ran up to the cab. The driver leaned across to open the door. 'Where d'you want to go, mate?'

'South. We're trying to get to Glastonbury.'

'I can take you as far as Swindon. Climb aboard.'

Martin looked at Branwen. 'Come on, it's all right.'

She mouthed a question, frowning.

'What?'

She gestured at the hugeness of the truck.

'I told you, it's all right,' he called, and glanced towards the ridge. The horseman had disappeared. Climbing up, he held his hand out. '*Branwen*. Let's get going.'

She came at last, with cautious steps, and let him pull her up into the cab. Martin shut the door, and took the seat beside the driver. Much better if he fielded any questions.

The truck sat throbbing, waiting for a gap, then rumbled forward. Branwen stiffened in her seat, with every muscle tensed. Martin peered past her, at the skyline. Isolated trees stood out against the cloudy light. But nothing was moving on the ridge. The muddy fields were empty.

As the miles were eaten up, she realized this was magic of some kind.

Of course she'd been afraid at first. The thing had seemed a dragon, clad in armour like a war-horse – and Martin had climbed up into its *helm*. But it didn't take her sharp mind long to recognize the truth. There wasn't any beast in here; the thing was just a wagon, as he'd told her. And yet it had the power to move – at speeds that made her stomach plunge inside her.

She felt a strange euphoria start to grow. Every mile she'd travelled up till now had been on foot; or on a horse, or in some jolting cart. This was like a miracle: the freedom of a bird.

Martin and the waggoner would speak from time to time. She had a childish urge to voice her awe but settled back instead, and kept her peace. Later would be time enough to ask about this power.

The ground raced by: so far below, so fast. The wagon's speed was lulling her, in spite of her excitement. Shifting in her seat, she closed her eyes. A pent-up tide of weariness flowed through her. The noise grew muffled, and began to fade.

Abruptly she was wide awake, as if she'd just been doused in icy water. She sat there, stunned and blinking for a moment; then realized that the saturating coldness was her sweat.

The road was passing through a town. Branwen's eyes grew wider as she saw it lay in ruins. The buildings were like burnt-out skulls: the brain-pans smashed and open to the sky. The silence of the charnel-house hung over everything.

The wagon sped between them, never slowing. Branwen stared in horror as the rubble-heaps slid by. She turned her head, to get a closer look, and almost gasped. The houses were complete again. Solid walls and friendly windows; gardens full of green. A mother led her child along the pavement.

She knew it was a Showing, then – a vision of the spirit. Looking forward once again, she glimpsed the devastation. Then her eyelids flickered, and the town came back to life. The brickwork wasn't even scorched. Not a tile was missing from the roofs. Still staring, she slumped weakly back, and cupped her cold white hands against her face.

Martin glanced towards her then.

'I hope you don't get travel-sick,' he said.

CHAPTER VIII

The Anger of God

I

They spoke in hard-edged whispers, as if afraid the man next door would hear them. Even those who questioned why they'd rescued him at all.

'The man's a holy *joe*, Carl. Bible-thumper, all that shit. What good's he gonna be?' Steve was leaning forward, eyes intense. His fist clenched on the tabletop, as if he had an urge to bang the wood.

'*Listen* to me, will you?' Carl snapped back. He paused to let the words sink in, flicking his gaze from face to face around the kitchen table. Steve and Neil and Julie. The inner core. The ones he *must* convince.

'He's got a way with people – like I said. These guys I've talked to couldn't hear enough. They said he made them want to *take* their freedom.'

Steve couldn't help snorting. 'You mean these nutters, right?'

Carl's face frosted over. 'Don't call them that,' he murmured.

Julie quickly backed him up – averting a collision as well as saying what she felt. 'You know why people end up in those places, Steve: because the state can't cope with *visionaries*, that's all . . .'

'Yeah, but come on, some of them are out of it, aren't they? Fucking mental.'

'Not these,' Carl said, still dangerously quiet.

'And one of them, remember, just got beaten up for getting off his backside.' That from Neil – the quiet one, who made his sayings count. A practical point, beyond the one at issue.

Steve slumped back morosely. For a moment they sat looking at the guns. The sawn-off four-ten shotgun, like a double-barrelled pistol. The bigger, wood-stocked farmer's gun, truncated in its turn. A Mosburgh pump-action, and a recommissioned Uzi, the latter with a clip of home-made rounds. Pistols and revolvers, too. The game was now being played for serious stakes.

The prospect was a daunting one: it weighed upon them all. Easy enough to talk of revolution, and fan the flames of hate among the poor. No big deal to scare the rich, or trash the BNP. But once they'd picked these weapons up, the State would move at once to wipe them out. One small guerrilla band against the forces of oppression. They had so much to do, and there would be so little time.

Unless they got the wider struggle going.

'So okay . . .' Steve came back again, with just a hint of give. 'He's got influence. So how're we going to use it?'

Carl scratched his cheek. 'Just leave that to me.'

'What's he gonna do, preach sweetness and light?'

'*Maybe* . . . to the people in the shit. He'll make them really want it, too. But then he's going to tell them how to get it. Not by voting, not by waiting and not by praying, neither. He'll get them off their knees at last. They're going to have to *fight*.'

'And what's religion got to do with that?' Steve grumbled.

'You should take a look at the Third World, mate. They know how to use it there. Hang its superstitions on the struggle. And with this bloke . . . Dominicain . . . we can do the same thing here.'

'Except that people here don't believe in that crap any more,' was Neil's objection.

'Maybe they will – if they're desperate enough. 'Cause that's the way religion *works*. People get infected when their system's running down. You've seen it breed; you've seen the power it has. Just think if we can harness that . . .'

The others listened, too absorbed to nod. Like him, they'd picked up echoes of that Third World gospel message – and focused on the call to arms, the struggle for the poor. And Carl was sure Dominicain was carrying that strain of the infection: a liberating pestilence of anger and revenge.

2

The voice had told him where to find the virus.

In fact, he'd crossed its carrier's trail before. Someone he knew had *heard* this preacher, raging in the streets. Carl hadn't been interested – despite the fact the man had got arrested. Such people wanted discipline: obedience to their god. Diverse, dissenting voices didn't feature in their plan.

New chains for old. And yet the guy who'd heard him was intrigued. The message had been full of anger: rage against the rich. More politics than piety. But Carl had simply shrugged that off, and cracked another can.

This had been a year ago, the other bloke recalled. The preacher man had not appeared again. Another martyr to the state. Carl hadn't been too bothered. But then the voice had made him think again.

The first time he had heard it, he'd woken up engulfed in sweaty dread. The thing was much too clear to be a dream – as if an unseen mouth had whispered wetly in his ear. Julie, there beside him on the mattress, had shifted once and murmured in her sleep; but Carl had sat and shivered until dawn. He didn't believe in ghosts, but he was willing to rethink that. Anything was better than the thought of going mad.

In the following weeks, the voice grew more insistent. He started to hear it in his waking moments too. He tried to shut the whispers out; they drove him to distraction. Just his name at first, as if someone was still catching his attention. Then words which formed as clearly as a thought inside his head.

Turn the black dog loose, and watch him run.

The dreams had started coming then. The voice was there behind them, he was quite convinced of that. Cause and effect, quite simple – like horror films and nightmares when he'd been a little kid. The dreams that racked him now were full of darkness: racing like a river under ground. The sense was one of chaos – liberation. The prison-hulk of state had broken up. He saw its rotting timbers swept away.

(Julie gave up soothing him, and made her bed elsewhere. Pissed off with being prodded, soaked with sweat and woken up.)

Another time, he saw the power had failed. The lamps had gone out *everywhere*. The world of rules was paralysed, its spying cameras blinded. And now the people rose to claim their due . . .

He began, despite his fear, to grow accustomed. The voice was like a pulse of intuition. It had shown him where to find two men. Both had been discharged from the psychiatric unit where the preacher was being kept. One by one he sought them out, and listened to their tales.

One was so inspired, he'd later tried to raise a mob and terrorize a middle-class estate. The cops had put that rising down, protected the rich bastards, but it showed the powers this crazy preacher had. Powers of insurrection and revolt. Whatever his religion, he needed to be out.

Turn the black dog loose, the whisper said.

Carl had called the group together; told them that a leader of the struggle was being held in hospital against his will. The phoney war was over. It was time to launch a raid.

And the voice had put those words into his head. *Domini Canis*. Where else could they have come from? He'd never studied Latin in his life. And sure enough, they'd had the right effect. The man had recognized them, and come at once. Carl had felt a heady thrill of power in that moment – even through the psyched-up buzz of leading the attack. The words had come from *outside*, and he'd used them.

As for *where* they'd come from . . . He didn't try to think on that too deeply. Perhaps there was some power in the general unconscious, at last reaching critical mass. Perhaps a mind like his could pick it up. Or perhaps there really was a god – more ruthless than his priests had ever dreamed.

Whatever, he was clear about one thing: he wasn't mad.

He gave the door a cautious knock, and pushed it open. The light from the room beyond flickered: a single candle burning on the salvaged chest-of-drawers. The Bible and the rosary lay next to it; the diamond glittered coldly in the glow. Carl guessed it wasn't real – it couldn't be. He wondered what it signified, but didn't really care.

Dominicain was sitting on the edge of the bed, still dressed as he'd been when they'd bundled him into the van. His face came up, eyes wary. He'd hardly said a word since he'd been brought here.

The man was clearly living in a world of his own. Fanaticism had stripped him to the basics of his cause. He'd been detained in hospital for a year, but he might as well have been locked up there since birth. His attitude to everything was watchful and suspicious. Everyday items seemed to strike him as bizarre.

Except for fags, of course. Carl produced a packet, and saw a dark light in the other's eyes.

'Heard you had a taste for these.' He crossed the room and proffered them. The Preacher took the packet – and noticed the revolver in Carl's waistband. His brows quirked down, intrigued.

'Anything else you want?' Carl asked.

'Some water and some bread,' the other mumbled, thoughtful. Carl nodded, and was heading for the door when Dominicain spoke again.

'What is the instrument you bear?'

'Try it yourself,' Carl told him drily.

The pistol was unloaded; he'd just cleaned it. He tossed the thing across the room, and Dominicain caught it smartly; sat weighing it for more than a moment, his gaze downcast. With his coat and stained pyjamas, his muffler and his gloves, he looked to Carl like a man who'd overslept beyond redemption, up and dressing with half his mind still senseless. But then he raised eyes which – in the shade of his tousled, grizzled hair – were agleam with cold, clear thought.

He'd never held a gun before; but his fingers fitted the grip as if by instinct. His curious thumb sought out a moving part that clicked beneath its pressure. The sound was sharp – and strangely rousing. He lifted the weapon to his ear, and listened. Then focused on the other man once more.

'This is a weapon, yes? A fire-arm.'

'Yeah.'

'You will show me how to wield it.'

'All in good time,' Carl told him, and went out.

Dominicain laid the gun aside, and leaned over to the candle: sucked living flame into a cigarette. He sat back, drawing smoke into his lungs. Still staring at the candle, as its flame grew quiet again.

The tongue of gold expanded, losing focus as he watched.

3

The sun was almost down behind the dark slope of the hillside; its light was pale and waning, like white gold. It shone right through the crumbled church, above him on the hill. The place appeared deserted, its window-holes like sightless eyes that glowed with borrowed light. But the Preacher kept on toiling up towards it.

He reached the gaping doorway, and peered through. The building's roof had fallen in; the nave was heaped with rubble. Everything was silent. He hesitated briefly; then stepped forward.

A glimpse of sombre figures, ranged around the gutted shell – and then a sword-blade flashed at him, and nicked his stubbled throat. It stayed there, pressing coldly on his skin. Swallowing, he felt the keen edge scrape some hair away.

Its owner held the weapon at arm's length. He had a cruel face, and sea-grey eyes. The Preacher stared back gravely. The other's clothes were mostly black, and caked with dust and ashes. The garments of a penitent – but he wore jewels too. A pearl on his gloved finger, and a pendant shaped from amber round his neck. Perhaps a cross; perhaps a pagan hammer.

'Easy, Rathulf. Let him through,' a man behind him said.

The swordsman smiled tauntingly, and moved his blade aside. The Preacher moved on past him. He knew these were the Carrion Knights. He'd found their lair at last.

Most of them had risen to their feet, ready to resist, in case he'd come here bearing terms for their surrender. The net was closing quickly now: the Cathar strongholds falling one by one. This church was just a temporary refuge. The stones were strewn with bedding, and the remnants of a meal. The men had the look of weary, cornered wolves.

All of them were wearing black – a livery of shadows. He might have passed for one of them himself, in his long cloak.

The one who'd spoken came towards him slowly, the ashy rubble crunching underfoot. This must be their leader, with his young-old face, and luminous blue eyes. The Preacher prostrated himself, as he might towards the Master of his Order. Face down in the dust, his arms outstretched.

'What do you want here, Priest?' the leader asked.

'God's mercy and yours,' was the muffled response.

The leader paced around him thoughtfully. 'You know who we are?'

'The French call you the Carrion Knights. Black English.'

'We fight for the Cathars . . . and make war on their persecutors. Neither side shows mercy – or expects it. Maybe we should kill you here and now.'

'If that is your judgement, then so be it.' The Preacher's voice was calm against the dirt.

'You want to be absolved – is that it?'

'Dominic preached *reason* to these people. He never dreamed to see this butchery.'

The English leader hunkered down. 'So you are blameless, then?'

The Preacher raised his head enough to shake it. 'We did not seek this thing, but we have played our part in it. I will make a reparation – if I can.'

The other rubbed his jaw, considering. 'You seek to ride with us?'

'Every band of soldiers needs its chaplain. Men who kill must needs have a confessor.'

The leader seemed to ponder that. The Preacher saw him toying with a well-worn silver coin. His grimy, half-gloved fingers turned and clasped it.

'What is your name?' he asked.

'You know how they call the friars of Dominic,' the Preacher said.

'*Domini Canes*, yes? The Hounds of the Lord.'

'Call me Domini*cain* now. My brothers' blood still cries out from the ground.'

The other stared at him; then nodded slowly. 'And I am Athelgar. These are the Raven's Breed. If you seek justice, then come with us.' Taking the Preacher's arm, he helped him up.

Dominicain looked round at his new brethren. Their faces were still bleak. Slowly they dispersed to settle down amid the ruin. The man called Rathulf had been counting coins, using a broken tombstone as a table. A dark-haired youth was sitting in an empty window arch, studying a skull as if he sought to read its mind. He sensed the Preacher's gaze, and turned his head – and suddenly the boy became a girl. Dominicain stood frowning in surprise. She wore her hair short, like a page; her face was calm and haunting. Her dark eyes must be deeper than the sockets of the skull.

Ne nos inducas in tentationem . . .

Discomfited, he glanced away, and turned to Athelgar. 'Why do you fight for heretics?' he asked uncertainly.

The other shrugged. 'Because they are in need.'

'They are enemies of *faith*,' the Preacher hissed. Even now, he couldn't keep that back.

'It doesn't matter what they might believe. They're poor and unprotected, so our swords are pledged to them.'

'They say *you* fight for payment too . . .' He looked around at Rathulf. The latter's cold eyes lifted from the growing stacks of coin. Dominicain looked curiously at Athelgar again. 'Some men say that you dwell among the stars; others, that you come from the grave. Why, then, do you need payment?'

'All things must be paid for,' said Athelgar drily. 'According to the wealth of every man. Where there is no silver, then our wage is bread and prayers. But every one must make his contribution. You know that even justice has a price.'

The candle-flame grew focused once again. Dominicain breathed smoke, and nodded slowly to himself. Then leaned towards the flame, and snuffed it out.

CHAPTER IX

Lightning East to West

I

You know what a wormhole is? asked Martin softly. *It's like when space gets folded, and you go right through the fold. Some people think that's true of time, as well.*

But that's silly! Fran protested – and woke up.

She sat up with a stifled gasp, convinced that he was with her in the room. The belief survived her dream for just a moment, then melted as she realized where she was. She sighed, and let her shoulders slump; her heartbeat still resounding in her throat. A cold, unpleasant tingle faded slowly from her limbs. It took another moment for the night's warmth to return.

The little garret window was half-open and uncurtained. She could see a brightly speckled patch of sky. Was Athelgar awake beneath those stars? Seeing them as she did, however many miles away he was? The breath of night was silent, apart from just the faintest city hum. She turned towards the star chart, but its glow had long since faded. All she could see was what the starlight showed her: a cluster of vague shapes, spread out like mould across the wall. Dead stars now. A galaxy in darkness. But the jewel at her bedside was still glimmering faintly, as if a spark was trapped within the amber.

She found herself imagining the tapestry of Time – all crumpled up and coated with a billion years of dust. Perhaps a moth had chewed its way from Athelgar to her, and linked them on that haunted Heaven's Field.

The image was absurd. She put her head down, snuggled

up again. But her mind was clear as crystal, wide awake. Martin's voice was silent now; his image had dissolved. She wondered if some outside sound had sparked the sequence off. A bat might have struck against the pane. Or maybe flown right in, and flitted round. The idea made her shift uncomfortably. But it was better than the darker one that niggled in the background. The thought that she'd been woken by a very different voice.

Fraaaaances . . .

Burying her face in the pillow, she tried to steer her mind down other paths. One of them was long-disused, but led her several years into the past. Back to another sleepless night, when she was still a student. She remembered she'd been suffering from 'flu – and somebody had called to say that Cruise was coming out. She'd felt an urge to struggle up, get dressed and go along, but Lyn was looking after her and wouldn't hear of it. She'd never missed a convoy yet; to be in bed while one was on the road was so frustrating. By 1 a.m., the mission would have started; she'd sat in bed, imagining its progress. She almost felt the convoy as it passed from east to west, a shapeless coldness moving through the night. She'd fancied she could *hear* the CB traffic, the mix of garbled voices growing louder . . . then slowly fading back into the dark.

Remembering, she thought about her flashback in Lyn's flat: that eerie radio message from the past. What if she had channelled it? Could her own *mind* have picked the signal up? Her thoughts groped further back, towards the car crash. She'd bashed her head – and heard that hateful gibberish, the radio squawking madly in the dark. The Ashman's mind? Its scrambled thoughts? Oh God, had she *attuned* herself somehow?

Maybe that was how she'd heard the prayers addressed to her.

But whose voice had it been, beneath the water?

Discomfited, she curled up tight, and courted sleep again; but her memories had spooked her. She had an awful feeling that the convoy was still out there – still haunting its old route. Still trying, in spirit, to complete its nightmare mission.

She'd heard that ghosts were formed like that: by some traumatic happening. Not tangible like Athelgar, but every bit as restless. And maybe it was her imagination, but she had a sense of *something* crossing country in the distance. Much colder than the mild summer night.

She sat up with a sigh of frustration, and squinted at her bedside clock. Past 3 a.m. already: it would soon be getting light. She glanced towards the window. She'd been awake so long, the stars had shifted. Newer, brighter ones were peeping in.

Hugging her knees, she listened to the stillness. Lyn was just a wall away; her parents were downstairs. She strained her ears, but couldn't hear them breathing. Just faint, sporadic noises from the house. She might have been alone up here. Forgotten.

Then somebody rapped sharply on the window.

She turned her head at once, but there was nobody there. How could there be? The ground was three floors down.

A night-bird, then. A bat. Nervously she rubbed her mouth, and looked towards the door. *Lynnie . . . can I come and sleep in your room?* The wistful thought was suddenly compelling. It very nearly got her out of bed.

Then the phantom knocked again: a single tap, so loud it made her flinch. The square of sky stayed empty – just tinged with the promise of day. Hugging herself, she stared at it, and heard a distant rattle: like a pebble kicked and rolling on a beach. Her mind picked up the image, and put two and two together.

Someone was in the garden, throwing stones up at her window.

The bare skin of her shoulders turned to gooseflesh. For a moment she was too afraid to move. Then the lodestone caught her eye. Its glimmer had become a vivid glow, as if she'd left a hot coal by her bedside.

One will call another: that's what Athelgar had said.

Breathlessly she scrambled out of bed, and went to the window. The garden was a grainy blur, with thick, misshapen shadows at the bottom – but a figure stood out clearly on the lawn. His black clothes almost blended with the dimness, but starlight tinged his head of pale hair.

His upturned face was indistinct – but she knew at once it wasn't Athelgar. Something sank, deflating, in her chest. And yet she felt excitement, too: a tingling in her nerves. This was what she'd waited for – looked forward to, and dreaded. Her respite from the shadow-world was over. One of them had come to fetch her back.

Reaching out, she waved to him; he gave a slow wave back. Not Leofric, either. This was one she hadn't met before. Ducking back, she stood quite still, and felt her stomach churn. The thought of going with him was unsettling. Off across the fields, in that unquiet night. But she only hesitated for a moment – and was almost dressed before she thought of Lyn.

Oh God, what will she think? The question – and its answer – were enough to make her pause. But she knew she hadn't any choice; nor time to tiptoe through, and wake her up to say goodbye. Besides, what explanation could she give?

She'd find a scrap of paper in the kitchen: write a note. Committed now, she pulled her jacket on. The worn, familiar denim was a comfort. She put the cold, bright lodestone in her bag; then touched her cross of nails, as if to check that it was there. Her icon was in place as well, still pinned to her lapel. She was as ready as she was ever going to be.

Heart in her mouth, she slipped out of the room, and crept down through the silent house. Every creaking floorboard made her wince. The kitchen, when she reached it, was immersed in bluish gloom. She groped round for a memo board or something; then heard a noise from overhead, and froze.

Bare feet on the staircase, coming slowly down towards her. She realized she must sound like a burglar – especially after that break-in the other day. They'd rifled through Lyn's wardrobe, and pinched her brand-new jacket. Fran had never seen her so upset.

She moved towards the fridge; she could always claim she'd come down feeling peckish. No reason to be fully dressed, but still . . .

The stairwell door creaked open, and she turned. A dim shape stood, uncertain, in the doorway. Fran opened her mouth – but Lyn spoke first, voice sleepy and bewildered. 'Fran? What is it?'

Fran let her breath out, crossed the room. 'Lyn, I'm really sorry . . . but I have to go, right now.'

Lyn peered back at her, frowning through her fringe. '*Frannie*. It's the middle of the night.'

'I know. I can't explain. But someone's waiting . . .' She could almost see the wheels going round inside Lyn's head. *Frannie's had a relapse, and she's started hearing voices*. Defying that conclusion, she went quickly to the kitchen door, unbolted it and pulled it open. The watcher stirred expectantly; they heard him. Lyn stiffened like a timid thing surprised.

'Who's outside . . . ?'

'The man who's come to fetch me. He's a friend.' Fran wavered with her hand still on the latch.

'Give my love to your mum and dad . . . say I'm really, really sorry that I didn't say goodbye.'

'What . . . what about your things, though?'

'I'll come back for them . . . in a few days' time. I don't know when. Don't worry.'

'Fran, where are you going? What's going on?'

Fran stared at her, not knowing where to start. After a moment she said: 'Remember that saying you told me once – that there are people still among us whose eyes have seen the Grail?' She moistened her lips. '*Believe* it, Lyn, it's true. Things are stranger than we ever guessed . . .'

Lyn took a step away from her. 'God, you sound like Martin.'

'Martin knows it too, I'm sure he does. It's like when history comes alive for *you* . . . except that there are parts of it which never died at all.'

Lyn just shook her head, not following.

'Magic's *real*,' Fran told her; 'ghosts *exist*. Not in my head – *out there*. I'm not mad, Lyn. I sometimes wish I was.'

Lyn made no response. Her silence was a wall of glass between them.

'I don't want to go,' Fran whispered. 'But I haven't any choice. I'll see you, right? I love you.' Stifled, she began to turn away.

'Fran – do you want my jacket?'

That halting offer breached the wall, and Fran could breathe again. 'What . . . your sheepskin one?'

Lyn nodded. 'It suits you. And you'll need it . . . if you're going on a journey.' She went across to get it from its hook. Fran took the opportunity to glance outside. Athelgar's man was waiting patiently. The gloom had grown more watery; the sky beyond the apple trees was paler.

Lyn brought her the big jacket, and Fran swapped it for her own; pinning her icon carefully to her blouse. They clasped each other's hands, and stood in silence. Then Lyn took a shaky breath.

'When I was small, I used to love the twilight. *Entre chien et loup*, so my grandmother said . . . but it seemed as if the past was getting closer. The woods and lanes round here are really old, and you could almost feel it breathing. Is that what it's like?'

Fran nodded. Lyn swallowed, and peered past her, at the figure in the garden.

'But he can't take you back there . . . ?'

'He carries it inside himself. I'll go with him, and share it.'

'Oh, Fran . . . I'd love to come – but I can't.'

Fran shook her head. 'It's not for you. You're lucky. Stay home safe.'

Lyn sniffed, and gave a rueful smile. 'You know what Doctor Who said once? I've always remembered it. "Come with me, or stay – and regret your staying till the day you die".' She squeezed Fran's fingers tighter. 'Please take care.'

'I will,' Fran said, and kissed her. 'Now lock up and go back to bed. Please, Lyn. I don't want you to see me go.'

Lyn stepped back reluctantly, and closed the door between them: shutting Fran out in her dark new world. And Fran turned round and walked away – towards the man who waited on the lawn.

His thigh-length coat was dark and double-breasted; he wore a pale three-button shirt beneath it. The growing light revealed his face, and something in her took to it at once. He looked her age, and amiable, with short hair and a growth of scrubby beard. Had laughter left those lines around his eyes? Perhaps – but he looked grave and wary now.

'Lady,' he said quietly.

'Frances,' she insisted. 'Call me that.'

He nodded slowly, touched his chest. An amulet hung just below the v-neck of his shirt. 'I am *Eldred*.' His accent was heavy. She guessed he wasn't used to modern English.

'Athelgar sent you?'

'He is in Wessexena. Come you south.' His tone was low and deferent, in contrast to the curtness of the summons. He led her out into the lane. Following, Fran glanced back at the house. It sat there, full of darkness, unaware. No sign of Lyn at any of the windows. A feeling of relief welled up inside her. Lyn might regret her staying, but at least she would be safe. It was Fran who had to go and face the Ashmen.

The prospect hadn't fully registered. There'd be time enough to worry once it had.

She found two horses waiting in the shadows of the lane, tethered to the hedgerow by their reins. Only one was saddled. His gesture said he'd brought that one for her.

Fran stared at it uncertainly. She hadn't ridden a horse for years – not since pony-trekking in the Peak. The main thing she remembered was how sore it made your bum. But after a moment's pause, she mounted up. He boosted her; she settled herself astride it. The twilight world looked different from up here.

Eldred's smiled flashed briefly in the dimness. He passed her the reins, and mounted his own horse. Then turned its head and walked it down the lane, the hoofs clip-clopping slowly through the stillness. Fran steered her own mount in pursuit, remembering to nudge it with her heels. It surged beneath her, moving smoothly forward: along the lane, towards the living past.

CHAPTER X

No Graves on Badon Hill

I

The lorry driver dropped them on the outskirts of Swindon. Martin turned, helped Branwen down. She looked subdued and haunted. He guessed this new experience had chewed deep into her nerves. She hadn't said a word throughout the journey.

The traffic rushed on past them like the soughing of the wind. 'Give my regards to Zumerzet,' the cheerful driver called, and Martin waved and watched him pull away. He'd been an amiable type – not cynical about their destination. No doubt he had them marked down as a couple of New Agers, but his attitude was *live and let live*. Martin had been grateful for such down-to-earth disinterest. He was wont to grit his teeth when Glastonbury was mentioned.

He'd only been there once, when he was twelve. They'd been holidaying in Somerset, and spent an afternoon there. Dad had explored the Abbey, and led them round the legendary sites. Lyn (of course) had thought the place was terribly romantic, but Martin had been bored out of his skull. The stories seemed absurd to him; the shops were full of superstitious crap. He'd stand by that opinion, even now. Nothing he'd seen in Glastonbury could touch on the *reality* of this.

But what would he find waiting there, this time?

He felt a sudden isolation, stuck here at the roadside, in this no man's land between the town and country. But Rathulf and his men were well behind them. He peered at the nearest road-sign. They needed to find someone who was going down to Exeter, or Bath. His stomach grumbled hollowly, reminding him they needed food as well. He looked around for Branwen, and saw her standing by the fence. She was gazing off across the open fields. He went to join her.

'Everyone goes by road these days. You'll get used to it.'

She glanced at him, a half-frown on her forehead, as if he was some stranger who'd intruded on her thoughts. Then she moistened her lips, and murmured: 'See . . .'

He followed her gaze, but nothing caught his eye. The country to the south-east looked deserted – right up to where the motorway lay seething in the distance. He spotted two birds circling above an empty field. Birds of prey, he guessed. But that was all.

Abruptly Branwen climbed the fence, and started off across the empty ground.

'Hey,' he called, then clambered after her. '*Branwen*.'

But Branwen scarcely heard him. The creatures in the air were swelling up; distorted and smeared, as if by tears, although her eyes were dry. She heard a muffled clattering, like beaten sheets of iron. And then her vision cleared again. She stumbled and collapsed onto her knees.

Two angels prowled the sky ahead of her.

One moment they appeared as giant insects – the next, as wolfish shapes with gaunt grey sides. Their wings were like great wheels. The noise was jarring.

Like the sound of rushing waters. Like the voice of the Almighty.

The sky behind them hardened to a colder, steely blue. Terrified, she crossed herself. The angels kept on circling. The battering of wingbeats came and went.

Martin caught her up again, and stood there, undecided. She didn't seem aware of him. Her eyes were fixed on the two patrolling birds.

One of the angels spurted fire: a gust of burning breath or searing vomit. Buildings in the haze ahead were chewed up and consumed. She scrambled to her feet and started running.

'Branwen! For God's sake . . .'

She weaved across the rough, uneven ground. One of the creatures swung around towards her; seen from the front, its body looked as bulbous as a spider's. She changed direction, gasping with distress. But something else was up ahead: a dark shape half-concealed by the next hedge. As she stared, it moved and started crawling. She thought it was a shield-burgh for a moment; but then it vented fire of its own. A burning serpent arched across the field, its tail still whole and glowing as its head plunged into bushes and exploded.

Martin, panting after her, saw nothing but a muck-spreader: spouting out manure in the next field.

Branwen fell again. He reached her, and crouched down to grasp her shoulders: stopping her from climbing up again. '*Branwen*. It's all right. What's wrong?'

She stared at him, then looked over his shoulder. The angels had vanished. The barren, windswept landscape was a fertile green again. Twisting round, she saw no flames ahead – just a clumsy farming engine of some kind.

'What is it?' Martin asked.

'Showings,' Branwen muttered. 'A settlement in ruins . . . and angels, like the ones Ezekiel saw.' She looked at him appealingly. 'Did *you* not see them, Martin?'

Martin could only shake his head, and help her to her feet. Her face was pasty-pale, her eyes unfocused. She looked as if she'd just been woken up.

'Sometimes I see happenings in other lands than this. And sometimes what will happen in *this* land . . .' She took a deep, uneven breath, looked round again – and stiffened. Martin's muscles tensed as well; but then she pointed off towards the south.

'That is the hill,' she said.

Martin could just make it out: a flat-topped hump, perhaps eight miles away. It looked to be a hill-fort. But what hill?

Branwen turned her anxious face to him.

'The things I have been shown . . . they are a warning. Evil things are coming on the land. So we must go to Badon Hill. We must confront them there.'

2

According to a finger-post, the fort lay on the Ridgeway, the prehistoric route through southern England. At this point it was just a muddy track. They hiked up onto higher ground with Branwen in the lead. Martin dawdled at her heels, still relishing the mellow afternoon. Birds were singing somewhere; the hillside was a sea of soft blue flowers. But up ahead, the rugged fort lurked grimly on the skyline.

A path branched off towards it on the shoulder of the hill. *Liddington Castle*, said the weathered wooden sign. The Ridgeway snaked on southward. Branwen peered along it, looking wary, then gestured to the fort. 'This is the place.'

'What happened here?' asked Martin, as she started up the path.

'A battle. The last great victory of the Country. We stopped the Saxon dragon here.'

'We?' he wondered, trampling the brambles in her wake.

She turned her head, but not to look at him. Her gaze went roving off along the landscape. 'My forefathers. My blood. Four hundred years before my mother bore me.'

Martin watched the ripples of the wind across the grass, and tried to catch the sound of swords and screams. All he heard was restless empty air. Time had stripped the past away, like rainfall leaching soil. Its voices had receded into infinite distance.

But something told him Branwen could still hear them. She'd turned her face into the breeze. It stirred her fringe, and ruffled her long skirt.

'*Arthur* was here,' she murmured. 'The Annals say he walked upon this hill. Carried Our Lord's cross upon his shoulders to the fight. But this was *their* Golgotha.'

That aroused his interest, though the hilltop felt quite lifeless. Clouds had crept across the sun. The day had grown more gloomy. The flowers were behind them now; they waded on through bracken and long grass.

'Arthur?' Martin prompted: imagining what Dad would say, if only he were here. But Branwen was still savouring the past, and didn't hear.

'They took it from us at the end, and thought to bind it with a Saxon name.' She glanced at him defiantly. 'But this was Arthur's hill, and it is *ours*.'

Martin nodded, not about to argue. Satisfied, she walked towards the fort.

Up close, it seemed much smaller than expected: just a lumpy, pitted rampart and a nettle-choked ditch. Martin was reminded of a World War One emplacement: desolate, and pulverized by shells. The breeze was stiffer here, and yet the silence felt oppressive. As if the fort had not yet been abandoned by its ghosts.

Branwen led the way into the scrubby central bowl. The whole place had a ravaged, gouged-out feel. Martin drifted over to the south, and climbed the rampart. There was no height advantage on this side. Beyond the ditch, a field of rape rolled off towards the downs.

'So why have we come here, then?' he called.

The breeze brought back her lilting voice. 'It guards the Old Path. The spirits of the dead still travel down it.'

An icy little tingle teased the fine hairs on his nape. He guessed she meant the Ridgeway, just the far side of the skyline. Over to the west and north, the hillside fell away, but here they only had the trench and rampart. Branwen came around the dike; it seemed she was assessing the defences. Reaching him, she shrugged into her jacket: the gesture like a barely muffled shiver.

'Enemies will seek to hold this hill,' she said.

He glanced at her sharply. 'Rathulf?'

'Not Rathulf. Worse enemies than he.'

Worse? he thought uneasily, and waited.

'So we must wait here, Martin, and keep watch.'

'What for?'

'We will know them when they show themselves.'

'Well, that's a help,' he muttered.

His tone provoked the faintest smile. 'Go you to the north-side now, and I will take the south.'

'Who are they?' he insisted.

Her brave face faded. 'Men saw portents in the air when Holy Island fell. The sea-wolves came that year, and laid it waste. *Wiking*-kind, they call themselves; the *witching*, in your tongue. It is in my heart to fear they are returned.'

He stared at her uncertainly; then looked back across the field. A few pale bars of sunlight were still poking through the clouds, but the grey air was a foretaste of the dusk. He thought he glimpsed a movement: a ripple through the rape, like yellow spume. Only the breeze, of course. He dropped his gaze to peer into their one line of defence. The ditch was flecked with dandelions, he noticed: toppling like stars into some great galactic trench.

With larks still in the air above the castle, and the sprawling town of Swindon in plain sight, he should have found it easy just to shrug off Branwen's words. He'd fallen in with people who were somehow trapped in time, and clinging to their ancient superstitions. But her earnest talk of visions had disturbed him. Crouching in the grass, he felt cut off from his own world – despite the mass of people just a mile or two away.

Dusk was coming down across the countryside, like dust. Mote by mote it misted up the fields. The lights along the motorway had started winking on: beads of pink that brightened into amber as he watched. A growing stream of fireflies passed east and west beneath them. The murky town itself was glowing now. Martin was reminded of a nebula in space; a gloomy coal-sack filling up with stars.

The distant hum of traffic carried clearly on the breeze. Yet when he stirred himself, and crossed the castle, it felt like he was stepping back through time. Round here the hill felt colder, and more ancient. The Swindon Nebula had set; the sound of cars was muted.

Branwen squatted, brooding, on the rampart. She glanced at him, unsmiling, then looked back towards the field.

'They are coming,' she said softly, speaking as if her mouth was dry. As if she was afraid.

Martin hesitated. 'Who are?'

'*Llychlynwyr*,' she replied. 'Dead men from the sea.'

He followed her gaze into the dusk. A prickly apprehension climbed his spine. 'Coming here?'

Branwen nodded sombrely. 'Along the Old Path.'

'And are they ghosts . . . or spirits? What?' His throat now felt as dry as hers had sounded.

'More than that, and less,' she said. 'They still wear flesh.'

The evening breeze was definitely colder. He dug out Dad's old garden gloves, and pulled them on. Waiting for her to straighten up. But Branwen didn't move.

'How close are they?'

'Very close,' she said.

A sudden shiver racked him. 'Come *on*, then . . .'

She shook her head. 'They must not take the hill.'

'*Branwen*.'

Now she rose, and turned to him, her face a pallid oval in the dusk. 'They *must not* take it, Martin. This castle holds a crossing of the ghost-roads. The Old Path, and the Rome-Straight from Corinium which goes south. If they take it, they have *power* over both.'

'So how're you going to stop them?'

'Badon Hill is *ours*,' she murmured doggedly. 'We held it once. We will hold it again.'

'What, just the two of us?'

'We shall not be alone,' she said – and walked towards the centre of the fort. She sat down in the heath again, cross-legged, and bowed her head. Minutes passed in silence then. He sensed her sinking deep into her thoughts.

A sudden burst of bluish flames engulfed her.

He stumbled back in horror, and felt a wave of cold against his cheeks. The eerie conflagration clung like napalm. Branwen stayed bolt upright, like a monk committing suicide by fire. Her face grew tighter, stretching like a mask. Martin watched her, petrified with nausea and shock. He couldn't drag her from the flames, the flames had come from *her*. His gorge rose as he waited for her tender skin to char. But Branwen's paleness didn't change. The spectral flames were burning without heat.

He backed away still further, away from their dancing halo. The fire was like a beacon in the brain-pan of the fort. Could it be seen outside the crumbled ramparts? Would Branwen's foes be drawn by it? He clambered back onto the dike to look.

He strained his eyes: saw nothing for a moment. The dark field whispered softly, like the sea. And then he saw them, rising from the skyline: a dozen shapes, advancing from the Ridgeway to the east. He realized he was back-lit; they would see him. And on that thought, the shadows started forward – lean and wolfish, sweeping through the rape. Like vikings wading hungrily ashore.

The *wiking*-kind.

The way that she'd pronounced it made them alien – and more real. No dry, historic concept now. Raiders from an unknown land were coming to destroy him.

The earthworks wouldn't slow them for a minute. Horrified, he skidded down, into the baleful light. Branwen sat and burned in chilly silence. 'For Christ's sake, girl,' he blurted out. 'You're bringing them straight here.'

He circled round her desperately, as if she were a martyr on a pyre. She'd gone and sacrificed herself; he couldn't save her now. Tearing his gaze away from her, he ran towards the north side of the fort. He wouldn't see the morning if he stayed on Badon Hill.

He stumbled through a breach in the old rampart. The ditch was like an open grave, just waiting to be filled. He groped across it breathlessly, and started to descend. The grass was short and slippery. He slithered downward, caught himself – and froze.

Something was moving about on the lower slope.

The figure seemed to realize he was there, and raised its eyes. The head was rounded, helmet-shaped; the dusk obscured its details like a scarf. But Martin had the sense of empty sockets, staring up – and felt the evil gaze of something rabid.

It made a muffled keening sound, sending Martin scurrying back. Other shapes were stirring in the longer grass down there. He heard them coming, climbing in his wake. The rampart loomed above him; he had a nightmare feeling that the pathway had been blocked, the castle somehow sealed against all-comers. But he found the breach again, and scrambled through.

Branwen was still sitting where he'd left her; but as he slumped into the bowl, she rose and spread her arms. Standing as if crucified, she cried aloud, and turned about herself – her arms described a ring, and the ancient dike caught fire. Blue flames rippled round it, encircling them both within the hollow of the fort. The flare lit up the figures at the near edge of the field. Martin glimpsed their iron masks and bony, gawping jaws. The *wiking*-kind fell back into the rape.

Three times in the next four hours, they tried to reach the fort. Branwen swayed, her arms outstretched – a scarecrow set aflame. He wanted to support her, but was too scared to approach. The fire round the walls became a flicker in the night; but then, like some grim weather vane, she'd turn around again, and fan the flames. Martin glimpsed the iron skulls, grimacing from the dark. But the weird, ethereal fire kept them at bay.

Towards the dawn, her strength gave out: she sank down on her knees and bowed her head. The fire was just a glow amid the grass. Her body had curved inward like a flower closing up, but still she kept her arms out in a cross. He couldn't tell if she was in a trance, or sleeping where she knelt.

The glimmer showed him nothing now. The hilltop lay in silence.

Sitting down quite close to her, he huddled up, and waited.

He must have nodded off himself – surprised by sheer fatigue, despite his fear. Someone touched his shoulder, and he woke with a start. Branwen crouched beside him. Her face was damp with sweat, her dark fringe sticky.

'The Grey Men have gone past us. Even they fear Celtic fire.' She raised herself, and moved towards the rim. 'They will follow the Old Path north and find another place to make their lair. But we must keep on south, to Glasynbri.'

Getting up, he followed her, and peered over the rampart. The slopes around the castle, and the rape field, were deserted. Beyond, the landscape was still dark; but the air was growing clearer.

Branwen gently tugged his sleeve. 'Martin: come you now.'

He glanced at her, bemused, then raised his eyes. The tide of night had long since turned, and most of the stars had guttered and gone out. But the Plough could still be seen near the horizon, like a scattering of jewels in the brightening sky.

V

RAIDERS

We have made a covenant with Death,
and with Hell are we at agreement.

Isaiah 28:15

Dear Craig

This letter's in my head: you'll never read it. Which I guess is just as well, because I know you'd follow me and try to fetch me back. But this is my road now – and you can't come.

Poor Lyn must be so worried seeing me just slope off with a stranger in the dawn. Eldred *is his name, and he's a warrior. There's no need to get jealous, though. He thinks that I'm a* saint!

I'm writing this from 'in the field' (literally!). I wonder if you felt like this, on exercise with Cruise. It's like we've been cut off from all the countryside around us; as if we're riding through another world. And all the time, you think you're being watched . . .

Look at me: I'm going to join an army! And I don't think I can ask them to make ploughshares of their swords. They're fighting things called Ashmen, which are like the walking dead. Someone's raised them up, and turned them loose. Even with the sun up, there's a shadow in the wind. A sense of evil, waiting to erupt. Sorry, but that's how I felt: when you lot were on exercise with Cruise.

I know you're thinking of me now. You'll never guess how much it means to me.

I'll see you, Craig. I will.

Love,

Fran

CHAPTER I

Land-Waster

I

The road to war was lined with summer flowers.

She saw hawthorn in the hedgerows as they went down narrow lanes. Poppies were growing in the long grass at the edges of fields. A wood they'd ridden through was full of bluebells.

Eldred led her south, avoiding busy roads and buildings. Each isolated farmhouse was occasion for a detour. Power lines disturbed him but he forced himself to ride beneath their towers. They heard the rumbling modern world, but kept it at arms' length. Sometimes it was even out of sight.

That first dawn found them riding down a shallow country stream, with trees and bushes blocking off the sunrise. Greyish mist was rising from the water. The day would be a scorcher, but the early morning air felt thin and chilly. Fran was grateful for the lining of Lyn's jacket. She turned in her saddle, staring back into the mist. Its pallid shapes were tinged with pink, like ghosts becoming flesh. Had Eldred come this way to throw pursuers off their trail? The jacket couldn't keep the chill of that thought out.

But perhaps it was his nature to be cautious. At times they seemed like pilgrims on a medieval way; but at others he was wary and alert. As if they were guerrillas, on the move through hostile lines. And Eldred was a warrior, there was no mistaking that. He had a sword against his thigh, its long blade wrapped in cloth.

The sun rose, and they splashed up from the river. Fran

felt her rider's instincts coming back: like swimming, it was something that you never quite forgot. She leaned over the horse's neck, then sat back as it came to level ground. Eldred turned his head, and smiled encouragement. Fran smiled back with growing confidence.

The day grew hot: she shed her outer layer, knotting the jacket loosely round her waist. Her clean white blouse looked radiant in the sunlight, but she guessed she didn't look exactly saintly. She'd undone the top buttons, revealing rather more than just her cross.

But Eldred didn't seem unduly bothered. He merely took his own coat off, and used it as a cushion. Fran moved up beside him as they went across a field.

'How far are we going?' she asked slowly.

'Many miles,' he said, face serious now. 'I left my Lord at Uffington. The *wulfas* comen from the south, and we go for to meet hem.'

She felt her spirits wane, despite the sunlight. The peaceful summer country was seductive – but the Ashmen were still waiting at the end of the road: as pitiless and grey as any winter.

She wished she hadn't promised to come back. Wished – and knew she couldn't bear to stay at home, waiting for news of an unknown war. Its outcome might affect her, if the hideous Ashmen won.

Her, and maybe everyone she knew.

His gaze had strayed away, towards her jacket. 'I see thou hast the *alyiz* for protection,' he said carefully. 'And yet . . . forgive me . . . it is upside down.'

Fran glanced down, and realized that he meant her CND badge. She'd brought that with her too, as if to strengthen her beliefs. He'd clearly read it as some kind of rune. 'We . . . wear it differently today,' she said, and offered him a rather sheepish smile.

The moment made her think of Craig again. She'd put a different badge on for their first weekend away. It had read:

We ♥ your faces, but not your bases

And Craig had shown up with a sew-on patch: it showed two brooding vultures and the legend:

Patience, my ass! I'm gonna KILL something.

Craig! That's horrible! she'd said, amid a fit of giggles. Her smile grew wider now as she remembered. Yet here she was, about to join a flight of killer ravens. Scavengers with swords. Her smile faded.

'How many battles have you fought?' she asked after a pause. Not making conversation; she was curious.

'Many battailes – yes,' he said. 'With Athelgar. Here in this lond, and over-sea.'

'Against the wolves?'

His calm face seemed to stiffen, closing up. 'First against the sea-men, yes. We did not slay enough.' He said that last with venom, watching her to see how she'd react. Fran waited; he breathed out and looked ahead. 'And then against those men who mocked the justice of the king.'

'But now the wolves are back again?' she ventured.

He looked at her sidelong. 'My Lord saith thou hast saved him, when they tried to take his life. Thou hast seen them, Lady. Is it true they are returned from Under-Earth? From Hell?'

'I don't know,' she murmured. But part of her was certain that they had.

2

The journey south took several days. Sleeping rough (she hardly slept at all), and stealing food. She actually nicked a loaf of bread from a sleepy village shop. The consequences didn't seem to matter. If caught, she might have said *The Master needs it*, as if it were some Biblical command.

Eldred pinched some apples from an orchard that they passed. He handed one across like a mischievous boy; his grin was sly, engaging, his thatchy blond hair almost in his eyes. She beamed her thanks, and crunched it as the horses jogged along. Such moments said much more than all their stilted conversations.

They didn't push the horses; but sometimes, when the ground was good, he'd nod to her and break into a canter. And Fran would flick the reins and follow, relishing the motion and the slipstream in her hair. Elsewhere, they proceeded with more caution. Down a woodland hollow way, now overgrown with shadows – and through a concrete underpass that boomed and clattered with the horses' hoofs. The claustrophobic tunnel made them crouch, and duck their heads. Eldred's hand stayed close beside his sword till they were clear.

They passed a battered camper van, abandoned in the middle of a field. Its windows had been shattered, and the doors were off their hinges. It looked to Fran like wreckage on a battlefield. But this felt very different from the hulks on Larkhill Range. Its sides were rainbow-coloured; there were curtains stirring faintly in the breeze.

The sight of it was mournful and unsettling. They rode on by, both looking: both uneasy.

The sky that day was low, and getting lower. By evening there was just a band of gold along the skyline. They'd crossed a disused railway line, its track long gone, and were plodding south along it. Fran had grown up near to one (some half-forgotten branch line), and used to watch it from her bedroom window. Bathed in evening light as it wound off into the hills, it had seemed like an enchanted road. But right now she felt knackered: drooping in her saddle like a flower in need of rain. Too tired to take much interest – until she heard a stealthy sound above her.

Startled, she raised her head. They were passing through a cutting, and its slopes were cloaked with undergrowth and trees. The twilight had come early here. Eldred reined in just ahead; her own horse shifted restively. She felt wide awake and nervous now. Adrenaline was buzzing like a dozen caffeine hits.

Another movement dislodged dirt: it rustled down the crumbled slope towards them. She glimpsed a crouching figure, ashen-haired and wrapped in black. Waiting in the treeline – staring down.

'*Hrafn*,' called Eldred softly. She sensed him sitting easier, and willed her own tight muscles to relax.

The other man came skidding down the slope, and landed on his feet beside the path. She felt a giddy surge inside herself: not knowing why until he straightened up. She recognized him then, although his face was still in shadow. Athelgar himself was here to meet them.

He came and greeted Eldred like a brother. They didn't speak, their gazes barely met. But each men grasped and held the other's wrist. The gesture said *I've missed you* more than words.

Then Athelgar came on, and took the bridle of Fran's horse, gazing up with pleasure and relief. It was clear that he had missed her just as much. Or maybe more.

'Wellcome, Frances. *Well* it is, now you are come to us.'

'I'm glad that you remembered me,' she said – and meant it, too.

He nodded back, still gazing at her face; then glanced aside. 'All things are made ready now. This night the Raven spreads his wings again.'

He held the horse while Fran got down and flexed her aching limbs. They'd been hours in the saddle, and the ground felt unfamiliar. 'And where are the Ashmen now?' she asked.

'South, along the Elderpath. A day's riding from here.'

'You're going down to fight them?'

'They *must* be stopped. The burnings have begun.' He wound the horse's rein around his fist. 'Our circle is complete again. And now we have our standard – and our saint.'

Fran looked at him, dismayed; then looked away. She'd tried to be a pacifist – and ended up inspiring ancient warriors. And worse, they took her presence as a *blessing* on their war. It flew in the face of all that she believed in.

Yet she had seen the Ashmen. How else could they be stopped?

Athelgar led the way on through the cutting, the weed-infested ballast crunching drily underfoot. Eldred had dismounted too; Fran gave him a shy smile. Not wanting to exclude him, now that she'd rejoined her Lord . . .

The notion came unbidden, and it took her by surprise. She felt a guilty flush, and bowed her head. The man was charismatic, yes; and handsome, that was true. But no, she didn't fancy him – how could she? His other-worldly aspect made him quite untouchable.

They left the track, moved up into the wood. The hush of it engulfed them: stillness and blue silence, though the topmost leaves were splashed with evening gold. Fran's neck began to prickle. It made her think of creeping up on Cruise. Except that here the guards were more alert. She glimpsed their stealthy figures, keeping pace between the trees.

They passed through the cordon, and reached the Ravens' camp. A dozen men were gathered there. Most of them were sitting round, like soldiers at the end of a gruelling march. One or two were huddled on the ground, as if asleep. A few were grouped together, tossing knucklebones like dice. All were similarly dressed: motley clothes, but uniformly dark. None of them wore armour; she couldn't see one helmet. But swords and heavy knives lay close to hand.

They turned their heads, and rose to meet their leader. Athelgar presented her; Fran dropped her eyes, embarrassed. But part of her was tempted to bask in their attention. Leofric was there, his smile as wry as ever; but the others were all strangers. Athelgar named each watchful face. She doubted she'd remember them, but one or two sank in. Harald, who looked handsome but disdainful; and Edgar, gaunt and grave as a Victorian gentleman.

One young man had black hair, and a lean and hungry look.

His dirty leather coat was midnight blue. 'Steffan,' murmured Athelgar. 'He was a Stranger once. Now he rides with us.

'And *Rathulf* keeps our silver. He rejoined us yesternight.'

She turned, and felt her stomach muscles twitch. The face was calm yet cruel, and the contrast was disquieting. But then she remembered where she'd heard the name before. She fumbled in her shoulder bag, and came up with the battered northern cross.

'*Rathulf* . . . This is yours, I think.'

He took it from her reverently. 'Athelgar has said you found the hoard . . .' He looked at her, a thin smile on his lips – then leaned towards her icon, which was peeping into view.

'I saw this script among the Rus: along the traders' road to Miklagard.' His eyes came up. 'Have *you* been thus far, Lady?'

She shook her head – and stood there, very still, as he touched one callused finger to the raised Cyrillic script. Trusted man he might be, but he set her nerves on edge. Then he remembered himself, and stepped back.

'There is no word of Branwen?' Athelgar asked.

Fran glanced at him. His face was set and shadowed, his emotions carefully veiled. Leofric, in the background, looked uncertain; and Eldred, at her side, seemed restive too.

'Not where I have travelled,' Rathulf said.

'She is at peace,' Leofric said. 'Accept it, and be thankful for her sake.'

But Athelgar kept staring for a moment; then turned away, and did not ask again.

3

The dusk was deep and full of rain: a dreary, hissing presence in the trees. The Ravens crouched against the trunks, or huddled round the single, sheltered fire. Someone came and offered Fran a bower made of blankets – but she declined, and sat out with the rest. Edgar was one of the others round the fire. She saw that he was fingering a shiny pocket watch: studying its gold casing as it caught the light. Perhaps it had come with the fur-trimmed coat he wore; or maybe he had looted it somewhere. Either way, she guessed its fascination. To him it was more talisman than timepiece.

'Can I see?' she ventured, hand extended. He looked at her, expressionless – then passed the thing across. She realized it was musical, and quickly wound it up. The lid sprang open at her touch, and elfin chimes went floating round the fire. The others stared in awe, as if she'd worked some kind of miracle. Feeling pleased, she closed the lid and handed back the watch. Edgar took it, full of reverence.

'Where did you get it from?' she asked; but Edgar's eyes grew wary. She realized that he didn't understand. Then Athelgar spoke behind her.

'The countryfolk say all rooks are thieves. And rooks are kin to ravens – as the Ravensbreed are brothers to the gravemakers who follow in their train.'

She looked around. He hunkered down to join her. His tone was calm: no kind of condemnation. 'Between two thieves, Our Lord died on the Tree.'

She dug into her bag again, and came up with his lodestone. The amber was alight – she almost dropped it. 'Thanks for trusting me,' she said, and put it in his hand.

He nodded, and replaced it in its pouch. Then raised his head, listening to the rain. Fran realized that the group had fallen silent. Outliers were drawing in, like shadows in the twilight. Everyone was waiting for his word.

'We all must make our peace with God, before we raise the Raven.' He raised his voice, and spoke in older English. She understood it, just about. 'Each man shall make confession to his brother!'

The group began to move apart. Athelgar's glance at her was wry but rueful. 'We have a priest no longer, as you see . . .' He hesitated. 'Lady, will you hear *my* confession?'

She stared at him: unwilling to say yes and quite unable to

say no. He gestured her towards the deeper shadows. Reluctantly she followed, and they knelt before each other. Athelgar bowed his head so that she couldn't see his face.

'Blessed Frances, pray for me, a sinner.'

'What are your sins?' she asked him hoarsely.

'That I have used the power of the Raven, in defiance of the laws of Holy Church.'

She let her gaze flick up for just a moment. Figures moved and murmured in the gloom. The Raven must be in the wood: somewhere in its tangled heart of undergrowth and shadow. Brooding there, as ancient as the trees . . .

'That I have killed too many men to count,' said Athelgar.

She bit her lip and waited. The pattering of raindrops filled the pause. But Athelgar hadn't finished. Something else was coming up, and clogging in his throat. She stared at him uneasily. And then he spat it out.

'That someone put her trust in me, and I betrayed her trust.'

She frowned, still waiting: wondering who he meant. But he offered nothing further. Clearly he had purged himself by saying that. Some of the tension left his frame. She realized he was waiting for her now.

Ego te absolvo was the only bit she knew. She raised her hand uncertainly – not sure if she dared. But suddenly he snatched at her, and took hold of her wrist. His eyes came up, like pale fire in the dimness.

'Know that I shall call upon the Raven yet again. Know that there are *more* men I shall kill.'

She swallowed. 'And someone else that you'll betray?'

He gazed at her, not answering. His eyes were haunted now. She gently freed her hand, and touched his forehead.

'God give you peace,' she whispered. 'May He walk beside us both.'

He closed his eyes, just briefly, then got to his feet. She followed suit. They moved apart in silence. Fran was left dissatisfied: the thing had been so intimate, and now it felt unfinished. She had a simple yearning to be cuddled. But there was only solitude and rain.

His confession kept on nagging her. So who had he betrayed?

A dribble of icy rain went down her neck. She shrugged her jacket closer, and went walking through the trees. The wood was ghostly, full of faceless muttering, while rain kept hissing downward through the leaves. At last she found Eldred, on his own. Nervous but resolved, she touched his arm.

'I need to be confessed as well,' she said.

He stared in surprise – then knelt down in the trampled mulch with her. She crossed herself reflexively, and put her head well down. It wasn't her tradition; but she needed to get some things off her chest.

'I'm not a saint, you know,' she said, wondering what was showing on his face. 'I'm trying to find my way, like you lot are. Please don't think I'm claiming to be good.'

Silence, apart from the rustling around them. There was a gap in the foliage overhead, and gouts of rain kept splashing on them both. She took another breath of misty air.

'Part of me says, trust in God and you'll never need to fight . . . But I'm not brave enough for that. I haven't got the *faith*. So I put my trust in Athelgar instead.

'Amen.'

A pause, and then his hand was on her head. Tenderly he fingered her damp hair. 'Thou art forgiven, Frances. Go in peace.'

Looking up, she stared at him. His face was hard to read, but full of feeling. Impulsively she kissed his cheek, then clambered up again. Eldred rose and looked at her, perplexed. They stood there for a moment, in the rain. And then a man's harsh cry rang through the trees.

'*Hwæt!*'

She knew it was a summons without needing to be told. Her heart began to beat a little faster. Without a word, the two of them went back towards the fire. The others were converging too – so purposeful and silent that they seemed to Fran like ghosts who'd heard the call. Athelgar stood waiting by the hissing, spitting flames, Leofric beside him with a torch. As the warriors gathered round, Fran slipped across to join them. Athelgar reached her with his eyes, but his face remained inflexible and stern.

He looked around the circle; then breathed out, and started speaking. Still in his old language, and yet Fran could understand it – as if, in this charged atmosphere, her brain could read the thoughts behind the words.

'This is the long night. This is the Raven-night. Let any man who comes with us have his sword in his hand, and the price of his own burial in his purse. Let each man swear to be his brother's keeper. The Lord will feed the ravens. This is the long night.'

(*Listen!* said the echo in her head).

'In memory of Edmund, king and martyr,' Edgar said. 'Who suffered cruel death and was beheaded by the Danes.'

A reverential pause; then Rathulf spoke. 'And lo, a wolf was sent, by God, to guard King Edmund's head. And as the king's folk wandered through the wood, they called: "Where are you, friend?" And "*Here! Here! Here!*" the head cried out. And thus they found the grey wolf, with the head between his paws . . .'

Leofric stepped forward, and took up the liturgy. 'That winter came Healfdene, Ivar's brother, into Wessex, with twenty-three ships. And there he was slain, with eight hundred of his men. And there the banner was taken which men call Raven.'

Athelgar nodded. 'And who possessed the field at Brunanburh?'

'The black Raven,' said Eldred, 'with the white-tailed eagle, and the grey wolf of the woods.'

She listened to their ritual, enthralled. And then Leofric raised his torch, and let the way into the deeper wood. The Ravens filed after him, like friars in procession. Fran stayed close to Athelgar; the thud of her heart was almost bruising now. The torch pushed back the shadows, though the rain unfurled a scarf of musty smoke.

They came to a deep hollow, still covered by the canopy above. The leaves were rustling dankly – and something big was moving in the dark. Athelgar had halted by Leofric, on the rim. Unthinkingly she took his arm; he clasped and squeezed her hand, still gazing downward. A wordless murmur went from mouth to mouth. Reverence or fear – she couldn't tell.

And then the Raven standard was brought up into the light.

One of the warriors carried it, of course; but that first moment flooded her with dread. The thing was like a head upon a pikestaff, with a trailing shroud attached. It seemed to hover, floating in the gloom. Then the bearer lifted it, and clambered up to join his fellow warriors. Overshadowed, Fran drew back. She felt its chilly aura, reaching out.

The Raven's curving head was more a beetle's than a bird's: a black and eyeless beak of polished horn. The *insect* look made something cringe inside her. The sombre cloth was wearing thin, and tattered round the edges. But power hung around it, like the smell of something foul.

This was the *Landeyda* that she'd read of in Lyn's book. The Viking battle-standard: the Land-Waster. All the summer flowers she'd seen would wither at its touch.

A second banner reared its head: suspended from a crosspiece, like a sail. This one was white, or had been once, with three black crosses on it. The middle one was largest, but all three were interlinked. The shapes were jagged, tapering to points. It could have been an image of three scarecrows, or three swords.

'Now is our time,' called Athelgar beside her. 'The Raven rises once again for us.'

Fran clung tight, still staring. The white banner was stained with mud, and maybe blood as well. The gathered warriors raised their swords, saluting the two standards. The spectacle was rousing and apalling. Eldred turned to look at her, his handsome face intense.

'Thou hast seen the portents, Lady Frances? Fiery lights in the southern sky. Omens of *war*.'

CHAPTER II

Bone Fire

I

The little girl was dawdling, with dusk at her heels. The wood was dense and hushed with it already. The way they'd come was fading, like a long-forgotten road. Humming to herself, she didn't notice. Ahead, the evening opened out: the hills seemed bathed with butter. But here between the trees, the day had withered – starved of light.

Her mother glanced back. A second girl was with her, even younger; holding hands. 'Come *on*, Sophie. Hurry up.'

Sophie trotted forward . . . and slowed again. Her little face looked sulky. She was holding a thin stick, and swiped at trees and bushes as she passed them. One backhand swing set bluebells nodding – and ruffled Eldred's hair. Prone beside the path, he didn't stir. Perhaps she even glimpsed him from the corner of her eye, but her idle, sullen mind made no connection. Just shadow, and a patch of straw. His eyes remained unblinking, as the flowers – just as blue – grew still again.

The mother smiled down at her younger daughter. *Nearly home*, her fond expression said.

Fran crouched very still, and watched them passing. Fear filled her throat like a nauseous lump. She could feel the Ravens waiting all around her, as motionless and patient as the trees.

Across the path, the wood was thick with twilight. Nothing had moved, nor made a sound. But the absence of noise just emphasized the *presence*. Over there, just yards away. They hadn't heard a bird for half an hour.

It seemed the mother sensed it too. Her pretty face grew troubled as Fran watched. The woman turned her head and looked towards her – and right through her. Fran felt almost spectral then: a part of all these shadows. The eerie hush, the brooding wood; the Ravens, barely breathing . . .

'Sophie!' the woman called again, her voice more brittle now.

For God's sake, hurry up, Fran thought.

Sophie came along, still dawdling. Still secure, within her small horizon. Fran risked a glance at Athelgar. Even knowing where he was, she had to stare before she saw him. He might have been a carving from the tree he stood against. His hair was grey as ashes in the twilight. His profile was like stone.

Something snapped and rustled in the undergrowth, quite close. Fran jumped – then realized it was just a stoat or something. Sophie heard it too, and paused again. Curiously, she peered into the trees. The darkness loomed behind her, like a wave about to break.

No time to think or hesitate. Fran slipped forward, crouching low: a stealthy forest ghost. Sophie saw her coming, and waited with wide eyes. Fran crept up close, and put her finger to her lips.

'Sophie – go with your mum now. *Hurry*.'

The little girl complied, and Fran drew back: crouching down again amid the leaves. God, she felt exposed here – right up against the edge. The path was like an ineffectual firebreak. A rush of flames could leap it in one go . . .

'There's someone in the trees, Mummy.'

'What?'

'A lady in the trees, I *saw* her.'

The mother grasped her daughter's hand, and hurried both girls off along the path. Fran raised her head and watched them go, heading for the afterglow beyond the funnelled gloom. She felt the briefest yearning to go with them; but the road would be too long – and much too hard.

A Raven stirred beside her; she glimpsed his pale eyes staring through the leaves. Once more she thought of stealthy special forces, on a mission from the past into the hostile modern world. That afternoon, with Athelgar, she'd felt like one of them. They'd crawled across a grassy field to peer towards the road. Cars were passing to and fro, oblivious. The sunlit countryside had the atmosphere of enemy territory.

Athelgar had pointed out the Elderpath – the Ridgeway. Nothing was moving on it. But scouts had said the Ashmen would be following that route.

'There is a giants' *bury*, near to Swine-Down,' he had said, while crickets chirped and rustled all around them. 'We thought they would await us there but they have kept on coming. As if they shun that hill . . .'

And then she heard a shifting in the undergrowth ahead, and came back to the present with a start. For a moment nothing moved beyond the path; there was just the veil of still, suspended dusk. Then a metal face rose up: sinister and eyeless, like an iron hockey-mask. Fran felt her muscles clench, and shrank away.

The sockets gazed towards her for a moment. Then twigs began to snap and pop; the shadows started moving. Death's head helmets leered between the leaves. Fran kept stepping backwards, her heart now pumping double-time. The nearest Raven rose, sword braced; retreating very slowly in her wake.

The meagre strip of No-Man's Land receded, step by step. The Ashmen crept from cover to reclaim it. She had her first clear sight of them: bony and grey, like hungry ghosts. Despite her mounting fear, she knew they could have moved much sooner. They could have had that mother and her kids.

For some reason she'd never know, they'd let them pass, and live. No time to wonder at it. Athelgar was at her side – from nowhere, like a ghost himself. He touched her shoulder, gripped it: draining off her tremble like an earthed electric charge. She looked at him, and swallowed hard, but now her face was calm. Back they eased together, with his Ravens keeping pace on either side.

Away from the path, denied its light, the undergrowth thinned out. Mulch and brambles rustled underfoot. The claustrophobic wood became more spacious. The air was bluish, misty, round the pillars of the trees. She sensed the Ravens closing up; and looking back, she saw why they'd withdrawn.

A lightning-blackened tree was there behind them, tall and gaunt. Its spread of naked branches breached the canopy of leaves, and gave a glimpse of vacant evening sky. And up in the boughs, the Raven banner brooded – black wings furled and twitching in the breeze. Like a prehistoric bird, Fran thought. An evil pterodactyl in its nest.

Edgar crouched below it, in the fork of the tree; his own black coat made him look like one of its offspring. The other Ravens ranged themselves around the blasted trunk, ready now to stand their ground and fight. A place of their own choosing, in the shadow of its wings. And here they'd have the room to use their swords.

'Guard yourself,' said Athelgar, and gestured her away. Sky-Edge was unsheathed now. Its naked length gleamed dully in the last gasp of the light. Despite the tightness in her chest, Fran shook her head.

'Athelgar, I *have* to stay.'

Perhaps she was beginning to believe in her own sainthood. Or was it a compulsion to be martyred at his side? The sudden notion left her sick and giddy – but more from wild euphoria than from fear.

There wasn't time to argue. The noises in the wood were coming closer. Deliberately she looked away; saw Eldred, breathing deeply, face intent. Rathulf stood against a tree, all ready to spring out. He swung his sword, as if in idle practice. Even now, his flinty face seemed calm.

She looked at Athelgar again; his own face showed his doubts. But when he saw she wouldn't budge, he turned back to his brothers – placing himself between her and the oncoming force.

'Rathulf . . . what say you that their play will be?'

Rathulf flexed his arm again, and slashed the greying air. 'They will charge us in the swine-wedge – as the Battle-bringer taught.'

'Swine possessed by devils,' murmured Eldred.

Athelgar hefted Sky-Edge, staring forward. 'Men who charge like swine can die like them.'

Leofric glanced at Fran, and smiled thinly. 'Rathulf serves two Masters still: Our Lord, and Odin Battle-bringer too.'

'It is not hard,' said Rathulf, still focused on the balance of his blade. 'The White Christ is my shield and the All-Father the strength behind my sword.'

She heard the dry amusement in their voices – and sensed the undercurrents, deeper down. Introspective, nervy and resigned. Perhaps all soldiers talked like this, in the final fleeting moments before battle.

The Ashmen were in sight. Dim figures coming forward through the twilight and the trees. No longer cautious; striding now. Now loping, wolfish, coming at the run – a terrifying, voiceless charge towards the Raven-tree.

Fran took one step back, just one; then dug her boot-heels in and clenched her fists. Her heart was bounding, robbing her of breath. One of her hands was at her throat, closed tight around her cross. The silver nails dug deep into her skin.

Swine-wedge.

The Ashmen closed the distance like a pack of wild boar; racing loose-knit through the trees, but grouped enough to smash the Ravens' line. The leaders had their shields braced; the others hefted battle-axes, swords. Leaves and briars crackled like a fire. Ghastly faces, mouths agape. She could hear their laboured breathing, smell it, *feel it* . . .

The hammer met the anvil in a spray of noise and sparks. The Ravens reeled beneath the charge, and both groups came apart. Fran ducked and wheeled to guard her back as the fight spread out around her. The wood was like a foundry now, all sparks and ringing steel and gasping men. It seemed they must be overwhelmed: the Ashmen too relentless to be counted.

Fran glimpsed withered flesh and naked teeth. Eldred hacked one down before her eyes – it folded up and crumpled like a scarecrow made of bones.

An anguished cry; she swung around. A Raven staggered like a drunk, still flailing with his sword. Blood as dark as wine came spurting out. Athelgar swung Sky-Edge, and it crashed into a shield, forcing the owner down onto one knee. The Lord of Ravens followed through, and kicked the Ashman over – then drove his blade in deep, and ripped him open.

Something grasped her shoulder, and she yelped – but it was Eldred. 'Climb, my Lady, *climb*!' he hissed; then let her go and spun to meet the next attacking shape. Fran backed away, and turned towards the tree. It seemed to tower over her, built up by all the years since she had climbed one. The Raven's ragged wings were flapping slowly overhead. But the chaos all around her now was impetus enough. She jumped to grasp the lowest branch, and clambered quickly up. The battle raged below her like a river in spate. She wrapped her limbs around the bough, afraid of falling in. The stench assailed her nostrils – a stinking spume of offal and decay.

Clinging there, she felt her spirits wither. Nausea and vertigo replaced them. The onset was so sudden that a part of her was ready to let go – to drop back down to earth and be devoured. But then an impulse made her turn her head. The Raven seemed to rustle with a life of its own – as restive as a shroud left in the treetop by a storm. It didn't want her close to it, she realized with a jolt. Its power was *resentful* of her presence.

Swallowing, she gripped the rough branch tighter, and looked down.

Bodies were strewn everywhere, most of them Ashmen. The Raven-ring was pushing slowly outward. Sword-strokes hard and rhythmic. Heavy blades that bludgeoned as they hacked.

A rusty helmet smashed; an arm came off. Bones were splintered, brittle as a mummy's. Fran grimaced and dropped her gaze – to find an Ashman's baleful mask below her. He was crouching there, about to leap and drag her down to join him. She gave a gasp of horror – drawing up her legs so fast she almost lost her balance. The Ashman groped with rotting gloves; he jumped, and almost had her. Fran stood upright, teetering, one hand against the trunk. The Ashman made to scrabble up, his empty eyeholes glaring.

Leofric came lunging in, and took him from behind. Slammed him up against the tree, and struck his skull clean off. Fran's reaction almost made her retch. Leofric peered up, his face exultant, then turned and waded back into the fray.

She braced herself, still panting, and looked round. The breeze was in the leaves and in her hair. She glimpsed more uptured faces, but they all belonged to Ravens; even as they fought, they kept on glancing at the tree. Seeking inspiration from their banner, she assumed; then realized they were looking up at *her*.

Blessed Frances, pray for us.

The Ashmen rallied fiercely, renewing their attack. The Raven-ring contracted, closing up. Suddenly the battle was below her once again. She wavered, with her stomach in her throat; then stood up straighter. The Raven's aura gnawed at her; she fought it. Drawing inspiration from each struggling warrior's glance.

This is blessed Frances, brother: Lady of the Ravens.

'*Hrafn . . .*' she called, as Eldred had before her. It sounded hoarse and timid in her ears. She saw a blade come flashing down, and flinched. It split an Ashman's helmet – and his skull – from crown to nose.

'*HRAFN!*' she yelled, with sudden eagerness. Now her voice rose cleanly through the twilight. Down below, the cry was taken up.

Rathulf circled round and round, his sword extended, drooping – a mocking invitation for his next assailant's blows. The Ashman hacked and hammered at the blade; then pressed too close, and Rathulf chopped him down.

Fran looked on in horrified excitement. The struggle was

ferocious: touch and go. From this high she could see the light, while those below her fought in growing darkness. She glanced across the canopy of leaves. Some way off, on higher ground, a single horseman waited: as sombre as a general directing operations.

She felt a lancing chill of fear, convinced he was the rider who'd appeared on Larkhill Range. It felt as if he'd fired a poisoned arrow at her heart.

A sudden hissing made her jump, and something struck the tree trunk right beside her. Fran recoiled, and almost lost her balance. A real arrow quivered there, protruding from the bark. A vicious little thing with wooden flights. She stared at it in disbelief. It was a crossbow bolt.

Abruptly she felt caught up here: defenceless and exposed. Looking round, she picked him out – the man who'd tried to kill her. He stood there at the edge of the clearing, detached from what was happening round the tree; already hauling back the crossbow's string. His shape was different from the other Ashmen: he wore a bulky, knee-length coat of mail. His face was just a shadow – but the nose-piece of his helmet caught the light. He looked just like a Norman ghost from Hastings.

Then he brought the crossbow up, and aimed it right towards her. She felt her stomach cringe against her backbone. The weapon gave a rusty twang that seemed to split the battle. The bolt streaked through the greying air; she dropped into a crouch, and it just missed her.

Jesus, what's he doing with the Vikings?

The battle was breaking up again, the Ashmen falling back. The Norman was undaunted. Mechanically, he started to reload. His unseen eyes stayed fixed on her; she glowered back in fear and defiance. *Have to keep distracting him . . . Oh Jesus . . . Athelgar!* He was reaching for his quiver when Leofric cut him down.

Something gave inside her, and she sagged against the tree. The wood was almost quiet now – just isolated rustlings and the lonely clash of swords. The Ashmen had been broken, like a wave against a beach: reduced to an exhausted, bloody swash. The last duel was decided as she listened. It seemed like every one of them was down.

From up here, she could only count a dozen. Had that been all? They'd fought like twice as many.

Athelgar glanced up at her. He looked completely drained.

She waved at him; then quickly clambered up. Above the trees, the day was almost gone. But the horseman was still waiting on the far side of the wood. Even as she spotted him, he turned his mount away. A few moments more and he had vanished from her sight, dissolving like a shadow in the dusk.

2

They brought the scattered bodies all together in a heap, covered them with kindling and set fire to it. The flames erupted hungrily, enveloping the pyre, then settled to a charcoal-burning glow. Fran stood back, but felt the heat against her bloodless face. The bodies burned like ancient stuff; like peat.

It was dark now – and darker in the trees around the clearing. Darker still outside the firelight. The Ravens formed a circle, as they had the night before: gazing, mesmerized, into the flames. Some knelt down, as if to pray, but others stood in meditative silence.

Two of the Ravensbreed were dead, and being buried somewhere in the wood. 'Pray for them,' said Athelgar. 'I will,' she'd said, and meant it. Looking around the faces now, she shared their weariness. Eldred hunkered down to poke a stick into the cinders, his face as blank as if this were a bonfire. Her gaze moved on to Edgar's grave expression. His hands were clasped against his lips, the pocket watch between them.

Athelgar put his arm around her shoulders. She pressed herself against him, and they stared into the fire. She still felt sick, and sweaty, and unpleasantly confused. She'd got a thrill from urging on the Ravens; a trace of it still lingered in her blood. But this was what their victory had meant.

'One of them was a Norman – did you see?' she murmured dully.

Athelgar nodded. 'One of William Bastard's men. It seems they have made common cause in this. The Normans are the enemies and blood-kin of the Norse.'

'A *furore nordmannorum, libera nos Domine*,' Leofric muttered grimly from beside her. Some of the other Ravens crossed themselves.

The bones were glowing, crumbling in the flames. Truly an *aeschere* now. It brought to mind the bale-fires of her childhood, burning on the village green on Midsummer Eve. A folky, smoky ritual she'd loved when she was small. But people called them *baal-fires*, too; and *baleful* was the word she thought of now. Woe. Destruction. Sacrifice. She turned her face away.

Perhaps one would be lit tonight – in answer to this beacon. But already she had lost track of the date.

Athelgar spoke up at length, addressing all his men. 'Some of them escaped the field, and Frances saw their captain. At first light, we must seek them out. *Longē lateque*: weald and field and river. Take what rest and nourishment you can.'

'Will it be over then?' Fran asked.

Solemnly he shook his head. 'This is just a raiding force. Their true strength will be mustered in the Dane-Law, to the north. The real war is only just begun.'

3

Far to the north, the bale-fire blazed, and heedless people watched it. The turnout had been good, despite the weather; the hot glow kept the drizzle and the gloomy dusk at bay. Children held their parents' hands, or played around the fringes of the crowd. Yellow flames licked up, and filled the cloudy sky with sparks. The old stones of St Mary's church looked amber in their light.

Older eyes were watching, from the darkened countryside.

At half a mile, the flames were just a damp smudge in the mist. The sombre figures crouched amid the trees, and watched them burn. They'd made no fire of their own, for nothing now could warm them. The rain of many centuries had soaked them to the bone.

The sheep that they were chewing on was tough and bloody-raw.

The beacon's light had drawn them, but they hung back at a safe, resentful distance. The village was a small one, but by no means undefended. Houses had been fortified: built up into robust familial towers. But more than that – this place was the abode of living men. People who had flourished while their old oppressors dwindled in the hills.

Between us, as the Scripture said, *there is a great gulf fixed.*

The leader of the watchers knew the gulf could not be crossed. His knights were exiled from the mortal world. They'd ridden north to terrorize and conquer, but never found the fortune they had sought. Instead, they had been spurned by Death and left to roam these wild northern hills. As restless as the ghosts of their own victims: the starved and bony refugees who'd rotted where they fell.

The beacon seemed as mocking as a damp November sun. He glowered at it, listening to his men devour their meat. Then something closer caught his eye: a patch of shadow, darker than the dusk. It sharpened into human shape: a cowled and muffled figure, standing silent in the mist. Watching them from mere yards away. Someone who had sought *them* out – and crept up like a phantom in the dark.

The leader felt a glimmering of long-forgotten dread. 'Who comes?' he growled. 'Who *dares* to look on us?'

'A friend,' the figure answered, from the dark pool of its face.

The knights had left off feasting. A couple of them straightened, with a creak of rusty mail. Swords and maces rattled as their owners took them up.

'What friend?'

'A pilgrim, who would share your travellers' tales.'

The figure spoke in Norman French. It felt like an eternity since they had heard the tongue. The language that they spoke themselves was gnarled, corrupted now.

'Come, then . . . *friend.* Be recognized.' The leader's weathered fingers found the handle of his sword.

The newcomer came forward – as easily as if this was a meeting of old friends. His robe and cowl were coarse black stuff: as if he were a mendicant or monk. Reaching up, he threw his shapeless hood back. The face beneath was gaunt and strong. The skin was deathly white.

'I would ask leave to share your fire, if only you had built one.'

'We have no need of fire, any more.'

A grim smile touched the other's lips. He hunkered down and looked around, from face to shadowed face. Raw meat glistened faintly in a Norman's bloody jaws. The iron of their helmets gleamed with rain.

'Except to put this country to the torch,' the pale man said.

The leader made a low, embittered sound. 'We laid waste to the northern shires, and let the rabble starve. An *age* ago – but we have found no rest.' He bared his teeth; they glimmered through the murk. '*This* is our Hell: to walk the hills of this forsaken country, and never to be warm or dry again.'

'And how much hatred have you treasured up?'

The Norman didn't answer, but an image filled his head. Of taking horse, and riding down into that scornful village. A hammer struck a wailing child, and crushed her fragile skull. A man was disembowelled by an ugly butcher's knife . . .

'Follow me,' the stranger said, 'and *justify* yourselves.'

The leader raised his dismal face. 'Why offer this?' he asked.

The other smiled. 'I seek my vengeance too.'

'These people – they are not like us. We are as outlaws in the realm of mighty men.'

The stranger laughed at that – and then leaned forward.

'You shall not be alone in this great fight. The Norsemen that you fought against will be your allies now. Kin of yours from Ely have been raised up from the fens. A warlord of East Anglia has risen from his barrow to serve *me*.'

The ragged knights were silent. 'You are a sorceror, I think,' their leader said at length.

'This *sorcery* can give you back the lands that you have lost.' The white-faced man glanced back towards the village. 'They store their power in houses set apart. Destroy those, and they stumble in the dark. Blinded, and unable to cry out. And you can cross their thresholds; cut their throats.

'Join me, then. Be justified. And you shall take far greater vills than this.'

'What would you have us do?' the Norman rasped after a pause.

'Take the Roman road, and journey south.' He dipped into the leather pouch which hung around his neck, and came up with a yellowed fingerbone. 'This relic will enable you to quit your place of banishment. I have my stronghold in the south; it needs an iron guard. The relic will lead you there. And you shall find me waiting.'

The Norman leader glowered for a moment; then took the bone, and clasped it in his fist.

As the knights broke camp in silence, the stranger stood and watched them slink away. Behind their backs, he faded and was swallowed by the mist. Reabsorbed into the boundless thought-world, he gazed out through the sockets of his captain in the south.

A battle had been lost tonight. It made no odds to him. The survivors would run wild, like rabid dogs. And while the Ravens hunted them, and fought to put them down, his army of the shadows would grow stronger.

His captain shifted restively, still glaring through the eyeholes of his mask. The pale man got a whiff of his confusion. This had been a warlord once, a king of the East English, but now he rode in thrall to someone else. Conjoured from his buried boat, to slaughter on command. The ravaged brain behind the mask could not quite work it out.

The pale man thought him into line, and focused on the light. The Ravens – and the woman in their midst.

Fraaances.

He knew she must be weary; he could reach for her again. Sink his claws into her mind, the way he'd done before. But no, the time was not yet ripe. Not yet.

First, the Ravens' magic ring: their gateway out of time. He flexed his senses, searching for a trace. The Chart was held by someone else. And he would seek them out.

CHAPTER III

Celebrant

I

Dominicain turned another page, fingering the text like a blind man reading Braille. A warm breeze tugged the corner. It brought a smell of fertile earth; the grating call of rooks.

With righteousness he will judge the needy. With justice he will give decisions to the poor of the earth.

A stutter of explosions ripped the afternoon apart. The Preacher flinched, despite himself, and slowly raised his eyes. The yard was wreathed in smoky haze; two outlaws were still brandishing their firearms. The others, grouped behind them, talked and chuckled. The scarecrow targets wilted, with their stuffing coming out. A sulphur-smell grew bitter in his nostrils.

(Julie let the Uzi's weight hang loosely from her arms; unable to stop grinning . . .)

Dominicain stayed sitting with his back against the wall. The echoes were receding all around them, like a ripple spreading out towards the edges of a pool. The flat, deserted farmland soaked it up, but the rooks took flight from distant trees, and spiralled up like cinders from a fire.

'Better than a vibrator, huh?' the man called Carl said cryptically. The woman's backward glance was wryly mocking. Dominicain felt strangely reassured. The language was distorted by the passage of the years – but the looks on people's faces stayed the same.

They'd been firing for an hour now – at paper targets, metal flasks, and now these rag-stuffed jerkins. Dominicain had sat and watched, with awe and apprehension. The firearms he'd seen in France were cruder things by far. It seemed that science had leaped ahead; this alchemy brought *power* to the poor. Not even the noblest lord could stand against saltpetre and shot.

The Bible rustled faintly in his grasp. Absently he smoothed the pages down.

Carl looked round at him, and smiled; then turned towards the man who'd just been shooting. 'Give us that a minute.' The surly Stephen handed him the firearm, and Carl walked over with it. Before the Preacher's very eyes, he broke the thing in two. Dominicain began to mouth a protest; then saw that it was hinged, and hung together. A pair of crimson husks fell out: still smouldering like cigarettes. Carl knelt before him, picked one up and handed it across. Dominicain frowned, and turned it in his fingers. Power had come forth from this shell – as if it were a chrysalis of sorts. He felt its heat, and sniffed its heady smell. Carl's smile was indulgent now, amused.

'These contain the charge, all right? The hammers here spring forward, set them off. As for the shot . . . you've seen what that can do.' He dug into his coat-pouch, and came up with two more vials; pushed them into place, and snapped the weapon closed again, like a physician resetting a bone. Dominicain watched, fascinated. Carl straightened up, and walked back to his fellows.

'Does this thing just fire single-shot?' the woman (*Giulia?*) asked.

''Fraid so.'

'At least I know how blokes feel when they come,' she told him sweetly.

'Holy Joe's impressed, I hope . . .' the one called Stephen muttered.

Their voices seemed to dwindle, like the echoes of the shots. Dominicain just sat there, with the Bible on his knee and the strange red shell still fuming in his fingers. He sniffed it again, like a vial of pungent salts – and recalled the other voice he'd heard, last night. The quiet, holy whisper in the darkness of his sleep. The words came back so vividly, he thought he might be hearing them afresh.

Tear down my house, and raise it up anew.

He looked away, across the empty country. The farmstead lay in splendid isolation. Whoever the lord of this manor was, he must live far away: oblivious to the plotters on his land.

A church tower caught his eye; there in the middle-distance, half-concealed by trees. Its weather vane flashed golden in the sun.

The scattered rooks were gathering again. Flying back in ones and twos to repossess the fields. They cawed and croaked like hanged men on the gallows.

Or like *ravens*.

He watched the creatures land and stalk about. Sinister black plunderers, despoiling common earth; as loathsome as *becchini* round the grave-pits of the Death. More of them were watching from the trees around the church. As if the sombre building was their lair.

A building topped with gleaming gold, while men starved in the streets. A nesting place for rooks. A den of *thieves*.

A tide of passion rose in him; a wave of hate went through it. The church was like a challenge, too complacent to be spared; but the gravedigger birds were a sign of something else. Sorcery. Hypocrisy. Betrayal.

Ravensbreed.

Without a word, he straightened and strode off across the field. Carl and his band were too absorbed to notice. Several minutes passed before they realized he had gone.

2

'What's the use of someone who just fucking wanders off . . . ?'

Steve again, complaining in the back. 'Pack it in,' Carl said, and put his foot down. The van bounced bruisingly along the farm track. 'Where is he now?' he snapped.

'Still in the field,' said Julie, peering out through her window. 'I think he's heading for that church . . .'

'Fucking bible-basher,' muttered Steve.

They'd already tried and failed to cut him off, hampered by the twists of the country lane. Dominicain was walking in a straight, determined line, and crossed the road before they had a chance to reach him. Swearing, Carl had steered onto the farm track. The others in the back hung on, and rocked from side to side. Clouds of dust rolled out behind them, settling in the sun.

They were moving parallel with him now. Carl craned across the wheel and caught a glimpse of him, a white and shining figure in the parched brown field. Pushing on, ignoring them – perhaps not even knowing they existed. His boots had raised a comet's tail of dust.

Julie settled back, and braced herself against the dash. It looked like she was right about the church. Another jouncing turn, and they were back onto the lane. The tower of the church was just ahead, amid the trees. They reached it and came scrunching to a halt.

Dominicain stood just inside the gate. He was staring at the building, not turning as they all piled out behind him. Carl was irritated now, but still ready to give him room. Julie's curious eyes belied her frown. But Steve was clearly well pissed-off, and brought the shotgun with him like a threat.

A yew tree in the churchyard was alive with croaking rooks. Their raucous calls were jarring, like a mantra of protection. They sounded both defensive and afraid.

The countryside around them was deserted: buzzing faintly, blanketed with heat. The rooftops of a hamlet were visible nearby, but the church was set apart. Carl glimpsed peeling posters in the shadow of the porch. Perhaps a dozen came here, every Sunday. The place was just a relic of the decomposing past.

The Preacher turned his head at last. He didn't seem surprised to see them waiting. His hospital pyjamas were dusty and discoloured, the tatty scarf still slung around his neck. He gripped his Bible tightly in both hands.

'Ready to go?' Carl asked him.

Dominicain stared back at him, eyes brooding and opaque. He didn't move. The others waited sullenly, impatient. Mac stifled a yawn, and leaned against a headstone.

'We need to move,' Carl tried again. 'No sense in being seen until we're ready.'

Dominicain came back towards them slowly. He halted in front of Steve, who bridled at that flat, obsidian stare. The scrutiny, this close, made him uneasy. 'What the fuck you looking at?' he breathed.

No answer, just that sombre gaze; but then the other blinked, and looked aside. Steve felt real relief, and tried to mask it with a grin. *Bible-bashing bastard*, jeered his mind.

And then the Bible smashed into his face.

The Book as bludgeon – a backhand clout that spun him half around. His legs gave and he slumped into the grass. Dominicain lunged forward while the others were still standing. He craned over his victim, face ferocious, brandishing the heavy book as though it were a weapon.

'*Dice il Signore*,' he snarled.

Steve just lay there, gasping: staring up. Dominicain stepped backward as the others started moving, and switched his burning gaze from face to face. The Bible's spine was bloodied now; but the zeal in his expression was what stopped them in their tracks. '*Dice il Signore*,' he said again. 'The day of anger comes. The day of blood.' Stooping down, he picked the shotgun up.

The group's mood changed at once. Shock, becoming anger, turned to fear. It was as if they were confronted by a child with a grenade. He cocked the hammers smoothly, in perfect imitation of the way he'd seen it done, and raised the gun one-handed. The Bible was uplifted in the other.

'Jesus,' Julie whispered.

'Will you see the poor set free?' Dominicain demanded.

'Will you build a bone-fire for the rich? *Yea?*' They nodded, paralysed. 'Then we will make a start of it this day.'

He glared at them a moment longer, then turned back towards the church; kicked the door open, and strode inside. Carl looked round at Julie, Neil – and glimpsed the same excitement that he felt. A manic, roller-coaster exultation. He followed in the Preacher's wake. The others came more warily, but didn't even pause to help Steve up.

Dominicain was glancing round the place's calm interior. Julie couldn't work out his expression: the rage in his eyes seemed to vie with a homecomer's hunger. But then his whole face twisted into hate. He levelled the gun at arm's length, and fired it down the nave. The blast, confined by cool stone walls, was deafening. Dust and splinters scattered from the pulpit, revealing instant wormholes in the wood. The recoil wrenched his gun-hand up, and seemed to startle him – but he hung on to the weapon, and forced it back down into line. The second blast destroyed a stained-glass window, exploding a kaleidoscope of fragments. Plain, austere light came streaming back into the church.

He kept the gun extended, but both triggers were now slack beneath the pressure of his finger. Dominicain's face came round again: a snarl carved into stone.

'It is the den of thieves,' he said. 'Tear it down, and put it to the torch.'

A dizzying euphoria overcame them. They raced back to the van for the rest of the guns, all but falling over each other in their haste to grab the choicest weapon. The silence of the church began to knit itself together; there was something almost pleading in the pause. But Dominicain just stood there with his shotgun and his Bible, raking the place with a stare that only promised what would come.

The volley of shots began a moment later. The Uzi was an easy gun to grow accustomed to, and Julie started wiping out the saints in every window. Carl thought again how good she looked; then turned the Mosburgh shotgun on the altar, building a momentum as he pumped the weapon empty. Others stood around with pistols, picking off the carvings round the place. The church filled up with smog and flying plaster. The noise was like a thick industrial roar.

Steve was fully recovered now; he'd brought a can of petrol from the van. As the shooting petered out, he began to splash it round in great stinking gouts that sparkled in the sunlight. Dominicain watched curiously – and backed out with the others when they went. Steve laid a trail along the aisle, and tossed the can aside. He struck a match, and flicked it – and the church was full of flames.

'Just like fucking Pentecost,' said Neil.

Fierce heat rushed out at them, as if this was the doorway to a furnace. It pushed the others backwards, but Dominicain stood watching where he was. Beyond the blazing portal, the church was like a bath of liquid air and molten gold. The whitewashed inner wall was turning black before his eyes. A sepulchre turned inside-out: exposed for all to see. He felt his hair begin to singe, and turned his face away.

'Come on, now,' Carl insisted, eyes still bright. 'We've got to get out of here.'

Dominicain complied at last, the last of them to leave the smoky churchyard, the gun's hot barrels resting on his shoulder. Despite the stained pyjamas and his tangled greying hair, the aspect of a sleepwalker had vanished. He loomed against the fire like someone truly born again.

He glanced back from the lych-gate, just as flames came licking out through one of the smashed windows. They flowed into the yew tree, and began to dart and crackle through its branches. The rookery erupted into panic, the dark birds flying high and wide across the empty fields.

CHAPTER IV

The Lych-Road

I

'I have seen men hanged,' he said, 'and I have seen men burned. And now the time is come for this to cease.'

The others sat and listened; hanging on the pause while he drew deep upon his smoke. The man had changed beyond all recognition – as if the torching of the church had lit a fire inside him. He'd shaken off his surliness, his stony-faced reserve, and spoke now with a dark, magnetic zeal. His tone of voice was quiet and insistent. The rich, Italian accent was compelling in itself.

Carl was in no doubt that he was speaking his delusions. But so long as *he* believed them, that was all that really mattered. True or false, the memories would serve to drive his engine.

Sitting back, detached again, he couldn't help but feel a tinge of admiration. The bastard had charisma, there was no denying that. Carl himself had been sucked in, the day they'd done the church. Julie, in the corner, had a rapt look on her face as if she'd swallowed every word he'd said.

Dominicain breathed out. His gaze was dark and brooding now. He looked from face to face.

'And I have seen the common men *betrayed*. Left to die, or live as slaves, by those who could have saved them. *Listen*. I will tell you who I mean . . .'

2

He remembered a great fire burning in the open. Its light bathed watching faces in a yellow-orange glow. He'd seen it from a distance, through the gathering dusk, and turned along the rutted lane towards it. The village that he came upon was dark and half-deserted; but the people of the fields had gathered here around the light. Thorns and brambles crackled in the heart of the fire, but rotten wood was heaped on it as well. The Death's decaying legacy was being cleansed at last.

The faces were relaxed, and some were laughing. Others seemed more pensive, staring deep into the flames. Sparks whirled up and hovered, like a swarm against the murky evening sky.

They greeted him warily, then saw the habit that he wore, still vaguely white beneath his caped black cloak. His friar's tonsure had grown out long since. Heartened, they let him share their meal: respectful of a preacher on the road. He sat and ate their rough dark bread, and chewed their *Englysshe* language. The Death had quit the land at last, a smiling woman said. She made it sound like dawn after the longest, blackest night. A grizzled ploughman told him that the life was better now; that commoners could claim a higher wage. See, the fields were planted and the dead wood being burned. And once again he heard the stalwart murmurs – that things must *change*, between the lords and commons.

It warmed his heart to be among these people; but none of them could help him in his quest. He asked, but got no answers. Perhaps they'd heard the rumours, but were too afraid to tell. A couple glanced away, into the darkness. And so, when he had rested and confessed them, he walked on.

Dawn found him on a hollow way, a track worn down by feet and hooves and wagons. It was overgrown and weedy now, as if no longer used. Mist hung in the trees on either side, muffling every wrinkled leaf. He trudged on through it, half-awake; digging in his staff with every stride. Dew had settled, dampening his hair. The spreading brambles snagged his trailing cloak.

Something clinked and snorted up ahead.

He stopped abruptly, blinking through the haze. A sombre mass was taking shape, approaching down the track. At once he was fully awake. He stood his ground and waited, still leaning on his staff. A horse-drawn cart was rumbling towards him, accompanied by shadow-men on foot. The veils of mist were pulled apart like cobwebs as they came.

The men could have been fellow-friars. Their cowls were up, and muffling their faces. The sight awoke grim memories of many such processions in the spectral morning mist. And then he saw the cart was heaped with bodies.

Convulsively he crossed himself. There must have been a dozen corpses, tangled up like firewood. The limbs of some thrust stiffly out, while others still hung loose. The woman had been wrong: the Death was rampant once again. He felt no fear, was long past that. But knowing she'd been cheated brought an upsurge of dismay.

The man who held the horse's bridle raised his shrouded head. He tightened his grip; the cart creaked to a standstill. 'Who stands upon the lych-road?' he asked drily.

'A pilgrim,' was the low response. 'And is the Death returned?'

A pause; and then the other showed a flicker of amusement. 'So it is,' he murmured. 'But blacker and less merciful this time.'

He led the horse on forward; and now the preacher saw the sheen of blood. The bodies had been doused with it, bright crimson in the colourless grey morning. Their clothes were gashed and tattered, and some of them were missing arms or heads. Once again he crossed himself, more thoughtfully this time. Then he stood aside and let the death cart past.

'And if I sought this Death . . . where should I find him?'

'Follow the road,' a muffled head advised. 'And you can find him drinking at the ale-stake by the well.'

The laden cart receded in the mist, together with its grave-digging cortege. The Preacher stood and watched them go; then glanced at the weeds beneath his feet. The lych-road to a burial pit. How long had it lain, disused and shunned, before this morning?

Once more he started walking – but this time with new vigour. After all the months of chasing after rumours, it seemed he had their scent at last. The stench of blood and filth they left behind them.

The path led through the ash-wood, and joined a broader way beyond its edge. He paused there at the junction, and spared the haunted road one backward glance. It faded in green shadows, like a way to nether realms. As if no living man had come along it.

A distant, raucous croaking reached his ears. He raised his head and listened, then turned along the new road, heading west. The sound of carrion birds grew louder, drifting across the open fields.

The inn was half a mile away. It stood there on the skyline, an isolated bulk against the clouds. The place had a rambling, ramshackle look: a pile of sagging wood and mangy thatch. The upper storey seemed about to topple off and crawl away.

The trees around the well were full of ravens.

The Preacher came up slowly. The ale-stake, with its bundled twigs, made him think of a broomstick: a witch's broomstick planted in the earth. He hesitated, glanced around. A derelict cart lay rotting at the roadside. The fields in all directions were deserted.

The ravens and the crows kept up their cawing. The branches were alive with them, as if this were a battlefield. The bodies had been hauled away – and yet the birds remained. Perhaps their instincts told them that more flesh was in the offing.

A line of horses waited on the building's leeward side. The

nearest had a rolled black cloak still tied behind the saddle. He walked across to look at it, then slapped the horse's flank and went inside.

The room was smoky, full of noise, confined by the low ceiling. Men sat and drank in dimness; diced and shouted; talked and laughed. No one showed much interest in the stranger at the door.

He turned his head to scan the crowded room; then ducked under a rafter and came forward. The air was thick and smelly, full of sweat and drying ale and mouldy straw. The open fireplace stained the nearest faces with its glare. But over by the corner, a window shed a damper, paler light. It oozed across a tabletop, and glinted on a scattering of coins. A group of men were gathered there, intent upon the next roll of the dice. The light showed up their pale hair – and tinged the dust and ashes on their clothes.

The fingers of one half-gloved hand were curled around a coin, and tapping its worn edge against the wood.

The Preacher moved towards them through the throng. The men were talking quietly, and none of them looked round. The restless silver coin was tapped and turned. He came up to the table-end, and raised his beggar's purse. It chinked and rattled dully as he shook it.

'Who will spare a penny for a preacher on the road?'

Their huddle opened smoothly, faces turning outward like a reflex of defence. A humourless smile touched Leofric's hard blue eyes. Rathulf looked up bleakly from beneath his lank fair hair. Aldhelm slowly wiped his mouth, his own pale stare unblinking.

'Behold our brother,' Eldred said, deliberately, to Harald. 'Come back to us from Italie, where even the dogs have souls.' The Preacher heard the mockery, and smiled thinly at it.

A cat mewled in the dimness of the corner. He turned and noticed Branwen, sitting watchful and aloof, the daylight shrunk to pinpoints in her eyes. The cat was cradled in her lap; her hand was gently massaging its fur.

The turning coin was tapped once more; the fingers closed around it. And Athelgar lifted his amicable gaze.

'So, my friend. You have returned, at last.'

'There were many miles to walk, and things to see,' Dominicain said drily. He looked down at the coins. 'I judge you have had work to do, this day.'

Athelgar shrugged. 'The people of this parish had no justice from their lord. His hirelings beat and robbed them – so they called on us for help.'

'And *no thing* shall be changed,' the Preacher said. 'The commoners elsewhere have no respite. Not until the rule of lords is broken.'

'That isn't work for us.'

'I tell you that it is.'

Athelgar stared up at him, then looked round at his men. 'Be ready to ride on,' he said. 'I'll be there presently.'

The Ravens clambered slowly to their feet. Silver coins were gathered up; the gold and copper ones left lying. Dominicain stood waiting as the men in black dispersed. A couple brushed against him, their sidelong glances veiled and suspicious. Only Branwen stayed behind, a watcher in the shadows, still cosseting the scrawny tavern cat.

Dominicain sat down on the rough bench, facing Athelgar across the table. The spill of coins looked out of place amid the mugs and bowls, the smears of cooling soup and stains of ale.

Athelgar took a hunk of bread, and tore himself a piece – then proffered the remainder to the Preacher. The latter took and broke it with a silent nod of thanks.

'Very well – Dominicain. You vanish from us . . . wander far and wide . . . and then return. And now you say we must resist our king.' Athelgar's tone was low and calm, but now his eyes were cool.

The other chewed and swallowed; shook his head. 'Not so. The commons will respect and serve a king who gives them justice. But the greed of lords and bishops must be ended.'

'Lords bring order to the land.'

'This is what I heard, upon the road. *When Adam delved, and Eve span, who was then the gentle-man?*'

'The Ravensbreed are called by kings. We shall not ride against one.'

Dominicain leaned forward. 'Your sword is pledged to justice and the poor. The richmen and the church are ranged against them. The Raven must stand on one side or the other.'

'The Raven takes no side. We serve the royal law, and come when we are called.'

'The commoners are calling now.'

'Enough of this. You know we will defend the poor, and fight to give them justice – but the land's estate is not for us to change.'

'Is this what you have come to, Athelgar? Fighting in *vendette*, like assassins? Dying over pigstys, when you could lead forth the armies of the poor?'

Athelgar just straightened up. 'It's time to find our rest again. Follow if you will.'

Dominicain stayed sitting. The gold coins were still gleaming at his fingertips. 'And what of your *hrafn-geld?*'

Athelgar smiled faintly. 'Give it to the poor. We have no use for it. Gold is a dross that men dig from the earth – but silver comes from the *sky*.'

He made his way to the door; the drinkers gave him room. Dominicain stared after him – then turned to look at Branwen. She'd risen to her feet as well, the skinny cat still stretching in her arms.

'You thought that he would listen, then?' she asked.

'Why should he not?'

'Athelgar is English, and the English are still Saxon. They have the hearts of warriors, bound in service to their lord. They would sooner die than break their oath to him.'

'And you are Welish. Who do *you* serve, Branwen?'

Her solemn gaze flicked past him; then returned. 'I have my lord as well,' she answered softly.

He watched her set the cat down, take her bundle of belongings and walk past him. He thought that she had more to say, that something lay unspoken on her heart. But like the cat, she crossed the room, and didn't look back once.

3

Even now, the memory was rich and full of detail; but Dominicain just shared the driest scraps – the barest bones. He spoke about the raven-men, betrayers of the people. Julie thought he must mean priests, which tied in with his burning of the church. The image was a fitting one – scavengers in cassocks, like big black crows. Figures that she'd loathed since convent school. But Carl was sure the reference was to coppers: the stormtroopers in black whom they'd be facing soon enough.

'They had a role as guardians,' so Dominicain explained – confirming each one's theory as he spoke. 'They foresook it. And now they are abroad again. Be wary of the Ravensbreed. We must show them no mercy.'

CHAPTER V

Fields of Blood

I

The days were close and muggy, that July. People in the wider world got on with all the trivia of their lives. The Ravens tracked an Ashman down, and killed him in a ditch.

Fran was there with Athelgar, a witness to the kill. The Ashman had been lurking near a building-site. They'd skirted it through knee-high grass and nettles, and crept towards the lumpy rubbish tip. The builders kept on working in the background. The tinny sound of radios carried clearly to her ears. Another life, so beckoningly real. Wolf-whistles and 1FM. She'd ducked her head, and kept on moving forward.

The Ashman was a presence, not glimpsed until the final moments. They sensed him like a shadow, fading back into the wood. They followed – and he sprang at them. Athelgar had brought four men, and one was disembowelled on the spot.

Fran stayed with him, gripped his hand; she was still nauseous and sweaty-cold with shock. The dying man's eyes burned into hers. Across the lane, the struggle was concluded: the Ashman borne down into the overgrown ditch. Muddy splashings and stifled blows. She didn't want to look, but had to see. Eldred was knee deep, his arms thrust into water to the elbows, his pleasant face disfigured by his rage. Athelgar thrust downward with his sword, like someone rodding-out a drain. The sunken body shuddered, and was still. The hand Fran held convulsed, as if in sympathy . . . and loosened. The Raven's last breath bubbled through his blood.

Athelgar climbed back onto the roadway. His boots were

squelching, full of slime. He gestured to his other man. 'Put *stones* upon his chest, and let him rot there.' Then he came across to Fran. 'And Edwin?'

Woodenly she shook her head, still clutching the limp hand. The sight of guts had left her feeling faint. She'd scarcely known the man, but he had smiled at her this morning; and now he was just road-kill, so much food for crows. Down on her knees in mud and mulch, she wasn't even sure that she could stand.

Athelgar knelt down as well. A moment's hesitation – then he touched her very lightly on the shoulder. 'It pains me that you see such things as these . . .'

'Why?' she almost snapped. 'In case I judge you?' She saw that she had got to him, and pressed home her advantage. 'This is where a saint should be: right here, in the middle of the *shit*.'

Now *there* was a good Old English word. He blinked; then nodded slowly, and got up. 'So,' he said, accepting it, and glanced back at the others. Eldred had his boots off and was pouring water out.

'Edwin we must bury. He has earned his rest at last.'

Fran climbed slowly up, on shaky legs. 'Where?'

'Deeper in the weald. It needs must be a shallow fosse, but all that we can give him . . . And we shall leave a cross beside the path.'

'What of his sword?' asked Eldred.

'It shall be buried with him.' He turned his grim face back to Fran. 'In former days, when Ravens fell, we drove the sword into the grave and left it standing there. For no man dared to touch a Raven-blade. It happened that I saw one once, all over-grown with ivy, still rooted in his resting-place, though four score years had passed. But latterly this was not so: for men no longer dread the Ravensbreed. I sometimes think they have forgotten us . . .'

It seemed his tone invited her denial. But Fran just glanced away, and didn't answer.

* * *

They scratched and gouged a shallow grave, and laid the body in it. No doubt it would be found in time. A fox might dig its bones up. Unsolved murder; unknown male. The file would never close.

A crudely fashioned cross of sticks was planted at the roadside. 'So those who pass can see it, and remember.' Athelgar surveyed it for a moment. 'We have left many crosses by the roads that we have walked.'

Fran stood there with her hands deep in her pockets. Lyn's jacket was the worse for wear, and reeked of grainy smoke. Her boots were scuffed and muddy, like her jeans. Everything she wore was stale and slept-in. She flicked a strand of lank hair back, and felt the briefest yearning for a bath.

Beyond the trees and vacant ground, the builders were still working. She doubted she'd get whistled now.

And buggered if she cared.

2

They killed again, before the day was out.

Stalking two more fugitives, they came towards an isolated farmhouse. A raw, burnt smell was hanging on the windless summer air. Fran saw blackened brickwork round the shattered kitchen window.

Apprehension filled her like an undigested stone. Wavering, she halted in the lane. Eldred stayed beside her, while the others crept around the silent building. Athelgar gestured silently, to one man, then the next. A tingling pause – and then they stormed the house.

She listened to the clash of steel, the splintering of wood. On impulse she went forward; stopped again. *Athelgar*. She bit her lip. Her stomach surged with dread.

Then the silence fell again, and Athelgar was standing in the doorway. She hurried forward, nauseous with relief. Then she smelled what lay inside the house. She stopped again; but

Athelgar was waiting. His face was frozen hard; his eyes were haunted. She saw his need to share this thing with her. Swallowing, she went inside to join him.

The kitchen was burned out, but the fire hadn't spread beyond the hallway. She glimpsed a withered body, black as coal. Not an Ashman; much too small. She whimpered with disgust, and looked away.

The others were still lying in the rooms where they had died. All had had their throats cut, or been bludgeoned to a pulp. One of the heads had been torn clear, to roll across the bloody bathroom tiles.

A family of five. *Oh, God.* She came downstairs, light-headed, close to tears.

One of those responsible lay crumpled in the yard, where Athelgar himself had chopped him down. She saw the coat of mail; another Norman. The corpse had lost its helmet in the struggle. Its sunken face was leathery and black.

One of the Ravens took a hoe, and prodded at the body as warily as if he thought it might begin to move. Fran looked on, grimacing. The Raven craned in closer, then glanced back.

'He has the look of something from a *slough*.'

'From Ely – I would wager that,' said Athelgar, beside her. He felt her curious look, and nodded grimly. 'We strove against the Bastard's knights in those forsaken fens. Some we butchered; some we burned. And some we led astray – and watched them sink.'

'What sorcery could make them rise again?' asked Eldred softly.

In the pause that followed, she realized they expected her to know. But all she could do was drop her gaze, pretending that she hadn't got the message.

Walking back across the yard, she veered aside and puked into the grass.

They sat there on the verge together: she and Athelgar. He'd wiped his sword-blade down, and now was whetting it again.

The rhythmic, abrasive sound was grating on her nerves; and yet she drew a comfort from his closeness.

'How ever did you get me into this?' she murmured dully.

His whetstone paused. He glanced at her. She thought he looked ashamed.

'You lent me strength, at Heofonfeld. You reawoke my *soul*. But as Our Lord will testify, I did not mean to draw you down this road.'

'What was . . . Heaven-feld to you?' she asked.

'As we rode north with Athelstan, we prayed to all the northern saints to aid us. At Heofonfeld, we called to mind the victory of Oswald, which saved Northumbria from heathen men.' He hesitated then, to pick his words. 'But as I knelt upon that field, I found *you* in my heart. A spirit light and carefree as a child's – but full of strength.'

Across a thousand years, she thought, and rubbed her aching head.

Heaven's Field had been a brutal battle. The earth round there was full of skulls and sword-blades. Even as a girl, she'd felt the irony of that. But now it came upon her with full force.

'And now you walk with us,' he said. 'My heart knew you on Waste-Down, between one beat and the next. And you have taken on a name that shows us that we may yet be redeemed.'

Startled, she looked round at him. His eyes were hooded, studying his sword. But how could her own name be something special? Like Francis of Assisi? Surely not.

'You *shall* be preserved,' he said, and went on with his work.

Fran just sat and watched in puzzled silence.

3

The hunt had led them far afield. The journey back was wearying: a drained, despondent slog. Fran walked next to Athelgar, but hardly said a word. And he seemed lost in thought as well – but flipped and caught his coin from time to time. Crowns or crosses; heads or tails. How many crosses in a row?

How many?

The slaughter-field of Brunanburh, with daylight on the wane; the autumn sky still flaming in the west. Harrying the fugitives, they'd taken one alive. Instinct said to kill the man, and keep up the pursuit. He still remembered how he'd felt: exhausted, bruised, and fiercely *alive*. His weary body driven by the thrill of victory, and gorging on the carnage of his blade.

Just as with a drinking-feast, the day would end in vomit and oblivion. But for now his mind was clear and burning bright. Weighing his sword, he'd watched the sea-wolf cower. And in that pause, he'd thought of her: the Saint of Heaven's Field. Amid the stench of gore and shit, she touched him like the clean air of the sea.

The memory transfixed him – while the pirate waited, panting, on his knees. The Ravens stood like elder-stones around them. The wind was now an evening breeze that ruffled cloaks and hair.

Edgar, standing further back, still held the Raven standard. It spread its gloomy wings, as if to swoop. But Harald, looking on as well, was bearing the Three Crosses. The fighting – toe-to-toe – had spattered blood across the banner. The jagged black designs looked more than ever like three swords.

Athelgar dug deep into the pouch around his neck. He drew out Holy Edmund's coin, and turned it thoughtfully. The sky above the forest was a blaze of pink and gold, the same as it had been at Heaven's Field. Three long years had passed since then, and yet it seemed so close: a memory that he could almost taste. A maiden's presence, full of life and laughter. Even here, on this foul field, he felt her in his heart, a challenge to the hunger of the Raven.

He turned his gaze towards the captured wolf.

'If Our Lord's sign comes up three times then you can have

your life.' He turned the penny one more time – then tossed the coin and caught it. Their captive flinched. The cross lay uppermost.

Carrion-birds were calling from their perches in the trees.

The coin flipped up and fell again, and showed the same result. The pirate took a rasping breath, but Athelgar's stern features never changed. He tossed and caught it one more time; stared down into his palm. Then made a fist around the coin, and raised his wintry eyes.

'Three crosses, sea-wolf.' He looked at Leofric, and jerked his head. Leofric and two others ambled forward. They bore the Norseman down, and started hacking off his thumbs. The others watched him kick and scream, unmoved. Osric was leaning on his sword, as if fatigue had caught him up at last. Eldred, just as weary, turned his head aside to spit.

Leofric, still impassive, clambered up. The Northman lay there, gasping now, his maimed hands gloved with blood. Athelgar stepped forward. He didn't doubt the saint approved of this.

'You'll get no more silver with your sword, you bastard. From now on you can beg for bread – and every day be thankful to another for your life.' He kicked at him. 'Now run. Rejoin your ships.'

The pirate struggled to his feet, and lurched across the field. Athelgar stared after him; then let his fingers open. Leofric moved to join him, and peered down at the coin. It rested with the king's inscription uppermost. The cross had gone face-down.

He raised his eyes, and shook his head, bemused. 'You are a strange man, Athelgar. Who can understand you?'

Athelgar just looked at him; then stowed the coin away. The glory in the west had turned to purple, like a bruise. Last light over Heaven's Field, and dusk was coming down. Her memory had faded too. His heart was dark again.

4

The others had made camp beside a river, under trees. Somebody had caught some fish to grace their makeshift meal; the rest was scavenged kitchen waste, and vegetables dug up from some allotment. Fran ate her meagre share without complaint. What mattered was that it stopped her stomach griping.

Strange, how quickly she'd got used to living like a tramp. But the evening air was sticky, and it felt like she'd been smeared with rancid butter. She had to slip away and try and freshen up a bit. Screened by leaves, she stripped down to bra and briefs, and sat beside the river for a while – letting the water soothe her aching feet. The cotton undies clung with sweat, but she didn't have the nerve to take them off. No place for skinny-dipping, with so many men around.

The river flowed past, cool and clear. She braced her arms, leaned back and closed her eyes. Then sensed someone behind her, and twisted quickly round.

Athelgar was standing there. He spread his hands. 'Forgive me.' Dropping his gaze, he came and hunkered down beside the bank a little way along from where she sat. Fran let herself relax again; still watching from the corner of her eye. But Athelgar was being careful not to look at her. He tugged at stalks of grass with the absorption of a child – then glanced away across the river. The breath of dusk lay on it like a mist.

'Tell me this,' he said at length. 'Will we be forgiven, for what we have done?'

His tone was almost musing – but he'd nerved himself to ask her that, she knew.

'For we have slain so many,' he went on, still gazing calmly out over the water. 'Their blood in the rivers . . . their bones in the earth. Sky-Edge was once christened the Sword of a Hundred Graves . . .' He turned his head and looked at her. 'You searched me out. You gave us hope. So can we be redeemed?'

'There's always hope – for everyone,' she murmured.

Athelgar merely gestured as if to swat the platitude away. 'We accepted the black martyrdom, and of our own free will. But we have lived a weary *age* since then. It is said that in God's house there are many mansions. Shall there be a garret kept for us, the Ravensbreed?'

Fran stared at him. His jaw was set, his gaze intent. The face of a man resolved to know the truth. The eyes of one who didn't want to hear it.

She drew her dripping feet up, and went to kneel beside him.

'What do you fight for?' She took hold of his shoulder. 'Tell me what.'

'Justice, and the poor,' he said.

'Which puts you on God's side, all right? "Those who aren't against us are *on our side*."' She moistened her lips. 'You say how many men you've killed. How many have you *spared*?'

He looked at her sidelong. 'Not many, Lady Frances. Not enough.'

'Even one might tip the scales. A man you gave his life.' She opened her mouth to gulp for words, and found them on her tongue. 'It takes vision to be just, you know – and courage to show mercy. Those are really special gifts; He's not about to waste them. I don't believe He's going to let you go.'

Athelgar breathed out, and glanced away – the gesture more frustrated than relieved. She tightened her grip and leaned in closer. He turned his head again. Their faces were a foot away: it seemed that she could count his every whisker. Each wrinkle in the pale discs of his eyes.

A moment passed. She was suddenly aware of her own warm breasts, grown fuller in their sticky white cocoon. Her cross hung in mid-air, as if to guard them.

Slowly, very carefully, he raised his hand towards her – and stroked his fingers gently down her cheek. Fran kept staring. A surge of heat rose up to close her throat.

'Have you been sent to tempt me?' He asked it softly, eyes

unblinking. A ripple of cold went down her spine. She thought that he might snap her neck, right now, if he believed it.

Her fingers found the hanging cross, and raised it to her lips. 'You know I haven't.' Her voice was small and husky, as if her vocal cords had been scorched dry.

His hand was sifting through her hair; its lankness didn't matter any more. She pinched her lips around the cross. Her stare was solemn, full of trepidation.

The fingertips against her face were roughened, callused, *old*. The hand of someone mummified in time. The notion sent a tingle through her flesh. And gentle though those fingers seemed, they made a brutal fist.

But what of the mind that wielded it? The strange and haunted mind behind those eyes?

'Frances . . .' he said quietly.

The sound of her name made her fine hairs stand on end. She kissed him, pressing deep into his arms. A minute passed before they paused for breath. He touched her face again, as if in awe – then rose, and drew her with him. Together they moved off into the twilight, putting distance between them and the murmuring camp. Beyond the trees, they reached a water-meadow. The light was turning grey across the soft, thick grass. They kissed again, more hungrily, and started to undress.

The song of birds was dwindling – as if the dusk was choking them like ash. The countryside was slowly losing focus. But the opalescent sky spread out benignly overhead.

She shrugged out of her bra and offered him her breasts, then gave a gasp of pleasure as he sucked them. The contact was electric, it convulsed her. Breathing through her open mouth, she stared down at his head. His hair was pale as ash again, but she could see the gold. She let him bear her down into the welcoming grass, and squirmed out of her briefs. He pulled his shirt over his head as if this was a race. Even on his knees, he seemed to loom against the sky. His breath was short and raspy-dry. His face was set like stone.

Sprawled there on her back, she felt a sudden apprehension. The grass was dark, and deep enough to drown in. Athelgar was naked now, his body lean and haggard in the twilight. It wasn't just desire that made her breathing start to quicken. Her bare breasts swelled and sank in growing rhythm.

The Raven-lord came down on her – and yet he was so gentle. Even as he poised himself, he cupped her face and kissed her mouth-to-mouth. Amulet and cross were hanging loose around his neck; she felt the ancient relics brush her chest. She spread her thighs to cradle him, and then he was inside, and she was full of him, engorged with him – a fusion of flesh that melted her thoughts like wax. She arched her spine, and made a guttural sound.

Eldred heard her make it, and a tic jumped in his cheek. He stayed where he was at the edge of the trees, still gazing at his Lord and Holy Lady. His pale eyes caught the dying light, as dead as stagnant pools.

Athelgar was almost reverent. He probed her body carefully, as if afraid he'd hurt her. Despite his need, he paced himself so she could share the pleasure. She wallowed in it for a while – then squeezed, demanding more. Athelgar began to thrust more deeply. She clung to him, adrift in time and space. This was some primeval field, and he a fallen angel who'd seduced her. She felt her climax coming, like a pan of boiling milk: a fizzing, seething rapture that rose up and overflowed.

She came with a squeal, and let her breath out slowly. The flame beneath the pan went out. The surge of froth subsided. She felt her body drifting: the meadow like a magic carpet, high above the earth.

Eldred forced his gaze away. The fields were very peaceful, the countryside dissolving into dusk. A bird was still calling somewhere – a lonely, distant sound.

Fran stretched, and drew one knee up. Athelgar breathed steadily beside her. The rush she'd felt was cooling now, as quickly as the air. Her langour faded with it, and she shifted with discomfort. The flattened grass was clinging to her back. The ecstasy had thickened to a glutted sense of guilt. As if she'd pigged herself at someone's party . . .

Craig.

The guilt leaped up inside her, and she winced. The man was half a world away – but surely he would sense this. Some instinct would alert him to his sweetheart's breach of faith.

I think about you every day, he'd said.

She rolled her head to look at Athelgar. He lay as still as she did: supine, spent. A warrior's body: muscle, bone and scars. She fancied she could *feel* his seed inside her. A part of him was struggling to take root in her womb. A part of the ancient past.

The thought snatched at her throat. *God, what if I get pregnant?* She raised herself to stare at him, then sat up straight and looked around. A soft night breeze came sighing through the grass. It chilled her drying sweat, and made her shiver.

It was dark, in the meadow.

They retraced their steps in silence, stopping by the riverbank for Fran to get her clothes. Both of them were pensive and subdued. She guessed that he was overawed by what he'd dared to do. What kind of man would screw a saint?

What kind of woman would?

Touché, she reflected, as she pulled her boots back on. She'd wanted this – perhaps before she knew it. A lot of things had drawn her, not just his lean good looks. His strong and solemn presence was a rock that she could cling to – and yet those haunting eyes were clear as glass.

But what was more desirable than *darkness* in a man?

Athelgar, already dressed, was waiting patiently. She couldn't help but glance at him as she laced her boots. A man of shadows, sinister and ruthless. The image was arousing – pointless to deny it. The myth of fallen angels turned her on.

Call yourself a peace campaigner? she thought morosely.

Memories of Cruisewatch crowded in. *Blood on your hands!* they'd shouted, as the Convoy thundered past. But here she was, with Athelgar – and God alone knew how much blood *he'd* spilled. Maybe part of her was in rebellion. A part that liked the thought of violent men.

And even now, despite her doubts, she realized that she wanted him again.

Pulling her jacket on, she went to join him. They'd come together naturally, and walked together now. Reaching down, she found his hand and gripped it in her own. The bond had not been broken. It was stronger.

The copse beside the river had a brooding, watchful look. She could almost sense the Raven at its heart. Once more she thought of missiles on deployment poisoning the shadows with their silence. Their highest code of readiness, she knew, was Black Alert.

There was no point being furtive. Whatever else, she didn't feel ashamed. Just short of the trees, she stopped and briefly kissed him.

'Stay by my side this night,' he murmured. She nodded, and they slipped into the wood. The beaten path was clogged with dusk, the branches cloaked in darkness. Neither of them saw Eldred where he crouched to watch them pass.

They passed quite close to Rathulf, overlooking him as well. He turned his head to follow them, a wry smile on his lips; his gloating eyes reflecting vacant sky.

4

The morning sky was pinkish-gold, the air already warm. Cautiously Fran stirred, and raised herself. The camp was wreathed in mist from off the river; people moving quietly around. She realized she was curled up naked, next to Athelgar. She must have shed her blanket in her sleep. Hastily she snatched at it, and wrapped it round her shoulders. Then she turned to look at him. Although he was still lying there, she thought he might have been awake for hours. His eyes were clear and lucid, full of light.

She smiled at him, still sleepy, and climbed to her feet. 'I'm going to wash,' she murmured. Draped in the old blanket, she picked her way down carefully to the bank. The water looked deep and deliciously cool, and she half-considered going for a swim. But in the end she just knelt down to splash and rub herself. She did it quickly, glancing round. Despite the cover of the mist, it was easy to imagine prying eyes.

Making her way back again, she came on Eldred kindling a fire. He glanced at her, but didn't smile. She drew the blanket closer, as if warding off a chill. Eldred's look was brooding and – it seemed to her – severe.

I'm not a saint, she thought. *I told you that!* Abruptly she felt sulky and defensive. She went on up the slope without looking back.

Athelgar had slept in clothes and boots. He was sitting up now, waiting. Fran knelt down beside him. She took his fingers, kissed them, turned them over in her own. One of his rings invited closer scrutiny.

'What's the design?' she murmured.

He looked at her sidelong. 'The head of a man, between wolves. A memorial for a warrior-saint. For Edmund, my first Lord.'

She hesitated. 'That story . . . is it true?'

'I had it from a man who saw and heard.'

The bit about the wolf she could believe. But did he mean the speaking head as well? Discomfited, she moved away and started to get dressed.

Eldred glanced up sullenly as Rathulf hunkered down beside the fire. The latter's face was sombre. 'I share your fears,' he said, without preamble.

'What fears?' Eldred muttered.

'A woman brought us down before. Our Lord's desire will threaten us again.'

Eldred glared at him, but didn't answer. Erik was standing close, he saw: leaning against the nearest tree.

'What befell *your* woman, Eldred?'

'You know that well enough.'

'And is it right that you should fast, while others of us feast?'

Eldred's knife came hissing out, to rest against his brother Raven's throat. 'Have a care . . . *Rathulf*. Or else I might remember that you were a sea-wolf once.'

Erik had straightened up at once – but Rathulf didn't blink. 'If she *is* a saint, he has defiled her,' he said calmly. 'But no saint loves the flesh like this. I think she has been sent as a temptation.'

Eldred sneered . . . but let his knife-hand drop. Rathulf leaned in closer.

'Perhaps *she* is a sorceress, as well. Athelgar is in her power. He cannot hold the Circle.'

'And so?' said Eldred, still contemptuous.

'So one of purer motives must unseat him.'

'How much purer?' Eldred spat. 'Would thirty silver pieces be a reason pure enough?'

Rathulf smiled, and didn't rise to that.

Eldred slid his knife into its sheath. 'A *thousand* silver coins would not be wergild for my Lord.'

Rathulf simply shrugged, and got to his feet. Eldred glowered after him, then turned his gaze towards the fire again.

He was racing through the summer grass, his long-sword in his hand. His brother and his labourers were running at his heels. The farmstead was on fire now – thatch and woodwork cackling like witches in the smoke. He heard a frantic screaming in their midst. Men on horseback milled about, grey shapes against the glare. One turned to meet him, sword upraised – but Eldred lunged beneath his guard, and thrust him off his horse. The raider hit the ground and rolled, and tried to struggle up. A backhand slash cut halfway through his neck. Eldred reared away from him, face spattered with his blood.

The hall was blazing furiously. The screams were now a single, keening wail. He staggered back, and spread his arms, and howled into the flames.

CHAPTER VI

The Fell Tale of the West

I

They'd stumbled on a battlefield, or so it seemed to Martin. A zone of mud and mangled trees, as ravaged as the Somme. He heard the cough and roar of heavy engines; the tank-like squeak and clatter of the caterpillar tracks. Bulky things were moving, just beyond the screen of leaves. People were shouting, somewhere close. Figures crept or scurried through the undergrowth around them.

They'd halted on the mulchy path that came down through the wood. Branwen had been leading, with the single-minded confidence that seemed her second nature. Now, as she looked back, her eyes were wary.

'You did not say the people were at war.'

'I didn't know they were,' said Martin, puzzled now. Uneasy.

She set the pace again, more slowly, drawn towards the fraying edge of daylight. There were people in the wood on either side, all staring in the same direction – as restless as soldiers who had pulled back to regroup. Another tree fell somewhere, crashing down.

They shouldered through some foliage and the woodland stopped abruptly, like a film set. Fallen trunks lay stripped and stacked, and then the barren land just opened out. A few trees stood forlornly, in unaccustomed silhouette against a soft blue sky. Pieces of tarpaulin hung and fluttered from the branches.

'Jesus,' Martin muttered. 'Bloody hell . . .'

He'd grown up with the country at the bottom of his garden,

and taken it for granted as some kind of ancient realm. Fields and trees were always there, despite their changing colours. He'd never seen such total devastation. Not a blade of grass remained. The earth was raw, and rotting like a wound.

He glanced at Branwen – saw her face. She looked as stunned as if she'd just been slapped.

JCBs were clawing at the edges of the wood. Security guards were drawn up to protect them: it seemed that there were hundreds of white helmets. Their opponents were less numerous, a ragbag of resistance. Like partisans defending their last refuge.

'Will the hearts of lordlings never change?' said Branwen bitterly.

Martin didn't blame her. 'They're trying to stop the road,' he said, by way of explanation.

She frowned at that, and looked at him. 'For why?'

'To save the woods.'

'The fugitives are hiding here?'

He gestured. 'No . . . the road's a link, they want to build right through it.'

Branwen's frown grew deeper. She'd thought that this was just some lord's reprisal – harrying the country-folk, or trying to unearth an outlaw band. The Normans hacked and burned like this; the savaged land was terrible to see. And yet the cause of it was not repression, but a *road*.

She thought about their journey in that magic iron wagon. Her mind's eye swept along the road: so swiftly that she felt her stomach churn.

'Best keep clear,' said Martin. 'This way, now . . .'

Branwen came reluctantly, still puzzled. 'The wagon that we travelled in . . . Such things could cross the land within a *day*. This is something wondrous. Why should men stand against it?'

Martin saw the irony, but didn't feel like laughing. In any case, the ruined land still shocked her. He saw that too.

They skirted round the carnage, keeping to the fringes and

the threadbare veil of green. They steered well clear of skirmishes and trampling reinforcements; but the sea of mud had spread this far, and plastered both their boots. Branwen kept on looking, with a haunted fascination, and Martin's gaze kept coming back as well. Each glimpse was of a battle in a graveyard – all churned-up earth and splintered wood and figures using fallen trees as cover.

They came to an encampment, and had their first hot meal for several days. They were treated with the casual acceptance due to veterans: muddy boots and slept-in clothes the proof of their commitment. One man started asking about news from other sites. Martin gave his answers through mouthfuls of stew, so that they sounded even vaguer than they were.

People wearing climbing ropes were in the trees above them, practising with harnesses and knots. Someone took the plunge, to hang suspended. Martin swallowed, and looked up. An urchin-headed girl grinned down at him. Sleeping bags were resting in the branches overhead. They made him think of an Indian burial ground.

'What people are these?' Branwen whispered.

Martin glanced around, and shrugged. 'Tribes against the government – the rulers.'

She sipped her coffee sombrely; then nodded towards the man who'd greeted them. He had a wild appearance, with his filthy clothes and dreadlocked hair and multi-pierced ears. Perhaps she thought he was an ancient Briton – like herself.

'How is he called?' she asked.

Martin snorted. 'Something like *Shagpile*, probably.'

She gave him a cool, enquiring look. 'And your heart is not with them?'

He hesitated. Not long ago, he might well have agreed: dismissing blokes like that as mere drop-outs. But now he'd seen the battlefield first-hand.

'I'm not quite sure,' he murmured. 'But I don't think it's against them any more.'

They finished their meal, their all-too-brief respite. Branwen was up and hanging round, impatient to get going. They left the camp as if to rejoin the fray, then veered off into the deeper wood. But Martin felt a curious reluctance. After a while he had to pause, and listen to the distant sounds of struggle.

'It don't seem right to leave, you know? To turn our backs on this.'

Branwen kicked the muddy path. 'The Rome-Straights were great highways once. But when the Romans left our land, the grass grew up between their stones again. The earth is stronger than the works of men.'

'That won't mend the damage *now*.'

'It will heal without our help. Our lifetimes are as nothing to the land.'

'And what about those people we just met?' He heard his own voice rising; it surprised him. 'They're living in the dirt back there, to try and save a little bit of country. And the people with the power are gonna come and kick them off it. I thought *you'd* understand that, but you don't . . .'

Branwen turned abruptly, grasped his coat and shoved him backward. He struck a tree and winced with pain; she tightened her grip, and hauled herself up close. Despite his height advantage, he could only stare with shock. Her size could not contain her strength – nor undermine her anger. Martin felt a quiver through his nerves. Once more she was the girl who'd stabbed a man before his eyes.

She spoke then, very tightly, through her teeth.

'The Saxons called us *welash* – that is "strangers" in their tongue. They drove us west, and said the land was *cleansed* when we were gone.' Her free hand pulled her collar down, as if to flaunt her throat. 'They would have put a rope around this neck, and seen me hanged. So never say to Branwen that she does not understand.'

She glared at him, still clutching his lapel. Then, easing away, she let her shoulders slump.

'We have our calling, Martin. We must go south. Unless I

meet the Ravens there, the outcome of this battle may not matter.'

She sounded spent and weary now. Chastened, Martin turned away. Branwen stood there, staring after him.

Her hand went to her throat, and gently rubbed it.

2

The noose was ready. Two men had her pinioned, with the rabble looking on from every side. Their foreign, Saxon language filled the market-place with spite. The jeering tone was clear enough, but Branwen knew the words. They called her *stranger-woman*, *whore* and *witch*. And there, before her eyes, the noose was ready.

Her captors thrust her forward. She squirmed and threshed between them. The gallows rope hung stark against the sky. In moments she would lose her breath: the air she took for granted. Her fear of choking made her struggle harder.

Another fair-haired brute joined in – the man who had accused her. Pretending to restrain her, he ripped her gown and clawed her naked breasts. Branwen hissed her pain through gritted teeth. Beads of blood popped up along the scratches.

Closer to the gibbet now, and closer. She twisted with such violence that her captors lost their grip – but she was caught off balance too, and pitched into the dirt. She had a heartbeat's grace, she knew, and then they'd be upon her. But several heartbeats thudded in her breast against the earth, without another hand being laid upon her. The market-place was silent – as if the watching crowd had been struck dead.

It was too much to hope for. Cautiously her eyes came up. The front hoofs of a horse were planted close beside her head. She rolled onto her side to see above them. The looming horse became its sombre rider, a tower reaching up to touch the sky.

It was a Saxon lord, of course. Looking down from his proud

seat the way they always did. She gazed up at his shoe, and saw the mud that caked its sole. A worm would see a man like this, the moment it was trodden down and crushed. Every nerve rebelled against the image. She tried, with all her strength, to struggle up. And then the Saxon came down off his horse. From that proud height, he dropped into a kneeling crouch beside her. Holding her, and helping her to sit.

The crowd kept silent. Their stares were like a spear-hedge all around her. Shrugging his strong fingers off, she clasped her gown together.

The Saxon's eyes were cold, but she could meet them. He wore his flaxen hair austerely short. His woollen cloak and smock – both black – were coarse and unadorned. And yet he had a sword behind his shoulder, like a thane.

Another black-cloaked man was there behind him, sitting on his horse and watching from the edge of the crowd. This one's hair was longer, collar-length, but roughly cut. His clothes were patched with poverty; his sword hung clean and sharp.

Branwen turned her head, and saw more riders. Half a dozen, ranged around the square. She knew them by their shadow-clothes; the silence of the crowd. Fear and revulsion filled her throat.

'How old are you, girl?' the Saxon asked her curtly.

'Sixteen summers. Lord.' The pause before that final word made deference defiant.

She glimpsed a spark in those pale eyes, as if he liked her spirit. Nonetheless, he didn't smile; his stare was grave and stern. 'Old enough to hang,' he said – and looked towards the crowd. 'What has she done?'

The one who'd groped her breasts was standing closest; her accuser. He gave the man in black a wary look. 'The king commands this punishment for witches.'

The ragged thane looked back at her; then reached towards her throat. Branwen wanted to recoil – but his gaze was like a snake's. Frozen with disgust, she let him move her hands aside, and open up the tatters of her gown.

Her mother's silver cross was hanging just above her breasts: sealed within its circle, as round as the moon. Carefully he took it in his fingers. Reverent: respectful of her flesh.

'*Croes Non*,' he said quietly. 'Isn't it?'

Startled, she just stared at him. His fleeting smile was almost sympathetic. 'The king respects your Celtic church,' he said, and straightened up.

'What kind of witch is this, who wears the holy cross?'

Her accuser spoke up gruffly. 'She casts her charms on men, to make them sick. And then she mocks us.'

The young lord's gaze grew bleaker. 'This is a serious charge,' he said – and Branwen knew she was alone again.

''Sides, she's just a Stranger. One who doesn't know her place.'

'Her place being in your bed?'

'Yes, my lord, indeed – by every right.'

The thane was looking pensive now. 'Her beauty makes you sick, with lust . . . and *she* mocks *you* by trying to fight you off.' He spoke as if unravelling a riddle.

'Temptation,' said the other, hastily. 'Just the same as Adam in the Garden.'

'And anyway – she's nothing but a Stranger.' The thane seemed satisfied by that. He looked towards the nearest of his men. 'What does Scripture say, about temptation?'

The man sat upright, smiling crookedly. 'That where there is temptation, the Lord shall also make a way out, that ye are able to bear it.'

'Truly,' said the thane. Turning, he took hold of her accuser, and drove his knee into the big man's groin.

Branwen's gasp was swallowed by the crowd's.

The man who'd pawed and bitten her slid, groaning, to his knees. The young lord grasped his cloak and *wrenched*, to lay him out full-length. Grim-faced now, he stepped away, and let him raise himself; then came at him, and kicked him flat again.

'Can you bear it yet?' he asked.

The other nodded, prostrate now, and gasping helplessly.

'That is good,' the young lord said – and glared around the crowd. 'Two months ago, you country-folk, we fought at Brunanburh. We didn't take that killing-ground for *this*. Steffan is a Stranger – there! A songsmith and sword-poet. He fought the *wiking*-kind at my right hand.'

Branwen twisted round to see. The horseman by the smithy wore a blue cloak, like a bard's. His face was gaunt, expressionless; his hair as dark as hers.

'Hear me, friends,' the thane went on. 'We have one king – and justice is his gift. Three summers past – while you were in your fields – the armies of one kingdom came together at his call. Four kings of the Northern Strangers joined our banners there. Danish earls rode northward at our side. Warriors from the far south-west were with us on the road. All of us united under Athelstan and God. We have not seen another king as wise and just as he. Whosoever preys on the least of his subjects will feel his wrath – and ours.'

He'd paced around the watching crowd, as if to will his words into their hearts. Now he turned, came back towards his horse.

Branwen clambered slowly to her feet. Gathering his rein, he looked at her. Cold eyes still, but thoughtful. 'What's your name?'

'Branwen . . .' *Wulfmar's slave*, she should have added. Instead, she fought her fear, and brought her chin up. 'Branwen, Morcant's daughter,' she said drily.

He nodded. 'I am Athelgar, who rides in the service of Athelstan, the king.'

'And what have the likes of us to hope for, from the Saxon king?'

'Justice, to begin with, Morcant's daughter. Remember that tomorrow, when you see the dawn again.' He studied her face; then swung astride, and turned his horse's head.

Suddenly a voice rose up, and snarled a word at him. Branwen's sour stomach clenched – it was the beggar woman.

One of her own people, old and wise. There she stood, beside the tree, her dark stare full of hatred and dismay.

Athelgar looked questioningly at Branwen. She moistened her lips.

'She calls you *Kicvran* – which has the meaning of *meat-crow.*'

'You know who we are, then?'

'I know men call you Ravensbreed – for wherever you ride, the hungry ravens follow.'

'You speak our language well,' said Athelgar mildly.

'I would not soil my mother's tongue by speaking it to you.'

The Saxon showed a glint of grim amusement, nothing more. Heeling his mount, he moved onto the road. His horsemen followed.

She found them camped on barren ground, beside the western way. The land round here was low and rough; the cold wind sighed across it. The Country's solid hills were like a rampart in the distance. This muddy merchant-track could take her home.

Instead she left it, crossed the scrub, and came towards their fire. The winter afternoon was bleak, beneath a livid sky. She hugged the stolen cloak around herself.

The Ravens sat and watched her come. Athelgar was waiting on the far side of the fire. His horse was close behind him, cropping grass. Even in this wilderness, its rein – and his sheathed sword – were close to hand.

'Morcant's daughter. What is it you want?'

She shifted nervously. 'A piece of my lord's bread, if he will spare it.'

An older, grizzled man spoke up; his craggy face was hostile. 'If you've left your master, girl, you'd better keep on running. There's good pasture here, and shepherds too – but if you're not content with that, the goats are over there.' He pointed off towards the gloomy hills.

'Stranger-land,' a lean man murmured, nodding.

Branwen kept her eyes on Athelgar. 'The old mother says it is my fate to follow you. Even my name constrains me. For *Branwen* means "white raven" in your tongue.'

Athelgar gestured her to sit, beside the windswept fire. She did so with exaggerated care. '*Sable-headed Stranger-girl*,' the lean man quoted drily. Branwen flashed a look at him, and tightened her furled cloak.

'So is it just the matter of a name?' asked Athelgar.

'And honour of the lord who spared my life.'

The one who'd quoted Scripture regarded her thoughtfully. 'You like the taste of justice, don't you, girl?'

She looked at him sidelong. 'Justice? What is that? Why are you come?'

'To keep watch on the border. Your countrymen are restless over there.'

'So they are,' she told him bitterly. 'A high summer we had of it – we *Strangers*. Our hopes waxed golden with the autumn sunlight, and burned with all the colours of the leaves. Then we felt the coming of the winter in the wind. A whisper from the north that spoke of *Wendun . . . Dinas Brunan*. And then your Saxon heralds came, to boast of *Brunanburh*.'

'We were there,' said Athelgar. 'We fought with Athelstan. And now his peace and his *justice* are secure.'

Branwen slowly shook her head. 'The sun is gone; the leaves are turned to mud. We *wept* to hear of Brunanburh, my lord.'

'So why come with us?' he asked.

She dropped her gaze, and was silent for a moment. A twig snapped in the fire. The cold breeze rustled round them on the heath.

'Tales are told,' she said at last, 'about you Ravensbreed. They say that you are murderers and thieves, who shall not rest until the Day of Doom.' She raised her eyes to Athelgar again. 'This is what I hear – not what I see. You rescued me from death, *then* spoke of justice. Let me seek it with you, on the road.'

'You don't know what you're asking,' he said quietly.

'Tell me, then,' she said. Her mouth was dry.

'To ride out with the Raven, you must turn your back on everything you know. And give all you have – including your soul, and your hope of life eternal – in order to be on earth forever restless, defending God's own justice and the poor.'

Branwen let the words sink in. The breeze kept slinking round them. She stared into the fire and swallowed hard.

'There are three kinds of martyrdom, so holy people say. The white and the green and the red. The white is self-denial – to set your face against the things you love. The green divides a man from his desires. The red is blood and butchery: the cross. But here I see black martyrdom: to sacrifice your *soul* for what is right.' She looked at him; then rose up on her knees. 'I am ready for this martyrdom, my lord.'

Athelgar's turn to shake his head. His smile, though grim, meant more to her than any that she'd seen.

'I'm no man's lord, still less a woman's master. Welcome, Branwen: sister to the Ravens.'

3

That evening, she and Martin crossed from Avon into Somerset. The sky above was ashy clear, but the western skyline brimmed with molten gold. They trudged in that direction, through a waving sea of wheat. The air grew darker, dustier. The light became the red glow of a forge.

Martin had first heard the name as *Summer-set*, of course. It still evoked an image of the year going down: a blaze of autumn glory, before winter came like night.

They went down an embankment and across a railway line. The signals glowed like beacons, but the cutting stayed deserted. Stepping between the points, he glanced at Branwen. Her face was sullen, eyes downcast. She'd withdrawn into herself this afternoon.

They found a copse on higher ground, and stopped there

for the night. Martin rooted round for sticks to build a make-shift shelter. Coming back, he found her with her back against a tree: huddled up, her arms wrapped round her knees. Her face was almost ghostly now: pale and tightly drawn, as if with pain.

'What is it?'

'The moon is dark tonight,' she muttered, in a small, pinched voice. 'Now turn your face away, and let me be.'

He did as he was told, but he didn't sleep. It wasn't just her silence, or the thought of that dark moon. Something cold was up ahead, just over the horizon: as if the year had aged before its time. The play on words was coming true. Summer set; and winter rising.

CHAPTER VII

Dark Moon Rising

I

Lyn paused, and bit her lip, and placed her palm against her belly. Gently, very gingerly, she rubbed around the pain. As if it needed further exploration. As if she even hoped that she could soothe it.

No question, this was going to be a bad one.

Pinching a face, she moved along the shelves. The sun was pouring in to fill the study; motes of dust stood out in it, like tiny golden sparks. But it couldn't reach the bloated ache inside her. Her long black skirt and polo-neck just magnified her mood; the pale fawn of her cardigan did little to relieve it.

She took another volume down, and started turning pages: aware that she was wasting time – or trying to. The study always called her back, whenever she was home, but today her mind was fluttery and restless. Bookworm into butterfly. She thought that with a rueful little smile.

It wasn't just the physical discomfort. She'd felt a dull anxiety for days. And something else, like envy, or a vague, unfocused longing. A niggling *if only* that just wouldn't go away.

Every day since Fran had left, she'd thought about her friend.

Standing in the sunlight now, she looked towards the window. The garden down below was in full bloom. She tried to re-imagine it in chilly pre-dawn darkness – with someone faceless waiting on the lawn. Someone who had led Fran off, across those sunny fields.

Somebody whose eyes had seen the Grail.

She knew what Fran was trying to say. The words evoked a feeling not a fact. But it nudged her on towards the books on Arthur. She fetched a couple down, and had a browse. Familiar, reassuring tales; but here and there she turned up something new – like the Cornish tradition that Arthur had come back as a raven.

Daddy hadn't looked at these in ages. She felt a dusty prickling in her nostrils as she read.

She knew the landscape well enough – but only in her daydreams. No way could Fran (or anyone) have found it. So who had really come for her? And where was she right now?

Regret it till the day you die. An echo in her head.

That strange, frustrated feeling started welling up again. She closed the book as if to cut it off. High time that she gave some thought to fine-tuning the thesis. Better that than simply moping around.

She let her fingers wander off, along the laden shelf. Here was a book containing medieval lives of saints – but that just took her thoughts back to square one. She couldn't help but open it, and re-read (for the hundredth time) the passage which had always haunted her.

It told of a place in King Athelstan's realm: *a certain royal island*, known as Glastonbury. Somewhere rich, idyllic and mysterious.

> *. . . where, by God's grace, the first Christians found a church built by no human hand – dedicated by Our Lord Jesus himself to his mother, the blessed Virgin Mary.*

Somebody had written that a thousand years ago. People even then believed that they had found a special, holy place.

That enigmatic *Athelgar* was stirring at the back of her mind. Here was the *South English Legendary*, another source she'd searched in vain for clues. The thing was an apocrypha of half-forgotten saints and weird tales. But not a word about him, even there.

She found herself reflecting on the rood-screen she had seen. The shadow-saint, his face erased. A phantom from the desecrated past . . .

Her fingers came to Martin's book and paused. *Myth and Magic in Medieval Europe*. She'd always think of it as *his* book, now. It sat there safely in its place, where she had put it back.

Make sure that you burn it. It has to be destroyed.

She hadn't even opened it, the day he'd come and gone. As soon as she had got herself together, she'd gone back in and put it on its shelf. Of course, it didn't scare her any longer – but the things he'd said had troubled her, and made the book seem tainted and infectious. She'd felt a little better once the thing was put away, absorbed into the library again. Paper to paper. Dust to dust.

Pensively she stroked its spine, remembering the chart which it contained. She could picture it so clearly, even now: the crooked shapes and crabbed, mysterious script. Real stars corrupted in a magical design. Could seeing *that* have screwed him up somehow?

Maybe she should blame herself: she'd pointed him towards it, after all.

Pulling a face, she moved along the shelf, and reached a book of Middle English Verse. She took that down instead and started reading. A nameless little poem caught her fancy. The past began to speak inside her head.

Wen þe turuf is þi tuur
And þe put is þi bour . . .

A gentle knock came on the door, although she'd left it open. She glanced around, and smiled. 'Hi, Daddy.'

'Everything okay?' her father asked.

'Yes, thanks. Just checking up some details . . .'

He seemed to sense her more immediate problem, but was

hesitant to put it into words. Not that she'd expect him to, of course. Mummy would know without being told. Lyn knew where she could go to get a cuddle.

'Give me a call if you want any help. I'll just be in the garden.' He had his jeans and jumper on, in contrast to her smart designer clothes. She smiled gratefully at him, already feeling better. Then looked back at the poem – unpicking its old characters and antiquarian spelling.

When the turf is thy tower,
And the pit is thy bower,
And thy skin and white throat
Are for grave-worms to note,
What profit thee then
All the world and its gain?

Behind her, Daddy knocked again – a single, muffled rap. She turned her head; the door was just ajar. She waited, but he didn't push it open. His reticence made her smile again.

'Come in.'

At once the door flew open, and a man she'd never seen before strode in and straight towards her. Lyn recoiled in shock and fright, the book of poems slipping from her hand. The stranger's skin was white as wax; his gaze was fixed and burning. He wore some kind of coarse black robe; the deep cowl framed his face. He glared at her then looked towards the bookcase. And then he disappeared before her eyes.

Her stomach seemed to leap up like a live thing. The balance in her belly was completely overturned – dissolving in a whirlpool of adrenaline and blood. She stumbled back against the desk, and gripped it with both hands. Gasping, doubled up with pain, she looked round the room.

He'd *gone.*

Faintly, through the open window, she heard the sound of Daddy chopping wood.

* * *

She went towards him timidly; he looked around and straightened up at once. 'Lyn?' He frowned. 'What is it?'

She couldn't answer. Her cheeks felt cold, and drained of blood. She knew she must look even whiter than the face that she'd just seen.

He laid the axe aside, and came and put his arm around her, leading her gently over to the bench against the wall. She realized she was trembling; without him there, she might have fallen over. He helped her sit, then sat himself beside her. Now his gaze was anxious and intense. 'What's wrong?'

'Oh Daddy . . .' Lyn began. She searched his face, and swallowed. 'Is there . . . Do you know . . . Did our house ever have a ghost?'

He frowned at that. 'Not that I know of. What on earth makes you think that?'

'But you do believe in them . . . ?'

He paused, and then spoke thoughtfully. 'You think you've seen one, don't you? Where – upstairs? Just now?'

Lyn nodded helplessly. 'This man with a white face. He walked into the study and just *vanished*.'

He put his hand on her forehead. 'Good heavens, girl, you're freezing . . .' Stroking her brow, he looked up at the study. 'You're sure he didn't just run out again?'

'Positive. He went into thin air. I *saw* him.'

'I think I'd better go and look. Will you come with me?' He took her hand and squeezed it. She hesitated, full of apprehension – but his grip was reassuring, like his eyes. 'All right, then,' she mumbled. They went inside and up the stairs together.

The study lay deserted in the sunlight. The dusty air was warm and undisturbed. Her father looked around, while she stood waiting on the threshold. Her stomach still felt scalded, but the sense of threat was fading. Daddy was wise enough to work this out.

He paced the room, and even sniffed the air; then picked up the book she'd dropped, and beckoned her to join him.

She did so cautiously. He put his arm around her shoulders.

'I believe you, Lyn: you obviously saw *something*. I'm not sure what it could have been. I've never felt anything strange about this house . . .'

'D'you think it could have been a ghost?' she asked.

'I'm not sure I believe in ghosts,' he smiled. 'But even if they *do* exist, most people seem to think they're only pictures. Projections of the past. They can't hurt you.'

'Fran believes in things like that,' she murmured. *And Martin, too,* she almost said, but stopped herself in time.

'I wouldn't pay too much mind to what Fran says. I know she's a nice girl, but she's had some problems, hasn't she? I really wouldn't worry, Lyn. This is your home, it always will be. You're safe here.'

Lyn nodded, feeling better. A part of her was even curious now. The apparition had been dressed like a monk – and weren't all ghosts supposed to look like that? She resolved to find out when the rectory was built, and what was here before it. Perhaps, in some uncanny way, she'd had a glimpse of living history.

But it hadn't been a pleasant glimpse, and she was still upset. That chalk-white face; those staring eyes. As if the man could see across the centuries between them. As if he'd risen up to seek her out.

CHAPTER VIII

The Sermon of the Wolf

I

The Ravens had found an empty house, and colonized its musty, wasted spaces. Instinct seemed to draw them to the attic and the cellar, as if they needed somewhere dark to nest – but blankets and equipment were soon dumped in every corner. The horses had been left in the nearby wood, with men assigned to guard them. Fran hovered in the hallway, while Athelgar put watchmen at the windows and outside. She couldn't help but think of Imber village, its houses taken over by the stealthy, sphinx-like monsters from the woods.

The state of Black Alert had not been lifted.

The building was detached, and on the outskirts of a town – its neighbours' roofs just visible beyond the hedge and trees. It wasn't derelict, just damp. Nobody had lived here for a while. The walls were white, the floorboards bare, the dusty rooms unfurnished.

For Fran, the most important thing was finding running water. The stopcock underneath the sink was stiff, but still connected. She waited till the taps ran clear, then filled the gritty bath and had a soak. The water had a penetrating coldness, enough to make her shiver with delight: a welcome contrast to the sticky day. It chilled her to the bone, and left her feeling purged and pure. She lay there for a long time, half-listening to them move around, upstairs and down below.

Athelgar. It seemed that she could feel him at her side. He might be walking round downstairs, turning the place into his *burgh*; but a part of him was with her in the room. A part that hadn't left her since the first time they'd made love. Absently she touched herself, and cosseted her breasts. The heart beneath them ached so hard. Her mind was miles away.

At length, when she was getting numb, she climbed out of the bath. Still naked, she walked down the landing to the room she'd been allotted, not caring who might see her – but the storey was deserted. No one else had a room of their own. She moped around it, letting herself dry. Its bareness made it seem austere, like a visionary's cell. The blank walls trapped the sour light, and lent a tinge of bleakness. Beneath the window, a patch of mouldy plaster stained the white: a gangrenous shadow, breaking through.

He came to her without being called. No doubts or hesitations this time round. They screwed without a wasted breath – as if the day since they'd last done so had been half an age too long. The plaster had a clammy feel against her drying back – but with his mouth between her thighs, she didn't care. She'd never dreamed a man of war could pleasure her like this. His loving tongue was careful as a cat's – lapping at its saucer without rippling the milk. Fran convulsed with pleasure; rolled her head from side to side. A glimpse of the damp, decaying wall and then the vacant ceiling. *God, he must have practised this.* But still she didn't care.

Afterwards, both drained and spent, they curled up on the floor and lay in silence. The sultry day turned gloomier outside. She realized he had drifted off, his breathing deep and even. Despite the spartan floorboards, she began to doze herself.

Then Athelgar woke up shouting.

The shock went thrilling down her nerves; she drew her arms and legs up. Then Athelgar sat bolt upright, displacing her sleepy head. His face was pale, still masked with sleep, his open eyes unfocused. The words he blurted out were harsh and foreign.

'Leofan men, yecnawath that sooth is, this worold is on ofste and hit nealacth tham ende . . .'

Fran lay blinking up at him; and after a moment he came

back to himself and to her. His tautened upper body seemed to sag: she saw the muscles slackening beneath his weathered skin. He rubbed his forehead, hand sliding back through sweaty hair – and glanced at her sidelong. His eyes now looked as raw as open wounds.

'What is it?' she whispered: afraid to raise her voice.

'No thing. A remembering.' He turned his face away, and shook his head.

'What was it you were you saying?' she insisted. Despite the alien words, despite the accent, she thought that she'd made sense of bits of it. *This world*, he'd said. *It neareth an end*. Or something very like it. Coming out of sleep, in that cryptic language, it had the chilling aspect of a portent. A prediction.

'High-Bishop Wulfstan's words,' he said. 'The sermon of the wolf to the English.'

Still lying there, she reached for him and drew him down beside her. He complied without resistance – almost dazed. Instinctively she cuddled him and waited.

'I heard it preached,' he said after a pause, his cheek against her shoulder. 'When all the land was being devoured by the Danes. The Bishop saw it was the wrath of God.'

He kept on in a subdued voice, the recollection coming out in fragments. And Fran could see it vividly, the scene that he described. As if she could recall it through his eyes.

He'd been in church, lurking near the back: a shadow from the wintry dark outside. The place was dim with candlelight – she could almost smell the wax. Local folk had crowded in, to huddle in the draughty flagstone nave. The priest was reading out the bishop's sermon.

'The year was thousand-thirteen,' murmured Athelgar beside her. 'The country was beset by many evils, and Athelred had summoned us too late. But worse, he willed that we should be his butchers. To murder *his own people* – though his real foes were visible and clear . . .'

Back in the church, the people listened, awestruck. She sensed their dread across the gulf of years. The sermon spoke of chaos and disaster, of law and order breaking down. Athelgar knew much of it by heart, or so it seemed – although she guessed he'd only heard it once. The sermon of the wolf had bitten deep.

But that was then, not now. She felt a need to put it in perspective. The call to repentance was familiar enough; apocalyptic threats were nothing new. Yet the images of crisis were persistent, and unsettling. The tirade evoked a landscape of evil; sorcerers and witches vied with murderers and thieves. And over them all, the shadow of the Vikings. It was more than pulpit rhetoric. The roots were deep and real.

History not prophecy, she thought. A voice from the past – not a vision of the future. But even so, her stomach wouldn't settle. The vacuum of anxiety remained.

This world is in haste, and is nearing an end. And the longer it lasts, so the worse it becomes . . .

Athelgar was fingering her nipple; as if it was a comforter, not something to arouse her. She stroked his cheek, and gazed into his face. 'What happened, in the end?' she asked.

'The *Witching* had the victory, and took the English crown.'

'But the . . . Witchings can't win this time. Can they?' She shouldn't need to ask, of course. As horrid as the Ashmen were, they'd be no match for guns, or planes, or tanks . . .

'I know not,' he said quietly. 'God saw fit to punish us before. Perhaps it is His will to make an end of things this time.'

And Fran began to realize that the Ashmen would be fighting no pitched battles. They'd raid at night – set fire to people's homes. Catch children unaware, and cut them up. The country would be turned into some Dark Age Vietnam. Every wood and empty house a death-trap. Every shadow full of fear. And nobody would know what to do. A modern, post-industrial state; but nobody would *know*.

Discomfited, she snuggled up against him. They lay in silence. Beyond the window, night was coming down.

* * *

When she woke, the room was full of darkness. She started and half-raised herself; then twisted round, and found the tall, dim window. Athelgar was still asleep – a softly breathing shadow, like a panther at her side.

The boards had left her feeling bruised and achy; they creaked as she got up. She hadn't a clue what time it was. Her watch was somewhere in the corner, with her clothes. The house was silent, very still. She tiptoed to the window, and peered out. The garden was a sea of gloom, but she knew the watchers were out there somewhere – ranged around the building in their hides and makeshift foxholes. For the first time she had an inkling of what the other side of Cruisewatch had been like. The Convoy on deployment, with its fences up and sentries on patrol. Craig would have seen nights like this. The thought stirred up the dormant guilt inside her.

But all *they'd* had to watch for was protesters like herself. Tonight, the ring was braced for much more sinister intruders. Nervously she peered into the dark, but saw no movement.

'All is quiet,' said Athelgar behind her, so close she felt his breath against her nape. She jumped with shock, and glanced around; he stood there, looking pensive. His naked skin shone faintly in the greyish light of night.

'*God*,' she said, 'I wish you wouldn't do that.'

He stroked a finger down her spine. 'And this?' he asked her softly.

She arched her back appreciatively. He took her shoulders, kissed her neck – and went completely still. His gentle fingers tightened till they dug into her skin. She felt a sudden chill. Her hairs stood up.

'Lady, what is this?' he breathed.

She turned her head, and realized what he'd seen. The butterfly tattoo on her left shoulder. She'd had it done during her rebellious phase. It had caused quite a stir in the changing rooms at school. *Frannie's had herself tattooed!* She'd basked in the attention then. She stood quite frozen now.

'This,' he asked her hollowly. 'Is this is your witch's mark?'

Jesus! 'No, it's not. Just done with ink . . .'

A pause: she sensed him pondering. His hands still rested close against her neck. Then he eased one down, to touch the delicate design.

She turned enough to let it catch the light; he traced its outline with his fingernail. Nervously, she craned around. His face was masked in thought.

'They said familiars followed *her*,' he murmured – still exploring.

She frowned, uncertain. 'Followed who?'

His eyes came up, and caught the meagre glow. 'You know that butterflies are restless souls.'

She didn't answer.

'Truly you have come to bless the Ravens,' he said softly. She watched as he pulled off one of his rings. The silver glittered faintly in the starlight.

'Put this on,' he told her. 'It will bind you in our circle. Wear it, so that *you* shall not be lost.'

Wondering at his emphasis, she let him slide the ring onto her finger, then raised her hand to study its design. The metal was worn and dark with age, but she could just about decipher the inscription. *IHS* ✠ *MAR*. It made no sense to her.

He slid his arms around her waist, and nuzzled at her neck. Warmth began to spread through her again. But then he paused, and held her tight, his head against her own. She fancied she could almost hear him thinking.

'Frances. Is this well?' he asked at length.

'Yes,' she said, not sure that it was.

2

'This world is coming to an end,' Dominicain said, pointing. 'Wolves and thieves are coming from the woods.' His grimy finger tracked from face to face. 'Behold the riches that shall not endure. Blessed be you poor, who cannot lose them.'

They were standing round a fountain, in the middle of a busy shopping mall. Dominicain paced up and down, his Bible in one hand; the black coat hanging open on his grubby white pyjamas. Carl was standing close at hand, his eyes as shifty as a bodyguard's. Others from the group were in support. They had the crossbones flag unfurled – a challenge to the spying precinct cameras. Few of the shoppers gave them more than a glance, but the gathering of street-people was growing.

Dominicain kept talking. He didn't stand haranguing them, but moved among the crowd addressing his appeal to every one of them in turn. Carl stood back and watched him with a cool and narrowed gaze. He couldn't help but marvel at the man. No matter that the words were shit; they came across with mesmerizing fervour. His sometimes broken English didn't hamper him at all. The wellspring of words just flowed and flowed, and forced his foreign tongue to give them shape. Even his strong accent added power to his speech – lending it a living, earthy flavour.

The banner leered behind him, like some prehistoric alien. And yet he had approved of it, with what struck Carl as Medieval relish. *Memento Mori*, so he'd said. *Remember thou shalt die . . .*

'Listen, you rich! The Lord says this. Sell what you have, and give the money to the poor. And you poor – use it *well*.' He strode across to where a man was swigging Tennant's Extra. His hand flashed out, and knocked the can away. Beer splashed the paving stones like piss. Befuddled though the drinker was, his face filled up with rage; then drained beneath Dominicain's fierce stare. The Preacher leaned in close, but spoke for all of them to hear. 'Do not buy *beer* with it – buy petrol! Fuel for the fires of Judgment Day. Buy petrol!'

He moved away, and sprang onto the fountain's low, flat rim. Glowering: transfixing them. More faces joined the crowd.

'This land will be laid waste,' he told them grimly. 'Those who have oppressed you will be punished.' And then his tone grew quieter, almost musing, so that his listeners had to strain to hear. 'But Our Lord also says that the earth shall bloom again, in fields of peace and plenty, and there shall you live for ever . . .'

The old lies were the best, Carl thought. The beggars who had come to sneer were looking pensive now.

'And how, then, shall this come about? The poor must rise, and take back what is theirs.'

Attaboy, Carl thought, but didn't smile. He'd glimpsed a copper from the corner of his eye. The bastard had his head inclined to speak into his radio. Now listening to instructions. They'd spotted the back-up transit van, parked just around the corner. Pretty soon this gathering was going to be dispersed. And what would friend Dominicain do then?

The law against the word of God. If Carl was right, it would force a confrontation. Not a shooting action, they weren't ready for one yet. But at least they'd get a chance to scrap, and kick a few fat heads in. Enough to show Dominicain the road he had to take – and make the right connections for his followers as well.

He glanced at Neil; the latter raised his bottle in a toast. The Preacher's voice cajoled and urged – but his dark, ferocious eyes bore half the message.

'Be mindful that Our Lord said this: *I have not come to bring peace to the earth, but a sword!* The Church has sided with the rich, but God stands with the poor. And through us, He shall cast the mighty down . . .'

The cops began converging, looking purposeful and tough, with cuffs and batons ready at their belts. The crowd closed up resentfully; the officers shoved through. Steve looked round, as if surprised – then let the first one have it with a half-brick. The copper stumbled back and fell. Blood burst like a geyser from his nose.

'They're scared of him!' Carl shouted. 'They don't want to hear him speak!'

The angry shout was taken up. People who'd been shoving back began to punch and kick. Somebody upturned a litter bin, providing ammunition in the form of cans and bottles. Pelted, the police fell back – then waded in again. The ruckus spread; a plate-glass window shattered. Rich, complacent shoppers scuttled clear.

'Put them to flight!' Dominicain commanded. 'Kill the fascist bastards!' shouted Neil. The death's head on the banner grinned to see it. A copper bawled for back-up on his radio. A spinning bottle smashed against his head.

They heard the barking dogs before they saw them. 'Leg it!' someone shouted, and the congregation scattered. Dominicain looked set to stand his ground. Reaching up, Carl tugged his coat. 'They'll put you in that hospital again.'

The Preacher seemed to hesitate, then followed at his heels. The dog-handlers had reached the mall. Alsatians snarled and strained against their leashes. Neil was stuffing rags into the bottle he'd been holding – labelled Beck's, but filled with paraffin. Lighting it, he threw it down to shatter on the paving. Liquid fire sprayed out into a lake.

Dominicain and Carl ran down the mall, with skirmishes caroming in their wake. Some among the dispossessed were playing cat and mouse – using hapless bystanders as cover. One of them tried talking to the coppers, even as he dodged and backed away. A young man with a serious face. His taunting tone was challenging as well.

'You're meant to protect the people – am I right? When you end up protecting the system *from* the people, you know you've lost the argument already . . .' At which point, outmanoeuvred, he got clouted round the head. They didn't even bother to arrest him.

Carl kept weaving through the crowds, and led Dominicain towards a side street. One of the cops had seen them, and came wheezing in pursuit. The Preacher kept on running, but Carl skidded to a halt around the corner – then lunged into the copper's path, and body-checked him like a rugby forward. The copper went down awkwardly; his radio handset clattered on the paving. Carl kicked him in the stomach, and the side.

Glancing round, he saw the Preacher striding back to join him. *Great, the bastard's got the bloody message!*

'Come on – help me break the scumbag's ribs,' he said aloud; then gave a startled gurgle as the Preacher seized his coat and wrenched him clear.

'Call no man worthless for whom Christ died,' Dominicain said harshly.

Carl stared back in disbelief. The Preacher glared, still grasping his lapels. From this close, Carl could see the haunted depths of those dark eyes. The ghosts of doubt were manifesting there.

Easing back, Dominicain let go. Carl felt anger pumping up inside him. It filled his throat, and bulged behind his eyes. The stricken copper groaned, and was ignored. The Preacher took a backward step, still glowering a warning. He turned along the street – and went quite still.

Fighting his rage, Carl looked as well. The fragment of a park lay at the entrance of the mall. A pocket handkerchief of grass, complete with some bedraggled-looking trees.

One of the trees was burning.

Dominicain stood staring – then went forward. Carl breathed out, and clenched his teeth, and turned to check behind them. Someone was still shouting in the distance. Dogs were barking hollowly; he heard the scream of sirens. But no one else had followed them down here.

The copper at his feet was reaching out for his dropped handset – fixed on it, as if it was the last thing in the world. Carl wavered, sorely tempted, then kicked the thing away from him, and strode after the Preacher.

Dominicain had reached the park; his face was full of wonder. The tree was burning fiercely, but it wasn't being consumed. The branches, sheathed in flame, were full of leaves. Instinctively he went down on one knee – hiding his face behind an upraised arm. Carl hung back behind him, puzzled now. There was no one else around; as if the tree had just spontaneously combusted. Someone from the riot must have set the thing on fire. He glanced around impatiently, not noticing that it was still unscathed.

A voice was welling up in Dominicain's head; the same voice that he'd heard inside the prison. But not a poet's words this time. The Messenger was speaking like a prophet.

What is the cross, but the shape of a sword? Take up your sword, *therefore, and follow me. The peasants shall rise up against their rulers. But first, the Raven's Breed must be destroyed.*

The grim words put a finger on his doubts. Confessing them in silence, he rose up and crossed himself. Turning from the miracle, he started off along another street. Muttering, Carl hurried to catch up.

Two men came towards them – one of them dazed and leaning on the other. His face was splashed with blood, his dark hair matted. Scruffy cords and waistcoat; muddy boots. Carl recognized the man who'd tried to reason with the law.

The Preacher spoke in passing: so absorbed by what he'd seen, he lapsed into Italian.

'Il regno di Dio è vicino . . . ravvedetevi e credete all'evangelo.'

Neither of them understood a word. But something about his tone of voice made both of them look round and follow him.

Behind, the burning tree began to char and shrivel up. The aura that had cooled the flames was sucked up like a cloud, and angry heat went searing through the leaves.

VI

MARTYRS

Let's talk of graves, of worms and epitaphs.

SHAKESPEARE

Dear Craig

You know when soldiers give a letter to their mates – in case they're killed? Well I've got nobody to give this to. It's in my mind – so if I die, you'll never know a thing. Everyone will just assume some psycho cut my throat.

You'll never know I've screwed . . . Okay, I'm screwing *someone else.*

You'll never know how sorry I am. I love you, and I miss you, but this is like another life. We're walking a knife-edge every day. Athelgar has nightmares, and he thinks that there's some crisis looming. The way he holds me . . . sorry, Craig . . . it's like he's scared that I'll be snatched away.

You'll never know how much I would have loved to meet your folks, and sit there in a rocker on the porch and see the mountains.

You'll never know how hard we fought to win this filthy war.

You'll never know a thing.

CHAPTER I

Massacre Is My Forgiveness

I

'What are we *waiting* for?' Fran asked.

The words came out with unexpected sharpness – brewed up like summer lightning in the closeness of the house. They'd been cooped up here for days now. The air was thick and stifling. *And* it was the wrong time of the month.

Athelgar just looked at her. A faint frown touched his forehead – like a shadow of frustration. Watching from across the room, she realized he'd been waiting for her word. They all were.

'Well don't look at me like that,' she snapped. 'This is *your* war, mate, not mine. Don't ask *me* how to fight it.'

He took that in morosely. Like her, he was sitting with his back against the wall. The floorboards of her room were like a barren field between them. The daylight was receding: ebbing slowly back towards the window.

'We *need* your guidance, Frances.' His voice was soft but urgent. He sounded like a man with a choice of roads before him – one of which, he knew, led straight to Hell.

If the blind lead the blind . . . she thought; but didn't say it. Resting her chin on her drawn-up knees, she stared down at the shrinking pool of light.

He looked away; she risked a sidelong glance. Wrapped up in his sombre coat, he looked like a shadow come early. Fran sat back uncomfortably, and pulled the big, bedraggled jacket closer round her. She'd screwed him several times now despite the chilly prospect of him getting her pregnant. The pangs of fear had worsened, but she couldn't let him go. All she could do was bite her lip, and hope, and maybe pray. *Please can I have my period. Please, God. Please.* And now it had begun, and she was miserable again.

The house was silent, full of tension, waiting.

She'd ventured out from time to time, to beg – and steal. Neither activity was beneath her now. She'd brought back what provisions she could get, but put some coins aside to make some phone calls. Huddled in the call-box at the corner of the road, listening to the distant numbers ringing, she'd felt like a medium making contact with the spirits of the dead.

Hi, Mum . . . It's me. I should have rung before, I'm really sorry . . .

Frannie! For God's sake, girl, where are you? We've been so worried . . .

She knew that only love could be so angry – but she'd cringed at the time, and she flinched from the memory now. Her mum had heard from Lyn that she had 'gone off with somebody'. The best that Fran could do was claim she'd fallen for some bloke. *We need some time together now . . .*

(Just, please, don't think I've had another breakdown.)

Athelgar was brooding with his fist against his mouth. Watching her. Still waiting.

Lyn . . . oh, Lyn. I'm sorry, but I can't get back there yet. I'm all right, though. Believe me. I'm okay . . .

And Lynnie had believed her: worried, but so wistful at the end of the line.

'*Frances . . .*' murmured Athelgar again. His grave face was appealing now; his low tone as insistent as he dared.

'I don't know yet!' she hissed at him, and turned her face away. A pungent silence thickened in the room. Between them on the floorboards, the pool of light dried up and turned to dust.

2

'Frances . . .'

The whisper woke her up at once. *Jesus, not again.* She turned her head, still half-asleep, but readying an irritable retort. Athelgar was lying on the far side of the room, his body just a vague shape in the dimness.

'What?' she asked.

He didn't respond. She listened to his breathing, then frowned and raised herself. The floor was no less hard beneath her makeshift nest of blankets, and the aching of her muscles made her wince. The air was dense, the silence hissing softly. 'I know you're awake,' she whispered, feeling peeved. 'And so am I, now . . . so all right, what?'

Still he didn't answer. Fran sat there, glowering; then settled down again. Enough of sleep still clung to her; she felt her mind begin to slip away.

'Frances . . .'

'What?'

She twisted round – and this time he was stirring. She watched him prop himself up on one elbow, his face just a blur in the gloom.

'What troubles you?' his voice asked warily.

Fran blinked in disbelief. 'Well *you're* the one who called me.'

He shook his head. 'I have not called.'

Silence fell between them. A sudden chill engulfed Fran's bare top half. She felt her fine hairs prickling like pins.

Your mind works in a funny way – that's all. Believe it, you're not mad.

Athelgar was waiting. She sensed his uncertainty but could he feel her fright?

'Sorry, I was dreaming,' she mumbled, and put her head back down, burrowing beneath the stale blankets. She listened to him shift, and settle. The room grew quiet again. The surge of sticky coldness didn't leave her.

Perhaps an hour passed – and then she heard her name again. An insubstantial husk of sound, as if the dark itself had breathed it out. And yet it seemed too real to be an echo in her head. She could almost feel her inner ear contracting.

The earlier chill was nothing to the icy surge of dread that filled her then. The door was shut, the creaky floorboards silent. No one had come in. But someone, somewhere in the house, was very softly calling.

Athelgar slept on. There was no sign of the other Ravens stirring. Why couldn't they hear it? *Why?*

'Frances . . .'

She sat bolt upright, listening. The voice seemed muffled: seeping through the door. She thought she heard a note of urgency. Like someone trying desperately to reach her, but fearful of waking up the sleepers all around.

She remembered the voice from the deep black pool – that night she'd gone diving for Athelgar's sword. The warning note had been the same.

Beware the Raven, Frances . . .

She waited, feeling sick and scared. The empty pause went on and on. And if she heard the call again – what answer should she give? *Speak Lord, for thy servant heareth?* That was what she'd learned in Junior Church, when Samuel was called . . .

But which Lord waited now, beyond the door?

'Frances . . .' Fainter now. 'Hear me . . .'

Gnawing her lip, she rose into a crouch. Athelgar had lent his coat towards her meagre bedding; she drew it on, and draped it round her shoulders. Wrapping it tight, she tiptoed to the door, and very gently eased it open.

The landing lay in blackness. The stairwell was a gulf she couldn't see. But the voice was rising from it, as it had from the bottomless pool.

'Come treading softly, Frances, this is the Ravens' lair.'

She hesitated, full of apprehension. A ghost was waiting down there, she was sure of it. But whatever it might be, it had something to tell her. And frightened though she was, she had to know.

Swallowing, she started forward: gliding like a shadow through the dark. Treading softly, as he'd warned – as if she, too, was scared to rouse the Ravens. The boards felt rough beneath her naked feet.

The phantom voice was silent as she ventured down the stairs. She was acutely aware of the sleepers in the rooms: their muffled breathing seemed to haunt the darkness. But others were awake, and keeping watch around the house . . .

She reached the ground floor and stopped again; stood huddled in the stiff and shabby coat. And then the whisper: *Answer me*. She thought it came from the first room on her left. The door was closed, a pale smudge in the dimness. Heart pounding, she reached down towards the handle. Her throat closed as she touched it. Every nerve was tingling as she turned the knob and pushed.

The room beyond was tinged with greyish light: a gluey phosphorescence, strung like slime between the walls. Its very touch was clammy on her face. Her muscles almost locked and left her stranded.

A brighter glow grew slowly from the centre, as if a sun was rising in the fog.

'Do not fear me, Frances. Enter now.'

She did so with reluctant fascination – drawn in like a moth towards a flame. The light was turning rosy, the mist and cobwebs shredding as she watched. And somebody was waiting there: a tall, imposing shape. She halted when she saw him, hands clutching at the collar of her coat. Her fists moved up against her mouth. Her wary eyes grew wide.

The figure dipped his head, as if in greeting. He wore a rough black hood that shrouded all his upper face. The lower part was lean, and sickly pale. A grizzled shadow roughened it which was somehow ugly and unnerving. It seemed to her like dead man's stubble, growing in the grave.

'Welcome, Lady Frances,' he said softly – and at last she

saw the moving lips behind that ghostly voice. She felt her prickling hairs stand up on end.

'Who are you?' she whispered back.

He raised his muffled head, so she could look into his face. The first glimpse didn't shock her as expected; his haggard look was human, in its way. But the stillness of those features made her flesh begin to crawl. Despite the graven lines and growth of stubble, it might have been a death mask, set in wax.

The eyes were still alive, though – and alight. They could have melted holes in any mask.

'My name is Brother Marcus, and I come to bring thee warning.'

'What about?'

'Of what must come to pass,' he answered grimly.

A chill went wriggling down her spine. She hunched her shoulders, waiting.

'I warn thee to beware the Raven,' he went on. 'I tell thee that its acolytes are faithless. I counsel thee to fear the man who leads thee to the bone-fire.'

'*What?*' she cut in sharply, her voice edged with dismay.

'Walk with Athelgar and thou shalt burn in earth as thou shalt in Hell.'

'Who *are* you?' she insisted.

'A man who knows all secrets, and all sins.'

She stared at him in queasy disbelief. Did it feel like this to use a ouija board, and find out things she wasn't meant to know? Voices from the dark side. From the demons . . .

A small, half-smothered instinct was urging her to back away and run. But no, she had to hear him out. To challenge and defeat him – prove him *wrong*.

'Athelgar's a man of God. I'd trust him with my *life*.' Fishing up her cross, she let him see it – trying to put defiance in her stare. The man called Marcus didn't even flinch.

'Others have said this before. Their bones still smoulder in his mind . . . perhaps.'

She swallowed hard to lubricate her throat. The brooding house of Ravens was forgotten. This chamber was a whole world in itself.

His tone was too seductive. Soft and grave – not hectoring at all. She felt a germ of doubt begin to fester. *He's trying to trick you, girl!* she thought. A *demon in disguise . . .*

'Show your real face,' she hissed, still clinging to the tiny silver cross.

'Wilt thou see it, Frances?' he asked bleakly.

Got him. 'Yes!' she said, and felt a surge of fear at once.

The eerie light began to fail; his features lost their focus. And sure enough, another face was there behind the mask. She had the briefest glimpse of it, and almost squealed with horror and disgust. The flesh was torn and bloody, its rags revealing bones. Some of it was scorched; the hair was gone. The eyes were still the same, though – watching her intently from above the melted nose and naked teeth.

Fran reared back, and felt her legs give way. She went down awkwardly on hands and knees. Nauseated, staring at the floor, she seemed to hear the roar of flames – but muffled, like the sea from a great distance. The stench of something burning filled her nostrils, so bitter that it nearly made her gag. And then the voice of Marcus came again.

'My face is fair no longer. Tell me truly.'

She sensed him move towards her, and jerked her head up. He loomed there in the murky light, his waxen features whole and calm again.

'Behold what men have done,' he said – and reached for her. She tried to scramble clear, but he took firm hold of her wrist and dragged her upright. His grip was cold and clammy, like the light. She wriggled ineffectually. His death-mask stare was much too close for comfort.

Stepping back, he drew her with him. The slimy glow engulfed them, and she felt a sense of void – as if the room had swelled to cathedral size. Marcus was at her side now, like somebody who meant to show her *sights*. She stumbled to keep up with him, holding the black coat closed with her free hand.

A gout of flame erupted through the half-light. She felt its brilliance bathe her without heat. A pyre of books was burning in the ectoplasmic fog. Marcus, heedless, reached into the fire, and plucked a volume out. The thing was scorched and smouldering; he let her go to open it. All the leaves combusted as he did so, but he kept hold of the book as if to read it while it burned. His pallid face looked radiant in its flare.

He dropped it then; it fell apart before it hit the floor. He grasped her arm again and wrenched her round. Her eyesight was still dazzled by the brilliance of the fires, but in the misty twilight she saw gallows and hanging bodies.

'Behold what *I* beheld,' he said. 'And then the same and more was done to me.'

Fran just stood there, lost for words. His false face turned towards her. 'And now I shall repay,' he said. 'Ye hunger for the dark, and ye shall *have it*.'

'What do you want?' she whispered, her voice squeezed small and tight.

'Justice for myself and for things past.'

'How?'

'To take this nation back into the darkness. Even to the *mire* whence it came.'

She searched his face. 'Was it you who called the Ashmen back?'

He didn't take her meaning for a moment. Then: 'There are wanderers with antique scores to settle – and dogs who do my bidding when I call them.' He seemed amused by that, but only briefly. 'Together they will teach this land the error of its ways.'

'No!' she blurted.

'Wherefore not?' he asked her, very softly.

'Can't you forgive . . . ?' She faltered. It sounded hopeless even as she said it.

'Forgive?' His smile became a sneer as he leaned forward.

'*Massacre* is my forgiveness. I am owed this retribution. Shall I not have it?'

'What *for*?'

He shook his head, ignoring her, relentless. 'My time is coming, Frances. It is even at the doors. Canst thou not feel it? Pestilence and war are all about thee.' He took her other wrist, and held her rigidly before him – those mad eyes burning down into her face. 'People will learn to *fear* the dark again. They will seek shelter in their houses and I will take the power that feeds their lanterns. *Then* shall they know what they have lost. And when I have the Chart of Stars, I will take thy Ravens too.'

Awed though she was, those last words struck a deeper chord. Athelgar had spoken of a star-chart . . . and Marcus seemed to sense her comprehension. 'Yes,' he said, 'thou knowest it. Its *stain* is on thee still.' And even as she gaped at him, he let her go and took a long step backwards. The atmosphere changed at once. The air grew thick and soupy, and her head began to sing. She felt a painful pressure in her ears, as if she'd just touched bottom at the deep end of a swimming pool. The whole room was imploding: collapsing to its normal size again. The transformation's violence sent her slumping to the floor – breathless, on the very brink of fainting. Marcus simply vanished, and the spectral light went with him. A fleeting afterglow – then inky blackness. When the door was opened moments later, and one of the Raven-watchmen peered in, he found her crouching there alone, still muffled in her coat. Trying, with all her stomach, to be sick.

3

'He shows us this – for why?' said Athelgar.

'Perhaps to taunt us,' someone muttered grimly.

Fran just sat in silence, with her head in her hands.

They had gathered in the spacious living room: sitting on

the concrete floor, their backs against the walls. Everyone was present now, except the outer watchmen. In that minimalist setting, with first light seeping bleakly through the window, it might have been a council of Japanese knights.

Fran had told them everything – including what he'd said about the Ravens as betrayers. She'd kept her eye on Athelgar: imploring his denial. But Athelgar had pondered, seeming genuinely perplexed. None of them had known this Brother Marcus. Nobody could say why he was seeking this revenge. Burning books and hanging men implied a persecution; but as Athelgar insisted, the Ravens always sided with the *victims* of a purge. The questions circled round themselves, and came to no conclusion. Which left them to consider why he'd shown himself last night.

'What say you, Frances?' asked Athelgar softly. 'Has he come to taunt us with his power?'

Fran was dressed again, but still felt naked; aware of all their eyes on her, as she sifted what she'd seen and heard last night. Eventually she raised her head, still frowning at the puzzle.

'No . . .' she said. 'It's like he *needs* to tell us. Like a deal he has to make with his own conscience.'

Eldred showed sardonic satisfaction. 'He has a weakness, then.'

'Or maybe a strength,' Fran murmured. She flicked her gaze from face to face: Eldred, Steffan, Rathulf, staring back. 'He looked just like a monk. A holy man . . .'

She'd meant it to sound hopeful, but Leofric gave a twisted little smile. 'You shall not find too many holy men in monkish dress. They feed on sins which men confess, as black flies feed on shit. Lechers, gluttons – yea, and *sorcerers*. Even Holy Mary's church has been corrupted now . . .'

Fran glanced round unhappily. Athelgar, beside her, was still gazing at the floor. 'Do you think it is his will that we should hinder his design?'

She mulled it over; shook her head. 'I think he needs to kid himself we could have, if we'd tried.' She couldn't help but think of a terrorist's coded warning – deliberately too cryptic to be understood in time.

'Therefore – if he shows his hand – he must believe the game is his already.'

She didn't want to think it through that far. Instead she said: 'He knows about your star-chart, but where is it?'

'None of us can say,' he said. 'On the night in which we were summoned, we were scattered to the winds . . .'

She forced herself to hear his words again. "When I have the star-chart . . . I will take the Ravens too." And then he said that I'd been *stained* by it . . .' As if she'd touched the thing, and found its ink on her hands, a magic taint that couldn't be washed off. Or as if it was contaminated somehow . . .

An sudden, icy flush went surging through her. *Contaminated.*

'*Jesus*, no . . .' she breathed

Athelgar looked round sharply. 'What?'

'Oh, God. Lyn's got it. Somewhere in her house.'

Athelgar sat waiting. She turned to him, eyes wide. 'While I was there, your lodestone kept on glowing – as if it was drawing power from somewhere close. And then her brother came back home from nowhere, and . . . and told her about an evil book, a magic book, and said she had to burn it.'

'Did she do so?' Rathulf asked intently.

'No, she didn't. It's still there. But if this Marcus wants it . . .'

Athelgar's hands were on her shoulders. 'Frances . . .'

'God, he'll send the Ashmen . . .'

'Does he know where the Sky-Chart lies?' His tone was firm, deliberately calm.

'He must do – he's a *spirit* of some kind! And he wouldn't let us know unless he thinks that we can't stop him.' She tried to clamber to her feet; he tightened his hold, and kept her there before him.

'Let me go . . .' *Oh, Lyn.* 'I've got to *be* there . . .'

'And so you shall – but faster riders need to go ahead. Men of war. We may yet reach the Sky-Chart first, and give your friend protection.' He glanced aside, at Eldred. 'Is it distant?'

'Cofentreium.'

'Eldred knows the way.' He looked back to his comrade. 'Choose your men, and ride there with all speed.'

Eldred nodded, rose at once and began to make his choice. Fran let her shoulders slump, and Athelgar relaxed his grip. She looked at him imploringly. 'I *have* to know that Lyn's okay.'

'Follow, then. Leofric shall go with you. The rest of us go north as well – tonight. We have lain here long enough.'

'You think they're on the move?' she asked.

'His *witching*-men will come down from the Dane-law. Now that he has shown himself, it must mean he is ready to begin.'

She thought of her own image: *like a Dark Age Vietnam*. But what Marcus conjured up was even bleaker. Like a nuclear aftermath, with people in the dark again – eking out a primitive existence. He'd claimed that he could take the power. And if that went, then everything else went with it.

People would fear the night again. And this time with good reason.

Athelgar released her, and she rose to her feet feeling hollow and drained. The circle of Ravens was breaking up. She looked for Eldred, but he had already gone. She found him outside, in the lane. He and three more swordsmen were already mounting up.

'Please, don't frighten her,' she said. 'She doesn't know about you – or them.'

Eldred stared down gravely. 'It shall be as thou sayest, Lady Frances.'

Reaching up, she tugged his sleeve. 'Good luck. Please get there soon.'

He nodded, gathered up the reins and started down the

lane. The others followed, each man glancing back. And Fran was left alone there in the half-light of the dawn, listening to their hoofbeats fade to nothing.

CHAPTER II

A Thousand Silver Pieces on the Black

I

Lyn hesitated, frowning; then heard the sound again. A stealthy rustling noise, beneath her window. She'd heard the like before on summer evenings. A fox had come to sniff around the house.

She sat still for a moment, picturing its movements in the velvet gloom outside, then went back to brushing her hair. When she paused again a minute later, the fragrant dusk was silent. Bre'er Fox had clearly given up, and slunk back to the wood.

She laid the brush aside and linked her hands behind her neck, stretching as she smiled at her reflection. Time to pick her supper from the freezer – a low-calorie lasagne, if there was one. She padded downstairs in her dressing gown, still feeling fresh and radiant from her bath. Her parents were away for the weekend, and she had the place to herself. A princess with a castle of her own. Part of her had been a little nervous, in case that ghost – that vision – might recur. But this was *home*: too comfy and familiar. A fleeting aberration couldn't sour it. Whatever it had really been, she hadn't heard a whisper of it since.

Besides, she had her mind on other things. Once she'd eaten supper, it was her turn to ring Simon. She'd put a quiet CD on, then curl up on the sofa with the cordless phone. Almost as good as having him there with her. The prospect brought a pleasurable glow.

She'd have to press some money onto Daddy. The phone bill for this quarter would be *huge*.

The kitchen lights were cosy and subdued. Pomfret watched her hopefully, although he'd just been fed. Ignoring him, she dug out a lasagne from the freezer, savouring the cold air as she peered at the instructions. Twenty-five minutes at gas mark 5. Behind her, Pomfret hissed.

'Shush,' she told him absently. She closed the freezer door, and turned towards the Aga. Pomfret caught her eye at once. He was crouching on the window-ledge, staring out into the dark. His fur began to bristle as she watched.

The sight was quite unsettling for a moment – but then she guessed the fox was back again. 'Come on, Pommie, leave it.' As she crossed towards the oven, he sprang down from the sill and darted past her – out of sight before she turned her head. She hesitated curiously, then detoured to the window. Her own reflection greeted her: a dim, transparent image of the kitchen. She leaned towards it, squinting.

A ghastly face sprang up beyond the glass.

Lyn gave a little shriek, and stumbled backwards. The head was in an iron mask, with sockets like a skull's. It left the lower face exposed, with shrivelled-looking skin around the mouth. The moment plunged her back into the terrors of her childhood: Old King Death had come for her at last.

The window shattered – deafening in the confines of the room. Galvanized, she jumped clean off the flagstones. The murky shape was reaching in, its shabby gauntlets groping for the catch. Shards of glass fell rattling to the sink. Clutching her cheeks, Lyn backed away still pasty-faced with shock. The horrible intruder raised his head and *looked* at her. She couldn't see his eyes at all; the down-turned mouth was loathsome in its promise.

And then she heard a pounding on the kitchen door behind her. The sounds were heavy – solid blows. Somebody was trying to break it down. Whimpering, she ducked towards the stairwell. Even as she fled upstairs, her mind a blur of panic, she heard the kitchen window-frame forced wide.

* * *

The noises carried clearly on the breathless evening air. Eldred reined his mount in hard, and heard them through the thumping in his ears. The tinkling cascade of glass; the crunch of tortured wood. He kicked his panting horse into a run along the lane. The lonely house stood out against the skyline, a tithe-barn silhouette against the deep blue of the sky. A golden lantern glow revealed the doorway.

His fellow Ravens thundered in his wake between the fields. The last dash felt like time turned back – once more that desperate race against the raiders. His own farm burning fiercely in the heat of harvest-tide, and dreadful screams still coming from the flames. A silhouette was waiting to confront him in the lane. He yelled, and hacked the man aside – the rage of past and present intermingled in the blow.

The *wiking* helmet spun away, and clattered to the road. The head was still inside it; the body toppled back into the hedge. Eldred dragged his horse around, and slid out of the saddle. Something else was moving in the field across the lane. One of the Ravens veered off, and galloped in pursuit. Eldred strode towards the door, which hung by nails and splinters. It gave onto a kitchen, suffused in dusky light – the magic glow which had no smoke or smell. He entered like a prowling cat, dropping to a crouch for fear of ambush. The room was empty. A skirmish had begun outside – he heard the clash of swords down by the orchard. But all his thoughts were focused on the charged air of the house. The raiders were above him. The ceiling seemed to quiver with their footfalls.

Another door gave access to the staircase. He ventured lithely up it – and found an Ashman waiting at the top. A sword came hissing at his head; he blocked the blow, returned it, and then pressed home his advantage. The Norseman reeled backwards, and he gained the topmost step. Before the grisly raider could recover, he lunged to split his helmet – and his skull.

Eldred took a breath, and wiped his sleeve across his mouth. His fingers flexed and tightened round the handle of his sword. Another lamp was burning in this chamber; but something else was moving in the dark wings of the house. Cautiously he started down the passage into gloom. Beyond the light, the place was like a warren: a burrow full of silences and voids. Starlight filtered into it where windows stood uncurtained; but that was little more than ghostly dust. His starved eyes strained for light enough to *see*.

He stole into a bed-chamber; the bed seemed quite the largest he had ever come across. A second door, across the room, was standing just ajar. As Eldred crept towards it, the Ashman pounced.

He'd been lurking in the shadows on the far side of the bed. His lunge was so ferocious that as Eldred tried to parry it, his sword was struck aside, spinning from his grip. He thudded up against the wall, and thrust himself straight back – springing at the raider, who was readying his blow. Seizing the man, he bore him down and dragged him to the floor – finishing on top, where he could put his knife to use. He plunged the narrow blade into an eyehole of the helmet. The wolf convulsed beneath him, and was still.

Eldred clambered to his feet, and listened, breathing hard. The house was hushed but fitful sounds of combat still rang out around the building. Where was the maid he'd glimpsed, that time before? Retrieving his sword, and sheathing it, he went back to the light. The oddly furnished room was as he'd left it – the Ashman's body lying in a pool of blood and slime. Again he paused to listen; peered around. And then he saw he'd overlooked the low door in the corner. He crossed to it, and gently eased it open. Another narrow staircase lay behind it. A blur of darkness waited at the top.

He knew that she was up there. The silence was alive, and full of fear. He started slowly up the stairs – as cautiously as someone trying to creep up on a deer. There was no door above him, just a bower. The room was full of dimness; but as he came up into it, he glimpsed a jerky movement in the corner. His eyes made out her crouching shape; her white gown stood out palely in the gloom.

Eldred stopped, and stared at her; then very carefully showed his empty hand.

Lyn was huddled on her bed, pressed back into the angles of the corner and the roof. Terrified, she'd listened to those grunting *things* downstairs; then ringing metal, thuds and scuffles . . . stillness. In the awful pause that followed, the first line of that poem started throbbing in her head: obsessively repeated, like a record with a scratch.

When the turf is thy tower . . .
When the turf is thy tower . . .
When the turf –

And then she'd heard the stairwell door creak open. Stifling a helpless sob, she'd drawn her knees up tighter; listening to the slow, ascending footsteps. A head came into view above the level of the floor. The dim light from the windows touched on hair as pale as frost.

'Frances . . .' he said softly. 'I am from *Frances* come.'

The voice was strangely accented, but urgent in its tone. Lyn stared back, her fists against her mouth. Her pent-up thoughts were racing now. The man who'd come for Fran that night had had fair hair as well . . .

He came no further up the stairs; just stood there with his hand extended, waiting. And down below, the lights were on; their afterglow just tinged his sombre figure.

'Come thou,' he invited.

'Who's downstairs?' she whispered.

'*Witching*-wolfs. But we have slain them now.'

Shocked as she was, the words had little meaning. What counted was his reassuring tone. The dry, firm voice of someone Fran had sent. Reluctantly – still feeling sick – she forced herself to move: getting off her bed, to stand forlornly in the middle of the room. Hugging her silk dressing gown around her, as if the summer night was winter-cold.

'Come thou,' he cajoled her, easing backwards. The soft glow of the living room was almost as inviting. She came at last, with timid little steps, and let him lead her down towards the light.

A foul smell was waiting to surprise her. She glimpsed a crumpled body, then he moved to block her view. Covering her mouth and nose, she looked at him instead. His face was drawn, but handsome, with laughter lines cracked deep around the eyes. Seen by proper light at last, it helped her to relax a little more. His smile now was earnest – clearly meant to reassure.

'Sky-Map,' he said carefully. '*Carta Astrarum*. We must have it.' He gazed at her imploringly: willing her to understand the words. She stared wide-eyed, not following at all – and then it came together in a flash. *The Enigmatic Star Chart*. Martin's book . . .

He seemed to sense her comprehension dawning. 'Frances needeth it,' he said.

Lyn nodded quickly, and led the way towards the study. Fizzing with adrenaline, enough to make her giddy, she went to where it nestled on its shelf. The stranger came in with her; she sensed him run his gaze along the rows of books. Perhaps he was impressed by them – but now, to her, they seemed like so much paper. History had come alive. The living, breathing past was at her shoulder.

Myth and Magic in Medieval Europe. She took it down with trembling hands, and turned to give it to him. He'd moved up close behind her, but he didn't take the book.

Instead he thrust a knife into her stomach.

The blow was blunt and sickening – enough to drive her back against the bookshelves. For a disbelieving moment, she thought that he had thumped her in the tummy. Her mouth began to open, and he clamped his hand across it, cramming sound and breath back down her throat. Her eyes stared, huge and frightened. And then he gave the knife a twist, and watched them close in anguish.

The book fell from Lyn's fingers as she flailed at him and squirmed. It thudded to the carpet by his boots and her bare feet. Eldred put his weight behind the knife-thrust and the gag – smothering the scream he knew was backing up inside her. A thin and high-pitched snorting sound was all that she could manage, and even that was more than he could stand. He forced the knife-blade upward with a disembowelling jerk, and Lyn felt life go out of her like water. She fought against oblivion for a horrid, choking moment – then crumpled like a puppet with cut strings. Eldred freed his bloody knife, and stepped away to let her slither down. Her trailing arm dislodged some books, which toppled after her and struck her side. She flopped onto her face, and never felt them.

Eldred wiped his mouth again – a quick, convulsive gesture. He stood there for a moment as if nailed to the floor, then knelt to clean his knife-blade on her gown. The silk absorbed the blood, and left it gleaming. He noticed the rings on her outflung hand, and hesitated briefly – then took it up, as if to kiss, and slid them off her fingers. Shiny silver; noble-looking stones. He put them in the relic-pouch he wore around his neck – then turned his grim attention to the book.

The lettering was only half-familiar; the language of the title was obscure. But this was what he'd come for, sure enough: the lodestone in his signet ring was picking up its power. He turned his hand to watch it glow; then felt his gaze drawn back towards the maiden. The wide eye in her profile seemed to watch him; her look was one of miserable reproach. Grimacing now, he straightened up, and tucked the precious book beneath his arm. Turning towards the doorway, he suddenly lashed out at the lantern – tearing through its paper shell, and snuffing out its light. The magic glass fell tinkling into darkness. He smashed the glowing lamp-stand in the other room as well, as if to cloak his own retreat – and cover up his deeds.

His brother-Ravens waited in the garden. 'I've killed two,' he told them, 'and we have the Chart of Stars.'

'Three have fallen here . . . the rest are scattered.'

'What of the lady?' Erik asked. 'Shall we not bring her too?'

'It is too late for that.' Eldred jerked his head, and they withdrew into the lane; two men bringing up the rear, and covering the shadows with their swords. The horses waited, nervous, though the countryside looked empty in the starlight. The Ravens mounted up, and headed back the way they'd come – still wary of an ambush from the hedges on each side. Eldred glanced behind him only once. The kitchen was still glowing in the dark shell of the house: its doorway open wide, as if to welcome a wanderer home. He turned his face away, and kept on riding.

2

Branwen woke at once, pursued by dread – a freezing wave that chased her up from whisper-haunted sleep. She sensed the walls around her, the ceiling like a coffin-lid above. The cell was stuffed with darkness, and it didn't have a door . . .

She sat up with a panicked gasp; then registered the softness of the bed. Sitting on it, panting now, she realized where she was: a lord's home farm, where they'd been given shelter. The murk took on a texture, and her eyes made out the dim blur of the window.

Sliding from the bed, she padded over to the curtains. The night beyond was bright and clear: the stars like distant fires. She wasn't used to sleeping with a roof over her head, and the sight of them began to calm her breathing. Like the campfires of a thousand guardian angels round the house.

She'd bathed herself, and eaten well. The flimsy gown she wore smelled clean and fresh. The bed itself was fit for a princess. And yet the rush of dread she'd felt still lingered – congealing, sick and chilly, in her belly and her bones.

Someone's soul had cried out in the darkness. Someone she was bound to in some way. Branwen strained her senses, but the night was silent now. She paced the room unhappily – then tiptoed to the door and eased it open. The room they'd given Martin was just there, along the passage. Staring through the dimness at the wood of its closed door, she felt her cold foreboding grow more bitter. And yet, whatever she had sensed, it hadn't woken him.

She stood there for a minute, undecided; then crept back to her bed, and curled up around the sourness in her stomach. The linen nest was comforting. But sleep did not return.

3

The horsemen moved through darkness, tracing paths they couldn't see – guided by their lodestones and the stars. In the last watch of the night, with the Raven's aura strengthening like dawn, they came upon an ancient, haunted barrow. Eldred watched his ring-stone changing colour; then called a halt, and nudged his horse upslope. The others waited on the trail, not speaking. He rode up through the screen of trees, until he reached the bare crest of the mound. The stars looked very bright up here, spread out above the earth. And Rathulf sat his bony horse and waited.

Eldred moved his mount up close, and handed him the book. 'Take it, Northman. Take it. It is done.'

'You know that this is well,' said Rathulf flatly.

Eldred only looked at him, the ghostly starlight tinging his bleak face. Rathulf weighed the book, then smiled grimly – almost mocking.

'His wergild is decided then?'

Eldred tugged his horse away – then wheeled it round again. 'A thousand, yes,' he said, with bitter sarcasm. 'So let that be my wager, wolf. A *thousand* silver pieces on the black.'

CHAPTER III

True Cross

I

They breasted the rise with dawn still fresh behind them, and saw the distant Rectory at last. The farmland looked idyllic – still drowsing in the day's first unspoilt moment. The wayside grass was glistening with dew. Birdsong drifted sweetly from the woods.

Fran knew at once that something had gone *wrong*.

She felt it like a stomach cramp, and almost doubled forward in her saddle. Clenching her fists around the reins, she looked at Leofric. Clearly he'd sensed something too; was staring at the building with a frown. His horse gave a snort, and shifted restlessly beneath him.

Impulsively, she heeled her own mount forward. Her heart was pumping thickly, like a bilge-pump in her throat. Down the quiet lane she came, Leofric close behind her. The clatter of his hoofbeats sounded half a world away.

The dark slot in the sunlit wall grew clearer. She saw it was the open kitchen door . . . Leofric caught her up then, and laid a warning hand on her elbow. 'Frances. *Ware* this place.'

'Where's Eldred?' she asked plaintively – and heard the frightened tremble in her voice.

They pulled up just below the little orchard. He looked around, and stiffened; then swung down, and made for a gap in the opposite hedge. Nervously she turned her head to watch. A fallow, weedy field spread out beyond it, and something dark was lying on the earth. It had a crumpled, flattened look; she thought it was a sack. But birds had gathered, pecking, all around it. They scattered as he reached them. Fran swallowed something bitter. She clambered down as well, on shaky limbs.

The early-morning silence yawned around them. The birds were croaking now, but barely scratched it.

Leofric strode back quickly, peering round. His hand was on the sword beneath his frock-coat. 'What is it?' Fran called squeakily, before he'd even reached her.

Leofric's face was grim. 'It is an Ashman.'

'*God* . . .' She looked towards the house again. The door was still wide open.

Again he touched her, wary and respectful. 'I will go, and see,' he said.

'I'm coming too,' she hissed.

He shrugged, and led the way along the lane. They reached a thin point in Lyn's hedge – ravaged, as if someone had struggled through it. It gave them stealthy access to the garden. And there beneath the apple trees, they came upon the remnants of a pyre.

Leofric hunkered down, and ran his fingers through the ashes; Fran just stared, her hand across her mouth. The flaky patch of greyness was still warmer than the day. Brittle, bony fragments lay like litter in the cinders. She saw the crumbled husk of someone's skull.

'These are wolves as well,' Leofric murmured. 'They do this to their fallen – once the slaughter-field is theirs.'

'Maybe Eldred did it, though,' Fran whispered. Thinking of the bone-fire that had followed their first battle. But Leofric shook his head.

'See how fiercely they have been consumed. The grass around has not caught fire. Some sorcery has done this.' He straightened up, and looked towards the house; its open doorway. 'Eldred may have slain these – but other wolves came here when he was gone.'

'He must have taken Lyn along,' Fran said, with sudden calm. 'God, she'll be so scared, poor girl . . . We have to catch them up . . .' Her voice tailed off.

'We must see inside,' Leofric said. He held her gaze – his own eyes grave, determined. Fran nodded, feeling cold and numb. Together they went up towards the house.

The back door had been smashed aside; the kitchen lights were on. He drew his sword, and stepped across the threshhold. Following, Fran sniffed the air, and pulled a sickened face. A smell like rotting excrement was coming from upstairs.

Leofric found the stairwell, and crept up it. Breathless now, Fran tiptoed in his wake. They came into the living room, and found a murky stain across the carpet. The stink was at its strongest here. She felt her empty stomach start to churn.

'One of them fell here,' Leofric said. Fran glimpsed a pulpy smear, and looked away. The silence of the house closed in around them. A cry began inside her swollen heart. Lyn's name rose to her lips and turned to dust inside her mouth.

She swallowed hard. 'I'd . . . better check her room . . .'

'Where is the Sky-Chart kept?' he asked her softly.

'Oh, Jesus, I don't know . . . I think the study's just through here . . .' She led the way, and stepped into the doorway. Then she stopped.

Lyn?

Leofric at her shoulder. 'Frances, *come* . . .'

'*LYN!*' she screamed. The word became a wail. She lunged across the room, and skidded down onto her knees. She seized Lyn's wrist – and let it drop at once. The flesh was cold, and stiffening like clay.

Another wail came surging up; she choked it with both hands. The effort made her shudder, and her eyes began to stream. Lyn lay there, crumpled, pasty-pale – her profile so forlorn. She looked like a girl with tummy ache, on the very point of bursting into tears.

Leofric looked on, helpless, from the doorway.

'Oh, *Lyn*,' Fran sobbed, 'I'm here, now. I'm *here* . . . You'll never be hurt like this again, I promise . . .' She reached out tentatively – and drew back despite herself. Lyn's body had a horrid, lifeless rigor. Her toffee-penny eyes were hard as glass.

A crimson, sieved-tomato stain had soaked into the carpet.

She heard Leofric venture in, but didn't look around. Lyn's gown had ridden up and fallen open, revealing all. She nerved herself to touch the corpse, and try and make it decent. Her tears fell on the body of her friend.

Leofric was beside her now, and kneeling down to check the scattered books. He looked up at the gap where they had fallen from their shelf. A separate gap, just one book wide, was further down the row.

'The Sky-Chart has been taken,' he said hoarsely.

Fran just wiped her dripping cheek. 'Oh, *Lynnie* . . .'

He grasped her by the shoulders then, and swung her round to face him. 'Leave her, Frances. By Our Lord and Lady, *come*!'

His sudden roughness shocked her into silence. For a moment she just stared at him with jerky, tearful eyes. Then he straightened up, and drew her with him.

'Athelgar must learn of this,' he told her, gently now. 'There is *none thing* you can do here. We must ride.'

Fran nodded raggedly, and rubbed her jacket sleeve across her face. *Lyn's* jacket sleeve. She felt the next pulse coming, like a sneeze; her woeful face began to crumple up. Leofric took her wrist and fairly dragged her to the door. She followed, stumbling, looking back. And then the ghastly sight was gone, and they were back in the living room; now creaking down the stairs towards the kitchen. The open doorway beckoned with its promise of fresh air. She reached the garden, gasping, convinced that she was going to be sick.

'Oh *Christ* . . .' She paused, heaved drily; nothing came. 'Why couldn't Eldred *save her*?'

Leofric spread his hands, and had no answer.

'Oh Lynnie . . . I'm so sorry . . .' Fran raised her head, pushed back her hair – and something caught her eye. Startled, she looked round and up.

A gargoyle shape was crouching on the flat roof of the shed.

Before she could cry out, the Ashman sprang. She flung herself aside, and he just missed her – landing like a spider, and half-scampering around. The caverns of his eyeholes fixed and held her. And then Leofric kicked at him, and sent him lurching back against the wall. A row of flowerpots was smashed to pieces. The Ashman tried to right himself, but Leofric was too fast. His sword was drawn already. He hacked the grisly figure into stillness as she watched.

Fran kept stepping backwards, numbed – and felt a sudden chill against her neck. What did she always think when she was watching scary films? *Don't walk backwards! Don't . . .*

She swung around but nobody was there.

Leofric turned about himself, sword levelled. The silence seemed enormous and unreal; the mellow light a mockery of what had just occurred. He beckoned her to follow. She wavered for a moment, then came forward. Another figure scuttled from the doorway right behind him.

'Look out!'

He spun at once, sword lifted – but the Ashman was too close. He breached Leofric's guard, and slashed the shoulder of his coat. Leofric stumbled backwards as the raider prowled around him. Another mantis-lunge, and he went down onto one knee. The Ashman raised his sword – and then Fran jumped him from behind, wrapping both her arms around his neck. He struggled to dislodge her, but she managed to hang on. His ragged clothes were stiff with mould; he smelled of rotting meat. He might have been gestated at the bottom of a bin.

Her gorge began to rise again; and then he overbalanced, staggered backwards. Like partners in a Dance of Death, they crashed against the woodshed. She took the brunt of that, and lost her grip; he shook her off, but then Leofric pounced. An axe had toppled into view; he grasped the thing and brought it swinging down. Fran rolled clear, and scrambled back, the awful *crunch* still ringing in her ears. Leofric kept on chopping, like a cold, demented woodsman; staving in his victim's chest, and shattering his skull. Then he threw the axe aside, and both of them retreated to the lane; he snatched his fallen sword up as he ran. The horses were still waiting – but Fran's mount shied away as she approached it. She tried again, and failed to catch its rein. Overwhelmed, she screamed at it, which didn't help at all. Leofric loomed above her, already in his saddle. Reaching down, he hauled her up behind him.

She linked her arms around his waist, and let her body sag, burying her face against his shoulder. As the laden horse went forward, and they left the house behind them, her silent, hopeless tears began again.

CHAPTER IV

Dead Men Ride

I

The Ravensbreed had gone to ground in woodland to the east. Leofric used his lodestone, and a hunter's instincts too, but it seemed to take all day to track them down. Deep in the trees, well off the beaten track, a couple of pickets showed themselves, and brought them to the camp.

Fran couldn't stop crying. She'd clung to Leofric, sick and numb, quite heedless of his careful navigation. Her sense of loss was physical – as if a lump of tissue had been gouged out of her midriff. And still the tears kept coming, like a rotten, streaming cold. The shoulder of his coat was soaking wet.

She sniffled as he helped her down. No one spoke. She sensed the Ravens hanging back, around the mulchy clearing. Perhaps it was respect, she thought. Or maybe it unnerved them all, to see their saint despairing. She wiped her eyes, and raised them – to find Eldred standing there. His face was pale. He couldn't meet her gaze.

'Forgive me, Lady. *Pray* for me. We were too late to save her . . .' He came and knelt before her: pressed his lips against her hand. Fran just stared, her mind a blank, not knowing what to say.

'Did they take the Chart?' Leofric asked.

Eldred rose, and glanced at him, and shrugged. 'We searched, but could not find it . . .'

'Where's Athelgar?' Fran mumbled.

'He comes,' a grave voice said. She looked, saw Edgar watching. His solemn, gaunt appearance was a comforter of sorts:

the way he still looked dignified, as well as down-at-heel. He gestured like a gentleman – a *knight* – for her to sit. She looked at him appealingly; then went and slumped down on a fallen trunk. The others kept their distance, but Edgar and Leofric came to stand on either side. More than guardians, though – or even servants. Their presence promised helping hands, to take her own and lead her through the dark.

The gloom of grief had blotted Eldred out. Some bitter little part of her was crying out to blame him – but the anger just kept smouldering, a spark that wouldn't catch. She sensed that he'd withdrawn, and didn't care.

Then Athelgar was kneeling there, and taking her limp hands. She felt the faintest glow of warmth inside her.

'Frances . . .'

'Lyn's dead, my best friend's dead!' she blurted out.

'It grieves us all, to see your pain,' he murmured. 'You foresaw this Marcus's move – and *we* failed to prevent it.'

She blinked at him. 'It's not your fault.'

'Eldred would have ridden like the wind,' he went on quietly. 'He would have saved your sister, if any man could.'

Deep inside, she realized that, and nodded miserably. She felt his strong hands tighten round her own.

He hesitated. 'Eldred could not find the Chart . . . Could it be hidden somewhere . . . ?'

'Oh, *sod* your fucking star-chart! Lynnie's *dead*!' She tugged one of her hands free, and wiped her eyes and dripping cheeks again.

Athelgar sat back and watched her gravely. She glared at him, and saw his face had hardened.

'There is a time to mourn,' he told her softly. 'But if tears could move the heart of God, I would have drowned the *world*.' His pale, bleached eyes kept staring for a moment. Then he rose, and moved away again.

Fran stared after him, perplexed; he didn't look around. Edgar waited next to her, with one foot on the trunk, watching over her without imposing. His calf-high boot was yellow with dried mud. She lowered her gaze, and put her head in her hands – as if to wash her face with her own tears.

That night they kept the campfire high to ward off phantoms from the murky wood around them. Fran just sat and stared into the flames. The firelight, hot and orange, dried her eyes and sticky cheeks, but couldn't reach the slimy cold inside her.

Beyond the black, enshrouding trees, the lamps would still be lit – towns and roads still winking in the distance. But here there was only naked flame, and sparks that flurried up to join the stars.

If tears could move the heart of God, I would have drowned the world.

She raised her head. Athelgar was nowhere to be seen. Other Ravens sat around, conversing in low voices. They'd given her some space to grieve, but Leofric was nearest. She caught his eye, and cleared her throat. He waited.

'How did you meet Athelgar?' she asked him.

'Athelgar came, a pilgrim, to my hall,' he answered simply. 'He shared my meat, and told his dreams, and asked if I would join him. And so it was we travelled on together.'

'Were you lords, or what? In your . . . old kingdom?'

He shrugged, and gestured off across the fire. 'Edgar is an *atheling* – a prince of the blood royal . . . Oswald was in servitude, a bondsman. Steffan was a Stranger, and our enemy in blood. But all of us are brother Ravens now.'

The man called Oswald glanced at her. 'Athelgar said this to me: "Whoever rides with the Ravens is a free man – and a free man never dies."'

Fran nodded pensively, and looked back at Leofric.

'When Athelgar said he would have drowned the world . . . what did he mean?'

The other's face grew sombre – but more from empathy than disapproval. The fire crackled, filling up the pause.

'There was once a rich young nobleman,' Leofric said at last.

'A thane of Wessexena. One night, so it is said, he dreamed a dream. In the meanest field of his estate, so it was shown to him, was buried a pearl beyond price. So when he woke, he went out to that fallow field, hedged all about with thorns . . . and he did search. But no pearl nor other hoard could be disclosed.'

Fran listened, frowning faintly. The other Ravens sat in silence now.

'The next night he did dream again . . . and saw that he was digging in the field. And digging, he disclosed a pearl, the richest pearl that he had ever seen. But it would not come freely from the earth, as though it had its roots within the soil. So in his dream, he dug still deeper round it and saw the pearl was set into the pommel of a sword: a great sword driven deep into the earth. And then he woke.'

A branch snapped in the flames. More sparks rushed upward.

'Now, the rich young nobleman was troubled by these showings. He was pondering their meaning when his wife was taken sick. He stayed beside her bed for many days and many nights, for she was fair and gentle, and he loved her very well. But notwithstanding all his prayers, she died. Then the rich young nobleman was mortified with grief, and said that now his soul had perished with her. He sold all things that he possessed, and gave the gold and silver to the poor. And one poor man, a beggar, gave to him a holy relic in return. And when this relic was unwrapped, he saw it was the longsword of his dreams. The blade of the *Bretwaldas* men call Sky-Edge, sword of souls.'

She stared at him. 'And . . . what about his pearl beyond price?'

Leofric's eyes were hooded now; reflective. 'He buried her in his fallow field, all hedged about with thorns – and went onto the road, a dead man riding.'

Fran absorbed that numbly, and looked back into the fire.

And out in the dark, beyond its light, a faceless shape sat

listening. Remembering *her* face, as if he'd kissed it yesterday; her hair, pinned up in waves of woven gold. Her cheeks and nose were sunburnt – a redness like the homely glow of having stared too long into the hearth. A well-made face; not beautiful, yet full of life and warmth . . .

And then his field, at twilight, with the cross of twisted branches. He used a stone to pound it into place. A piece of her fine needlework was fastened to the upright. It fluttered in the evening breeze as he walked slowly back towards his horse.

Athelgar sat silent for a moment, in the dark. Then the whetstone in his hand began to scrape again, his longsword growing keener with each stroke.

2

Eldred, too, had kept back from the light. He knew that Frances was no saint – but maybe she had power enough to see into his heart. Especially if she really was a witch.

Restless now, he prowled around the fringes of the camp. Out in the gloomy undergrowth, he heard a stealthy rustling, and froze. 'Who comes?' challenged Erik's voice, and he started to relax. Then someone pounced, and seized him from behind.

He groaned as he was slammed against a tree trunk. The hands renewed their purchase on his coat, and flung him down. Winded, he rolled over and reached for his knife. Shadow-figures hemmed him in, like spirits from the black heart of the wood. One of them leaned forward hungrily.

'Where is the Sky-Chart?' Rathulf hissed.

'Call your dogs off me, you *wiking* bastard.' His hand moved from his knife to wipe his mouth. 'I put that cursed book into your hands.'

'It is not here,' said Rathulf fiercely.

Eldred spat, and clambered to his feet. That was Aldhelm,

looming up beside him. A pulse of firelight showed him Erik's sneer.

'She knew what I was asking for – and gave me that book. The paper's *stained* with shinecraft. The lodestones know their own.'

'A page has been torn out – *behold.*' Rathulf held the book out, where the fitful glow could reach it.

Eldred looked, and raised his eyes. 'I haven't got it, Rathulf,' he said flatly.

They glowered at each other. The filtered light grew stronger as more fuel went on the fire. Eldred noticed Harald, who was lurking in the background. A man considered brave enough to bear the Three-Cross standard; yet here he was, conspiring in the shadows.

As I am, he thought sombrely; feeling as resigned as Harald looked.

'What if there's another answer?' Erik murmured slowly.

'Give it, then,' snapped Rathulf.

'The Summoner went back in secret: stole the thing away.'

A startled pause; then Rathulf thumped the book. '*Bastard.* We must find him – and the witch.'

'How?' said Eldred sourly.

'Athelgar will seek her out . . . and she will come to him. All we need do is wake and wait.'

Sounding satisfied with that, he turned towards the fire. Eldred suddenly reached out, and took hold of his cassock. 'I can see her eyes,' he rasped. 'Still watching me.'

'Blind them, then,' said Rathulf, unconcerned.

'It was not *right*. She had no part of this.'

Coldly Rathulf shrugged him off. 'The lady had possession of the Chart, which was not hers. Her fate was sealed already. Your kindness would have killed her just the same.'

3

The farmer and his wife were up while dawn was still a promise; but they found the Welsh girl downstairs in the kitchen. Sitting at the table, with her jacket on over her borrowed nightie. Waiting, like a cat, to be let out.

Martin found her standing in the yard. The eastern sky was glaring, but the air was thin and dank. Yet Branwen was still barefoot – her jacket round her shoulders and a nightdress on beneath it. She was studying a crumpled sheet of paper.

'Morning,' he said – then gave a sheepish smile. 'Sorry, but I can't remember it in Welsh.'

Yesterday, along the road, she'd taught him a few words of her old language. They'd started off with basic stuff, like *haul* and *dŵr* and *dafad*. Then on to hawking CH sounds, and phlegmy double-Ls. She'd listened to him choke on them, and giggled like a girl. He thought of her sitting on that stile, indulgent and delighted. '*Bara a chaws* . . .' she'd prompted, teasing him. Even as he'd shared her joke, he'd felt a sudden flutter of arousal. But now her face was tired and grave again.

Chickens were pecking in the yard. A chained dog sat and watched them. Breakfast would be ready soon. He smelt the bacon, sizzling in butter.

He'd been surprised at the warm welcome they'd been given by the Tribes: the fellowship of travellers and protestors. And now he'd been surprised again, to get this hospitality from a farmer.

He went across to join her, and saw what she was holding. Something icy filled his throat, and lodged there.

'What's that?' he croaked – already knowing.

'A copy of our Circle, which we spoke of before.'

He swallowed. 'You've had it with you all the time?'

'Since before our ways met.'

'Where did you get it?'

She shrugged. 'A house near Cofentreium. A high-born lady lived there.'

'What was she like?'

'Beautiful, and cold,' she said.

'Jesus, that's my sister.' He took a rueful breath; then glanced at her. 'She isn't cold, she's really nice . . .'

'Your sister?' Branwen murmured. 'Then this was the chart *you* used?'

He nodded, feeling angry and frustrated. *Lyn, you silly girl: I said to* burn *it!*

Branwen watched him carefully. She moistened her lips . . . then pinched them closed again.

'It is a necromantic chart,' she said, after a pause. 'A gateway for the lost ones: the black martyrs.'

'Hold on . . . *You* were summoned.'

'We are all of us black martyrs: dead to this world, although we walk and breathe.' She chewed her lip, still looking at the map. 'The Ravensbreed have flown now – but there may be other things the Chart can tell us.' She sounded slightly wary at the prospect.

'About this call you've had?' he asked.

'Some thing is arising in the south. The Raven has moved northward now, away from his old nest – but the evil is still flowing up the road. It may be that my brothers have not sensed it. So I must find the source, and make them know.'

'What sort of evil is it? Can you tell?'

'Some thing dead, and in his grave – but restless, as we are.'

'And buried at Glas . . . tingabury?'

'Perhaps.' She started folding up the map again. 'There are many secrets sleeping in the earth around that place. Many years ago, the monks dug up an ancient tomb. A skeleton was found, his brain-pan smashed. They claimed that words were graven on a cross. *Hic iacet sepultus rex Arthurius in insula avallonia* . . .' She raised her eyebrows, as if that said it all; then crammed the chart into her jacket pocket, and turned back towards the house.

Martin stayed where he was. 'You're not saying that it's Arthur's *ghost*?' he muttered.

Branwen paused, and gave him a disdainful backward glance.

'Arthur is not dead,' she told him tartly.

CHAPTER V

In Search of Holy England

I

Fran stood there at the centre of the ruins, oblivious to the tourists milling round her. She might have been the statue of a long-forgotten saint miraculously left standing when the roof came crashing down.

To the glory of God this cathedral burned. She'd picked the phrase up somewhere, and it hovered in her head. The last time that she'd been here – just a month ago, with Lyn – they'd marvelled at the building's peace and silence. Today, despite the carefree faces round her, it seemed she heard the roaring fire of fifty years ago.

Oh, *Lynnie*.

The rubble had been cleared away long since, to leave a gutted shell. The reddish walls – still grimed by smoke – were like a jagged frame around the sky. Their skeletal arched windows made them even less substantial. The traceries of stonework looked as delicate as lace.

The nave had been paved over, with just the stumps of pillars to be seen; interspersed with benches now, where students read, and lovers talked, and office workers ate their sandwich lunches. They came and went, but Fran stayed where she was, the still point in a time-lapse film. Gazing east towards the sanctuary and altar.

She'd had to come to Coventry again. Two days after that awful, awful morning, she *needed* to know what was happening about Lyn. What had been reported; what theories people had. When and where the funeral would be.

A cross of blackened roof-beams had been mounted on the altar: a skewed silhouette against the bones of blown-out windows. Two words, inlaid with gold, stood out behind it.

FATHER FORGIVE

I can't, she thought. *I can't forgive whoever did that.*

Lyn's mournful, martyred stare was there before her. Fran swayed, and dug her fists into her pockets. She must look like a beggar, she thought, with her scruffy, dirty clothes and unwashed hair. Or maybe like a junkie, with her pale and dull-eyed face. No wonder everyone was walking round her.

Athelgar was restless, and had drifted out of sight. She realized he had gone, but didn't care. The medieval ruin had left him awestruck: a whole cathedral, derelict and shattered. Amazingly, the spire still stood – tall and gaunt against the summer sky.

'Who razed this place?' he'd asked, as they approached it.

She'd looked the spire up and down. 'The Germans.'

'*Germanii*. The Old Saxons?' He shook his head, as if in disbelief. 'Our *own kin*?'

'Things have changed a bit,' she'd told him sourly, and walked on through the gaping western doorway. And here she'd been for nearly half an hour. Still searching for a peace she couldn't find.

The local paper had had plenty to say on the city's latest murder. They'd printed Lynnie's graduation photo; she looked so proud and happy. Fran had cried again, right there in the street, but she'd managed to keep reading through the tears. Talk of 'distraught parents' made her wince with real pain.

Nothing had been said about human remains in the garden. What of the ones Leofric had killed? Had other Ashmen come for them, and given them a sorcerous cremation? Forensics must have found *some* trace . . . but clearly they were keeping very quiet.

Police would like to interview a group of undead Vikings. The thought brought up a bitter laugh. She stifled it behind her hand; it turned into a sob of tears and snot.

Pigeons whirred contentedly above her. A pair of them took flight, spattering the sunlight with their wingbeats. Fran sniffed, and wiped her cheek, and turned away. She walked towards the gateway in the north wall, where a great porch linked the ruins with the splendid new cathedral. Coming down the steps, she saw that Athelgar was standing in its shadow. Like her, he was a fixture which the passers-by ignored, despite his murky clothes and shroud-like coat. His back was turned towards her as he gazed up at the window: the wall of glass that screened the new interior.

Fran trudged down to join him, eyeing the ghostly figures frozen in the panes. Saints and angels, row on row, engraved into the glass. Again, she'd been impressed last time, and felt unsettled now. The figures loomed above her as she moved up to his shoulder. Images of frost and bone, with empty holes for eyes.

'Shinecraft,' he said softly, as if sensing she was there. 'What wraiths are these, which guard God's house?'

'They're pictures,' she said tiredly. 'Just images, that's all. There's Alfred the Great . . . and Thomas à Beckett . . .' (*God, he had a sword stuck through his head*) '. . . Mary in the middle . . . and the angels all around . . .'

'Which of them is Alfred?' he asked, frowning.

'There,' she told him. 'Second row. They made him a saint. And who remembers *you*, any more?'

He must have heard her bitterness: the dead note of despair. But he kept on staring at the screen – until she took his sleeve, and drew him with her.

2

The summer sun was bright, but there were demons in the city. Edgar heard them wailing to each other. The vile sound made his stomach clench; he reached behind his shoulder for his sword. And yet the folk around them kept on walking, unperturbed. He gazed at them, and checked himself, but left his sword-hand resting on his shoulder. The blade was slung, and wrapped in cloth; it might have been the bedroll of a tramp. Once or twice a person met his eyes – and hurried past.

Oswald backed towards him; turned to stare. 'Blood of Christ,' he muttered, 'what are *they*?'

Slowly Edgar shook his head. He was thinking of the tales he'd heard: round campfires, or the hearth-stones of great halls. Tales of such as Beowulf, the mighty men of old – and of the evil creatures that they'd fought. The sons of fallen angels. Kin of Cain.

They'd banqueted on horrors, down these Ages of the Raven; but always crossing swords with human foes. He'd never dreamed to face a thing like Grendel. Its race had died out long ago – or so he had believed.

The demon whooped and wailed again. A passing woman glanced behind her, back along the road. Edgar turned to look as well; the crossroads, with its ghostly lights, was empty. Oswald shifted, foot to foot. His hand was on the sword beneath the heavy cloak he wore.

They'd come with Athelgar and Blessed Frances. The city, huge and roaring, had engulfed them; they'd crept through street and underpass, observed from every side. The saint looked sickly and distressed: perhaps there was a relic in the high-church that could salve her. Edgar threw a glance at the cathedral. Its spire rose beyond the roofs: a burnt-out torch against the cloudless sky. The sight of it distressed him even further. What evil had taken Cofentreium of Mercia, where churches were destroyed, and demons walked?

'Where are they?' Oswald wondered, through his teeth. 'Athelgar, and the Lady. We must *go*.'

Once more they heard the banshee: it was closer. Edgar's face was hard as stone, although his mind was racing. Should they stand, and meet it here – or look for hallowed ground to hold against it? People had stopped in ones or twos, but still looked deathly calm. He realized what had happened, then. The giants who possessed the town had manacled their souls.

Lord, he thought – and heard small feet behind him. A little girl came running up; dodged round him without looking. Hiding from a playmate, as if no one else existed. As if she hadn't even heard the demon.

He stared at her; she seemed to sense his gaze, and turned her head. Her eyes were wide and clear. He forced his rigid face to smile; she smiled shyly back. The giants hadn't claimed her yet: he saw that straight away.

Then she ducked away, and scurried out into the road – just as the beast careered into view.

'Holy Mother Mary . . .' Oswald hissed.

Edgar's heart became a fist, bunched hard against his ribs. The monster's shell was burnished white, like ivory or bone. Bluish lightning flickered from its forehead and its jaws. It screeched at a demented pitch. The little girl went stiff with terror – frozen in its path. The demon hurtled forward to devour her. Edgar's muscles clenched as well, then flowed to let him lunge and scoop her up. The howling monster filled the world, and missed them by a hand's-span. A phantom wind swirled round him but he kept his hold, and hauled the girl to safety. The monster sped on, screaming; he glimpsed the fiery eyes in the back of its head. And yet it moved on wheels, like some great engine out of Hell.

Instinctively he hugged the child; then heaved her up, and looked her in the face. Pale and shocked, she peered back. Again he found a smile to offer her.

'Katie!' someone shouted, more in anguish than relief, and running feet approached him from behind. He was still turning when a white-faced woman snatched the girl out of his arms – jealous and defensive, like a cat about to claw him. The child burst out crying, but wrapped her arms around her mother's neck. The woman glared at Edgar, and strode hurriedly away.

Edgar stood and watched her go, still shaken with reaction.

The beast had almost had them both. And he'd been treated like an outcast for his pains. The lot of every Raven, and he struggled to accept it. But something deep inside him felt the hurt.

They could hear more demons taking up the cry, gathering like wasps around their nest. He turned his head as Oswald crossed towards him. 'What shall we do?'

'Find Athelgar, and leave this place,' said Oswald, low and wary.

'What kind of thing was *that*?'

His brother shrugged – still shaken. 'A name was written on its side: Woleeche, or Poleeche . . . but it passed me by too quickly.'

'I think their lair is near,' said Edgar slowly. 'And Athelgar will wish to know their strength . . .'

Oswald wavered but Edgar was resolved. The demon had brushed him with its wings, and now he felt an impulse to pursue it. Perhaps to challenge it again – and dance out of its reach. Defy it as only dead men might. Let commoners disdain him if they would.

They set off down a side street in the direction of the sounds. The wailing came and went above the rooftops. Edgar felt the atmosphere changing. The next road that they came to was deserted, with the preternatural stillness of a storm about to break. The calm before the onset of a battle. His instincts knew it right away. Out of sight, but somewhere close, the men of war were waiting.

He unslung his bedroll and unwrapped it. The sword gleamed bright against the dirty blanket. Oswald turned to scan the road – and stiffened. 'Look.'

Edgar did so, straightening. A man was standing watching them from fifty yards away. They could see his greying hair and unkempt beard. His grubby clothes had once been white, although his coat was dark. To Edgar he looked austere and unworldly: like a hermit who had crawled out of his hole. For no good reason, something quailed inside him.

Oswald was staring. 'Dominicain,' he said. 'It is the *prester*.'

Edgar frowned – and the watcher stepped from view.

'It's *him*,' insisted Oswald, starting forward. Edgar followed, sword in hand, the blanket draped around it. The man had seemed familiar, yes – but was his brother right?

They heard shouting in the distance. A dog was barking somewhere. The sound of breaking glass came on the breeze. The battle had been joined, perhaps a street or two away. Men against the demons? Or had the demons driven them to fight among themselves? Whichever, he and Oswald were behind the battle-lines. The empty road was waiting; the silence desolate, and yet expectant.

They came up to the corner where the watcher had been standing. There was no trace of him there. But others were standing in the road – a clutch of yeomen armed with makeshift weapons. They were staring in the opposite direction, as tense as levies waiting in reserve. A couple glanced around at them, but didn't make a move. Edgar heard a distant sound, like missiles hitting shields. A monster screeched, in fury or distress.

A narrow passage led between two houses. They strode along it, anxious now to catch the stranger up. The battle was a loose-knit one; they seemed to hear its noises all around them. Men were running somewhere – in a charge or a retreat. They came into an alleyway, a gulley lined with crumbling reddish bricks. Houses rose to left and right. The *eremite* was waiting for them there.

'Dominicain . . .' said Oswald – and a crack of thunder split the air around them. Smoke burst from the pair of pipes the grim-faced Preacher held. Oswald was flung backwards, spouting blood. He slumped against the wall and slithered down it. His dropped sword rang out dully on the rough stones of the path.

Edgar stared in disbelief. The bitter smoke engulfed him, stung his nostrils and his eyes. Oswald's chest was torn apart – his heavy cloak in shreds . . .

His head snapped round; the pair of pipes was levelled at him now. One of them still smoked with devil's breath. The Preacher's face was pitiless; disdainful. Edgar made to raise his sword. Dominicain just braced himself behind his fire-arm.

'Drop your sword, or likewise be destroyed.'

Edgar heard men coming up behind him. He turned, to find them blocking his retreat. The yeomen who'd been waiting in the roadway. Their faces, like the Preacher's, showed no mercy.

Every noble instinct balked at giving up his sword. But all his warrior's strength had turned to sickness. He'd come to test his mettle against demons. Instead, he'd found a brother who'd betrayed him.

He loosened his grip, and let his longsword fall. It clattered in the gutter like the base metal it was.

'Take him,' said Dominicain behind him, and they did.

3

'Something is amiss,' said Athelgar.

It didn't take a visionary to work that out. Another back-up transit hurtled past them, blue lights flashing. The sirens were converging to the north of the cathedral. It sounded like a riot was in progress.

'Maybe they went to look,' suggested Fran.

Athelgar fished his lodestone out, and cupped his palm around it: peering into shadow, like a man about to light a cigarette. Fran waited, feeling irritable and restless. 'What?' she asked, after a pause; his puzzled frown had deepened.

'The light is different.'

'How?' she asked, not bothering to look.

'As the fire in a smithy, when the iron is not pure. There is another lodestone here.'

'Whose?'

'I know not,' he said slowly. 'Some of us are scattered yet. Still wandering . . .'

Oh, God, she thought sulkily. Tracking down an errant member of Athelgar's band was the last thing she felt like doing. But then he closed his fist around the jewel. 'We must go.'

Despite herself, she blinked at him. 'So what about the others? Edgar?'

'They will make their own way back. There is danger here.' He said that with the wariness he'd shown at Imber village. The sirens had unsettled him, but this was something more.

Whatever it was, she felt it too. The sunny afternoon had failed to pierce the night inside her – but now the heedless city seemed more hostile. She looked around uncertainly, then let him set the pace. The sooner they were out of it, the better.

CHAPTER VI

Night in Gehenna

I

'Five hundred *years* have passed, since last we met. What news have you to tell me, brother? Speak.'

Edgar heard him dimly, through the grinding in his head. Even his brains felt bruised and swollen now; it seemed his skull must split along the seams. He brought his face up, blinking blood. Another fist drove into it. The blow felt oddly shapeless: a surge of pressure rather than a punch. But hard enough to knock him to the floor.

Carl stepped backward, massaging his hand. The others waited with him, as their battered victim tried to clamber up. It was like watching a drunk in the gutter. He strained, and slumped – then flailed around: as if no longer aware that they existed. His torn white shirt hung open, stained with blood. His face was doused with crimson; his blond moustache now matted and bedraggled.

A *betrayer of the poor*, so the Preacher had told them. *His brotherhood are plotting our defeat and execution*. Carl wasn't really sure who the arrogant bastard was – except that he was rich enough to lug a *sword* around. The weapon was a contrast to his shabby, unwashed clothes; he was clearly an eccentric of some sort. But the bones of his disdainful face betrayed his high-class background – and Carl was going to fracture every one.

Edgar reached his knees, and paused for breath. Head down; panting hoarsely. The air was thick with sweat and hate – the latter just as acrid, like a taste on Julie's tongue. She hung back in the doorway, her face a mask of morbid fascination. Disgust was playing at her mouth, without her being aware of it.

The room was lit by candles, which increased its greasy feel. They'd been placed around the floor, in dirty jars. The mottled plaster seemed to bubble in the glow, as if it was decaying while she watched.

Edgar straightened, swaying. Steve moved in to take his turn – and Edgar's own fist lashed out without warning. It clipped Steve's jaw, and spun him back. The blow was a vindictive one, without hope of escape. Edgar was still clawing back his balance as Neil brought a pickaxe handle down across his shoulders. The brutal impact felled him like a tree.

Steve lurched forward, spitting blood; the punch had chipped a tooth. Livid now, he kicked the fallen Raven. Edgar's body humped around the blow. Julie flinched instinctively. The Preacher didn't blink.

He was leaning up against the wall, drawing deeply on a fag. The hot ash flared and faded in the bleary candle-glow; his dark eyes watched the beating without pity. He spoke into the breaks and breathing spaces: talking to their victim as if no one else but them was in the room. Mixing up his English with a language that they couldn't understand.

Steve steamed in again, with vicious force. 'Okay,' said Carl, and snatched his sleeve. 'Just leave him for a second.'

Edgar lay there, struggling to writhe. Julie hugged her elbows. The Preacher breathed out smoke.

'Where is *Athelgar*?' he asked, as calm as a confessor.

Gasping, Edgar raised his head, but couldn't get his gaze up off the floor.

'Where is the Raven now?'

Dominicain took a slow drag while he waited for an answer. To Julie he seemed part of this old room. His off-white clothes were like the filthy plaster; his dark coat like the shadows in the corners. With his greying hair awry, and a bandolier of shotgun cartridges slung over his shoulder, he had an atavistic look. He might have been the ghost of this derelict house.

As if her thoughts had prompted him, he straightened and came forward to stand next to Carl. Again he spoke in dialect – some weird form of English that she barely recognized. A couple of the others exchanged glances.

'Brother Edgar. Do you hear me now?'

Edgar nodded once.

'Speak for them – or you shall speak for me.'

'I say *this only* . . . brother,' Edgar gasped; and even now, that last word was a sneer. 'Athelgar's saint is with us in the flesh. The Lady of the Ravens keeps us now.'

'*Ubi Corvus est?*' Dominicain demanded.

Edgar shook his head. 'I shall not give my *darling* to the power of the *dog*.'

The reference to a psalm wasn't lost on the Preacher; and nor was the defiance. He stood in pensive silence for a moment, sucking the life from his smoke. Then dropped the stub, and crushed it with his boot.

'I pray you, tell me brother,' he said softly. 'Confession shall do better for us both. Together we have ridden far. I will not see you suffer.'

'Our Lord said we should not give pearls to swine.' Edgar glanced around him, still defiant through the pain. 'And *certes*, you are a swine-herd now.'

Dominicain's face twitched; then formed a mirthless smile. 'Perhaps you speak the truth . . . my friend. These people are no match for Raven's-breed. They think that they are hard, but they are soft. They never were in Languedoc. They never saw the things that we have seen.' And saying that, he won his first reaction. A muscle jumped in Edgar's ravaged face.

Dominicain kept staring for a moment; then straightened up and gestured to his men. 'Bind him to the chair.' The circle closed in tighter, and they hauled their victim up. The wooden chair was the only piece of furniture in the room. They put him on it; tied him to it. Ankles to the chair-legs, and his arms behind the back. Dominicain had turned away, came walking back to Julie. He didn't even glance at her; just bent down for the plastic bag he'd brought. Something he had scavenged from the ruins round the building. He'd been out there until dusk, amid the rubble – creeping round, and crouching down, and filling up the bag. Like someone harvesting a crop. She caught a glimpse of greenery, and frowned.

The torturers moved outwards, leaving Edgar trussed and slumped against his ropes. The Raven's heart was pumping faster now. An icy stream pulsed through it with each beat. He peered through his blood at Dominicain's back. The Preacher was standing with his head bowed, as though deep in contemplation – or summoning strength.

Then he turned, eyes blazing, full of darkness. The stream of cold congealed in Edgar's heart. He thought of what they'd seen when they campaigned in Languedoc. The heaps of charred and mutilated corpses. As if they'd raided into Hell, like the heroes of fireside myth . . .

Dominicain came forward slowly. He was holding a shiny sack in both gloved hands. The others watched in silence, as if *they* were nervous now.

'Know you of the fate of Hugh Despenser?' Dominicain asked grimly. 'An English lord as arrogant as you. He was crowned with nettles for his crimes; his private parts were cut from him, and burned before his face. And then he was hanged, cut down again, and quartered.' Standing in front of Edgar now, he opened up the bag. It was full of nettles: bulging with their ragged, withered leaves.

'Where is the Raven's nest?' he asked.

Edgar took a jerky breath, but offered no reply.

Dominicain pulled the bag over his head.

Edgar writhed in blind, convulsive silence – like someone in the death-grip of a crude electric chair. The white hood of the plastic bag compounded the impression, and Julie felt her gorge begin to rise. The old wood creaked alarmingly, and Neil and Steve moved in to hold his shoulders. The Preacher grasped the bobbing bag, and pressed its contents inwards.

Edgar arched his back, and let a muffled sound escape him. Dominicain kept squeezing, his face a mask of bitter resolution. Then he pulled the bag off, spilling nettles to the floor. Edgar's jaw and teeth were clenched, his eyes were still screwed shut. His bloody face was blistering already.

Dominicain leaned close, as if confiding with a friend. 'Now shall I cut your *couillons* off, and roast them on a spit?'

Edgar's face came round to his. He grunted once, to vent his pain; then spoke through gritted teeth. 'Do what you will, but Athelgar shall kill you. Not even blessed Frances will plead your cause.'

'Frances. Who is she?'

'The Lady of the Ravens, sent from God. And you have damned your self.'

The other's fierce stare appeared to flicker – then grew firm. 'Not so. God stands with me, betrayer. I live. *You* are damned.'

'Yes, we were in Languedoc,' said Edgar to his face. 'You scavenged like a dog among the martyrs. You said you had no part in it – but now we see you *lied*.'

The Preacher hit him – forehand, backhand. His face was white with rage. He broke away, and strode back to the corner. A couple of plastic petrol flasks were standing by the wall. He snatched one up, unscrewed the cap and turned again to Edgar. 'For fuck's sake . . .' someone murmured; then '*Jesus!*' as Dominicain began to douse their prisoner. The others shrank away at once. The giddy stench of petrol filled the room. Julie glanced in horror at the naked candle flames – blurred by glass, but open to the air.

Edgar gave a retching cough. The liquid pooled beneath him, as the cracked and dusty floorboards drank it up. The Preacher dropped the empty can, and fumbled in his pocket.

'Listen . . . hold on . . . *Jesus*,' Carl protested. He was already by the doorway, and the rest of them were jostling to get past him. Dominicain had found his box of matches. He turned his head and looked, as if surprised to find them there.

'*Leave us*,' he said flatly.

They stumbled back beneath his gaze: more frightening than the petrol. He let them all withdraw into the passage, then looked back round to Edgar.

'The alchemists have mixed this brew to feed the horseless engines. *Petrol* is the name they give to it. It burns as lamp-oil does, but hotter. As hot as Hell's own flames.' He held the match against the box. 'Now will you beg for mercy?'

Edgar took a breath, and coughed again. 'I will not.'

Dominicain began to back away. 'Then pay for your transgressions.'

'Just as the Cathars paid?'

The Preacher grimly shook his head. 'I tried to stop that butchery. You *know* this.'

'I know you seek to *burn* your fellow man.'

Dominicain had reached the door. He laid the match against the roughened paper. 'Sometimes spirit must be cleansed of flesh.'

Edgar fixed him with his one good eye. 'And what of the one you tried to save? Will you see another die as she did?'

Dominicain went very still. They stared at each other, with no sound save for Edgar's laboured breathing. Then the Preacher came at him, grasped Edgar's head and twisted it around. The neck gave with an ugly crack; the body spasmed, and slumped. Julie, watching, winced in sympathy.

Dominicain breathed out, and let the Raven's head loll forward.

'This is the only mercy that you shall receive from me,' he murmured bleakly.

Retreating to the door again, he struck his match and tossed it at the body. The petrol caught and blazed at once, engulfing man and chair in yellow flames. A wave of heat came rushing out, and broke against their faces. And then the door was slammed on the inferno.

Dominicain stepped back from it: staring at the panel, as if waiting for the fire to crackle through. Appalled, the others shrank away – retreating off the landing, stair by stair. When he turned to look at them, his glare was just as full of pent-up flame.

'Which of you has killed before?' he asked.

None of them – not even Carl. But no one dared to say so.

'So. You shall grow used to it. Acquainted with the *smell*.' Gesturing, he followed them downstairs.

'Take the cannons. We must leave the city.'

The guns were in the shell of the front room, with their provisions. Hastily they got the stuff together; an acrid haze of smoke was in the air. Pausing, Julie heard a muffled sound upstairs. The burnt-up chair collapsing with its body. So she hoped.

She glanced at Carl. His face was pale, but set. The others, although shaken, moved efficiently enough – and so did she. They were all of them committed, now. Perhaps Dominicain was right: the first death was the hardest one to stomach . . .

'Where to?' Neil asked, slinging the old carbine they had recently acquired.

'Woodland. We shall watch, and wait for other folk to join us.'

Julie wiped her mouth, still folding blankets. Still straining her ears for a movement from upstairs. The corpse was surely charcoal now – and yet it felt that someone else was with them in the house. A brooding, gloating presence in the void above the flames.

CHAPTER VII

Requiem

I

Fran knelt – or rather, slumped onto her knees. A heavy, hollow weariness came over her at once. She felt as drained as someone with ME.

The afternoon was scorching hot. The grass felt dry and prickly through her jeans. But the pile of floral tributes still looked fresh. Lilies, and carnations (which had been Lyn's favourite flowers), and a wreath of white, expensive-looking roses. The mound of fresh-turned soil was almost hidden.

She gazed at them with dry, sore eyes, then added her own tribute to the heap. Flowers she'd gathered on the way: fading bluebells, vivid poppies, buttercups and daisies. They'd wilted in her sweaty hand, but made a pretty splash. Leaning back, she sniffed and clasped her fingers in her lap.

'Hi, Lynnie . . . Sorry I'm late.'

The crickets kept on whirring, in the longer grass beside the churchyard wall. The air was warm and windless. All around, the countryside was drowsing in the haze.

'I couldn't be here yesterday . . . I couldn't face your poor mum and dad. But look at all these flowers . . . you can see how much we loved you . . .'

The card with the roses was slightly smudged, although it hadn't rained. *Sleep tight, darling. Love for ever. Mummy & Daddy*. Another smudge appeared on it, like magic, as she watched. She cupped her hand across her face, to stifle her own tears.

'*. . . Lynnie . . .*'

A faint, uneasy movement from behind her. She knew that it was Athelgar, and didn't turn her head. The pulse of weeping spent itself – a shower of summer rain. She sniffed away the dregs, and knelt there with her head bowed low. No feeling but the sun against her neck. At length she raised her eyes again, and looked towards the lych-gate. The Welshman, Steffan, stood there – keeping watch. Another of the Ravens was on the far side of the churchyard. They had the place staked out for her, like sombre guardian angels. A country church, amid shady lanes . . . who knew what might creep up?

She looked around at Athelgar. He was leaning on the drystone wall, his coat hung from his shoulders – as if he were impervious to the heat. His face was grave, his eyes full of concern.

'How did *you* feel?' she asked him. 'To lose a person that you really loved?'

The pale eyes grew hooded – then flicked up at her again. 'As if my life was ended,' he said softly.

'Do you still feel that?' she ventured. Right now, she could believe her grief would last a thousand years. The thought was too dispiriting for words.

Perhaps he'd just been screwing her in order to *forget*.

'No,' he said, still watching her. 'It *was* ended – and it is begun.'

She didn't know what to say to that. But something warmed her belly, and began to soothe its pangs. No matter that they couldn't have a future. This war was all the future she could think about, today.

She realized he was looking at her breasts. He glanced away.

'Do you hate, as well as love?' he asked after a minute.

The answer rose like vomit, and she tried to fight it down again. In vain.

'Yes,' she hissed. 'Of course I fucking do.' Gazing at the flowers, she had promised Lyn she'd come back in a year: to see and touch her gravestone – and to tell her that the Ashmen were destroyed. Them and their evil master, Brother Marcus.

Just the thought of his name made her guts convulse with hate.

Can you hear me now, you shit? I'll let the Ravens bury you. Massacre is my *forgiveness too.*

Athelgar looked round, into her eyes.

'I wished that *I* could do so, once. I dared to wish my lady had been murdered by the Danes – so that I could abhor them, and be purged. But she was slain by *sickness*. It came upon the summer wind and took my love away. My sword could not protect her, nor avenge her. I was helpless. And so my grief stayed in my heart, like poison in a wound.'

'Maybe you should take it out on God,' she muttered. Half-musingly; half meaning it.

A thin smile tinged the grimness of his face. 'I have reasoned many times with God – and wrestled with Him too. I do not claim to understand His wisdom and His wyrd. But one who hates God, hates himself – and all the goodness in him.'

She shrugged, and shook her hair back. 'So would you have felt better – if they'd killed her and you'd taken your revenge?'

His face grew solemn once again. 'Eldred's wife was murdered. He killed many in revenge. And still he hates. And still he does not rest.'

Fran stared at him, eyes widening. She thought of Eldred's boyish grin – and how he'd cooled towards her, once she and Athelgar had started screwing. She had an inkling why now. His leader had found love again, while he was still alone. A twinge of guilt went through her. She'd have to make her peace with him when she got back.

'This murderer,' said Athelgar, 'this *Marcus*. Does *he* hate?'

She frowned at him; the name was still revolting. 'Well, obviously. I *told* you.'

'So you did. He seeks revenge. And what is he become?'

Fran moistened her lips, and didn't answer. Watching as he straightened up and came to crouch beside her. He laid his gentle sword-hand on her shoulder.

'Hate not for your dear sister, Frances. Let her rest in peace

– and rise in glory.' His hand moved up to stroke her cheek. 'And we must journey on.'

She nodded stiffly, and clambered to her feet. ''Bye, Lyn,' she whispered, and plodded with him back across the churchyard. A sudden weakness took her as she went out through the lych-gate: she slumped against the wooden post, and clung to it for balance. Athelgar stood by, but didn't move to her assistance; and after a pause she forced herself back upright, and walked on.

Steffan was now waiting with the horses in the lane. Seen against the backdrop of the sunlit Norman wall, he seemed to turn the place into a pocket of the past – despite the modern saddles, and his shabby blue suede coat. He offered Fran the reins of her new mount, his haggard face as hard to read as ever. She nodded, and he held the horse while she swung up astride it. Lyn's jacket was still slung behind the saddle. She couldn't help but turn around and touch its matted fur.

'Go with God,' said Athelgar, still claiming his own mount. 'Steffan and I will follow.'

Fran gazed down at him, frowning. 'Aren't you coming now?'

He shook his head. 'We must scout around. We still know not what fate befell our brothers – Edgar, Oswald. Perhaps another Ash-force is abroad.'

She rubbed her arm uneasily – then glanced at the fourth Raven, as he came around the churchyard wall towards them. Athelgar followed her gaze. One of the horses shook itself and snorted.

'Harald shall ride back with you,' he said.

Harald dipped his head with grave respect. His lean young face was stony and unsmiling. Fran registered discomfort, and had to chide herself. He mounted up beside her, and moved off into the lead. She let her horse pace after him, along the dusty lane – leaving Lyn, and Athelgar, behind her.

CHAPTER VIII

Dominion

I

Harald wasn't one for conversation. He followed the paths like a sniffer dog, absorbed in the old landscape; glancing back from time to time, but gesturing more often than he spoke. Fran was content to let him pick the pace. She felt drained and lethargic – just as she had in the worst days of depression. The evening seemed to match her mood: clouding over, cooling, turning grey. A moist wind stirred the long grass as they crossed a fallow field. It seemed an effort just to pull her jacket on.

Beneath the gloomy slag of clouds, the country looked abandoned. There was just that row of pylons on the skyline. She remembered Marcus's threat again – and recalled a film called *Threads*, about the aftermath of nuclear attack. It had scared her as a schoolgirl, but had never seemed more real than it did now, with that lonely wind against her face, and the clouds above them bulging with black rain.

Harald had reined in beside a solitary tree. His pensive stare unsettled her; she shifted in her saddle. 'How much further, then?' she asked.

'Not far,' he said, still watching, narrow-eyed. As if he searched for something; then he blinked and glanced away. Her horse came plodding up to his. She saw his sword, tucked in beneath his thigh. The handle there for him to grasp. Her stomach did a roll.

No reason. He was on her side. But instinct said that something wasn't right.

The empty field spread out in all directions.

Harald looked at her again. 'What think you of the Danes, my Lady Frances? Shall they all be damned as *wiking*-kind?'

She frowned, a little warily. 'Why do you ask?'

'I seek to know our enemy,' he said.

Fran hesitated. His tone was bland, his face inscrutable. She dropped her gaze, and stroked her horse's neck. 'They killed my friend,' she said at length. 'And how can I forgive them, when I'm hoping that they'll finish up in *Hell?*' She looked up almost guiltily. His grim face hadn't changed.

'You would condemn them all?' he asked.

Yes, her mind retorted – but something in her shrank from such a judgment. Some crippled remnant of her better nature. She shrugged.

'Yea or nay?' he pressed her.

'The Vikings were a bunch of ruthless bastards. We still remember that today, you know?'

Still he waited.

'*No*,' she said, like someone spitting bile.

He drew his sword abruptly; she jumped as if a snake had tried to strike her. Her horse picked up her fright, and shied away. Then Harald's mount was nudging it, and his sword-point was an inch from Fran's shocked face.

'That is wisely answered, Lady Frances. A damned man would lose nothing if he cut a woman's throat – even if that woman were a saint.'

'Jesus . . . you're a Viking too?'

He shook his head. 'The son of one; so I am still a Dane. But many Danes have ridden with the Ravens.'

'Rathulf . . .'

A grim smile touched his mouth. 'I was farming English soil when he was not yet fathered. I was *born* in this land, Lady. My father was a raider, so that I had land to plough, and *my* sons could be artisans, or skalds. Athelstan, the Saxon king, gave justice to us too. But Athel*red* gave orders that the Danes should all be killed.' He gestured with the sword again. 'Is this your judgment too?'

She swallowed hard, and shook her head.

'You said the same in ignorance,' he mused between his teeth. 'Perhaps you *are* as holy as they say. A churchman would have said the Danes are damned.' He spat the last with cynical contempt.

Fran waited: stomach knotted up, heart thumping. Lightning flickered silently behind him – on the skyline, as if the pylons were short-circuiting. As if the lights were going out already. A single windblown raindrop hit her cheek.

'Are you truly blessed, Lady Frances?' he asked softly. 'Or have you come to tempt us to our doom?'

She took a breath, her hands clenched round the reins. 'I'm here to guide you through my world, and help you win this war. And if you don't believe me, you can *kill* me.'

He let his sword-blade waver, almost teasingly, before her. The polished steel looked very sharp. Her muscles wouldn't function for a moment – but then she pulled her jacket wide, and glowered back at him. Her breasts were unprotected, apart from by her blouse and by her bra. Her Cross of Nails gleamed dully in the decomposing light.

'Cross my heart and hope to die,' she said.

He stared into her eyes for what seemed ages – then lowered his sword, and heeled his horse away. Fran slumped, as if a current had been switched off; she almost slid out of her saddle. Giddily she hung on tight, and straightened up again. Harald looked uneasy, almost shamefaced.

'Christ forgive me, lady. I should not have doubted you.'

Unthinkingly she offered him her hand. He moved his horse back up to hers, and stooped to kiss her fingers. She managed not to shudder. His eyes, when he looked up, were bleak and haunted.

'Now we must make haste,' he said. 'And when we meet with Athelgar, there are things which he must hear.'

He led the way on across the empty field. Fran pulled herself together and got going in his wake – still feeling numb and nauseous with shock. The lightning kept on flashing in the distance, but she couldn't hear the thunder. It might have been the spectre of a storm.

2

The rain held back, a mist on the horizon. Dusk was seeping down instead as they reached a sunken lane – and abruptly Harald pulled his horse up short.

'What?' Fran asked, her throat still dry.

Harald's head was turning, side to side. The fields to left and right were grey and silent. The lane dipped down ahead of them, and went into a bend; as far as she could see, it was deserted. Twilight had congealed between the hedgerows, and clotted round the roots of wayside trees. The black mass of a wood was looming up to their right front.

Her own mount raised its head, and gave a snort. She moved herself uneasily – and not just to relieve her aching bum. But then Harald went forward once again. Fran gave a little sigh, and followed him. She guessed such wariness was second nature to him now – until he was could be sure the way was clear. The man was a professional; his presence reassured her. It didn't seem to matter that he might have cut her throat.

The evening breeze was rustling in the hedge. She tracked her gaze across the fading farmland; it seemed to rise around them as they rode into the dip. The rustling was behind her now, as if the breeze was chasing its own tail. The hedgerows on each side of her were silent . . .

She swung round.

No one was behind her. The empty lane rose palely to the skyline. She felt her clenched heart loosen as she turned around again.

A rusty-sounding *twang* came through the twilight – and

Harald's mount cried out in shrill distress. The sound was almost human, but more anguished. The horse went down before her like a foundering ship. Harald slithered clear of it, and fetched up on his knees.

That sudden, evil gin-trap sound still echoed in Fran's ears. Her nerve-ends were reacting while her mind was still a blank – but then she realized where she knew it from. The solitary Norman in the battle of the wood. The one who'd fired a crossbow at her face.

Her horse was panicked, almost bucking now. She struggled to control it, as Harald scrambled up. The saddle's firm and lofty seat was suddenly precarious – a peak from which it seemed she had to fall. She dug her knees in, gripped the reins, glimpsed movement from the corner of her eye. Despite herself, she glanced in that direction – saw figures coming down across the field. Three dark shapes were scurrying towards her. The half-light made a dull sheen of their helmets.

Fear snatched at her throat. She craned around, and saw two more in the other field. *God!* she thought – a pure prayer – *they'll trap us*.

Harald's sword was sheathed against his saddle. He drew it now, and swung around towards her. The fallen horse was whickering behind him. His face was white as flour in the dusk.

'Fly, my Lady! Never let them take you!'

Her nerves sang out to follow his advice – but still she kept her frightened mount in check. 'Come on, get on with *me*,' she called, voice cracking.

'Go you, Lady! Christ!' he shouted back.

She looked and saw the Ashmen coming up towards the hedge. They'd lurked well back, too well-concealed to spot; but now they'd closed the distance in a rush. With a last despairing glance at Harald, she kicked her horse's ribs and let it run.

The surge of speed was dizzying; she crouched, and clung on tight. Straight ahead, along the gloomy lane. The crossbowman was somewhere close, but things like that took ages to reload. She came into the bend, full-tilt – and suddenly the world turned upside down. She felt herself flipped forward, like a jockey come to grief. Over the horse's neck she went, still clinging to the reins – a glimpse of sky, and then she crashed to earth. The numbing impact almost knocked her senseless; for a moment all was aching dark and disembodied nausea. Then panic crackled through her like a jump-start. She opened her eyes, disoriented – and realized she had landed on the verge. She flailed and tried to struggle up, grimacing with distress. The roadside grass had cushioned her, but every bone felt bruised.

Her horse was lying on its side, still paddling the air with one good leg. It whinnied pitifully. She looked towards it, gasping – and saw the rope strung out across the lane.

Somebody was coming, lurching down the road towards her. She squirmed around in fright – but it was Harald. He'd hurt his knee or ankle, and was limping, lunging, stumbling to join her. Two of the Ashmen had reached the lane behind him; she had a glimpse of others in the field. Moving round to cut him off, and catch her.

Adrenaline boiled through her, but her body couldn't run on empty lungs. Again she tried to scramble up – and slipped. She might have been a new-born lamb. The Ashmen came like wolves.

Harald's face was skeletal and bloodless. He threw a glance behind him, looked at her, and raised his sword. 'Forgive me,' he said breathlessly – and swung it at her neck.

Fran squealed, and floundered backwards. The hissing steel missed her by an inch. She gawped at him; he shook his head, his face a bitter mask. 'They shall not have my Lady,' he said fiercely.

'Jesus, please . . .' she said – then rolled aside. His down-swing slashed through dandelions and grass. She scrambled back on hands and heels. 'You can't . . .' she gasped. 'You *mustn't* . . .'

'Frances, *please* . . .' He staggered in pursuit. 'They are my kin, I *know* what they will do.' Again his sword slashed out at her. She ducked the blow, rolled clear of him, and struggled to her feet. Harald overbalanced, and went down onto one knee. He looked at her imploringly: begging her to let herself be killed. She backed away, her fist against her mouth.

The hungry wolves were racing for their prey.

'*Lady* . . .' he said desperately. The horror in his eyes was all for her. It crossed the gap between them like a gust of forest fire; she felt it springing up inside herself. He risked a glance behind him – then took his sword, and twisted it around. 'Forgive me, Athelgar!' he yelled, and fell onto its point.

Fran mewled between her fingers.

His body twitched, and slumped onto its side. Stupefied, she almost stopped; then spun around and ran. The Ashmen were just yards away – she heard their raspy breathing. The leader's visor filled her mind: grotesque as goggles; insect eyes. She heard the shadows scuttling through the fields on either side. As pitiless as hunting dogs. *I know what they will do*.

She pelted headlong down the lane, her aching joints forgotten. Terror drove her engine now. She reached the wood, and veered off to plunge into the trees. They followed, crashing after her. Here it was night already; just rags of grey sky visible amid the spiky murk. She collided with a tree trunk, snagging her jacket on some thorns. Sticks were snapping all around. She heard the withered whisper of the leaves above her head.

It took all the nerve she had to stop and listen. She crouched amid some bushes in the shadow of an oak, her hands against her mouth to stop her breathing. The wolves were ranging through the trees; she heard one passing close. Sword-blades hacked through undergrowth. Startled woodland creatures scurried clear. Peering through the screen of leaves, she glimpsed a sombre figure. His helmet glinted briefly, then he melted into gloom.

Gradually, the sounds of searching faded. All she could hear was the thumping of her heart. But it was fully half an hour before she let her limbs unfreeze, and straightened up.

A fitful wind was soughing through the branches overhead, but otherwise the wood was dark and still.

She wavered, undecided: not knowing where to turn. Tangled darkness loomed on every side. The aftermath of shock was engulfing her in clammy, shivery cold. She didn't have a lodestone. How the hell would she get back?

Harald. He had *killed* himself, he'd been so scared of them. *Never let them take you*, he had said.

Cautiously, she started creeping forward. Straining her ears with every step, but hearing only silence. The wood began to thin at last – but then the ground ran out.

She'd come to the rim of an overgrown chasm. It opened up before her like a shadowy moat, cutting her off from the open fields beyond. The sloping sides were thick with grass; the bottom was a mass of gloomy brambles. It might have been an obstacle for soldiers: a gaping trench or tank trap, full of wire. She knew at once she wouldn't get across.

Shit!

The countryside lay empty in the twilight. She thought she might be looking east, but couldn't really tell; the sunset had been smothered by the clouds. But as she watched, a light came on: an isolated glow-worm in the distance. A window into somewhere warm, if only she could reach it.

She made her way along the edge, hoping for a crossing of some kind. Judging by its width and depth, the gully was another disused railway. The bats were out – she glimpsed one swooping past her. Its high-pitched squeaking made her eardrums twinge.

The cutting deepened gloomily and ended in a tunnel. The bricked-up arch was half submerged in brambles. She squinted through the dimness and saw where shadow drained into a hole. Bricks had been knocked in, like teeth: just there, below the level of the leaves. The tunnel had been opened. And stealthy things were creeping in and out.

Adrenaline shocked through her. Bathed in sweat, she eased into a crouch.

The brambles rustled fitfully. Shapeless movements churned the dusk like silt. She couldn't see them clearly, but she knew that they were Ashmen. The group of them who'd ambushed her had made their hideout here.

Or was this where they crawled into the world?

We are climbing Jacob's Ladder . . . all the way from Hell. The image made her stomach cramp with cold. Backing off, unbreathing, she withdrew into the trees. Shadows overwhelmed her, thick with silence. Every crunching step was a betrayal. She froze and listened helplessly; then steeled herself, and started groping forward. All she had to do was circle round them. Now, before it got completely dark.

A minute or so later, she came to a clearing. The light was very muddy, but she saw enough to stop her in her tracks. She'd almost wandered right into some kind of weapon-dump. Shields and war-gear lay around, all ready to be taken up again. Three spears leaned together, like a frame for cooking-pots. A cloak was draped round something in the middle of the clearing: perhaps a sword stuck in the ground, or maybe just a post. Charms were slung around it, and a helmet had been balanced on the top. The look of it unsettled her, and doubtless it was meant to. She guessed it was a totem of some kind.

A stepped-on twig snapped drily.

The totem turned its head.

She stifled a gasp – and saw it was a guard. His metal skull looked round, the sockets glaring. She didn't move a muscle as they tracked past her position. It felt like being scanned in infra-red.

Her nerve-ends must have been glowing – but the Ashman didn't see her. His helmet kept on turning, like a turret. She forced a thaw into her frozen muscles. Step by step, she started to retreat. The grey haze of the clearing slipped away . . .

Don't walk backwards. Don't.

Something heavy cracked against her skull. The impact

snuffed her mind out like a candle. Her sense of taste was last to go – a bitter tang of bile upon her tongue. Then she crumpled face-down in the mulch, and lay there like a discarded doll.

After a moment a hand reached down, and gently started fingering her hair.

VII

PILGRIMS

If we are to be pilgrims of justice and peace, we must expect the desert.

DOM HELDER CAMARA

Dear Frannie

I'm thinking of you now: but can you feel it? I'm reaching through the dark, because I don't know where you are.

I'm sending this to Lyn's place, in case you go back there. I've called a dozen times, but no one answers. I called your parents, too, and they're as worried as I am. They say you went off without a word – just like you told me Lyn's own brother did. The thought that you've just vanished makes me sick, and very scared.

Is it your voices calling you again? Listen out for mine instead. They'll try and trick you, Frannie – but they can't fake what I feel.

I hope to God you're somewhere safe. I'm thinking of you now.

Love,

Craig

CHAPTER I

Liberation

I

She was running naked through a field, and being chased by wolves. Above her frantic gasps for breath, she heard their racing paws. An eerie howl went up and seemed to linger in the air – hanging like a ghost above the farmland. But when she glanced behind her, there were human figures pounding in pursuit. Shadows with no faces, though the evening sky was clear.

She kept on fleeing, through the long dry grass. The men had turned to wolves again: she felt their panting breath against her legs. Muzzles full of fangs and drool were snapping at her thighs. She swerved and skidded, tried to shake them off, but it was hopeless. A wood lay on the skyline, but it seemed to come no closer. The countryside was opening out. She'd never felt so dreadfully exposed.

The end came in a final rush. She knew it had to happen (though it *couldn't*) and it did. The fastest wolf sprang up, and brought her down. Paws – or were they human claws? – seized hold of her bare shoulders; voracious teeth bit deep into her neck. Stumbling, she tried to scream, and pitched full length beneath its grasping weight. Her mouth was filling up with blood. The wolf-things pounced on her defenceless flesh.

'*Please!*' she wailed – and everything dissolved. Her spirit left her body, and flew upward. The air turned foul and crimson, thickening around her like a soupy menstrual murk. Ethereal though she was, she felt a nauseating pain. And then, before her eyes, she saw the cross.

It hung there like a vision, and she stared with bleary awe. A glowing figure slumped on it – radiating light into her stinging, squinted eyes. A faceless man with shining skin, his arms spread out in welcome . . . And then perspective kicked back in, and shrank him to a toy: polished silver gleaming with the light from somewhere else. She found that she was gawping at a common crucifix.

Suddenly the ground was there, beneath her knees and elbows. The shock was almost physical, as if she'd plunged through space. Her stomach shrank, and then convulsed; a bitter lump thrust upwards. She turned her face away, and spewed it out.

'*See*,' a rough voice leered. 'She has a devil.'

'Let her be,' a woman said, her tone detached and flat. 'It's the knock on her head, that's all. It could be she's concussed, let's have a look . . .'

They might have been two voices on a radio; she ignored them. But then someone was crouching down, to grasp her by the arms and sit her upright. It had to be the woman who had spoken; she took Fran's head in both her hands, and looked into her eyes. Fran just peered back, stupefied. It felt as if her skull was cracked, all ready to cave in. She had a sudden image of those fingers pushing through to touch her brain.

The woman drew back thoughtfully, and held one finger up. She looked about Fran's age, with cool grey eyes and a gold stud in her nose. Her hair was lank and fair beneath a pushed-back army cap.

'Follow my finger with your eyes . . .' She moved it side to side. Fran had to frown, but managed to keep focused. The woman nodded sombrely. 'You'll live.'

Fran herself wasn't so sure. She still felt sick, and had a splitting headache. But details of her surroundings were beginning to soak in. Trees rose dark on every side, but misty yellow light was slanting through them. The embers of an open fire were smouldering beside her.

At least she had her clothes on now; the jacket thick and smelly as the hide of a dead sheep.

The hard-faced girl had sat back on her heels. She was wearing an old army coat, its camouflage like seaweed. A watchful man was standing there behind her, resting a hand against the nearest tree. The daybreak was behind him, and his face was mostly shadow, but Fran could sense the patience in his stare.

And someone else was on her left; she turned her head to see. This man had the crucifix – still dangling it before her by its string of worry-beads. She registered his scuffed black coat; the dirty white pyjamas. And then his scowling face dipped close, the eyes like molten tar.

'What is your name?' he growled at her.

It seemed that she'd forgotten it. Befuddled, she spat bile, and wiped saliva from her mouth.

'What is your *name*, I ask!'

His sudden anger made her flinch. 'Fran,' she mumbled. 'Frances . . .'

Shadows seemed to gather in the contours of his face. He nodded grimly. 'So you are the witch who leads the Ravens now.'

She didn't rise to that at first; her attention had been captured by the diamond. It glittered in the rosary, incongruous among the rough wood beads. A jewel held by somebody who knew about the Ravens . . .

Lodestone, she thought suddenly.

Then: *Witch?*

He lifted up the cross, as if to taunt her. 'You come out of that Hell-mouth. You have been to meet your master.'

She realized what he meant at once – remembering the Ashmen with a rush of inner cold. She tried to shake her throbbing head. 'No,' she panted. '*Athelgar*. I've come to you from *him*.'

'Athelgar is damned,' he said, with infinite contempt.

Fran just stared at him, wide-eyed. He cocked his head,

considering – then offered her a smile of cruel indulgence. 'Perhaps you shall return to him – and tempt him to the judgment he deserves.'

'I'm not a *witch*,' she said belatedly.

'Confess it,' was his bleak response. 'Or we will have to put you to the question.'

Instinctively she snatched his cross, and pressed it to her lips. He stiffened, caught completely by surprise. She drew back, glaring up at him. 'So can a witch do that?' Hooking up her Cross of Nails, she let him see its silver. 'Athelgar's not damned, and nor am I. We're all on the same *side*, you stupid sod.'

The other glowered back at her; then took her hand and twisted it, examining her rings. Fran sat still and let him – her temper brewing up despite the dizziness and pain. The ring she'd had from Athelgar was the one that held his interest. He rubbed it round to pick out the inscription; then lingered on those broken words for what seemed half a minute. At last he let her hand drop back, and straightened up again. His face had grown inscrutable as stone.

'We will speak of this again,' he said, and turned away.

Fran gazed after him; then gingerly reached up to feel the back of her head. Her fingers touched a flashpoint, and she drew a hissing breath. Her hair was matted, sticky. Her heartbeat fluttered briefly as she realized it was blood.

The other man had straightened up. She saw he had a stubbly beard, and medium-length black hair. A narrow, knotted headband kept his fringe out of his eyes. He stared after the man in white as well; then came and hunkered down beside the girl.

'Were you a nurse or summat, then?' He sounded interested.

She shrugged. 'I did two years of training, then I chucked it. It's all about conformity and systems. People get ill because they're poor, but no one questions that . . .'

Reluctantly Fran's fingers had crept back into her hair – as if she thought the pain might go away. It didn't, and she winced again. The woman turned her head.

'Shep just clouted you, that's all. I'd try and sleep it off if I was you.'

She nodded towards a pile of blankets at the edge of the clearing. Fran hesitated, frowning; then clambered up unsteadily, went over and lay down. The blankets were soiled and threadbare, and the ground was rough beneath them . . . but a murky swamp of weariness was waiting to engulf her. She knew she wasn't safe yet, but she felt too stunned to care.

The other two were talking in an undertone. It seemed they were receding, although none of them had moved. Curling up, she closed her eyes – and heard the girl's low murmur.

'Remember that poor sod he burned? If he thinks she's a *witch* . . .'

'Jesus,' the man breathed. 'He couldn't, though . . .'

'He would,' the woman muttered. Her distant voice was cheerless with conviction.

Alarmed, Fran tried to listen, tried to keep herself awake. Then she lost her grip and darkness sucked her down.

2

When she woke, the wood looked very different. The day was bright, and well-advanced: already afternoon. The shadows had been watered down – the dimness in amongst the trees seemed tranquil and unthreatening. The clearing itself was full of sun and sparks of summer dust. Every leaf and line of bark stood out in perfect focus.

Her head still pounded dully, but the edge of pain was gone. Her mouth was parched, her stomach contents stagnant; the nausea, it seemed, had passed as well. Lying there, moving nothing but her eyes, she tried to get a grasp of her surroundings.

There were several people lounging round, within the

deeper wood. They had the look of people used to living out of doors. Well-worn clothes, and stoic, weathered faces. As if this was a travellers' camp or something. None of them seemed interested in her.

The nearest group were chuckling together. Someone swigged a can of beer, then gestured with it as he went on speaking. And yet she was reminded of the Ravens in *their* camp: strangers to the land, and to the time.

She sat up stiffly, cautiously, and looked towards the smell of rusty smoke. The fire had been rekindled, and refuelled with bits of wood. An ancient stovetop kettle was balanced on the nest of licking flames.

The dark-haired man she'd seen before was squatting down beside it. He was watching her expectantly; she'd clearly given signs of waking up. His youngish face was grave, but not unpleasant.

'Welcome back,' he said. 'You want some tea?'

She almost rubbed her head again, but stopped herself in time. 'Yeah . . . please.'

'Something to eat?'

She shook her head.

He wrapped a cloth around the kettle's handle, and poured into a battered metal pot. 'My name's Shep,' he said. 'You're Frances, right?'

'Mm.'

'And you think you can do the cops' work for them?' He put the question wryly, but she heard the challenge in it.

She scowled, puzzled. '*What?*'

'You're with these Ravens, aren't you? Playing vigilantes, thinking no one's going to see. Well now the rules have changed, all right? And if you want a dirty war, you'll have one.

'Hope you don't take milk, 'cause we ain't got none.'

Fran blinked at him, still floundering. He poured a mug of tea and brought it over. His chest was bare, beneath a shabby waistcoat; an amulet was hanging on a thong around his neck.

She realized that his headband was a makeshift-looking bandage, and wondered if the girl had done that too. Then she saw the pistol in his belt.

Bloody hell. She stared at it – then took the proffered mug.

'That other bloke,' she asked, as he went back to pour his own. 'Who was he?'

'He calls himself Dominicain. You'd better watch yourself when he's around. The guy's a fundamentalist. A *Christian*.'

'I try to be a Christian too,' she muttered, slightly piqued.

He smiled flatly. 'I don't.'

'So how come he's in charge, then?'

'He knows what has to happen. Of course, he has to see it in his own religious terms . . . but what the hell: the end result's the same.'

She took a wary sip. 'Which is?'

'To turn this fucking country upside down.'

She looked around, then back at him. 'What . . . all fifteen of you?' There didn't seem to be too many more.

He shrugged. 'Someone's got to light the fire. The tinder's dry enough. Believe me, it'll spread.'

'So how're you going to light it, then?' she asked, with some disdain.

'Sabotage to start with. Hit and run. But then we up the ante – start to make some proper raids. I'll say this for Dominicain: he may be a fanatic, but he knows guerrilla warfare. I think he was in Salvador, or Bosnia maybe.'

Marcus, she thought giddily. *The bastard's got his hooks in them somehow.* A second raiding force turned loose, to slash and burn through unsuspecting country. God, perhaps the Ashmen were their *allies*.

She pulled a face, and forced herself to drink. The strong tea had a smoky taste, as if it had been flavoured by the campfire.

Shep leaned forward, earnest now. 'Listen to me, Frances. Humanity's not going to *survive* – not unless we pull the plug on this whole fucking system. Pollution's getting out of hand, and no one's gonna stop it. Every country wants its nukes – and one day they'll be used. We need to put things back two hundred years, or we have *had it*.'

Fran tried to find an answer, but there wasn't one to hand.

Shep took another drink, and shook his head. 'You know what I think sometimes? That we really need a *plague*. Something like Ebola spreading right across the world. And Christ, I wouldn't want that . . . but what if it's the only way? Nuclear war's no good, 'cause that would trash the fucking planet . . . but something has to take the cities out – the *governments*. Stop those fucking factories, and junk the nukes, the chem-and-bio weapons. And yes, I know that *people* don't deserve to die like that. But Jesus, girl, we're going to lose the *earth*.'

'Stop it,' she snapped back at him: unsettled by the chord that he had struck. She'd thought like that herself when she was sunk in her depression – giving up all hope of peace, all faith in human nature. *Let's have a fucking war, and start again*.

'You have to face it, Frances,' he said softly.

No I bloody don't, she thought: resisting the compulsion like an obstinate child. She stared into her black and bitter tea.

'. . . 'Cause if you cross Dominicain, he'll kill you, girl – all right? Don't think I could stop him – and sure as hell, Carl won't.'

She raised her eyes. 'Who's Carl?'

'He's sort of like our military commander. He might have had a vision once, but now he's too hung up on trashing things. Hate's what keeps him going now. But then, you need good haters, if you're gonna win a war . . .'

She had to vent her growing desperation. 'What about those things last night? You're taking sides with *those*?'

'Hardly. Christ.' He seemed amused. 'Army on manoeuvres, that lot were. We kept good and quiet, they didn't see us. Maybe they've been told to keep a lookout; maybe not.'

Fran just sighed defeatedly, and turned her face away.

Dominicain was standing very close.

Shock jumped through her nerves, and bunched her muscles. She sat there as he came across the clearing – gripping her mug so tightly that a part of her expected it to break. His grim face was forbidding. His eyes burned into hers.

'Think I'll leave you to it,' murmured Shep, and straightened up. She looked at him imploringly; he gave a mocking smile. 'Make your choice,' he said, and walked away.

Dominicain crouched down beside the fire, still watching her. His rosary was round his neck – the cross and beads contrasting with the belt of shotgun rounds. He dug into his pocket, and came up with a packet of smokes. She frowned at them, surprised – and felt a half-forgotten craving stir again. He put a fag between his lips, and lit it with a splinter from the fire; then raised his eyes, and read her hungry stare.

She moistened her lips. 'Can I have one . . . ?' she asked.

He looked at her impassively; then came across and offered her the packet. She fumbled out a cigarette, her fingers trembling slightly. He let her light it from his own: the gesture like a proxy kiss that almost made her cringe. She drew the smoke down deep, and breathed it out.

Dominicain stayed standing. She felt him looming over her, and didn't want to look – but in the end, despite herself, she had to.

His face was still inscrutable. The bearded jaw looked set into a sneer. Her heartstrings tightened nervously. And yet it seemed those eyes betrayed a craving of his own.

'Who *are* you?' he demanded.

'Frances,' she said sullenly. 'I told you.'

'And are you come from Heaven – or from Hell?'

She took another drag of smoke to ease her prickly nerves. 'Neither. I'm not special. Just a pilgrim on the road.'

'And yet you wear that ring,' he murmured darkly.

She raised her hand, and looked at it. The metal barely glittered. 'Athelgar gave it me,' she said.

'Yes,' he said, and squatted down before her. 'He took it from the ashes of a saint he could not save.'

She stared at him – then back towards the ring. A sudden chill flowed up her arm, like phantom septic shock. *Cut it off*, an instinct hissed. She winced.

Dominicain was watching her intently. He saw her doubts, and smiled at them, his dark eyes full of spite.

'Put not your trust in Athelgar – for he will let you die like all the rest.'

'Why do you hate him, anyway?' she burst out. Shaken up now: feeling scratched and scared.

He sat back on his creaking heels, and sucked his cigarette until it glowed.

'Listen, while I tell to you a parable,' he said – his wry tone almost mocking. 'There was once a rook, that followed the plough. The farmer did not hinder him, for he rooted up the worms that lived in the field. And so he ate of *vermin*, and did think himself well blest. And the crops grew, and were harvested to fill the farmer's barn.

'There was also a dog, who had left his own master and who now lived in the wild. He made a friendship with the rook, and warned him that no master could be trusted.

'"But I call no man master," said the rook.'

Dominicain broke off to draw another breath of smoke; watching her from under his brows. His tone of voice was grimly serious now.

'It happened one day that the black rook saw a pure white lamb which the farmer meant to kill and share with the master of the dog. His heart was moved to pity, and he asked the dog to plead for it. But the dog was beaten back, while the rook and all his brethren looked on and gave no help. And the lamb was killed and eaten just the same.'

Fran sat there, staring back at him. Her own cigarette was smouldering, forgotten in her fingers.

'I rode out with the Ravensbreed,' he said, no longer preaching. 'I was their counsellor and their confessor. We lived to mete out justice, in defence of the defenceless. But then, after the Death, we were divided. The poor had risen in revolt and Athelgar had betrayed them. He held the Raven back, and let them fall.'

Something inside her almost winced. 'But . . . why?'

'Because he thought his duty done. Because he owed his loyalty to *lords*. Though he might defend a peasant, yet he would not lift his yoke.'

The Preacher paused reflectively, watching fiery ash go flaking off his cigarette.

'In truth, he tried to make a reparation: to settle this old conflict between justice and the law. In France, there was a war that lasted lifetimes. Men were born, grew old and died, and still the strife went on. The Ravens took this penance: to fight and keep on fighting, until all of them were dust.'

Fran could picture that, all right: the Ravensbreed as medieval shock troops. Always coming back for more, though kings and captains changed. Perhaps they'd fought at Poitiers – and Agincourt as well. Their dreadful secret handed on, like nuclear missile codes . . .

'He could still have redeemed himself,' Dominicain went on. 'The call to justice came again – and this time he obeyed it. He broke loose from the bonds of blood and honour. Then he sent to me once more, to plead for his liege-lady. But when my words were not enough, the swords which could have saved her never came.'

She snatched a nervous drag, her eyes still wide.

The Preacher watched his words sink in; then sneered through the smoke. 'By rights, the Ravens should be dust and ashes. Consumed by guilt, they challenged a whole army with their swords. They should have gone to God on English gibbets, and great pyres. Their memory has been wiped out. And yet they still endure.'

Fran felt like someone stranded in a thorny maze at night. He'd planted it around her: hedged her in. Dismayed, she tried to force her way back out.

'Did you see those things last night? Hiding in the tunnel? Shep believes they're soldiers . . . the Queen's Men. But you don't think that, do you?'

He seemed to hesitate – then shook his head. 'I saw them. They are devils, out of Hell.'

'Athelgar is fighting them – right now.'

'Then may he find the end he seeks, this time.' He blew another stream of smoke. 'I have mine own war now. This time the poor will be revenged. We will upturn this country, as a man upturns his garden with a spade.'

'And what'll you do afterwards?' she challenged. 'Will you rebuild the homes that get burned down?' She gazed at him insistently then clambered to her feet as if to take advantage of some moral higher ground – but her weary tone was anything but gloating.

'And wipe the *tears* away?' she said. 'And bring the ones who've died to life again?' She filled her lungs with calming smoke, and paced around behind him, staring down. 'And stop the hate from going on and *on*?'

His face came round, expressionless. She looked at him, then slowly shook her head. 'In that case, we don't *want* your revolution.'

A dry twig cracked behind her, and she turned. Another man was coming up. Cold blue eyes, and short-cropped ginger hair. His face was hard and hostile.

'Who the hell are you, then?'

Carl, she thought at once – and felt her own face closing up. But she stood her ground.

Dominicain rose up to stand beside her. 'She is Frances, of the Ravens.'

Carl nodded, smiling sourly now – as if he'd heard of her. 'Shep told me that he'd caught her sneaking round. Come to spy on us, has she?'

Dominicain seemed pensive. 'She has come to seek our aid.'

'Yeah?' Carl looked at her. The smile became a sneer. 'See that badge she's wearing? It's like . . . a *mark*, that people give to cowards – and to traitors. People who don't want to fight our war.'

Fran glanced down at her CND badge. Dominicain had turned to look as well. She felt a sudden pang of fear, and knew she mustn't show it.

'You think he cares about the poor?' she said – and glared at Carl. 'He wants a war that nobody can win.'

'Better than tying ribbons to a fence, and singing fucking *songs*.' A sly look crossed his face then. 'Dominicain . . . you know what that sign means? It's a cross, see? Upside down, and broken. She's one of *them*.'

Jesus, she thought helplessly. *You bastard*. She'd heard that one before, from fundamentalist opponents. The ones who thought that nuclear war would be the will of God.

Dominicain's eyes bored into her. 'Is this the truth?' he asked.

'No it bloody isn't!'

He kept on staring, silent now. Carl was looking smug. She felt her heartbeat thumping. At last Dominicain spoke again – in a musing way that made her nerve-ends itch.

'Edgar said you are a saint. A saint would drive those devils from their nest.'

She glanced at him, and frowned. '*Edgar*? What happened to him?'

'I burned him, Frances. A fitting doom for liars and deceivers. Shall I burn you as well?'

Fran went completely cold. *Oh, God.*

. . . The ashes of a saint he could not save . . .

Carl gave a malicious grin. 'Yeah, come on then, *Frances*. Fucking pacifist. Let's see you take those army bastards on.'

'All right,' she said, beside herself with fury. 'I will.'

CHAPTER II

Inferno

I

'So why not torch it now?' Shep asked.

'Because,' she said, 'I think they're still inside.'

He glanced at her, then back into the gully. Drowsing in the daylight now: it seemed a different place. The placid whir of crickets hung about it. A bee buzzed close, and drifted off again. But the tunnel's crumbled arch was still in shadow. Fran could feel the cold down there – despite the summer heat against her neck.

He ambled back, and squatted down against the nearest tree. As she watched, he opened up a clasp knife, and started whittling at a piece of wood. Fran remained sitting, her legs tucked underneath her; the heavy jacket draped across her knees. The countryside was hazy and deserted. It might have been a picnic they were on.

Except her skin was crawling, and her heart was beating hard.

He offered her a crooked, sidelong smile. 'I can't believe you're doing this,' he said.

She swallowed. 'Like I told you – they're not soldiers. Mercenaries, more like. Hired to massacre and burn. I've got to stop them *somehow*.'

'So who're these Ravens, then?' he asked.

'Dominicain belonged to them. They're like, a secret army – and they're fighting for the poor.'

He flashed a mocking smile – still scraping wood. 'You're living in a time-warp, girl. The poor are fighting for *themselves*. We don't need anyone to do it for us.'

'Didn't someone say about the Mexican revolution, that it was like a bullfight where the bull gets killed and the matador gets brain damage?'

The knife-blade paused; his glance was just as sharp. 'Don't patronize us, Frances.'

'I'm not.' She sat up straighter. 'But there's a whole new battlefield out here; whichever side you're on. And whoever gets involved is going to *suffer*. Maybe neither side will walk away. You want to share the grief out? 'Cause I don't.'

He stared at her; then went back to his whittling. His metal pendant caught the sun, and winked. She thought it was a wheel of scythes – or maybe sheaves of corn. But the handle of a pistol still protruded from his belt. She looked towards the trees again. The rebel camp was out of sight, but hardly out of mind.

'You've given up on Carl, I see,' he murmured drily.

She snorted. 'I might as well argue with someone who thinks the world was created in seven days.' Turning back to him, she made a face. 'I hate that Class War crap of his. The way he *dehumanizes* his enemies. The last time we did that, it was so we could bulldoze their trenches and bury them alive. Drop bloody *napalm* on them. Do you want that? What *do* you want?'

'I want our bloody planet back,' he said.

'Jesus, so do I. But not like that.'

'If there was any other way . . .' Shep said. He wavered then, like someone on the verge of a confession; then went on, staring fiercely at her. 'I was into *peace*, as well. It never changed a thing. And I've had it up to here, all right? Not running *any more*.'

She held her hands up. 'Shep, you'll do his bloody work *for him*. This bloke called Marcus that we're trying to fight. Once you've gone and smashed things up, you'll never make the pieces fit again . . .'

Stubbornly he shook his head. 'You can't defeat the system from inside it.'

'The system's made of *people*, Shep. It's like the Universe: there's *no* outside.'

'Very profound.' He shook his head. 'I suppose you vote, as well.'

'I was on a psychie ward,' she said. 'They wouldn't let me.'

Carl had been seething with mistrust. As she'd started getting ready, he came to her and roughly grasped her wrist.

'What's your fucking game, girl? Eh? We don't need this, not yet.'

She'd yanked her arm clear, glowering. 'Your *leader* thinks you do.' She nodded at Dominicain, who was watching the proceedings. Carl glanced round; then leaned in close and hissed.

'Listen to me, you silly bitch . . . this is the *army*, right?'

'No they're not,' she muttered. *Bloody worse than that*, she thought.

'Let her purge the demons' nest,' Dominicain said grimly. 'If she is false, then she will fail – and be devoured by them.'

'*Dominicain* knows what they are,' she said, and smiled sweetly. 'Or would you be suggesting that he's mad?'

His lip curled, but he kept himself in check. Suddenly he snatched at her, and tore the CND badge off Lyn's jacket. 'Not fit to be wearing this then, are you?'

She'd made to grab it back from him – then let her shoulders slump. 'Maybe you're right,' she'd said. 'Why don't you keep it?'

Her sarcasm hadn't quite concealed the come-down that she'd felt.

The first bat of the twilight gave a warning. She glimpsed it, rising upward like a bubble of blurred wings – a fleeting shape against the sallow sky. She swallowed and looked back towards the tunnel.

Nothing moved.

She was lying on her stomach now, and peering through the rank grass of the verge. Minutes passed. More bats emerged like scouts being sent ahead. She only saw one flutter through the brambles; it seemed the rest appeared out of thin air. Two and three; now four and five. They spiralled up and circled, then swooped down into the trench. One swerved at speed and flashed above her head. Prone though she already was, she couldn't help but flinch.

Shep came up to join her in a crouch. He'd put a dirty cotton shirt on underneath his waistcoat. 'Shhh,' she hissed, and waved him down. 'I think they're coming out.'

The guerrillas were all ready to move northward, getting clear of the area under cover of darkness. The word was, they were taking on the army: torching a fuel dump, while the troops were out on night manoeuvres. She'd sensed their mixed emotions: excitement and unease. Tonight they would commit an act of *war* . . .

A rustling came from deep within the brambles. At once her eyes were focused once again. The leaves were stirring faintly, but that could have been the breeze.

The bramble thicket seemed to breathe and *bulge*. The first dark shape came groping into view.

Ashman.

He crawled out of the bramble bush like something given birth there: pushing through its spiky stalks, quite heedless of their hooks. Slowly he rose upright, the helmet-sockets scanning left and right. Fran lay rigid, motionless, her hands against her mouth – as if her shallow breathing might alert him. Once again she felt as if she'd stumbled on a hidden gate of Hell.

Shep was staring, frozen too. At this range, through the rising dusk, the figure could have passed for a soldier. Someone in chemical warfare gear, all flaps and gloves and goggles. But something in the way it moved was utterly inhuman.

Maybe they're the ones who murdered Lyn . . .

The thought sprang out of nowhere, and it almost made her sob. Lyn had been caught alone by one of these. The past she loved had risen up, and dragged her down to join it in the grave. The last things she'd have felt were fear and horror.

More of them were coming out; the bramble bush contracting like a womb. Biting her lip, Fran forced herself to watch. One by one the gargoyle helmets thrust up through the leaves. Shaggy clothing snagged, and then tore free. Swords and axe-heads caught the dregs of daylight. A couple carried blackened leather shields across their backs. And though the bush kept rustling, and a loosened brick gave way, they crept out of their hole in nightmare silence.

Satisfied the way was clear, the leading raider started down the trench. The others followed: wading through the nettles and briers. She thought that there were eight or nine, but couldn't keep a count. They passed beneath her, single file, and faded in the gloom along the cutting.

'Christ,' breathed Shep, when silence fell at last.

Breathless, Fran sat up and looked around.

'How do we know there's no one left inside?' he asked.

She glanced at him, and swallowed. 'We don't.'

Shep grimaced, and pulled his pistol out. She saw it had two barrels, like some junior sawn-off shotgun. He cupped the hammers: clicked them back. She'd never have dreamed the sound could reassure her. Turning her head, she listened to the breeze. It rustled drily through the wood. She heard no other sounds.

Time to move: right now, or never. She picked a flask of petrol up, and clambered to her feet. The bats were flitting overhead. The air was growing denser.

With Shep at her heels, she crept along the edge, and came to a crumbled place beside the tunnel. No time to stop and think, not now; she eased into a crouch and ventured downward. The earth was dry and treacherous. A clod of it broke loose beneath her tentative boot, to drop and skitter down into the brambles. She froze with apprehension: precariously balanced on her boot-heels and her bum. The rustling from below her seemed to go on for too long.

With agonizing slowness she continued her descent, glad of her boots and well-worn jeans as she finished in a knee-high patch of nettles. The wall of bricks looked mournful, like a blank, disfigured face. Moss and lichens made her think of features – the same effect as patches on the surface of the moon. And down behind the bushes, she could see the broken mouth: a dim snarl, full of emptiness and cold.

The cold was real, was physical. Up top, the air was cooling, but still sticky with the last heat of the day. Here, it had a chill in it, like something being breathed out of the depths.

If she raised her head, right now, she might see something carved above the entrance. Perhaps an ancient, grinning skull. Or just the worn-out words *Abandon hope . . .*

Shep slid down to join her, the gun back in his waistband and the other petrol flask in his free hand. He passed it to her, and drew the gun again. Both of them surveyed the wall. 'Okay?' he asked her softly.

No, she thought. *Of course I'm not.* They didn't have a torch, of course, and naked flames would be a bad idea. So she would have to creep inside, and splash the petrol round in total darkness.

The black mouth waited, sneering at her hesitation. The evening air was absolutely still.

Feeling sick, she moved up to the wall. Shep went sidling round her; his pistol held two-handed now and aimed towards the hole. The thicket had been mangled where the Ashmen had come through. She shouldered through the bramble-stalks, and heard them scrunch a warning. The trench was full of shadows now. The tunnel's depths were infinitely black.

Filling her lungs like a diver, she ducked her head and forced herself inside.

Cloacal gloom engulfed her – deep and cold and thick enough to drown in. The stink was like a sewer's, too; she pinched her lips tight shut. A sewer choked with carcasses, piled up and left to rot. Her mind could see them festering around her.

Something shifted warily then scurried through the darkness. She almost dropped the petrol flasks, and very nearly squealed. Not an Ashman, much too small. It had to be an animal. A rat?

Oh, *God*.

She undid the first cap, and sloshed the contents round in all directions. The activity was something she could get a focus on. She urged herself in deeper, as if this was a crazy schoolgirl dare. The unseen ground felt lumpy underfoot. The plastic flask grew lighter with each frantic jerk she gave it, each gout that she sent splashing up the brickwork. It took her several moments to accept that it was empty. She tossed it ahead of her, into the murk. The tunnel amplified its hollow clatter.

Now where was the second one? She turned around, disoriented – and felt a rush of fright. No way to tell which way was which. The walls had vanished; she'd somehow wandered through into an underground cathedral. *Fuck*, she thought, and wavered – then reached out. The air was as dense as liquid mud, yet offered no resistance. Her sightless hand groped left and right. Her muscles itched to snatch it back again.

Nerving herself, she took a slow step forward. Then another. Reaching blindly out again, she touched the curving wall. The bricks felt cold and slimy. Turning, she sensed something brush her hair: a ghostly touch, like dead, ethereal fingers. She gasped and cowered, then realized that she'd walked into some cobwebs.

She reared back, hands scrubbing through her hair – *not spiders, Jesus, please*. She thought she felt them on her scalp, and crawling down her neck. Spiky giants, fattened by the dark . . .

She stumbled on the second petrol flask, and almost fell. 'Fuck!' she sobbed, aloud this time, and fought her panic down. She took the thing, unscrewed the cap, then simply poured the petrol as she backed towards the entrance. Suddenly it struck her that she'd chosen the wrong way; retreating with each step into the depths of the tunnel. But then she sensed its stopped-up mouth behind her, and saw a smudge of greyness in the murk.

'Shep?'

'All clear,' his voice came back. He sounded quite keyed-up.

Instinct said to drop the flask, and make straight for the breach. But she forced herself to walk those last few steps, still spilling out the petrol. Reaching the hole, she scrambled out, and splashed the brambles too; then staggered back, and took a gulp of air. Night air, fresh and clean, to purge the vileness from her nostrils.

'Okay,' Shep murmured. 'Let's get out of here.' He fumbled in his pocket, and she realized he was reaching for a match.

'No,' she said, and snatched his sleeve. 'We need to wait until they're back inside.'

He looked at her. '*Frances*. For Christ's sake . . .'

'They're not *human*, Shep. Not any more. You *saw* them.'

'You're crazy,' he said flatly – but he let the matches be. Just stared at her in silence. The dusk hid his face like a camouflage veil.

She hoped that hers was hidden too. As if, without a face, she could escape the blame for what was coming next.

The summer night was short, and she was screwed up with reaction; but even so, she almost nodded off before they came.

The ooze of sleep had filled her head already. She felt like someone drowning in an inch or two of water. Then Shep touched her shoulder, and she surfaced with a start. They were lying above the tunnel now; the gateway and the brambles right below them. Swallowing, she raised her head, and saw them in the cutting. Ghostly figures, creeping back. Behind them, light was seeping up the sky.

She glanced at Shep; he was squinting at the Ashmen. It was still too dark to make them out in detail. But surely he could see they weren't just soldiers.

One by one they reached the wall, and crept into their nest.

She felt her heartbeat thud against the ground; what if they heard it? But the shapes remained oblivious. She watched the last ones wait their turn. They seemed not to communicate at all.

They're dead, her mind insisted: *walking dead.*

They'd murdered Lyn. These revenants. These *things*. She shuddered with revulsion – and realized it was turning into rage.

I know what they will do was Harald's warning. She knew that he'd meant rape and mutilation. But Lyn: what had they done to *her*? She couldn't bear to think it.

She rose up on her knees. Shep took her sleeve. 'Frances,' he said hoarsely. 'Listen, now . . .'

A part of her was grateful for the doubts she should have shared. But then she freed herself. 'I *have* to do this.'

She'd crammed the empty petrol flask with grass; a flammable scum still lingered at the bottom. She picked it up, and breathed the spiky stink. 'Give us a match,' she murmured, and reluctantly he did so. Swallowing, she struck it, dropped it down the open neck – then quickly tossed the flask towards the brambles.

The flames came licking out at once: following the petrol through the leaves. Fran dropped back, and listened to them crackle. Her stomach was a chilly lump of dread.

The hidden gate erupted, belching yellow-orange flames; lighting up the cutting like a premature sunrise. The brambles burned ferociously. Leaning out, she forced herself to watch. The tunnel had been turned into a furnace. Smoke boiled up into the dawn, but nothing else emerged.

It felt as if she'd just wiped out an ants' nest – but doing so had never brought such bitter satisfaction. 'That's for Lyn!' she hissed, and scrambled back.

As she rose, Shep grasped her arms, and swung her round to face him. 'What was it you said, about us using fucking *napalm?*'

His voice was harsh, and edged with disillusion. She felt it cutting deep into her conscience. A moment's pain; but then she steeled herself. Stony-faced, she shook him off and walked towards the trees.

The encampment was deserted now. The group had slipped away. But Dominicain still waited by the ashes of the fire. Fran walked straight towards him, ignoring Carl and his pit-bull sidekick. Her face was dirty from the smoke. A single tear had streaked it.

'*Now* do you believe me?' she demanded.

Dominicain stared back at her; then glanced at Shep, who'd followed in her wake. Shep must have nodded. *Yes, it's done.* The Preacher took a long drag on his smoke.

'And those were just the scouts,' she went on tightly. 'There's an army of them coming. The Ravens have to fight them, and they need all the help they can get.'

'If Satan drive out Satan, then his empire cannot stand . . .' He said that almost musingly – then jerked his head at her. 'So. It seems you speak the truth. What message do you bring?'

'Let me go to Athelgar. The Ravens need your help.'

'The Northern Bear and Southern Dog have all the gulf of heaven in between them.' Dominicain glanced upward – as if the stars could still be seen, beyond the muddy sky. His pensive gaze returned to her. 'Another sought to bridge it, and could not.'

'Let me try,' she murmured.

'You will return to us?' he asked.

She nodded quickly. 'Yeah . . .'

'Go, then.' He gestured, flicking ash at her. She wasn't really sure if it was blessing or dismissal. She glanced at Carl – warding off his glare with a cold little smile; then turned and hurried westward through the trees.

Carl stood staring after her, fist clenching. Shep gave him a veiled glance, and went to get his bedroll. Dominicain had turned to watch the sunrise. Steve stood ready, waiting for Carl's word.

'She's going to screw this whole thing up,' Carl hissed after a moment. He glanced at Steve. 'Go after her, and *do* her. I mean fucking take her out.'

Steve nodded once, not smiling. 'Be my pleasure.'

CHAPTER III

The Rage of Killing

I

What had Craig said, at the gates of Greenham Common? Hugging her against him, in the shadow of that Neolithic junkyard. *It feels like the end of the world.*

That was what it felt like now. And how she wished his arms were still around her.

The countryside seemed desolate, made bleaker by a fitful, doleful breeze amid the grass. The sky above was overcast, with sunlight soaking palely through the grey. She knew that there were farms around her; towns and cities over the horizon. And yet it was too easy to imagine that Marcus had fulfilled his threat already. As if the day she'd spent with Dominicain's band had been a fatal *age* outside the wood.

And Athelgar had journeyed on long since.

Somehow she could feel that he had gone, he hadn't waited. No matter how close the Raven's camp, it would be deserted now, with circles of cold ashes as the only trace they'd left. She halted on the country road, examining his ring – turning it around her middle finger. It would bind her in their circle, so he'd promised. But the tarnished band of silver now felt tainted and inert. If the thing was like a lodestone, it was picking nothing up.

He took it from the ashes of a saint he could not save.

Dominicain's words flowed through her mind, discharging icy rills into her system. The metal was discoloured by its age, so she'd assumed. But what if smoke had blackened it? Or fire?

She felt her arm turn cold again. Had someone *burned* while wearing this? She tugged the ring up tight against her knuckle, imagining some woman full of terror crying out. But Athelgar had not saved her. Had stood by with his Ravens, so Dominicain had claimed.

She tried to disbelieve it – but his parable had lodged itself inside her. He'd preached it with a passion that was real, and persuasive. And now she felt like someone in the middle of a swamp, who realizes the map she's got is false. The sense of being abandoned was unnerving.

Fatigue was piling up on her, putting grit in her eyes and mud into her mind. She still felt drained, revolted by the fire *she* had set. The bleakness of the landscape matched the wasteland of her heart: in both, she was entirely alone.

If only Craig were with her now. If only he could rescue her from this. *Christ, if my love were in my arms, and I in my bed again . . .*

And then, amid the emptiness, she had a sense of presence. She looked around her quickly – but the road and fields were dismal and deserted. She shifted restlessly; her heart began to throb on tightened strings. There was nothing to be seen, and yet her instincts were insistent. The feeling was of being watched, and followed.

She wavered for a moment, looking back towards the wood: the trees were just a dark blur in the distance. Had Dominicain had second thoughts? She'd only seen his anger once, but latent threat hung all about the man: brooding black as thunderclouds behind that slaty stare. His passion was mercurial – like madness. But she believed he'd keep his word. Or wanted to believe it.

She walked on down the road, a little faster. Looking back from time to time. Still no one at her heels. And then she saw the horseman in the field to her left.

The first glimpse made her heart leap up. The man's coat draped the horse's flanks – as sombre as a Raven's. But then she saw the chequered band around the rider's helmet. *Police.* She felt her spirits drop. His presence might protect her, if

Dominicain was coming. But maybe he was searching for the renegades himself. And she was an outsider too: an *outlaw*, in her way . . .

He'd turned his head to look at her, and now he turned his mount. Fran kept walking, trying to ignore him. A queasy guilt was growing in her stomach. The ground rose up, then dipped again, towards a wider road. A couple of police vans waited by the junction.

For a moment she was tempted to turn back the way she'd come. But that would look suspicious and make them keen to follow. The horseman in the field was coming up towards the fence. She glanced at him; his young face looked unfriendly. A long black baton hung beside his saddle. For no clear reason, she thought of that wrecked van she'd seen – an age ago, while riding south with Eldred. The one with battered bodywork, and roughly smashed-in windows.

She walked on towards the junction: trying to appear all unconcerned. The rider followed, pacing her. A couple of policemen had stepped out into the road. Their interest was obvious, and she knew what she must look like – but if they wanted her to stop, they'd have to say so. She pinched a smile, and made to walk right past them.

'Hang on just a minute, *Miss*,' said one. His cap was in his hand, revealing short, receding hair. His mocking eyes belied his skin-deep smile.

Fran looked at him, and waited. A WPC was standing by the roadside, further back, her own expression neutral and detached.

'You a traveller, then?' the copper asked.

'No,' she said, 'I always dress like this.'

His gaze grew sharper. 'Don't get fresh with me, my girl. We're looking for some mates of yours, they're lurking round here somewhere. Maybe you could tell us where they are?'

'I don't have any mates round here,' she murmured.

'Where've you come from?' the second copper asked. His

greying stubble beard made him look older; shrewder, too. Fran felt a moment's panic, and then inspiration struck.

'Our van broke down . . . I'm looking for a phone.'

'How far?'

She shrugged. 'About five miles.'

'What's the licence number?'

'Sorry . . . don't remember.'

He studied her for a moment. 'Got any ID on you?'

Her grubby benefit book was still stuffed down in her hip pocket. She dug it out, and waited while he checked it. He didn't seem to notice that she hadn't claimed for weeks.

'All right then . . . Miss Bennett.' He handed it back. 'There's some nasty people hiding out round here. Not into peace and love at all. I'd stick to the main road if I were you.'

'I'll do that,' she said meekly; but the other man stayed blocking her way.

'Got any dope?' he asked, as if inviting her to share it. She curled her lip at him, not even bothering to shake her head.

'Think she's got a stash inside her knickers? Maybe we should search her.'

'Leave it out,' the other copper muttered.

'Yeah? What do you think, Solly?'

'I think you should stop behaving like an arsehole,' the woman said.

Stung by that, he stepped aside, and Fran walked quickly past. The woman stayed expressionless, but her cool eyes offered something: as wordless and as welcome as a soft touch on Fran's arm.

A man in a blue sweater was sitting on the verge behind the van, smoking a cigarette. This one had a beret on, set squarely on his sandy, close-cropped hair. And then she saw the rifle in his lap.

She gawped at him; his eyes stared flatly back. She didn't know much about guns, but this one had its magazine behind the pistol-grip: more like an army rifle than the sort that coppers used.

'Don't alarm the natives, Stu,' said someone, and they laughed. Fran joined the wider road, and walked along for several yards – then gave in to her jangling nerves, and glanced back at the checkpoint. The sniper was still smoking, and the other three were pacing on the road. How many more were in the vans? How many more had guns?

Despite their bored demeanour, she could feel the danger there. Dominicain was being hunted now: an undeclared guerrilla war already being fought. And what if Marcus struck as he had promised? Law and order might collapse completely. How long before they started shooting people at the roadside?

The horseman was still watching her, immobile in the field: rising like a statue from the sea of windblown wheat.

2

Fifteen minutes down the road, the sense of being followed was still with her. She stopped and looked around again, but there was nobody in sight. The sky was lower, greyer now. The wheatfields soughed and rippled in the breeze.

She felt her strength congealing as she stood there. The same effect as stopping on a school cross-country run – except it wasn't physical this time. Despondency had got a grip. It seemed she'd never start to walk again.

If the Ravens had flown north, she had to follow. But which way was she headed now? She didn't have a clue. A town was in the distance, as hazy as a sailor's glimpse of land. She really hoped it wasn't Coventry. Perhaps she'd need to double back – go past those cops again. They'd doubtless be more interested this time. *Where did you say your van was*, *Miss?* And all the while, the distance would be growing. She didn't know how fast she'd have to run to catch him up.

'Athelgar,' she whispered. Her own voice sounded petulant, a mask for her dismay. Then she heard a scrunching to her left, and turned her head.

Somebody was in the field, and wading straight towards her.

She recognized the face at once, and understood its vehement expression. Her stomach flipped, and flopped again. He reached the fence and straddled it, while Fran just faltered backwards. And then he *smiled*, which left her in no doubt of his intentions. Her muscles came to life again. She broke into a run.

Steve sprang down onto the road, and pelted in pursuit. She heard his boots come scuffing up, his breath against her neck. She glanced behind her, tried to dodge; no way could she outrun him. He overshot, but grasped her collar, swinging her round with him as he turned. She almost tripped over her feet, the tarmac veering close – but then, with frantic strength, she wriggled free. Steve lurched back and nearly fell; she lunged across the road into the field. He followed at her heels, like the wolf-things of her dream. Whimpering, she flailed through wheat, his panting mouth behind her. And then he pounced, and dragged her down, his fingers in her collar and her hair.

Oh PLEASE! she thought, face shoved into the stalks – but this time she stayed trapped inside herself.

'Bitch!' he hissed, and punched her in the head. Despite the stunning pain of that, she kept on pressing down against the ground: desperate to deny him what he wanted. But Steve just rolled her over, and then sat himself astride her. His face was flushed, and shiny with his sweat. The sky looked vast and pitiless behind him.

'Reckon you're a Christian?' he asked thickly.

Fran just lay there, gasping, staring up.

'Well try forgiving *this*,' he said, and ripped her blouse wide open. She squealed and tried to fend him off; he clamped his free hand down across his face. She lashed out blindly, struck his head. And suddenly he screamed.

The sound was hoarse and shocking – enough to send a chill through her, in spite of his distress. His hand was snatched away, and she could see and breathe again. He was clutching at his own face now, his left cheek dark with shadow. And then her eyes grew wide: it wasn't shadow. He'd been *burned.*

A tiny shoot of flame broke through the cracked, corroded flesh. It might have grown and flowered, if his clawing fingers hadn't snuffed it out.

What the *hell?*

He toppled off her, scrambling back: retreating like a crippled crab. His hand was still pressed tight against his cheek. His eyes were blazing, full of pain, and hate – and something else.

Stupefied, she raised herself, not caring that her breasts were almost bare. For a moment they just stared at one another. And then she felt her throbbing hand, and turned her face towards it.

The ring she'd had from Athelgar looked just as plain as ever; but now it squeezed her finger like a silver tourniquet. Her whole hand seemed to bulge with pulsing blood – or latent power. And more, the ring was searing hot, like something from an oven. A fleeting touch without the glove: impossibly prolonged. Impossible, because she wasn't burned.

Steve snarled, and came at her again. Instinctively she swiped at him, her fingers hooked like claws. The ring didn't make contact – but her touch sank through his jacket and burned deep into his skin. She heard the muffled sizzling as he yelled and floundered back. Smoke spread palely outward, from the leather, or the flesh.

Oh God.

His face – the bits not charred or scorched – was white with pain and shock. He flopped across the verge, and slithered down onto the road. Fran straightened, and stalked after him. He saw her coming, tried to rise; she brought her right hand up. The gesture was unthinking, but she knew it in her bones. The fire was focused in the ring, and now she could direct it. A swipe into thin air, and he would *burn.*

Steve had clearly sensed it too. 'For Christ's sake, don't!' he gasped.

Fran kept coming, hand still poised, her mind a fug of rage. He'd put his dirty hands on her, and meant to do much worse: no fault of hers, and yet she felt *ashamed.* One of her breasts was scratched, the furrows stinging. Her narrowed eyes filled up with tears. His face became a blur.

'It was *Carl's* idea,' he wheezed, 'not mine . . .'

'You *bastard,*' she hissed back at him, and felt her muscles tense in preparation. The shame and anger swelled inside her, bursting for release. She blinked, and saw him cowering, and knew that she had *power.* The giddy realization went like vodka to her head.

Be so easy. Purge yourself. And make the bastard pay.

She drew a breath; he ducked his head. And then she swung away from him, and vented all her fury in a scream. Her empty hand flailed outward, and the power was unleashed – to scatter, like her cry, across the fields. With no flesh to attract it, it decayed into the wind and was dispersed.

Gasping, she looked back at Steve. 'Get out of here!' she blurted, the promise of another scream already in her voice. Steve just lay and gawped at her; then struggled to his feet. Fran stood watching, weeping now – and when he risked another look, she lost her rag completely. The screams that she'd been fighting rose like vomit from her stomach. 'Run, you bastard! Run away! Just *run!*'

And run he did, in limping, veering panic. She gazed at his retreating back; then let herself slump down onto the verge. Reaction overwhelmed her – so numbing that she couldn't even sob. But then, with sudden urgency, she grasped the ring and wrenched it off her finger. She flung the thing away from her: down hard against the road. Its tinny rattle sank into the stillness. And all her thoughts dissolved in bitter tears.

CHAPTER IV

Mystic and Severe

I

Something sighed across the fields, and whispered round her head. It slipped into her mind the way a draught invades a house. A still, small voice: not God of course, but *Marcus*.

'Frances, I salute thee . . . thou art worthy to be called.'

She gasped and jerked her head up, convinced that he had risen from behind her. Heart in her throat, she twisted round. But nobody was there. Just grey wind, and a loneliness that pressed on her like lead. In that despairing moment, she half wanted to be mad. Someone to be cosseted, and stupefied with drugs. She felt a sudden *yearning* for the psychiatric ward.

'It is *good*,' the wheatfields whispered, 'that we two have common cause.'

Outrage snapped her out of it, and brought her to her feet. 'No, we don't. Fuck off. You killed my *friend*.'

Silence then. She listened to it, panting. The empty country mocked her, but she knew that he was there.

'Thy friend is blessed, Frances. She has been *spared* from that which is to come.'

She couldn't help but turn again. Still nothing she could focus on. And yet it felt quite natural, to spit into the wind.

'We haven't anything in common. Not one thing!'

'Thou hast put my servants to the torch,' he told her softly. 'And did their fatal pyre not warm thy heart?'

'But they're just *ghouls*,' she snapped, after a moment's hesitation. 'They're already dead.'

'Thou didst not hear their *screaming*?'

'*No!*' she blurted: more than just an answer.

'Softly, Frances. Be thou not ashamed. For thee and me, the pleasure is revenge.'

She could almost sense him circling around her, a ghostly, gloating presence in the breeze. She pressed her hands against her ears, as if to crush her head.

'And thou hast burned thy brother,' Marcus taunted, 'in thy *heart*.'

'I *didn't*,' she said fiercely. 'I bloody let him go.'

He kept his peace – and let her mind complete what he had started. She thought of Craig again, in Greenham's shadow. Saying that the missiles there would never have been used.

Maybe not, she'd told him; *but the readiness was there*.

And then imagination joined the fray. It showed her Steve as she had almost left him: a black, mutated carcass, like an alien's, in the road. A picture from Hiroshima, to peer at through her fingers. She'd come within an inch of doing *that*.

'I wouldn't have . . .' she whispered.

'Thou liest,' said the voice.

Perhaps he reached into her mind, and plucked the next thought out. A simple quote that always used to haunt her.

The real horror isn't that we might be bombed ourselves, but that we'd think of bombing someone else.

She had. She knew she had. She'd wanted him to burn.

'Thou *liest*,' hissed the wind, and said no more.

Fran just stood there, breathless, lost for words. Her arms fell to her sides. She felt quite gutted: disembowelled. No stomach to be sick with anymore.

Go on, get moving (Her voice, now). *Keep going, or you'll die*. She forced herself to take a step – and glimpsed a wink of brightness on the tarmac. The ring, where it had come to rest.

The relic of a saint who'd died by fire.

She hesitated, staring down; then stooped to pick it up. The silver had grown cold again; she turned it in her fingers.

Instinct said to lose the thing, to throw it far away – and yet she couldn't. It seemed that to discard it would be to reject its owner too; betray the poor girl a second time. So after a pause, she put it in her pocket and wiped her palm across her jacket front.

She strained her ears against the breeze, but Marcus had withdrawn. Or was he watching? She looked around herself once more; then started down the road.

2

As she trudged, he caught her up, and came at her again. She felt him stalking round her: as if he was her partner in a slow and formal dance. Her mind's eye saw him clear enough – a sombre, hooded figure. Darker than a shadow, and much harder to shake off.

'The world must be cleansed. The land must be purified. Thou *knowest* this,' he said.

Fran kept going, staring at the road. It felt like she was walking through a rainstorm with her hood up: nothing to see but the next two feet of tarmac, while cold, wet greyness beat against her head.

'Men will never live in peace. Always shall they steal, and kill, and plunder. And now the earth is turned into their midden. Thou hast *seen*.'

She'd seen the pictures, right enough: the wars, pollution, famine. The planet being disfigured as she watched. Again she felt the lack of power; the terrible frustration. And yes, the anger too. The helpless rage.

'When I began to grope out from my grave,' his voice went on, 'I found the hearts around me had not changed. I came on souls so empty that they would cremate whole *peoples* at a word! My servants crept in close, and saw what engines they possessed. Perhaps I should have seized them, Lady Frances?' She sensed him shake his cowled head in mockery and spite.

'I had no need. Those empty hearts will rend thy world apart!'

Ashmen on the Plain, she thought – attracted by the evil chill of Cruise. Scouts from the forgotten past, encountering a barbarous new world . . .

'So let it come down,' he whispered. 'Let it all go up in flames.'

She swayed like someone half-asleep: immersed in her depression and fatigue. Part of her was tempted now. Part of her was itching to say *yes*.

'Doest thou presume to hinder Armageddon? Wilt thou resist the judgment of thy God?'

Dimly she saw what he was trying to do. Trying to break her spirit by undermining her beliefs. She made to swat the words away like wasps.

'God *forbid* we'll have a war,' she told him through her teeth.

'Thou sayest. Thou art rich, and livest well. And what say the poor, my Lady? The nations doomed to pestilence and hunger? Are *they* content to see the world grow older? Or do they pray, at every dawn, for Judgment Day to come?'

'No!' she snapped instinctively. Then she sensed an obstacle ahead, and looked up with a gasp. Marcus stood there in her path, as solemn as a monument in stone.

'The living must die so that the dead can live,' he said.

She yelped with fright, and turned to run; he caught her in three strides. Clutched at her with real hands. She squealed and tried to squirm away. His fingers grasped her hair and pulled her head back. His voice was slaty-sombre in her ear.

'Listen, thou who call'st thyself a *saint*. The bliss of Heaven was bought with blood and tears. Thou canst not taste the sweetness, save by swallowing the gall. Where are *thy* stigmata, then? Disclose thy holy wounds!'

He flung her down; she rolled, looked back – and whimpered with dismay. He'd disappeared. To left and right, the country road was empty.

Sobbing now, she scrambled up and tried to keep on walking. The outskirts of a village lay ahead. The murmur of a motorway had risen in the distance. Perhaps she was emerging from the wilderness at last – and the world was there to welcome her back. But now it seemed a different place: untrustworthy and tainted.

'Resist me not,' breathed Marcus, like a ghost inside her head. 'Resist *God* not. Thou art *in* the world, not *of* it. Let it burn.'

She stumbled, veered, and caught herself; kept moving. She barely had the strength to walk – still less to argue back. But worse, she had no words with which to do so.

And Lyn was dead. And Athelgar had left her. She was suddenly convinced that he was dreaming of his wife; still mourning for his lady of a thousand years ago. She herself had been a passing fancy. Jealousy stirred feebly and collapsed into despair.

Mechanically she walked into the village. As people came in sight again, so Marcus eased away and let her go. His voice and all its echoes were sucked back out of her head. She might have just imagined every word.

And what if she had?

The thought was so enormous that it stopped her in the middle of the road. What if she was *really* schizophrenic, as she'd feared?

While she'd been in hospital, she'd read up on the subject: scared to death but desperate to know. She'd managed to convince herself that she was in the clear. Voices were a symptom, sure, but so were other things. They hadn't fit the jigsaw then. But maybe they did now . . .

A car horn blared behind her. She jumped, and scurried sideways; then let herself sag back against a wall.

Schizophrenic people had unshakeable delusions. They couldn't tell the unreal from the real. Athelgar was real, of course. 'I've *slept* with him,' she murmured. Yet where could she find proof of that? He didn't bite like she did. His sperm had long since withered in her womb.

She couldn't have dreamed the Ravens up – yet how could they exist? The village shop, that pub, seemed much more real. And now there was this evil voice; that vision in the road. Urging her to crucify herself.

She turned to look the way she'd come, across the empty fields. Hadn't she nearly burned a man back there? Standing here, right now, she couldn't even swear to that.

So had she dreamed the whole thing up? Oh God, she didn't *know*.

Perhaps it would be better if she had.

A phone box stood outside the shop. Fran stared at it for several minutes, chewing on her nails; then very slowly crossed the road towards it. Dry-mouthed, she dialled the operator, and let her have the number.

She listened to it ringing, in the distance, in her ear. It seemed that nobody was there; and then her mother answered. Would she accept the charges? 'Yes, of course.' Fran heard the eagerness in that – as if her mum had guessed who this must be.

And so she had. She spoke at once. 'Is that you, Frannie, love?'

'Yes,' Fran mumbled tearfully. 'Hi, Mum.'

'Oh, *love*. Are you all right? Where are you?'

'Somewhere down by Leicester.' She gave as many details as she knew; then sniffed and wiped her nose. 'Can you or Dad drive down and pick me up? I'm sorry, Mum. I've had enough. I'm ready to come home.'

CHAPTER V

Hell's Ditch

I

The lowlands around Glastonbury were filled with pre-dawn mist. The Tor was in the distance, its tower silhouetted by a pearly strip of sky. But cloud still lingered overhead, and night clung on like cobwebs to a ceiling.

'There,' gasped Martin. 'Made it. Satisfied?' They hadn't slept, she'd been so keen to get here. He felt like sitting down, right now – and never getting up.

Branwen kept on walking, glancing back. 'When the Ravensbreed are here, then I shall be content.' She looked as tired as he was – her eyes like cinders in her ashen face. But her voice remained determined: its softness worn away to leave a harder, brittle tone. Martin stretched his weary limbs, and plodded after her.

The country road meandered gently downwards. Away to their left, the old Fosse Way still murmured in the dimness: a trunk road now, with speeding lights like underwater spirits.

They'd rested last at Shepton Mallet, begging enough silver for an unsustaining meal. Martin's shrunken stomach was still grumbling to itself. He'd put some coins aside, and felt them burning in his pocket. Branwen had gone off to draw some comfort from the churchyard; and he had found a call box, and rung Claire.

The burring had gone on and on – then ended with a click. Her voice had answered, full of sleep. 'Hello?'

He'd opened his mouth, and found he couldn't speak. 'Who's that?' she'd asked uncertainly. Then: 'Martin?'

Convulsively, despite himself, he'd broken the connection. The line went dead, and came back as a buzzing in his ear. And then he struck the handset on the hard edge of the coin-box – until he'd cut the buzzing off, and smashed the phone to bits.

She'd talked about an island, and the Tor had that appearance – surrounded by a spectral frozen sea. They came to its shore and took the plunge, down into the greyish depths, still following the road. Divers, on their way to some drowned village. The growing visibility was suddenly curtailed. The air congealed around them, damp and dense. A hollow silence spread beyond the fields that they could see. But then he heard a rusty cry, which grew into a chorus. Crows were out there, calling as the newcomers slunk past.

He sidled up to Branwen, but she didn't turn her head. Her pale face looked preoccupied. He saw she was uneasy.

'You think we'll find someone you know?' he wondered, more to get her talking than to have the question answered.

Shrugging, she just stopped to check the silver brooch she wore. He couldn't help but think of Claire, examining her fob watch.

'The lodestone has no life in it,' she muttered, sounding fretful. 'I cannot be the only one who senses peril here!'

Martin looked both ways along the road. It faded off into the haze within a dozen yards as if they'd come from nowhere and were heading for oblivion. The mist hung low over the fields, and turned them into insubstantial marshland. Trees were like dim figures at the limits of his vision. Somewhere beyond, the crows kept up their cawing.

Then he heard another sound, a thudding. Muffled and arrhythmic, like a dying person's heart. Branwen heard it too, and raised her head.

The thudding moved across their front, and faded in the mist. Martin frowned, went over to the hedge. The stagnant greyness hadn't stirred. He looked around at Branwen. She was standing there behind him, very still.

'Let us go forward, *now*,' she whispered hoarsely.

Unsettled, he rejoined her, and they hurried down the road. After a minute, the sound began again. The misty air distorted it, obscuring both its distance and direction. But then he glimpsed a movement in the field on their right. A murky horseman cantering across it.

'*There*.'

The shape kept moving, ghostly in the dawn – but the thudding of its hoofs on turf was solid and substantial.

Branwen slowed: her stride became a prowl. Then they heard another horse, directly up ahead: iron horseshoes ringing on the surface of the road. Martin moved aside, towards the verge. The animal was closing fast – was coming at the gallop. They heard it panting, snorting with exertion. A spectre in the mist, and then a thundering dark shape. And Martin felt his heart convulse with shock.

The rider wore a knee-length coat of chinking iron mail. His helmet had a nose-piece that obscured half his face. The image was familiar from a dozen of Dad's books; he'd seen a hundred pictures of the Normans. But none of them had put across the *terror* of their charge.

Stupefied, he stumbled back and cringed into the hedge.

Branwen seemed to waver, like a rabbit in the road. The horseman surged towards her. He had a hammer, poised to swing: a medieval pick-axe. She stood her ground, and drew him on – then dodged at the last moment. He tried to strike her as he passed: a backhand swing that ruffled her dark hair.

She rolled, and scrambled to her feet. '*Come!*' she shouted, gesturing to Martin. The knight was dragging on his reins, feet thrust into the stirrups. Martin stood and gawped at him, unable to believe what he was seeing. The chain mail had a stiffened look, as if the links were rusting. The horse's sweaty stink was in his nostrils. And then the rider craned around to focus on his prey. His face, where it was visible, looked greasy bluish-grey; the sockets of his eyes were full of shadow. Horribly impassive, he began to turn his horse.

Martin lunged across the road, and fled into the field in Branwen's wake. The mist had soaked her up like a windblown rag: a flitting shadow, somewhere up ahead. But then she looked behind herself, white-faced, and came up short. He put on a spurt to catch her up, his breathing hoarse and raw.

He heard the horse's whickering, and then its pounding hoofs. The impacts quivered through the lumpy ground. Branwen waited, poised to flee, then snatched his sleeve, and on they ran together.

The mist flowed past, and eddied in their wake. The horse was drawing closer all the time. Martin risked a fast glance back, and saw its looming shadow. Then Branwen yanked him sideways, and went down on hands and knees, moving off at a tangent, lithe as a cat. Martin followed, panting like a dog. The rider missed them in the haze, and slowed – then came around. His hoof-beats seemed to echo off the denseness in the air. *No, not echoes*, Martin thought, still crawling through the dirt. Another horseman, somewhere in the field.

Oh God.

Disorientation pushed him close to panic. The field felt huge, expanding by the moment. The disembodied hoof-beats circled round them. Then a ragged hedge took shape amid the vagueness. They came to it, and struggled through, and slithered down onto another road. Branwen grasped his wrist again. '*Dewch!*' she hissed, beside herself, relapsing into Welsh. He stumbled to keep up with her, then twisted round to look along the hedge. They'd made enough noise getting through. The hunters must have heard it.

'*What* . . .' he panted, winded. 'What the *fuck* . . . ?'

'The Men in Iron Coats,' she gasped, still towing him along. 'The Bastard's mailed fist . . . which Myrddin saw . . .'

Merlin? he thought stupidly – and then a horse came crashing through the hedge. It overshot the narrow road; the rider dragged it round. He picked them up at once, and dug his spurs in. The horse surged forward, nostrils flared – its rasping snorts as rhythmic as the noise of hoofs and harness. The rider sat bolt upright, like a statue come to life. And yes, this was a second one: he didn't have a hammer, but a sword.

They sprinted down the stony road – so frantically that Martin thought his feet would trip him up. The horse came up behind them, fast. He sensed its humid breath against his neck.

Abruptly he was pulled around, as Branwen swung to face it.

'*No!*' he yelled instinctively, still floundering for balance. She didn't turn her head. Something silver gleamed in her free hand – he recognized her brooch as it was thrust towards the rider. The Celtic cross lit up, as if the hidden sun had touched it – or had she channelled power down her arm? A cross of light was thrown against the Norman's sombre face. It found the shadowed eyes, and made them glare. The horse reared up in panic, pawing at the air with its front hoofs.

Branwen gasped, and seemed to slump; then gathered herself, and pulled Martin off the road – down into the marsh of mist. The horse was bucking, kicking now; the rider hanging on one-handed. His other hand was clawing at his face.

Off they flailed, across the field. Martin glanced back, and tugged against her grip.

'Circle . . . can't you make one?'

'There is no *time*,' she panted. And even as she spoke, he heard the other horseman coming. Other horse*men* coming.

She let him go, so they could both run faster; the sudden loss of contact was unnerving. The riders followed, spacing out, and calling to each other as they came. Their voices were distorted, harsh as rooks. He looked back again. There had to be four or five of them, as indistinct as shadows in the murk.

They stumbled on a drainage ditch, beside a stony track. Branwen glanced behind, then gestured downward. She looked exhausted, as if whatever she'd done with the brooch had spent her strength. Martin wavered, loath to pause. The hoof-beats were approaching once again. His nerves and muscles itched to move. He stared at Branwen's ashy face; wisps of damp hair clung to her forehead. Then they both ducked down, and cowered low.

One of the riders caught them up a mere moment later. He reined his mount in at the edge of the field, and sat there as if brooding. Sniffing the dismal air perhaps – or listening for a heartbeat.

Martin lay quite motionless, unable to look anywhere but up. Horse and rider loomed above him, sheer as a cliff. The knight turned in his saddle, staring off into the mist. His mount was breathing very fast; once it tossed its head, eyes rolling. As if it was in terror of the creature on its back.

Branwen huddled close, but kept her face against the earth. Her eyes were shut, but her mind was full of pictures: images she'd struggled to forget. Hammered skulls, and faces slashed wide open. Children lost and crying by the roadside. The Saxon country ravaged in its turn.

Men shall come, in iron coats and timber, and take vengeance of the Saxons for their wickedness. Myrddin himself had prophesied as much. She should have rejoiced, to see their kingdom fall. Yet the old oppressors' fate had left her grieving . . .

Horseshoes scraped on stones, a yard away. The Norman's armour rattled with the shifting of his mount. And then the horse was off again, along the misty track. Martin closed his weary eyes, and wished that he could sink into oblivion – never to stir from this sodden, weedy ditch.

Minutes passed, and Branwen raised her head; then took hold of his coat and urged him up. They stepped onto the trackway, both shivering now, as much from reaction as from the dankness of the air.

'Come,' she whispered. 'We must not stay.'

The milky mist hung undisturbed – but the hunters were still out in it, and Martin didn't think they'd given up. Which way to turn? Even Branwen seemed unsure. She looked around them, fingering her mouth. Her brooch was still clutched tightly in her hand.

Then she set off down the track, in the opposite direction to the one the knight had taken. Martin followed, looking over his shoulder as he matched her wary pace.

Dawn was creeping damply up, but the world was still asleep. They reached a farm, and stole across the yard. The buildings dripped with silence, wrapped in mist. It felt as if the owners had been smothered in their beds.

A cock crowed somewhere. Martin jumped. And then they heard a horse's hoofs again.

'*Fuck*,' he hissed, to vent his fear. It didn't drain the coldness from his chest. Both of them moved round behind a piece of farm machinery: an ugly metal monster in the dawn. Branwen put her back to it but Martin couldn't help but take a look.

The rider clattered down the lane, imposing as a dreadnought. The mist was thinner, more dilute, and Martin had a clear sight of his face. It had a dark, encrusted look, the teeth like yellowed bone. The eyes were sunk in blackness, but he remembered what he'd glimpsed. That maddened stare, reflecting Branwen's cross . . .

The horseman tugged his rein, and paused. The helmet-head came round to scan the yard. Martin watched him through a spider's web. The strands were strung with beads of dew, like tiny perfect pearls. The Norman lingered in the net – then cantered on; the mist received him back. The pacing hoofbeats faded in the fog.

Martin breathed out hoarsely. 'Let's just stay . . .'

'No,' she told him flatly. 'They will *find* us.' Distractedly she ran her hand into her mist-slicked hair. 'We need to gain a place where they cannot follow. I know of one, I think. If I can find it . . .'

Reluctantly they left the farm, and struck off through the trackless waste of mist. The sound of horses came and went. They heard the riders calling. Panic breathed down Martin's neck; but Branwen seemed to know where she was headed.

Several minutes later they came to a stream: its surface pewter-coloured under clinging whorls of mist. The banks were steep and grassy, overgrown. They scrambled down and crouched there, out of sight.

The Normans must have seen them go to ground. Their hoof-beats grouped, and started to converge. Martin cowered lower, as helpless as a soldier facing tanks for the first time. Massive, looming, clanking things, advancing through the fog . . .

'The Saxons call this place Hell's Ditch,' said Branwen in his ear. If that was meant to reassure him, it did anything but. She hesitated briefly, as if drawn into herself, then clambered up the grassy bank again.

What?

Martin tried to grab her ankle – missed – and slithered back. She reached the top, and stood there in full view. The riders saw, and kicked their mounts towards her.

'*MALFOSSE!*' Branwen yelled.

The effect was instantaneous and startling. The line of charging horsemen came apart. Martin raised himself, to see them sheer off in confusion. One of the horses plunged and kicked. And yet it seemed the *riders* were unsettled, not the mounts.

'*MALfosse!*'' Branwen cried again. Her voice cracked with the effort – but the Normans flinched from it. As Martin watched, they withered, melting back into the mist. Suddenly the field ahead was empty.

Branwen stood there, swaying; then slumped down again beside him. '*Malfosse* . . .' she said bitterly, but to herself this time. Then she doubled forward and was sick into the grass.

Martin waited, too surprised to speak, or offer comfort. She spat until her mouth was clear, then wiped her lips, and glanced at him. Her face was drawn and paper-white, the cheekbones showing through. A little girl grown old, he thought. But her look was wry and rueful.

'Time has passed,' she muttered. 'The Raven gave me stomach for such things.'

He hesitated. 'What things?'

'At Hastingas, when the field was lost, the Normans gave pursuit . . . and in the dusk, they rode into our trap. A gully, overgrown – they saw it not. And in they rode, and down they plunged. And then the Raven swooped.'

Her eyes were dark with memory, not seeing him at all.

'And to this day, the place is called *Malfosse*, the Evil Ditch. Because of the great slaughter – but also for the shadow of the Raven. You see, they dread it still.'

She slid down to the water's edge, and scooped herself a mouthful, swilled it round, and spat it out again. Martin stayed near the top of the bank, still keeping watch. But it seemed that she was right. Somehow the living dead had been scared off.

After a pause he looked at her again. 'Hastings? You were there?'

'Yes,' she murmured bleakly. 'I was there. I was at Malfosse, and I went down among the dying. I cut their throats, and pushed my blade into their moving eyes.' She raised her head, her face composed and calm. 'Does this disturb you, Martin? Will you sleep less soundly, knowing this?'

'How come you didn't win then?' he asked dully. 'If you were there, at Hastings.'

She shrugged. 'The Raven cannot hold the field, if God has not ordained it.'

The sky was brighter overhead. He guessed the sun had risen now; the mist would burn away before too long. 'How long should we wait?' he asked.

'They will not show their faces to the sun. By the time the mist is gone, they will be hidden in their holes. And we shall walk to *Glasynbri* unhindered.'

Martin nodded, slumping back. He closed his eyes, and tried to think of Claire.

And Branwen saw the horses crashing down, and heard

their screams – a noise that even warriors couldn't bear. The riders yelling, howling too; the dead-wood snap of bones. They'd gone into the gully like a dark, collapsing hillside, the riders crushed, their horses crippled, limbs wrenched out, and bellies bursting open. She seemed to see it from below, as if the sky was falling – to bury her in tortured flesh, and drown her thoughts in excrement and blood.

CHAPTER VI

Winter Runes

I

It might have been another world; an ancient, distant time. Not half-a-dozen miles away, and seven hours ago. Glastonbury was teeming, full of traffic, full of sun. Martin couldn't get his head around it. Part of him was hopelessly adrift, like a swimmer getting glimpses of a murky sunken city. And sensing sharks around him in the water.

'Why are they *here*?' said Branwen's voice beside him. He looked, but she was frowning into space. Pale and puzzled: worrying the question. 'As if this were their castel to be kept . . .'

'Maybe they've been tracking us,' suggested Martin vaguely. He shifted then, as another thought occurred to him. 'Or maybe *Rathulf* sent them.'

'No . . .' she murmured. 'No: they know this ground.'

Martin raised his eyes again. 'Spare some change, please?'

Another person passed without a glance.

'Christ, I'm starving.' He settled back against the wall. 'How about you?' They were sitting here like refugees who'd walked until they'd dropped. This might as well have been a foreign country, where no one spoke their language or was ready to receive them. While homes were burning, over the horizon.

Branwen had her knees drawn up, her forearms draped across them. Her head was bowed in thought – or weariness. 'We shall not eat,' she murmured.

'It's beginning to bloody look like that . . .'

'No,' she said, and fixed her gaze on him. 'Today we must fast, and pray. Prepare ourselves. Tonight we turn the Wheel of Stars again.'

He thought of the map, still folded in her pocket. Flattened, creased, reduced – and yet still active. Being held by somebody who knew how to control it; and yet – or so it seemed to him – still volatile and threatening.

'And do what?' he asked, after a pause. His own voice tasted thick and grey.

'Summon the Ravens. Call them home. Some great evil gathers here – and yet they have not come.'

People kept on walking by, but Martin let them pass. Money for a bite to eat was quite forgotten now.

'What, you think those knights are guarding something?'

She shrugged, like someone with a great weight on her shoulders. 'Perhaps. It could be they are outlaws, who will raid and ride away . . . but it thinks me they were *waiting*, they were sent to *hunt us down*.' She tipped her head back pensively; then let it roll towards him. 'The air around this place is changed. You cannot smell it? No?'

'Smell what?'

'It is like a midden that has burned. Scraps and shit and rotted meat, that have not been consumed. Still stinking, under smoke and flies. And yet the wind plays tricks . . .'

Martin smelled exhaust fumes, nothing worse. She read the blankness on his face, and looked away again.

'Perhaps we shall see more within the Circle.' She didn't seem delighted by the prospect.

'We're safe inside the town, though . . . aren't we?'

'Yes,' she said. 'And safest on the abbey's holy ground. So that is where we go, this night – to summon back the damned, my brother Ravens.'

2

Someone took pity on them, and bought them soup and coffee at the Assembly Rooms café. Martin wolfed his portion down, despite the chill she'd put into his belly. Best to keep his churning stomach busy. But Branwen wouldn't touch her bowl; just sat there, looking glumly disapproving.

'Mind if I have yours as well?' he asked, and helped himself. 'Look – whatever you aim to do tonight – I'm going to need the energy. All right?'

She didn't reply, just slipped her crusty roll into a pocket of her jacket. Something for later, then. He took it as a sort of vindication.

They went outside, and down the steps into the inner courtyard. She glanced up at the square of sky, then fumbled for the map and brought it out.

'Study this,' she told him. 'There are words which you must learn.'

He stared at it uncertainly, then took it from her hand. His mouth grew dry as he unfolded it. The daylight put a flat sheen on the paper. *A photograph*, he thought, *that's all it is*. A frozen moment, sealed into the page. And yet it could thaw out again: perhaps beneath his gaze . . .

The Chart was a web, full of spidery words. He picked out names he recognized, and found they were no comfort.

'See the words around the rim,' she murmured. He guessed she meant the five in the outermost ring: evenly spaced, with crosses in between.

ROTAS ✠ OPERA ✠ TENET ✠ AREPO ✠ SATOR

He frowned at them, and realized that they read the same way backwards.

'These words have power,' Branwen said. 'Have them in your heart when I am opening the ring.'

It hardly seemed the place to be discussing magic rites. Not with bright sky overhead, and pigeons cooing softly in the shadows. The bustle of the High Street carried clearly down the passage. Martin rubbed his hand across his mouth.

'What do they mean?'

'*Pater Noster*, spoken twice; and Alpha, and Omega. The letters mixed, to blend into your spirit as you taste them.'

This didn't seem the time to say, *I don't believe in God*. He paced the yard uneasily; she turned around to watch him. 'Why Glastonbury, though?' he asked.

'This has always been a sacred place.'

'You said the Chart was drawn up here?'

'Yes,' she said. 'In secrecy and darkness. There is much learning here, at Glasynbri. The monks have books from many lands. Wisdom from far places. They tamed the *wiking* Raven, which the Wessexmen had caught. Snared and seeled and hooded it within this sacred ring. By its power, we winter in the nameless fields between this world and Hell.'

Martin halted, staring at the map. The web was there for him to fall right into.

'Its nature is still evil: it is carrion-bird and battle-hawk and wolf. Three in one.' She crossed herself. 'Once the hood is taken off, it lives to feast on flesh. The Ravensbreed are but its beak and claws. Few men are as charmed as you – to raise the thing in ignorance, and live.'

Her gaze was introspective now. He thought of what she'd told him at Hell's Ditch. 'And you . . .' he said. 'Are you its claw as well?'

'I am skilled in healing craft. I thought that I could share it. But the Raven . . . it puts gall into your soul.' She pulled a sour face, as if that gall was on her tongue; then turned away from him, and said no more.

3

The abbey, around 4 p.m . . . The air was warm; still hours of daylight left. But he could feel the night's first spores already – growing from his stomach like the tendrils of dry rot.

Branwen turned about herself, her face still blank with shock. Of course she hadn't known about the abbey's dissolution. The building stood in fragments now, wide open to the sky. The nave beneath her boots was new-mown grass, muffling her steps as though to mock her.

Does this mean we can't do it, then? he thought.

The ruins had a cutaway surrealism, as if two worlds had intersected here. It seemed his mind had learned to stretch: he could picture them completed in some parallel dimension. Intangible, unseen, and yet still present.

He was standing by the site of Arthur's tomb – according to the sign, at any rate. An oblong of grass with a plain stone kerb. The monks (he read) had found it in 1191, and moved it from their ancient cemetery. Dad had disappointed Lyn by calling it a medieval hoax. Martin glanced at Branwen now, and thought it would be best if he kept quiet.

She came slowly back towards him, her look almost accusing. 'Who has done this?'

He shrugged. 'The king closed all the monasteries four hundred years ago.'

'For why?'

'So he could have their property, I think.'

Branwen's eyes grew narrow. Still gazing at him, she nodded to herself. 'Then it is *well* that we did what we did.'

She didn't enlarge on that; just looked around herself once more. 'No matter. It is holy ground. And we must be prepared.'

She took out the roll she'd saved from lunch, and twisted it in two.

'What?' he asked uncertainly, as she offered half to him.

'This shall be our sacrament,' she said.

'I don't believe in all that stuff.'

She seemed nonplussed by that, but rallied quickly. 'Then I needs must believe for both of us. But you must take this, Martin. Share the bread, to make us one.'

They went to where the altar had once stood. The walls this end were down to their foundations. It felt as if the world was looking on. Without quite knowing why, he let her draw him down to kneel on the green grass. Facing him, she tore a piece of bread and proffered it. He took it in his mouth like a child being fed, and then returned the gesture.

A pair of hippies, sharing their communion. Some people paused to stare then wandered on. Nothing would surprise them in a place like Glastonbury.

4

They climbed the Tor to watch the night come down. The calm air round the abbey was deceptive; up here the wind was vigorous and bracing. It tugged Martin's coat, and ruffled Branwen's hair. Clouds streamed past to left and right, as if this was a boulder in midstream. Shadows slid like ghosts across the Levels. Weather fronts collided as they watched.

The Tor's got its own weather. Somebody had told him that, the last time he was here. In a way, he thought it might be true.

Branwen hunkered down to brood; Martin waited at her shoulder. Down below, the lights were coming on. The town was turned into an orange constellation. Lamps spread out along the roads, to dwindle in the dusk. And still the wind kept buffeting, while clouds the size of mountains drifted past.

'The way is dark,' said Branwen. 'It is time.'

They came down through the twilight, and crept back into the abbey. The ruined walls rose stark against the purpling sky. He'd had a sense of peace before, but now the place seemed harsher, almost hostile.

'It matters not that churches fall,' said Branwen in the dimness. 'The wind of God keeps blowing through the ruins.'

They came to the old grave, and walked around it. 'So who *was* buried here?' he asked – whispering, without intending to.

Branwen barely glanced towards the spot. 'Who can say? I think it was some English plot, to take heart from we *Welsh*. But there may be other secrets. Other graves . . .'

They were deep inside the abbey now. The air was hushed and shadowy, as if the crumbled walls could still contain it. The brightest stars were glinting overhead.

'Think upon the irony of this,' she went on drily. 'Whenever we were roused again, I heard new stories told among the people. Tales of Arthur, and his sister Morcant; of Myrddin his wise counsellor as well. And yet they grew from *our own deeds* – the wars of the Black Saxons!' Turning, she looked up, and pointed skyward at the Plough. 'See? The sign of *Athelgar*. The people call it Arthur's chariot now . . .'

'So which of you was Merlin, then?' he asked. She didn't answer.

Down they went, into the undercroft. It felt like a descent into the deep end of a pool. Dusty gloom closed over them. The vault was open to the sky, but the recessed shrine was like a tunnel's mouth.

Branwen knelt before it; so did he. Even through his jeans, the stone was cold. She moved around to face him. He heard the paper rustling as she unfolded the map and spread it out.

'*Hibernacula*,' she murmured. 'A Latin word; we know it from the war-dukes. An army's wintering place. The Ravens sleep in winter signs. The houses of the stars are *hibernacula* for us.'

Settling back, she crossed herself twice over, and raised her gun-sight pendant to her lips. Then she reached for him, and took his hands. Fingers clasping hard in his.

'We call upon the High King of Creation,' she said hoarsely.

'May His presence be around us in this place. As deep as the earth that holds us up; as steadfast as these stones; as watchful as the spirits of the air.'

Martin tried to keep his thoughts in neutral. He could smell the night around them now – the subtly changing flavour of the fields. His fear had just been simmering, but now he felt it coming to the boil. The Chart was still an inert square of blackness. How long before it opened up and sucked him in again?

Branwen sensed his rising dread. 'Do not be afraid,' she breathed. 'The saints are all around us.' She drew herself up closer, and he felt her gentle voice against his cheek. 'Cleave to the living world. You shall not fall.'

It felt as if he'd passed some kind of barrier, uplifted by the strength of her conviction. He heard – or thought he heard – distorted voices, crackling and splintered at the edges of perception. They mingled in the trees around the foot of the Tor, and hovered in the void beyond the fields. Distant, eerie gibberish – like spirits raised by radio.

Branwen's fingers tightened as he listened, full of awe. 'Be silent now, within your soul, for I must call the Raven.'

Martin simply nodded. His mouth was dry but his mind was full of a strange, objective calm.

'*Hrafn . . . Guthhafoc . . . Wulf*,' she said.

He sensed the thoughts behind her words spread outward like radio waves. Then: '*Yn Enw'r Tad, a'r Mab, a'r Ysbryd Glân . . .*' she whispered. He somehow guessed what those words meant: one Trinity invoked against another.

The air was thicker, darker now. The abbey felt more solid, more *substantial*. Martin risked an upward glance, but couldn't see the stars. The sky had clouded over with frightening speed.

And yet there was no wind round here. The air was cool and still.

A blink-and-miss-it flash of blue; he glimpsed a solid sky. A vaulted, stony ceiling overhead . . .

Oh my God.

Branwen's fingers clenched round his. 'Regard the Chart,' she hissed.

Staring down, he saw the map was glowing: a whirlpool of reflected stars and bottomless black water.

The voices he could hear were different now. Clearer, more harmonious, but they made his hackles rise. A soft, mesmeric plainchant from five centuries ago. Whether it was in his mind, or in the real world, the abbey had come back to life again. And dawn was here.

They knelt there, bathed in multicoloured light. Red and yellow, green and blue – as if the sun was streaming down through medieval glass. The wonder of it caught him up and he struggled to keep focused on the Chart. The gleaming of the stars was undiminished.

A faint vibration started, half a universe away. A beating like the slow wings of a bird. He felt it in his bloodstream, like the rhythm of his own pulse. A sudden, sickly chill welled up inside him.

Branwen also felt it, and it caught her by surprise. Her hands closed tight round his. He heard her gasp.

The light grew bleak and searing: melting down the coloured glass – then blowing out the frames. The building was engulfed by fire; they both looked up in horror. A face was there amid the flames, blistering and leathery.

The voice that Martin heard was raw and mangled in his head. 'Who is this who *dares* to enter here?'

The abbey fell about them, collapsing back into the ruined darkness. Branwen screamed. The flames went out. The shadows overcame them like a tide.

VIII

WARRIORS

His bursting from the spicèd tomb,
His riding up the heavenly way,
His coming on the Day of Doom
I bind unto myself today.

THE HYMN OF ST PATRICK

CHAPTER I

Forgotten Ground

I

The sky was bright, beyond the bathroom window. The bland sounds of the village carried faintly through the casement. Familiar sounds: a passing bus, the distant hiss and rattle of a train. But Fran lay silent in the bath, as if she'd drowned long since.

The room was all familiar, too. The carpeted but creaky boards, the stripped-wood door she'd locked behind herself. Dad's shaving things, still lined up on the sill. The light-pull made of conkers, which he'd helped her make when she was in her teens. The bathroom she'd grown up with – its various colour schemes like changing seasons. The walls were summer yellow now. Mum had painted them last year, trying to make the house a bit more cheerful for her daughter. But today it seemed like so much wasted effort. The whole world had a washed-out, winter feel.

The bathwater was tepid; the foam had turned to scum. It seemed as if she'd lain in it for ever. Her aching head was propped against the rim: a leaden helmet, much too hard to lift. Her fingers clasped her squeezed-out sponge against her drying chest. Perhaps, if she lay here long enough, she'd quietly dissolve and be forgotten.

A gentle tap against the door. Ignoring it, she stared up at the ceiling.

'Frannie?' came her mother's cautious voice.

'What?'

'What would you like for lunch?'

'Nothing.'

A moment's hesitation. 'You've got to have something, love.'

White fire flared inside her then: a flash of rage that almost made her swear. But vacuum snuffed it out again before it reached her mouth.

'Not hungry,' she said flatly. It was true enough. She'd been back home a week, and still not eaten a square meal. Just nibbled and picked, with anorexic languor.

Long pause. She sensed her mother struggling with the silence and the locked, unyielding barrier of the door. The thought left her unmoved. It might have been a stranger on the landing. Or one of her Voices, seeping through the wood.

'You've been in there a while . . . is there anything you need?'

Fran almost said, *A razor blade*, but stopped herself in time. Dad's razor was in here anyway. She felt too apathetic to consider using it.

'Well . . . whenever you're ready to come down, we'll be happy to see you.'

Fran just sighed, and waited for her mum to take the hint. The sullen silence did the job: that nagging, stifling presence went away. She listened to the footsteps plodding wearily downstairs.

Leave me alone. Just let me be. You haven't seen the things I've seen. You haven't got a clue! She shook her angry thoughts until they seethed inside her head. White and fizzing, blotting out the guilt, the part of her that felt her mother's pain.

But even the rage had lost its roots. The things that she had lived through left her cold. They belonged to some previous existence. Marcus had discarded her, as if she were a chess piece. Athelgar had vanished into history again. If either had existed independent of her mind, they were nothing more to do with her now.

Somewhere miles away beyond the window, they could still be pursuing their secret war. Ravens fighting Ashmen, like two factions in a book: a story she could put away half-read. One side might win, or neither would; it didn't really matter. The world would go its merry way regardless. Down to Hell.

It felt as though all her hopes had died with Lyn.

She lay here like a corpse herself, with both hands folded neatly on her chest. She raised her right hand and stared at the ring – the only physical evidence she had.

IHS ✠ MAR

She'd put it on again, although she wasn't quite sure why. The metal seemed innocuous, like something cheap she'd picked up in a market. She braced her nerves, and tried to feel its power. One tingle, that was all she asked. And then she'd thrust her hand into the water, and hope it had the same effect as dropping in a live electric fire. Her body would squirm and kick, and then shut down. No need to drag the past round any more. Or face the future.

But the band of tarnished silver stayed inert.

The bathroom echoed briefly with the giggles of a ghost. *Her* ghost. Sitting in Craig's bath, in his apartment, on the Base. At this remove she sounded like a silly little girl, delighted by the sense of her own daring. Then his ghost came in as well, and sat down on the rim of the tub. He put his camouflage cap on her head, and grinned at the result. 'Mm,' he said, 'it goes with your eyes.' Then he clambered smoothly in to join her.

The phantom lovers faded. The bubble bath was ditchwater again. Lying there alone, Fran bit her lip.

Eventually – against all expectations – she found the strength to clamber from the bath. Towelling herself listlessly, she thought about the last time she had talked to Craig. Hadn't he promised to come over, sometime soon? The prospect failed to move her. He seemed as unreal as Athelgar – much further than four thousand miles away. Both of them had screwed her; but now they were both memories, and she was just screwed up.

* * *

She came down in her dressing-gown, and slumped onto the sofa: fixing her attention on the TV in the corner.

'Would you like a cup of coffee?' asked her mother from the doorway. Fran shook her head, not bothering to turn it. Boredom, more than anything, had driven her downstairs. She felt too flat to read or listen to music in her room. Daytime TV was the best way left to disengage her brain.

After a minute her mum came in and sat down in the armchair. Instinctively Fran closed her gown. The skin over her breastbone was stippled with red marks: tiny puncture wounds, like insect bites. She'd taken to fiddling with her cross – and jabbing its fine points into her chest. More and more obsessively, she'd mortify herself. And dig a little deeper every time.

'I'm sorry, Fran,' her mother said. 'I know how bad you're feeling, but I have to say this. Your father and I think you ought to see someone.'

Now she looked round, scowling. 'Like who?'

'Someone from . . . the hospital. You're really getting down again, and they can help you up.'

'There's nothing *wrong* with me,' Fran snapped.

'Oh, Frannie, love, of course there's not. You're just depressed – we know that. A bit more than the rest of us, that's all. But there's no need just to sit it out. You've had the drugs before, you know they work . . .'

'It wasn't the bloody drugs that helped me last time. It wasn't you two, either.' A poisonous barb; she saw it hit and hurt. 'Lyn was the one who got me back, and *she* can't help me now.'

She turned back to the TV screen, and glared into the picture. Trying to escape from where she was and what she'd done.

'It's no wonder that you're feeling down,' said Mum after a long and fragile pause. 'To have your best friend killed like that . . .'

You don't know the half of it. I found her body, *Mum!*

'. . . And it hurts us both, it really does, to see you down like this.'

'Don't then. Go away, and leave me be.' Saying it, she felt just like the scorpion in that old fable: stinging the person trying to save it. *I can't help it, it's my nature . . .*

Her mother got up and left the room abruptly. Fran settled back, still staring at the screen. After a moment she reached for the remote, and thumbed the volume up. But the soundtrack couldn't quite drown out the muffled sound of crying from the kitchen.

2

'I don't know what to *say* to her. I really don't.' With Fran upstairs and out of sight, her mother could give vent to her frustration. All the hurt she'd tried to hide was raw and naked now. Perhaps she didn't care if her voice carried. And Fran was on the landing, and could hear every word.

'Let me have a word with her,' her father murmured. He'd just got in from work, and sounded tired. The car keys rattled as he hung them up.

A floorboard creaked beneath her scuffed DMs. She'd just got dressed, all ready to go out. Black jeans and a stone-grey sweater, summing up her mood. She couldn't stay in here another minute; it felt like being crammed into a doll's house. She was gasping for fresh air, and open sky.

Best to make a move, or she'd be stuck here. She started briskly down the stairs, and met him at the bottom. 'Hi, Dad,' she said flatly. 'I'm just going for a walk . . .'

He thought on his feet. 'Why not wait till after tea . . . I could do with one myself.'

'No, thanks. I'd rather be on my own.' Passing him, she walked towards the door.

'Frannie,' he called softly. She wavered with her fingers on the latch. After a moment she turned her head. His gaze was warm and anxious, like his tone. 'How's it going, girl?'

She shrugged, and tried to smile: her facial muscles twitched, and failed to form one. Staring at him, she glimpsed herself – a girl in this same hallway. Off to catch the bus to school, or meet friends for a disco. But time was like a telescope, and she was looking down it the wrong way.

Her father hesitated. 'I've got tickets for the first game of the season . . . if you're interested.'

She moistened her lips, and shrugged again. 'Maybe. I don't know.' She saw him clutch that *maybe* like a straw. And then she was out, and the door was closed between them.

After being cooped up there all day, she almost gulped the breezy afternoon. Above the roofs, the uplands rose in slabs against the sky. Higger Tor loomed like a tumbledown turret. She stared at it; then turned away, and took a different path.

An hour's listless walking brought her up to North Lees Hall. It sat there in its hollow, like some isolated fragment of her college, complete with kitchen chimneys and a crenellated roof. A rookery still flourished in the clump of trees behind it. Otherwise the solitude was total, as if she'd swum a mile out to sea. She gazed back down the valley, then slowly climbed the lane towards the house.

Mum had brought her here when she was younger, to see one of the settings for *Jane Eyre*. Fran had been impressed – but then she'd noticed Stanage Edge, the great escarpment rising to the north. She turned to look towards it now: a massive, crumbled rampart on the skyline. It still awoke a glimmer of her awe that afternoon. Back then it had seemed like the rim of another world.

From that day on, she'd yearned to see beyond it. Eventually she'd walked up there with Dad – to find a sea of heath that sloped away to the next skyline. Despite the view, it seemed an anticlimax. But Dad had sensed her bafflement, and put his arm around her.

It's part of the fun of walking, Fran. Come to one horizon, and you'll always find another one beyond it . . .

The lane led onward, past the house and onto rising ground. She climbed some steps and reached a muddy path. Stanage Edge was there ahead, imposing as a wall across the world. Behind it lay the Hallam Moors, wild and lonely, waiting for the night. She wanted to keep going, past the point of no return; in search of the horizon she was never going to reach.

She took one pace – and then she heard the call. It rose from some vast distance so far away that she could feel it coming. A keening note that grew into a single shouted word.

'*HWÆT!*'

She heard it in her head, and yet the rookery exploded into noise, taking up the cry in all its harshness. Fran swung round in disbelief; then cowered as the croaking birds took flight, spreading the word across the open fields.

hwæt . . . ! hwæt . . . ! hwæt . . . !

Athelgar had used that word when summoning the Ravens. Lyn had had it framed above her desk. *Listen!* it commanded. *Come and hear!*

Her hand went to her open mouth, and she snatched it back. Something like a dentist's drill had buzzed against her teeth. She stared into her open hand, and realized that the ring had come to life. Vibrations started spreading through her nerves. Before she could try to pull it off, the itch of power had crept along her arm.

Panicked, she turned back towards the house – and came up short. A sombre shape was waiting in the lane, beside the wall. It looked like a ghost against that gothic building. But then she saw and recognized his face.

Coldness filled her body, and squeezed out through every pore.

Athelgar's skin had a faint, unhealthy sheen. He raised one hand towards her like a beggar. His eyes were empty hollows.

'Frances . . . Come, and help us.'

Fran stayed frozen, staring down. His face stood out too

clearly, as if starting to decay. His distant, husky voice was full of ashes.

'Help you how?' she blurted.

'Wait for me at *Weondun*,' he said. The final word was snatched away, as if the wind had changed.

'Where is that?' she whispered. The ring still squeezed her finger like a vice.

His figure glided closer to the bottom of the steps. Petrified, she waited at the top. The brooding house and empty nests all magnified the silence.

'You *know* where, Lady. The field of crows, around the Holy Hill.'

Helplessly she shook her head. 'I don't remember it.'

'South of where the waters meet. At Brunanburh,' he said.

Her skin began to crawl beneath her clothes. If he put one foot on the steps, she knew she'd break and run.

'Are you a ghost?' she asked in a small voice.

He shook his head; she glimpsed a grim amusement. 'See me *shine*,' he said – and disappeared.

Fran just gawped: he'd gone into thin air. For a terrifying moment it was proof of her psychosis. But then she thought about the rooks. Something real had scared them off. The branches overhead were still deserted.

The aching in her finger faded slowly. That was something real, as well. Gingerly she touched the ring, then turned it. It was dead.

The sun was down behind the hills, the air was thinning out. Shadows had crept up around the house. As she stared, a light came on: a window lit with gold. It made her ache to be at home again. But the road back into Hathersage was lonely and unlit, and what she'd seen would haunt her all the way.

She stood there for a minute, staring down the empty lane. Then very slowly she started to descend.

3

Dad had all the local OS maps. She spread them on the table, once the tea was cleared away, and searched them for the clues that she'd been given.

Frances, come and help us. She was needed: she'd been called. Even as she looked, she felt the bite of apprehension in her belly. Life had meaning once again, and now she wished that she'd been left in peace.

The TV winked and murmured in the background. Dad was in his easy-chair, absorbed in an edition of *Horizon*. She could hear Mum in the kitchen, setting up the ironing board. It felt just like Fran's schooldays: homework to be done, before she went out with her friends. But now the atmosphere was soured, the homely comfort gone. And all her friends had carried on without her.

South of where the waters meet, so Athelgar had said. The rivers Don and Rother came together east of Sheffield, but she couldn't find a place called Weondun. Nor was there a Brunanburh, although the name was naggingly familiar. She chewed the word, and felt it give: he'd mentioned it before. One of the battles he'd fought a thousand years ago.

How much had the landscape changed since then?

No battlefield was marked here. She scowled with concentration, then glanced towards the door. Why not ring up Lyn, she'd know . . .

Oh. No, she wouldn't.

Tears were in her eyes before she knew it. She bit her lip and blinked them back. The smudgy blur resolved itself again.

She heard her mum come in – and pause. Fran kept staring downwards, but part of her was yearning for a cuddle. *Tell me that I'm pretty as a pixie. I won't mind.*

Her mother went back out without a word.

Fran just sniffed, and glowered at the map. Everything was modern: just a mass of streets and buildings. Reservoirs and steel works; the coking plant at Orgreave. But then a detail caught her eye – a flyspeck in the middle of it all. The plain word *Moat*, in gothic script: there, in a chink of open ground between Rotherham and Sheffield. The remnant of a stronghold of some kind? She couldn't tell.

Whatever, it was something *old* – the only ancient landmark she could find. An outcrop lay beside it, where the river Rother snaked around its base. Was this the hill that Athelgar had meant? This tiny fragment, cut off by the tide?

She went and got the *South Yorkshire Street Atlas*, which showed the area on a larger scale. She found the page, but couldn't see an earthwork. Just farmland, and a sewage works, and Brinsworth Switching Station. Brinsworth was the suburb that had spread across the hill. She studied it, frustrated now, and saw another name.

White Hill.

It looked to be the name of an estate. Fran sat back uncertainly. *The field of crows . . . around the Holy Hill.* White could be a synonym for that.

Wait for me at Weondun. The dead sound of his voice was still a whisper in her ears. It put a chill into this cosy room. How had he appeared to her, and what did he want?

She knew their cause was lost now; perhaps the final battle had already taken place. The last stand of the Raven, in a spinney or a rubbish tip somewhere. Athelgar had fallen – and come back to her in spirit. Hopelessly appealing for the help she couldn't give.

The poignancy was sharp enough to prick her. She found herself decided: she would try and seek him out. Her faith was smashed and splintered up, like china in an upturned packing case. But if she gripped its jagged shards, she might just find the strength to lay his ghost.

She reckoned that she owed him that. He'd laid *her*, after all.

CHAPTER II

On the White Hill

I

She left right after breakfast, which for her was just a fruit juice and some coffee. As usual, she'd turned down toast and cereal – but not through listlessness this time. Her stomach was too churned-up to accept them.

Where will you be going, love?

Just into town, she'd shrugged.

She caught the train to Sheffield, where she changed for Rotherham. The ground between the cities was a barren no-man's land: all factories, scrapyards and derelict sheds. The shadow of the battlefield loomed closer.

Brooding now, she took a bus into the southern suburbs, wrapped up in her silence while the conversations flowed, and sunlight winked and flashed across the aisle. She got off near the hospital, and carried on on foot. She'd brought along Dad's map to find the way. It led her through a fringe of woods, and down into the open Rother valley.

Her first sight of the hill was unimpressive. There it was, on the far side of the river: beaten down and built on, with council houses covering the top. The motorway ran right across its shoulder, east and west. The steady roar of traffic carried clearly.

The switching station at its foot looked rather like a city in itself. Clean, efficient, busy, and quite lifeless. Pylons marched across the fields, in pilgrimage towards it.

The past had been ploughed over. Even the most tenacious ghost must lose its hold round here.

She felt her spirits wane, but kept on going – over the ring road, and down into the fields. The traffic roar was louder now, like breakers on a beach, but once amid the water meadows she found a strange, uneasy kind of stillness. Placid cows were grazing here and there. The boggy ground looked good for little else.

She wandered through the scrubby fields, but couldn't find a sign of any moat; just a lumpy-looking earthwork that was probably a dyke. Thistles sprang up thickly, but they'd withered in the soil. The place had a contaminated feel.

The motorway embankment barred her way. She turned her face into the breeze, and watched the cars come rushing down the hill. The river slunk away between its overgrown banks. Athelgar might well have come – and been scared off again. The traffic was a torrent, and the power lines a web. He didn't belong here: there was nothing to belong to.

She'd put Lyn's jacket on for this. Mum had had it cleaned for her – wiping out the smells of ancient woodland. History had vanished just the same.

'*Where are you?*' she shouted, but the words were swept away. They carried off her meagre hopes, and left her feeling empty and resigned. So what did it matter if this motorway fell silent, and thistles grew in every poisoned field? Dispirited, she started back, along the muddy path.

A pylon towered above her in the middle of the meadow. Thousands of volts flowed overhead, to feed the switching station. She couldn't hear the humming, but she felt it in her water and her bones. Subliminal, elusive, and it set her teeth on edge. A tang of static crackled in the air.

The ring began to tingle on her finger.

She swung around, and saw him at the edge of the field. He was crouching like a crippled rook: the same as when she'd first met him. But he wasn't digging for bones this time. His perch was on a little cobbled bridge that crossed a stream. Self-absorbed, he gazed into the water. It seemed a bitter parody of some romantic tryst.

She approached him slowly, half-afraid he'd disappear again. Still hunkered down, he raised his head and waited. The setting grew more real with every step. The bridge was like a sewer arch; it spanned a weed-clogged ditch. And poison ivy crawled across its stones.

Athelgar sat watching her, impassive. His eyes were like a stranger's, not a lover's any more. They caught the light, opaque as polished stones.

'Why have you abandoned us?' he said.

'I didn't,' she protested. 'You left *me*.'

He looked into the ditch again. 'I thought that you would follow.'

'Why should I?' she snapped suddenly. 'Why should I *follow* you?'

His head came up and he straightened. 'Forgive me, Lady Frances,' he said softly. 'Remember what I said to you on Waste-Down.'

Sobering, she gazed at him. 'Come *with* me . . .'

'No man may ask more than that,' he said. 'I ask it now.'

'Last night,' said Fran uncertainly. 'I thought you were a ghost.'

He shook his head. 'Mine hour is not yet come. I sought you out with shinecraft. The Raven gives us power for such things.'

She hesitated, listening to the silence. The world was turning, rushing past, but this was like the still point at the centre.

'Come,' he said, and beckoned her. 'Behold the great memorial built for us.'

He led the way across the grass, and up onto the dyke. It might have been the grave mound of an army; the thistles had their roots in something foul. They went along the riverbank, and halted by a gloomy concrete bridge. From here the station looked more ominous: a field of metal gibbets, row on row against the sky.

A medieval fortress; a necropolis; a *shrine*.

'Who was it you fought against?' she murmured.

'The Witchings and the Scots. They came along this valley from the north. Eastward . . . *there* . . . the Mercians stood. And *here*, upon this Holy Hill, the men of Wessexena.'

She looked where he had pointed. His voice was full of memory, and yet it was so hard for her to *see*. The traffic kept on racing past, a blur on the horizon. She turned back to the scaffolds and the citadel of power. Marcus could destroy this place and pull the plug on *cities*.

Athelgar took her gently by the arm.

'One more battle, Lady. We have one more war to fight.'

'I'm not your *saint*. I'm no one's saint.' She shrugged him off again. 'I'm sorry . . . I can't help you any more.'

'Frances. Wherefore not?'

'It's going to happen anyway. Just let it.'

'Let what thing happen?'

'What that bishop preached about. The Sermon of the Wolf.'

He stared at her. 'You think we cannot win?'

She thought of Marcus gloating, like a dark, all-seeing god. And what he'd said about the world; about the hearts of men.

'No,' she said, 'I don't believe you can.'

He nodded gravely, studying her face.

'Thus we came to Brunanburh, with foes on every side. And thus we fought – and *thus* we won the day.'

Seizing her, he swung her round to face the open fields. Instinct made her try to squirm; he held her close against him, squeezing tight.

'Can you feel the *power*?' he hissed. 'The shadows of the dead are sleepless here.'

The hum became a buzzing in her head. Memories were lingering like marsh gas all around them. A stagnant pocket of the past: invisible and foul. Then the static sparked it off – and set the whole of history ablaze.

Images exploded through her mind. She felt herself fall backwards, though he kept her body braced. Everything was blurring and collapsing. The switching station folded up; the houses disappeared. The wasted land renewed itself, and she was in the middle of a *war*.

She tried to raise her arms, and couldn't move them. Warriors lunged at her face – and passed her by like ghosts. Armies came together, their shield-walls crashing and locking. Axes hacked in frenzy, like machetes through a hedge.

She glimpsed the Raven banner, rearing up above the scrum. And there, drenched in blood, were the Three Crosses. Other standards fluttered and contended on the wind. Voices howled across the centuries.

The fighting was more horrible than anything she'd seen. Skulls burst open as she watched, and bodies spilled their guts. Men were struggling everywhere around her, the battle breaking up into a score of skirmishes. Somebody drove forward with a press of warriors round him. Sunlight from the racing sky picked out the crown he wore.

Athelstan, she thought: *The king*. That snarling dragon standard must be his. And even as she stared in awe, the blue-faced Scots repulsed him. The sight of them was terrible, like men who'd just been hanged. The Saxon horde began to come apart. Everything was chaos and confusion. It sucked her in, so close that she could see into their eyes: the wide eyes of the desperate and the dying. Athelstan's sword was knocked aside, and vanished underfoot. His guards closed in around him. The moment hung suspended as the Celts drew back to strike.

Athelgar came plunging in from nowhere. He raised Sky-Edge, and flung it over the mêlée towards the king. It landed on a trampled patch of earth. The king himself crouched down to pick it up. Their eyes met for a moment, then Athelstan rose up to his full height. He thrust the dawn-bright steel into the sky, and looked around. When he spoke, Fran understood the words.

'*Men of Wessex! Who will come with* me?'

The army rallied round him, and surged forward. Athelgar

took up a fallen sword. Fran felt the sheer elation of the moment, as if his blood was pumping through her veins.

'*RAVEN!*' shouted Athelgar, and charged.

The Ravensbreed came down the slope, an avalanche of black. Terror came before them like a shock wave. It swept her up, and knocked her to the ground with winding force. Her body in the real world just buckled at the knees; she swooned, and felt him slumping down behind her. He hugged her close, and held her up, and still he kept on murmuring. An ardent whisper in her ear, but now the words were meaningless again.

'*Letan him behindan . . . hra bruttian . . . saluwypadan . . . thone swearten* hrafn . . .'

She felt a plunge of nausea, and everything dissolved. A sense of falling back through space – then stillness, and the traffic on the skyline. Athelgar was holding her in silence. She thought she heard a helicopter, miles overhead. The clouds absorbed its clatter as they soaked the sunlight up.

Drained, she let her head fall back to rest against his shoulder. She realized she was cold with sweat. Gently he reached up to stroke her hair.

'That is what the Raven does. Its hunger grows and grows. And we shall slay and slay, until our souls are drowned in blood – unless we have your pity to preserve us.'

It sounded like some kind of chain reaction. Something which, if not contained, would keep on till the whole world was consumed.

'Come with me,' he urged again. 'For we have found the *æschere* at last. They are mustering in fenland to the east of Lincolonia, and soon they will be ready to move south: to haunt the wealds like wolves, and feast on flesh. This will be *our* Brunanburh – the greatest battle of this generation. The Raven gives us battle-lust. But will you balance justice with your mercy?'

'Lincolonia? That's Lincoln, right?' Sitting up, she frowned at him. 'Why there?'

'Something has drawn the ash-ships to that coast. It is as if our foe has built a bale-fire for them there. And Lincolonia was a witching-burgh, in Alfred's time. There is much empty land where they can lurk.'

'Do you think we'll find *him* there?' she asked.

He gestured. 'I know not.'

She rubbed her brow. If felt as if her mind was bruised: as if she'd really walked right through that battle. But seeing it had purged the gluey fog of her depression. The thrill she'd had from Athelgar had shocked her awake. Her heart and lungs were clear again; the summer breeze was blowing through her head.

'Yes,' she said. 'I'll come.' She scrambled up. 'Just let me go back home and see my parents . . .'

Rising too, he took her hands, and gripped them. 'You cannot put your hand upon the plough and then look back.'

The hardest of hard sayings. She wouldn't swallow it. 'My mother and my father, and I'll *honour* them – all right?' She stared into his face. 'Or don't you trust me?'

He nodded, face still sombre. 'I trust you, Frances. With my life and soul.'

'Wait for me at Lincoln, then. I'll find you.'

Together they walked back towards the road. A couple of horses were grazing in the first field. A third, already saddled, had been tethered by the hedge. She hadn't noticed.

'Athelgar . . .' she said, as he untied it. 'That isn't a memorial over there. No one knows what happened here. Nobody remembers what you did.'

He seemed to hesitate. She bit her lip. 'And that's what really scares me,' she admitted.

Now he turned to look at her. His face was still impassive, but his eyes were calm and clear.

'It matters not if men forget our battles – so long as they are nourished by the victories we win. For justice will roll on into the future, flowing like the river out of Eden for our folk. *They* gain from the warriors' loss. For warriors always lose.

'But *we* shall not be lost: we twain,' he said.

Reaching out, he cupped her face, and drew her in to kiss. Startled, she relaxed and let him taste her, then clutched at him, and kissed him fiercely back. Blood went rushing through her, bringing warmth to cold, forgotten places.

She wanted to go with him *now*, but knew she had to wait. They parted, and she watched him mount his horse and ride away, leaving her alone beside an overgrown, forsaken killing field.

CHAPTER III

Saint and Sorceress

I

The woman stood and listened to the night.

The land around her cottage was a deep morass of hush. An owl hooted distantly, at least two fields away. But something unidentified was closer – very close. She sensed it like a solid mass; a physical distortion of the dark.

The wind-chimes in the kitchen tinkled faintly. Each note was a gem of ice that melted into silence. She went on through, but didn't turn the light on. A faint, ethereal glow suffused the kitchen. Beyond the trees, the starry sky was clear.

The garden was a gloomy swamp. Trees and bushes, fence and shed were indistinct and lumpy. She stood there, trying to focus in. Whatever it was, the thing was yards away.

The breeze was imperceptible, the music very faint, as if one chime was sounding on its own.

Her mind went darting back two days. She'd had a *weird* encounter then – more startling than any since she'd moved here. Heading home with her dog at the end of his evening walk, she'd been coming down the lane beside the Tor. Someone on a horse had crossed her path – emerging from a clump of trees, and galloping away across a field. Dusk was laid on thick by then. She hadn't seen much detail but everything inside her had recoiled. Cabal, her dog, had snarled and started barking. Crouching down to comfort him, she'd felt his bristling fur beneath her hand.

He was watching her now, from his basket in the corner, the starlight sheening his big, unblinking eyes. She had the clear impression he had sensed the presence too, but this time he was silent – almost solemn.

She spoke his name; he rose, and crossed the kitchen to her side. Tightening the belt of her long cotton gown, she unhooked the torch from its bracket by the door. Instinctively she touched the silver pendant round her neck then opened the door and slipped into the night.

Cabal went forward slowly. Following, she thumbed the torch and flashed the beam around. Familiar features surfaced, and then sank from sight again. She tracked the patch of light onto the woodshed. The door was slightly ajar.

Once more her fingers found the pendant. Still holding it, she moved across the garden. Reaching the shed, she took a shallow breath. Cabal was crouching at her side, a reassuring shadow; she heard him panting softly through the hush. Her nerves were tuned as tightly as the strings of a guitar, alert to what was lying up inside. Denser than the darkness: something solid and alive.

She curled her fingers round the handle – then yanked the door open and shone the torchbeam through.

A bloodless face lit up and seemed to hang suspended in the dark like a jaundiced moon.

The woman felt her heartstrings twitch. The face's eyes were hooded like a death-mask's – intent on something hidden in the gloom. She saw it was another woman, younger than herself. The other didn't flinch, just looked up slowly. Her features were impassive yet resentful. The torchlight caught her eyes and made them glow.

Cabal growled very faintly in the depths of his throat.

The tableau lasted seconds, though it seemed like half a minute. Then the older woman let the torch's beam slide downwards. The girl was crouched or sitting, with someone else reclining in her lap. A second face soaked up the light. A man's this time, though scarcely any older. His eyes stayed closed; he looked exhausted, spent. The girl's arms were around him in a tight, protective clinch.

Cabal growled again. The girl hissed softly through her teeth, and glowered at the dog.

'Cabal,' the woman murmured. 'Quiet, now.' Her jerky heart was settling again. It hadn't been a prowler that she'd sensed, still less a restless spirit. Just a couple of New Age nomads: flesh and blood.

'Comfortable?' she asked after a moment, and managed to put some dryness in her tone.

The girl stared back at her, moistening her lips. 'We need this shelter. Do we have your leave?'

She had a strong Welsh accent, and her choice of words was strange. The woman smiled faintly. 'Yes,' she said, 'of course you do.' She searched the girl's strained face a moment longer. 'You can come into the house if you prefer.'

The other seemed to hesitate, running her fingers slowly through the young man's tousled hair. 'Better we stay out here,' she said, like someone in two minds.

'I mean it. You'd be welcome.' Something here was out of place and yet she felt a growth of empathy. That dark, internal glow she rarely felt. 'My name's Kathryne . . . and this is Cabal.'

The last name seemed to strike a chord; the girl's face showed a trace of animation. 'Branwen is my name,' she said. 'And this is brother Martin.'

Kathryne eyed her shrewdly. 'And what is it you need to shelter from?'

'The Iron-Coats,' said Branwen. And Kathryne's mind flashed back two days, and showed her that weird rider in the lane. A chill went tingling through her nerves. She let it spend itself, and then spoke calmly.

'Come on in then, both of you. Get warm.'

'*Diolch.* We will follow. Let me rouse him, he is tired.'

Kathryne nodded, turned away, and gestured for Cabal to follow her. Walking back towards the cottage, she switched the torch off. She knew the garden path, of course; but the flash would carry far across the unlit countryside. And who could tell what was riding round out there?

'Martin . . .' Branwen whispered in the darkness of the shed. She gently dipped her face to kiss his hair.

Claire was getting frisky now: squeezing him, and purring in his ear. Martin stretched, luxuriating – and then his cosy world slipped out of joint. He fell through with a jolt, and woke in darkness, stiff and cold. But her arms were still around him; her body soft and warm against his back.

'Martin . . . you must waken, we must move.' But the voice was wrong, not hers at all. Disoriented, he tried to struggle clear, then realized it was Branwen, and went limp. A wave of disappointment swilled inside him: whatever else, he wasn't getting laid. And yet her musky closeness brought an upsurge of arousal. Currents crossing, sucking at his stomach.

'Martin . . .'

Fear made a grab for him. 'Jesus, are they after us again?'

'*Hist*,' she murmured, holding on. 'We are safe here. Someone will shelter us.'

Martin slumped, still drained by what had happened at the abbey. She kissed the top of his head chastely, like a sister. Unfulfilled, he shrugged her off, as gently as he could.

'Who?'

'Kathryne is her name, and we can trust her.'

He flexed his shoulders, glancing round. The dark was thick and musty, with a creeping, cobwebbed feel. The starlight from the doorway couldn't reach them.

The hand of fear was looming up, and poised to lunge again.

'How come you're so sure, then?' he muttered.

'Because she is a witch,' said Branwen softly.

2

Kathryne got them settled down, then went to make some soup. Seen clearly, she was younger than expected: a woman of twenty-five or so, with dark hair and a fresh, attractive face.

Branwen sat and listened to her working in the kitchen, then got up from the sofa and moved restlessly around. The cluttered room was full of books, lined up on every shelf. Moving to the mantelpiece, she let her finger trail along the spines.

'What was it?' Martin muttered.

She turned her head enquiringly.

'That *thing* we saw. What was it?'

'Some thing out of Hell,' she answered flatly.

Martin just sagged back, and didn't argue. 'Did you . . . reach your friends, do you know?' he asked.

She shook her head.

'I've got some elderberry wine,' called Kathryne from the kitchen.

'I'll have some of that,' said Martin, getting up and going through. Kathryne seemed to read a lot; there were more books in the hallway. 'What do you do?' he asked, as she poured him a glass.

'Freelance writing, mainly. Bits and bobs . . .' Her modest smile was friendly. 'Are you two on a pilgrimage or something?'

'Sort of, yeah . . .' He took a gulp of wine. 'Cheers, by the way.' Still smiling, she looked back towards the pan.

He couldn't quite believe she was a witch. She seemed like any other girl, and timider than some. The only outward symbol was the pentagram she wore on her left hand.

Witche.

He'd shied away from thinking that of Branwen ever since the day they'd met, despite her obvious powers. Rathulf's man had used the word – and she had stabbed him dead.

He realized she had nothing on beneath her cotton gown. 'Thanks,' he murmured awkwardly, and went back out again. A framed print in the hallway caught his eye. It looked like a circular local map, but with dark shapes spread across it. Strange, mutated figures of some kind. *The Temple of the Stars*, the caption read. The paper it was printed on was yellowing with age.

Branwen was still browsing through the library of books.

'Get yourself a drink as well,' he urged her, and she shrugged. Sipping his wine (not nearly strong enough), he took her place and carried on from there. Some of the spines were cracked with age, while others looked quite new. Most of it was history, or pseudo-science, or both. Various takes on Arthur and the legend of the Grail. A *Guide to Glastonbury's Temple of Stars*. Curiously he picked that out, and started to flick through it.

Branwen wandered through into the kitchen. Kathryne smiled, and gave the soup a stir.

'Have yourself a shower if you want . . .' She glanced towards the door. 'The two of you . . . you said he was your brother?'

Branwen's smile was tired. 'In his way.'

'Well . . . There's just the one spare bedroom, but I can make a bed up on the sofa.'

Branwen nodded gratefully, and started nosing round. Kathryne looked her over. The travel-stained black clothing was evocative enough, but still she had the sense of something deeper. Something *ancient* going on, behind the Welsh girl's eyes.

'You follow the Old Way, don't you?' She asked it almost shyly, but her eyes were confident.

Branwen nodded cautiously.

'I *knew* it. I could feel it in your aura . . .' Her pleasure made her hesitate, bemused. She was older than Branwen by several years, but now she felt as if she were a novice.

'I suppose you could call me a hedge-witch,' she went on. 'Not part of any coven.'

She poured the soup into three bowls, and brought it through into the living room. Martin put his book aside; but Branwen had paused by a picture on the wall.

'Who is this?' she asked.

Martin had found it striking too, no doubt for different reasons. An arty, vaguely Sapphic print of winsome girls in medieval armour.

Kathryne gestured. 'It's just from a *Redemption* calendar. Joan of Arc – supposed to be.'

'Jeanne D'Arc?' said Branwen. '*La Pucelle?*'

'That's right. You know she really was a witch? A mistress of the Craft.'

Branwen came and sat down at the table. 'Jeanne was no *sorceress*,' she murmured. 'She spoke with saints and angels, sent from God. Even on her ring, she bore the holy names of Jesus and Maria . . .'

Martin had raised his spoon to start. He hesitated now, between them both.

Kathryne frowned. 'I thought the church just hijacked her, to cover up her powers.'

'Her strength came from another,' Branwen said. 'He who is king and beggar, lover and lord.' She gave her head the smallest shake. 'There are no words to tell.'

Kathryne sat back, puzzled. 'So *you* follow Jesus, then?'

'As far as I may. There is no *mansion* for the Raven's breed.'

A sombre pause. Martin glanced from face to face, then shrugged, and dipped his spoon into his soup.

'You know a bit about her? Joan, I mean. Jeanne . . .'

'I was there,' said Branwen. 'When they *burned* her.' She spoke with such conviction that Kathryne felt a twinge of sympathy. She had done some shamanism as well; she knew how intimate the visions were.

Branwen looked away, her soup untouched. Kathryne reached across and took her hand. Whatever her beliefs, she had a visionary spirit, and that was something worthy of respect.

'What about these . . . Iron-Coats?' she asked, after a while.

Branwen kept her hand entwined with Kathryne's. 'They guard some evil thing within the abbey.'

'We saw it,' Martin added. 'And it's fucking horrible.'

He thought back to the abbey, and the ghastly face they'd glimpsed – and then the surge of power, which had stunned and crippled them. Somehow she had dragged him out; he felt like he'd been rescued from a fire. Except there'd been no flames, no heat – just hungry shadows licking at their heels . . .

'I need to send a message to my brothers,' Branwen said. 'When we have drawn a little strength again . . .'

'In the daylight this time, right?' said Martin.

She shook her head. 'It must be dark. A clear night. *Una notte serena . . .*' She said that with a twisted little smile. He didn't know the language, and supposed that it was Latin; but something in her tone of voice intrigued him. A twinge of bitterness, perhaps. An echo of regret for something lost.

Only Martin slept that night – behind them, on the sofa. Branwen, though exhausted, was still up to see the dawn. And Kathryne, after hours of talk, was there to watch it with her, although her head was nodding and her eyes were full of sleep.

CHAPTER IV

Reprisal Weapons

I

Lincoln: a place she hadn't visited for years. Fran left the station forecourt, and wandered out into the city centre. She didn't have a clue where she should start.

The shopping precincts round the hill were full of heedless people. She picked her way among them like a lost evacuee – made to feel the more so by Lyn's big jacket, and her Traidcraft duffle bag from student days. She'd packed it for a night or two; and who knew what would happen after that?

To come here was a leap of faith. She wasn't sure in whom.

Her parents didn't know of course. They'd only have tried to stop her. This morning, very early, she had slipped out of the house. *I've got to go away for a few days*, said her note on the cold fridge door. *I'll be all right, I promise. Please don't worry*. They would, of course – and with more reason than they knew. Athelgar had called her to a battle with the Ashmen. Maybe she'd get hurt . . . or killed. Or captured. The last thought was the one that made her shudder.

But she hadn't had the heart to write a proper farewell note, with all the things that needed to be said. They'd think she'd gone to kill herself or something. So if she didn't make it back, that hasty little scrawl was all they'd have.

See you soon. Love, Fran. And that was it.

She paced around, feeling a little queasy; but it was too late to do anything about it now. She rubbed her hand back through her hair – then swallowed hard, and started up the hill.

She'd come here to find Athelgar. Whatever happened then was up to him.

2

She'd hoped he would be waiting in the older parts of town: the medieval streets, or the cathedral. She walked into the latter with her stomach squeezing tight, convinced he would be lurking in its shadows. But Athelgar was nowhere to be seen. She drifted round the building like a jaded tourist, and sat for half an hour on a hard-backed plastic seat. He didn't come and touch her on the shoulder. The only saints she saw were glass and stone.

Back into the light again; less confident, less *faithful* now. It was like that time at Tilshead village, half an age ago. He'd watched and waited long enough before appearing then. As if he got a kick from it. As if it were a game. Her burgeoning frustration turned to anger at the thought.

Don't piss me around. I said I'd come, I'm here – so where are you?

She had a frugal lunch, and let it stretch to fill an hour. It wasn't just a case of not being hungry; she didn't have much cash in her account. Enough for two days' stay, perhaps. This afternoon she'd have to find a guest house, not too pricey. It promised to be a chore, but also a distraction she would welcome. Better that than hang around and wait.

But something else was nibbling at her thoughts.

Four years ago, she'd come here for a demo. There'd been a march to Waddington, the RAF base a few miles to the south. Nuclear bombers used to fly from there. Remembering the bleakness and the bunkers, she felt a nagging impulse to set eyes on it again. A weird feeling; morbid, maybe. It called her like the Imber Ranges had.

Perhaps *he'd* sense the atmosphere, and hear the call as well.
Fran pushed her coffee cup away, and looked round for the waitress. Whatever. *Shit, why not?* she thought. It seemed as good a place as any other.

3

It wasn't far: a few miles down the road. Fran walked slowly, chewing on her thoughts. The day was mild and cool, beneath a milky overcast – the same weather as last time. As the hangars came in sight again, it felt as if she'd slipped into the past. The runway stretched away to meet the sky. But this time she was on her own – encircled by the level, empty landscape.

There wasn't much security in evidence: just an ugly wire fence beside the road. It seemed to whisper thinly in the breeze. She came to a halt, and gazed towards the buildings. The airbase looked deserted, like the others that she'd been to. But this one was still active, she could feel it.

The row of concrete bunkers had a compound of their own, set amid fields on the far side of the road. Concrete lintels, grassy slopes: they looked like Greenham silos. Or barrows from a prehistoric age. She turned around to stare at them, imagining their gloomy interiors. Then hunched her shoulders up and looked away.

It seemed as if she'd had a wasted journey. Athelgar was nowhere close – she'd sense him if he was. Her ring would start to radiate or something. She touched it rather warily, and turned it on her finger. Not a twinge.

She didn't realize how far she'd let her hopes creep up, until she felt them slither down again. Now it was a five-mile walk just to get back to square one. She swore under her breath, and kicked the verge. She'd only come here on a whim, but it felt like being stood up.

Adjusting her bag, she turned – and jumped. Somebody was

standing on the far side of the road, maybe fifty yards behind but clearly watching her. She couldn't make his face out, but it wasn't Athelgar: his hair was dark, his jacket brown not black. Apart from them, the road was empty. She stood her ground uncertainly and waited.

He started forward then, along the verge. Walking briskly: focusing on her. Studying his scrawny frame, she realized it was Shep. A muscle quivered in her thigh, inviting her to run. But everything seemed deadened by a fatalistic calm. She'd found a doorway after all. One way or another, she was going to leave her dreary world behind.

Shep glanced up and down the road, and crossed it. His face was tight and bloodless. Her heart began to pound as he came stalking up to her. He'd hauled his pocket shotgun out. Perhaps he'd pull the trigger and the thing would just go *pop*. Or maybe not. Her stomach sank. The gun was pointed right towards her navel.

'Fancy meeting you again,' he said between his teeth.

'Small world, yeah . . .' she said. Her mouth was dry.

He gestured with the gun. 'I ought to kill you here – right now.'

Calm or not, her heart convulsed. 'What for?'

'Oh, don't play *fucking* innocent with me. You told the coppers where to look. It's your bad luck they didn't get us all.'

'I never said a *word* . . .'

'We thought we'd never shake 'em off,' he went on, right across her – leaning in so she could smell his breath. 'They came with choppers, dogs and guns – the same day you left. You call that a coincidence? I don't.'

'It *is*, though,' she insisted, more indignant than afraid.

'Save your breath. Steve saw you going off with them.'

'Steve? Who's Steve?' Her eyes grew wide. 'Is he the little shit who tried to rape me?' Even as she said it, she remembered the ring: the ghastly first-strike option on her finger . . .

Shep was frowning, startled by her outburst. 'That's what he said to us, all right? That you had gone and grassed.'

The ring was tingling faintly now, as if charging up its power from her emotions. Instinctively she clenched her fist, and thrust it deep into her jacket pocket. *Don't put me to the test like this*, she thought. *Oh Jesus, please*.

Another car was coming up the road. He moved in close to shield the gun, and waited while it passed; then jerked his head. 'What's in the bag?'

'Just my overnight things.'

'Empty it,' he said.

She shrugged it off and did so, spilling out its contents on the turf. He squatted down and rooted through the heap. She watched him turn her towels up, and then her change of undies. He fingered those deliberately, gazing up in mocking provocation. Fran stared back in silence and disdain.

Satisfied, he straightened up again. 'Seen anyone on your way here?'

'Like who?'

'They've got mounted patrols out looking for us now. Punishment units. Beat you up as soon as look at you.'

'What are you doing here, then?'

'We've had enough of running, so we're going to hit back. I came out here to check this place. See if there's some oil tanks or something we can torch . . .'

'I'd give it a miss, if I were you. See those bunkers over there? They've obviously got something worth guarding.' She looked towards the fence, and pulled a face. 'This used to be a V-Bomber base, you know?'

'V for what?' he asked.

'Dunno. Vengeance, probably.' She knew there'd been a range of planes whose names began with V. Sinister, forbidding names. Vulcan. Vampire. Voodoo . . .

'Come on,' he told her tersely. 'Let's get going.'

She nodded at a sign hung on the wire. 'Armed RAF Guards on Patrol', she told him pointedly.

He jabbed his gun into her belly and she winced. 'They wouldn't hear a thing,' he muttered grimly.

Fran could feel her stomach trying to get out past her spine. Shep's face was as sour as his breath. Her hidden fist was throbbing with the power of the ring. The windswept airbase echoed at her back.

Then he moved away, one step. Swallowing saliva, she turned aside to gather up her things.

'Leave them. You won't be needing them were you're going.'

Her nightshirt lay between them, twitching on the grass like a moribund ghost. He placed his grimy boot on it, and scuffed it to one side.

'I came to find the Ravensbreed,' she murmured urgently. 'I know they're round here somewhere.'

'Tell that to the Preacher,' Shep retorted. 'If you get the chance, before he burns you.'

CHAPTER V

The Saying of the Swords

I

She kept on glancing round as they moved eastward. Not just because of Shep, who walked behind her, his pistol pointed loosely at her back. Waddington had slipped away, beyond the low horizon, but she had the eerie feeling it could still reclaim them both. As if, at any second, she would see a Vulcan bomber rising from the landscape like a silhouette of doom. She'd seen one at an airshow once. Its monstrous roar had made her want to scream.

But the countryside stayed empty, the silence only broken by the hissing of the breeze. They were walking down a minor road, with hedges on each side. She could still see the cathedral, like a finely detailed model on the skyline.

'Hoping that your mates are gonna rescue you?' he sneered.

'Maybe they will,' she murmured sulkily, imagining his expression if they did. Especially if they chopped his bloody head off . . .

'You'd better hope they don't,' he said. 'I'll fucking kill you first, be sure of that.'

She looked at him, and back along the road.

'Maybe I'll just fucking kill you anyway,' he said.

'Look, I never sold you out. Okay?'

He shook his head, his anger flaring up. '*Half* the group we've lost because of you. Savaged by the dogs, or beaten up. Now they're being held without trial somewhere.'

'I've not seen any mention on the news.'

He snorted. 'Well you wouldn't, would you?'

Open cropfields stretched to left and right. The sense of isolation was unnerving. He could shove her off the road, right now, and find a drainage ditch. Maybe shoot her in the head or pull his clasp-knife out and cut her throat. Doubtless he would rob her too. When they found her body, she'd be just a mash of flesh. They'd have to identify her by her tattoo.

'How far is it?' she asked, her voice a croak.

'Not far,' he told her grimly.

She could picture that dark Vulcan, still pursuing. The image in her head became the evil Raven banner, spreading its black wings across the sky. Mocking her for touching it and hoping to stay pure.

2

They reached the unmarked turn-off to a farmhouse. He urged her up the rutted track. Glancing to the left, she saw a scrappy little copse, a shadow in the greying afternoon. Somebody was standing at the edge of the trees: so drably dressed, she almost overlooked him. He kept on watching, faceless at that distance. For a moment she assumed it was the farmer. Then Shep waved behind her and the figure gestured back.

They came up to the farmyard. A scruffy-looking, bearded man was waiting for them there. Fran recognized him vaguely. He in turn seemed pleased enough to see her – but in a way that made her flesh go cold.

'Look what I've found,' Shep said drily.

'Excellent,' the other gloated. 'Bring her to the barn.'

She darted a glance towards the house. The place was clearly lived-in, there were curtains in the windows; she glimpsed a line of washing round the back. But everything was swamped in gloomy silence. Had the people here been murdered by Dominicain's band? Or were they being kept as hostages, to fob the hunters off? She hadn't got an answer by the time they reached the barn.

She walked in with her shoulders hunched, her hands deep in her pockets. The place smelled overwhelmingly of damp, decaying straw. It offered shelter from the wind, but didn't feel like any kind of refuge.

'Shit,' said someone. 'Look who's here.'

Most of them were in there, sitting grimly round the walls. They had a keyed-up, harried look, like soldiers in retreat. Half-a-dozen faces turned to stare. Instinct made her glance round for the girl called Julie; she found herself confronting Steve instead. Her stomach shrank defensively, for all that she had humbled him before. But Steve just stood and gawped at her, his eyes grown wide and scared. A makeshift dressing covered half his face. *So how did you explain that, then?* she thought.

The one who'd spoken – Neil – was coming forward. He wore an army surplus coat of faded, filthy colours. One of his hands was bandaged, and he had an automatic in his belt. She stood and watched him nervously: his steely calm was setting off alarms. Shep was right behind her, still. And Carl was on his feet as well, advancing from the gloom beneath the loft.

She couldn't see Dominicain. Oh God, perhaps they'd ditched him.

'*Bet* you never thought that you'd be seeing us again.' Carl's face was a mask of grime, as if he hadn't washed it for a month. Camouflage, she realized. It made his beady eyes seem all the brighter.

Julie was still with them, sitting over in the corner. It seemed as if she'd shrunk inside her parka. The peak of her cap left her eye sockets in shadow. Fran could feel her gaze, but couldn't read it.

Her eyes flicked round to Steve again. He flinched, despite himself.

'And so she has returned to meet her fate.'

Now they all looked round and up. Dominicain was watching from the loft. He stood and glowered down at them, a preacher with a captive congregation. He'd exchanged his white pyjamas for a scuffed black boiler suit. It made his hair look greyer; or perhaps it really was.

She wondered who he might have killed to get it.

He swung onto the ladder and descended. Fran just waited, listening to her heart. A whirlpool of emotion swirled inside it. Relief that he was still here to be reasoned with; and dread of what would happen if she failed.

'*Cannone*,' said Dominicain. Someone picked his shotgun up, and lobbed it. The Preacher caught it deftly: the slap of flesh on metal made her wince. He glanced around, then turned and prowled towards her. His eyes were black, like bits of coal. He aimed the gun one-handed . . . then tipped the weapon up and back, to dangle by its guard behind his shoulder.

'You come here empty handed,' he said darkly. 'How, then, can you buy back your lost soul?'

Before she could reply – although her mind had gone quite blank – someone seized her from behind. She gave a squeal of panic as he dragged her to the floor; then groaned as he dropped hard onto her back. '*Bitch*,' he spat into her ear, then raised his face and voice towards the others. '*Watch* her. She's fucking dangerous.'

Steve, she realized queasily. He had hold of both her wrists now, and was pinning them to the floor.

When Carl spoke, his voice was almost mocking. 'Jesus, mate – afraid she'll beat you up?'

'Sold us out, the little cow. I *told* you.'

'Let her speak,' Dominicain said flatly.

An aching pause, which Steve filled with his panting, while Fran just strained to breathe at all. Then the weight was lifted from her back. Steve got up and moved well clear, but Fran stayed where she was. Cautiously, she raised her eyes. The Preacher's muddy boots were planted there.

'What do you seek here?' his grim voice asked.

'God's mercy and yours,' she muttered quickly.

She knew that was a Dominican response; it seemed to

leave him nonplussed for a moment. She could feel the floor resounding with her heartbeat. Then she heard him slap his palm against the shotgun butt. The sound was curt, peremptory – and yet she had the sense of a reprieve. Pushing herself up from the greasy floor, she drew one knee up under her: slowly, as if scared that she'd provoke him. But Dominicain stayed silent. She saw Carl watching bleakly, from the corner of her eye. Settled on both knees, she straightened her back: trying to look humble, but determined not to cringe.

The Preacher's face was stony. 'Have you word of Athelgar?' he asked.

'I saw him . . . yeah.' She wet her lips. 'He says the Ashmen's force is out here somewhere. There's going to be a battle.'

'And what has this to do with us?' he said.

'There's someone evil leading them. Some kind of monk, called Marcus . . .' She hesitated, seeking a reaction. There was none. Quickly she pushed on, before she lost him. 'He wants to wreck the *country* – not to save the poor, he'll make them suffer like the rest.' She shot a bitter glance at Carl. 'Just like *him*, in fact.'

'Shut it, bitch,' Carl murmured.

Dominicain began to pace around her. Uneasily she turned her head. He'd fished a cigarette from his breast pocket, and paused behind her now for Neil to light it. She watched him drawing on the flame, as if his mind had drifted. It felt like she was balanced on the brink of being dismissed.

Dominicain breathed smoke. 'And you. Why are *you* here?'

She swallowed. 'I promised that I'd join him.'

'Yes – to cast your spell upon his warriors. To send them into battle full of rage.'

Twisting round, she shook her head. 'He says he needs my *mercy*.'

A fleeting smile twitched his mouth, but never touched his eyes. 'What place is there for mercy in times like these?'

She thought of Lyn's drained body on the carpet; the gnarled and goggled faces of the Ashmen. Her wellspring of pity had dried to a drop in the desert.

'It fights against the hunger of the Raven,' she said slowly. 'He said they need the balance – like a scales.' But the hunger was a greedy fire, and she just had this droplet of compassion. She might as well try spitting in a furnace.

The Preacher had resumed his walk around her. His tone of voice was musing, but she sensed its mockery. She faced ahead, and listened to his footfalls on the concrete.

'You wish for us to take the field *against* this Brother Marcus?'

Hostile faces, watching her. She took a deep breath. 'Yeah.'

'Thought you were a pacifist,' came Shep's dry voice from over by the doorway.

She didn't turn her head, and couldn't answer.

Dominicain came round into her line of sight again. 'This is what Our Lord has said. "Let him who has no sword sell his cloak and buy one."'

'". . . And he who takes up the sword, will die by it,"' she muttered.

'We have prepared ourselves for that.'

'So have I,' she said, before she knew it.

The Preacher's eyes were searching: scouring. 'What do you *want*?' he asked again.

'Athelgar needs both of us – and anyone who'll join him. Anyone who knows the *real* enemy.' She glared at Carl and saw his patience fraying. She looked back to Dominicain again. 'You think you're fighting for the poor, but this is Marcus's war. If you help him win it, you'll be bringing back the worst things that you've seen. All the death squads. All the ethnic cleansing . . .' Shep had said Dominicain had fought in other wars. She hammered home the images, and hoped they'd strike a chord.

Someone shifted, restless, in the background.

'Haven't you heard enough?' Carl said. 'Like Steve said – she's a traitor.'

Again she turned to glare at him. 'No – *you* are.'

'She's a fucking liar, and you know it. The cops have got us cornered, and they're playing with us now. If we let our guard down, they'll destroy us.'

'What then must we do?' Dominicain asked coldly. His caustic stare still focused; the shotgun balanced idly on his shoulder.

'Take the fascist bastards on. Slip through the lines, and hit them in the rear.'

Dominicain looked round at him then back at Fran. 'And her?'

'Hang the bitch,' said Steve.

Fran's throat tightened. She glanced at him, and felt it close completely. Steve had found a length of rope. Even as he glared at her, he was fumbling a slip-knot into shape.

She stared in horror at the noose.

'I mean it. String her up right now, and let her choke.'

Fran already felt like she was choking. She looked at Julie. The girl was leaning forward – but her face was wan and bleak.

Steve was breathing quickly now. He threw the rope across a beam. The noose dropped back: a mocking O. Fran tried to scramble up, but Neil was ready. He grasped her arms, and wrestled them behind her – then brought his knee up hard into her back. She squeaked and writhed in breathless pain; then sagged. She forced her smarting eyes to find Dominicain's again. 'Oh, please . . .' she gasped. And Neil hauled her upright.

Dominicain stared back: a hanging judge. Steve had wrapped the free end of the rope around his arm. Ready to take the weight – *her* weight. Something made her look for Shep. His face was grimly set.

'You know the last thing that you'll feel?' breathed Neil in her ear. 'Your knickers filling up. You'll piss yourself.'

Squirming, she looked round the barn. A couple of people wouldn't meet her eye. Then the Preacher stepped aside, and Neil shoved her forward.

The worst thing was, she'd *mused* about this moment. Years ago, she'd wondered what she'd do. Walk to the scaffold with her head held high – or kick and scream with all the strength she had?

Dominicain reached out and grasped the collar of her jacket. 'Have you foreseen your fate?' he asked her sternly.

Nothing wrong with screaming. Scream all the way to the gallows. Let them know that doing this is wrong . . .

Panic was swelling, bulging to get out, but an answer came from nowhere, ready-made. She forced it out between her teeth. 'They always hang the ones who tell the truth.'

The Preacher didn't let her go. He stared into her face. Fran waited, panting shallowly. Then he cocked his head to take in Carl.

'This *mercy* that she speaks of. It will weaken us?' he asked.

'Yes, it *will.*' Carl came forward, brandishing his fist. '*This* is gonna win the day. Class war, class violence – not bleeding hearts like her. Wankers holding hands and singing "We shall overcome . . ."'

'So wrath must be our weapon, then? And violence with no pity?'

Carl gave her a derisive glance, and nodded fiercely.

Dominicain just nodded. 'So,' he said. His free hand brought the shotgun up, and fired it at Steve.

The confines of the building seemed to magnify the blast. Fran convulsed in startled fright; Dominicain held on. The burst of pellets riddled Steve and seemed to burst him open. He floundered backwards, drenched with blood from collar-bones to crotch. His face, beneath its pads of gauze, went flour-white with shock. Mouth still open soundlessly, he crumpled to the floor. The rope came coiling down on top of him.

'*E cosi sià*,' Dominicain said flatly. Still holding Fran, he pivoted and swung the smoking shotgun onto Carl. The latter was too stupefied to make a single move.

Neil was just as stunned, it seemed – still clutching her

as well. But then he let her go and stumbled backwards. She slithered to her knees, as he began to draw his pistol. But Shep had hauled his own gun out. 'Just *drop it,*' he said.

The others had scrambled up, but made no move to intervene. A pump-action shotgun was propped against the wall. Carl gave it a helpless glance, but nobody was going to chuck it over. Steve lay twitching weakly where he'd fallen. Foggy gunsmoke stung Fran's nose. She coughed, and kept on coughing.

Dominicain ran his gaze around the remnants of his band – and jerked his head. The gathering moved in without a word. One of them bent over Steve, and started to unwind the length of rope. Three of the others closed with Neil, and seized him by the arms.

'Oh my God,' Fran whispered, and the Preacher hauled her up.

The rope was flung across the beam again. The noose hung down and dangled, like a mouth without a face. Neil began to struggle as his captors dragged him forward: digging in his heels, to no avail. Shep was walking close behind him, kicking at his boots. Julie watched, expressionless. The pistol in her hand was aimed at Carl.

'Look at you!' Neil blurted, as they forced the noose around his twisting neck. Even now, he sounded scandalized. 'You've thrown your fucking rights away! Just following a leader, like the rest . . .'

'Don't you get it, yet?' said Julie tightly. '*You're* the one who's driven us to this. You and your hate. It's poison, and we're fucking sick of it.' She nodded at Dominicain. 'The Preacher tried to *stop* us . . .'

Horrified, Fran glanced at him. He looked at her implacably; the cigarette between his teeth flared scarlet. And then the hangmen took the strain, and Neil was lifted, threshing, into space.

Fran mewled, and clapped both hands against her mouth.

Carl's hard face was bloodless now; he knew he was alone. His frightened eyes moved jerkily; then he fixed on Shep.

'So how're you gonna save the world, you *wanker*?' he burst out.

'Here's a start,' said Shep, and pulled the trigger. The gunshot made Fran jump again. Carl spun back, and crashed against the wall. Grimly, Shep took aim at him, and fired a second time. The pistol's roar was thunderous, and everybody flinched. A bloody hole exploded in Carl's jacket. Flailing out, he toppled to the floor.

I'm dreaming this, Fran thought. *It's just a nightmare*.

But Dominicain's rough grasp was real enough. Letting her collar go at last, he took hold of her hand. Raising it, as if to kiss, he scrutinized her ring. His level gaze came up again. She clenched her muscles, trying not to shake.

'Well did you say – as *she* did – that the ones who tell the truth are those who hang.' He glanced at Neil, whose body was still kicking. 'Better we should save this fate for those who would deceive us.'

He loosened his grip and she almost snatched her hand back. The barn looked like the climax of a Jacobean tragedy: one man hanged, two blown apart, and blood spilt everywhere. The rest of the cast looked on, white-faced. Shep was gazing at his gun as if its power had caught him by surprise.

Dominicain surveyed the corpses. 'They break, but cannot build again. They are no help to us.'

'These are the only ones we've killed,' Shep murmured flatly. 'Bit of a fucking useless revolution.'

'There is more killing to be done,' Dominicain retorted. He moved away, and left Fran where she stood. Shep looked up, then came across and took hold of her jacket.

'Look!' he said. 'And *there*. You see? *You* did that. You talked about a balance . . . well, there was a balance here. And you're the one who walked right in and tipped it. Don't talk to me about mercy. You wanted this.'

'I *didn't*!' she protested.

'You knew it had to happen, though,' he said.

Dominicain was pulling on his coat – an extra layer of dusty, scruffy black. He looked from Shep to Fran. His eyes were cold.

'Go your way. Find Athelgar. Tell him that the Dog would meet with him.'

'Want me to go with her?' Shep asked. The Preacher nodded grimly, and shrugged into his shotgun bandolier.

'Glad to see you trust me, then,' Fran muttered.

'I don't,' he told her evenly. 'But I think it's time we met these friends of yours.' He paused. 'And I'd rather have an argument with *you*, than swallow what Carl said. At least we'd have a world with you in charge.'

That sounded like a sort of compliment. Bemused, she watched him go and talk to Julie. The others were getting ready to decamp: stepping carefully round their former comrades. The smell of blood was thickening in the air. Still shaken, she turned round, and found Dominicain behind her. His face as grave as granite – like his voice.

'Athelgar is a man of war. Be you at his side or no, there shall be *no mercy* shown.'

He wasn't trying to warn her off, she realized, just seeking to prepare her for the war she'd called him to. The hunger of the Raven she was going to see unleashed. She thought of Brunanburh, and didn't argue.

3

They reached the level crossing at the bottom of the hill, and waited while a train came clunking past. People crowded round them, not caring who they were. Fran stood watching glumly: sensing Shep, and smelling him, but trying to pretend he wasn't there. His silence felt sardonic, yet they'd reached a truce of sorts. She'd *needed* a companion on the road back into town.

The train was a portentous thing, its heavy rumble ominous as thunder. Its wagons overshadowed them. The slowly turning axles rasped and squealed.

'Where do you think you'll find them, then?' Shep asked.

She glanced at him unhappily, then back at the cathedral. It rose up like a fortress on its hill. 'Maybe up there somewhere. I don't know.'

The train was through and the barriers rose again. They crossed the tracks, and walked into the centre. It was late afternoon, but the precinct was still crowded. Fran felt like an outcast now and Shep looked like an outlaw – tense and sullen, restless as a fox. The chickens clucked and strutted round, and he just slunk right through them. No one sensed his pistol, which was barely out of sight.

Fran stopped in the middle of the square, rubbing her hands distractedly as if about to pray. But her gaze kept tracking round like a radar sweep from face to carefree face. None of them was known to her, and nobody looked back.

Thumb and finger found the ring, and pressed it gingerly. No response. Dead metal. She trudged on up the hill with Shep. They moved wide apart, like strangers to each other. The rising incline made her muscles ache.

They halted on the high peak of the city. Surely they'd be met here in these medieval streets between the castle and cathedral. A quarter of an hour passed. No sign.

'What if they don't show?' insisted Shep.

Fran just shrugged, and glanced away again.

'I'm not hanging round much longer,' he said grimly.

She wondered if her ring could draw their lodestones. 'They're hiding out, like you lot are,' she muttered. 'Maybe it'll take a while for them to realize that I'm here.'

'The cops are on the lookout too. We don't blend in round here.' He looked round as he said it. The bandage in his lank black hair might be passed off as a headband, but that wasn't much help. Traveller or fugitive, he'd draw a second glance.

'I'll take another look inside the cathedral,' she suggested.

'Suit yourself – but hurry up, all right?'

She went across the forecourt, and slipped inside. The evening sun had broken through, to scatter rainbow colours down the nave. She wasn't going to linger; just a quick walk down the side-aisles to the Angel Choir and back. She didn't really think that he'd be in there but Shep was getting on her nerves; she had to have a breather.

But what would happen if he *didn't* show? She found she couldn't face up to the prospect. Seeking a distraction, she paused at a display in the north transept. A series of drawings showed the growth of the cathedral. It rose up through the centuries. Might Athelgar have witnessed every stage?

Her eyes strayed to a piece of text: a written meditation of some kind. Cities came in many types, according to the writer. Some were secretive, and some surprising. But some stood up against the sky, and called you from far off.

Lincoln is one of these.

Something made her frown at that; it struck some kind of chord. Perhaps it was the starkness of the image. *Nakedly, against the white sky* . . . Preoccupied, she turned away – and glimpsed a figure rising from his seat. Recognition sparked in her – she swung around, heart leaping. And then she gasped in horror.

It was Craig.

CHAPTER VI

Wilderness

I

She didn't speak; just grasped his wrist, and dragged him out the back way – leaving via the coffee shop, which gave onto a narrow cobbled street. He made a show of stumbling to keep up then dug his heels in, took hold of her sleeve and pulled her round. 'Hold it, Fran. Just wait a minute, will you?'

'What are you doing *here*?' she hissed.

He snorted. 'I could ask you the same question.' His shrewd eyes searched her face. She could almost feel how pale she looked, how drained by what she'd seen that afternoon.

'Fran, your folks are worried sick,' he said. 'What's going on?'

She stared at him; then glanced over his shoulder. The cathedral loomed against the evening sky. Shep, already restless, was bound to come looking for her soon.

'I told you I was coming over,' Craig went on quietly. 'Your mom told me how down you'd been. I thought that I'd surprise you.'

She shifted nervously. 'How did you find me?'

'Military intelligence,' he grinned.

'*Craig*.'

'Okay . . . When you were checking train times, you went and left your notes beside the phone. And I know you like old churches, so I just kept coming back.'

Her eyes flicked to the doorway of the coffee shop again. This time he looked round as well. 'What is it?'

I'm with another man, and he might kill us.

'Nothing,' she said hastily. 'So listen, are you staying here, somewhere?'

'Down by the marina, yeah . . .'

Swallowing, she tugged his arm. 'I think you'd better take me there,' she said.

Back in his hotel room, he tried at last to put his arm around her. She wriggled, shrugged him off and stepped away.

'Leave it, Craig – I don't feel *clean* enough.'

Something flickered on his face. His eyes seemed bleaker now. 'Have you been seeing someone else?' he asked after a pause.

Yes, her mind crowed bitterly, *of course I bloody have!*

'Nobody like you,' she answered dully. 'Nobody I've got a future with.'

He chewed on that, then swallowed it. 'So come on back with me.'

She looked towards the window. The sky above the river was as faded as she felt. She thought of Shep. He must be going *spare*.

'I can't,' she said. 'There's . . . things I have to do.'

'Like what?'

She looked at him again, and shook her head.

He moved a little closer. 'You've got yourself caught up in something, right? And you want out.'

'Yeah . . .' She smiled bitterly. 'I think you could say that.'

'Let me help you, then.'

'You think you can?'

'You think that I don't love you?'

'Oh, Craig . . .' She bit her lip tight shut. Her pent-up grief was bursting to get out. It made her realize just how tired, how *desperate* she was. She sat down on the well-sprung bed, and tried to get a grip.

He eased himself down gingerly beside her. A pause, and then his arm crept round her shoulders. She didn't try to shrug him off this time.

'Come on, Frannie. Let me take you home. Have yourself a good long bath . . . then come to bed and let me hold you tight. Nothing more than that, unless you want it. Tomorrow you'll be back safe with your mom and dad again. And next week we can fly out to the States, just like I promised.'

Listening with her head down, she was suddenly so tempted. The world had stopped, and now she could get off. It could start again without her. She was mad to think that she could make it turn the other way.

Sanctuary was there, across the ocean. She could almost feel the purifying sunlight; drying out the dampness and decay. She'd lie back in his rocking chair, and smile beneath her shades, and let her pallid body soak it up.

She turned her head; looked right into his eyes. The dying light was in them. She thought that they had never seemed so clear.

'Have you been sent to tempt me?' she asked softly – as Athelgar had asked *her*, on that evening by the river.

Craig just frowned at her, and shook his head.

'Please,' she said, 'I just need to lie down.'

All the miles and misery were catching up at last. Abruptly she was dopey with fatigue. Craig eased off, and helped her with her jacket. She pulled her muddy boots off too, and curled up on the bedspread, fully clothed. *You want something to eat?* his voice asked vaguely. She mumbled something negative, and let herself sink deeply into sleep.

2

When she woke, the room was full of darkness. Craig lay slumped beside her, fast asleep. He hadn't undressed either. She guessed it was the jet lag catching up.

Fran listened to him breathing, then raised herself, and peered towards the clock on the TV. The luminous red figures had gone out.

She blinked and squinted. The sooty silence whispered in her ears. No hum of air-conditioning now. And yet the room felt cold.

Sliding carefully off the bed, she padded to the window. A weird light was leaking round the curtains. She parted them, and peered through. The marina was engulfed in mist. She could just make out the nearest boats, like fly-husks in the shroud of some vast cobweb.

The deathly, muffled silence seemed to press against her ears.

An awful trepidation overcame her. Without a thought, she turned away and walked towards the door. It melted at her touch, and she was moving through the city. Everywhere was silent and deserted. Litter from an upturned bin lay rustling in the square. Every streetlamp had gone out; the shop-fronts stood in darkness. But high above the rooftops, the cathedral was lit up.

It felt as if the Bomb had dropped while she had been asleep.

The building's glow was spectral, almost putrid. It rose up sickly pale against the lowering black sky. She peered at it uncertainly and started up the hill. Something dark was gurgling in the gutters as she climbed. Like treacle in the gloom, but much too runny. Here and there it overflowed, to stream between the cobbles. She stepped across a delta of the stuff and came up short. The ghostly light had tinged it red. She realized it was blood.

Sickened though she was, she kept on climbing. The flow was like the run-off from a slaughterhouse up there. A thousand sleepers butchered in their beds.

The cathedral rose above her, as stark and white and naked as the bones of some great beast. A hooded shape was waiting on the forecourt, brooding on an open book as if absorbed in prayer. She caught her breath and froze – but he had realized she was there. Slowly the black cowl came round. The white face lit within it, like a frosty moon emerging from the clouds.

'Well met, *blessed* Frances,' Marcus sneered.

'We know you've called the Ashmen here,' she burst out bitterly. 'The Ravens are here, too. We've caught you now!'

He nodded. 'It is fitting that these Wickings serve my cause. For these men, saith the Chronicler, *made that which once was great, become as nothing*. And now they shall avenge a kindred crime.'

'So what do you want?' she hissed. 'For us to *stop* you?'

'We cannot be stopped – not even by thy Ravens. But somebody must *know* why it is done. For how else shall the past be justified? Someone who is wise enough. Could it be *thee* . . . my *Lady*?'

He tore a leaf out of his book, and offered it to her. She tried to read it, picking at the medieval script. Suddenly the page flared up and turned to ashes in his fingers. Whatever the words had been, they were lost to her now. She stared at him, frustrated and perplexed.

'Doest thou still not understand?' he taunted her.

'Tell me, then! Stop pissing me around!'

'Reflect upon this wisdom, lady Frances. When once a land has lost its past, its future dies as well.'

Something moved behind her, and she swung around to see. An Ashman stood there, grinning with its mouth of naked teeth. It had a doll's head balanced in its hand. Fran drew back, disgusted, but the figure came no closer. The plastic head looked shiny in the half-light. The eyelids were half-open. A fine gold curl stirred gently in the breeze.

Nausea ballooned inside her belly. She looked again, in disbelief, and saw the blood that soaked the Ashman's glove.

Not a doll's head. Not a doll at all.

'*NO!*' she screamed – and catapulted herself back onto Craig's bed. The vision was consumed by dark and silence. She sat straight up, as if she'd bounced. The mattress barely creaked.

Craig's breathing, deep and steady, never faltered.

The TV clock was lit again and the room felt warmer now. The shock of the transition left her weightless for a moment.

Then her hollow stomach surged. Scrambling up, she bolted for the bathroom to be sick.

The choked sounds of her nausea didn't wake him. She pieced herself together, crouched in misery and darkness, then ventured weakly back into the bedroom. He hadn't stirred. Bitter-mouthed, she groped round for her jacket and her boots. The smell of field and farmyard helped her find them.

Sorry, Craig. I have to go. I promise I'll come back.

The first pale gleam of day was seeping faintly through the curtains. By its light, she saw his Zippo, lying on the table. A moment's hesitation, then she crept across and took it. Cool in her hand, substantial in her pocket. It was the only keepsake she would have.

She knew she couldn't touch him, couldn't even risk a kiss. It hurt so much to leave like this: going off to war without the chance to say goodbye. She might die in a ditch today – with everything she felt for him still trapped inside her heart. Congealing with her blood. And it would rot there.

She hovered like a faceless ghost, as if she meant to wake him up, to *warn* him. But dawn was here already – and like a ghost, she knew she couldn't linger.

Craig . . . she mouthed; then slipped away and left him to his dreams.

Outside, the breaking day was quiet; but the city, still alive, had started stirring. Warily she went back up the lanes to the cathedral. The forecourt was deserted. No ghostly monk, no grinning corpse, no gutters full of blood. She walked around the barred and silent building. Still no sign of Athelgar or Shep. She lit a cigarette, and smoked it down to the filter. Then ground it into ash beneath her boot.

The æschere are mustered to the east.

Lingering, she looked both ways – then started down the road in that direction. The Ravens wouldn't come to her. It seemed she'd have to go and look for them.

CHAPTER VII
Black Cavalry

I

She thought she'd glimpsed a movement – too distant for her eyesight to discern its source. Something in a field, beside an isolated copse. And then she saw, or thought she saw, a sudden wink of light.

Fran halted by the roadside, on the brow of a hill. Half a mile from Lincoln now, with rolling fields of crops on either side. The road curved sharply downwards here, and stretched into the open countryside. She picked out knots of villages along it. The landscape was a flat expanse of fields and boggy ground. Copses stood out, dark against the drabness. Further back, to left and right, the river's brooding bluffs were cloaked with trees.

The flicker didn't come again. It might have been a sunbeam on something bright. But the sun had gone; the sky was clouding over.

She frowned and kept on walking, willing her eyes to see another flash. Like looking for the lightning in a distant thunderstorm. Her neck was prickling, right enough – as if it felt the static.

Something *clicked* beside her, very close.

She froze at once, and slowly turned her head. Shep had risen from the roadside grass. She looked into the barrels of his gun.

'We must stop meeting like this,' he sneered after a moment.

'Aw,' she managed drily. 'Must we?'

'Reckoned you could dump me, didn't you?'

'I was looking up old friends – all right?'

He came down off the verge and stalked towards her. Bits of grass were clinging to his coat. 'At least you're still out searching. I thought you'd set me up, you little cow.'

The pistol was still pointed at her chest. She slid her hands deliberately into her jacket pockets. 'Athelgar said the enemy was gathered to the east. It could be that his men are out here, too.'

She forced herself to glance away, towards the distant copse. That glimpse had stirred up something, a memory she couldn't put her finger on. But it made those murky clumps of trees compelling – and repulsive.

When she looked at him again, he'd tucked his pistol back into his belt. His dark eyes watched her narrowly beneath his bandaged fringe. Pissed off though he clearly was, she saw the threat had passed.

'Where did you sleep last night?' she asked.

'Under a fucking hedge, of course.'

She dropped her gaze; then fumbled in her pocket. 'Would you like a cigarette, or . . . ?' He snatched the pack away before she'd finished. She dug the Zippo out as well. He lit a cigarette and breathed out smoke.

'Nifty lighter, girl.' He tossed it back. 'So, now what?'

She pointed off along the road. 'I saw something just now, in those fields down there. Something flashed, just once – but like a signal. It seemed familiar, somehow. I reckon we should go and take a look.'

He nodded, and she smiled despite herself. She felt a little safer, now he'd caught her up again.

A footpath took them past a church, and down along the river. Following the dyke, they headed eastward. A watchful-looking wood slipped past, then an empty, shuttered house. The river was wide and quiet here and the calm began to grate after a while. Nothing but the hissing reeds, and ducks that splashed and spattered into flight as they went past. The horizon opened flatly all around them. The cathedral rose in gloomy silhouette. From down here, it looked almost ominous – like a horned and crouching monster on the skyline.

The copse looked much more ominous from fifty yards away, especially now the day was overcast. A muddy track led past it from the road. She studied it uneasily, then glanced back west again. Lincoln was a mound of shadow underneath the clouds. The spires of the cathedral seemed to brush them, about to snag the mass of filthy wool.

Where was Craig right now? What was he thinking?

They'd moved up from the riverbank, rejoining the deserted country road. The countryside was sodden, green, beneath a low horizon. Another wood came right up to the near side of the road. A clearing had been made for some dilapidated sheds. Something made Shep pause, then he carried on to join her.

She squinted at the copse again. It had a hostile aura, as if it were a stand of trees on Larkhill Range, or Imber. She'd felt that way before, about the copses where the Ravensbreed were lurking.

'Come on,' she said, and started up the track.

A huge black shape erupted from the trees.

She cowered back in sudden fright – then registered the horse, the rider's cloak. *Raven*, she thought instantly, and felt her nerves relax. But then she saw the helmet, its tinted visor open on a staring, bloodless face. The 'cloak' became a long black coat. She'd run into a copper.

He had his baton drawn and raised.

Oh shit!

The horseman surged towards her. 'Stand still!' he barked, 'stand *still*!' Her instincts clashed: to freeze at his command, or turn and run. Behind her, Shep was falling back already. And then she heard a scuff of hoofs, as other horsemen moved to cut them off.

She whirled, and saw him dragging out his pistol, as two more riders spurred into the road. '*No!*' she yelled, so sharply that he wavered for a second. Before he could complete his move, a baton struck his shoulder. The gun went jumping from his grasp, and clattered to the road.

The horseman brought his mount around, and clobbered him again: the baton made a wooden sound on bone. Shep collapsed onto his hands and knees. The rider urged his horse over the pistol – securing the weapon, though its owner was in no fit state to reach it. Then, as his victim tried to rise, he leaned down from his saddle, and backhanded a blow that knocked Shep flat.

Three police riders were now blocking the road. They must have used those rusty sheds as cover. Fran heard the fourth come stamping up behind her. The horse's shoulder struck her back, and pushed her roughly forward.

'Hands where I can see them!' bawled the man. She did so, keeping them shoulder-high to signal her surrender. He drove her on ahead of him, to where the others waited. Their riding coats hung loose, like shrouds on scarecrows.

Shep, still dazed, crawled out from underfoot. The nearest rider towered over him – gesturing with his stick, to make him flinch.

'Where's the rest of you?' snapped someone.

'There's no one else,' she said.

'Sure.' One of them dismounted, and pushed Shep onto his stomach, then tied his wrists behind him with a loop of toughened plastic. The other blokes kept glancing round. Fran stood still, heart pounding. The horse behind her snorted in her ear.

Then her wrists were tied as well. The plastic loop was drawn too tight: she hissed between clenched teeth.

'Names?' the man demanded.

'Number?' she shot back over her shoulder.

Framed by his helmet, his face looked doubly grim. 'Suit yourself,' he muttered. 'You won't be getting bail anyway.'

He searched them both, then retrieved Shep's pistol, very carefully, and mounted up again. Shep had struggled upright

– no mean feat with his hands behind his back. His face was splashed with blood, already bruising. He glowered at the coppers. Instinctively Fran moved across to join him.

The one with sergeant's chevrons was reporting in; he wore a hands-free headset, like a pilot's. Fran heard herself pigeon-holed as an *IC1 Female*. Finished, he gestured up the road: away from Lincoln, off towards the fens. 'All right then, let's get going.'

She and Shep went stumbling ahead. The horses paced unhurriedly behind them. Dry remarks passed to and fro; a radio crackled briefly. Glancing back, she tried to gauge their mood. They had a tense and wary look, despite their conversation, as if the empty countryside was getting on their nerves. Like a cavalry patrol out searching for Apaches, and hoping that they wouldn't be successful.

The image underlined the sense of wilderness out here. And what if a party of Ashmen were lurking in ambush? They'd be cut off and overwhelmed in no time. The wind wouldn't carry their screams as far as Lincoln. And what chance would *she* have, with both hands tied?

The ghost of Harald's voice again: *I know what they will do . . .*

They turned along a farm track, the four black riders stalking in their wake. Fran glanced at Shep. 'Okay?'

'No fucking thanks to you,' he muttered back.

'Sorry,' she said – meaning it, and knowing how inadequate it sounded. 'Listen . . . what'll you tell them, when they question us?'

'No talking,' someone shouted from behind them.

A police Range Rover, bristling with aerials, was coming down the muddy track towards them. An incident control vehicle; she'd seen the kind before. Bumping past, it flicked its headlights once. Fran thought at once of Cruisewatch, her memory unblocking like a drain.

She'd climbed up to White Barrow, on a murky afternoon, to try and spot the Convoy's new position. Looking towards

West Down, she'd glimpsed a flicker in the grey – a movement near a copse three miles away. Binoculars had shown a pair of MDP Land-Rovers, meeting up. *That* was where she'd seen the flash before.

A bit too bloody late to realize now.

The track led to some isolated buildings. Four more mounted coppers sat their horses in the yard. A transit van was parked outside, a yellow-coated officer beside it. Someone senior, judging by his cap and silver pips; but his boots were good and muddy, and he wore black overalls.

He had the face of somebody in charge: long and craggy, with dark eyes and a black moustache. She found its strength appealing – and hoped she could appeal to him in turn. To no avail. He looked her over like a piece of luggage.

'They say anything?'

'Not much,' the sergeant said.

'Right . . . get them aboard the carrier.'

Two more men climbed down from the vehicle. Fran was taken firmly by the elbow and led to the back door. The transit was compartmentalized for prisoners: the rear section caged with wire, and fitted with two benches. It stank of disinfectant: mortuary-strength. Shep was made to sit across from her.

'Back to Lincoln nick?' the driver asked, about to close the doors.

The Inspector shook his head. 'Ops centre first – the boss'll want a word. Then I think he'll send them south. It's a job to keep the lid on as it is . . .'

'Who do you think you're looking for?' Fran asked him suddenly.

He turned his head, as if really noticing her for the first time. Then smiled bitterly. 'Your *comrades*, girl. Your anarchist brigade. What do they think this is, the bloody Spanish Civil War?' Nodding to the driver, he stepped back.

'I know about that murder down in Coventry,' she said.

He looked at her again. 'Which murder?'

'Lynette Simmons.'

The PC was unmoved by that – but the Inspector leaned in, frowning. 'What do you know?'

'What killed her.'

It hooked him, as she'd guessed it would: that *what*, instead of *who*. He stared into her face. 'Have you got some evidence? Or something to *confess*?'

'You've classified the details, right? Because there's something *weird*, that doesn't fit.'

'What was she to you?' he asked.

Fran swallowed. 'My best friend.'

'Who killed her?'

'Who do *you* think did?'

'Not my patch,' he came back flatly.

'You've heard something, though – haven't you?'

He seemed to hesitate over his answer. But when he spoke, his voice was firm enough. 'I heard she was gutted like a fish, and some of her jewellery was stolen. We're looking for a petty crook. All right?' He glared at her; then slapped the driver's shoulder. 'Okay, let's shift, before we lose the light.'

The doors clunked shut. Fran winced.

'Well, something's got him rattled,' murmured Shep. She glanced at him. His eyes were shrewd, suspicious. The Inspector had climbed in beside the driver, not giving them a backward glance.

The van set off along the lane quite slowly so the riders could keep up. All eight of them were following like an escort. The countryside slipped by outside the windows – a montage of monotonous green fields and muddy sky.

'What *do* you know?' Shep asked her.

'The Ashmen that we've got to fight – they killed her.' And robbed her too, it seemed. She couldn't say why they'd bother taking jewels. It had to be their nature: in the blood.

She thought of Edgar, with his shiny watch. *All rooks are thieves*, as Athelgar had said.

The van pulled up abruptly, and just sat there. Fran looked

towards the front. The coppers were exchanging puzzled glances. She felt a sudden tension in the air.

She peered between their shoulders, looking through the dirty windscreen – and felt her mouth drop open in an O.

Another horseman waited in the middle of the track: sitting there, as patient as a statue. *Athelgar*.

'Who the bloody hell . . . ?' the driver murmured.

The Raven Lord was thirty feet away. His black coat curled and fluttered in the wind from off the fens. He hadn't drawn his sword.

The Inspector raised a handset from the dashboard. 'Okay,' he said. 'Go forward. Check him out.'

His men moved past on either side, their batons coming out. Fran sat very still, her heart galumphing. Locked in here, her wrists bound tight, she had an urge to squirm with sheer frustration.

The sergeant walked his horse ahead, the other riders mustering behind him. 'Got a problem, mate?' he called, his baton braced.

Athelgar inclined his head, the gesture almost mocking. His face remained impassive. His hands stayed resting on the saddle-horn. The copper closed the distance warily.

It felt as if Fran's stomach had been screwed into a ball. 'Oh please,' she breathed at Athelgar. 'Don't kill him . . .' The Inspector heard, and looked around – then brought his radio handset up again. But before he could speak, the sergeant had spurred forward. No doubt he hoped to call the other's bluff; but his baton came up, ready for resistance.

Athelgar drew Sky-Edge in a blur of polished steel. The sergeant was too close to swerve, and lashed out with his stick. The sword blade cut straight through it. The sergeant recoiled, and lost his balance, sliding from his saddle to go sprawling on the ground.

'Jesus Christ,' said someone. Then: 'Quick, rush him!' The horsemen jostled forward but the track was still too narrow. They'd have to come against him two on one. Athelgar had drawn a second weapon – a club with a segmented iron head. He gripped his horse between his knees, and waited. The next pair took him on, their batons flailing. Athelgar feinted with his sword, and one of them sheered off. The other took a swing at him; but the Raven used his mace to block the blow. For a moment, as the weapons locked, the rival horsemen strained against each other. Then the sword flashed out again, and cut the other's reins. Pulling hard on nothing, the copper tumbled backwards off his horse.

'Yes!' Fran yelped. 'Oh, God . . .'

The third policeman came again. Athelgar ducked his frantic blow, and let him overshoot – then twisted round to club him in the back. 'Aaah!' the copper shouted. '*Fuck!*' A moment later, he was down as well.

And then the fields on either side erupted. Fran felt a moment's panic as the muddy shapes appeared – as if the fens were giving up their dead. The figures rushed the road with weapons drawn. But then she glimpsed Leofric's face, and realized who they were.

The remaining horsemen tried to mill, but found themselves hedged in by swords and spearpoints. Something struck the side of the van. Fran looked at the Inspector and found him staring back, searching her face for some kind of explanation. Then he swung back round, and raised his handset – but before he could make his call for help, someone reached in through his window, and laid a butcher's knife against his throat.

'Be *still*,' a gruff voice ordered. Fran saw that it was Steffan.

Someone else was struggling with the doors. Rathulf's grim face peered in through the window. Fran never thought she'd be relieved to see him. The doors were opened roughly, and she gulped a breath of air. Rathulf clambered in, and used a knife to cut her bonds: sawing through the taut, resilient plastic. He looked at Shep askance. 'And who is this?'

'He's on our side,' Fran muttered, and sat there massaging her wrists while Shep was freed as well.

Outside, the riders were being forced to dismount. Climbing

down, she saw Eldred looking on, sword ready. He sensed her gaze, and turned his head – then quickly looked away.

The Inspector and his driver had been set afoot as well. Athelgar, still mounted, paced towards them. Sword and mace were sheathed again, half-hidden by his coat.

'Are you the captain here?' he asked.

The Inspector hesitated; then nodded grimly.

'And I am Athelgar, Lord of Ravens. Now you must yield to me.'

The officer just stared at him in anger and dismay. 'Who are you?' he asked, as if he hadn't just been told. 'Friend of that Arthur Pendragon bloke, or what?'

Fran realized who he meant, of course: the self-styled medieval king who lent his weight to demos at Stonehenge. But Athelgar smiled cryptically, as if he'd found a meaning of his own.

'Be thankful that your knights have kept their heads,' was all he said. Swinging down, he walked on past, to Fran.

'I knew that you would come to us.' He took and kissed her hand. His eyes betrayed a need to taste much more of her than that. Fran felt a glow inside her, but was still too tired to smile.

'I was looking for you,' she murmured, 'when we ran into this lot.'

'We fought against the Bastard's knights in fenland such as this.' He glanced back at the sullen, grouped policemen. 'Who are these? Oppressors like his own?'

'Not that bad. I'm glad you didn't kill them.' She shrugged a little deeper into her jacket. 'What about the Ashmen? Are they close?'

He nodded. 'Very close. The lines are drawn.'

'Marcus came to me last night,' she muttered.

Athelgar's eyes narrowed. 'And what news did that necromancer bring?'

'He wanted me to understand,' she told him. 'But I don't. He said that it was *fitting* that he'd brought the Ashmen back.

He quoted from a chronicle. It said that they'd made something great become as nothing . . . ?' She looked at him appealingly. He gave a sombre nod.

'Aye, the Chronicler wrote that when Edmund's kingdom fell. The Ashmen burned its glories to the ground. We fled. We shall not flee again. But *this* is not the cause of his revenge?'

'Something else . . .' Fran murmured; she was frowning. 'In my dream, he was up by the cathedral. The whole building was glowing. You know the place stands out for miles. Perhaps their ships can see it in the dark?'

'Their beacon, and their bale-fire. Who can say?' He looked away, across the empty fields.

'I've met Dominicain as well,' she said, belatedly.

His grave face went as stiff as if she'd slapped it. She saw his pale eyes flare, like cold blue suns. 'And what word do you bring from *him*?' he asked, after a pause.

'He says he wants a reconciliation. I told him about the Ashmen. Marcus has been using him but now I think he's seen the real threat.'

Athelgar rubbed his tight-lipped mouth. When he spoke, his tone was wry but mirthless. 'I have not spoken with the Dog since what befell at Rouen. I fear our meeting would be over-warm.'

She felt her own doubts rise again. What if she talked him into this, and found it was a trap? But something else was stirring, even deeper: the doubts and fears Dominicain had planted. *Put not your trust in Athelgar, for he will let you die.*

'Who is he?' she asked carefully. 'He said he was your counsellor, and used to ride with you.'

'A man has no worse enemies than those who were his friends.'

Behind him, Steffan and Rathulf were opening the side door of the van. Fran glimpsed a stack of full-length riot shields inside.

'He's got a band of fighters, now,' she said. 'And powerful

weapons. If you're taking on the Ashmen, you'll need all the help you can get.'

A flicker of something crossed his face. 'There are other Ravens with him?'

'I don't think so, no.'

'No dark-haired woman?'

She shook her head, intrigued.

Rathulf held a shield up, and Steffan swung his sword. The blade bounced off the tough, transparent plastic. The noise made Athelgar look round.

It seemed that Rathulf's eyes lit up. He glanced at Fran. 'What sorcery made these?'

She shrugged. 'It isn't glass, just sort of see-through armour. The cops . . . these sheriff's men . . . they use it.'

Athelgar looked pensive. 'Truly, we have need of every man – especially horsemen. These riding-knights have courage – challenging a swordsman with their sticks. Speak to them, and bid them join us.'

'*What?*' she said.

'They will respect a saint,' he told her.

She didn't share his confidence, but found she couldn't think of an excuse. Swallowing, she started down the track. The coppers had been herded back against the grassy verge; the three who'd taken falls were sitting down. They all looked round towards her: shaken up, uneasy and resentful. The shadows of the Ravensbreed stood guard.

She stopped in front of them, her mind a blank. Mocking phrases rushed into the vacuum. *Unaccustomed as I am to public speaking . . . You may not recognize me, but I'm a saint . . .*

'My name's Fran,' she blurted. 'I'm here to ask who's able to forgive me.'

That awoke some curious looks, at least. 'What for?' asked one man flatly.

'For getting you involved. These are my protectors, and they came to rescue me. We're taking on an enemy you haven't *dreamed* about. You want to walk away? I wouldn't blame you.'

The flow of words dried up again. She stopped and licked her lips, not knowing what on earth she could say next.

'What enemy?' asked someone else.

'*Your* enemy. Our enemy. They make those anarchists look like beginners . . .'

The group of coppers stared at her. She saw their leader scowl in disbelief.

'Let me get this straight, all right? You're asking us to *join* you?'

'*Yes.*'

The sergeant forced a mocking laugh. 'Well, doesn't that beat *everything*?' He glanced round at his colleagues, then grinned fiercely back at her. 'Sorry, love – we didn't realize you'd skipped from a mental hospital.'

That barb reached the bone. She almost winced.

'I bet you think that *someone* has, though – don't you?' she bit back. 'A bunch of bloody psychopaths were on the loose, down south.'

His leer began to fade.

'No motives, and no mercy – right? You've tried to keep it quiet.' She searched their hostile faces for a glint of comprehension, and here and there she thought she might have glimpsed it. 'So how many farms did they burn down, before these people stopped them?'

'What do you know?' the grim Inspector asked.

Fran shrugged the question off, and started pacing. 'The murderers wore armour. Don't tell me no one's told you. They killed with knives and axes. And when you checked their bodies out, you found that there was something *strange* about them.'

She hoped there'd been enough remains to go on. Every raider that they'd killed, they'd burned or dumped in water in case the grisly corpses rose again. But she got her confirmation from his silence, and his eyes. She turned to him, accusing and imploring. '*Now* will you tell me what you think about what happened down in Coventry?'

He seemed to shift uncomfortably, very aware of the stillness of his men. 'It's just a rumour, right?' he said at length. 'There were bits of other bodies in the garden. They'd been burned. And a stain of something upstairs in the lounge. The samples buggered up the lab. And some of the photos . . . came out looking strange.'

'So what if someone told you that the murderers weren't human any more?'

'I'd laugh at you,' he said – without conviction.

Fran gestured to the Ravens. 'This lot won't.'

There was an edgy pause. Waiting horses flicked their tails, and snorted at their unfamiliar handlers. Fran rubbed her forehead tiredly – then gestured eastward, off across the fields.

'Out there – where it's getting dark – there's more of those things waiting. And *here* . . . these men are all that stands against them. If we lose, they'll sweep across the country like a plague. And that's why we need brave men to stand beside us.'

A few of them were turning now, and following her gaze. Another shook his head: still trying hard to cling to disbelief. 'You really think we'll swallow that, and join the revolution?'

'Forget the bloody *anarchists*. We're going to have to talk *them* round as well.'

'You're giving us a choice?' the Inspector asked. His face was flinty: difficult to read.

'Nobody can force you. If you want to run, you can.'

'I'm not bloody running,' someone muttered, sounding irked.

'What do we do, Sir?'

She shook her head. 'Don't order them. They need to make their choice.'

The coppers moved uneasily. No one was quite ready to step forward. She had a sinking feeling that at this rate they were never going to be.

Then somebody beside her lobbed a helmet at the group. It clattered like a bucket to the road. The only man still sitting took a look – and scrambled up. The others shrank away. Fran glanced down in puzzlement, then gasped against her hand.

The helmet still encased a severed head. A gnarled, grimacing Ashman head. The visor was down, the baleful sockets staring. Wisps of desiccated hair escaped the metal shell.

As she stared – before their eyes – the jaw began to move. Convulsively it flexed, and closed. And then the skull was still.

'Jesus, *fuck*,' the sergeant said.

Fran swung round, her eyes still wide. Athelgar was standing there beside her. 'Blessed are they who have *not* seen, and believe,' he muttered drily.

'Where did you get *that*?' she hissed.

'It is one of their scouts. We found him very close to here.' He glanced up at the murky sky, then gestured to his men. 'We must find safer ground.'

She looked back at the horrified policemen. '*Now* do you see what we're up against? So do you want to come with us, or hang around out here?'

They needed no more prompting, following the Ravens who were leading off their horses. They could have passed as carrion birds themselves, in their long coats. The inspector and a couple more went over to the van. Shep had got his pistol back, and watched suspiciously. 'Let them drive,' Fran told him. 'You can keep an eye on them.' He nodded, still uneasy. Not really sure what was going on.

She turned to scan the countryside. The fenland, like the cloud above, was brewing something up. It wasn't just the cold that made her shiver.

'What about Dominicain?' she muttered.

'He will find us when he wishes to,' was Athelgar's flat answer. He took her shoulder, squeezing it. 'Come now.'

They stepped back as the transit van rolled forward. Its

nearside wheel went right over the Ashman's severed head. The battered helmet crumpled, and the ghastly skull was flattened like an egg.

CHAPTER VIII

Hard Standing

I

The headlights came towards them through the darkness: flickering and bobbing over potholes in the track. Fran waited, feeling gutted with unease.

The transit van just sat there, ticking over. Its own lights bathed the next few yards of lane. Standing by the driver's door, she glanced into the night. Beyond the fringes of the glow, the land and sky alike were one black gulf. It felt like the edge of a precipice here. She pressed herself against the van's cold skin.

The oncoming vehicle came in range, and showed up ghostly white. The Range Rover she'd seen before: it trundled up and halted, nose-to-nose with the van. The patch of road between them was suffused with glaring light. Was that the safest place to stand, protected from the darkness? Or was it just the most exposed: a beacon in the night?

She swallowed and looked round again. Murky figures waited at the roadside. Others, she knew, were out there in the fields: standing guard in lonely, blinding gloom. She felt her stomach churn on their behalf.

Behind the van, the track glowed red, receding in the dark.

The Range Rover's crew were getting out. The Inspector went to meet them. She listened to the newcomers' excited, frightened talk. 'Someone moving round out there . . . We didn't see them clearly . . . Some of them were following, on foot . . .'

The Inspector started trying to explain. Fran waited with

her jacket zipped up tight. The whirring of the engines was a sort of reassurance, but it couldn't drown the restless, sighing wind.

The Inspector paused to pick his words. 'We've stumbled on something ugly here. Guerrillas of some kind . . .' (*You know what kind*, she thought, but let him do it his own way.) '. . . We've got a chance to stop them now, before they do more damage. These people here are sort of vigilantes: they can help us . . .'

Fran peered into the dark again. Someone must have seen the light; this glimmer in the vast expanse of blackness. Someone, or some thing.

'. . . Shouldn't we call for back-up . . . ?'

'We haven't time,' the Inspector answered flatly.

Still looking round uneasily, she turned to see behind the van – and froze. A figure had appeared in the road back there: right at the edge of the tail-lights' crimson glow. As she watched, it started coming forward, soaking up the wash of bloody light. She saw it was Dominicain, and let herself breathe out. Her heart kept up its pounding, like a drum.

Steffan eased out from the verge, taking a stand with his hand above his scabbard. But he made no move to block the other's path. Dominicain stalked past him with a grim, defiant glance. The Welshman turned his head, his face impassive. Other men were drawing in to see. She glimpsed more figures, looking on from further down the track.

'*Se swartan hund* . . .' breathed someone from the darkness.

He came down past the waiting van, acknowledging Fran with a cold flick of his eyes. He had his shotgun resting on his shoulder. She sensed and saw his tension: as if he were a gin-trap, poised to spring.

Passing her, he moved into the stark glow of the headlights. The coppers took one look, and backed away. She heard a plaintive voice ask: 'Who the *hell* . . . ?'

The Preacher halted in the melting-pot of light and drifting mist. Then Athelgar stepped forward to confront him. Fran wavered for a moment with her heartbeat in her throat; then sidled out to join them in the road.

The two men faced each other, silent. Then the shotgun's maws came swinging down. Fran caught her breath, and found she couldn't move. Athelgar stayed motionless as well. If he sensed the shotgun's danger then he didn't let it show. His sword was in its sheath; his hands were empty.

She glanced from face to face. Athelgar's was sombre and resigned. Dominicain's expression seemed less stable. She realized he was weighing up the options – one of which was just to pull the trigger.

Oh please don't.

'Your time is finished, brother,' said the Preacher. 'Go you to your judgment, and your rest.'

Athelgar calmly shook his head. 'It is not yet time for that.'

'And who are you to say?'

'It is not I who says it.'

Dominicain gave Fran a sidelong glance. She met his eyes, hoping that she didn't look as nervous as she felt.

'So how shall this be proved?' he growled.

Athelgar dug deep into a pocket, and came up with his well-used silver coin. He held it up beside his face. It glimmered like a tiny tarnished moon.

'Three crosses,' he said softly.

The Preacher glowered back at him, then slowly shook his head. '*Five*.'

Something flickered in Athelgar's gaze: as if the number had some special meaning. Then he nodded slowly – and flipped the coin across. The Preacher snatched it from the air, and stared into his palm. Then raised his eyes, impassive. 'That is one.'

He tossed the coin himself, and caught it deftly; the barrels of the shotgun barely wavered. One by one his grimy fingers opened. Heart in her mouth, Fran craned her head to look.

Two crosses.

Up the penny spun again, and back into his grasp. She

winced, and thought that Athelgar did too. Once more the cross was uppermost; her heart kept squeezing tighter. She didn't know the odds, but they were long, and getting longer.

The fourth cross screwed her nerves to screaming pitch. Dominicain's own face was bleak with tension. Everyone was watching from the edges of the light, but it seemed as if the three of them were standing here alone.

The Preacher flipped the coin one final time. It struck his hand, and spun onto the road. Fran gasped – then dropped into a crouch, and watched it settle. Horror surged inside her as she made out the inscription. EADMUND REX. The coin had come down Crowns.

She glanced up at Dominicain, and knew that he had seen. Instinctively she tried to grab the coin but the Preacher was too quick for her. His heavy boot came down on it. Fran recoiled and snatched her hand away.

The Preacher trod down sharply, as if to grind the coin into the road. He glared at Fran, then raised his eyes to Athelgar again.

'That is five,' he said, and let his shotgun droop aside.

Fran stayed crouching, open-mouthed. Dominicain allowed himself a fleeting, sombre smile. He hunkered down, retrieved the coin, but didn't give it back. He put it in a pocket of his coat.

'So. And you are with us, then?' said Athelgar.

The other nodded heavily.

'Until your debts are paid at last,' he said.

2

The anarchists were less than pleased to find their new-found allies were policemen. They came to join the gathering – then backed away again. The cops were just as hostile; it made Fran think of two opposing magnets. The little force fragmented into small, dissenting groups.

If she'd had the strength, she would have knocked their heads together. Instead, she had to try and talk them round. Wading in, she looked for Julie; found her with a couple of her mates.

'Remember what I told you at the farm? It's happening *now*. We need these people: need them on our side.'

A bloke with dreadlocks shook his head, more pitying than angry. 'You think that you can trust them? You're a fool.'

Voices rose and mingled all around them. Dominicain had joined the fray, with all of his charisma. He moved among his erstwhile flock, cajoling and berating. A copper tried to muscle in, and found himself included in the sermon.

'We're all in this *together*,' Fran insisted.

'Don't give us that crap. I've had enough mates beaten up by fascist shits like them. I remember the Beanfield, even if you don't . . .'

'Watch your bloody mouth, chum,' a policeman called. It seemed that some of them were having second thoughts, as well.

Athelgar was at the roadside, drawing people round him with the power of his words. They came to her in snatches, and she felt her spirits lift. It sounded like a speech at Agincourt.

'This isn't our fight,' said someone.

She rounded on him. 'Yes it is. You can overthrow the State another day. Right now we've got worse enemies to fight.'

'To keep the system just the way it is? Fuck *off*.'

'You want to see things go to hell? Then join the other side. Go on, they're out there somewhere. When we hear you start to scream, we'll know how far away.'

'Who are they?' he asked, after a moment's hesitation.

'The same things that we burned in that old tunnel.'

'That doesn't tell us *who*.'

'Not who but *what*. They're Viking raiders. Ones who never died.'

The nearest faces stared at her, but no one tried to mock.

Perhaps it didn't sound so strange. They'd all been out there, waiting in the dark.

Julie jerked her head towards the watching Ravensbreed. 'And these?'

'Their enemies. My friends.'

'If you seek justice, come with *us*,' said Athelgar behind her.

Someone else had joined Fran's group: a craggy, older man. 'Whoever they are . . . why should we take them on? Vikings? They were pagan oak, free spirits . . .'

She almost lost all patience. 'Oh, for God's *sake*.'

'*Yes they were*. It was Christian propaganda made them out to be barbarians. And now you think we'll swallow it again.'

She thought of Harald then. The question that he'd asked her, and the sacrifice he'd made.

'I know,' she said, more quietly. 'But this lot are berserkers. They'll maim and murder anything that moves – poor as well as rich. And no one's going to stop them except us.'

The arguments continued. At length . . . it seemed like hours . . . they reached a settlement of sorts. A rough alliance, fragile and uneasy. Fran stood back, and wiped her cheeks, and found herself in tears of sheer exhaustion.

Athelgar touched her shoulder. She almost shrugged him off; then leaned against him. His arm went round her shoulders, squeezing tight.

'Frances. We have forged the bond. Now rest.'

She looked at him with brimming eyes. 'You think I've done enough yet?'

'Hush,' he said, and gently kissed her forehead. The engines kept on whirring in the background. She clung to him, but kept on gazing out into the dark. While they'd been standing here arguing – all lit up by the lamps – what might have crept in close, to gauge their weakness?

She crawled into the van, and curled up on a couple of the seats. Before she could get comfortable, the side door rattled open. The inspector clambered in, and spread a large scale map across the floor. Someone helped to hold it down, and lit it with a heavy-duty torch. Athelgar surveyed it from the doorway. Others gathered round to see, Shep leaning over the back of the driver's seat. Fran drew up her feet, and sat there watching.

Somebody leaned forward. 'What's that place?'

The copper bent his head to check. 'Disused psychiatric unit. Been closed about three years.'

'Somewhere we can make a stand against them?'

'What if they just go past?' Fran asked.

Athelgar shook his head. 'They will not pass. They know that we are here, as Marcus knows. They cannot have us at their backs. They must defeat us first, and then pass on.'

'It may be they will try to take the Raven,' Steffan said.

'God forbid,' another swordsman muttered. Fran echoed that in silence. She barely had the strength to prop her head up.

Hoof-beats carried on the breeze; she glimpsed two horsemen gallop past and on along the track. Somewhere in the distance, where the skyline ought to be, she made out winking lights like fireflies.

'Here we will meet them,' Athelgar said, his finger jabbing down towards the map. 'We will meet them *here*.'

In the distance, something else was burning.

CHAPTER IX

Legion

I

They came to the hospital just before dawn, and turned along the access road towards it. The Range Rover led the way, in circumspect first gear; the crowded transit followed behind. Mounted men kept pace on either side.

Fran was in the front seat of the transit, slumped there with her boots against the dashboard. Despite the fuzz of tiredness, she felt her stomach churning. Beyond the Rover's faded lights, the buildings looked as dismal as a ghost-town.

They drove towards the forecourt, very slowly: the chug and whine of engines was the only sound that carried in the twilight. The vehicle lamps seemed weaker now, like torches with drained batteries. An isolated building came up on the left, a villa with its windows boarded up. Black-draped riders walked their horses round it.

She felt as if they'd turned off down a trackway to the past – *her* past. It could have been the road to Imber village, or the hospital where she had been a patient. The fence round the perimeter recalled the miles of wire at Greenham Common.

The vehicles pulled up facing the front entrance. They dismounted and Fran stood there, gazing up at the facade. The long drive down towards it had unnerved her, with the gatehouse looming larger by the moment. She shook a shiver off, and looked around. Every aspect of the place seemed ominous and threatening. The massive water tower had the grim look of a crematorium's chimney.

A group of rooks took off from it and circled, croaking hoarsely.

'*Per me si va ne la città dolente*,' Dominicain said softly from behind her. She glanced at him. His face was closed and wary.

The Inspector passed her, gesturing. 'Get the vehicles hidden. They're bound to send a chopper out to look . . .'

The ground-floor windows were all nailed shut but there were gaps between the buildings, giving access to the centre of the complex. Nerving herself, Fran ventured through. More birds – pigeons, this time – clattered up into the sky. Otherwise the hospital was desolate and silent. She roamed it like a ghost herself, through mouldering cloisters and overgrown quads. This was Christ Church fallen into ruins, in some parallel world which never saw the sun.

She came across the vehicles, being driven into a works yard round the back. Some of the cops stood ready with a tattered old tarpaulin that they'd found. The Inspector was directing operations. The tower loomed above them, square and sombre. She saw that it had windows, like the belfry of a church.

The Inspector turned to look at her, and seemed to share her thoughts. 'Might be a good vantage point, if we can get inside.'

She nodded pensively, and drifted past. Athelgar and Leofric were standing in the road. Clearly they were checking the defences. The notion sent her heart-rate up a notch. Half-a-dozen outbuildings were ranged around the rear of the site. More villas, she realized, with self-contained wards. But now she could see them through Athelgar's eyes – as a line of border posts between the city and the fields.

He found a small, tight smile for her, then turned to Leofric. 'Do you remember Orléans, my friend?'

Leofric nodded bleakly. 'As it might be yesterday.'

A cold resolve had sharpened Athelgar's gaze. He pointed to the nearest villa. '*Bastille* St Jean le Blanc.' And then the next: '*Bastille* Saint-Loup.' And now the yard: '*Les Augustins* – you see?'

'Yes,' Leofric murmured, like someone staring deep into the past. Then he glanced at Athelgar. 'But we are much too few to hold them all.'

'They must find us, ere they fight us.' He looked at Fran. 'These houses, all around the citadel. The Ashmen will not know which ones we hold. Thus we can divide their force – and lure it.'

She hesitated. 'Lure it how?'

'If they find one fortified.' He pointed at the nearest house. 'See, they are like farmsteads – not so hard to overthrow. So we shall let them breach the place. And then ensure their welcome is a warm one.'

The dungeons were all empty now; the men possessed by demons had been scattered. But the breath of evil spirits still remained. Dominicain could feel them as he paced around the walls. Shadows watched behind the upper windows. The chill of empty cells was in the chambers of his heart.

He came upon an isolated building. A bell hung from a bracket on the roof above the entrance – as if it was a chapel of some kind. The windows had been boarded up; the heavy door was locked. The Preacher reared back and kicked it in. Light spilled through the building's dim interior. He paused upon the threshold, then walked in.

Even in this colony, some pioneering saint had built a church.

The place had been stripped bare, and smelled of damp; but an empty cross was hanging on the wall at the far end. The thing was four or five feet high – and dark, as if the wood was full of rot. The Preacher went towards it. His boot-heels clicked and scraped across the gritty concrete floor.

A shadow sprang up in the light. Dominicain swung round. Athelgar was watching from the doorway. The two men stood in silence, face to face. There was too much to be said. It went unspoken.

'And Branwen?' asked Dominicain at length.

Athelgar stared back at him. His eyes were clear and cold. 'I had that in my heart to ask of *you*.'

2

Martin pelted down the lane. The cottage was in sight, he'd nearly made it. Another thirty seconds and the girls would know his news. He saw their faces in his mind already. He felt just like a little kid again.

The road was slick and puddled from the afternoon's rain, but now the pools reflected clearer skies. The landscape looked idyllic in the mellow evening light. No sign now of what he'd just seen lurking in the woods.

He came to Kathryne's gate and had to pause there, waiting for his heart to slow, his lungs to settle down. Then he hurried up the path, and hammered at the door. Kathryne came to answer it, looking less witchy than ever in her *Goddess Bless* T-shirt and faded jeans. 'Hi . . .' he gasped, and squeezed his way in past her. 'Where's Branwen?' Saying it, he turned and saw her coming down the stairs. His heart snagged for a moment as if he'd glimpsed a ghost. But her black clothes were too lived-in, her bloodless face more tired than tormented. She didn't have her jacket on. The floppy jersey made her look forlorn. Staring up, he thought that she'd been crying.

'What is it?' she asked dully.

'Those knights are on the move again. The Normans . . .'

She came up short. 'They saw you?'

He shook his head, and shuddered to remember. Walking back from town, he'd glimpsed a movement in the trees, and then a mounted shadow on the skyline. The Norman hadn't seen him, but was clearly on patrol. Martin hadn't moved or breathed until the shape had vanished.

'Something is afoot, this night,' said Branwen, pensive now. 'And we are not the only pieces waiting on the board.'

'What else is going on, then?' Martin asked.

She turned towards the window. 'The Raven has been raised,' she said. 'To feast in some great battle, at the far end of the road.' When her face came round again, her eyes were bright and hard. 'Whatever foe my brothers face, it thinks me that we face its master here. And therefore he must watch tonight; be with his wolves in spirit. He has unchained his iron dogs again, to guard his lair.'

Martin watched her, frowning now. 'So . . . ?'

'So we must work our craft again – while his thoughts are elsewhere.'

He sucked a breath through gritted teeth. 'Not that bloody star-chart. Not again.'

'Martin, yes we must . . .'

'I'm not setting foot in that abbey again. *All right?*'

She moved to put her hands on him, placating. 'We need only find some open place. The air is cleanest after rain. The stars will all be there.'

He stepped back to evade her. 'And what about those *iron dogs* of his?'

She hesitated. 'This is a chance we needs must take.'

'Oh, must we? Like, who says?' He gazed at her resentfully, then shook his head. 'You don't care if you live or die, do you?'

'Do I not?' she snapped. 'I have prepared myself, this day. The sky is clear tonight. And I am *frighted*, Martin. I do not want to leave this place, and go into the dark.'

She glared at him, then shook her head. Her tone of voice grew quieter, more resigned. 'I *will* not, but I *shall*. The Ravensbreed, my brothers, must be summoned down the road.'

Saying it, she longed to be there with them. Why should she be here, alone, a lantern-bearer on this desolate headland?

'What if they lose this battle, though?' asked Martin sullenly.

Branwen flinched. Her brown eyes flared. 'Do not you even *speak* of it,' she hissed.

Martin turned abruptly and went out.

Branwen sniffed and swallowed, fighting back her memories

along with the tears. He'd stirred her doubts again, and they were seething. Win or lose, the tide could turn against them.

They'd held the field at Stamford Bridge then crossed the country, north to south, to fight *another* battle at Hastingas. But victory had sapped their strength. The road had been too long. The second strife had ended in disaster.

And as it was, so might it be again.

The stars were like a turning wheel, and so were all the chronicles of men. She'd learned that from her mother, very young. All things came around again. The future had its image in the past.

Kathryne's hand was on her arm. 'All right?' she whispered gently. But Branwen didn't answer; just reached up for the witch's hand, and leaned her weary head against her sister's.

3

In the drying splash of daylight, on the far side of the room, Athelgar was sharpening his sword.

He held the blade across his knees, to catch the amber glow. As if the steel could draw from it, and still be shining when the darkness came.

As if.

Fran turned glumly back towards the window. They were up in the old water tower, in some kind of control room. It gave onto all corners of the site. Beyond the glass, the grounds appeared deserted.

I have a rendezvous with death, at some disputed barricade. The line came ghosting through her head, and made her hunch her shoulders. Wasn't it a poem from the First World War? Abstract when she'd studied it, but cold and concrete now.

The whetstone in his hand kept up its rasping. The sound made her grit her teeth, but that was just a symptom of a much deeper unease. He glimpsed it when she turned to look at him.

'The sword must be our saviour now. There is no other way.' He studied her, imploring. 'Do you see?'

She crossed the room, and hunkered down beside him. 'Yes, we've got to fight them here: I *know* that. The sword can win the battle, true. But not the war. It'll never win the war.'

They both looked round as someone's boots came trudging up the stairwell. The Inspector joined them, looking tense and haggard.

'The villa by the access road's set up. The wood's bone dry, the place is full of rubbish – and we used a bit of petrol.' He glanced at Fran uneasily. 'I never thought I'd *set* a fire trap.'

'How will they know it's occupied?' she murmured, getting up.

'They will know,' said Athelgar beside her.

'There's someone with a radio tagging on to every group. We can give directions from up here.'

Just like chess, she thought. Except the opposition didn't have a vantage point. A watchful mind behind their moves. Or did they?

Athelgar stood up, and turned to her.

'You must stay above us, in the tower. Leofric and his chosen men will guard you.'

'What about you?'

'I shall lead the riding-knights, with Eldred.'

The horseman had been gathered in the central quadrangle. She'd watched them filing past her, down the walkways. The noise of hoofs on concrete had resounded in the cloisters, and echoed from the faces of the ward-blocks all around.

'When will they come?' she whispered.

'Living men attack at dawn – but these will wait for nightfall. And they will come all through the hours of darkness.'

The sun could still be seen from this high up: a molten flare between the distant trees. It would soon be gone now. The people waiting down below were mired in dusk already.

Athelgar moved over to the door. Impulsively she turned and caught his sleeve. 'Do you trust Dominicain?' she asked.

He nodded, once. 'I trust him.' He touched her hand, and stroked it – then went out.

Listening to him go downstairs, she thought of what Dominicain had said standing in the road, his shotgun aimed, Athelgar unblinking in his sights. What had passed between them then? What memories of violence and betrayal?

What were the debts still needing to be paid?

4

'The sun is down,' said Branwen. 'Let us go.'

She pulled the leather jacket on, and rummaged in the pockets. A pair of velvet gloves were pushed inside them. *Posh girl's gloves*, thought Martin. The sort that Lyn might wear . . .

It seemed that Branwen put them on with ritualistic care.

'Let me come,' said Kathryne.

Branwen glanced at her, and shook her head. 'The thing is ours to finish.'

Kathryne seemed to hesitate; then took a book down from its shelf. It had a pretty cover, and a craft-shop look to it; the sort of thing a girl might use for recipes, or flowers.

'This is my Book of Shadows: all the spells and charms I know. Take it, if you think that it can help . . .'

Branwen's smile was grateful, but she shook her head again. 'We need no book for this. Stay in safety by your hearth. And pray for us tonight.'

'Where do we go?' asked Martin edgily. Despite his doubts, he'd put his coat on too.

'An open field is all we need.' Branwen rubbed her fingers through the velvet. It felt as if the dark girl was still with her – hand in glove. Martin's sister. The notion brought a flicker of unease.

'Good luck,' Kathryne murmured. 'Goddess bless . . .' She was fiddling with the pentagram that glinted on her finger.

They went outside, and started down the lane. The verge

was wet and the air smelled clean. The scent of night was rising from the fields. Martin turned around himself. The country looked deserted in the dusk. He put on a spurt to catch her up again.

'Branwen . . .'

'Yes?'

'Are *you* a witch?'

'Some would call me so,' she answered briskly.

'You worship Nature too?'

They'd come to a stile. Climbing it, she paused to look at him. 'I worship my Creator – not Creation. Kathryne pays great honour to the earth, and that is *good*. But there is more to life than just the land.' She straightened up to look around; then glanced at him again. 'This is a saying which Athelgar had. Gold is a dross that men dig from the earth – but silver comes from the *sky*.'

'So what does that mean, then?'

She smiled, almost slyly and sprang down onto the path. 'Who can say? The Saxons like their riddles and their word-play.'

Crouching, she scooped up a piece of mud. He watched her mould a ball from it, and offer it towards him in her palm.

'This is how I see it,' she said softly. 'This is *all created things*, to God. See how small, how delicate it is. And yet it shall endure – because He loves it.'

She turned it in her fingers; then stooped to lay it gently in the grass. *Fragile earth*, thought Martin, and lost it in a universe of dusk. Branwen rose, and went on down the path. He followed her in silence.

The air was thickening like smoke; the land was dark. But overhead, the brightest stars had started breaking through.

5

Last light. Still no movement. Fran had her nose against the dirty window. The hospital below her was dissolving in the twilight. Further out, towards the trees, the blackness was as glutinous as tar.

The vehicles were out again, and parked around the front.

'Victor Two to Control. Can you see anything up there?'

The Inspector raised his handset. 'Bugger all.'

'We'll drive around . . . See if anything's moving.'

'Roger. Watch yourselves.'

A pause, and then the Range Rover went forward. Fran watched it moving slowly off, then looked towards the villa. Steffan and a group of men were lying up in there, breathing mould and petrol fumes; and waiting.

She felt as blind and bottled-up as they were. Nervously she stepped away, and started pacing round. Leofric stood watching from the doorway. His calm expression had a hint of awe. She realized that the sorcery of radio still impressed him.

Back to the window. The Rover was more distant now, a pale blur in the dusk. Following the access road. They hadn't switched their lights on.

'Something right ahead of us . . . Ohhh, God!'

Even as she gasped in shock, the vehicle came bumping to a halt. Distantly they heard its windscreen breaking. A banging on the bodywork. Then silence.

The Inspector swallowed. 'Control to Victor Two, come in . . .' The empty channel crackled in response.

'Control to Victor *Two* . . .'

A harsh, unearthly scream rose through the dusk. Fran went cold beneath her clothes, her fine hairs freezing upright. The scream kept building, raw and atavistic; then tailed off and faded in the hissing of her ears. The twilight was still unrelieved. The air vibrated, waiting to be filled.

'Shit!.' said the Inspector. 'What the hell . . . ?'

Fran wiped her mouth with the back of one cold hand. Another sound had started, at the limits of her hearing. Slowly getting louder, clearer . . . closer. The rhythmic, croaking chant of many voices; a single word, mechanically repeated. Gradually she made it out and felt her stomach curdle.

Hrafn . . . Hrafn . . . Hrafn . . .

She looked around at Leofric. His face was like a death-mask in the gloom.

'The Norse tongue is akin to ours. They are calling to their Raven.'

The Ashmen kept advancing, still unseen. Their outcry was inhuman – a demented choir of Daleks. Another noise now underpinned the chanting: the measured thump of weapons against shields.

The Inspector's handset crackled into life. '*Visual contact*,' someone squawked. '*A group of them crossing the access road now . . .*'

'Who's that?'

'*Three-oh-six . . . They're coming from the south.*'

The Inspector moved up quickly to the window. Fran pulled her jacket closer as she peered over his shoulder. Southward, in the open fields, she got a glimpse of movement. A patch of shadow spreading, like an oil slick in the dusk.

'*Someone coming up towards the strongpoint . . .*' Another voice, as keyed-up as the first.

'All ready, there?' the Inspector snapped.

'*Yessir . . . Jesus . . .*'

'How many?'

'*Can't say. More than five . . .*'

'Hear that, Frazer? Ready with the horses.'

The villa was an unlit hulk; it was hard to believe that someone's voice was coming out of there. Harder still to picture the scene within: the claustrophobic darkness, the ghastly isolation that the waiting men must feel.

HRAFN! . . . HRAFN! . . . HRAFN!

'Any other contact?' the Inspector asked; instinct made him glance round at the bare walls of the room.

'*Negative, sir . . . no movement round the back . . .*' Whoever that was, there'd been a nervous pause before he said it.

The Inspector flicked his gaze at Fran. The knuckles of his ungloved hand were white around the handset.

'*Two-six-eight: the villa sir. They're trying to get in!*'

'All right, don't lose it . . . Stick to the plan.'

The handset lapsed into a hiss. The Ashmen kept on shouting. Fran could hear – or thought she heard – the sound of crunching wood. Looking down towards the villa, she could see the darkness crawling. The Ashmen had converged on it. Her mind's eye was right there to see them pounding on the door, and clawing at the barricaded windows. And what must it be like inside? The blacked-out rooms and narrow stairwell full of hungry noise . . .

Someone would be waiting in the hall, ready to cross swords with the first one through the door. Steffan himself, maybe. He'd fight across whatever junk they'd used to block the hall; and then pull back, retreat upstairs . . . and draw the Ashmen in.

'Two-six-eight,' the Inspector said. 'Is your escape route clear?'

'*Christ, I hope so . . .*' A pause, and then the voice burst out. '*They're inside now, they're trying to get upstairs . . .*'

'Okay, Frazer, tell our friend to *move*.'

Cavalry to the rescue. Fran realized she was biting on her finger. One of the poor sods in there would have to cover the retreat: fighting on the staircase, and defending down the passage. Holding up the Ashmen while the others scrambled out. Whoever it was, her mind was in there with him. She could see the sword-blades clashing. Striking sparks . . .

'*Jesus!*'

'What?'

'*Petrol's caught!*'

'Oh my God,' Fran breathed. The house was still in darkness, with the fire sealed inside – but her mind was full of pent-up, searing flame.

'Get out, out, out,' the Inspector rapped.

'*Oh Jesus, we're on fire . . . !*' The voice broke off abruptly. Horrified, she stared towards the villa: not a flicker. Beside her, the Inspector raised his binoculars.

'Come on,' he grated. 'Get your arses *out* . . . *That's it!*'

Someone had emerged as planned, dropping from a window to the out-house roof below. Another scrambled after him; she only glimpsed them vaguely in the dimness. The third man she saw clearly. The third man was on fire.

Oh *no*.

He landed on the roof, and started writhing. One of the others sprang at him, and tried to beat the flames out. The window's glow grew fiercer above them. Chinks of light began to show, around the darkened house.

Another burning figure came erupting into view – through a different window, round the side. She heard the chipboard panel burst apart. The body plunged to earth, a falling comet: it could have been a Raven or an Ashman. Sparks and blazing splinters showered with him. Flames gushed skywards, sucking at fresh air.

The three men on the back roof were clambering down. Whatever the third one's injuries, at least he could still move. The building was a lighthouse now, its unblocked windows glaring. Reflections flickered off the Ashmen's armour. They'd loosened their grip on the shuttered house, but now they saw the fugitives and moved to intercept them.

The cavalry came riding out, and spurred towards the scene. Fran watched them pass below her. The coppers had their helmets on, the metal gleaming dully – but Athelgar and Eldred rode bareheaded in the lead.

The Ashmen turned to meet the charge – and fell back in confusion. Athelgar's sweep cut some of them off; she saw one fleeing figure ridden down. A sword flashed in the firelight. The coppers used their batons with a fury born of fear. The skirmish was too distant for the crunch of bones to carry, but Fran could swear she heard it, even so.

The survivors from the villa struggled clear. The horsemen pulled back with them. A shroud of smoke had folded round the building. The ground floor was a furnace now. How many Ashmen had they lured? And who had they lost?

The Inspector thumbed his handset. 'Two-six-eight? Malone, are you receiving?'

The channel hissed emptily back at him.

'Shit,' he murmured. 'Frazer . . . ?'

'Yessir.'

'Where's Malone?'

'He's out, but he's got burns . . . dunno how bad. We got three of them away from there. No casualties with us . . .'

'Pull back to the courtyard. We'll see where they try next.'

Fran, still at her window, thought of Marcus. Was he out there somewhere, with his army of the damned? Brooding on his strategy. Deciding his next move. Perhaps this was just sport to him: a game of knuckle-bones. With every bone the relic of a saint.

She had the ugly feeling he was relishing each throw.

Dominicain was kneeling in the chapel. The place was as bleak as a burnt-out grate. Sooty darkness breathed against his neck. But his mind was ablaze with golden light – enough to lick these shadows up, and burn them to the wall.

He'd stepped into a sunlit, cloistered garden: a quiet square of long, green grass, and rosebushes in bloom. She was sitting on an archway-sill, her knees drawn up, her face turned to the light. As ever, she was dressed in black, from skirt to ragged shawl; a shadow in the garden that refused to flee away.

Ne nos inducas in tentationem . . .

He wore his plain white habit, the coarse cloth bleached by sunlight. She opened her eyes, as if she sensed its brightness.

A wry smile curved her lips. 'Greetings, brother Preacher. Have you come to save my soul?'

'A maid as wise as you can save her own.'

She knew he meant it seriously, and couldn't hide a flattered little smile. 'Athelgar sets great store by *your* learning.'

The Preacher shrugged. 'Faith is from God – but so is *knowledge*. Dominic sold all he had, to benefit the poor. But he kept his books. He could not sell his books.'

'You speak like one in love,' she teased him softly.

'*Sophia* has my heart. The Holy Wisdom.' His gaze was calm and quizzical. 'And who is *your* love, lady?'

Her fingers touched the cross around her neck. 'Mary's son. He has courted me long. And he shall win me . . . in due season.'

Her voice tailed off, but her dark eyes didn't blink. Dominicain gazed back at her in silence. Bees were buzzing in the open roses. The silence of the abbey was a wall against the world.

Outside, the snarling Ashmen charged again.

A group of men rushed forward like a snatch-squad: holding up their long, transparent shields. The shock of the collision sent an echo round the site. The Viking swine-wedge broke apart. Axes struck and scratched the toughened plastic.

The defenders backtracked quickly, their shields still held high. The Ashmen took advantage with a primitive compulsion. The shield-wall broke – a move both planned and panicked. Back they ran, with shadows at their heels, retreating through the entrance to the quad. The Ashmen followed: crammed into the passage. And as they choked the narrow gap, the Ravens turned at bay.

A fire door above them was kicked open, and someone thrust a bed out. The rusty metal skeleton plunged down onto the crush. The Ashmen writhed like beetles underneath it. It rose up like a ship beneath the black swell of their fury. Shep came running forward with Carl's shotgun. He started to fire, at point-blank range. Bodies came apart like papier-mâché. Mouths gaped open soundlessly, as if to mock the sockets of their masks.

Domincain heard the echoes. His bowed head came up sharply.

The cavalry surged out into the fields around the chapel. The Ashmen waiting in reserve were hacked and ridden down. But then more hoof-beats joined the fray: other horsemen racing in like waves beneath the wind. A grey sea running. Storm and steel. Every Raven recognized the shapes.

'Guard yourselves!' cried Athelgar.

The men around him scattered, but the leading knight latched onto one, and chased him like a dog. The copper tried in vain to shake him off. The Norman moved abreast of him, and lashed out with his mace. The toughened visor turned opaque; the policeman's head flew back, and snapped his neck. He somersaulted backwards off his horse.

The others wheeled, returning to the fray. The field became a mêlée of confusion. The coppers laid in furiously – but batons were no match for swords and maces. Someone's arm was hacked clean off, to leave a spurting stump. More blood sprayed the inside of his visor as he screamed.

Athelgar chopped a Norman from his saddle. Eldred split another rider's skull. But the cavalry had too much weight behind them. The defenders were pushed back towards the chapel.

Some of those on foot came rushing out to reinforce them. Shep was there, still breathless with a sick exhilaration. He blasted at a horse as it surged past him, and sent it ploughing headlong through the grass. The rider landed awkwardly, and tried to clamber up. Shep swung round and fired from a crouch. The stricken horseman flipped onto his back. But that was it, his final shot. He threw the gun away.

Dominicain inclined his head, still listening.

* * *

Julie had her pistol out; her face was bleached with fear. She'd just seen someone skewered by a lance. The rival horsemen milled around, still slashing at each other, but if the iron knights broke through, the footsloggers were fucked. Only three or four of them were left: stuck up against the chapel, like a last stand round some grimy public toilet. Shep had drawn his pistol too, but he was moving, looking for a gap.

'Where're you going? *Shep!*' she called.

He glanced at her. 'The Range Rover got ambushed round the front. They're past it now; I reckon I can make it. *Not to run away*,' he said, and grasped her shoulder tightly. 'Trust me, Jules, all right? Let's see them stand against a set of wheels.'

Fran was at the window, staring down into the void. The night was alive with the sounds of death and horror. Faceless armies struggled in the darkness. No way of telling who might win, and who was going to lose.

Was Marcus any better off? He must have sensed her presence. If he took the hospital, his *Witchings* would be right up here to get her. The windows were all locked, or jammed. She couldn't even jump.

'Get off your knees and *help us*!' blurted Julie from the doorway.

Dominicain looked round at her; then climbed to his feet and went over to the cross. It was screwed against the brickwork, but the fixings had come loose. He gripped the thing and wrenched it from the wall. Teetering, he hefted it and turned to face Julie. She watched him open-mouthed. He stared back like some sinister messiah – complete with scruffy clothes and catridge belt. His eyes were zealous, burning now. The vigour of his movements gave the lie to greying hair.

He manhandled the cross towards the doorway. She stepped aside, and saw his shotgun propped against the wall. Impulsively she picked it up, and followed him outside.

Everything was chaos and confusion. People were falling back towards the chapel. Armoured horsemen rode at them, like drovers herding sheep. Dominicain strode forward. A rider galloped past him, and he swung the heavy cross: it caught the knight, and knocked him from his saddle. Julie gasped in disbelief. The Preacher raised the cross again, and smashed the rider flat against the earth.

Another horseman thundered in, his broadsword poised to strike. Dominicain swung to meet him, levelling the cross like a battering ram. The crosspiece blocked the other's blow, the sword-blade biting deep into the wood. Checked, the Norman jerked his rein, and tried to keep his balance. The Preacher lunged, unhorsing him as well.

Julie darted forward. Dominicain released the cross, which thudded to the grass. The knight began to struggle up, only to find himself confronted with the shotgun.

'*Prega*,' sneered the Preacher, and fired from the hip. The Norman's skull exploded, the empty helmet spinning from his shoulders.

Other riders loomed out of the darkness. They barked and snarled like dogs; the horses whinnied. Someone's head was hammered, splitting open with a crunch. Julie gripped her aiming wrist to stop her pistol trembling. She fired twice, to no avail. The third shot hit a rider's shield, and sang into the sky.

Dominicain aimed lower. A crippled horse plunged forward, and the knight went flying off. She hesitated even then, but fired at the last moment. Another horse screamed out and dumped its rider.

One of the horsemen snatched at her attention. Taller than the others, and more threatening somehow. Then a flare went soaring up, to cast a ghostly light around the chapel. The rider stood out starkly in the middle of his men. He wore a different helmet, with a metal mask that covered all his face. It caught the light like gleaming bone. The socket eyes looked up towards the flare.

The defenders, too, were frozen by the light. A mounted copper, tugging at his rein; a wounded man retreating on his knees. And Athelgar, astride his own pale horse.

Then the spell was broken, as the Iron-coats came pushing in again. Ravens and policeman surged to meet them. Dominicain backed slowly to the chapel door, still firing. Another horse came crashing down. The rider tried to crawl away. A copper trampled him.

'Warlord! Turn and fight!' yelled Athelgar.

Metal face came round to meet the challenge.

'Who are you? What brings you from your barrow?' Athelgar spurred forward. Their swords clashed in a spray of sparks. Athelgar ducked, and dragged his horse around. It slithered, skidded down onto its haunches, and sprang up. The other tried to wheel – too late. Sky-Edge smashed his helmet, disfiguring its supercilious mask. The contents spurted out and oozed, like pressed, putrescent fruit.

The warlord toppled, bouncing like a dummy in the grass. The surviving knights lost impetus, and pulled back in confusion. Someone crabbed out, triggering the Uzi. Other shooters joined the enfilade. Horses fell as if they'd just been trip-wired.

Julie was still pulling her own trigger. The cylinder rotated, *click, click, click* . . . There was no one left to shoot at. Dominicain came up to her, and pulled the empty weapon from her grasp.

'Leave this place,' he told her gruffly. 'Carry on our struggle for the wretched of the earth.'

'I'm not running out!' she blurted back.

'Someone must live to spread the word. That is the harder road, if you can take it.'

She stared at him uncertainly. 'What about you?'

He turned his head as Athelgar rode past. The Raven-leader glanced at him; it seemed like a salute. His face remained expressionless. Dominicain stood watching him – then looked at her again.

'My work is not yet done,' he said. 'There are some who still have need to be absolved.'

The Inspector had given her his torch, and gone to join his men. Fran paced round the darkened room, entirely alone. The stars were out and hovering like sparks at every window; their light was bleak, and dirtied by the glass. Despite the gloom, she didn't switch the torch on. Better she should hide her face. She felt like a prisoner trapped up here, a princess in the tower.

The broken sounds of battle reached her ears. Smashing noises; sharp, sporadic gunshots. The worst of it was over on the far side of the buildings. She saw a flare go up, and sink to earth. White light tinged the gables and the leads.

Footsteps, racing up the stairs. She turned towards the door, levelling the torch in both hands like a gun. Something rose towards her through the darkness. Her heart-rate peaked. She thumbed the switch without intending to. Light flashed out, and bathed Leofric's face.

'We are *betrayed*,' he hissed at her. 'The Ashmen are inside.'

6

'So are we going to stare at it, or what?' said Martin tersely.

Branwen left off pacing round the field, and looked at him. She'd been gliding like a shadow, but the starlight made a grey mask of her face. He'd stopped walking too, although the air was getting cold.

The map was there between them, lying somewhere in the grass. She'd spread it out, but left it well alone. Time had passed, while she stood in silence. Martin had grown restless, and begun to move around. The night was clear and bright up here, unspoilt by light-pollution. A breathless storm of diamond dust hung frozen overhead. Round and round he'd wandered, staring up into the sky. Branwen had started roaming too, and suddenly he realized they were circling the map. Drifting in, despite themselves, like satellites around a lightless sun.

'Prepare yourself,' she answered now. 'Be ready to receive.'

'Receive what?'

'Power on earth, as Athelgar would say.'

He guessed that she'd been praying. A waste of breath and brain-power – or so he would have thought a while ago. Now he felt frustrated: as if she'd found some path he couldn't follow.

The field spread out around him, vague and grey. Hedges of blackness cut them off. The night glowed overhead.

'Still you do not hear the voice of God?' she asked him quietly.

He shook his head, not sure if he felt wilful or abashed. He couldn't read her smudgy face, but her voice was gentle and full of understanding.

'It does not matter, Martin. See the beauty of the sky, and draw your strength from that. Glory in created things, if not in the Creator. Come you, now.'

She walked up to the map, and knelt before it. Cautiously he came and did likewise. A pause, and then she bowed her head; began to murmur softly. Communing with her God or with the light inside herself. He clasped his hands uncertainly; then let his head tip back.

The earth plunged into darkness, and he soared.

A sense of wonder raised him, as strong as when he'd first looked up and seen those diamonds winking like crown jewels. Then his adult mind kicked in – but still the awe remained. The Milky Way flowed overhead, and tumbled from the zenith. Stars that he'd grown up with shone like beacons everywhere: low on the skyline, amid the trees – or surging and sparking in patterns of force. The deep summer sky was alive with their light, the universe crackling with fire and ice. And underlying everything, the miracles of physics, and distances too infinite to grasp. *I'm a* part *of this*, he thought.

'*Dunamis on eorthan*,' Branwen breathed.

Reaching out, she grasped his hands; their fingers interlinked – and suddenly he felt that Lyn was with them. It might have been *her* hands inside those gloves. And yet she couldn't reach him. He sensed her groping through the dark, as frightened as a child.

It's okay, Lyn. Don't worry. I'll be home when this is over . . .

Branwen's upturned face was rapt – as if this was a sacrament of sex. Claire's eyes went as soft as that, when she was going to come. Martin felt a rush of warmth; but Branwen was completely in control. Her voice rose, rich and fierce in its assertion.

'Man is *born* unto trouble, as the sparks fly upward . . .'

And up they flew, as if the map was burning. For a moment they just hovered in the updraught, then scattered like a streaking meteor shower.

Part of Martin's startled mind went flying in pursuit.

The swarm of fireflies raced ahead, eating up the miles of darkened landscape. Here and there, he glimpsed one veering off: homing in on lodestones by the wayside. Here, a man who'd lost his mind, a wanderer who never heard the call. There, an undiscovered corpse. Deep in tangled woodland, like a long-dead soldier waiting to be found. Martin picked up flashes, just enough to understand, and then his mind was up and off again.

Far to the north – he sensed that much – the swarm fell on a group of unlit buildings. He felt his mind begin to disengage. The void in his body was dragging it back, like light towards a bottomless Black Hole. But in those final seconds, he saw one spark reach its target. It fizzled in the darkness, and turned into a dot of brilliant light. The radiance was unnatural, it seemed to shed no glow. It could have been some weird thermal image.

A lodestone going critical, he thought: as if its nucleus had just been split.

And then he had a glimpse of Rathulf's face.

7

'Rathulf has deserted us,' said Leofric.

Fran gawped at him. 'But what about the others?'

'The tower is unguarded. You must *come*.'

She felt a plunge of vertigo which emphasized their awful isolation. Swallowing, she raised the torch, but Leofric clearly meant to lead the way. He took a downward step – and hesitated. He didn't turn his head, but she could sense what he was feeling. The countryside of Wessex was unfolding in his mind – and over it, the kingdom of the stars. Everything recoiled from going down into the pit. He didn't want to perish under ground.

Her mind's eye shared his vision for a moment but then he took a breath and kept on going.

'Shield the light,' he hissed as they groped downwards. She clamped her palm across the lens, and watched her blood glow scarlet.

A shapeless heap lay tumbled at the bottom of the stairs. She let the torch sweep over it, and saw it was a Raven. His throat was gaping, drooling blood, but the Ashmen weren't here yet. She heard them blundering about on the next level, still searching through a boneyard of beds.

They were right down in the basement now. The corridor ahead of them was choked with total darkness. Its very hush sent ripples down her spine. She shone the torchbeam into it. The light was swallowed up. The ceiling was made up of pipes, like glinting metal guts.

'Go,' Leofric urged her. 'And I will hold them here.'

She stared at him. 'You can't!'

'I must.' He shoved her forward. She stumbled; then began to walk. The torchbeam slid ahead of her, a luminous amoeba. The darkness pushed against it. She realized she was breathing very fast.

The Ashmen were still rooting round upstairs. Sharp

sporadic clatters reached her ears; then something smashed. It felt like she was trying to creep beneath a haunted ward.

'*De profundis . . .*' Leofric cried behind her. Twisting round, she heard the clash of swords. God, he would be fighting blind – against things that could see him in the dark.

The steely ringing petered out. Silence flowed towards her down the tunnel, like a breath. Biting back a sob, she kept on going.

The corridor went right beneath the building. She might have walked a hundred yards; it felt like half a mile. The sense of being buried grew more stifling with each step. Every time she glanced back, she expected to see red eyes in the darkness.

Surely she was clear by now. She reached an access stairwell, and ran up it. The ground floor was no lighter, just distorted in the torchbeam, like a murky flooded maze. Groping down a corridor, she reached the central hallway – and stopped dead.

The hall was full of shadows and moving shapes. It might have been a stirred-up nest of mutant soldier ants. She backed away in horror. And then a blaze of light came streaming in through the main doors.

Shep just put his foot down, and the Range Rover surged forward. A ghastly figure showed up in the headlights: the clearest glimpse he'd yet had of an Ashman. Nauseous, he flicked the wheel and smashed the thing aside, sending it splintering. Other shapes went scuttling clear as he swung into the forecourt. The headlamps flashed across a figure aiming from the shoulder. Then something punched his window in, and hit him in the neck. It felt as if an icicle had lodged in his throat. It melted in a blaze of pain – and scalding, salty liquid filled his mouth. Gurgling, he fought the wheel. The transit van was parked across his path. Instinct sent him powering towards it. Anything to free himself from this.

The Rover hit the van full on, and slewed into the entrance. Both vehicles exploded, filling the central block with blazing petrol. The gathering of Ashmen was engulfed.

The fireball didn't linger to digest them. Figures were still writhing as it billowed on towards Fran, down the hall. She felt the air being sucked from her lungs. The brilliance scorched her cheeks, and singed her eyebrows. And yet it had a rippling, nightmare beauty.

She stood there, mesmerized for an instant, then tore herself away. Round a corner: back into the dark. The flashover had missed her, but the sounds of conflagration filled her ears.

And she'd taken the wrong turning: this corridor must surely lead to Hell. Black as pitch, it smelled of smoke and burning. But then she heard the noises from behind her. Hungry things were coming at her heels.

Gasping, she ran on, and reached a foyer at the rear of the building. Something huge was looming there: a monstrous, snorting shape. It lurched towards her clumsily. Fran recoiled, and realized she was trapped.

'Come on!' someone shouted. The shape was a policeman on his horse. He'd ridden in, and now seemed twice as tall. The animal was terrified: she smelled the reek of shit. She circled carefully round it – and the Ashmen caught her up.

The horse's clatter filled the hall as it stamped and reared in panic. The copper fought it down again, and bludgeoned at the nearest gargoyle-face. His baton clanged on iron, but the onslaught smashed the desiccated skull.

'Run!' he bawled at Fran. 'Get out!'

Something down the corridor gave way and then collapsed, stirring up a gust of burning wind. The horse reared again, its front hoofs smashing down onto an Ashman. Fran was loath to leave him but her nerves were too insistent. Turning, she fled on towards the doors.

The air outside was just as hot; the night revealed a universe of sparks. Stumbling clear, she twisted round and gazed at them in awe. And then she saw the Raven banner, flying from the roof of the main building. The firestorm wind made its black shroud flap like wings. It looked like it was frantic to escape. As she watched, it wilted – and burst into a gout of orange flame.

Somehow, in her inner ear, she heard its evil scream.

'*Control to all units . . . Pull out, get well clear . . .*'

She looked around, but couldn't see which radio that had come from. Perhaps a corpse's handset, somewhere close. Dazed and sick, she carried on retreating. A pair of shapes were struggling in the uncut grass. She saw a copper rear up and beat an Ashman down, staving in its head with vicious blows. *Beasts of the field*, she thought, and hurried on – passing the deserted, brooding villas. She reached a narrow lane, and turned along it.

A shuddering *boom* drifted over the fields. Fran looked back, and stumbled to a halt – gasping with reaction, and the stitch beneath her ribs. The hospital had turned into a real crematorium, a complex with its ovens at full blast. Windows gave a glimpse into the furnaces within. The sky above looked sunset-red, and low enough to touch.

She turned, and kept on slogging down the lane. A horse's hoofs came pounding up behind her. She swerved aside, and shrank against the verge. The rider passed, his coat-tails flying; she glimpsed his numbered helmet, and allowed herself to breathe. The copper kept on going, like a bat out of Hell.

A streak of dawn was showing, at the far edge of the dark.

She left the lane, and struck across a field. Another muffled rumble reached her ears. Glancing back, one final time, she thought of the *Titanic*. The sound of bulkheads giving way, and engines breaking loose . . .

A horse without a rider galloped past. Its rasping breath grew loud, then faded out. And then a horseman cut across her path. She hesitated, poised to duck and run. Then straightened, as she realized who it was.

The Inspector wiped his forehead with the back of one gloved hand. 'We're heading back to town to face the music. You coming?'

She shook her head. 'I've got to find the others.'

He sat there, staring down at her. 'You led us into this, my girl. You're the only witness that we didn't just go mad.'

Fran shifted uneasily – aware that she was *evidence* and proof. 'You think that they'd believe me, then?' she muttered.

His dark face was unreadable; but then he nodded stiffly.

'Luck to you, then . . . Frances. Whoever you are.' He tugged his horse's head around, and rode off through the twilight.

She realized that she didn't know his name.

And what about the anarchists, if any had survived? She guessed they would be scattering as well. The overnight alliance had disintegrated now. Older scores were still waiting to be settled. Men who'd fought together would be enemies again. Unless the things they'd shared could somehow bond them.

Away to the east, where the cloudy edge of night had come adrift, she saw a stripe of pallid-looking sky. Athelgar sat waiting, like a silhouette against it; his sword now sheathed and slung across his back.

'Someone calls us from the south,' he said.

'Haven't we done *enough*?' she almost wailed.

'*Marcus*, lady! Marcus is still thriving. The body has been burned, but the head still lives. And now I see how he has worked his craft.' He twisted round to gesture in his saddle. 'The old Foss Way runs south from Lincolonia. It leads a man through Mercia, to Wessexena Land. The Rome-Straights are still haunted roads; a sorcerer can send his power along them. It is as you envisioned it. He lit the hilltop minster with his shinecraft. A beacon for the dragon ships. A bale-fire for the dead.'

'So what's at the far end?' she asked.

'The Vale of Avalon itself. *Glastingabury*,' he said. 'So we must journey south, as best we might.'

She looked around uncertainly. 'Who's we?'

'You and I, my Lady – as it was when we began.'

'What about the others?'

Something flickered in his eyes, although his jaw stayed

firm. 'The Raven is consumed at last. My brothers rest in peace.'

'Rathulf: he ran out on us.' She scurried up to him. 'He killed one of your men, and then he let the Ashmen in. There was nobody to guard the tower. They *left* us.'

Athelgar's horse shifted, as if sensing his dismay. 'Eldred I sent back to you, with news – you did not meet him?'

She shook her head.

He frowned, and glanced towards the burning building. Then gestured to her. 'Come, we must make haste.'

He pulled her up behind him; she wriggled close, and wrapped her arms around him. But his sword was still between them . . . like a long, gaunt crucifix against her breasts.

CHAPTER X

Snake

I

Five shadows rode through the gathering light, in single file across the misty fields. The burning fortress rumbled in the distance, its reddish aura like a misplaced sunrise. The horsemen glanced back, one by one, and kept on heading southward.

The place was well behind when they came upon the dyke. It rose up from the landscape, a forbidding pagan earthwork. Even as they halted, a train of ghostly wagons hurtled past along the top. Yellow windows glowed in them, much brighter than the sky. Even Aldhelm crossed himself; Franchisca mouthed a curse. The swift, metallic rattle drove them back towards the far edge of the field.

'There is a gateway, see,' said Erik, pointing. And so there was, with lintels made of stone. A patch of sky was visible beyond it.

Rathulf was studying his lodestone. He raised his eyes to Aldhelm and nodded grimly. 'Branwen. She is far unto the south.' He turned towards the others, and saw Eldred looking back. He heeled his horse across. 'We are pursued?'

'Athelgar comes,' said Eldred sombrely.

The countryside behind them was still dark, but Rathulf didn't doubt that he was right.

'Then take your stand,' he said, 'and stop him here. The Raven-lord has followed far enough.'

The sun had almost risen now. The sky was flushed with dissipating clouds. Athelgar rode through some trees, and drew the horse up sharply. Still hanging on, Fran looked over his shoulder. A railway embankment crossed the level ground ahead, imposing as a medieval rampart. A single horseman waited on its crest.

'Who is it?' she murmured. Then she recognized him. '*Eldred*.'

Their own mount waited patiently beneath them. Athelgar sat motionless, bolt upright; she felt the dull vibration of his heart. Then his head came half around. His profile gave her nothing to relate to.

'Now you must step down,' he told her calmly.

She felt a sudden throb of dread. 'Listen, let me talk to him,' she said.

'The time for speech is done.'

She held him tighter round the waist – anything to modulate the flatness of his voice. 'Let me *try*,' she pleaded. A wild, unspoken thought was taking shape behind the words. Better she should risk *her* life, than see him risking his.

He simply nudged the horse towards a bank beside the path. She hesitated, then slid down awkwardly. The other horseman hadn't moved. Athelgar gathered up his reins.

'Can't we just go *round* him, though?' she blurted.

Athelgar shook his head. And now his face and voice betrayed his feelings. Bewilderment, and anger, and a dreadful sense of loss.

'Eldred is my *friend*,' he said. 'Who else but I shall kill him?'

He galloped out into the field, his sword still sheathed behind him. Fran came walking slowly in his wake. Eldred saw them right away, and turned his horse's head in expectation.

Athelgar rode back and forth, as if to tempt him down. But Eldred had the high ground, and he wasn't going to leave it. Athelgar must realize that. She guessed this was a ritual to whet their appetites.

'Why have you betrayed us, friend?' he called. And that

was real; no ritual. His voice was hungry with the need to know.

But Eldred didn't answer. His face was mostly shadow in the pearly pre-dawn light. His silence might be sullen, or ashamed. She couldn't tell.

Athelgar's horse reared up, and plunged again. He hauled it round, still glaring at his brother.

'You sold me. Just like Judas. Like a *snake*.'

He veered away, came back to the middle of the field, then drove towards the embankment once again. He forced his mount to scale the slope, and crested it a hundred yards from Eldred. And now Sky-Edge came flashing out: as bright as if it caught the sun from over the horizon.

Fran ran forward, and stopped again. The two riders sat facing one another, poised in silhouette against the sky. And then they started moving, like two jousters converging down the railway tracks, full tilt.

Their sword-blades clashed and locked. The horses wheeled. Athelgar hacked at Eldred's guard with brutal vehemence. The latter tried to break away, misjudged his stroke, and lost his sword completely. Fran saw it spinning through the air. Elation fizzled through her. *Yes! That's it!*

Athelgar went straight in for the kill. Eldred ducked beneath the blow, and launched himself across the gap between them. He grasped his leader's coat, and bore him backwards. Athelgar lashed out, and lost his balance. Both men fell, still struggling, and tumbled down the slope.

The second bounce broke Eldred's grip; they came apart and plunged towards the bottom. Athelgar rolled awkwardly, and turned a somersault. Fran stifled a cry, convinced he'd break his neck.

They slithered to the foot of the embankment, and lay winded. She started forward, full of apprehension: a fall like that had surely broken bones. But then, to her amazement, they began to scramble up. Neither had a weapon now – which wasn't going to stop them. Eldred had scarcely found his feet, when Athelgar sprang forward like a cat. The two men went down, grappling. She watched them claw and punch and kick – on the ground, then on their knees, then struggling back upright. Eldred hauled a dagger from his belt. Athelgar retreated as the weapon slashed and stabbed. He started backing up the slope, then dived from it head first. Down they went, with force enough to empty Eldred's lungs. She couldn't help but flinch in sympathy.

Athelgar rolled sideways. Snatching up a piece of stone, he brought it slamming down on Eldred's skull. Rearing back, he struck again. *Again.* The clubbing sound became a liquid crunch.

'Oh Jesus, that's *enough!*' Fran called.

He threw a vicious glance at her, his face drained white with fury. Wide-eyed, she stared back, and saw the madness burning out. The rock descended one more time, but shakily, as if he'd lost his strength. Eldred was no longer even twitching. Fran grimaced, and fought her gorge back down.

Athelgar knelt upright, and tossed the bloodied hunk of stone aside. He tipped his head back, dragged fresh air down into his lungs. Fran came inching closer. Eldred's skull was crumpled and misshapen, a mess of gore and matted golden hair.

Athelgar wiped his sweaty face, and bent over the body. She watched him rummage in the pouch still hung around its neck. Relics, trinkets, coins came spilling out. She glimpsed a silver ring with a colourless stone. It seemed familiar, somehow. She stared at it; her eyes grew huge. She made a muffled sound behind her palm.

Athelgar looked round. 'What ails you?'

'It's *Lyn's*,' she almost whimpered through her fingers.

He picked the ring up and held it out towards her. 'You see?' his hoarse voice told her. 'It was *his* blade in her belly.'

Fran lurched back unsteadily. It seemed that Lyn was lying there between them, staring up in miserable abandon, her blood still oozing out into a scummy crimson pool. But the utter shit who'd killed her had been faceless up till now: a man who crouched in shadow, shaped from nightmares. Unmasked, he had a name – a quirky smile. A character she'd got to know and like.

Eldred, her confessor: brother-gentle. He'd butchered her best friend. Try as she might to disbelieve it, the evidence, in silver, was right there. Acceptance seared like acid down her throat. She gagged on her revulsion.

Athelgar clenched his fist around the ring. 'Do not say I slew my brother for no reason,' he warned softly.

Fran jerked her gaze up – glaring. 'You said my tears couldn't bring her back. So can his blood? His *brains*?'

Athelgar regarded her coldly for a moment, then let his breath rasp out and turned away. Adjusting his ripped and rumpled coat, he went to fetch Sky-Edge. The sword was lying on the slope, a dozen yards away. Fran stood watching, nauseous with reaction. Then a horse whinnied from the top of the bank, and both of them looked up.

Dominicain stared down at them, a vision in black apart from where the dawn breeze stirred his tangled, greying hair.

Gazing back, Fran felt a nervous spasm. Athelgar seemed to hesitate, then reached out for his sword. Domincain sat upright in his saddle, and threw something. It glittered in the early light; she saw it was the coin. Athelgar snatched it from the air and looked up from his palm.

'You *know* what it is for,' the Preacher said.

IX

RAVENS

And where I wrote my name, and then you carved
  yours,
Black smoke will rise up to cover the stars.
Nothing's said to be for ever –
Except for the night that'll come when we burn you
  down

THE LEVELLERS

Dear Craig

Whatever else, I know you're safe: two hundred miles *and more behind the lines. We're going to meet* Marcus *now. We're going to finish this. And when it's over – if I live – then I'll come after* you.

Promise that you'll wait.

I love you

Fran

CHAPTER I

Book of Shadows

I

Branwen felt her head begin to swim. Renewing her grip on the toilet bowl, she waited miserably. But nothing came. Still nothing. The sickness in her belly wouldn't stir.

Channelling the Spirit always drained her, but this was worse than anything she'd known. In spite of Kathryne's pampering, she still felt weak and feverish. And the sickness kept on coming back: a deep, insidious nausea. Ever since they'd used the Chart, she'd felt as if a part of her was dying.

Kneeling on the bathroom floor, she wiped her clammy forehead. A horrid fear was lurking, but she wouldn't give it room inside her head. She knew the Chart was sorcerous – a nightmare-catching web. A demon might have scuttled in when she had bared her soul. And *that* was why the sickness wouldn't go.

She pressed her cross against her lips – until the thought had lost its shape again. The summons had been sent and she'd played her role. Now they could only wait.

Wait, while something evil lay and festered in the earth.

Wait, while iron horsemen searched them out. She remembered tales she'd heard of the Great Harrying: people being rooted up, and massacred, and raped. Her mind's eye saw the Normans through a haze of wattle smoke – a dirty fog lit up by burning buildings.

But this time they might come in stealth, to rape and murder sleepers in their beds.

Swallowing, she raised her head and looked round the room.

Had even the Old Romans known such luxury as this? Basin and bath were the colour of jade, offset by ferns and ivy. The four walls had an eggshell tinge, and now they felt equally fragile. The gloomy weight of afternoon was building up behind them. Yet two whole nights had passed, without a whisper from outside.

Except for the dreams.

The bowl was trying to draw her down, and she felt a surge of giddiness again. The shadow in the water gave a hint of unplumbed depths. It seemed the thing was bottomless, though Kathryne said it drained into a midden under ground.

The master of the Iron-coats was lurking down there somewhere. Dormant, like a dragon in its cave. Her thoughts had scoured the abbey grounds, and failed to find an entrance. But her sleeping mind had crept into his lair.

It stank of blistered flesh, that place. A cavern full of darkness and decay. But her spirit-sight caught glimpses of a white, distorted face as mournful as the moon's and just as cold.

Her instincts always woke her then – before she could be caught. Her stomach would be curled into a ball. As if her flesh had followed where her dreaming mind had led.

Who is this who dares *to enter here?*

He hadn't broken through, the second time they'd used the Chart. He must have been distracted by the battle in the north. The outcome of that strife was cloaked in silence. The summons had been sent, but who would come?

Rathulf! blurted Martin in her head. *I just saw Rathulf. You've only gone and told him where we are!*

The Star-Chart puts its power in every lodestone, she'd replied. *All the Ravensbreed will hear, and come in answer.*

How many, though? He'd asked her that – and now she asked herself. No way of knowing who was still alive. Leofric had stood and died with Athelgar, of course. So maybe Edgar was their leader now. He would surely get here. She pictured his strong, wise face. Eldred must win through, as well; and Steffan. And who else?

She felt a sudden twist of pain – enough to make her bite her lip, and fill her eyes with tears. The loneliness of centuries welled up into her throat. As bitter as the taste of bile, and just as hard to purge.

How many, then? And who would get here first?

At last her stomach settled (or the demon fell asleep). Wearily she clambered up, and went over to the basin. She worked the taps as Kathryne had shown her, and splashed metallic water on her face. Light had almost faded from the frosty window now. There were unlit candles all around the room. Melting wax had fused them into place, like fungal growths.

Someone rapped on the door. 'Yes?' she answered huskily, still staring at the wan face in the mirror.

'There's someone creeping round outside,' came Martin's voice.

She fumbled with the door and opened it. He beckoned her across the passage, into Kathryne's room. The lamp was off, the chamber full of dusk. Kathryne was peering through the window. She glanced round, looking pale. 'He's over by the copse.'

Branwen went to join her. The sky was low and filthy, and the night was coming down – but *there* was someone, moving in a crouch. Her tender stomach tightened as she watched him cross the field. No question, he was circling the house. His shape was mostly shadow, but his pallid hair showed up.

He scurried forward; stopped again. And someone else came creeping in his wake. This one moved more cautiously, a rabbit to his fox. Despite the veil of twilight, she could tell it was a girl.

'Are these your friends?' asked Kathryne, sounding doubtful.

Branwen didn't answer, just turned and hurried back towards her bedroom. Her coat was lying crumpled on the bed. Even through its blackness, she could *feel* the lodestone's light. By the time she turned the brooch up, the sardonyx was glowing like a star.

She gazed at it intently – then quickly turned her head. Martin had followed, and was watching from the threshold.

'Open the door,' she whispered. 'Let them in.'

The three of them went cautiously downstairs. Cabal was in the hallway, hackles raised. Kathryne switched the hall light on, and went to the back door. She hesitated, glancing back, awaiting Branwen's nod. Then turned the latch.

The lamp outside had come on too. The dusk congealed around it. It seemed that minutes passed, and then the garden gate creaked open. Kathryne hunkered down beside Cabal, and stroked his fur.

The fair-haired man came warily towards them. He was dressed in black, like all the Ravensbreed, his greatcoat slung around him, like a cloak. Martin glimpsed a sword, and felt his nerves begin to tingle. Branwen saw his face, and gasped aloud.

Martin turned his head, surprised. Her eyes were wide and staring, the irises as full as hazel moons. His instinct was to panic: she'd recognized this man, and was *afraid*. But when he looked around again, the newcomer seemed just as stupefied.

He'd halted on the threshold, staring in. His companion moved up cautiously behind him. Martin saw an anxious-looking girl, wearing a bomber jacket with a matted sheepskin lining. She seemed familiar, somehow. He stared at her. She looked back at him blankly.

Then Branwen went rushing forward, and flung her arms around the stranger's neck. He held her tightly, rocking her, murmuring soft words into her hair. 'Branwen. Oh, my sister. How I hoped you were at rest.'

The other girl slipped round them, and smiled a little awkwardly at Martin and Kathryne. Her jacket had a lived-in look, the leather dark as treacle. Though tired, she had a fresh, appealing face and wide pale eyes. Martin searched his memory, while trying to keep from staring.

The others eased apart at last. Branwen's cheeks were wet, but she was radiant with pleasure and relief. 'This is Athelgar,' she said. 'The *Lord* of Ravens.'

The man's enquiring gaze came round to them. Kathryne gave her name, and so did Martin. Athelgar nodded solemnly to each. Branwen had thought him dead, of course. But why had she believed he'd gone to Hell?

Martin mulled it over, still uneasy; and Branwen's face had grown more earnest too. She tugged at a handful of Athelgar's coat. 'What of Dominicain?' she asked.

'He comes by his own road.'

She drew her breath in sharply – then covered her mouth as if ashamed of her delight. Martin didn't notice; he'd looked back towards the girl. He'd placed her face, or thought he had, unlikely as it seemed. 'Frances . . . isn't it?' he ventured.

She stared at him. Then: '*Martin*.'

He thought he'd only met her once: in Oxford, years ago. A cheerful and vivacious friend of Lyn's. She'd been on her way out, and said hello in passing. Neither of them had *dreamed* this far ahead . . .

'Seen Lyn recently?' he asked, as if they'd just met socially again.

Fran just stood there, open-mouthed. *Oh God, he doesn't know*.

'Rathulf will come,' said Athelgar beside her.

She forced her mind to move again: engaging with the future. Deliberately she looked at the two women. 'We hitched down here. We think he's still behind us.' Martin was still watching her. *Oh Jesus, has he seen it in my face?*

'What about his men?' said Martin. 'Aldhelm and the others . . .' His voice was dry, but didn't sound suspicious. She began to feel relieved, then frowned. 'What others?'

'Erik, and Franchisca.'

'Four of them,' said Athelgar. His tone was flat and bitter as he counted his betrayers. 'They will follow us as fast as they can ride.'

'Who are you talking about?' asked Kathryne.

'Enemies. They come in search of Branwen.'

'How far've *you* come?' she asked, after a slightly nervous pause.

'From Lincoln,' murmured Fran. Dominicain had ridden on, after their dawn encounter. But she'd suggested following the tracks, and seeing if they could get aboard a goods train. They'd found one going south, and ridden down to Birmingham huddled on a chassis while the countryside clanked by. A couple of truckers had brought them the rest of the way, with Sky-Edge wrapped discreetly in Athelgar's coat.

'The two of you look famished,' Kathryne said. 'Close the door, you're welcome here. Come and sit in the living room, and let me make some supper. I guess that you've got lots to talk about . . .'

2

Once the meal was finished, and the plates were cleared away, the five of them stayed sitting round the table. Athelgar was staring down into his empty mug, his coat around his shoulders, and his sword slung from the chair-back. He seemed to Kathryne like some resurrected warlord turning her house into his feasting hall. She couldn't help but stare at him in awe. Across from him, Fran waited with her chin in her hands. The journey south was catching up with her; she'd barely slept. Martin glanced at her again, imagining what Lyn would say, if only she knew.

Branwen rose, went quietly upstairs. She brought the crumpled Star-Chart down, and spread it out between them. Athelgar looked up at her as she resumed her seat.

'You think I did not keep my word?' he said.

Branwen shook her head. 'It does not matter.'

'The king's men did not meet us, though we waited on the road. Darkness came, and swallowed us, although it was full lay. We slept, and when I woke, I was alone in this new vorld.'

'It was the same with me,' she told him dully. 'I placed the word in safety – where you found it. I thought my duty done, and went my way. But darkness snatched me up while I was valking.'

'This is the Black Rapture, which Dominicain foresaw. The Raven claws his servants back, to feed his bloody unger.'

'It's burned though, now. I saw it,' Fran put in.

'We are not free,' said Athelgar. 'Not yet.'

'Whom do we face?' asked Branwen, wary now.

'His name is Marcus. We know not who he is.'

'We roused him, when we used the Chart to call you. His hade was in the abbey, which is utterly cast down.' She gesured to the map. 'This opened up a gateway to the shadow-vorld, his realm.'

'The Zodiac,' said Kathryne suddenly.

Branwen looked around at her. 'What Zodiac is this?'

She hesitated. 'There's a ring of giant effigies, all laid out n the landscape. They're moulded by the contours and the oads . . . The High History was based on it.'

'History of what?' asked Fran.

'The Holy Grail.' They stared at her. 'Symbolically, I think,' he added lamely.

Martin was shaking his head. Fran turned to him. 'What?'

'I've read that book of yours,' he said to Kathryne. 'I've earned to believe a lot of things . . . but not in this. There *is* no zodiac, it's just a half-baked fantasy. I've seen enough *reality* o know.'

Fran just shrugged. 'I wouldn't know what's real any more.'

'Well, *I* believe there's something in it,' Kathryne came ack levelly. 'And I think it's the key to the power round his place.' She glanced at Branwen. 'You can feel it, can't ou?'

Branwen nodded. 'Some thing,' she said quietly.

'Marcus is here,' said Athelgar. 'Whatever else, this is *hi*
anchor-hold. We have destroyed his Ash-force, and hi
knights. Now we must needs put an end to him.'

'By entering his realm.' Branwen's voice was low with resig
nation.

He nodded grimly. 'How shall it be done?'

She pondered, with her eyes downcast; then she looked a
him again. 'You must relinquish every thing you value. Ever
thing in which you place your trust. Then, within the shadow
world, you must regain them all. And *then* you can confron
him, at the centre of his maze.'

'What then?' he asked. 'One cannot lay a spirit with
sword.'

Branwen sat back sombrely. 'You will be shown the way.
It seemed that she was trying to convince *herself* of that.

'I've studied this,' said Kathryne. 'I can help to guide yo
through it. You said this ghost, this sorcerer, was using th
Fosse Way. That cuts across the circle – right through Scorpio
Antares – that's the scorpion's *heart* – lies almost on th
road . . .'

'*Kathryne*. It's all bollocks!' Martin said.

Fran looked at the Star-Chart. 'That one's real, though
isn't it?' she murmured.

'Yeah. That's real all right.'

'And this shadow-world . . . It's maybe not so different.
Her stagnant mind was silting up, but something broke th
surface. 'Perhaps, if you *believe* in it, you'll find a differen
sky.'

Martin still looked unconvinced. Kathryne shifted, toyin
with her pendant. Then Athelgar tapped his coin against th
tabletop: bleakly, as if calling them to order.

'There is one thing more to do, before day comes.'

'What?' Fran asked.

'To take my leave of you, my Lady Frances. You canno
follow me into the shadows.'

She clasped his hand. 'I've come this far already.'

He glanced across at Branwen from under his brows. She gave her head a solemn little shake.

'*Every thing* I value. Do you see? This, the coin my first lord Edmund gave me. Sky-Edge, my companion on the road. Even the Cross, by which we are redeemed. A sword, a coin, a gallows-post: and all my world was built upon these things. Yet Branwen bids me leave them . . . and I shall. But now she puts her finger on the cup you offer me. The loving cup. And *now* I would resist – and so must not.'

'Feelings. *Love.*' She squeezed his hand. 'You *have* to take those with you.'

He returned her grip, took Branwen's hand as well. 'Find me in the shadows; I will seek you. Both of you, be with me on this road.' He looked at Kathryne. 'Lady, will you lend your wisdom too?'

Kathryne nodded eagerly. She'd never felt so honoured, or so awed. Part of her was sure he was an aspect of the God, Cernunnos, come to her as Death and Winter.

'It isn't long till dawn,' said Fran. 'We'd better get some rest.'

3

Weariness came down on her, as soft and thick and heavy as a snow-slip. It was all that she could do to get upstairs. 'You have my bed,' said Kathryne, 'I can bed down somewhere else.' Despite her fatigue, Fran wouldn't hear of it. They finally agreed to share. Fran stripped down to her underwear, and had a listless wash. Watching, Kathryne cleared her throat, a little sheepishly.

'Um. Normally, in summer, I sleep . . .'

'Sky-clad?'

'Starkers, I was going to say. But yeah.'

Fran just smiled blearily. 'Don't worry, I'm too knackered to seduce you.' Yawning, she went through into the bedroom and was practically asleep before her head had touched the pillow.

She dreamed of Craig.

Athelgar was just as drained, but didn't sleep. He sat on the floor, at the foot of Branwen's bed watching with his back against the wall. And Branwen shared his vigil, sitting on the covers with her arms around her knees. They gazed towards each other through the darkness, listening to the silence of the house. A clock was ticking distantly downstairs; the dog, Cabal, growled softly in his dreams. They sensed the others drifting off, like candles going out.

'Has my lord forgiven me?' her voice asked quietly.

He shook his head. 'You know that there is *no thing* to forgive. You saw the truth, and brought it back to us. We did what we were called to do. There was no other way.'

She lapsed back into silence, still muffled by the gloom. But Athelgar could see for centuries. The distant past grew brighter, like a bubble in the dark. Once more he smelled the dust, and felt the sunlight.

Branwen stood there in the road, the Ravens gathered round her. Her sombre clothes were pale with dust, her boots were caked with dirt. She'd walked for days, avoiding French patrols, to meet them here. Fatigue was like a burden on her shoulders, but fierce excitement sparkled in her eyes.

'I say that we must break our oath,' she told him.

He stared at her in disbelief. 'And fight an English king?'

'I am not English,' Steffan said.

'Nor I,' said Rathulf calmly.

Athelgar glanced round at them, then back at her. The others looked on pensively. He knew that they were pondering her words.

Branwen's voice was soft, appealing now.

'You never fought for *kings*, but for the justice that they gave. Your swords defend the people – not the land. A king grows old and dies like other men. Even Athelstan is dust and bones.'

'*In pace requiescat*,' Edgar said, and crossed himself. Every Raven echoed him. Branwen paused, and dipped her head in honour of the *Mechteyrn*, then started pressing Athelgar again.

'Athelred you disobeyed.'

'We didn't join his foes!'

Athelgar was scowling now, though he was more perplexed than angry. Branwen's eyes were willing him to *see*. Their brother Ravens watched them both, and waited. He sensed the indecision in their silence.

'I sent you out to find their *strength*,' he chided.

'And so I did,' she answered him. 'I *know* what makes them strong. And that is why the Ravensbreed must join them.'

Branwen's inner eye saw something different; a sight that made her own eyes fill with tears. A barren country crossroads, and a gathering of hunted, hungry men. Their coats – already battle-worn – were ripped and filthy now. She looked from face to grimy face, expecting condemnation. And some stared back resentfully, but most were just resigned.

All her dreams had turned to dust and ashes. (*Ashes, yes!*) And now it seemed the End-Times were upon them. Everything was sliding, like a loosened, muddy slope beneath her feet.

Athelgar had lost his horse but he still carried the saddle across his back. He lifted Sky-Edge in its sheath, and offered it to her.

'Take this back to Meon; hide it well. Someone else will find it in due season. Plain steel's the only trophy that the king will have from us.'

Instinctively she took the sword – then stood and stared at him.

'Go,' he urged her. 'Search for him. Grow old and die in peace.'

The prospect was so tempting, but she couldn't turn away. 'And you?' she whispered faintly. 'What of *you*?'

'The time has come to take my stand, at last.' He looked round wryly at his men. 'If any of you wants to stay, he's welcome. If not, then go with God. Every sword is turned against us now. The gallows and the pyres are prepared. But if some of you win through, my bones will know it, and rest easy.'

All her strength went out of her. She slumped onto her knees. '*Athelgar*. You are a saint! It cannot end like this.'

Reaching down, he stroked her hair; then raised her tearful face towards his own. His features were grim, and firmly set, and yet she saw his eyes were full of love.

'I'm no saint,' he told her, 'just a false knight on the road. And whoever meets me can kill me.'

Martin kept the sofa, but he hardly slept all. Towards the dawn, he floated off – and found himself with Claire. She'd opened the door to let him in, and now her face was shining with delight. Her hair had never been so blonde, her eyes so crystal blue. Something tore inside him as he realized he was dreaming. But when he came awake again, his groping mind was reaching out for Lyn.

Kathryne, snuggled up with Fran, dreamed of someone with a hood over his head, advancing through the mist towards her cottage. The hood was white and featureless, the kind they put on people being hanged. But as she watched, two mournful holes appeared – as if his eyes were burning through the cloth.

4

The four horsemen came to the crest of the rise, and saw the misty Levels spread below them. They halted and sat watching, as if savouring the moment. Dawn was just a promise, spreading dimly from the east. But the birds had started singing in the trees.

The ride south had been punishing. Aldhelm's bones felt cold and bruised, despite his heavy coat. But now a glow of satisfaction warmed them. He glanced across at Rathulf. 'How do you feel, returning here once more?'

'Like a shipman who has seen the lights of land,' said Rathulf drily.

The others started forward, but he kept his horse in check. Realizing this, they turned, and saw him studying his ring.

'Athelgar is here,' he told them calmly.

Franchisca frowned in disbelief. 'Behind us *and* in front?'

'It's Branwen's magic.' Erik crossed himself, and spat.

Franchisca walked his horse around, still surveying the shrouded landscape. 'We should have known she'd come back here. The Strangers held this place when it was *young*.'

Smiling grimly, Rathulf flicked his reins, and moved to join them. 'It is our fate that brings us round full circle. From here the Ravensbreed rode out; from here they will go back into the darkness. We shall our ends by our beginnings know.'

CHAPTER II

The Betrayed

I

Fran hesitated sickly for a moment, then gripped the latch, and opened the back door. A wave of chilly air flowed in, and soaked her to the bone.

The two of them stepped out into a spooky, curdled twilight. Mist lay thick and white around the cottage. She felt its dampness in her fringe, and breathed its musty smell. The hush was like a blanket on the world.

Athelgar's face looked bleak and grey like stone in this dead light. She looked at him, and swallowed.

'You'll make it back,' she said. 'I know you will.'

He didn't react, just stared into the mist. The nearest trees were indistinct as phantoms. The rest was nothingness.

Take up your faith and walk, Branwen had said. *The gate stands open for you*. Fran turned to see the Welsh girl watching now, but hanging back, half-blurred into the dimness of the passage. As if she was afraid to see him go.

Athelgar went forward a few paces. The grass was heavy, soaking, underfoot. His coat was hanging open round his shoulders; she tugged at it, and came around to face him.

'Let me come.'

He shook his head. 'This is the warrior's way.'

'No road for me? You said that once before.'

He gently took her upturned face, and kissed her on the lips. 'That is so, my Lady. But this time you must guide from higher ground.'

Fran wrapped her arms around him then, and pressed her

mouth to his. She had a mind-eye's image of the moment: two lovers saying farewell before a mission in the dawn. Except that *she* was in the scruffy bomber jacket.

She let him go at last – like a drowning woman, losing strength. He put his finger to her lips: she nibbled at the nail, and it was gone. His face was set, unsmiling.

'You cannot come, and yet you shall be there.' He glanced across at Branwen, who had ventured to the door. 'As you shall be, my sister. In my heart.'

'*Yn oes oesoedd*,' said Branwen softly.

Athelgar just nodded, once. '*Amen*.'

He turned and walked downslope into the mist. As he dwindled to a silhouette, Fran saw him gesture sharply, and realized he had flipped away his coin. His shadow was dissolving as he tugged the cross from round his neck, and cast that off as well.

The depthless grey had swallowed him by the time he'd unslung Sky-Edge, and thrown the sword and scabbard to one side.

She turned away, and went back in – shutting the door on the void around the house. Athelgar had gone, as if he'd never existed. The world was blank and still again. But somewhere in the distance, she could hear the rasp of crows.

Her hair was wet, and clinging to her forehead. Droplets had spilled down into her eyes. She wiped them hastily, and blinked at Branwen. The latter's face was grave, but there was understanding there. Fellow-feeling, soul to soul. Although she hardly knew the girl, Fran very nearly hugged her.

'Come,' said Branwen, drawing back. 'We must make all things ready.'

Wearily Fran followed her upstairs. A musky smell of incense tinged the dim air of the landing. The nearest door stood open. The other two were waiting in the unlit room beyond.

Kathryne's face was solemn. 'He's away?'

'Yeah.'

The room must have been the smallest in the cottage: tucked into a corner, with its window in the eaves. No furnishings, just cushions round the walls, and a little wooden table in the centre. It was clearly Kathryne's sacred space. The place she cast her spells.

The star-chart had been spread out on the table, with various items placed on it like paperweights. A small jar in the middle, with the burning joss stick in it; a saucer full of soil, and one of water. Fran sat herself down, still looking. An ivory comb was there as well, along with a silver thimble and a plain gold earring. Unlit beeswax candles stood in holders.

Kathryne was dressed in black now, kneeling on a cushion in her velvety long dress. A ceremonial dagger lay before her on the varnished wooden floor. She kept her hands clasped in her lap, waiting until Branwen too was settled. Then she gave a nervous little smile.

'Ready, then?'

Fran just shrugged. Her mouth was dry. Branwen's face was full of sombre thoughts. Martin was still standing by the window, a shadow on the edge of misty light.

'What do we do?' Fran asked.

'We need to form a link with him to guide his steps across the Otherworld. There are clues in the High History . . .'

Fran's stomach rumbled. She felt hollow, but not hungry. No one had had breakfast, just a token bite to eat. Kathryne had given her a small piece of bread, and a morsel of meat to Branwen. She herself had sipped a little wine. Had that been a part of the ritual too? Fran rubbed her fingers nervously together.

The joss stick kept on burning, a fleck of fiery scarlet in the gloom.

Kathryne took the earring from the table, and handed it to Fran. 'That's for the Sun,' she murmured. Fran held it, feeling awkward. The thimble went to Branwen, 'for the Pole Star'.

The comb – 'The Moon' – she picked up for herself.

Fran glanced at Martin. He didn't seem impressed.

'Now be still for a minute,' Kathryne said. She struck a match, and started lighting candles. 'Breathe the incense in, just let it soothe you.'

'What is it?' Fran asked.

'Frankincense.'

'They're all the same to me,' said Fran. 'A bit like Indian meals.'

A wry smile sparked on Martin's face.

'From Nagasaki,' Kathryne said, not unamused herself. She lit another candle, then looked at Fran, and saw she'd struck a chord. 'That sort of makes it different, doesn't it?'

Fran nodded slowly.

Kathryne kindled one more flame. 'There's a witch who lives round here. She's part of Nukewatch. Tracking the warhead convoys south to Plymouth.' She smiled faintly to herself. 'And people say that *we're* in league with evil.'

The candle-glow infused the bleary light. Kathryne sat back, surveying the table, then nodded to herself. She picked the ornate dagger up, and pointed at the saucers.

'This is sacred earth, from the lands of the Shoshone. The water's from the Chalice Well. Living flames. And our own breath . . .' She tracked the dagger round the room. 'Now put in something of yourselves. Something you keep close, which means a lot to you.'

She took the silver amulet that hung around her neck: two interlocking circles, like a seal. Leaning forward, she placed it on the chart. Branwen laid a silver brooch among the odds and ends. An interwoven Celtic cross, with a dull stone at its centre. Fran hesitated, staring at the map. They might have been three gamblers, putting all their worldly goods into the pot. Staking everything on one last throw. She was about to unclasp her Coventry Cross, when Branwen reached across and grasped her wrist.

'That ring. Where is it from?'

Fran hesitated, startled. Then: 'Athelgar. He gave it to me.'

'It is *Jeanne's*.'

She frowned. 'Who's . . . Zhan?'

'Jeanne, *la Pucelle*. Let me see . . .' Branwen leaned in close – then drew back. 'No, offer this – for all of us. You must.'

Fran stared at her, then pulled the ring off. Branwen seemed to take it with exquisite caution – as if she knew its power, its latent heat. She turned it in her fingers. 'Yes,' she breathed.

'What does the engraving mean?' Fran asked in a small voice.

'*Ihesus Maria*, in the French tongue. This was Jeanne's, she wore it. And Athelgar has got it from the ashes of her pyre.'

Fran just gasped. 'Joan of *Arc*, you mean?'

'Yes. Jeanne d'Arc. We pledged ourselves to *La Pucelle* and yet we could not save her. And that is why we have not found our rest.'

Fran wet her lips, and felt a little sick. 'There's power in it. It burns. Oh . . . bloody hell.'

Branwen nodded solemnly, and put it on the chart. Fran sat frozen, staring. Somewhere in the distance, she thought that she could hear the roar of flames.

Oh God, she thought, *and I've been* wearing *it*. Cool sweat bathed her shoulders. She thought about how close she'd come to sharing that same fate.

'All right, then,' Kathryne said, quite awed herself. 'Now we can begin. The Zodiac's a map, and we can use it.' She put the dagger down again. 'Join hands.'

Fran looked around. 'Martin?'

'Sorry. Count me out.'

'It is enough: we three,' said Branwen quietly.

'Weird sisters,' Martin said. Ironic, yet not mocking.

'You can bring us coffee,' Fran suggested in a last attempt at levity. She moistened her lips again, and looked at Branwen. 'How long will it take to do what he has to do?'

'Who can say?' the Welsh girl shrugged. 'Perhaps as long as we have left to live.'

And how long's that? Fran almost asked, then pinched her lips together. Suddenly she didn't want to know.

Darkness when she closed her eyes; the cloying smell of incense. The room was hushed and still. If it hadn't been for Kathryne's hand and Branwen's, she might have been alone in empty space.

Minutes passed and melted in a sluggish stream of time. She felt her heartbeat slowing down. Her thoughts began to float. And then a glow came seeping through her mind. For a moment she thought the sun was out, and shining through the window. But then an image formed: murky still, and unrelieved, but with a sense of *depth*. Her mind went forward, wading in. She was still dimly aware of the hands she held but it seemed as if her arms had been severed. Left behind in Branwen's and Kathryne's grip, transmitting phantom signals to her nerves.

And she was in the mist, with Athelgar.

The murk was thinning, drifting past, although she sensed no breeze. The world beyond was desolate and grey. A landscape like the Peak: just heath and stone. As barren as the view from Stanage Edge.

Come to one horizon, and you'll always find another one beyond it.

And yet it was still Glastonbury: the Levels. The Tor was looming, very close, a dim shape in the haze. Its lonely tower stood out against the low, oppressive sky.

Only her mind had ventured here, but a sudden chill spread back into her body. She'd always pictured Chernobyl like this. Tor and tower recalled that ruined building, but what obscene sarcophagus was decomposing here? She knew that she was much too close, a ghost in no man's land. Ashes and waste on every side. Even the sky looked dead.

Athelgar had turned his head. She could see him from the

corner of her eye. She wanted to reach out for him but she had no arms. All she could do was pray that he could sense her.

And then the vision faded, and her body sucked her back. She came to herself, head reeling, and thought that she was going to be sick.

'Okay?' asked Kathryne anxiously. She nodded, trying to ignore the clamminess of her skin.

'How are we going to guide him?' she asked hoarsely.

'By the Royal Star Cross. It's something that bisects the Zodiac.'

'What's that?'

'Aldèbaran, in Taurus, to the east. Antares to the west – in Scorpio. Regulus, in Leo, to the south. And Fomalhaut, north of the Tor.'

A snort from Martin. 'Fomalhaut's the Southern Fish – it isn't even *in* the zodiac.'

Kathryne didn't seem perturbed. 'So maybe that's the starting point: the one outside the ring.'

'Martin, which one's brightest?' Fran asked, swallowing.

'Aldèbaran, I think. They're all first magnitude or less.' His tone became sardonic then. 'I don't suppose we've got a book that tells us things like that.'

'And which is closest?' she added suddenly.

'Fomalhaut's close. Twenty-something light years.'

'That's close?'

'Andromeda's two *million*.'

'But this is medieval, right? So, no one could have known that.'

'Couldn't they?' asked Kathryne, very softly.

Fran hesitated – glanced at her. Then disengaged her hand to take the antique silver ring, and move it to the star marked *Fumalhut*.

Outside, the light was growing: seeping through the shroud of mist, like much-diluted blood.

Rathulf halted in his tracks and reached up to muffle his horse's nostrils. They were in a lane, beside a low stone wall. The dripping mist hung low on every side.

He murmured something to his mount, then took a few steps forward, hitching his scabbard up across his midriff. The hilt was angled, ready to be grasped. A shadow wavered in the mist, and crabbed its way towards him. He recognized Franchisca's shape before the face was clear.

'Sight or sign?' he challenged, but Franchisca shook his head.

'And yet they are close,' said Rathulf, gazing past him. 'There is shinecraft in the air.' He paused and stood in silence – as if it were a scent that he could savour. Then he tugged his horse's rein, and started prowling forward.

'Does *Fomalhaut* mean something?' wondered Fran.

'Mouth of the Fish,' said Martin, still aloof.

She turned back to the chart. The bright flames of the candles were a living constellation in themselves, gilding Kathryne's face and Branwen's cheek. Fomalhaut lay dormant in the centre of Joan's ring.

Fran closed her eyes again. Nothing happened. Her head was clear. It felt as if she'd woken up, and wouldn't sleep again. But then her mind flowed out of her once more – so suddenly, so unannounced, it took her by surprise.

She found herself with Athelgar again. Walking in his footsteps, almost breathing down his neck. The effect was claustrophobic, much too close, like a hand-held camera trying to keep up. Athelgar kept moving, at a grim, relentless pace but suddenly she knew he'd sensed her presence. Again he turned his head, as if to glimpse her.

'Frances?'

He rounded on her then – but she just swung around behind him. It seemed she couldn't look into his face. He stood there, gazing back the way he'd come. The landscape was still draped with mist, but then she saw the Tor again, more distant than before.

It's working, she thought giddily. They'd managed to compel him to go north. But once he'd got to Fomalhaut, what then?

Distantly, the others squeezed her fingers.

He'd given four things up, and now he had to win them back. Sword, and coin, and cross, and cup. The four Royal Stars were guiding lights. But which thing would be where?

Mouth of the Fish, she murmured. It sounded like a riddle of some kind. One they had to solve, on pain of death.

Athelgar had resumed his course. Fran glimpsed something looming through the mist. A rugged shape, imposing as a pinnacle of rock. But although its lines were crumbled, they had once been cleanly drawn. She saw it was a building, an isolated castle of some kind.

Athelgar saw it too. She hovered at his shoulder and felt his apprehension flowing back into her veins. Something about that murky fort distracted and dismayed him. But then he seemed to nerve himself, and started moving forward once again.

The land ahead was flooded: a lake of steely water stretched away into the mist. The castle stood a little way offshore, as sombre as the remnant of a drowned, forgotten city. From this close it looked gloomy and imposing, and yet it was much smaller than she'd thought. Two turrets, and a gateway in between them. The latter had a gabled roof, but that had fallen in. A few charred rafters poked towards the sky.

Athelgar had halted on the shore to stare at it. The place was like a barbican, the gatehouse of a medieval bridge. But nothing else was visible above the misty surface. The towers themselves seemed derelict, deserted. And even if they weren't, the lake had cut the building off.

Hanging back, she peered across the water. It seemed to have the faintest phosphorescence. Was this the lake in which he'd find his sword?

Mouth of the Fish, she thought again. It struck an echo somewhere. Athelgar stood motionless, awaiting inspiration.

The barbican had drawn his gaze again. Once more she sensed the pangs of his unease. It was as if he knew the place from somewhere.

A ripple stirred the soggy reeds. She felt a growth of pressure on her heart. Something was demanding that she choose. The image of a sword being lifted from the depths was a beguiling one – and yet it rang false somehow. Perhaps it was too obvious; too *easy*. So what else might be hidden here? The cup, for all this water? Or the coin . . . ?

A sudden thrill went through her. *Look in the mouth of the fish!* she blurted out.

He understood her somehow, and went wading slowly in. In spirit, she moved right up to the edge, but couldn't follow. The water that swirled round him seemed quite dead. Beyond the sloshing of his strides, the silence felt as curdled as the mist.

Fran gave the barbican a glance. There was no sign of life.

Athelgar was knee-deep now. She saw him hesitate, and then hunch forward. Suddenly he plunged his hand into the water and came up with a glowing silver fish. It wriggled in his grasp as he stood upright.

Open up its mouth, and you shall find a piece of money – enough to pay the tax for thee and me. A fragment of the Gospels which she'd long ago forgotten. As she watched excitedly, he prised its mouth apart. The silver coin popped out into his palm.

For thee and me.

'Yes,' she gasped, then squealed with fright as something broke the surface right behind him.

She thought it was an Ashman for a moment. But no, this figure was a knight encased in rusty armour. Water dribbled from the joints, along with something darker and putrescent. Its helmet was an upturned bowl, with just a slit for eyes. Its jaw dropped down below the rim; more liquid overflowed, to spill like vomit down its front.

Athelgar had swung around, and now flailed back in horror. The figure lumbered after him, its ragged surcoat trailing like a shroud across the surface. '*Traitor!*' croaked the drooling mouth. 'Come down to join us now!'

The muffled words were taken up across the misty lake. Petrified, Fran looked, and saw more figures rising up. Drowned men who'd been ages in the water. The flesh she glimpsed had rotted into goo. Their clothes were decomposing too, their armour all corroded. Some had lost their helmets, and their heads were black and swollen. They retched and gargled, floundering towards her, but it was Athelgar they wanted. The nearest ones caught hold of him, and tried to pull him down. He thrashed in panic, fought them off and lurched towards the shore. The putrid figures crowded in his wake. More bloated heads bobbed up, and bodies followed. Oh God, there were a dozen of them, maybe more. And all the time the cries rang out: 'Thou traitor! Thou betrayer! Join us now!'

Athelgar broke free and fell, to scrabble through the shallows. He looked around for Fran, but it was clear he couldn't see her. And Fran was just a phantom, with no strength to pull him in. She could have wept with fear and frustration.

Then Branwen's voice was in her ear. *Your name. Tell them your name!*

Fran just stared, not knowing what she meant. The drowned men waded after Athelgar. One still gripped a lance in bony fingers. He aimed it now, as if to spear a fish.

Tell them who you are! hissed Branwen fiercely.

'Frances!' Fran burst out – and saw their faces turn towards her. Even those with holes instead of eyes. She stared at them with loathing for a moment, then realized they'd stopped moving. As if they'd been unnerved by just her name.

'I'm *Fraaaances*!' she yelled bitterly, and this time they recoiled. She stood and watched them lurching back, unable to believe it. Disfigured though their faces were, she saw them fill with hatred and alarm. Rotting fingers stabbed at her, as if to guard against the Evil Eye. One of the corpses even crossed itself.

A word was passed between them, thick with dread. She

heard it go from mouth to gaping mouth. A desperate accusation, and a warning.

Witch!

Spitting it, they shrank away, and sank into the lake. She watched them disappearing, one by one. Bubbles surged and spent themselves, like bursts of noxious gas. A rusting sword was brandished by a disembodied hand, as if to mock her earlier idea. And then that too was gone beneath the surface.

Athelgar had crawled ashore. He rolled onto his back, and lay there gasping. 'Jesu . . .' he said hoarsely. 'God forgive me.' His face was grey and drawn with an unfathomable despair. But after a pause he raised himself, and opened his clenched hand. The coin was lying safely in his palm.

Fran felt drained enough to faint, her spirit reeling with horror and relief. The turmoil turned to giddiness, the scene was snatched away, and she was back in Kathryne's room again.

The impact tore a sob from her. She slumped, and Branwen squeezed her hand, then squirmed around to grasp her arms before she could collapse. Kathryne looked on anxiously. Even Martin registered concern.

Taking a deep, unsteady breath, Fran raised her face to Branwen's. 'Where was that?' she whispered. 'Who were *they*?'

'The gate of the *Tourelles*,' said Branwen softly. 'The bridgehead which the English army held, at Orléans. Jeanne led the attack on it, and we the Ravensbreed were at her side. Glasdale and his men fell back, the bridge gave way beneath them, and they drowned. We stood and watched; it was our victory. Yet these were men who we had *ridden* with, the soldiers of the king who conjured us.' She shook her head. 'It had to be. But Athelgar has not forgotten it.'

And Marcus knows his weaknesses, Fran thought. She swallowed hard. 'So what about my name?'

'Your name is Frances – *française* – do you see? They thought you were the *Pucelle* come again.'

Fran just nodded mutely. She realized she was bathed in

sweat. Sitting up, she pulled her jacket off. The air felt cool against her naked arms.

'He's passed the first test, hasn't he?' asked Kathryne. Fran nodded again, and clasped hands with them both.

Martin straightened up. 'I could do with some fresh air. Reckon you can spare me for a bit?'

'Certainly,' said Kathryne. She cleared her throat. 'Could you bring some bottled water from the kitchen? It's in the fridge.'

'Sure.' He stepped around them, heading for the door; then turned his head. 'Can I make some phone calls in a while? I need to ring my girlfriend to let her know that I'm okay. And my sister.'

'*No!*' Fran burst out. 'Don't . . .'

Startled, he just frowned at her. She squirmed, and tried to think of a way out. There wasn't one. She'd trapped herself. In any case, she saw it was too late.

'What is it?' he asked warily.

'Martin . . . Lynnie's dead.'

Silence in the room. The other women sat and watched, like statues. Martin's face had frozen up; but when he tried to speak, she saw it quiver.

'*What?*' he whispered.

'Eldred killed her. Rathulf had her killed.' She heard a gasp from Branwen, but she couldn't look away.

Martin lurched, and slumped against the door-frame.

'Oh no,' he said. 'Oh Christ. To get at *me*?'

'To get the Chart,' Fran mumbled. And saying it, she realized she'd been *used*.

Marcus had appeared to her, and told her that he meant to have the Chart. Of course, he must have known about the traitors in their midst. And so he'd goaded her, until she'd guessed its whereabouts. And given poor Lyn away, to Athelgar – and *Rathulf*.

How he must have laughed, to see the outcome.

She sat back with a sobbing gasp. But Martin was staring

at Branwen now. 'Those gloves,' he said. 'The gloves that you were wearing . . .'

Branwen stared back helplessly. Her eyes were sheened with tears.

'They're hers,' he said. 'You stole them. And the jacket? Jesus *Christ*!' His own face was a mask of disbelief, becoming rage. Branwen opened her mouth – but before she could speak, he'd turned and blundered out. She started to get up; Fran took her arm.

'*Leave* him. Let him go.' Tears were stinging her eyes too. They listened to him storm downstairs, and out through the back door. Fran sniffed, and wiped her sticky cheek. 'Oh . . . *shit*.'

Releasing Branwen's sleeve, she knew who'd stolen Lynnie's present, the leather jacket that she'd been so pleased with. She stroked its ravaged surface now, then raised her eyes to Branwen's. She felt no accusation; just bewilderment and hurt.

'You took the Chart. Why couldn't you have warned her?'

Branwen had a haunted look. 'I thought she would be *safe*, once it was gone.'

So both of us are guilty, then. But no, of course they weren't. *Marcus* was the cause of it. And Athelgar was going to make him pay.

She straightened her back, and took a shaky breath. 'All right. Where next?'

'Around the circle. Widdershins, I think.' Kathryne saw her puzzled look. 'That's anti-clockwise, sorry.'

'Against the sun,' said Branwen dourly.

Fran leaned towards the map. 'Aldèbaran's the next one, right?' (*Aldabaran*, according to the chart). She glanced at Kathryne, saw her nod, then took the ring and moved it like a chess piece. Sitting back, she took their hands again.

'I wish he hadn't gone. He might have told us what it means.'

'Aldèbaran's in Taurus,' Kathryne murmured. 'But Gemini's right next to it. The effigy's this giant figure, sleeping in the earth . . .'

Fran flexed her fingers, keeping them enmeshed. She felt a tingling in her nerves, as Kathryne's voice grew quicker.

'Orion falls on Gemini. His stars on Dundon Hill. Orion's *sword*.'

2

Martin had plunged deep into the mist. The cottage fell behind him, and foundered like a ghost-ship in the murk. Out here, there was nothing. Just a cold and dismal sea. And nobody to see him if he wept.

He thought of Lyn the last time he had seen her. The love and longing in her eyes. The hurt on her sweet face.

'I said to *burn* the bloody thing!' he yelled into the mist. 'Why didn't you *listen*, you *silly* girl.'

His legs gave as his voice broke up; he slumped onto his knees.

'*Lyn* . . .'

A twig snapped, somewhere close.

Panting, Martin raised his head. The trees were hunched and shadowy – like weeping willows, sharing in his grief. He listened, but could only hear the dripping in their branches. Gluey greyness everywhere, as if the world was melting.

Then he heard a squish of mulch, as something rushed towards him from behind. He swung around, and gave a startled yelp. Aldhelm's face was spectre-grim, and every bit as grey. Even as he struggled up, the Raven was upon him – kicking him back down into the grass. Winded, Martin rolled, and tried to drag himself away. Something like a cricket bat was slammed against his spine. He kicked and writhed convulsively, his bowels full of fire. Then Aldhelm seized his coat and hauled him upright.

Another harsh, familiar face was waiting in the mist. Franchisca held a shotgun in both fists. Martin stared in wheezy disbelief. But then he saw the weapon had been emptied and abused: the barrel out of true, the breech jammed open. Clearly his opponent didn't understand the thing. Except that it was heavy, with the balance of a club.

The butt whacked hard into his solar plexus. The pain was paralysing: Martin groaned, and tried to double forward. But Aldhelm held him upright like a target. Franchisca swung the butt again, and struck him on the jaw. Lightning flashed through Martin's head, his limbs slipped out of joint. When Aldhelm let him go, he simply crumpled to the grass.

'Have a care,' came Erik's gloating voice. 'Or Rathulf will not know his face again.'

Martin lay there, gasping, too stunned to find his feet. He had a skewed and blurry glimpse of Erik coming forward. Aldhelm and Franchisca towered up into the mist. But then a fourth shape joined them and Rathulf squatted down by Martin's side.

A finely pointed knife was in his fingers. He seemed to hold it carelessly. His face was stony calm. But his eyes were windows on an empty soul.

Martin gagged, and tried to squirm. Aldhelm's boot came down beside his head. Rathulf stared, expressionless. He touched the knife-point to his lip, as if to scratch an itch.

'Foolish the man,' he said at last, 'who does not heed *my* words.'

(*Slowly you will die*, the echoes said.)

Panic surged through Martin's nerves. 'Branwen made me go with her,' he hissed.

Rathulf smiled behind the blade. 'And where is Branwen now?'

'Oh Jesus . . . I don't *KNOW*.' The last a whoop of agony, as Rathulf slammed the hilt against his stomach.

'Branwen. Frances. *Athelgar*. Where are they?'

'Hiding out in someone's house. I couldn't find the way

back in this mist.' It seemed the only straw that he could clutch at.

'So wherefore should I spare your life?' sneered Rathulf. 'Better I should offer you to Odin, with this knife. Cut the sark from your back, and the skin from the flesh, and the flesh from the *bones*, and the heart from the whole.'

'Odin's Eagle,' Erik said, like someone who had seen it and enjoyed it.

Martin flinched. 'All right! I'll try . . .'

'Will you?' Rathulf nodded. 'That is good.' Sitting back, he jerked his head, and Aldhelm hoisted Martin to his feet. Rathulf rose as well, and sheathed his knife.

'You shit,' said Martin, close to tears. 'You killed my *sister*.'

Rathulf gave a twisted smile. 'So,' he said. 'And what is that? Hela's realm is but a kiss away.'

Turning, he went over to his horse. The gallows-rope was hanging like a lariat from the saddle. He brought it back, uncoiling it, and Martin flinched away. Aldhelm's grip grew tighter. Martin tried to duck, but it was hopeless. Rathulf put the noose around his neck, and drew it tight.

He stared at Martin – face to face – then drew back, smiling coldly. 'Come then, Summoner. Be our hunting hound. This time you *shall* lead us to the Chart.'

The stone in Branwen's brooch had started glowing.

None of them noticed it at first. Kathryne had remembered something else. 'There's a legend about Dundon church. It's haunted by a knight with a great sword . . .'

Fran sat listening, entranced. Then Branwen's fingers tightened. They both looked round; the Welsh girl nodded downward. The lodestone's gleam grew brighter as they watched.

'Someone draws near,' said Branwen.

Instinctively, Fran glanced towards the dagger then at Kathryne.

'It's not for *killing* people!' Kathryne said.

*   *   *

Rathulf kicked him forward like a dog, taking up the slack around his wrist. Martin stumbled, almost fell, and felt the rope close tighter round his throat. The iron mask of numbness was beginning to wear off and pain was throbbing in his teeth and jaw. Something warm had smeared his clammy skin.

Kathryne's cottage was just ahead, a vague shape in the mist. He hadn't had a chance to misdirect them. He hadn't had a *choice*.

He could see no sign of life. No lights were on. But he could almost feel the others start to salivate around him, like foxes slinking in towards a sleeping chicken coop.

Rathulf drew the choking noose still tighter, giving Martin no chance of trying to shout a warning. They reached the ragged treeline; halted there. Rathulf gestured silently. Erik scurried up to the cottage, and crept along the end wall to the corner. His sword was drawn, and Aldhelm's too. The grizzled Raven circled round to cover the front lane.

Franchisca glanced at Rathulf, and strode towards the cottage's back door.

'Rathulf. He is *here*,' said Branwen hoarsely.

They were halfway down the staircase when Franchisca started smashing down the door.

CHAPTER III

The Field of Blades

I

Out in the wastes, in the fields of drifting fog, Athelgar came up short and looked around. There'd been no sound, no movement in the mist. But a sudden chill had settled on his heart.

Frances was no longer at his shoulder.

He felt his heartbeat quicken, forcing sweat from his pores like moisture from a cheese. He recognized the fear, and tried to fight it. Clutching his coin, he waited for a sign.

The emptiness remained unfilled. He sensed no breath of comfort from her lips.

He reached for his cross, and remembered it was gone. Everything was gone. He might have been a seafarer, adrift, his lifeline snapped. Left behind to sink into an endless slaty sea.

2

Franchisca's boots came creaking up the stairs. He stepped onto the landing, hatchet poised. A smell like incense spiked the air: the musky tang of mystery and faith. He listened for a moment then strode towards the nearest door, and kicked the panel inward.

The room was lit by candle-flames, and most of them blew out. He saw a low-topped table, and cushions strewn across the polished floor. The tabletop was bare but the items scattered round it made him think it had been covered, and the cover had been hastily snatched off. A broken saucer lay in gleaming wetness. The incense-stick still smouldered in the fragments of its jar.

A silver talisman lay close to his foot. He stooped to pick it up, and let it dangle by its chain, frowning at its mystical design.

The room was empty.

Rathulf stood and waited in the garden, gazing at the building's upper windows. Absently, he tightened Martin's leash, not blinking as his prisoner gagged for breath.

Martin fell to his knees, clawing at the noose until it let a pinch of air into his lungs. His panting seemed to fill the stagnant silence. Guiltily he raised his head. The cottage looked reproving. He risked a glance at Rathulf.

The latter's cruel face was smiling faintly.

Erik paced from room to room, rooting through the shadows with his sword. A jittery frustration grew with every fruitless thrust. In the half-light of the living room, he swept a row of books down off their shelf, pivoting away before the last of them had landed. The stillness seemed to mock him, and he hissed between his teeth.

The women were still hiding here. They *must* be. He slashed a sofa cushion as he passed it, and moved into the silent hall again.

Fran just glimpsed him through the crack. The sight of his ferocious face sent panic leaping up from deep inside her.

Kathryne hugged her closer in the dimness. They were squeezed into the boiler-cupboard underneath the stairs. The door did not quite fit the frame and they could see into the hallway through the gap. See and *be* seen. She felt her muscles knotting up as Erik came on past.

He's seen the door. He's got *to check behind it* . . . Her nerves were singing, loud enough to hear. But Erik kept on walking.

Kathryne's heart was thudding next to hers. The air was thick and stifling. Heavy footsteps creaked about upstairs.

It had to be a miracle – or magic. As they'd looked in panic for somewhere to hide, Kathryne had said something about *glamours*. But could she really hide them both? Or was this Erik's game?

Fran swallowed wetly, trying not to breathe. She forced herself to peep out through the crack. Erik was in the kitchen now, upsetting pots and pans. The angry clatter bounded through the house. She could see across the hall, and through the doorway of the living room. The murk in there was shapeless, like a pall of hanging dust.

Then Branwen blinked.

Even then, Fran had to keep on staring until the image seeped into her brain. Branwen seemed to grow out of the shadows, although she'd been in plain sight all along. Motionless, unbreathing, with her power wrapped around her – and Erik had stalked past her, unawares.

A patch of paleness turned into her contemplative face; she raised her hooded eyes, and looked at Fran.

Aldhelm watched the rear of the house: standing there as patient as a gnarled and weathered oak. The wall was ivy-covered here, with roses on a trellis. The mist was thinning, melting into dew. Above the roof, the sky was getting clearer.

Crows were cawing hoarsely all around.

Franchisca shoved the next door roughly open. The room beyond smelled faintly of the sea. The bath in it was carved from solid jade. A curtain hung above it; he hooked it with his axe and drew it back.

Still nothing.

Back onto the landing, his axe still raised and ready. Silence hung about him, though the noise of Erik's searching carried clearly from downstairs. Moving down the passageway, he raised his boot, and kicked the last door open.

He glimpsed a bed, and something crouching on it, and then a great black dog was up and coming for his throat. The

Raven took a backward stride, and tried to aim his blow. Too late: the dog was faster. Snarling now, it sprang at him, its claws against his chest. Franchisca yelled and stumbled back, flailing at the creature as it chewed into his coat.

Erik heard, came running back, and pounded up the stairs.

Kathryne made her move at once, pulling Fran back out into the hall. Instinct made the younger girl resist for just a moment; the staircase was still shuddering above them. She felt her gorge fill up with ice and bile. Then Branwen was beside them, her fingers taking hold of Fran's bare arm.

'Come on!' hissed Kathryne. 'Both of you. Get *out*!'

Fran turned saucer eyes on her. 'And you?'

'Someone has to keep the glamour earthed.' She looked at Branwen, wavering, then kissed her on the cheek. 'Just keep going straight. And blessed be.'

Branwen nodded, took Fran's hand, and pulled. They fled along the passage, through the kitchen, to the door. 'More of them outside,' Fran gasped; but Branwen seized the latch, and wrenched it open.

Aldhelm heard a rustling behind him, in the hedge. A stealthy, timid rabbit-sound; but then it seemed to swell – became man-sized and threatening. He swung around, sword ready, and the unseen shape retreated. One of them was out here, she was trying to escape. He started grimly forward, and the clinging mist embraced him. Absorbed in his pursuit, he didn't see the back door open. Fran and Branwen flitted past, like ghosts into the grey.

The sounds began to fade at once: dwindling to rabbit-size again. Baffled, he looked round himself, then back towards the dim shape of the house.

Everything upstairs had stopped. The flounderings and yells and snarls had ended with a whimper. The upper storey brooded, like a thundercloud above her. But then she heard a floorboard creak and something soggy tumbled down the stairs. Kathryne's turn to whimper, as she recognized Cabal. His eyes were blank, his belly slit and bloody. Nausea filled her throat and turned her cold. But she stood there in the hall – *her* hall – and waited.

A blond man with a broken nose came slowly down the stairs, treading in the dead dog's greasy wake. His clothes were brightly splashed with blood, his sword was dripping red. His flat blue eyes caught sight of her. His wide-lipped mouth drew wider in a leer.

Kathryne's courage almost failed. She glanced towards the door. But that way out was blocked now. Martin stood there, helpless, with a rope around his neck. Another fair-haired man was at his shoulder. His face was calm, his eyes were frost and fire. Kathryne knew at once that this was Rathulf.

O Goddess help me.

Someone else was on the stairs; she jerked her head around. This man had Fran's jacket, and was trailing it behind him like a trophy.

'Where are they?' asked Rathulf, like a reasonable man.

She looked at him and swallowed. 'Away where you can't catch them.'

'And Athelgar?'

'Gone into the Otherworld. Try following him *there*.'

Even as she sneered at him, the swordsman grasped her hair. The agony brought tears to her eyes. He hauled her through into the living room. Gasping, she was flung onto the sofa. Broken-nose stood over her, his fixed expression humourless and hungry. His eyes burned through his unkempt fringe – as dangerous as sparks in dirty straw. Kathryne tried to squirm away; the other man moved round to hem her in. He let his hatchet slide down through his fingers, and slowly pushed the handle through his belt.

Staring up, she heard a groan from Martin in the hall. His body slumped and slithered to the floor. A moment later, Rathulf crossed the threshold.

Then the axe-man growled, and pounced on her. Horrified,

she kicked and wriggled, clawing for his face. His foulness almost made her gag: millions of bacteria decaying on his breath. He slapped her down, and ripped into her dress. And suddenly he reared back, his mouth clamped tight with pain.

Rathulf stood behind him, a fist clenched in his minion's mop of hair. His bony face was rigid and severe.

'Stop this,' he said coldly. 'You must have *respect* for the Wise.' Levering the axe-man up, he slung him to one side. Kathryne lay there: panting, petrified. Even when she saw the noose in his free hand, she couldn't move.

He raised the rope and showed her it. His face was like a death-mask. 'Have no fear,' he said after a moment. 'The Gallows-Lord is waiting for us all.'

Then, with one quick movement, he had dropped it round her neck. The slipknot tightened smoothly, like a thumb against her throat. 'Oh, please . . .' she croaked. *Oh, let me see the sun.* But Rathulf's hand was on her chest already. He put his weight on it, and heaved. Kathryne choked and gurgled as the rope drew bowstring-taut. Rathulf clenched his jaw, and kept on pulling. Her body threshed beneath him for a minute, and was still.

Rathulf's breath hissed out; he looked around. Franchisca waited sullenly. Erik feigned indifference, wiping down his sword-blade on the sofa's rumpled throw. Aldhelm had rejoined them and was watching from the doorway.

'Bring the Summoner,' said Rathulf grimly.

Martin let himself be dragged, his stomach still aflame from Rathulf's punch. Nausea was a bubble in his throat, about to burst. The noose was gone from round his neck, but that was no relief. He felt too sick and shaken up to care.

Aldhelm heaved him round, and let him flop into a chair. Martin slumped there, panting shallowly. But then, as Aldhelm moved aside, his lungs seized up completely.

Kathryne was spreadeagled on the sofa, facing him. Rathulf's noose was round her neck. Her tongue protruded, dark and stiff; her eyes were white and blind.

'Oh my *God* . . .'

And then he saw what occupied the other easy chair. Kathryne's dog was piled up there, a ruptured bag of offal. Bits of it were dangling. Blood was slowly soaking through the rug.

Martin had a freezing flush, and very nearly puked.

'Three gifts for the offering,' said Rathulf, right behind him. 'So three can follow Athelgar into the shadow-place.'

Erik, by the doorway, looked uneasy. 'Is this your *wise-craft*, Rathulf?' He made it sound like some kind of perversion.

'So it is,' said Rathulf affably. 'And with it you shall hunt him down and kill him.'

'I have no wish to walk among the dead.' Franchisca, by the fireplace, was having doubts as well.

'The mystics saw three drops of blood: a symbol for the Name of the All-Mighty. That is the secret I have heard, the key to the enchantments round this place. And thus we shall unlock the shadow-gates.'

He walked around to where the dog lay bleeding, and stooped to dip his fingers in the gore; then flicked the droplets at each man in turn. It looked like an anointing – or a baptism. Erik flinched, and Aldhelm pulled a face. But no one turned away.

'Now you are prepared,' Rathulf said. 'Go – cut out his heart, and bring it back. The gates will open. And thus you shall repay your lord for all the *gold* he gives you.'

The others shifted restively, then turned towards the door. Martin watched them, breathless now. *Three gifts for the offering*. And two of them had been sacrificed already . . .

The three men left the cottage. Martin sensed them move away, spreading out into the fading mist. His mind's eye seemed to watch them from the rooftop. Off they went, three different ways, the shroud of mist engulfing them. But they left their shadows hanging there, like flies strung out around a funnel web.

Something stirred; he came back with a jolt. Kathryne's milky eyes were fixed on him, but it was Rathulf who had moved. Martin watched the Raven take a fourth chair for himself – drawing it up, as if to join their group.

Sitting down, he studied Kathryne's pendant, swinging it like a hypnotist's medallion. Then he raised his head, looked round at Martin. And though his face was blank, his eyes were burning.

3

Fran and Branwen ran, until they couldn't carry on another yard. They found themselves in someone's field. The ground was still wreathed in mist. Startled sheep went scuttling away: glimpses in the haze, like dirty ghosts. Higher up, the air was clear, and Fran could see the Tor.

She slumped across a fence to get her breath. She hadn't had a stitch this bad since childhood. It felt more like a stab-wound in her side.

Branwen was beside her, staring back the way they'd come. Her hand was at her mouth. Fran guessed who her thoughts were with, and knew how she was feeling.

'Kathryne?' she asked faintly.

Branwen shook her head. 'He will not spare her.'

'Oh God. We shouldn't have . . .'

Branwen took her arm, and squeezed. 'She gave her life for us. Shall it be wasted?' She pulled the folded star-chart from her pocket. 'Athelgar is waiting for our lead.'

Fran had started shivering, and not just from reaction. The morning damp had soaked into her T-shirt. She watched while Branwen peered at the map. 'Al-dabaran?' – Fran nodded – 'So we must be there to meet him.' Branwen raised her eyes. 'You have the ring?'

Fran dug into her pocket, and brought it out. Joan's ring. She put it on her finger without needing to be told.

'What if Rathulf follows us?'

'He has not found us yet.' Branwen gestured her to kneel, and spread the map between them. Then she took Fran's hands and raised them up.

'I can't do this,' Fran blurted. Her mind was still in turmoil, but her heart felt clogged and blocked.

'Yes you can,' said Branwen, leaning close. 'Reach out with your spirit. He is waiting.'

Rathulf's knife was out again. Pensively he breathed against the blade. Martin risked a glance towards the doorway.

'Are you in haste to meet your God?' asked Rathulf. He didn't even raise his eyes, still staring at the items on the floor. Fran's jacket was spread out there, like a fresh-skinned hide; a spattering of canine guts compounding the impression. Kathryne's pendant lay in blood, along with Branwen's brooch. The lodestone glimmered fitfully, as if its power was waning.

'You're going to kill me anyway,' said Martin, resigned to sharing Lyn's fate – and her murderer as well. The symmetry was comforting, somehow.

Rathulf gave no sign of confirmation, or denial. Martin felt a spark of hope which mocked his resignation. Why had he been left alive? He thought of past encounters. Maybe Rathulf *liked* him, in some patronizing way.

'What about the girls?' he asked.

'Once Athelgar is dead, they will be hunted down and slain.' Rathulf gave a rueful shrug. 'Branwen is *wise* – a mistress of her craft. Would that she had been my friend, instead of my opponent.'

'I don't think you can beat her. She's too *pure*.'

The other gave a bark of harsh amusement. 'Not so pure, Summoner. She has a taste for fruit that is forbidden.' His grim smile lost its humour then. 'And she it was who brought the Ravens down.'

'So what's this? Your revenge on her?'

'I seek to hold the Star-Chart, that is all. Some believe it is a map, to guide men to the hidden wealth of Britain, but *we* know what its real treasure is. Power to voyage as an unbound soul. To cross the bridge from one world to the next. To sleep among the stars and never die.'

'Don't you know you're being used?' said Martin helplessly.

Rathulf smirked. 'Who *uses* me?'

'There's someone evil . . . lurking round this place.'

'Odin Slaughter-Father is my lord. The White Christ is my brother. Whom then shall I fear?' Rathulf waited mockingly, then looked back at his magical design. Leaning down, he used his knife to sift the chunks of meat.

'Take him: he is yours,' he breathed, to no one in the room.

In spirit, Fran slipped through the gates, and moved into the shadow-world again. Athelgar was up ahead and she willed herself to catch him. Suddenly it felt as if she was flying. She brushed against his neck like a butterfly kiss, ethereal as a fairy. He didn't look around, but he had sensed her. Relief eased every muscle of his frame.

'Blessed may you be, my Lady Frances.'

Fran would have embraced him if she could. Her naked soul was warm and glowing now.

The shroud of mist was subsiding to a curdled, milky fog. Sky-Edge must be somewhere close. She looked round for a clue, and then she saw them. Scores of them. A *field* of planted swords.

Athelgar moved forward, and she drifted at his heels. The sight ahead was like some rusty graveyard: iron crosses growing from the earth. Wherever she looked, they crowded in, receding to the misty middle distance. They came in every size and type: giant double-handers next to Roman stabbing swords.

She thought of how the Ravens marked a grave. An army must have fallen here. A thousand soldiers buried where they fell.

Have a care, warned Branwen in her head.

Athelgar stopped, as if he'd heard her too. The croak of

ravens filled the pause that followed. Fran could see them in the nearest tree. Black and watchful: waiting for their meat.

'Can you hear me, Frances?' murmured Athelgar. 'Which shall I choose? And what if I choose wrongly?'

Fran felt Branwen's hands in hers, a link between the worlds of flesh and spirit. She knew the other girl could share the vision. After a moment, Branwen spoke again.

This is a place where evil warriors sleep. If the wrong sword is withdrawn, the corpse shall rise again.

'How shall we find it then?' Fran whispered, as if afraid that Athelgar would sense her indecision.

Silence in her head. Athelgar waited, fingering his coin. Fran glimpsed bones amid the nearest sword-blades. Curls of mist were rising from the sockets of a skull.

Five crosses! Branwen said, and then her thoughts came in a rush. *Jeanne's blade was graven with five crosses. Put that thought into his heart. The fall of the coin can lead him to his sword.*

'Five crosses,' Fran repeated. Dominicain had made that challenge too. Athelgar heard, or got the message somehow. He raised his coin, considering, then flipped it. Crowns came up. He faced another way, and tried again. This time it was crosses. Cautiously he started out, across the misty field.

Fran followed, full of trepidation. More bones were scattered underfoot, along with bits of armour. Although she had no substance here, she felt a chill of dread.

Athelgar moved slowly through the blades. He stopped at random; tossed the coin again. Crosses, and he set off at a tangent. Fran looked at the swords they passed. A woman's tattered veil was caught on one.

Something whickered faintly in her ear. A fizz of fright went through her. Athelgar ducked, as if reacting with her nerves. A throwing-axe just missed his head, and spun into the haze.

Fran looked round in horror. Franchisca stood among the blades, a dozen yards away. He had a second axe already drawn. He lifted it and lined it up. Athelgar stepped back slowly, his body tense and poised to dodge again.

Fran just looked on, powerless; then sensed another presence in the mist. Something stirred behind her. Erik's scarred and grinning face was there when she turned round.

Oh shit.

Athelgar glanced from one man to the other, his own expression stony and resolved. Any doubts he might have had were battened tightly down.

Fran was at the centre of their triangle now. She watched as Erik started moving sideways. Sauntering, still smiling, but his sword was drawn and ready. Athelgar eased back and round, to keep them both in view.

'Have you no sword?' leered Erik. 'Remember what Our Lord has said: that he who has no sword to wield, should sell his cloak and buy one.'

Athelgar's hands were raised to shoulder height: his hanging coat spread out like sombre wings. It didn't seem a gesture of surrender, more likely it was readiness to catch Franchisca's axe. As if he could.

'I see your Lord is Rathulf now,' he growled.

'Rathulf *shares* the money we have fought for. He pays us gold out of the raven-purse.'

Athelgar smiled bleakly. 'Your grave-goods will be fine ones, then.'

Erik kept on pacing slowly round him. His own smile had gone out like a snuffed candle. 'You wish for a sword? Come, and take this one.'

Athelgar's eyes flicked back towards Franchisca. The hatchet was still aimed. His gaze moved to the nearest sword. The wired hilt was waiting to be snatched.

'Oh, don't!' Fran hissed, and Branwen echoed her.

Athelgar retreated once again. Erik was converging with him now. Franchisca eased around to block him off. It seemed to Fran as if they moved in time to solemn music. The raven-tree was very close, its occupants as raucous as a Colosseum crowd.

'Is this your honour, friend?' said Athelgar.

'We are Death's men already. Why resist him?' Erik said that calmly – then he lunged. Athelgar scooped something up, and blocked the other's blow. A hollow metal clang rang round the field. Fran saw Athelgar was holding a battered piece of armour. He sprang backwards. Erik snarled, and went for him again. Again his sword-blade struck the makeshift shield. Then Athelgar flung the armour in his face. Erik lurched, and almost lost his balance. Athelgar went scrabbling through the mist, and came up with some ugly kind of club. As he raised it in both hands, Fran realized what it was.

A human leg-bone, long and gaunt. He came at Erik, clouted him, and knocked his sword aside. Franchisca started forward, with his hatchet poised to fly. Instinctively, Fran tried to block his view; he stared right through her.

Athelgar seized hold of Erik, twisting him around as a human shield against Franchisca's axe. Erik tried to struggle, but the length of bone was wedged against his windpipe. Athelgar held it there with both clenched fists, choking off all efforts to resist. His own face was ferocious now, teeth bared and eyes ablaze. A warrior's face, quite merciless. It even frightened Fran.

Erik made a gagging sound; his eyes were on Franchisca. Already widened by distress, they bulged with sudden fear.

'Come, now,' taunted Athelgar. 'Your hunting skills have not deserted you?'

The other's face was tight with indecision. Fran could see him gnawing at his lip. But the axe stayed up, still tilted back, still ready for the throw.

Even the hungry ravens in the tree had fallen silent.

Athelgar hauled Erik back a step – and Erik twisted suddenly, and jerked his elbow backwards. Athelgar hunched up around the blow. His fists began to open round the leg-bone, and Erik's head moved quickly to one side.

'Now!' he croaked, as Fran cried 'No!' The axe went spinning, hissing through the air. And Athelgar reared back again, the bony lever forcing Erik's head up. The axe struck home between his eyes, and split his skull wide open. The harsh cry of a raven seemed to mock his gaping mouth.

Athelgar gave way beneath the impact of the blow, and let the body tumble to one side. Franchisca snarled an oath, and drew his sword. He charged at once – a mangy, maddened dog. Athelgar looked round for Erik's blade. The mire of mist concealed it. Fran went wading forward in a frantic bid to help; she didn't feel ethereal any more. Then she heard the flap of heavy wings. A great black raven fluttered down, and landed on the pommel of a sword.

She took it as a sign, and so did he; quick as thought, he sprang towards the weapon. The raven screeched, and lifted off again. Athelgar gripped the handle, drew the sword up from the earth, and spun around to meet Franchisca's charge. Fear sparked in the other's eyes, but now he was committed. He flailed at Athelgar, who ducked. Then Sky-Edge ripped him open.

She wished her mind's wide eye could look away.

Franchisca toppled soggily to earth. Athelgar stared down at him, then drew a bitter breath and turned around. Erik lay as shapeless as a grave-mound in the mist. And up above, the raven was still circling.

With all these swords to perch on, it had chosen Athelgar's. As if some instinct told it that this blade had given most food to its kind. This Sword of a Hundred Graves . . .

Athelgar had pocketed his coin; he touched it now. Then he began to pick his way between the crosses and the bones. Fran stared sickly after him, then turned to follow.

Something furtive caught her eye – a stirring in the mist. Someone else was with them in the field. And then the scene was swallowed up, and she plunged into her body once again.

Her arms were wrapped round Branwen, who was hugging her as tightly. They were both still on their knees, in dewy grass. Fran swallowed, and drew gently back. Branwen's face was trickling with tears.

The field was such a contrast to that grisly killing ground.

The morning light was golden now, the grass was fresh and green. Some of the sheep were grazing nearby. Living flowers blossomed in the hedge.

Although she hadn't moved, she felt exhausted. Water in her muscles, and an anaerobic weakness in her joints. A pool of nausea in her stomach, too.

'He found his sword – you saw?' she said. 'That's *two* things he's got back. And two to go.' Tired though she was, she knew they had to carry on. Had that been Aldhelm, lurking in the mist?

Branwen sniffed, and wiped her cheeks. Her face and eyes were desolate, despite their victory.

'Shh, what's wrong?' Fran whispered, leaning forward. The highlights in the Welsh girl's eyes were flecks of molten gold.

'No thing,' Branwen murmured. 'It is Fate. We are a dying kind, we Ravensbreed.'

CHAPTER IV

The Cat, the Wolf and the Dog

I

Here and there, where people were awake, they heard the horse. Its iron shoes clipped slowly down the lane. Getting up, a teenage girl went over to her window, and glimpsed the rider going past the house. An old man with a dog saw something moving in the mist. A mother in her kitchen didn't look up from the stove.

Two children camping out in their front garden saw him pass. A tall man, dressed in black, with greying hair. He had a cross around his neck; a belt of bullets too. A shotgun's butt was braced against his leg. He turned his head and looked at them, unsmiling. The children watched with solemn fascination.

The horse paced on unhurriedly, and took him from their sight.

Blue was breaking through the mist; the air was getting warmer. It was going to be a beautiful day.

Rathulf hissed between his teeth, and picked up Branwen's brooch. He studied it in silence for a minute. The lodestone was still flickering, but Martin couldn't tell if it was brighter.

The offal had grown colder, no longer steaming faintly in the chill air of the room. The frigid atmosphere belied the growing light outside.

Kathryne's body lay in lax abandon. And still he kept expecting her to move . . .

Then Rathulf raised his eyes and looked at him. 'Erik's star is set; Franchisca's too. Does that please you, Summoner?'

Martin quickly shook his head. Rathulf kept on staring – then closed his fingers round the brooch, as if he meant to crush it in his fist.

'Athelgar moves onward. Branwen is still guiding him, and Frances. It seems I must do *all* things for myself.'

Standing up, he kicked apart his magical design. Fran's jacket twitched, as if possessed, then crumpled to a boneless piece of skin. Bits of meat went spattering away. Kathryne's pendant rattled in a corner. Rathulf turned to her corpse next. Lifting up one wax-pale hand, he started prying off her signet ring.

Martin launched himself towards the doorway. But Rathulf was much faster, much too fast. His hand caught Martin's collar like a snake, and dragged him backwards, flinging him back down into the chair. Martin aimed a kick towards his crotch, but Rathulf dodged it. And then the knife was hovering above him, poised to plunge.

'And so,' said Rathulf through his teeth, 'the time comes for the parting of the ways.'

Martin gripped the chair-arms, a reflex from the dentist's surgery. The knife came stabbing downward, and he yelled – in startled disbelief as well as pain.

'It profits a man, to sit and think awhile,' said Rathulf.

Martin gasped, grimacing at the knife. It had gone right through his braced right hand, and pinned it to the chair. He watched his fingers quivering. They'd gone as white as Kathryne's.

A jumping muscle moved his arm. The pain flashed to his shoulder, and he groaned. Blood welled up between his straining tendons.

Rathulf straightened up. His face was sombre. 'You summoned us,' he said, 'and so we came. The Ravensbreed will never come again. Remember us.'

With that he turned and walked on out. Martin heard him leave the house. Shudders of reaction started building up inside him: each tremble fraying nerves against the edges of the knife. He gritted his teeth, and tried to keep from howling.

2

'Regulus is next,' Fran ventured, 'isn't it?'

Branwen nodded pensively. Fran leaned forward, staring at the map. Regulus, in Leo. She saw it had been Edgar's sign. His name was written there. Now it was an empty house: she knew its tenant wasn't coming back.

Cross or Cup? She didn't have a clue. Without Kathryne or Martin to advise them, they would have to feel their way.

And Marcus? What's he *doing?* Had he lost his fix on them, or was he simply waiting?

Fear twitched like a finger in her throat. She gulped it down. Then reached for Branwen's hands again. 'Come on, we're nearly there.'

The wasteland opened out once more, still grey with drifting mist. She picked up Athelgar again, and flitted to rejoin him. Although she had no body here, she still felt clean and naked. A sprite with gauzy wings, perhaps.

Athelgar kept walking, his sword-blade tilted back across one shoulder. Spots of blood had dripped onto his coat, growing slowly darker as they dried and soaked up dust.

Fran looked back the way he'd come. A thorn tree stood beside the path, snagging the mist as if to shred it. She saw no trace of movement in the haze.

Athelgar looked round as well. She hoped he'd caught a hint of her unease. At least he'd sensed her presence. Still looking back, he spoke to her, his voice a murmur in his lover's ear.

'Frances . . . is there danger? I saw three figures, cowled in white, who showed the way ahead. Now there are but two. Where is the third?'

Don't worry about us, she whispered back. *You have to keep on going.*

He glanced round for a wary moment longer, then went on. A lonely, crumbled building broke the skyline up ahead. He left the path, and climbed the slope towards it. Following, Fran saw it was a chapel. The roof was gone; the windows, gaping holes. They reached a broken drystone wall which gave onto a graveyard. Or rather, to a yard that was one grave.

Athelgar brought the sword down off his shoulder.

Insubstantial though Fran was, she gave a gasp of horror. Bodies had been heaped into a rotting, greasy mass, piled up like drifted snow in every corner. A trench beside the chapel wall was full to overflowing. Some of the dead were wrapped in shrouds, but most had been stripped naked. She saw the clustered tumours, then; patches of decay. Pallid flesh was turning black. She realized they'd been struck down by the *plague*.

Athelgar had frozen too. Again she sensed his fear. A medieval dread, but she could share it. Whatever might be hidden here, the chapel was contaminated now. He could walk in, and out again, only to die in agony a few hours later. She could almost sense the microbes in the stagnant air ahead. Her mind was like a Geiger counter, picking up the crackle of electrons. Except this was a *living* death – far worse than radiation.

The chapel was in ruins, its shadows overgrown and full of rubble. Wood and metal crosses grew up starkly through the tangle of dead limbs. Instinctively she hugged herself, and felt her wings of thought begin to wilt.

Athelgar grew tense – and then went forward. She almost snatched at him, although she knew he had no choice. This was the test: it tried his faith, and hers. Reluctantly she followed at his heels. It felt as if her soul could be infected by this place. The skin of her own body must be pimpling with fear. The plague bacilli thickened in the air.

He began to pick his way among the markers, peering at

the carvings and inscriptions on each cross. Whorls of mist slunk past his legs, as if the dead were breathing. Fran glanced toward the chapel's empty doorway. It opened like a throat into the gloomy maw beyond.

Spooked, she started searching too, gliding up and down among the bodies. The corpses stared at her with glassy eyes. There must be something hidden here. There had to be a clue.

Athelgar had halted on the far side of the graveyard. Fran came up behind, and swung around him. And then she saw it, standing out against the sombre building. A plain white cross that glimmered with a pale, unhealthy light.

He sensed what she had seen, and turned to look. Fran moved up beside him, staring too. The cross was weirdly out of place in this macabre setting. Its lines were clean and smooth, its surface spotless. But its light was like the aura of decay.

Athelgar stepped forward – and stopped again. Fran drew closer, sharing his unease. She tried to push her mind back through to Branwen. *What should he do?* But Branwen didn't answer.

The cross looked much too *modern* for this place. It made her think of pictures from the First World War. Row on row of crosses, in a wilderness of mud. And then she realized why she knew the image.

The Sandham Memorial Chapel, with its murals. She'd gone to have a look at it, one day when she'd been down at Greenham Common. One wall showed a field of soldiers, rising from the dead. Pulling up crosses just like this one.

Yes! she told him. *That's the grave you want . . .*

Cautiously he walked towards the marker. Fran glanced round the yard, surveyed the corpses. Not one twitch of movement. No one blinked. She looked back at the grave again. So what was buried here?

Branwen squeezed her distant hands, a universe away – and then she was as close as Fran's own breath.

Remember Badon Hill, she said, her thought-voice strong and fervent: *Where Arthur bore the Cross of Our Lord Jesus Christ on his shoulders for three days and three nights, and the Britons were* victorious . . .

Not the grave, the cross itself. The symbol of a soldier's resurrection. She willed the thought into his heart, and felt it taking root. He grasped the cross, and dragged it from the soil.

She came back to her body with a jolt.

Everything was muzzy for a moment, then Branwen's face came into focus, inches from her own. The Welsh girl's eyes were wide.

'Rathulf comes,' she whispered.

Fran's sick stomach turned again. 'Oh, God . . .' Still on her knees, she looked around. The field was empty now, as if the grazing sheep had fled.

Quickly Branwen picked the Star-Chart up. 'He will come for this, so I must take it.' She looked at Fran, her face quite bloodless now. 'And while I lead the wolf astray, so you must guide my lord, and bring him to the end which is prepared.'

She straightened up. Fran stared at her. 'How *can* I, without that?'

'You can reach him with your love, and by Jeanne's strength.' Reaching down, she touched the ring, and fingered its cool silver. Then she took Fran's hand, and squeezed it tight. 'Your name has bound you to him, as did mine. For *Fran*' – and she pronounced it *Vrahn* – 'becomes a name for "raven" in my tongue.'

She spread the chart for Fran to see. 'There is but one star left now. *Antares*, in the Scorpion's heart. It is a fatal gateway, but through it he may pass into the centre of the circle. And only you may open it for him.'

Fran realized she was terrified of being left alone, of having to do this thing with no one's help. But looking up at Branwen now, she realized what the other girl was risking.

'Be careful,' she said faintly. 'He might catch you.'

Branwen forced a pallid smile. 'Perhaps,' she said, and swallowed. 'But an Other has his hand upon us both. And how can anything be done, that is not done well?' She pulled Fran to her feet again. 'Now *go*.'

Fran backed away unsteadily, then turned and ran. Branwen's wistful gaze went after her – and fell behind. Wiping her mouth, she looked around for Rathulf.

The countryside lay dormant in the clear morning light: the last, pale mist still rising from the meadows. Hedgrerows seemed to trap the hush. She thought the grass had never been so green.

No one else was stirring between here and the great Tor.

Let me see another dawn like this, she prayed. *One to share with you, my Lord . . . my* Love . . .

Rathulf was getting closer – behind that hedge, or over in that field. She felt his nearness crawling in her flesh. And though she'd lost her lodestone now, the Chart would draw him on. She looked towards the clump of trees where Fran had disappeared; then set off in the opposite direction.

She reached a road; a car swept past; she crossed. Rooks were calling, somewhere in the distance. She lingered on the grassy verge to scan the fields again. The smell of summer flowers teased her nostrils.

Instinct said to *use* the land, to make the most of every ditch and hedge. Maybe she could double back: evade him. Beside the road, another meadow opened out. Broad and flat, no cover there. She wavered, with her apprehension pounding in her throat, then went striding off across it.

Come, now, Rathulf. Follow me.

Halfway across, she knew that he was with her in the field. Her back turned cold and sweaty, as if she'd glimpsed a mad dog at her heels. But she didn't look around until his harsh voice called her name.

Branwen came up short, and slowly turned. A leaden calm had settled on her now.

Rathulf was advancing at a walk. His sword was slung across

his stomach, ready to be drawn. His eyes were cold and narrowed.

She stood her ground and waited, her arms at her sides. Rathulf was confused by that: he slowed and stopped, a dozen yards away. Stillness then. They searched each other's faces. The Star-Chart rustled faintly in a whisper of breeze.

Rathulf spread his empty palm. 'Give to me the Chart, for I have *earned* it.'

She stared at the rotting glove he wore: like black, decaying flesh around the bone. 'You shall not have it, Rathulf,' she said grimly.

He took a slow step forward; she eased back. His eyes on her were sharp and watchful, wary of some ploy.

'We could have shared this power,' he hissed. 'You are not *wise* but foolish.'

'*Rathulf!*'

Both of them swung round, and Branwen gasped. Dominicain was watching from the edge of the field.

She thought he was a ghost at first, a dusty shadow risen from the earth. But then he looked at her, and she knew better. No one dead could touch her heart like that.

He stepped down off the verge, and stalked towards them. His right hand kept the shotgun trained on Rathulf. The latter glowered back at him, his sword hand poised but helpless.

'It is finished, bandit. Call to your gods and die.'

Rathulf showed no hint of fear; he spoke disdainfully. 'Shame on you, to wield that devil's weapon. Have you no courage? Have you no *faith*?'

Still staring at Dominicain, he unslung his scabbard and held it up. 'You, who call yourself a priest – take up the cross.' He flung the sheathed sword down.

Branwen felt a pang of apprehension.

Rathulf raised his hand towards his shoulder, ready to grasp the handle of the blade behind his neck. 'Steel against steel – and the Christ shall choose between us.' His face was calm and earnest, like his voice.

Dominicain seemed to hesitate; then looked down at the sword. Rathulf flicked his gaze at Branwen then. His calm face didn't waver, but she glimpsed the baleful chill behind his eyes.

'*No*,' she murmured tightly. 'Do not trust him.'

Rathulf, still impassive, scratched his neck.

Dominicain looked round at her. 'It is not *him* I trust,' he said – and laid the shotgun down. He picked the Viking sword up by its scabbard, and brandished it as if it *were* a cross. A demon might have been repelled, but Rathulf just smiled thinly. The two men started edging round each other. Branwen, full of dread, went creeping closer.

The Preacher held the scabbard poised, his right hand hovering just above the hilt. Rathulf's hand moved back another inch. Round they sidled, step by step. Slowly they began to circle inward.

Branwen's hand was at her mouth; her heart throbbed like a drum. Dominicain risked a fleeting glance at her. Memory leaped between them like a spark. For a moment, as they walked the field, the two of them were centuries away. Still in that cloistered garden, though the air was dim and cool, the sun was down, the roses closing up. The words were all exhausted now. Their lips could meet in silence . . .

Et ne nos inducas in tentationem,
Sed libera nos a malo . . .

The Preacher grasped the hilt – and gave a startled, anguished yell. The binding wire was searing hot. Incandescent pain blazed up his arm. He stumbled back, still clutching at the sword, still trying in his agony to draw it. Rathulf snarled with triumph, lunging forward. His own blade caught the sunlight as he hauled it out and slashed. But Branwen sprang between them, and her flesh absorbed the blow. She groaned aloud as Dominicain reeled backwards. The sword fell from his grip at last. He went down on one knee.

Rathulf freed his blade, and shoved Branwen's drooping body to one side. He waved the bloodied steel in Dominicain's face. 'Now call on *your* God, *Prester*.'

He strode in for the kill at once. Dominicain snatched at the fallen sword, trying to grasp the scabbard in both hands. His right, although unscarred, could barely close. He raised the weapon just in time to block the other's swing. Rathulf kicked him in the chest, and sent him over backwards.

'*In nomine Patris . . .*' Rathulf sneered, and came at him again. The Preacher tried to rise, then rolled aside. The sword hacked into soil where he'd been lying.

'*Et Filii . . .*' Rathulf prompted, mocking now. Dominicain was trying to struggle up. Rathulf aimed another kick that knocked him to the ground. He raised his sword. '*Et Spiritus Sancti . . .*'

Dominicain rolled over – and came up with the shotgun in his hands. '*AMEN!*' he yelled, and fired at point-blank range. The double blast tore Rathulf's chest apart. Bloody fragments filled the air like petals of dead roses in a sudden gust of wind.

Rathulf crumpled spinelessly. The shot had chewed his face as well, and burst one glaring eye. The other didn't blink as he collapsed into the grass.

Dominicain lay there panting for a moment, then sat up. The empty shotgun fell aside. He crawled across to where Branwen lay face downward. He grasped her arm, and rolled her over. Her body moved as limply as a sack of boiled bones.

Her eyes were closed, her lips still slightly parted. And as she turned, a stream of blood went pulsing down her chest. Its brightness made him catch his breath, and still it came like wasted wine: a river from her heart. He pressed both hands against the wound, and felt her gentle breasts. But Branwen's lovely face stayed blank and white.

His gloves grew sodden as the flow was staunched. But when he dared to move his hands, it didn't start again.

He felt his heart and stomach plunge inside him. The gulf of Hell itself could go no deeper. Convulsively he crossed himself, his bloody fingers stigmatizing his forehead. A cold voice said her soul was leaving now; he had to pray and win it a safe passage. But first he had to guard them both from Rathulf's evil power.

He didn't want to leave her. He wanted to embrace her flesh, and wallow in her blood. But he forced himself to rise and turn away from her limp body.

Taking Rathulf's fallen blade, he hacked off the dead sorcerer's right hand.

CHAPTER V

Scorpion Gate

I

Fran stopped beside a fallen tree, and turned to look behind her. There was no sign of Branwen now, nor any trace of Rathulf. Beyond the fringes of the copse, the green fields were deserted.

She sat down on the trunk to get her breath back, then touched her thumb and finger to Joan's ring. Turning it, she studied the inscription. Even though she'd seen its power, it still required an effort to believe. Not just in its great age, but in the person who had worn it. Yet somehow, in her blood and bones, she felt the other's presence as if that distant fire had forged a link.

One more thing to find now. The loving cup that somehow stood for *her*.

Clasping her hands against her mouth, she closed her eyes and thought of Athelgar.

She found him on the road again, alone in that grey landscape. He'd rolled his coat and tied it round his body, like a sling. It held the soldier's cross against his back. Sky-Edge was still ready in his hand.

'Frances . . .' He looked round for her. 'What happens, while I wander here? I saw *one* figure walking up ahead.'

Even in her spirit-state, she felt the pain of that. *Oh Branwen, no.* She looked along the road, but it was empty. The ground on either side was flat: water-meadows turned to lifeless marshland. The Tor lurked in the distance, like some prehistoric beast.

But Branwen isn't guiding him. It doesn't mean she isn't still alive.

Athelgar kept walking. They came to a roadside shrine of sorts, bedecked with long-dead flowers. A spring rose from the ground here. A wooden cup was sitting in the niche.

They stared at it together. 'Is this your gift?' he asked her.

Not mine, she said, and wondered if he'd heard her. His lips were dry; his tongue came out and licked them.

The crystal splashing made Fran thirsty too. Her spirit-wings had withered, like the flowers round the shrine. She wished that she could share the drink to refresh her soul again. And what if it were poisoned? She found she didn't care. The prospect seemed as harmless as a drug that promised deep and dreamless sleep.

He glanced around, then took the cup and hunkered down to fill it. And Aldhelm rose behind him like a corpse on Judgment Day.

Fran was so absorbed herself, she almost failed to notice. Then she sensed his rush, and swung around. Aldhelm's clothes were soaked with slime, as if he really had come from the grave. Thatchy marsh-grass clung to him, like make-shift camouflage. But his eyes were unpolluted – blazing blue.

It seemed that she was screaming underwater; then Athelgar reacted, rolling clear. Aldhelm's sword-blade fanned his hair, and rang against the shrine. The cup spilled out and clattered to the road.

Athelgar was hampered by the cross against his back. It turned his roll into a clumsy sprawl. He kicked and tried to scramble up. Aldhelm swooped, and swung at him again. Athelgar spun round, and let the cross deflect the blow. The impact pushed him forwards, but he got his feet beneath him. As Aldhelm followed through, he turned at bay.

Their two swords rang and rasped against each other.

Athelgar spoke through his teeth, still straining at his grim opponent's blade.

'Friend, why are you here?'

Aldhelm glared at him, but didn't answer. The weapons came unlocked again – and Athelgar thrust deep beneath his guard. Aldhelm gave a stifled cry, and let his own sword fall. As Athelgar stepped back again, he crumpled, to lie gasping on the road.

Athelgar was breathing just as hard. Staring down, he wiped his sweaty forehead. Fran watched from the roadside, feeling numb. Aldhelm was too weak to crawl, and lay there like a dog. His face, already ravaged, had a death's head ugliness.

She didn't say a word, but something welled up in her heart: an instinct that transcended things like anger and betrayal. She let the feeling out of her, and felt it rise in Athelgar as well. He wavered, full of bitterness, then turned away, took the cup, and filled it at the spring. Coming back, he crouched beside the man who'd been his friend, supporting Aldhelm's head to let him drink.

Fran just stared with haunted eyes. She wanted to grip her aching skull, to rake her fingers back into her hair.

Aldhelm took a gulp of water, closed his eyes, then coughed. Blood spilled from his mouth into the cup. He gave a palsied quiver, and went limp. Athelgar kept holding him, his face as hard as stone, then let him slowly down onto the road. He studied the cup distastefully: a mockery of water into wine. Then he poured it out, and straightened up.

Coin and sword and cross and cup, Fran thought. *That's it, he's got all four . . .*

Athelgar set off again, his comrade's blood still glistening on his hand. Fran made to follow him – and found she couldn't move. Not only had she lost her wings, it felt as if she'd walked into a mire.

Wait for me! she called, and felt a sudden wave of dread. But Athelgar didn't hear, and kept on walking.

Then something loomed behind her, breathing down her

neck from out of nowhere. Before she could begin to turn, her spirit had been seized. She tried to wriggle clear, and found she couldn't. The clutching arms were real. Their grip was crushing.

'Well met, *blessed* Frances,' whispered Marcus in her ear.

Back in the copse, Fran's body toppled sideways, collapsing like a doll into the dirt. Part of her rejoined it for a moment, to wallow in a semi-conscious blur. Then the world dissolved again, and vanished like a dream.

Dominicain found her lying there. He stared, as if unwilling to approach her, then ventured through the slanting light to crouch down at her side. The bloodstains on his black coat glistened wetly. His gloved hand on her shoulder left a smear across her skin.

'Frances . . .' he said hoarsely, shaking her. Fran didn't stir. Her head lolled as he tried to raise her up. But he saw she was still breathing, just about. He cupped her face, and stared into its blankness. Then put his arm round her, and hauled her upright.

'*Francesca . . . vieni qua.*' Supporting her, he paused to glance around. Apart from motes of sunlit dust, the copse was still. A warm breeze stirred the leaves. No birds were singing.

He brought the shotgun up in his free hand.

Fran had bowed her head again. He pressed her to his shoulder, like the love that he had lost. 'Tell me where is *Athelgar*,' he muttered. His tone was strained and ragged, almost fretful. But Fran was far away, and never heard him.

CHAPTER VI

The Fire of the Dove

I

Her mind came into focus very slowly. She'd hovered in the limbo between one world and the next, but now she felt substantial again. Back inside her body – though she couldn't move her cold and crippled limbs. She raised her head, and forced her eyelids open.

Everything was dead and grey around her: a world of rubble ghostly in the mist. Its borders were colossal walls, which loomed on every side. She glanced round in confusion and saw it was the shell of some great building, floored with crumbled masonry and open to the sky. A church, she realized. Ransacked and destroyed.

The silence had the presence of a spectral congregation. Gothic windows opened onto void. Sheets of mist like spiderwebs bound stones and sky together.

A spasm of panic racked her. This was still the shadow-world but now she was a *part* of it somehow. The air felt clammy on her skin; her arms and legs seemed trapped. And something rough was pressing on her spine.

She turned her head and realized she was up against a post. A sturdy baulk of timber at the centre of the nave. Her arms were twisted back and tied behind it. Her ankles had been bound as well. She dropped her gaze to see.

A gout of dread erupted in her stomach.

The makings of a bonfire had been heaped around the post. Dry, dead wood and brittle thorns came almost to her knees.

A gooey liquid – black as pitch – was daubed across the pile. Straight away she knew this was a *stake*.

The dread flowed into every vein. She tried with all her will to wake from this. But in the distant world of flesh, her body barely moved; a sluggish twist, and she was still again.

(*Rouse yourself!* the Preacher urged; but she was deaf to him.)

'This day shalt thou *earn* thy place in Paradise,' said Marcus.

She'd closed her eyes with effort; now they opened with a start. The spectre monk was standing there before her. His waxen mask was calm and pale as death. Four dishevelled Norman knights were drawn up at his back, their features dark as leather, gnarled with age. One man held a broadsword, one a spear. The other two had arrows notched to bows.

The arrowheads were bound with oily cloth.

Fran just stared in horror. Marcus smiled.

'Have I not told thee so before? To be a saint, thou must be *mortified*.'

'I might get to Heaven, but you'll finish up in *Hell*,' she blurted out.

'This is my Hell. I am already here.'

'Oh, God,' she gasped. 'Where is this place?'

'The Great Church of St Mary, Glastonbury. It standeth here forever in the twilight of the world. The king's men came, and cast it down, profaned this holy ground. They brake and burned my body, too. But that was not the worst.'

She swallowed hard. 'What was?'

In answer, he held up a tattered breviary. 'See this thing. None other is more precious. A man may write, another man can read. Thus does wisdom pass from age to age. There was a treasure in this place, more valuable than gold. Its library of books, its wealth of *words*. Wisdom such as England has not seen, before or since. But then *they* came, and took the books. They tore them up and burned them. I tried to reason and resist. They did the same to me.'

'When was this?' she asked faintly.

'Thousand and five hundred, nine-and-fifty. They put my bones into the ground, and thought that I was gone. But I was skilled in hidden arts like many of my brethren. A necromancer's bones do not rest easy.'

Fran was still grappling with the date. 'But listen . . . that was centuries ago!'

'What is *time* but flowing sands and melting candle-wax? It cannot heal a wound which crieth out to be avenged.' His arm swept out around the devastation. 'Our wealth was turned to ashes here, the voices of the past stopped up for ever. In that year, Holy England turned its face away from light. So let it be: ye shall *deserve* the dark.'

'Athelgar's destroyed your men! He's going to stop *you*, *too*.'

Marcus smiled bitterly at that. 'Athelgar of Meon – yes. I thought he was a myth. There was an ancient book which men called *Clavicula Corvi*, a key whereby – so it was claimed – their lair could be unlocked. I read it in our library. It burned with all the rest. But copies had been made of it, and one of these was used to set them free. The key turned by a heedless youth. The irony is rich.'

'Oh please, just let me go,' she said. 'I know what books are worth.'

'Athelgar will come, as thou hast said. He knoweth he must save thee from the pyre. For thou hast named thyself *Française*, in honour of the Maid whom he betrayed. So let him come, for all things are now ready.'

The knights behind him stirred themselves at that. The spearman ambled forward, raised his weapon at arm's length, and moved the rusting point towards her face. She tried to twist her head away, and felt the spearhead prod against her throat. Its pressure pushed her chin right up, the iron cold and hard enough to choke on.

The swordsman turned away from her, to stare along the nave. The other two moved off to left and right. Marcus spread his arms as if to bless them – and the rags around the arrowheads caught fire. Like torch-bearers, the bowmen slipped away into the mist. The oily flames grew smudged and pale then vanished through the breaches in the walls.

Marcus stayed there, staring up at her. She'd never felt so naked but his gaze betrayed no lust. 'It is a fitting end,' he told her softly. 'A false saint, and a traitor knight, consumed like all the learning we have lost.'

The closeness of those hidden flames set all her nerves alight. But the spear was right beneath her jaw; she couldn't shout, or even shake her head. 'What's worse, though?' she gritted out. 'To make a fire of paper, or of *people*?'

Marcus shrugged. 'All flesh shall pass. But words will last for ever.'

'You're just like *them*,' she hissed. 'You realize that?'

Marcus smiled, and turned away. The cowl eclipsed his face. Breathless, Fran looked down the nave. The west door was an empty arch, the gateway to a sump of mist and shadow. Athelgar was coming – she could feel him drawing near. And here she was, a second Joan, just begging to be saved.

You bear a name which shows us that we may yet be redeemed.

The heap of wood was tinder-dry. One shot would set it off. She couldn't shout a warning, only stare one. He'd read it in her eyes when he was climbing up the pyre. But that would be too late for both of them.

Dominicain sensed movement, and swung round. A flicker in the trees, and it was gone. Still hanging on to Fran, he aimed the shotgun. The thing he thought he'd glimpsed was like a taunt beyond belief.

Fran squirmed again, as if in sleep. He started forward slowly, and she stumbled at his side, her body still responding though her spirit was elsewhere. And then the shadow crossed the light again.

He froze in disbelief, the gun extended. The fleeting shape was formless, and had melted in the sun. But all his instincts said that it was Branwen.

The Preacher would have crossed himself, if either hand were free.

An eerie pause and then another glimpse. His pounding heart leaped up. He'd laid her breathless body in the slow grave of the river but now her ghost had sought him out again. If he could just get closer, he would *see* that it was her.

The shadow seemed to beckon through the dancing motes of dust. He hesitated briefly, then let it draw him back, towards the town.

Athelgar was standing in the doorway. *Now* he could see Fran; she watched the colour leave his face. 'Stay *back*!' she squeaked, above the choking spike. He didn't hear.

The spearman glowered up at her, his sunken eyes like holes behind the nose-guard of his helmet. The other knight prowled forward, sword upraised. Athelgar braced Sky-Edge as his gaze flicked round the church. It lit on Marcus, lingering, becoming grim with promise, then focused back on Fran. She saw his *need*.

Don't look at me! she thought at him. *This is a trap, and I'm the bait, you have to* realize *that!*

The Norman swordsman lunged at him. Athelgar's distraction cost an almost fatal moment, but then he swung, and fended off the blow. Sparks flew in the dimness, the clash of steel went ringing round the walls. Marcus stood impassive, like the statue of a mourner on a tomb.

The sombre swordsmen clashed again, and skittered round each other in the rubble. The Norman raised his blade, and lumbered forward. Athelgar fell back – then plunged towards him. Sky-Edge breached the other's guard, and hacked into his neck. The Norman clattered down into the debris.

Athelgar retreated, breathing hard. Then his eyes came round towards the pyre. Fran stared back in horrified entreaty and realized she was *pleading* with her eyes. The spearman hadn't even flinched. His master stood as silent as a phantom.

'So,' said Athelgar. 'And you are Marcus.'

'So I am.' His cold voice, from the cowl.

'Who are you?'

'A seeker after justice – as are *you*.'

'*Justice?* There is death on every side, because of you.'

'No more than what this rotting land deserves.'

Athelgar came forward, very slowly. Fran tore her gaze away from him, jerking it to left and right, in frantic hope that he would get the message. But Marcus had begun to move. He was circling away, around the pyre. Step by step with Athelgar; then the two men paused together. Fran was there between them now, with Marcus out of sight. She felt his gloating presence at her back.

Oh, God, she thought. *Oh, please.*

Athelgar looked back towards the spearman. 'Coward – will you save yourself, and use that point on *me*?'

The Norman stood immobile for a moment. Then the spear-head left her throat, and swung around to bear. Fran let go a croaking gasp – then whooped to fill her lungs. The Norman aimed one thrust, and missed; the Lord of Ravens swung his blade, and didn't. Rage flamed in his features, putting strength behind the blow. The spearman's helmet crumpled like a can.

Athelgar was on the pyre before the other man had finished falling. He thrashed into the tangled thorns, and climbed the heap towards her. His gaze was full of feeling now, and Marcus was forgotten. 'NO!' she wailed into his face. 'He wants to burn us both!' Athelgar frowned, teetering, and then she saw the flare. A fiery comet, arcing through the mist. He sensed her horror, turned his head, and sprang into its path. The burning arrow hit him in the back.

'*No!*' she blurted out again, her voice pitched high with anguish. Athelgar lurched forward, caught himself, and looked at her. A flash of desperate humour bared his teeth. She realized that the shot had struck the cross upon his back. The arrow had stuck fast. He wasn't hurt.

She caught the whiff of burning wood. The thing was catching fire. Ignoring it, he floundered round behind her. She felt his fingers struggling with her bonds. Twisting her head, she saw the next shot coming.

'Look out!'

He'd glimpsed it too, and lunged again to catch it. In his side. The impact sent him reeling, and he clung to her for balance. No humour now; his teeth were clenched, his face as tight as leather being cured. The shaft protruded from his ribs. His shirt was smouldering.

Fran just cried out wordlessly. He heaved himself back upright, and went stumbling down the pile. Another arrow hissed across the church. This one was unlit, but it combusted in the air as Marcus worked his magic from behind her. Athelgar took that one, too. His folded coat caught fire.

Fran was sobbing, fighting to get free. The archers were advancing now, still trying to get a shot into the pyre. The next shaft was deflected by Sky-Edge, and flipped away. Athelgar swung round, and stopped the fifth one with his thigh. She saw him grit his teeth with pain, and go down on one knee. He gripped the shaft and snapped it off, but tongues of flame went licking up his leg.

'*Finish him!*' snarled Marcus from the shadows.

The Normans cast their bows aside, in favour of their swords. The *rasp* of baring metal was a grim, decisive sound. Athelgar was down, as if to grovel in the rubble. The cross he bore was now alight, the white wood charring black.

They closed with him together, as he tried to find his feet. The first man made to cut him down but Athelgar, still burning, scrabbled backwards. He tried to rise again; his leg gave way. The swing that should have split his head just missed him. And then Sky-Edge went slicing up, between the Norman's legs.

The blade was keen, the leverage inhuman. The Norman doubled forward, disembowelled. Athelgar collapsed as well, and dragged his weapon clear. The second knight came wading in. Athelgar just flailed at him, a prisoner of his pain. His arm was sleeved in flames, and scattered sparks. The Norman flinched away, like some spooked beast.

'Get *up*!' screamed Fran, still squirming as she watched.

And Athelgar rose up, as if empowered. He shrugged out of his burning coat; the fiery cross slipped down into the dust. The coat unfurled and became a blazing shroud. He flung it at the Norman as the knight strode in again. It cloaked the man, and sent him rearing backwards. Athelgar lurched after him, and hacked into the flames. The knight kicked out convulsively, and dropped, to burn in silence.

Athelgar swung round to glare at Marcus.

The shirt was burning off his back; his arms and legs were sheathed with yellow fire. The blaze lit up his blackened face, and Fran could see the blisters on his skin. His flaxen hair was singeing. But his eyes were icy cold.

The arrowheads had bitten deep. He staggered like a drunk as he came forward. Death was in his system now; the gnawing flames were keeping him alive. Fran could only stare, wide-eyed. And Marcus stood and waited, unperturbed.

'You think to slay me, Athelgar? I am already slain. Your sword may cut me down but I shall rise again to make this country *grieve*. You may have put my army down but I shall raise another, just as foul.'

Fran's gaze went from face to face: the one begrimed, the other ghastly white. Athelgar was stumbling now, as if about to stop; and once he did, the fire would just consume him where he stood. But Marcus's tone, though sneering, had the awful ring of truth.

What was it she'd said herself? *The sword may win the battle, but shall never win the war . . .*

She gave a little whimper of frustration and despair. And then she felt a presence, right behind her.

'*Listen!*' whispered Branwen in her ear.

They'd reached the ruined abbey, still deserted at this hour. Dominicain looked round, but there was no sign of the shadow;

just dewy dimness, clinging on, as sunlight flooded through the shattered walls.

Fran's body writhed against him then, like someone trying to waken from a nightmare. He stumbled back, and almost let her fall. She gasped aloud, and quietened again.

His hairs rose up.

Branwen was here. He felt it in the ruin's holy stillness. Her spirit was as close as Fran's own flesh.

Her hands gripped Fran's bare shoulders, willing strength into her soul. 'As Jeanne died, she cried out for a cross,' the Welsh girl hissed. 'And so an English soldier offered one.'

And then, from some great distance, came Dominicain's grim voice. *We saw it*, said the Preacher. *We were* there!

'The cross!' Fran cried. 'Joan's cross! It's all you need!'

Athelgar veered towards the burning wooden cross, throwing his sword aside. As he picked the marker up, its flames engulfed his hands. Fran saw them tightening like claws. His face had tightened too, enough to split. But his stare remained implacable. He raised the cross, and started to advance.

This time Marcus seemed to quail. He flashed a dreadful look at Fran; she felt its hate, like venom in her veins. But Branwen was still holding her, and now her hands moved down to free her bonds. Fran was only half aware, her mind transfixed by this last confrontation. Marcus was retreating but the ancient blackened stonework barred his way. The flaming cross lit up his face, and bleached it like a skull. And Athelgar bore down on him, relentless, all ablaze. Full of accusation now, and speaking as he came.

'Wound for wound . . . and stripe for stripe . . . Burning for burning . . . *Root* and *branch*.'

Marcus lashed out with his book; it spun away, unscorched. Fran felt horror coming to the brim. Then Branwen took her arms and raised them up.

'Lady Raven, spread your wings and rise up like the dove!'

'Athelgar!' screamed Fran, and felt her footing slip away.

Marcus snarled in fury and despair. And Athelgar thrust the cross against his chest, to slam him back and pin him to the wall.

'Your cross, Jeanne! Your *cross! PARDONNEZ MOI!*'

Even as he yelled that out, the flames engulfed them both. Fran's mouth became an O, but no sound came. She'd turned ethereal once more, her spirit rising up. Branwen was a shade, ascending with her. The gutted abbey fell away below them. The burning men still grappled with the cross. And then the ruin vanished in a flash of brilliant light.

She watched the fireball expand. It was as blinding as magnesium, but she couldn't look away. A ghostly ripple spread across the landscape from its heart. Floating there, she saw it reach the shadowy horizon. And then the light rose up to swallow her.

'Frances. Child, *arise*,' the Preacher said.

She was grovelling in darkness and the sky was full of smoke. The fireball was gone, but it had stripped her of her wings, and brought her plunging back to earth again. The air was cold, and everything had turned to soot and shadow. And yet there was the feel of *grass* beneath her knees and elbows. Her mind sank into glue again, although she had a disembodied sense of someone holding her. A whiff of summer, far away. But then the dark returned.

Nauseous, she raised herself, and squinted through the gloom. There was no sign of Branwen. Just blackened slag on every side. And up ahead, the ruins of the abbey.

Most of it had been reduced to what was standing in the distant, real world. Crumbled cloisters; bitten chunks of wall. She clambered up, and made her way towards it. Athelgar was still inside. No matter that the blaze had razed the building to the ground. She'd left him there, and now she had to find him.

She crept in through a gothic arch: the gateway to this

chilly, burnt-out Hell. A skull was half-submerged amid the ashes of the choir. Her heart convulsed, but then she saw the battered Norman helmet. Shuddering, she turned around. A breathless silence filled the smoky air.

Then she heard a rasping breath behind her.

Again she wheeled, and saw him crouching there. A black lump in the dimness, but a glimmer of his pale hair remained.

She sobbed, and hurried over, but he waved her back and turned his face away. His shadow-face. She slumped onto her knees.

'*Athelgar* . . .'

'Frances,' he said hoarsely. 'Oh, my lady . . .'

She reached for him instinctively, despite the awful damage. He tried to fend her off again, then took her hand and gripped it in his own.

'So,' he rasped, his head still bowed. 'And is it finished now?'

Fran just nodded, choking on her tears.

'The land will be at peace tonight,' he told her, ashen-voiced. 'The common folk have won, though we have lost.' She sensed his wry and bitter grin. 'The warriors always lose.'

'You've paid your debt,' she whispered. 'You can rest now.'

Athelgar stayed silent, but she felt his grip grow tighter. She stared down at his shrivelled leather glove.

Frances . . .

The voice was small with distance, but it echoed in the hush. Hearing it, she felt a spark of panic. But then she realized who it was. Dominicain was calling out for her.

She raised her tearful eyes and saw the looming clouds of smoke begin to break. A spectral wind was blowing, east to west. The dismal gloom became a starry twilight: a million burning snowflakes spreading out above the church. She gazed at them, entranced, then sensed a movement and looked round.

Branwen stood there, watching from the arch of the west doorway.

Somehow she'd retrieved her brooch; it glinted in her hand. The lodestone shone more brightly than the brightest of the stars. The filthy air was limpid now. The Universe itself was there behind her.

Her face was ghostly pale, but calm. She smiled at Fran, with love beyond expressing. Then she raised her glowing brooch, and looked to Athelgar.

'Come,' she murmured gently. 'She is waiting for you now.'

Her voice filled Fran with yearning, like a summons into splendour without end. It was dusk on the skyline and night overhead; the pastureland of stars stretched out for ever. And who was there to greet him in their glow? Her mind's eye glimpsed a fresh-faced girl as full of life as *she'd* been at nineteen. Her armour cast aside at last. A country maid again.

Athelgar began to stir; she sobbed, and clung to him. But then she heard her name again; Dominicain's faint voice. Something hooked her soul, and tugged. She knew she couldn't come.

Athelgar had raised his head. 'Frances?' he asked softly. 'Is it well?'

'Yes,' she almost whimpered. 'You can *go*.'

His blackened fingers squeezed again and then the stars went out. Sunlight flooded through her head, and bathed her in its warmth. Looking up, she saw the sky. The vault of heaven, blue and blank and empty.

Her body threshed one final time; Dominicain lurched backwards, and they both went down together. She looked around her desperately and realized they were in the real abbey. Sunlit walls, and soft green grass. She wailed into the wind.

Apart from them, the ruins were deserted.

Fran began to sob and squirm. Dominicain wrapped both his arms around her. She fought him for a moment, then slumped back. 'The thing is finished now,' he said. 'Our foe has been *consumed*.'

His voice was gruff. A single tear was glistening in the stubble of his cheek.

She swallowed. 'Branwen saved us. She's . . . been taken, hasn't she?'

The Preacher nodded sombrely. 'And Athelgar has found his rest at last. The debts are paid; the Ravensbreed are free.' He gently touched her face. 'And so are you.'

CHAPTER VII
The End of the River

I

The wells behind her eyes were dry. No water left for tears. Sitting on the bed, she stroked her hand through Kathryne's hair, then stooped to kiss her gently on the forehead.

Dominicain had brought the body up here, and laid it on the pretty counterpane, but Fran had stayed alone to finish things. She pulled her sweaty clothes off first – disgusted by the staining and the smell – then undressed Kathryne too, and washed her clean. The dead girl's face looked peaceful now. Martin had already closed her eyes.

They'd found him sitting on the stairs, a bloody towel wrapped around his hand. Fran had found a first-aid kit, and bandaged him more firmly; a distraction for her bleeding, crippled mind. He was somewhere downstairs now, as shocked and drained as she was.

She wasn't really sure of the formalities for pagans. A vase of flowers was blooming in the sunlight from the window. She'd plaited them into a makeshift garland, and settled it round Kathryne's brows, then eased her head back down onto the pillow.

The ache was still inside her, needing tears for its release in the same way that her body needed sweat.

Getting up, she pulled on Kathryne's cotton gown, and went droopily downstairs. Martin was slumped numbly at the table, as if he hadn't left it since last night. A dark red smudge was seeping through his bandage. Fran wondered if she'd done it right; it had been so long since she had learned first aid.

Dominicain stood waiting at his shoulder. The blood on his clothes was drying, turning blacker. Blending in.

'What about Branwen?' she asked.

'I gave her to the river that runs westward from this place. Perhaps its flow will take her to the sea . . .' A wistful pause; but then he shrugged. 'It matters not,' he said. 'Her soul is safe.'

'And Rathulf?'

'The foxes and the crows will make his grave.'

Fran just nodded, fingering her cross.

Dominicain took a folded piece of paper from his coat. Fran and Martin stiffened as they realized what it was. The Preacher spread the Star-Chart on the tabletop between them, then let his rosary spill out across it. The crucifix and diamond lodestone fell outside the circle. He nudged the blackened string of beads and raised his eyes to theirs.

'See the pattern. *Eridanus*. River through the stars.'

She saw the constellation marked. It twisted and meandered off the map. Dominicain reached down, and took the diamond.

'And this is Achernar, the river's ending.' He snapped the lodestone off its thread, and handed it to Fran.

She swallowed. 'Won't you need it?'

He smiled gravely. 'Not where I am going.'

They came outside with him to say farewell. The afternoon light was clean and hot; Fran felt her body glowing through the gown. The garden grass was dry beneath her feet.

Dominicain had taken a blanket, slinging it behind him like a bedroll. His Bible was stuffed into a pocket of his coat. He'd finished Kathryne's bread and drunk some wine, but taken no food with him. *A friar preacher on the road must earn his keep*, he'd said.

He paused there in the garden, as if suddenly enchanted by the hush. Insects were still humming, but the world had gone to sleep. Cautiously Fran sidled up behind him.

'Branwen didn't *really* bring the Ravens down?' she said at length.

He shook his head, still studying the fields.

'What happened, then?' she ventured.

'Branwen met Jeanne, called *La Pucelle*. She saw the Maid was touched by God, and that her cause was just. She made the Ravens see this truth and so it was they turned against their country, and their king.

'Then Jeanne was captured. The Ravens could have rescued her but Athelgar still doubted. The shame of the forsworn was in his heart. Branwen he sent to seek me out; I was estranged by then. Rising when the Ravens did, but following *my* way . . .

'She begged me, as a Friar Preacher, to plead for *La Pucelle*. I tried, but all my efforts were in vain. And after she was burned, all hope was lost.

'The Ravens were condemned. Their name was blotted out from every book. The last chance to redeem themselves was lost. I hear they tried to make an end – to stand against the king and all his army. But the Land-waster enraptured them, and drew them back to join it in the dark.'

'They're free today,' said Martin sombrely.

Dominicain struck a match and lit Fran's final cigarette. *Condemned man's last request*, she thought; and yet his face was calm. When he spoke, his tone was almost musing.

'Branwen was a Welsh-woman, yet she joined an English lord. And Athelgar, an Englishman, he sided with the French. They found a cause more precious than the call of blood and soil. For *Justice* was the Lady they both served.'

He breathed out smoke. 'Your future lies behind you now,' he said.

She hesitated. 'How do you mean?'

'I learned this from a wise man once – a scholar of the Jews. The past is there before our eyes: we see it, it is *known*. But the future lies behind us. We do not see, we cannot know, until we turn, and face it.'

She nodded slowly, trying to take that in. Then tensed, as he began to move away.

He hadn't ditched the shotgun – it was tucked into the blanket. The butt-end was just visible. She stared at it, then looked down at his Bible. 'You need them both?' she asked, uncertainly.

The Preacher shrugged, as if resigned. 'You know there is no easy road to freedom.'

He raised his hand and blessed them with two fingers held together. '*Addio*,' he said, and turned away. Lingering, they watched him go, departing like a shadow through the drowsy summer haze. Martin was beside Fran now. Unthinkingly, he put his arm around her. Fran just snuggled close and hugged him back.

CHAPTER VIII

A Roof for a Skyful of Stars

I

Walking from the station, through the heady summer dusk, she found herself remembering a rhyme. Something she'd read in a childhood book. Something that had made her cry and cry.

The village hadn't changed that much since then. Its fringes had pushed out a little further, but the houses round the main street were the same. She raised her eyes above their roofs and lichen-speckled chimneys. The uplands hadn't changed at all. *The old, eternal rocks.*

Some kids were in the road ahead, scuffing a football round between the kerbs. They paused just long enough to let her pass. She felt them staring after her, but then the game resumed. No wonder they were curious. She must look quite a sight.

She'd tried to wash the bloodstains off her Levis and Lyn's jacket – working in the cool of Kathryne's kitchen. The soiling was less obvious now, the foul smell a little less pronounced. The jacket was ruined anyway, but she kept it round her shoulders. It had seen her through the journey. It was *her*.

Of course, she looked like someone on the road. Her muddy boots were scuffed, her T-shirt sweaty. Her cowl of hair was lank and tangled now. She hadn't washed her body, or her grubby face, for days.

But somehow she had made it home – with money which she knew poor Kathryne wouldn't have begrudged her. Somehow, here she was in safe, familiar Hathersage.

That rhyme. She tried to piece its words together. The story of a little girl who'd lost her favourite doll. She'd wept and searched for weeks but never found it. Even now, the memory was poignant. As she turned into her street, Fran felt her eyes start stinging.

Faltering, she came to the front door. She hadn't phoned; they weren't expecting her. She hesitated, heart in mouth; then reached out for the bell.

In the achy pause that followed, she went on with the rhyme. The girl had found her doll again – years later. It had turned up at the bottom of the garden: broken up and filthy and bedraggled.

The front door opened slowly. Fran tried to smile, and say, *Hi, Mum* – but her voice broke, and her eyes filled up with tears. Her mother almost snatched her from the step, and hugged her tight. And as Fran sobbed, and clung to her, she thought about the ending of the rhyme. The damage and defilement didn't matter. In the eyes of the girl who'd lost it, she was still the most beautiful doll in the world.

2

Martin stood and stared into the past.

The stars were like a snowstorm in midsummer. The air was hushed, and crystal clear. The city sounds were muted, far away.

Vega flashed like fire overhead. That brilliant light had left the star a quarter of a century ago. The flames that reached his eyes tonight had burned before both he and Lyn were born.

Lyn . . .

He glanced towards the Rectory. The window of the living room glowed softly. He guessed that Mum and Dad were still sitting where he'd left them. Still weak, of course, still deeply scarred. They must have felt like they'd been left with nothing. But now they'd got one child back from the dead.

He'd never seen his father cry before.

The sky was full of far more distant stars, much older ghosts. He was seeing some now as they'd been in Branwen's time. Someone in a future age would see them as they really were tonight. He found the notion weirdly reassuring.

Whatever happened here on earth, the cosmos would survive it. In time – about twelve thousand years – bright Vega would be up there in the north, the changeless star, as Thuban and Polaris had once been. The Universe was infinite – and maybe every part of it would somehow last for ever. Every precious atom. Every thought.

Nothing ever dies, he told himself. He waited for some instinct to gainsay him. But his scepticism drew back, and didn't argue.

Claire had answered the door, just as he'd dreamed. Her hair was full of gold, her eyes like sapphires; the bloom of coming motherhood was on her. He'd stood there, looking sheepish, as a tide of warmth went through him. He'd waited for her smile.

She'd slapped his face.

Not a testy, girly slap. She'd almost knocked his head off. Stunned, he'd reeled back, then tried again. 'Bastard!' Claire had gasped, and started flailing with both hands. Martin lurched into the hall, then dropped his arms and took his punishment. '*Bastard!*' she exclaimed again. 'I *hate* you . . .' She forced him back against the wall; he slithered down beneath a rain of blows. But Claire was sobbing now, and she had lost co-ordination. Down she slumped, on top of him, and took hold of his coat. Her head nudged his. She splashed him with her tears. Martin drew her down, and held her close.

'You *shit*,' she sobbed at last. 'Where have you *been*?'

He could have said, My *sister's dead*, and wriggled off the hook. But that would leave her plunged in guilt for laying in like this. Better to be her punch-bag, then – and soak up all her anger and her pain.

Crazy instinct. Maybe it was love.

He managed a smile, although his face was aching. 'Is this how you treat *all* your patients, then?'

She swiped at him again, half-heartedly. She looked more hurt than angry now. He thought he saw a glimmer of relief, and maybe something deeper. Something *more*.

He cupped her tearful face and smiled, a little groggily. His cheeks were stinging now and he tasted blood. He'd never dreamed a nurse would beat him up.

'I really think it's time you met my parents,' he had said.

In my Father's house, there are many mansions . . .

Branwen had alluded to that haunting Gospel verse. She'd feared that there'd be no place for the Ravens. But as he gazed into the night, he realized there was somewhere for them all.

The cloud of stars above his head was just one galaxy. Others, by the billion, lay beyond it. The spiral of Andromeda had risen in the east. A lake of light, two million years away. He saw it through the picture in his room, and felt its warmth. None of the rest were naked-eye, but telescopes revealed them. Some like whirlpools. Some like rising suns.

Radio waves kept going on for ever. Maybe thoughts – and memories – could follow where they led.

He took the dog-eared Star-Chart from his pocket. Striking a match, he touched it to one corner; a ghostly bluish flame began to spread. He held it at arm's length as it began to shrivel up. Burning bits of paper floated skyward, firefly orange; sparks into stars. Martin watched them rise towards those great galactic mansions, and knew at last that nothing ever dies.

Epilogue

SO CLOSE THAT THERE IS NOTHING IN BETWEEN

Farewell now, my sister;
Up ahead there lies your road.
And your conscience walks beside you:
It's the best friend you'll ever know.
And the past is now your future,
It bears witness to your soul.
Make sure the love you offer up
Does not fall on barren soil.

DEAD CAN DANCE

The sky looked oddly colourless, the summer sunlight filtered by her shades. The old, familiar, reassuring plastic. Fran reached up and took them off. Her eyes were clear and dry.

'Hi,' said Martin. 'Frances, this is Claire.'

Fran just smiled, and took the blonde girl's hand. Claire squeezed back, her own smile shy. She'd picked a smart grey suit for the occasion. Its formal cut just emphasized the freshness of her face.

Craig's arm tightened briefly round Fran's shoulders.

'We've got a son now,' Martin said. 'He's back with Mum and Dad this afternoon. But we'll bring him when he's older; let her see him.'

They went in through the lych-gate, and down the path to stand around Lyn's grave. The crickets were still buzzing in the long grass by the wall. A stone had been erected in the year since she had been here. Polished marble, chiselled with a name.

Martin knelt to place his flowers, still holding hands with Claire. Rising, he looked round at Fran.

'We'll see you in the Coach House. I'd like us all to raise a glass to her. Then Craig and I can sink some beers, and *you* can have a gossip. I reckon she'll approve.'

'. . . And listen in,' Fran smiled. 'Take care; we'll see you later.'

The two of them went back towards the cars. Craig hesitated briefly, then put his own flowers down. Fran's fingers brushed his collar: the musty brown suede jacket that he'd always used to wear. He straightened up, and kissed her.

'I'll go wait by the car. You'll be okay?'

She nodded. 'We'll be fine.'

He gazed at her, a half-smile on his face; then turned away. Fran just stood there, savouring the stillness.

Your future lies behind you, now. She glanced around, and it became the past. Athelgar had stood beside that wall, while she had wept. The patch of grass was empty now, the air too bright for ghosts. The churchyard lay deserted, and at peace.

Crouching down before the grave, she laid her bunch of flowers with the rest.

'Hiya, Lyn,' she whispered. 'I told you I'd come back when it was over. Has it seemed a year, to you? I've missed you every day . . .

'I thought you'd like to hear my news. I've just been to America, with Craig. We spent a month out there. You should have seen us. It's wonderful, that place, it's like a dream. Even the sky looks bigger there. You feel that you can travel on for ever. There's so much sun – it's really hot. And I just *wallowed* in it, every day.' Smiling now, she leaned a little closer. 'You know my white bikini? *It still fits.*'

A pause; then she confided her Big Secret. 'He's *asked me*, Lyn; the last night we were there. He said he wants to share it all with me.' She took a breath, and glanced around the churchyard. 'But this is home. I'm part of this. The roots go down much deeper. Oh Lynnie . . .' She smiled ruefully. 'I don't know what to do.'

Church and field and hills: forever England. *A richer dust*, or so the poem said. Recalling it, she nodded to herself. Breaking off a blade of grass, she rubbed it in her palms.

'No one knows what happened,' she went on after a while. 'We fought a *war* . . . we risked so much . . . and people are no wiser. They'll keep on digging up the bones, but nobody will piece them all together. There may be rumours here and there – but who believes them? *I* wouldn't.

'You never met Dominicain – but he's the only one who walked away. He's out there somewhere now, among the homeless and the poor. There's been no word . . . but, who knows, we might hear of him again. From some disputed barricade, maybe.'

Another pause. She listened to the hush. Then spoke as if unwilling to disturb it.

'I would have gone with Athelgar, you know? If I'd been able. That place I saw was lovely – like the brightest summer night. But Dominicain said I wasn't ready yet. I'm only twenty-four and I've got so much left to do. So many things to see. So much to feel.'

She glanced at Craig. He was chatting with the others by the car. A little spasm of pleasure tugged her heart. Somehow Lyn was there, and smiling with her. Fran looked at what she'd written on the card with her bouquet.

Our summer will come again.

'I'll see you,' she said softly, and stood up.

As she crossed the churchyard, a breeze went sighing through the grass, and rustled in the trees. She paused and looked around, but it had faded in the heat. She listened to the silence for a moment; then smiled fondly to herself, and went on through the gate.

AUTHOR'S NOTE

The seed for this whole story was planted in the early 1980s by the BBC TV documentary series *In Search of . . .* These were eight brilliant 'Dark Age detective stories', presented by Michael Wood, which made the medieval past immediate and real. The programme on King Athelstan was particularly evocative and gripping, with many resonances in these pages. More recently, on Radio 4, Michael Wood presented an equally haunting programme on the Glastonbury legends, which added to the substance of this book.

Many factors influenced the story's long gestation. The black-cloaked 'watchmen' of the Ravensbreed owe much to Fields of the Nephilim, while the restless goth romanticism of All About Eve helped develop many characters and themes. The Levellers lent their zest for life and feeling for the land – and there's my usual large debt to the myth, magic and music of the Italian Western. I didn't know that Joan of Arc would play a role *at all* – until I joined a Holts' Tours trip, led by Ian Powys MC, which traced her life and times; and heard Richard Einhorn's *Voices of Light*, a marvellous choral work about her fate.

A special mention must go to the Atomic Mirror Pilgrimage, organized in 1996 by Janet Bloomfield and Pamela Meidell. This linked Britain's sacred and nuclear sites: from Avebury to Aldermaston, Glastonbury to Greenham. Many ideas were cooked up here. Warm regards to all I met, especially Tim Knock, Sophie King, Rob Green, David Lane, Charity Scott Stokes, Scilla Ellworthy and Kia Miller.

Though this isn't a historical novel, the characters remember real events. The capture of the Danish Raven banner in 878 is noted in the Anglo-Saxon Chronicle – just months before Alfred's victory at Edington. Athelstan ('the Glorious') established his rule with campaigns in 927 and 934, before the decisive battle of Brunanburh in 937. Following the Norman invasion of England, a rebellion in 1069 was ferociously suppressed in a campaign which became know as the Harrying of the North. Hereward the Wake, meanwhile, led resistance in the fens around Ely during 1070–71. The Albigensian Crusade, to destroy the Cathar heresy in southern France, lasted from 1209 to around 1226. The Black Death struck England in 1348, and the Peasants' Revolt followed in 1381. By then, the Hundred Years War was already under way; the siege of Orléans was raised in 1429, and Jeanne d'Arc herself was burned in 1431.

Books. You want books? Too many to remember (and of course, I've treated facts as I see fit); but I'd particularly mention *In Search of the Dark Ages* and *Domesday: A Search for the Roots of England* (both by Michael Wood); *The Anglo-Saxon Chronicles* (translations by G N Garmonsway and Anne Savage); *The Warrior's Way*, by Stephen Pollington; *Strange Landscape*, by Christopher Frayling; *The Trial of Joan of Arc* (transcript introduced and edited by Marina Warner); *Jeanne d'Arc, par elle-même et par ses témoins*, by Régine Pernoud; *Enfolded in Love* (Sheila Upjohn's translations of Julian of Norwich); A *Guide to Glastonbury's Temple of Stars*, by Katherine Maltwood; and – as a healthy dose of scepticism – *The Demon-Haunted World*, by the late and much lamented Carl Sagan.

Some of the locations used are open to discussion. The site of Brunanburh is still not known, but Brinsworth is one of the leading contenders, and Michael Wood evoked the scene to powerful effect in his Athelstan film. The site of Badon Hill (a historical battle later associated with Arthur) is also still debated, but Liddington Castle in Wiltshire is favoured by many. Again, Michael Wood's description of its strategic importance as 'like a Dark Age Spaghetti Junction' was completely irresistible, I thought. The bounds of the old estate at Meon, however, are set out in a 10th century charter and can still be traced today: land granted by king Athelstan to his loyal armour-bearer – Athelgeard.

Many thanks are due to Dr R. Telfryn Pritchard (Hi, Dad!) for medievalist advice; to Mum, for showing me the pictures in the stars; and to Ann, for cheerful company on sundry field trips. Also to Huw Pryce, for the usual wit and wisdom; Véronique Duvergé, who once accompanied me to a Michael Wood lecture for entirely the wrong reason ('I think he's *really dishy*, John!'); Beth Elgood ('Come on you Cobblers!', and other insights); Suzy Holloway and Lesley Heath, for assisting the General in his strategic planning; Roger & Jean F, for hospitality in an inspiring house; Jane and Jim at *Voyager*, for editorial encouragement; Nicola, Marilyn, Sue and Helen, for being the office angels; and Barbara, Jane and Christina, for bribery and corruption.

Special regards to the Oxford Blackfriars Affinity Group, the Upper Heyford Vigil crowd, and everyone from Cruisewatch who I stayed up late with between October 1987 and July 1990 – especially Bob, Roger, Caroline, Jill, Indra, Richard, Linda, Jean, Torquemada & The Inquisitors, and that nice WPC who nicked me on Fore Down.

Musical influences on the writing are too numerous to mention; but for the benefit of people who (a) like making lists of things, and (b) ask 'where *do* you get your ideas?', here are ten pieces of music which helped create and shape the book you've read. Some of them inspired entire scenes.

Theme from *Silent Witness*, by Alan Hawkshaw
Moonchild (from *The Nephilim*) by Fields of the Nephilim
Sell Out (from *Levelling the Land*) by the Levellers

The Second Chase (from *The Big Gundown*) by Ennio Morricone
Torture (from *Voices of Light*) by Richard Einhorn
Shine (from *Zoon*) by the Nefilim
Luisa Rojas 1852–1870 (from *The Land Raiders*) by Bruno Nicolai
The Chamber/Hibernaculum (from *The Songs of Distant Earth*) by Mike Oldfield
Mystic and Severe (from *Death Rides a Horse*) by Ennio Morricone
Peace Returns to Mimbres (from *The Return of Ringo*) by Ennio Morricone
Particular thanks also to Dead Can Dance, Richard Souther, Pink Floyd, Steeleye Span, Enya and The Mediæval Bæbes.